Mav Caid

The Complete Story

Mav Caid

The Complete Story

Eugene Stonefield

DEDICATION

I dedicate this book to my wife, Pat, whose patience, and encouragement has been invaluable.

Published by Great Fiction Publishing

Printed in the United States of America

ACKNOWLEDGMENTS

I want to acknowledge the people contributing to the preparation for publication of this book whose attention to their role I appreciate. For their patience and endurance, and for their efforts to read the various iterations of the book that I have presented to them, I thank them. The names of these patient and helpful individuals are: readers Pat Denny, Gail Simmons, and Laurel Scott.

GENERAL STATEMENT:

This book is a fantasy-fiction of the life of protagonist, Mav Caid, and readers should recognize that all incidents and characters of action are fictional and solely the product of the writer's imagination. Any resemblances to persons living or deceased, or resemblances to actual events are completely coincidental. References to protagonist interactions and/or claims of protagonist's interactions in this book with historical persons are creative fabrications. I seek, by their inclusion, to add texture and highlight the time-frame of the story occurring between 1867 and 1939 in and around the fictional town of Beaton, Arkansas. Dates of historic events referenced are generally true, but the chronology of a few are fictional. It is the author's wish that the reader enjoys the book for the story it tells. The three books that are consolidated into this Mav Caid — The Complete Story are, Mav Caid — The Early Years, Mav Caid — The Middle Years, and Mav Caid — The Final Years.

Cover Image Information

Cover image:
By John C. H. Grabill - This image is available from the United States Library of Congress's Prints and Photographs division under the digital ID ppmsc.02638.
Credit:
Library of Congress, Prints and Photographs Division, John C.H. Grabill Collection, [reproduction number, e.g., LC-USZ62-90145]
General statement:
Photographs in this collection were deposited for copyright between 1887 and 1892. Works copyrighted in the U.S. more than 95 years ago are in the public domain
Photo information:
Title: "The Cow Boy" / J.C.H. Grabill, photographer, Sturgis, Dakota Ter.
Creator(s): Grabill, John C. H., photographer
Date Created/Published: c1888.
Medium: 1 photographic print.
Summary: Photograph shows side view of a cowboy on a horse, looking towards the camera.
Reproduction Number: LC-DIG-ppmsc-02638 (digital file from original photo) LC-USZ62-13227 (b&w film copy neg.)
Rights Advisory: No known restrictions on publication. No renewal in Copyright Office
Call Number: LOT 3076-12, no. 320 [P&P]
Repository: Library of Congress Prints and Photographs Division Washington, D.C. 20540
Notes: Copyright deposit; 1888. Title from item. Forms part of the John C. H. Grabill Collection

A word from the author:

The story of the life and times of Mav Caid is a fantasy-fiction with touches of history to flavor the story and give the reader a sense of the time in which Mav Caid lived. It is a story that spans the age from the last decade of the nineteenth century into the third decade of the twentieth century, and I present this consolidated story of a series of three volumes titled The Life and Times of Mav Caid. Maverick Caiden, the true name of the protagonist, comes from a family of subsistence farmers in the heart of Texas who seeks adventure on the cattle trail moving cattle to markets in the north but cannot change his roots as a farmer. Some of his adventures are fantastical, others common to the age, when outlaws confronted society and law-abiding citizens had to use their ingenuity to counter them.

It is my sincerest hope that the reader of Mav Caid — The Complete Story will enjoy the tale as much as I have enjoyed telling it.

Table Of Contents

Chapter 1

Tragedy in Bandera

The annals of history will not record the events in the life of Maverick Caiden, a young cowboy riding from Ogallala, Nebraska in 1889 with an uncertain destination. Yet, he has just completed a drive of over three-thousand two and three-year-old longhorn steers from Texas under the direction of Captain John T. Lytle whose earlier pioneering of the Great Western Cattle Trail will be recorded for posterity. Lytle's trail, beginning south of the small Texas town of Bandera near San Antonio, then winding northward across open range through Oklahoma Indian Territory, western Kansas and into Nebraska, ends in Ogallala. The Great Western Cattle Trail is one of the preferred pathways for the movement of cattle to northern markets where, upon arrival, the cattle are sold, fattened, and eventually transported west to California or east to Chicago by Union Pacific railway, the first transcontinental railroad created by the linking of the Central Pacific Railroad line and the Union Pacific Rail Road in

Eugene Stonefield

Utah on May 10,1869.   The other primary trails supporting the commerce in cattle from Texas to points north are the Goodnight-Loving to Cheyenne, the Chisholm to Abilene, and the Sedalia and Baxter Springs trail to Sedalia, Missouri.   For the young cowboy, youthful enthusiasm and newly-found freedom had determined the trail he followed for five years.   Now, freshly released from his trail obligations, he follows his own.

Maverick Caiden, whose name was shortened to Mav Caid by cowboy orthodoxy, had little experience working with cattle or horses when he began with the Lytle company in 1884, but was a Bandera farmer's son who was looking to experience something other than farming.   For the young farmer-to-be, farming seemed routine and dull.   To Maverick, romance and excitement glittered in his dream of going 'up the trail,' with a herd of longhorn steers to markets north, to be a drover.   Upon his turning seventeen, Captain Lytle had employed Mav as wrangler, the entry-level position, and he progressed through positions with increasing responsibility until he excelled at all duties required of a seasoned cowboy, from managing cattle, to selecting and managing the remuda for the drover's specific needs during herd assemblies and on the trail drives.   And although he recognized that he had a natural knack for working with animals, the ending of the drive, with all wages due paid in full and in his war-bag, along with an unexpected bonus, the young man seeks something new but will find something old.   In typical fashion, at the end of the drive, Lytle released all hands to return to Texas or to go wherever inclination dictates. Maverick made the decision to ride eastward and return through unfamiliar territory to get a feeling for the country.

The route taken brought him through eastern Kansas through Abilene into Missouri, then turning south at Sedalia, due south into Arkansas to an appealing valley just outside the small town of Beaton, in the foothills of the Ouachita mountain range.   Here he found a place abundant with wildlife, water, near mountains, and grassland, and welcoming nature to the people he met in the area.

A chance meeting with a family of easterners wanting to sell their property and return to their old home in Virginia offered an opportunity to Mav that he found he could not resist. He bought the property, consisting of twenty acres of cleared land with a partially built cabin constructed of pine logs cut from the surrounding forest. For the next several months, Maverick felled trees, cut the trunks into logs and finished the cabin. When he was not engaged in those activities, he was hunting or fishing to furnish his everyday needs for food, or, occasionally, riding to Beaton to obtain whatever staples needed that he could not provide himself.

As he visited Beaton, Maverick met several of the residents engaged in the business of supplying the goods and services that he will always need. One of the services was the postal service that he needed to send news of his activities to his family in Bandera and receive news of his family there. The Arkland Stage line, whose station is under the management of station-keeper Chauncey Wilson, is the entity contracted by the U.S. Postal Service to deliver mail in Beaton and the surrounding area. Chauncey has taken the Oath of Mail Contractors and Carriers and, being of advanced age, depends upon his daughter, Macy to assist in his duties. Chauncey and Macy reside in a small cottage behind the Arkland Stage line's facility in Beaton.

Today, young Maverick Caiden is riding aback Biscuit, a horse that he trained personally under the direction of Lytle's expert horse trainer, Charlie Hale. When Mav left the drive in Ogallala, he purchased the horse out of the Lytle remuda selecting Biscuit because of a special affection Maverick had for Biscuit and knowing that, as a one-person horse, he is less useful to other riders. Biscuit had demonstrated a temperamental nature and simply would not permit others to ride him.

Eugene Stonefield

It is nearly a year later, and as he rides toward Beaton, Mav recalls his first visit to the Arkland Stage line office shortly after his arrival to post a letter to his ma and pa to let them know his whereabouts. That visit had resulted in his meeting Chauncey's daughter, Macy, who was substituting for her father and distributing mail received on the last Arkland stagecoach into postal boxes for the residents of Beaton. As Maverick stepped to the counter, ambient noise had prevented Macy, from hearing Mav's arrival, and as Macy placed the last letter in its proper box and turned to face the counter, her hand accidentally swept an uncapped inkwell across the counter onto Mav where it began its indelible stain waist to boot. Mav paused to watch the flow of blackness down his pant leg, then looking up at the horrified Macy, and found himself face to face with his future. He could not have known it then, but if the truth were told, Macy did.

"I…I'm so sorry, Mr.…Mr.…" stuttered Macy, while her eyes transfixed those of Maverick, who endured their power for but a minute before replying:

"No harm done, Ma'am. These here ain't my Sunday-go-to-meetin' duds, nohow. An', my name is Maverick Caiden, an' I'm a-hankerin' to hav' a mailbox, ifn you don't mind."

Macy, keeping her gaze steady, asked: "Are you new to Beaton, Mr. Caiden?"

"Yes, ma'am. I reckon I am. I bought th' Mallory place 'bout six miles out," while thinking: 'Where did those eyes come from? And that hair.' Immediately, Maverick turned scarlet, sensing an unease that was not familiar to him, a feeling as if he was violating some unwritten rule, then nervously repeated: "I jes' come to post this here letter to my folks an' rent me a mailbox."

"Certainly," answered Macy, "I will assign you postal box number sixty. That will be one dollar for the first six months. If you would please sign on this form." Macy looked at the completed form, then said: "I've never met anyone named Maverick, mind telling me how you came by that name since I thought maverick defines a wayward person who is unruly. Is your name a family name or something?" Macy gives Mav a questioning look.

"Well, 'wayward' does kinda fit, as far as I hav' larn'd," returned Mav. "Thar is a story about it down Texas way. A cattleman by th' name o' Maverick — thet wuz his last name — had this here large herd thet ranged south of San Antonio to th' coast. Twicest each year th' cattlemen aroun' San Antonio held roundups together to collect th' unbranded calves an' brand 'em ifn th' owner wuz known. Ifn th' calf wuz already weened frum its mother, th' calf's owner couldn't be figger'd. Thet's when th' finders-keepers rule wuz used. But durin' th' war betwixt th' states, hirin' cowboys wuz hard, an' Sam Maverick couldn't brand-up them found cattle, an' folks 'round San Antonio an' south to th' coast knowed he couldn't, so started assumin' them unbranded cattle wuz th' property o' Sam's or had been so, so began callin' any unbranded cow a 'maverick.' Wunst thet name wuz giv' to any unbranded cattle, it wuz sorta natural thet folks would come to name a boy child, Maverick, cause thet child is like some unbranded wild thing." [1] Mav went silent.

"Wild thing, huh?" replied Macy.

The posted letter to his parents in Bandera was to inform them of his intended visit within a month, the time required to travel from Beaton to Bandera. Mav arrived back at the cabin before sundown with an expectation of leaving for Bandera the next day. He will travel with most of his possessions, the sum being Biscuit, a western saddle with a blanket also for Biscuit, a bridle with reins for Biscuit, a hat for Mav, saddlebags, a bedroll, tarpaulin, two blankets, one war bag, foul weather poncho, saddle holster for his Henry, an 1847 Colt Walker six-shooter with holster, boots, two pair of pants, one leather vest, gloves, bandanna, four shirts, several pair of socks, two pair of long johns and several pair of short drawers, braces, and one lariat. Also, Mav would take the necessary food, or 'chuck' in the language of the trail.

With those trail necessities, Mav set out the next day to travel to Bandera, the town of his upbringing and a home he has not visited in several years. As he rides, he wonders just how big his brother and sister have become now, and he rides with great anticipation. He knows that he, himself, has filled out a great deal since he left Bandera and has gained weight. Mav feels that he is a man now, not the way he felt when he left the home place. 'Ma and Pa may not recognize me,' he muses, trying to imagine how they will look to him. 'Will they appear older? Will they be turning gray? What will they think about me?'

Mav recalls the last advice his papa gave him before he left home: "Son, when I left Carolina, I went to New Orleans, not really a-knowing whut I wanted to do. I found three things: yor mama, freedom to make my own choices, an' thet leaving yor roots is hard to do. Yor mama's folks wuz plantation folks. My folks grew goobers an' corn. We both knew farming, an' Texas was th' frontier whar a man could do whut he wuz a-wantin' to do. I want no less fo' you. To choose yor own way in life is true freedom. But, Maverick, you won't be able to avoid yor roots. Farmin' is in yor soul, know it or not. Go an' foller th' trail with Lytle, larn all you can o' life, then find yorsel' a wife and settle down. An' don't worry 'bout us. We will be fine. I'm still strong an' yor brother is getting strong enough to hep with th' chores."

Nor was his ma silent when he was leaving. Her advice was to stay away from saloons where there is gambling and dancehall girls to turn a boy's head. Keep to the ways they taught him at home and in church. Keep to the narrow path. Her last words were: "Come home when you can," she said, wiping tears from her eyes.

Mav Caid — The Complete Story

He relives the twenty-five days riding twenty-five miles each day toward his destination bringing Mav to the barbed wire gate across the narrow path leading around a hill to the home place. Mav dismounts and walks to the gate to lift the wire loop from the 'belly-buster' latch, a short piece of wood whose ends secure the wire gate to the cedar gatepost by looped wire at the top and bottom. Anyone whose grip on the gate has faltered after lifting the top loop from a tensioned wire gate and experienced the jolt of the loosed end against an unsuspecting torso understands the designation of 'belly-buster.'

His anticipation grows as he leads Biscuit through the opening and re-latches the gate across the path. Remounting, Mav sets Biscuit in a canter toward the house. The sight before him as he rounds the bend is distressing and traumatic. Rather than a familiar farmhouse with wraparound porch and curtains blowing through open windows, he sees only rubble, the remains of a burned-out house and barn. With growing despair, Mav dismounts Biscuit and walks around the burned remains of his history. At first, he scans all around for sight of some temporary structure where his family may be occupying after some obvious tragedy. He discovered none. He knows he will have to ride into Bandera and seek the sheriff to gain some understanding of what he has found. As he prepares to ride out, his eyes fall upon the small family cemetery in the distance that looks different from what he recalls. He starts to mount Biscuit, then decides to walk. It was a walk of sorrow as he approached and counted the number of crosses standing where just one stood before. Erected white crosses named and marked the eternal resting place of his ma, his pa, his sister and his brother, and another without a name. Mav stood before the wooden memorials, standing upon graves that had already collapsed and were almost level with the surrounding ground. He had no explanation, no comprehension of the cause; he had only the rude shock of unexpected discovery. After the passing of an hour, Mav mounted Biscuit and rode out to find the sheriff in Bandera.

"Sheriff Partin, I'm Maverick Caiden."

"Maverick Caiden," repeated the sheriff. "You belong to the Caiden family who is now deceased. Is that right?"

"Yessir. I jes' come from th' home place an' they are all gone." Mav shook the sheriff's hand.

"I'm guessing you would like to know what happened," began the sheriff. "Truth is, we don't know for sure what happened. A neighbor saw smoke from the place and went to investigate. By the time he got there, the house and barn both had nearly burned to the ground. I looked around some, but couldn't be sure how your folks died until Doc Monroe came to pronounce them deceased and noticed the bullet wounds. The bodies were charred. We don't know who the fifth person is. He could even be the killer who died in the assault. We just don't know. We did what we could at the time. It is a real tragedy. You may want to talk to Preacher Branch at the Baptist church. He told me someone had given him some things that belong to you."

Mav rode to the church and tied the reins to the hitching post, then went inside where he found the preacher placing new hymnals out for the next Sunday. Removing his hat, Mav said: "Howdy, Preacher Branch. I'm Maverick Caiden, and I jes' come from th' sheriff's office. He tol' me you had somethin' fo' me."

"Mr. Caiden," began Preacher Branch, I am so sorry for the loss of your family. It is a true shame what happens to people sometimes."

"Yessir," returned Mav. "I'm a-wantin' to larn who wuz responsible whilst I'm here."

After a few minutes discussing the event, Preacher Branch left for a few minutes then returned with a package which he gave to Mav. "This here was found under a dead horse near the barn. I suspect it should go to you, being as you are the heir.

"Yessir. I'm th' only heir," returned Mav, taking the package from the preacher.

"Now, since you have not gone through anything like this before, I feel obligated to mention that you will have to speak with the county judge about the property. You will need him to certify your right to the property before it can be transferred into your name." Preacher Branch then asked: "Perhaps I could offer a prayer for the departed, now that you are here to join me."

Mav shook his head that it was ok to have a prayer offered for his family and bowed his head as the preacher offered the prayer. As Preacher Branch began his prayer, Mav experienced the strange sensation of emotional disconnectedness that often accompanies instances of sudden loss. The preacher's voice rose and fell in volume without adding understanding or assuaging the growing feeling of aloneness now felt by Mav Caid, the orphan. He sensed himself an outsider looking in at a scene that perplexed and discomforted. Upon finishing, Mav thanked the preacher and returned to Biscuit.

Mav did what Preacher Branch advised and spoke with the judge who referred him to a lawyer to handle the paperwork. Mav spoke again with Sheriff Partin, asking him how he thought the killings happened and discussed several possibilities, such as an attack by renegade Indians, Mexican banditos, robbers and finally, Sheriff Partin said he would notify Mav by letter when he knew more. He accomplished all these activities with little cognizance of accomplishment. With nothing more to do, Maverick Caiden left his address with all those who needed to know how to write to him and returned to the trail back to Beaton.

Chapter 2

A Maverick Returns

Under a brilliant sapphire sky flaunting its hue behind the marshmallow clouds adrift, Mav rode up to the hitching rail outside the Arkland office, and dismounted from his sorrel gelding, Biscuit, and threw the reins across the rail. For the people of Beaton, Mav Caid is a tabula rasa, a blank page yet to be written upon. His nature unknown. Today, for one citizen of Beaton, begins the filling of that page.

As he entered the local Arkland office, Mav saw Station-keeper Chauncey Wilson sorting the recently received mail into the several letterboxes behind the counter. Mav looked beyond Chauncey to his personal box, which was empty. Knowing what he knows now, it is not unexpected. The only letter that could have been there is a letter in answer to his to his ma and pa that he was coming to visit. There was no such letter posted, he supposed, or they never lived to receive his. For a moment, Mav suffered a pang of conscience, a feeling that somehow, he had betrayed them by not being there in their time of need. He turned to leave but the soft musical voice of Macy Wilson who was entering from the back room halted his leaving.

"Mornin' Mav. We haven't seen you lately. Too busy to visit us or just gone for a spell?" she asked, being the only one in Beaton with awareness enough to note his absence.

"Gone for a spell, Miss Wilson. Back now. Things normal 'round here?" answered Mav with a side glance at Macy whose sea-green eyes demanded the attention of any warm being that fell under their sway for the briefest moment. Mav was not unaware of their unsettling power and made an effort not to engage in direct contact for the unease they unleashed in the mind of this private man.

Macy sensed Mav's obvious reluctance to engage in anything but momentary eye contact but failed in her attempts to understand why. Was it only shyness? Why did he always look away? Am I so unappealing? Did he hide some deep secret that would explain his discomfort? Does he have a wife somewhere? She couldn't say what it was and that intrigued her more than anything else. Maybe it was just that he defied characterizing as this kind of person or that kind who behaves this way or that way. She wanted the opportunity to be with him more so she could explore Mav Caid more closely, and finally solve the riddle of Mav Caid. It would also be the opportunity to discover the mystery about herself - of why she cared. What did she know about him? Hardly anything at all. Well, only that he is tall, at least six-foot in height, broad shoulders, muscular arms, medium brown shoulder-length hair, hazel eyes, clean shaven, bronzed skin, commanding chin, ungodly handsome. But that's the physical. Beyond that, what did she know? His speech, his drawl is out of the heart of Texas. Is he intelligent? What is his past? Can he love? Or, more specifically, can he love me?

Macy is two months beyond eighteen and still unmarried. She is not desperate to find a mate, but she is not unaware that people are wondering why they have seen no courtship from anyone. Perhaps her criteria are too lofty for many to vault, some say. Too high a requirement in a prospective mate can lead to spinsterhood, others say. But no one thought Macy to be cold to romance, and everyone liked her sunny disposition and assertiveness.

Today, in a just realized acknowledgment to herself, she contemplates strategy. How does she gain more attention from Mav Caid? She considered a demure approach but discarded that idea when she realized that if his is shyness, two with the same mien will not likely find the level of amity that she believed she may want. He may not respond to anyone he isn't around often and just turn away. But, being too flirtatious risks the chance that a girl gets the label of wanton. What would be his reaction to a girl who others may perceive wantonness to be her character? What does he think of me now? The more honest, unassuming posture would be best, she decides if she can initiate it and stay with it. Be friendly and helpful. Show enough assertiveness to show self-confidence but not so much as to infer superiority. Above all, be patient! In that, there was no guarantee given her self-assured nature. Of course, on the other hand, she thinks, 'a little aggressiveness never hurt in a girl's stalking of an objective.' Macy wouldn't characterize it as stalking, instead just showing interest in a new person in her sphere who is not someone she has grown up with in Beaton. Mav was the mysterious unknown, therefore, exciting. Finally, putting aside those special considerations, she brushed back her auburn hair and advanced toward Mav.

"Why, about as much excitement as watching red paint dry on a barn," Macy replied, smiling, then continuing, "although, Sheriff Bonney did have to arrest Mitchell Ormsby again for shooting up the ceiling of Charlie's stable. And, by the way, just call me Macy."

"Drunk again?" returned Mav while moving closer to the door. "I've heard stories."

"Not more than very. Mitchell has a history of drinking and picking fights. He's quite a bully. And Molly Avers, she's getting hitched to Sid Kincheloe and moving to Pea Ridge where he is taking over the family farm. Oh, and we have two new residents who have moved into the old Horace Mitchel place, down the road."

"New residents? What are they like? Have you seen them?" Mav asked while keeping his voice level so as not to show too much interest.

"Two men. A man about forty and his brother, I think, about age thirty-five. They look like anyone else around here. I don't know about any women. I think they are by themselves." Macy completes her answer as she responds to an inner urge to get closer to Mav.

Mav glanced up at Macy who had come around the counter to continue the conversation and was now inside his personal zone which, to Mav, had a radius of five feet.

"I'm a-thinkin' I'll git some mail soon, Miss, uh, Macy. Might you tell yor pa an', mayhap, he might could send someone to tell me when it arrives, ifn I don't come in within a few days? It's sorta important." Mav edged closer to the door and turned to exit.

"I'll tell him," Macy said, thinking that such an event was indicative of a change that, itself, heightened the intrigue in an otherwise dull life of the daughter of the station-keeper of Beaton. "By the way, here's a copy of the Beaton Gazette if you care to take one."

As Mav mounted Biscuit, he heard Macy shout to her father that Mav was expecting a delivery and wanted to know when it comes. Receiving no response from her father, Macy shouts louder: "I said, Mav is getting a delivery, so let me know, and I will take it to him when it comes!"

Chapter 3

Mystery of the Diary / The Grief of Bandera

Mav turned his horse south and rode past the various businesses that have endeavored to serve the needs of the town's citizens for longer than Mav has been in Beaton. Those businesses were of the typical kind for a village like Beaton, a general store, blacksmith and livery, saloon, law office, barber, physician, mercantile, bakery, feed store, an apothecary that was in competition with Edna at the general store, and a weekly newspaper. Improvements to the post roads to and from Beaton resulted in the Arkland Stage-line becoming the primary method of communicating with communities beyond.

Representing the religious community are three churches, notably, First Baptist, Methodist, and Church of Christ. In all, Beaton is a quiet town of about eight hundred residents, and the local weekly Beaton Gazette struggles to find news to report and fills its pages with whatever publisher Wallace Zentner can dig up to cover the white newsprint. Wallace receives other newspapers from around the country through the mail, and a good portion of news printed in the Gazette is an understandably delayed reprinting of news taken from those subscriptions. Zentner reprints news from the State Government primarily from the Arkansas Gazette published by William Woodruff in Little Rock. New residents always represent fodder for the Beaton Gazette. Mav expects that the newcomers will have half a page devoted to their story printed in the next edition of the Gazette. He makes a mental note to pick one up next Thursday.

Three miles out of town, Mav turns his horse toward the old Horace Mitchel place with a quiet order to Biscuit, his trusted cutting horse that he trained from its wildness one year ago. This achievement was an accomplishment that Mav was proud to claim, considering that his roots were in farming and the training of a cutting horse was a far stride from farming. Mav rebukes himself softly for making this side journey. Those in his past who might seek to harm were most likely far away and will not know where he is anyway. But there were threats made. Mav and Biscuit approached the house cautiously from the covering of the pine thicket just north of the house but stayed within its cover. Dismounting, Mav looks for activity but sees nothing. After twenty minutes, the door opens, and two men exit the house and move to the covered porch. They seem to be in an animated conversation, but they are too far away for Mav to hear their conversation. It is enough to know that they are strangers to him. That he can discern from a distance, so remounting Biscuit, Mav doubles back to the main road and heads home to his cabin four miles further south.

They arrive in a short time and, after a quick look around, both rider and horse approach the barn where Mav unbridles Biscuit and removes the saddle and blanket. He immediately waters Biscuit and treats him to a brushing then gives him his oat feed. Mav walks the twenty yards to the front door and enters, a fresh pot of coffee on his mind.

Mav Caid — The Complete Story

It felt good to be back in his comfortable cabin. It is also good that it hasn't become a warm shelter for anyone else who might have wandered by while he was gone. So many have been on the move since the war between the north and the south that any seemingly empty cabin has become an enticement to squatter and fugitive alike. Reconstruction, which added to the migration issue, ended just a decade ago, and many of the state governments are still in the process of rebuilding. Resettling of the native tribes on reservations has encouraged the movement of people from the east into areas previously considered unsafe, though these are still troubled times in some areas of the frontier.

Mav replaced his rifle in its rack near the door and moved his saddlebag to the table where he opened it and removed a sealed package. Taking his bowie knife, Mav carefully slit the binding tape and opened the package. Inside lay a bound diary, mud-stained and with a cover partially detached from the pages. Lettered in large, carefully crafted letters the title: <u>Diary of Wendell Forda, Captain, 4th Cavalry, USA</u>. For a few minutes, Mav allowed himself to stare at the cover before opening it to the written pages. Within the pages of this diary is the answer to a mystery and possibly the reason for his personal grief. The sheets appeared the same in size and texture, and the lettering looked familiar. Is it possible that they would match?

Rising from his chair, Mav walked to the pot-bellied stove where the coffee pot with the boiled coffee summonsed by its fragrance and poured a cup. Returning to the table, Mav placed the cup down and proceeded to the small rock fireplace where he removed a stone from above the rough-hewn cedarwood mantel. Reaching into the void, Mav retrieved a leather wallet and returned to the table. From the wallet, he removed a couple of pieces of paper that he compared to the pages of the diary. In his hand were two pages, possibly taken from this very diary. Two pages of unknown import which he had received several years ago in such a strange manner that he retained them folded in his wallet. He recalled that it was on his birthday his mother gave him a package addressed to Maverick Caiden from her brother. It contained the two pages, one of which had a hand-drawn map, and four unusual rocks which his mother said she would explain to him when she found out herself from a letter she expected to receive from a brother. That explanation never came, either because the message never came or she forgot to tell him. But to a young boy, a mysterious map stimulated an imagination of some buried treasure just waiting for him to find. He recalled burying the rocks pretending they were a pirate's treasure then forgetting where he hid them. In his mind, the mysterious map hinted at something valuable enough to document but not sufficiently described to give certainty of its location or nature.

Whatever its character, the map alone presumed an intention to return at some future time to explore it. On the second page was the beginning of instructions on how to interpret the map. Only the phrase 'from Indian Territory and Fort Sill go east to approx. Long…' could he read easily, the rest of the text either indecipherable or meaningless. The one curious thing about the first page of the map was three small ink-filled triangles at the leftmost edge of the page left ragged from being torn from a bound book of some kind. Between these triangles, drawn lines pointed to four unidentifiable symbols at four points on the map. The other page had no such markings. Mav set the two pages aside and began to read the diary that began with the commissioning of Captain William Forda into the service of the United States Cavalry, a service that would last for five years under the command of Colonel Ranald Slidell Mackenzie at Fort Richardson in Jacksboro, Texas. Captain Forda was with Colonel Mackenzie in the Battle of Blanco Canyon and the Battle of the North Fork of the Red River upon the Llano Estacado but had resigned his commission sometime after that and disappeared from the land of the Comanche.

Several years have passed since his disappearance. Mav had never met the captain that he could recall but understood that he was his uncle, given that his mother's family name was also Forda. Mav inspected the diary cursorily looking for a location that would accommodate the two loose pages among the written upon which could shine light upon the symbols and lines on the map. In this, he was unsuccessful. Nevertheless, he did note that several pages had been torn from among the blank pages near the end of the diary, pages torn out and possibly used to pass information on to someone in a note. Perhaps that is where the map pages were torn from. As he fingered the pages and tested the texture and thickness of the paper, he became increasingly confident that his map came from this diary. Somewhere in this diary is the key to comprehension. Presently, Mav began to read the slanted cursive of Captain William Forda.

[Diary entry for August 12, 1871. Colonel Mackenzie has ordered Major Grierson to mount an incursion into Comancheria to confront recalcitrant Khotsoteka and Quahadi bands of Comanche warriors causing trouble in Texas and territory west. These bands are out of compliance with the standing order to the Comanche to relocate to the Fort Sill reservation in Oklahoma territory following the Warren wagon train raid of May 18 on the Salt Creek. I am to accompany Grierson in this endeavor. This action is to show force and to punish those who refuse to obey that lawful order just as Satana, Satank, and Ado-ete will receive punishment for their part in that wagon train massacre at Salt Creek. They must comply, or they will hang, according to Mackenzie. The Comanche problem must cease. The powers in Washington have mandated it. The pressure of the western migration of settlers pushing beyond the protective chain of military fortresses across the western frontier rings loudly in the ears of powerful people in Washington, and they are not shy in passing that pressure down to the commanders on the frontier. Settlers want the security to establish homesteads in Texas and avoid attacks by renegade bands of natives. Much of the mischief would mitigate if the Comancheros in New Mexican territory and west Texas were not supplying a bad mix of liquor, weapons, and ammunition to the Comanches and other tribes of the plains. Not so long ago, the Comanche and the Cibolero buffalo hunters were happy with hunting the buffalo. They have hunted the Llano Estacado for centuries, when the buffalo were plentiful. Their method was to kill by lance, or stampede buffalo over cliffs to kill them and supply their needs. Today, the white buffalo hunters roam the plains to kill the buffalo with long rifles for the hides alone, leaving the skinned buffalo to lie in the sun in their pinkness to rot. Is it any wonder that the natives hate these hunters? They are killing the food source of the natives, wastefully. Clashes between the natives and the white hunters must add to the sources of weapons and ammunition the natives acquire. If it is the policy of Washington to starve the Indians, it is a wrong-headed policy that I cannot condone. I was foolish to have left my life on the sea for this.]

✳✳✳

Mav's pathway to maturity was like many young boys smitten with the romance of trailing cattle to markets in the north. His upbringing taught him farming. He wanted excitement. Lytle gave him the opportunity to grow as a man. Mav began working with horses, becoming expert in managing the remuda and learned to train them under guidance of Charley Hale. Eventually, he became a full-fledged drover, complete with experience beginning with riding drag, the dusty job at the back of the heard, and after three years working as a drover, Lytle appointed Mav *Segundo*, second to Lytle's foreman, 'Cinch' Pendergast. Although Pendergast was in charge, Lytle sometimes went along to execute contracts for future drives.

After five years of gaining knowledge and skills, he left the Lytle outfit and eventually found himself in Beaton. Having the money to buy some acreage and build a cabin at such a young age, suggests he is not a poor man. Mav has money in the Beaton bank. He has pretty much lived off the land since, hunting and fishing and using his time to clear the twenty acres of trees and undergrowth. Although he has met many of the farmers and ranchers around Beaton, he has no close friends in Beaton, and he wonders from time to time if his solitudinous life might be a pathway to future regret. Maybe he should participate more in the activities in the town, a thought that surfaced now and then but never seriously contemplated to the point of doing something about it. Thoughts of the future were ephemeral, never lasting long. He lived in the present, and that was enough for him. He was not an unfriendly man, just one that does not warm quickly to new acquaintances. In the time he has been in Beaton, only one person has penetrated his thoughts enough to shape them in the least. "Thet filly, Macy, at the Arkland Stage line office is a real purdy gal, a real looker," he has said to himself and to his confidant, Biscuit, but has done nothing to say more than, "Howdy, Miss Wilson," in his Texas drawl, and ask for his mail.

Time moves on even for Mav Caid, and by today he is well experienced as a cowhand but is longing for something in his past that is unresolved. He will not return to that life. Awakening to these unsettling feelings, and not having heard from his ma and pa for a time, last year he returned home to visit his family he was so anxious to leave just after his seventeenth birthday. The trip did not go well and it haunts him still. To his sorrow, he found five upright crosses on collapsed graves not far from the charred remains of the modest farmhouse of the home-place of his youth. Each cross displayed a name - one each for his pa, Elmer, his ma, Celine, brother, Travis and Sara, his sister. The other cross had no name.

In Bandera, Sheriff Partin had offered his condolences and thoughts relating to the deaths as a possible renegade attack, and Preacher Branch gave him the few items found in the ruins after the fire, one of which was the diary found in a saddlebag under a dead horse. Preacher Branch could not explain how the diary survived the inferno nor recall who had found it and passed it on to him for safekeeping should Mav return. Everyone in Bandera knowing the Caiden family had expected Mav to sow a little wild-oats and return home to continue farming with his pa. Now, home is Beaton. His trip had been painful, especially learning how his younger brother Travis and still younger sister Sara died from such savagery. He knew his papa would have put up a strong fight and his ma could handle a rifle with the best, so he expected they went down fighting. The identity of the fifth person in the grave without a name is puzzling and the sheriff suggested, could even be the killer himself who could have died from injuries received from the defenders. Someday it may be known.

Initially, as he learned of the tragedy, he became saddened and enraged at the unknown killers. His first inclination was to believe their killers were renegade Apache or Comanches. Many attacks have happened over the years on the frontier and even though Cochise made his peace years ago and moved to the reservation in the Chiricahua mountains and has since died. Goyaalé, or Geronimo, medicine man of the Bendonkohe, in alliance with other bands of the Chiricahua Apache nation, is rumored to be hiding somewhere in Mexico with a strength of seven hundred braves. His fleeing from his reservation was reportedly because of a Washington policy change that required the people of his reservation to move to the San Carlos reservation in Arizona territory. Where in Mexico is his band of warriors? And then there is Victorio. Where is he? Could he and his warriors have come east to the border between Texas and Mexico? Texas is Comanche territory. Could or would any of them mount a raid so far as Bandera? How many are there? And, only a raid on one farm didn't make sense. Maybe a small band was passing through and seeking to join Apache Geronimo or Victorio, or to join renegade Comanches. Yet, there seemed to be no corroborating evidence. No Indian weapons, no scalping, nothing to support a conclusion that natives were involved. Possibly Mexican banditos fleeing the Texas

Rangers makes better sense. It could even be an attempted robbery by some outlaw gang. Who will ever know other than the perpetrators themselves? Without a specific entity to rage against, his anger devolved into the blackness of despair and feelings of insufficiency and numbness.

People are supposed to grieve the deaths of loved ones. What is grief? He doesn't know, and he wonders when he will begin to grieve for the family that he now feels that he abandoned. He grieves now, he just doesn't know it, nor can he avoid it. Grieving comes, and there is nothing that intensifies grief more than a visitation of memories. He will relive those memories and regret leaving, regret the time lost being with them. He will come to blame himself, believing that he could have protected them had he been there. He will know all stages: disbelief and shock, denial, anger, self-blame, depression – some that he has already felt. At times he will try to bargain the event away. He will feel anger toward God, whom he has considered a friend and protector since childhood. Finally, he will accept what he cannot change.

To shake from a growing feeling of despondency, Mav picks up the Gazette and reads a few items of interest. Susan B. Anthony opened a Congress for Women's Rights on March 25, 1888, and in April the International Council of Women assembled to promote human rights for women. Also, in April, the Texas State Capitol building opened in Austin at an astounding cost of three million dollars. Benjamin Harrison and Levi P. Morton won nominations for President and Vice-President. In New York, engineer B.C. Miller moved an entire hotel over five hundred feet utilizing six steam locomotives. From the News from Abroad section, he reads the Buffalo Bill Cody's Wild West Show has performed for Queen Victoria in London in celebration of the Queen's Jubilee year. Cody will be taking his show to Europe for tours there this year. In London, a strike began by local matchgirls protesting the dismissal of three co-workers

Eugene Stonefield

from the Bryant and May match factory, presumably for interviews on working conditions at the factory they gave to journalist Annie Besant. A serial killer, known by the nickname of Jack the Ripper, plagues London. His targets of choice are the night ladies of London. So far, Mary Ann Nichols, Annie Chapman, Elizabeth Stride, and Catherine Eddowes have succumbed to his brutal attacks. There are no witnesses or suspects. Setting aside the Gazette, Mav went to the barn to check on Biscuit, then turned in for the night.

Chapter 4

A Visitor's Soft Interrogation

Autumn was quietly approaching, and the trees were beginning to turn to their unique color from their various shadings of green. Hardwood trees of different types can be depended upon to provide enough splendor across the landscape and to instill awe in anyone with a modicum of sensitivity to the beauty of nature. Mav had more than a fraction, so was subject to urges to stand before the colorful vista and admire its beauty. Today he was engaged by just such a call and was standing upon his small porch outside the cabin's front door watching several Mississippi kites soaring on unseen currents of air above the changing trees when he heard a friendly: "Hullo, the cabin," shouted from a distance.

The voice was the voice of a woman. Mav stepped off the porch in the direction of the call, shouting back: "Over here, come on ahead," and recognized the auburn hair of Macy Wilson falling from under a wide-brimmed hat to embrace the shoulders that were clad in the gingham dress he had first seen her wear as he returned from his sad trip home. Her locks seemed to be two feet long and swept back and forth across her bosom as she cantered up, sidesaddle on a roan mare. He was unprepared for the feelings the sight of Macy encroaching into his personal sanctuary engendered. In one way he felt threatened, by what, he didn't know. In another way, only exhilaration would explain the feeling. Macy reached the cabin in short order and dismounted, dropping the reins to the ground in front of Penny, her mare.

"Good morning, Mav." Macy ventured her greeting with a smile and glance at the angles of shadow to assure herself it was morning still. "I was mighty sure I had the right place but called out just in case I was wrong. Didn't want anyone to start shooting at me thinking the wrong thing."

"I cain't imagin' anyone shootin' at you Macy! They'd hav' to be plumb loco." Mav moved toward Macy but stopped five feet away. "I boiled a fresh pot o' Arbuckle's an' was a-fixin' to pour some. Do you drink coffee?" Inwardly, Mav marveled that he could be so bold as to ask if she wanted coffee.

"I do, and have been thirsty for a cup," Macy replied while removing her hat to display her beautiful crown of color in full competition with the colorful trees. Her green eyes focused steadily on Mav whose own eyes met them briefly before dropping.

"I'll fetch a couple o' chairs to th' porch then git th' coffee. Feel free to water yor horse. I'll jes' be a short spell." Mav turned quickly and went inside to accomplish his stated tasks as Macy led Penny to the trough of water.

As Penny began to drink, Macy returned to the porch where two unmatched chairs awaited occupants and took a seat. As she waited for Mav to bring the coffee, she cast a glance at the surrounding acres of cleared land and noted a sizeable vacant expanse of level land about twenty yards from the house and thought: 'how nice a garden would look there.' Turning in another direction, Macy thought: 'over there would be a great place for a chicken coop,' then wondered why her thoughts dwelled upon such things. Wondered why her heart beat so strangely as Mav stepped from the cabin with two cups of coffee. She felt as if she had been running.

"Mav," she began, "I've mail for you that came yesterday and the Gazette from last week. Seems some lawyer sent you a letter from Bandera County down in Texas. I'm thinking it is what you were expecting."

Looking at the sender's name and return address, Mav replied: "It shor is, Macy. Jes' a land deed." Mav shuffled his feet but offered no other explanation. Finally, after an awkward silence, he sat down next to Macy, perhaps as close to her as he has ever been, and unavoidable, considering the smallness of the porch. A sudden move by Macy, were it to occur, might be enough to bring him out of the chair with equal suddenness, such was his anxiety. Amid his nervousness though, was a sense of comfort, a feeling that enduring happiness was near.

"How's th' Arbuckle," he asked with some nervousness in his voice. Being the host was not something he had experience in and engaging in small-talk with a woman was not a developed skill. Sitting next to beauty was not within his experience.

"Coffee's good," responded Macy as she lifted the cup for another sip. It would have been good had it been kerosene. "I never had a chance to ask if your last trip – which I assume was to visit family – if your trip to Bandera was good." Macy purposefully looked out at Penny so not to look directly at Mav but quickly looked back to assess his reception of so intrusive a question. She sought to avoid any perception that her inquiry was anything other than small-talk but desired greatly to learn anything he might be willing to reveal willingly or unwillingly. His receiving a deed to property must mean he purchased a place that he intends to go to at some point or has acquired it through an inheritance, which also could say he may be leaving. Macy felt a slight chill rising from that thought. She had looked forward to bringing Mav's mail to him. The notion that it could mean he was leaving placed a dark cloud in Macy's mind. For a moment, she suffered a chill and shivered.

"Well, I.., not so good, Macy. Family's all gone." His face revealed more than he would have intended had he had more control, but the suddenness of the question took him by surprise, and his native honesty forced the revelation that had plagued his mind since he returned. His family was indeed, gone. He was alone with the knowledge that he could not bring himself to share with anyone even if he had someone to share it with. Now he has shared it in some part with someone who unsettles his thoughts.

"Oh," interjected Macy, not certain if it meant they had left for some other place or if a more tragic meaning is meant. Her reading of his face confirmed the latter. She sensed that she must probe carefully for more information if she wanted to avoid making Mav feel that it was an interrogation. Hesitatingly, she asked: "Are you thinking of moving back down there?"

"No, no need." Mav looked down at his boots and said no more. Macy's dark cloud swept away.

"Mav," began Macy, strategically changing the subject, "the congregation is planning a picnic on the lake on Sunday. Might you be interested in coming in? You won't have to bring anything because I will be taking enough for two. Papa's not attending, and I thought it might be a good time for others to get to know you, and you to know them. The new residents will be coming. You don't have to decide now – just think about it. We would be honored if you would come."

Sensing that she had delivered her message and her stay had grown longer than propriety would suffer, she stood to leave.

"Well, I guess Penny has had her fill of water. The coffee was delicious. I'll leave you to your day. Please think about coming. I wish you would."

Mav Caid — The Complete Story

Mav, jumping to his feet stuttered: "Macy, uh, thanks fo' a-bringin' me my mail. I'll ponder 'bout th' picnic some." A strange feeling of loss crossed his mind as he realized this unexpected visit was ending. He didn't know how to react to his emotion, it was so unusual to feel loss when all that was happening was that his visitor was leaving. He has left family and friends behind, and drover and wrangler friends and trail bosses before and not felt a loss, indeed, often felt exhilaration at the thought of moving on to something or someplace new. He was feeling the loss of his family, but this was different. This feeling was uniquely disquieting, a feeling that merged his sense of abandonment with a fear that it was the last time. Even though he knew that all goodbyes may be forever as it was with his family in Bandera, he did not want to contemplate that when Macy rode off, it would be the last time he would see her. He watched Macy as she rode away, hair blowing, her shapely body riding comfortably, and he felt disquieting apprehension.

Returning to the house, Mav found his mind lingering on Macy's visit and found a reluctance to turn his thoughts to other matters. He picked up the cups to take back into the cabin and looked at Macy's cup, thinking, 'her lips touched this cup' then poured another cup of coffee into Macy's cup and returned to the porch to sit in Macy's chair. Finally, with his thoughts subsiding, he picked up the Gazette Macy had brought. He read that the two new residents of Beaton living in the old Horace Mitchel place are planning to open a sawmill on the site to provide sawn lumber to build houses and barns in and around Beaton. When asked why they chose Beaton for their business Carleton Graves, simply answered: "Why not? All thet wuz needed wuz timber an' warter!" to which his brother, Henson nodded his agreement with the answer in the typical reticence of a Texan to engage in lengthy explanations when short ones suffice. Further reading revealed that they recently moved from Nacogdoches, Texas, its oldest town, where they had a similar business for ten years which they sold when their contracts for timber dried up. Neither had wives or children. Their interests are working, fishing, and hunting.

Turning to the section reporting news from abroad, Mav read that Mary Jane Kelly, a woman whose profession of sweetheart for the hour, became another murder victim of Jack the Ripper in Whitechapel. This makes a total of five killings linked to the person who named himself Jack the Ripper in a letter called the Dear Boss letter he sent to London's Central News Agency. "All this killin'!" said Mav to himself. "Where might it all end?"

The problem with such a question is that there is only one answer, and that is that killing ends when there are no more people to kill. It is a sad tragedy of humanity that we have not learned how to live together with our differences and to reject the pervasive idea that objectionable differences deserve resolution by killing. We continually make victims of ourselves through our actions. Greed, power, lust, hate – the instigators of all bad behaviors. Only the most optimistic can believe that love and understanding will someday conquer. Mav is just such a man, believing that every person is worthy until they prove themselves otherwise, and believing there are more good people than bad. Yet he wonders how and when events will somehow – not right the wrong of his family's murder, for achieving that is not possible – but, bring some sense of the prevailing of justice over the injustice that occurred. He envisions the possible actions his parents may have taken as they were under attack in Bandera – actions they would have taken to protect his brother and sister and themselves. He imagines heroics that fell short of success in their efforts, and he wonders what would be his action were he in their position. Would he fight or flee? He hopes he will never have to find out.

For a time, Mav examines his thoughts and feelings on how he might behave were he faced with some life-threatening situation. From personal experience and what he has read in the Gazette, Mav knows that there are threats of many kinds surrounding people at every turn. Some are natural, such as tornados and flood, and people cannot address them in the same way that they address threats from other people. How is a person to protect himself or protect those he loves? Some people perform better than others when faced with a threat. What do they do that is different? Do they have more natural courage? More knowledge and skill? Can their greater success be the result of blind luck? Some people claim their success in a threatening situation is to have a good defense. Others say that they must employ a superior offence. Mav concludes that there is no guarantee that either strategy will infallibly produce a positive result. Either can fail. His childhood years imbued him with the concepts of the Golden Rule, to treat others as you would want them to treat you. But others don't follow that rule. He reasons that the better pathway is to avoid those situations, if possible, but if avoidance is not possible, employ as much calm reasoning as likely to be successful in structuring both a defense and an offense. Review the landscape of the threat, plan a reasonable counter to an attack, determine when changing from defense to offence is appropriate, and when the opportunity arises, counterattack with confidence and force.

Chapter 5

The Strategy of Picnics

Today is decision day, the day contemplated, put aside, reconsidered and finally, surrendered to as only a marginal introvert can do. Mav will make his decision whether to attend the picnic or make an excuse for staying home. But the hour being early, and with morning chores completed, there is time for diversion. He will first read more on his uncle Wendell's diary.

[Diary entry for Sept. 27, 1872: Pawnee Scouts have located the band sixteen miles south-southwest from our temporary encampment. They estimate their strength at ten Apache warriors with rifles, twenty armed with bows, and an equal number of women and children. Orders are to mount up for a nighttime ride to be in place for an early-morning raid. Perhaps today is the day of retribution. Colonel Grierson has given me the honor to be the first to engage the enemy when we reach their position. He doesn't mean I should meet them to negotiate a surrender. Reconnaissance has told us that there are women and children in their encampment. How can we justify raiding a camp with women and children present who are in danger of injury or death from the crossfire? What have women and children to do with the actions of the men? I have lately noted a growing sentiment among senior ranks holding that 'to break the men, break the women first.' I cannot subscribe to that policy.]

Mav closes the diary and sets it aside. Today is Sunday – picnic day in Beaton. He has been in a quandary for days trying to decide if he is ready to meet new people or even engage with those he already knows. And then there is Macy. Macy. How can he ignore her invitation without hurting her feelings? He thinks to himself, 'she has always been nice to me. What harm can come from picnicking with people of Beaton?' Still, they are basically strangers. Perhaps going won't be so bad. Maybe he will enjoy it. He recalls going to church picnics when he was a child. Perhaps it will be like that. Music and laughter and fun. Perhaps he should go. Eventually, his decision made, Mav mounts Biscuit for the trip to Beaton. As he arrives, he hears a pianist playing familiar tunes on a piano borrowed from a local church and taken to the bandstand near the lake where it joined an assortment of instruments.

"Mav! Over here!" shouts Macy as Mav rides up to the lakeside picnic site. "Join me! It's such a nice day!"

Mav dismounted and walked toward Macy who was wearing a long sleeve white dress with blue frilly tatted trim and a white bonnet tied under her chin. Mav recalls his ma tatting and crocheting and wonders if Macy had done the tatting, or if the work was that of her mother or grandmother. Macy held a blue umbrella in her hand and motioned to the handmade quilt spread upon the ground. "How was your ride in?" she asked while masking her pleasure at his coming.

"Tolerable," Mav replied, in keeping with his habit of not revealing much of his thinking. "Yor papa didn't come?" he asked, knowing that Macy previously said he would not attend but feeling a need to begin a conversation. His discomfort in doing so stemmed from his recognized inexperience in knowing what subjects might be of interest to a young lady. What was unknown to Mav is that it would not matter to <u>this</u> young lady, who would hang on every word and search each sentence for something that she could use to formulate another question and keep him talking about himself.

"No," she replied. "Papa doesn't like crowds much now that he can't hear the conversations. He's somewhat self-conscious."

"Yes. I savvy thet. My grandpappy wuz like thet. We all hav' our portion o' pride. I don't much cotton to crowds mysel'." Mav voluntarily surrendered his personal space to Macy who had moved almost within touching distance on the quilt. Mav inspected the quilt which is a wedding-ring pattern made of scraps of cloth from many worn-out shirts and dresses that Macy's mother had set aside for just such use. "I see children swimmin' in th' lake. Do you swim?" a marginally pertinent question but one that Mav would not know to be so.

"I have, but not in a long time," Macy stated, "I find it more a thing for children than for adults."

"Me too, 'specially when thar's othern 'round. Quiet places without all th' hoopla is more in keepin' with my druthers. Not much dif'runce twixt swimmin' and bathin' to my way o' figurin'," he added, thinking to himself, 'but with swimmin' with othern, one has to wear those gosh awful swimmin' suits!'

"Yes. My thought too." Macy conjured a mental image of Mav swimming in some quiet place as she silently looked on. Presently she added her own image swimming in that quiet place with Mav beside her. She imagined Mav coming closer and closer until he was almost touching, then he…. Sensing her face becoming warm with a growing blush, and shaking her head to rid herself of that suggestive image of Mav and herself swimming together in some isolated cove, Macy asked: "Mav, could I get you some lemonade?"

Eugene Stonefield

"Lemonade? Great! I ain't had no lemonade since Methuselah wuz born. I've plumb forgot about it. I recall my mama makin' lemonade fo' everybody. We used to go to church picnics at times. I near forgot 'bout th' hootin' an' hollerin' an' the fun afore you asked me to come. Y'all had a good idea. I reckon I am a-glad I come." Mav waited as Macy filled a dipper from the crock and filled a glass for him, then exclaimed: "Macy, when are we eatin'? I had me some breakfast before sunup in th' way of some eggs an' bacon an' grits, but I'm a-thinkin' I might be a might hungry again. I swan, I could stand me a taste o' some o' them banes an' chicken an' ribs."

There is an old saying that the way to a man's heart is through the stomach. Macy had internalized that adage and has cooked accordingly. Without a doubt, when it is not known the preferences of a man, it is prudent to prepare for anything. That she has done and owing to strategy and pre-planning, Macy has managed to guide that heart by helpfully loading Mav's plate with food of her own preparation, with few exceptions.

"Lordy! I've ne'er been so full," stated Mav as he rubs his stomach and leans back against a convenient maple tree. "My mama couldn't cook so well. You have outdone yorsel', Macy. Yor mama must've been a good cook to larn you so well. An' lordy! Thet rhubarb cobbler was somethin'. I swan, it wuz jes' larrupin'!"

"Well," returned Macy while privately enjoying exhilaration from the praise. "The picnic is a coming together of all the local folks, so some of the dishes you may have had could be from someone else," fully knowing that they consisted of the lemonade and that 'larruping' rhubarb cobbler, which she had to allow was good – just not hers – but something now on her list of skills to acquire. All else, she had made sure by excellent guidance and gentle suasion, was from her own efforts.

"Did you hav' some o' them banes, Macy?" asked Mav. "I've et many meals of banes alone whilst on th' trail an' I ain't ne'er had sech good banes!"

"Oh, Mav, I did. Those were my beans. I am so glad you liked them," returned Macy.

"Well, there wuz somethin' in them banes thet I didn't recognize. Might you tell me what you put in 'em to make them so cotton-pickin' good?" Mav asked, not realizing that he was touching a universal no-no.

"Won't say," responded Macy, lifting her chin in defiance.

"Why not?" asked Mav, somewhat flabbergasted at Macy's answer.

"Mav! An unmarried girl must have some secrets to take to her marriage. After all, it's different for a girl than for a man. A girl can't just order a husband like a man can order a bride from some catalog or wherever men order brides from. A girl must await the asking, and it is important that they have something special to offer. A girl needs to have some mystery about her, even if it's only her cooking." Suddenly, Macy realized her own faux pas in saying the word marriage to someone she must now admit, at least privately, that she is pursuing. Self-reproach troubled her thoughts.

"I don't rec'lect ever bein' tol' thet," replied Mav, a look of amazement in his eyes. "Are you a-plannin' to git hitched anytime?" Mav followed up with what he believed was a reasonable question.

"May someday, Mav, but a girl has to find the right person – one that she feels, in her heart, she can make happy and one who can make her happy. It takes a little strategy too, sometimes." Macy looked intently into Mav's eyes for a moment. He didn't look away.

"Have you foun' th' right man, Macy? I mean, ifn it won't trouble you none to tell me," Mav continued with what he believed was another reasonable question. He was unsure what answer he wanted to hear but was leaning toward wanting the answer to be no.

Eugene Stonefield

"Oh, I don't know, Mav. Time will tell, they say." Macy smiled at her inquisitor. Both went silent for a while as each sought to analyze any hidden meaning to the conversation. In the west, the sun is streaming golden spikes through the trees across the lake, and long fingers of reflected light interlace the cast shadows of the trees all shimmering on the glassy surface of the water. Various singers sang popular songs of the day such as <u>Beautiful Dreamer</u>, <u>I Gave My Love A Cherry</u>, <u>Skip to My Lou</u>, <u>Home Sweet Home</u>, and even the <u>Yellow Rose of Texas</u> to the delight of the audience.

Macy had listened attentively to the song, <u>Yellow Rose of Texas</u>, with rapt attention. What are they talking about, she wanted to know? Was she just a blond beauty of whom some smitten songwriter wanted to memorialize? Eventually, she leaned over to ask Mav: "Do you know about the Yellow Rose?"

"Yaller Rose? Well, my pa tol' me a story 'bout her when I wuz a boy on th' farm. Pa wuz a young boy o' seventeen in 1835 an' 36 when Santa Anna attacked th' defenders o' th' Alamo in San Antonio an' gave no quarters. Santa Anna's order wuz to pound th' walls with cannon an' mortar, then when th' wall wuz breached, to put ever man to th' sword. An' he had thousands o' soldiers around th' Alamo. Th' defenders wuz stayin' to fight when defeat wuz certain. Only one hundred an' eighty-three against five thousan' is poor odds even if thar wuz a wall betwixt them. Anyways, Sam Houston wuz gatherin' supporters o' th' revolution an' needin' time to recruit. All those folks at th' Alamo died, includin' William Travis, Davy Crockett, and Jim Bowie. He, my pa, wuz, as mos' wuz in Texas, angry over th' Goliad massacre as well, but Santa Anna had so many more soldiers thet, standing toe-to-toe in battle wuz, mayhap not gonna hav' a happy outcome. Folks could see thet what wuz commin' wuz like th' Goliad massacre, where over four hundred Texian captives includin' their commander, Colonel Fannin, from the battle of Coleto wuz put to death by a firin' squad an' th' wounded killed by knife or club by Santa

Anna. They wuz needin' a miracle or somethin' to change th' odds o' winnin'. Thet somethin' turned out to be a mulatto woman named Emily Morgan, as I rec'lect pa sayin'. Emily wuz beholden to th' wealthy James Morgan family, whar she gits thet name o' hern. She wuz prob'ly th' daughter o' a slave or freedwoman, he didn't know. Anyways, she, being mulatto, wuz called a 'high-yaller', which wuz to say, a black person who had light golden skin, an' wuz said quite beautiful. She wuz captured an' wuz spotted by Santa Anna an' he wuz smitten by her. Eventually, he brought her into camp as a, uh, special guest o' hisn. It wuz his dalliance with Emily thet delayed thet army o' hisn in a dangerous position down at th' San Jacinto River near Houston. Whilst Sam Houston 'massed th' troops o' hisn, Santa Anna wuz with Emily thet tent o' hisn eatin' choc'lates, an' those troops o' hisn wuz at siesta. Santa Anna's 'scape wuz blocked by th' Texian army led by Sam Houston, an' by th' San Jacinto River an' marshes. Houston's army wuz blocked by th' bayou behind an' Santa Anna in front, plus a burned bridge thet my pa tol' me Houston destroy'd hissel'. They hadta fight. Both sides had cannons which they used, then it wuz han'-to-han' fightin'. Santa Anna lost thet fight in only eighteen minutes an' fled th' battlefield. Pa said they found him th' nex' day wearin' th' uniform o' a simple Mexican soldier, an' a-holdin' a box o' choc'lates. No one has seen Emily Morgan since. Only th' song speaks o' her livin'. Mos' Texans, hold Emily in high esteem, even though her morality mayhap be questioned by some. Some say Emily is a ghost thet walks along th' river on quiet summer nights there, among th' stones of th' fallen at San Jacinto. Thet's whut my pa tol' me." For a moment Mav became pensive, then added: "I ken almost hear my pa singing about the Yaller Rose as he did his plowin'. Papa would sing:

    'Where the Rio Grande is flowing
    And the starry skies are bright
    Oh, she walks along the river

In the quiet summer night
And she thinks if I remember
When we parted long ago
I promised to come back again
And not to leave her so.'

Funny how one recalls little things like thet." Mav went silent, thinking of his murdered papa.

Macy was fascinated with the richness of his voice and wondered about songs he may know, wondering if a sweetheart somewhere ever thrilled to the sound of his voice. Wondering if he knew a love song.

Finally, the hour approaching sundown, musicians were tuning up to send people off with a special request for a new song called, <u>Oh Promise Me</u>, written by Reginald De Koven and Clement Scott just last year and sent to churches everywhere. By special request, the announcer of the request said he would not reveal the name of the requestor in favor of letting all the young ladies in the crowd claim the words. The announcer of the song said that the song is becoming a favorite song requested at weddings, leaving folks to wonder if there is a wedding to be held sometime soon in Beaton, and to wonder who might be tying the knot. On the piano was Mable Rhodes from the Beaton Methodist church accompanied by singer Sally Miller from the same. The words flowed effortlessly:

"Oh, promise me that someday you and I
Will take our love together to some sky
Where we can be alone, and faith renew,
And find the hollows where those flowers grew,
Those first sweet violets of early spring,
Which come in whispers, thrill us both, and sing
Of love unspeakable that is to be;
Oh, promise me! Oh, promise me!

Oh, promise me that you will take my hand,
The most unworthy in this lonely land,
And let me sit beside you in your eyes,
Seeing the vision of our paradise,
Hearing God's message while the organ rolls
Its mighty music to our very souls,
No love less perfect than a life with thee;
Oh, promise me! Oh, promise me!" [2]

As the last note ended and the band began to pack up their instruments, Mav turned to Macy and said: "I reckon, mayhap, I should orta git on back home afore dark, so I ken git my chores done. Let me allow thet th' day has gone quickly, so, I'm a-reckonin' thet means I had fun. Y'all know whut folks say – time flies when yor a-havin' fun. Tell yor papa howdy fo' me."

With that, Mav turned to leave but in doing so, a sudden move by Macy placed her in direct contradiction to his turn, and they touched. His arm brushed Macy's breast only so briefly, but in that moment, a tremor surged through his body and introduced a sensation unfamiliar yet pleasant. Macy smiled. Mav turned red and mumbled, "pardon, miss."

"Yes," she returned and laid a hand on his arm. "Come back soon. I predict that you will receive more mail."

Mav felt heat rush into his face, and all he could do was nod his assent. As he walked toward the hitching post where Biscuit waited, Mav felt that his legs were not feeling the same as when he came. They felt weak like he recalled they felt when he was suffering an illness as a child. They shouldn't feel that way.

On the trail back to his cabin, Mav talked to Biscuit about anything but what was on his mind. Some thoughts just may be too private. Biscuit played his role as an understanding friend, but without knowing the unknown, offered no advice on the quandary that is quietly and assuredly building in his friend.

Chapter 6

A Disconcerting Letter

Morning broke, and Mav began his day performing the tasks required of a man of the land. He had bought a hand plow to turn a small garden which he would plant when the moon advised, and bought some chickens which have already provided eggs for his breakfast. He had a hog now and a sow ready to farrow, and one cow. He didn't quite understand why he bought the cow, not being an avid milk drinker but it seemed right somehow. But he did buy a churn to make butter for his pancakes and biscuits. If Clarissa gives more milk than he needs for making biscuits and pancakes, Mav is certain the hogs will love it. He guessed growing things and raising animals was in the soul of a farmer's son. Mav found himself getting excited thinking about the vegetables he would plant when the time came. Wildfowl and a deer now and then gave him the meat he needed and there were special fishing holes that he visited when the desire came to brace himself against an accommodating tree on the bank of the river in which he dropped a line. Overall, Mav was self-sufficient though he went into Beaton for vegetables he was not yet growing in his not yet planted garden and for items like kerosene, lucifers, salt, pepper, coffee, flour, sugar, air-tights of tomatoes, and dried herbs, which Macy has told him can add flavor to his still uncertain cooking. Recently, he has given himself praise for his cornbread, and he has made clabber milk from some of Clarissa's milk, but his beans miss the mark when compared to Macy's.

Occasionally, he visits the Arkland office to check his mailbox in which he has arranged to have a copy of the Gazette placed when printed for distribution. As for mail, he would have had difficulty explaining to himself why he felt the need to check for mail when there was no one to write to him. Last week, though, he received a hand-written letter in his postal box at the Arkland Stage-line office. Given that his family was gone, he was surprised to find that he had mail, that not being the typical occurrence when he dropped by the Arkland office. Also, not typical was the scent he smelled when it was handed over to him by the station-keeper himself.

'Surely,' he thought, 'Mr. Wilson is not wearing lavender or some such cologne.' No, but the letter carried the fragrance of some unknown flower. He didn't recognize the writing on the envelope, so a certain curiosity accompanied its receipt and he opened it to assuage that curiosity. He saw the flowing cursive and the evenly spaced lines that filled the single page from the initial 'Dear Mav,' down to the closing phrase 'Forever Yours. Sincerely,' followed by the writer's name, 'Macy.' Oddly enough, he didn't read the letter itself, only its salutation and closing.

His business in town finished, Mav remounted Biscuit and started for home. On the way, he kept repeating to himself, 'Forever Yours, sincerely.' When he reached the cabin and removed Biscuit's burdens and gave him water and oat feed, Mav went to his cabin and sat down to read the letter in its entirety. He thought about it. It was his first real letter from someone that was not family. He had written home several times when he was on the trail with Lytle and had received a few in return which he carried in his war-bag while on the trail. Occasional rereading their letters gave Mav comfort in times he began to miss them. This was not from a lawyer like he had received in Beaton a year ago. This was a real letter from someone he knows. Someone he hasn't seen in three months. Not since the picnic. But here it is, and it smells good, and the writing is beautiful in its flowing linked letters, and he can't read a word of it because his hand is shaking. Mav drops the letter on the table and rubs his hands together then flexes his fingers. Must be the cold he murmurs to himself. I should build a fire, he says to himself. Maybe boil some coffee. Finally, when all reasons to delay were exhausted Mav read the letter in its entirety.

Dear Mav

It has been in my mind for several days now — no, that's not true — it has been for several weeks that I have wanted to write to you to ask if all is well with you. I have looked for you at the Arkland office every day thinking that you might come by. If I had to be away, I always asked Papa if you had come by. But I am always disappointed. Honestly, I am worried that since you live alone that some harm might happen to you and there would be no one to help you. You could break a leg or something worse. It would so relieve my mind if you stopped in. If I am not there when you come, there are paper and pencils on the table inside the door that you can leave me a note. Papa will give it to me when I return. Before I close, I want you to recall how much pleasure I had at the picnic because you came. Of course, I hope that you also found pleasure in my company and of course the other friends there. I feel that I don't speak falsely in saying that they miss seeing you but certainly not as much as I. I will close now before I say too much.

Forever Yours, Sincerely.
Macy

Eugene Stonefield

Mav has read Macy's letter. And has read it a second time. And a third. Mav folds the letter and lays it on the table and repeats its close again 'Forever Yours, Sincerely. Macy.' Mav knows that he must respond in some way. He must drop by the Arkland office in a few days or maybe write a letter to Macy. But what will he say? What does a man say to someone like Macy? What words are appropriate? What does he feel about Macy? Why are his hands shaking again?

The next morning snow was falling, and from the look of the sky, it would continue for some time. Crisp, blowing wind was already creating drifts, and trees were carrying a heavy load of snow from the previous day. Mav completed his chores and prepared breakfast of bacon, eggs, coffee and would have had toasted bread with Clarissa's butter if he had any bread. That, he regretted. He recalled the smell of freshly baked sourdough bread his ma made and wished he could smell it again. And cakes. He could smell the vanilla that permeated the house when his ma made cakes or cookies. He missed that. Vowing to buy some baked bread in Beaton before long he went back to his breakfast as unsatisfactory as it had become. After he finished, Mav began a list of items he wanted to get when he went to Beaton. At the top of the list was bread followed by salt-pork, beans, pepper, vinegar, potatoes, soap, and Wellington's Bayberry-Lavender After Shave lotion. The last item on the list was a reminder to drop by the Arkland office. He would keep the lavender water in his saddlebag.

It snowed all day, and the drifts were becoming tall and deep, but the rate of snow falling lessened late in the afternoon. Mav had been inside part of the day reading the diary and searching for clues to where the pages with the map came from. He recognized that his assumption could be wrong and the pages may not have come from the diary of

Captain Forda, but what else did he have? All that he knew at this time is that the diary hid a key to understanding the map. He did not know the nature of the hidden key, so reading the diary, with the hope of perceiving the key was all that he could do. He continued to read:

[Diary entry for Sept. 28, 1872: This morning we mounted a charge into the camp of the enemy. They were entirely unaware of our presence, so were unprepared for an attack. Out of thirty warriors, only five remained alive to return to the reservation or to trial. There were many women and children killed or injured. The company recovered thirty-two stolen horses and three cows. Major Grierson congratulated the men on a successful campaign and visited with the wounded, I being one of the unfortunates who took an arrow to the thigh. Luckily the arrow missed bone and artery and removal was easy, but not without pain. We had three fatalities and six wounded in all. I will provide a full report to Colonel Mackenzie when we get back to headquarters. I will not include how sickened I am at the carnage. In the past, I have seen people receive praise, even in their failure, when the task was difficult. I question: If one is praised and admired who perseveres through his failures, should he receive praise and admiration for persevering through his loathsome successes also? When asked about the desirability of ending the war with the natives, Custer said that officially, at least, he would be glad to see an end, but personally, would prefer to see the war continue. Presumably, he meant until the last native dies. I cannot subscribe to that. This was their land before we came. Anyone would fight to preserve and protect what they feel is theirs. Annihilation cannot serve justice. On another occasion, Custer placed himself in the moccasins of the natives and said that, if he were a native, he too would prefer life on the plains rather than confinement to a reservation. I can agree with that. Who would not want to preserve a way of life? It is not our way of life that is under pressure to change, it is the native's. Everyone hates, or should hate the brutality of war. War is a failure to come to a just accommodation. On our last raid, five children died. What have the children to do with war?]

Mav set the diary aside and picked up his letter again. The fragrance remained, and he held it up to his face to receive the full effect as he inhaled deeply.

The next day found Mav and Biscuit walking carefully through the drifted snow toward Beaton. The trip to town was slower than usual but comfortable, and the sun had emerged from the cloudbank to the east allowing sharp shadows to fall across the trail. Mav talked to Biscuit as he rode along and asked questions of him which Mav voiced answers to himself which he then followed up by questioning Biscuit on whether he was right in his response. Biscuit whinnied now and then to keep Mav satisfied that he was listening.

Beaton appeared from its hidden valley, and Mav suddenly realized how much he had anticipated coming in. Usually coming to Beaton was a bit of a chore, something he needed to do to purchase staples or ammunition, but this time it was different, yet he couldn't exactly put his finger on that difference. Mav tied up outside the S & E General Store, owned and operated by Sidney Gill and his wife Edna where he proceeded to request the items on his list. All were available, and Mav placed them in his saddlebags, but before closing the bag, he uncorked the bottle of lavender water and poured a small amount into an ungloved hand which he then used to slap his face on one side then the other causing Biscuit to register his strong displeasure with a notable snort. Mav looked at Biscuit and said: "Ifn thet's th' way yor a-feelin' about it, none fo' you!" That done, Mav remounted Biscuit and rode to the Arkland office.

"Mr. Wilson, howdy. Y'all doin' well?" Mav signaled his entry in a voice out of character and waited for the elderly station-keeper to appear at the customer window. Silently he hoped another face would appear.

"Well, hullo Mav," expressed Chauncey Wilson, somewhat surprised. "Here to check yor mail?"

"Yessir, had to come fo' some chuck so reckon'd it a good idea." Mav looked past the aging station-keeper but saw only the postal boxes with mail for several townspeople. "I ken see my box. Looks a might empty though."

"True enough," Chauncey replied. "Mebbe nex' time," then adding, "No, wait – I do have somethin'." Chauncey began sorting through all of four letters that he had not placed in their proper boxes.

For a moment, Mav's pulse quickened, and once again, he felt an unusual sensation. "What is it?" he asked, but instead of an answer was handed another letter which he quickly brought to eye-level to check the handwriting, and surreptitiously, its fragrance. "Shor obliged, Mr. Wilson. Guess I'll be a-headin' out now. Tell yor daughter I'm right sorrowful I missed seein' her." With that, Mav walked outside and mounted Biscuit for a return to his cabin. Half-way there he reflected: "Mayhap, I orta left a note."

Regret has a way of eating at a person, even regret for small things like forgetting to leave a personal note, even when the prospective writer of that unwritten note had no idea what he could have written anyway. But that was a minor aspect. He could have said that he did find pleasure in her company at the picnic and that her cooking was outstanding or that maybe he would come to another if the opportunity arose. Never did he think that he could have written about his desire to see her again. That might have been the bridge too far for someone who hadn't come to grips with those strange sensations that kept cropping up when he thinks of Macy or re-reads her letter or finds disappointment in not seeing her at the Arkland office. No, that just might have been that bridge too far for an independent Mav Caid.

Arriving at the cabin, Mav performed his duty to make Biscuit comfortable and sat down to read his new letter. For a moment, he just held it in his hand. Then he held it to his nose and inhaled deeply.

Opening it carefully to preserve the envelope, he felt something drop out onto the floor. Reaching down, he picked up a small curl of auburn hair tied with a small white bow. For a moment, he was confused. In the next, he changed.

Mav read the letter then replaced it in the envelope with the curl of fragrant auburn hair and placed the letter with the first in his secret vault behind the fireplace stone. Before going to bed, he must have retrieved the lock of hair a half dozen times just to hold it in his hand. Imagination is a toy for children and adults alike, and in the imagination of Mav Caid at this moment, as he holds a lock of Macy's hair, he holds the girl, in her completeness, and although he could not say it, he became her silent lover.

Chapter 7

A Nice Day for an Ambush

Mav rode into the clearing with the sun shining strongly from thirty-degrees off the horizon and shadows of himself and Biscuit stretching out to the west. The day was windy but seasonably warm, and he looked forward to reaching his favorite hunting ground three or four miles ahead. He was unprepared for the report of a rifle from an oak mott forty to fifty yards to the northeast. 'Hunters!' he thought and was about to say good hunting when the second rifle shot kicked up dust just ahead of Biscuit. Mav didn't pause to analyze the shooter's intent. He and Biscuit were entirely in the clearing, and no hunter would misidentify a man on a horse as a deer or any other game. In the distance was a dense cypress bosk that promised safety. Immediately, Mav spurred Biscuit toward the bosk bordering a small creek on the west side of the clearing. The run was hard ahead for a hundred yards in the direction opposite from where the shooter had to have been.

Distance, he knew, would provide a diminishing target to the shooter and the cover would give him time to assess what it all meant. Mav heard two additional shots, but he saw no results, so he assumed the shots fell short. Biscuit brought Mav to the most advantageous spot as if he had analyzed the situation and made a choice himself. Mav dismounted and pulled his Henry rifle from its saddle scabbard. Taking Biscuit's reins, he led him into the creek and behind a bank of projecting rock where he tied him loosely to a branch of a small tree that overhung the water. He then returned to the place they had entered and knelt behind a tree with a good view of the clearing. There he waited.

A half-hour later he heard a horse shuffling slowly in his direction just outside the line of trees along the creek. He shifted his position to get a better view. Leveling his rifle in the direction of the sound, he waited. The sound of the approaching rider stopped, then reversed and became quieter as the rider rode in the other direction. Mav stood up and moved cautiously out to the edge of the tree cover that secreted him and Biscuit, far enough to see the receding image of a rider in a dark hat atop a pinto horse. Mav thought of sending a warning shot in the direction of the man on the pinto, and could easily have killed him for his attempt on his own life was it in Mav's nature to shoot a man in the back, which it is not. The back of the receding rider offered too little information to identify the person to whom it belonged. All that Mav could discern was a rider clothed in a brown coat, brown trousers and wearing a brown medium-high crowned hat with a wide brim. Around his neck was a red bandanna.

In time Mav retrieved Biscuit and carried on to his destination and brought a six-point white-tail buck home for his efforts, the fortune of Mav and misfortune of the deer consisting of both choosing a well-worn path through the brush leading to the salt lick. On the way back, Mav reflected upon the mysterious rider who shot at him and Biscuit. He also thought about a statement Macy made in a postscript to her letter that an unknown man on a paint was asking about someone named Maverick.

'Could be a coincidence,' he thought, 'lots of people from Texas are named Maverick – especially those who may have the cattle business in their blood.' Then thinking: 'It's silly. Why would anyone want to kill me? I wonder if it was that whomperjawed polecat Slade. Could be Slade, but that varmint is probably still running from the marshal in Ogallala once Lytle filed the charges against him for the robbery attempt. Slade could be harboring a grudge against me for alerting Lytle of his and his partner's plan. His partner certainly would since he is still in jail for his part. How could Slade have found me? If it is Slade, that is. Could be just mistaken identity. I guess I need to ask folks around Beaton myself. See what I can learn.' His decision made, Mav and Biscuit came home. Immediately upon entering his cabin, Mav put the coffee on the stove to boil and retrieved the diary. He began to read:

[Diary entry for April 18, 1873: My leg wound has healed with no residual disablement, and I have decided to resign my commission. I must admit if only to myself, that I have developed a sense of pity for these natives from whom we newcomers have taken so much. I wonder if I would act the same as they have, were the roles reversed and I was forcibly relocated onto a reservation that would not support my way of life. I can't do it anymore. Chasing renegades is not what I want to do in my life. Many of the whites migrating west have done as terrible a thing to the natives as the natives to them and the whites suffer no retribution. I will leave as soon as possible, and head to Tennessee and spend time with some of the family that is now living in Memphis. Maybe I'll go back to sea and make a living as a mariner. My navigation skills are always needed on the sea. Someday, I will go back to Texas to see my sister in Bandera, whom I haven't seen since she married and moved from Louisiana to Texas. Time will tell.]

The next several entries dealt with his daily activities before an official acceptance of his resignation. These entries Mav read quickly until the entry for June 23, 1873. Here he read:

[Diary entry for June 23, 1873: On the road today, I met with an unfortunate accident when my horse stepped into a gopher hole and broke a leg. Sorrowfully, I had to kill the animal and resume my trek on foot. By nightfall, I was feeling a bit footsore, so I stopped and built a lean-to for shelter and built a fire. I have been carrying my bedroll and saddlebags with the hardtack and some salted meat and some pemmican that I got from some friendly natives who were trying to avoid having to live on the Ft. Sill reservation, so that's what is on the menu tonight and tomorrow. I hope to run across some game that I might bring to tomorrow evening's campfire.

An unusual thing happened yesterday as I walked through a narrow pass into a valley lushly covered by grass with several clear-water streams running through it. It is my concept of perfection. I have drawn a rough map of the location, which is in this diary. The unusual thing is that I ran across a streambed with numerous – too numerous to even estimate the number - of small clear or nearly clear, oddly shaped stones swirling around in pools carved in the rocky streambed. It looked like these stones had eroded the bedrock into almost perfect circular patterns. There were hundreds of circular indentions with the rocks that rotated around the edges of the indentions as the water streamed over and among them. Given my situation, I could only trace the streambed for a few miles before I drew the map and carried on toward my destination. Someday I will return to collect more stones and learn what they are. To obscure its location, I have removed the page with the map and have drawn a copy. I will keep one and send one along with a few of the stones to my nephew Maverick as soon as I find a town. Maverick is young now, but if anything happens to me, he may want to follow up on this strange discovery when he gets older. I will explain this to my sister in a separate letter. I don't know if they have value or not, but I think they may be d....]

The last word was damaged and undecipherable.

'So, that is why I got the map,' thought Mav. The letter to ma must never have come, or she would have told me. Putting aside the diary Mav went outside to attend to the gathering number of chores attendant to farming. As Mav milked his brindle cow and slopped the two hogs with their several piglets and chased an offending rabbit from the vegetable garden, he thought to himself: 'the life of a drover looked pretty good in comparison.' It was Deja-vu, but Mav did not recognize it as being so.

Chapter 8

A Grudge's History / Finding the Key

While riding into Beaton Mav was careful to scan ahead for a possible ambuscade. He knows that the advantage of a killer thrives in each turn in the trail, each dense growth of trees, each rock outcropping or rise in the terrain. Mav had finally resolved in his mind that the only people that could possibly have a grudge against him were Slade and his jailed partner, Fenner Korn. He recalled the night vividly in Ogallala just after the Lytle sold the herd and announced that the next day, he was to receive payment at the Ogallala bank and would be giving the drovers and others that had brought the herd from Texas their pay in hard currency. The pattern was the same as on earlier drives, when the drive reaches destination, and the cattle buyer accepts delivery, all drovers receive their salary depending upon how many days they worked and are free to go wherever they chose. Some would return with Lytle, but others would drift around as they desired. This was the day to which all had looked forward since the drive up the trail began.

Everyone except for Lytle and the cook, Manuel, were in their bedrolls sleeping soundly. Mav had chosen a spot away from the group and was in his bedroll near some trees but had not gone to sleep. He heard the voices of two people talking low a few yards away but out of his sight. They were speaking of the money that Lytle would be carrying back to camp by noon the next day and how all the drovers would be bathing in the stream and getting ready for a day and a night on the town. Mav could not fully comprehend their conversation but, what he could hear suggested a plan for a robbery. Mav continued to pretend that he was asleep and kept his eyes closed even when someone struck a lucifer match near him and waved it before his face.

Eventually, the two cowhands returned to their own bedrolls near the center of the camp. Mav got up and moved around the camp to approach the cook's wagon where Lytle and the cook were discussing provisions needed for the return trip to Texas. Five drovers have chosen to stay with Lytle for an overland trip, and two wranglers, who are to return with the remuda, which consisted of 76 horses. The rest of the boys will avail themselves of the special cowboy rate for returning to Texas by rail. From Ogallala, the Union Pacific line will take them to St. Joe in Missouri, then to Kansas City, then south to Nassau, where they may purchase tickets all to way to San Antonio on the MK&T, the Missouri, Kansas, and Texas railway, otherwise known as the Katy. The other route is to travel down the Mississippi from St. Louis to New Orleans then to Galveston or Corpus Christi and on to San Antonio by stage or rail.

Lytle greeted Mav as he came into their presence and asked the reason for the visit. Mav then reported the conversation. The rest is history. Lytle informed the marshal of the plan, and a trap was set for the two conspirators. One was Henry Slade, the other was Fenner Korn, both, replacement hands hired to replace two others who had left the drive in Dodge City. It wasn't much when it transpired. The marshal, accompanied by Mav to identify Fenner and Slade, plus four deputies, located the two plotters where they planned to intercept Lytle with the money. Marshal Haversham shouted to Fenner to drop his gun and fired a shot or two for emphasis at which point Fenner complied but not without uttering a few death threats when he saw Mav and deduced Mav had told Lytle about his and Slade's plan. The marshal arrested Fenner, but Slade lit out on a fast horse stolen from the remuda. There was no sustained effort to chase him since the robbery was not successful and Captain Lytle would not be in Ogallala to testify in court should the marshal eventually arrest Slade. When Marshal Haversham checked the 'wanted' bulletins he found a posting for Fenner in another jurisdiction on a robbery charge and there was a five-hundred dollars reward for his capture. The marshal determined that Mav earned the reward.

Lytle and his drovers left the following day, but before going, Lytle called Mav in to reward him personally for notifying him of the robbery plan. His reward matched that of the marshal's five-hundred, giving Mav a substantial total reward of one-thousand dollars in addition to his pay. A thousand dollars is a considerable amount of money – more than a full year's salary - enough to encourage him to follow through on a developing dream to be totally free of employment by someone else. He thanked Captain Lytle for allowing him to work for him for five years and saddled up to become an independent man, one who can follow his own dream.

Mav drifted around for a while just looking over the country between Ogallala and wherever he found himself next. Eventually, he found a place that met some unspoken criteria, and he stopped. When Mav settled outside of Beaton, he immediately deposited one-thousand dollars in the bank. The rest that he had saved, he used to buy some land and build his three-room cabin.

Eugene Stonefield

✳✳✳

Mav arrived in Beaton at a time of celebration at the church where a couple was being married by the Reverend Mr. Smedley, pastor at the local Methodist church who had come from Virginia in 1887 rumored at the instigation of Dr. Andrew Hunter, often called The Grand Old Man of Arkansas and The Patriarch of Methodism. Mav didn't know who the couple might be so he decided to stop first at the Arkland office and ask for his mail, should he have any, and possibly could learn the names of those jumping the broom, a term he often heard used when he was younger for those getting hitched.

"Good-mornin', Mav," came the wavering voice of the station-keeper. "Come fo' yor mail?" the question was always the same.

"Howdy, Mr. Wilson. Yessir, ifn I hav' any today." He was becoming more hopeful of receiving a short letter from Macy if he has not been in for a length of time. Today he was to be sorely disappointed as none was waiting for him. Finally, he asked: "Macy here?"

"No, sorry, Mav. Macy is over to the church. They're havin' a weddin' today."

"Who's gittin' hitched?" asked Mav, hiding his disappointment with a question for which an answer is immaterial. A year ago, Mav would not have asked that question but since the picnic, the word 'marriage' itself stimulates an interest in the people choosing to marry.

"Why, it's Jenni Weldon an' Lance Cole. They musta been sparkin' for oh, two or three months now. Everyone's wishin' them th' best." Chauncey went back to his duties sorting mail, and Mav waved his goodbye and left the Arkland office. Mav didn't know Jenni other than that she was a comely girl of about eighteen with big hazel eyes and slightly buck teeth and a scattering of freckles across her nose. Macy introduced Jenni to Mav at the picnic. Lance's pa, Harmon, had

60

sold Mav his cow, and they see each other now and then when they pass on the trail. Mav had only seen Lance when he was with his pa or his brother Billy. Thinking back, Lance seemed only a boy just a short time ago. Time runs on fleet feet. Now he is a married man. Mav shook his twenty-two-year-old head and mounted up for the short ride to the S & E General Store. On the way, Mav ponders about what the life of a married man might be and wonders if the world is passing him by while he remains a bachelor.

"Howdy, Mav," Edna ventured as Mav came in the door. "Hain't seen you ina month o' Sundays, it seems. You been ailin'?" Edna is the town's original erstwhile pharmacist who was unchallenged before the Claymore Apothecary shop opened last year. She keeps a special cabinet stocked with every concoction and physic known to man and then has a personal pharmacopeia of recipes for home remedies she learned from her ma, who said she acquired them from the Indians.

"Naw, Edna, all's good with me. I hav' a good stock o' physics at home, so I got no need to come by fo' thet. I'm jes' needin' to restock some victuals, so here's my list. Whate'er y'all don't hav', well, I'll jes' hav' to bear it." Mav handed the list to Edna.

"'Lo, Mav," greeted Sidney as he entered from the back. "Yor lookin' fit. Edna got yor order? Need any huntin' ammo?"

"She's got it, Sidney. No, I don't believe I need… Well, I might orta take a box o' rim-fires fo' my Henry rifle. Ne'er ken tell when thar might'n be a need."

"Right thinkin' Mav, you ne'er ken tell when a wuf or a catamount might need shootin'. Say, by the way – some feller I ne'er seed before come by an' axed if you wuz in town. I told him you lived a might way out to the south, couldn't say how far."

Sidney had a characteristic that always amused Mav when he witnessed it. Sidney wore a long beard that was brown but is now mostly gray which he continually encircles in his hand and strokes downward. He does this continuously until it becomes necessary to employ both hands in whatever task is at hand. The effect is to make one believe that tugs on the beard manipulate the mouth. Mav cannot understand why all the long whiskers are not pulled out with all the stroking. In the main, Sidney is as honest as anyone Mav has ever known. Edna, on the other hand, just might sell you a pig in a poke when those concoctions are concerned. Mav bought a vial of something made of sassafras and horseradish which turned him three shades of green when he tried it to cure his cough that he developed last winter. It never cured the cough but took his voice away for a full hour each time he took a dose of the concoction. Since then, he has been reluctant to reveal any ailments to Edna.

Upon receiving his order and loading all items into his saddlebags, Mav ventured a question to Sidney: "Did y'all get a peek at th' stranger's hoss when he asked 'bout me?"

Sidney, stroking his beard thought a minute, then stated: "They wuz two hosses tied out front, a paint an', uh, Edna, wuz thet a bay or..."

"It wuz a strawberry roan, and it belonged to Macy. She was takin' a ride to visit some ailin' friend and stopped by for a little gift for her an' some ergot for her headaches and some Lydia Pinkham. You 'member, — she asked if we has seen Mav here."

"Thet's right!" assured Sidney, a roan, a paint an' Macy. Thet's what they wuz."

"Whut wuz he wearin'?" queried Mav as he picked up the items he purchased.

Sidney thought for a second, the replied: "He wuz all brown, 'cept his kerchief, that wuz red."

Mav thanked both Sidney and Edna and mounted Biscuit to return to his cabin. He wanted to get back before it began to get dark so he could do all his chores in the light of day. It takes planning to be a farmer, he admitted to himself.

Mav Caid — The Complete Story

✱✱✱

He kept the pace fast enough to return before dark and completed his work before the sun had dropped behind the trees to the west. After preparing a meal of venison and corn from an air-tight he bought at the general store, he returned to reading the diary of Captain Forda:

[Diary entry for July 25, 1874: I have been walking now for a month without finding a town. My health is in decline as I have picked up a severe cough along the way which exhausts my strength long before it should. I have a concern that I won't make it much further if I don't find a town soon. I fear the discovery I made will perish with me. If…When I find a town, I will try to send it to my sister and young nephew to exploit if, in fact, it is what I surmise it to be.]

Mav began to feel a little regret creep into his mind. Here is a man, an uncle, the brother to his ma who is failing and seemingly, near death. The feeling merged with those feelings about the way his family died. But, he realized, he had the diary and the map now and freedom to find out what the discovery really is.

Reading further, he noticed that it began to be strange, like his uncle's mind may have been wandering like one who is delirious from thirst or severe fever. The thoughts written seemed jumbled or incomplete. Several times he mentioned a specific date. On a hunch, Mav went back to the entry for the date to reread the entry. Then he noticed something he had not seen when he thumbed through the diary before. There, next to the bound edges of the diary Mav could see a line of numbers and characters written close to the spine from bottom to top that included three small triangles and groups of characters enclosed within parentheses. A ragged edge of paper near the spine identified where pages, possibly those with the drawn map, had been removed. He immediately rose and retrieved the map which he inserted in the diary to align the triangles on the map with those in the diary. The rambling message began to make sense. The alignments formed diamond shapes that pointed one to the map, the other to the diary. Letters and numbers enclosed by parenthesis in the diary connected to lines drawn on the map, seemingly to identify a mark or character on the map. The diary entry reads: '3 6nlt-9 4lg (1 mt▲nw12dfmnores12m) (2 mt▲se150dfmnores3m) (3 mt▲sw190dfmnores15m) D runne>sw' and can now be coordinated to the map. Although the map had lines and symbols that aligned with the strange gibberish in the diary, the meaning is obscure. He returns to Wendell's entries for 1874 and continues to read:

[Diary entry for Aug. 12 or 13, 1874: Very sick. Severe chills. See town ahead. Believe I am near Little Rock. Will seek doctor in town. Chilblains so bad I can hardly walk. Don't know name of town but will mail…Ran across a man calling himself Chico who pointed to the town but would not take me in or go in for help himself. Suspect he was running from the law. He gave me quite a jolt. I was having a tough night with my fever and all. I fear I had been babbling in my sleep and awoke with a start and found this, Chico, watching me. He had been rummaging through my saddlebag, but there was nothing to take, my food had run out two days ago. He could have killed me easily. He asked a lot of questions about where I came from and where I was going. I hadn't the presence of mind to answer falsely. I hope I don't pay a price for telling him about my sister and her family in Bandera.]

Mav closed the diary. The rest is known, or at least, assumed.

Chapter 9

An Appeal for Information / First Letter

Mav's schooling ended after he turned eleven, and he had learned about Christopher Columbus and other famous explorers of earlier times, and he knew that they found their way across the seas by celestial navigation. He knew that to navigate a ship a person had to know coordinates called latitude and longitude and that they used instruments to read the stars to help them determine their position on the earth when all that was available to them to observe was the vastness of the sea. He just didn't know what latitude and longitude really were or how they allowed explorers to get around. He had read about the pole star, and he knew that there is something called magnetic north or something like that and that geographic north and magnetic north are not the same. He needed help but didn't know where to get it. After some thought, he realized that what he had learned was likely, still taught in schools and a new school had opened last year in Beaton staffed by a new Schoolmaster, Marcus Vale. The opportunity was primarily through a grant by the Peabody Education Fund, a philanthropic effort of financier and philanthropist, George Peabody. According to what Mav had read in the Gazette, Marcus Vale is a graduate of the University of Nashville, from a college referred to as the Peabody Normal College which focuses on teacher preparation.

Mav decides that he will visit with Mr. Vale when he goes back to Beaton. In the meantime, Mav will test his skill at letter writing. He began:

Dear Miss Wilson… (This beginning he realized was too formal so, he threw it away and got another piece of paper to try again.)

Dear Miss Macy

I have received several letters from you over time but have not written one to you. I hope this will correct that slight, which wasn't meant to be a slight. If anything, it was because I seldom write letters to anyone. I will be coming to Beaton next Friday to speak with Schoolmaster Vale about another subject and will stop by the Arkland office then.

My best wishes,
Mav Caid

As he was in the mood for writing, Mav took another sheet of paper to write to Sheriff Partin in Bandera.

Dear Sheriff Partin

A while back, I returned home after being gone for several years and found my whole family had been killed by unknown persons. You told me the story of

Mav Caid — The Complete Story

how they were killed, and Preacher Branch gave me some personal property that included a diary which fortunately had survived the fire that took the cabin and barn. Now, there were four marked graves for my ma and pa and brother and sister. What I want to know is whether you now know the identity of the fifth deceased person found and buried there whose name was not known at the time? Please write to me and tell me what you know about this. It is possible that the unknown person is my uncle, Wendell Forda.

Maverick Caiden

The tasks completed, Mav folded and stuffed them into envelopes which he addressed. Having no stamps or place to post the letter to Sheriff Partin, he would have to wait until he could take them into Beaton himself.

Fortune sometimes smiles upon even the least of us, and this was just such a day in the life of Mav Caid. A passerby stopped at Mav's cabin.

"Ho! Hallo! Mav, are ya home?" shouted the arriving young man on the bay horse. Mav was not unaware of his coming toward the cabin, because since the attempted ambush, Mav had been watching closely for the appearance of strangers. As the rider came nearer, Mav lowered his rifle which he had picked up when he saw the rider and waved him in.

"Howdy, Billy, whut brung you out this-a-way?" queried Mav before Billy dismounted. "You ain't lost, ere you?" Mav attempted to tease the visitor, knowing well that Billy knew every hill and valley in the area.

"Naw, not lost! Come to see if I could bring ya anythin' from the Gen'ral Store, seein' how I gotta go there mysel' and yorsel' bein' on the way."

'A neighbor being neighborly,' thought Mav as he leaned his rifle against the post.

"Coffee, maybe blackstrap molasses, a couple o' air-tights of tomatoes and green banes, an'…Oh, I have some letters to post. Mayhap you could take 'em by the Arkland office? I'll give you th' money to pay fo' it." Mav looked at Billy.

"Will do," returned Billy, Uh, any message for…for Macy?"

"Macy?" taken aback, Mav glanced at Billy, then thought he probably shouldn't give Billy the letter to Macy. People talk. "Ah, no, message, jes' these here letters," he said, thinking to himself that 'Billy will read the names of the addressees, but will not open them.' The fact that he asked the question suggests that some must be talking about Macy's and his friendship. 'Well, so what? I ain't ashamed of writing to Macy.'

Presently, Mav went into the cabin and returned with his letters to Macy and to the sheriff of Bandera, Texas, and cash for the postage and general store purchases. "Much obliged fo' thinkin' o' me, Billy, I'm down to 'most nothin' in th' coffee can. By th' way, Billy, I'm a-thinkin' o' diggin' a well. Do you know a diviner thet would hep me locate th' water?"

"I know one Mav. His name is Willard Finley, and his fee is reasonable. I'll let him know that ya wanna see him. He prob'ly can come by next week."

"Much obliged, Billy. I'll be right here," returned Mav.

Billy continued: "Are ya lookin' for someone ta help you dig tha well? It is always better to have two people in case something goes wrong during tha digging. If you are, I will come help ya when ya are ready ta start. If a neighbor didn't help another neighbor, where would we be in this world. Pa won't care if I'm gone for a while. Neighbors helped him when he came ta tha area and staked his claim. They helped with raising tha house and tha barn. Why, heck, they even built an outhouse for him and ma. That was before either Lance or I was born. Lance came along a year later, and I came along two years or so later. There was a baby, a little girl, lost in between. Ma still talks about her."

"Billy, I shor would 'preciate yor hep with th' diggin'."

"Well, I'll be off. Prob'ly, won't be back 'til late. Don't shoot me if I ride up after sundown," he said, laughing and motioning toward the Henry rifle Mav leaned against the porch post.

"My swear-on-th'-Bible promise thet ifn I did, I would do it gentle like! Not so's it would hurt you none, anyhow. An', cross my heart," answered Mav, laughing with Billy.

Chapter 10

An Unexpected Visitor / A Partner Gained

Another month has rolled around, and Mav has come to Beaton to buy provisions he has run short on and is now entering the Arkland office where Macy is on duty, relieving her pa who is ill. Contrary to his earlier behavior, the Arkland office is now his first stop.

"Oh, howdy, Macy!" Mav exclaimed when he stepped to the Arkland postal window expecting to see station-keeper Wilson. "I didn't 'spect you to be sortin' the mail. Is yor papa ailin'?"

"A little, but mostly just needing a day of rest. He has been working hard lately, and, at his age, it is exhausting. I guess you are looking for your mail?" hoping to hear him say that he was just coming by to see her. She would be disappointed with his answer.

"Yes'm, I'm 'spectin' a letter directly. A letter from th' sheriff down in Bandera." He realized by the look on her face that it wasn't what she wanted to hear, but it was too late to recover the moment.

"Well, you are in luck," announced Macy showing some disappointment. "Here it is." She pushed the letter toward Mav. "I hope you get whatever you are looking for. By the way, Maverick Caiden, your letter Billy delivered to Papa while I was away was sweet. I want to thank you for it."

Raising an eyebrow, Mav queried: "Maverick Caiden? Yor'e usin' my 'fficial name?" his question of her using his full name hanging between them for a full minute.

Displaying a severe countenance, Macy replied: "Well, you deserve it! I have written at least FIVE letters to you, and you have answered only ONE!" her sea-green eyes leveled at Mav's hazel, and with her feigned anger accompanied by stamping of a foot. Then, changing tone suddenly said: "But you can make up for it. I will expect you to come to the village dance on Saturday in the park. They will have a three-piece band and a dance floor and punch, and you…will be there! Or else!"

"Cain't I jes' 'pologize 'nstead?" he asked in a subdued tone.

"Absolutely NOT! Your punishment must fit the crime, and your inattention is becoming criminal at least…at least four times over," replied Macy, showing her mock fighting ability.

"But I cain't dance! I ne'er shook a hoof b'fore." His response returned as if that should settle any question about a dance. "On top o' thet, Billy an' me wuz fixin' to start a-diggin' me a water well."

Ignoring the second objection, Macy continued: "No one is born knowing how to dance. I will teach you. So, at six o'clock on Saturday. I will see you. OK?" exclaimed Macy with a finality that Mav was not prepared to counter.

"Well… Well… I s'pose th' well diggin' ken wait. Saturday at six then." Mav turned to leave, feeling that staying longer might chance a rethinking of his punishment and a harsher penalty. It never occurred to Mav that his submitting to her discipline was his choice.

✳✳✳

As this unbalanced negotiation was proceeding, back at Mav's cabin, a trespasser was searching for something with a purpose but finding nothing. He has searched for Mav for a long time, so waiting a little longer to get what he came for is a small price.

Taking his *pistola*, an 1886 Army Colt forty-five revolver, from his belt, the intruder laid it on the table behind which he sat down to wait and watch the door. The stranger had made a special effort to hide his horse and walked to the cabin when he saw Mav leave earlier. The sun will be down soon. He thought about an easy success, and waiting in the dark, should it come before Mav returns, gives him an advantage. After all these years, he has the patience to wait a little longer.

Mav rode in as expected by the intruder about an hour after sunset. After taking care of his late afternoon obligations to Biscuit and the other animals, Mav walked through his door into a dark room and felt for the kerosene lantern that always hangs next to the door. Taking a lucifer from his shirt pocket and striking it on the door Mav lit the lamp and turned to set it on the table. He immediately froze as the *pistola* in the hand of an unknown person was pointing at his face from five feet away.

"*Bueños noches, Señor* Maverick!" stated the stranger, "I hav' ben lookin' for you everwhere."

"Jes' who are you? Why are you a-pointin' thet hog-leg at me?" asked Mav while trying to decide if he should throw the lantern at the intruder and escape to the outside. He decided his arm was not faster than the bullet that could come his way. "Hav' we met?"

"Th' thin' is, I know you. An' you have somethin' I want." The intruder interjected, smiling in the dim light that flickered from the lantern still in Mav's hand.

"Put the *lámpara* down, *Señor* Maverick. On the table. Carefully. *Siéntese, por favor*...sit down, please." The intruder emphasized his words by tapping with the *pistola* barrel on the table indicating the spot where Mav was to place the lantern. "*Señor* Maverick, why don't we keep this frien'ly. *Como amigos*...Like friends. I tell you what I want, and you give it to me. Is that a deal?"

"I hanker to know who I'd be dealin' with in sech a transaction if thar should be one," returned Mav, seeking to elicit some information from this stranger.

"Fair enough, *Señor* Maverick. Let's say my name is Chico. And let's say Chico was a Comanchero in those troublesome days when the Army wanted to keep us Comancheros from trading guns and whisky to the Comanche. And let's say Chico had to leave Comancheria. And let's say Chico took a map from an *hombre* who was fortunate to meet Chico who maybe was kind enough to leave him *vivo*...alive, a while ago, and let's say that Chico, he does not have a certain *diario* that Chico wants. And let's say that Chico *sabe...sabe*...Ah! <u>knows</u> that *Señor* Maverick does have that certain *diario*." The intruding stranger named Chico smiled knowingly and fell silent, his eyes, glittering in the lamp light.

"Whut gives you to '*sabe*' thar's a diary an' I've got it?" asked Mav, thankful he had put it and the map in his hidden vault behind the stone on the fireplace.

"Ah! What makes Chico *sabe Señor* Maverick has the *diario*?" He spoke slowly emphasizing each word. "Because, *Señor* Maverick..., a kind and thoughtful *hombre* and his *mujer* with *muchacho y muchacha* said there was a *diario* that gives *comprensión*...gives meanin' to the map, but that diario has been *perdio...perdio*...lost. But another brave *hombre* who give Chico the map told Chico that *el sobrino*...a nephew, had *el diario*!

Mav Caid — The Complete Story

Quién era Chico para creer? Who was Chico to believe? But then, you see, that brave *hombre* tried to tell Chico that you were *muerto*. Isn't that funny? Do you not think that funny? You are not *muerto, Señor* Maverick. *Estás vivo!* You are much alive! But Chico, —he does not believe those people, so Chico, he made those people *muy muerto*...very dead, and then Chico, —he searched and searched but could not find it. So, Chico,—he asked around and learned that you, *Señor* Maverick are not *muerto*. Chico, he is very smart. No?"

Feeling anger rise to the point that safety was the least of his concern, Mav gripped the table and leaned toward Chico. Here before him is the man who murdered his family in Bandera, making demands. Realizing the impact his words had on Mav, Chico attempted to refocus his captive by the sound of his *pistola* butt slamming against the table, but with little success.

Rising from his chair and leaning forward, Mav shouted: "You murderer! Thet *hombre* an' *mujer* wuz a livin' man an' livin' woman, — my papa an' mama! Thet *muchacho* an' *muchacha* wuz a young boy an' young girl, —my brother an' sister! They had life an' names! They wer' mine! You killed my fam'ly!" As his vocal outburst subsided, the immediacy of his anger abated slightly, and Mav returned to his chair, yet, both hands remained clenched into fists, his face, a mask of hardness; his lips a thin line; his skin, reddened by anger. In his heart, a resolve to bring this evil man to justice.

"Now, now, *Señor* Maverick. Calm yourself. *Lo hecho, hecho está!* What is done is done. *El tiempo avanza!* Time moves on! We have *mucho* bizness to atten' to today. We should be *compañeros*...partners! We should be *amigos!*" Chico changed his tone slightly to emphasize that he did not want to shoot Mav just yet.

"Ifn I had sech a diary an' thet diary pointed to some riches, would I be a-livin' ina cabin o' such low means? I fancy sech a man to be a-livin' ina big city ina big house, or ownin' cattle or be a-travelin' someplace like Chicago or New York." Again, Mav sought to draw out more conversation and buy valuable time.

"Strange are the ways of rich *hombres*," returned Chico, "but maybe *Señor* Maverick needs my map to be that rich *hombre*. Yes?" Chico smiled at his logic and displayed large crooked yellow, tobacco-stained, teeth to his captive before continuing. "But you see, *Señor* Maverick, if you have no *diario*, Chico, he does not need *Señor* Maverick as a *compañeros* just as Chico did not need the other *hombres* in Bandera." His smile faded to a stony stare through dark eyes flashing in the flickering light from the lantern, his meaning, as clear as water from a spring. As the intruder stared at Mav, his jaw muscles tightened and relaxed beneath swarthy pox-marked skin with a regular rhythm and his black mustache moved in concert. Chico began to tap his *pistola* barrel against the table. Tap, tap, tap, mimicking the sound of a pendulum clock.

For an extended period, Mav stared at Chico, as if to burn into his mind the image of ultimate evil, evil that had robbed Mav of his family, and to plan retribution by a partnership of heart, mind, and soul. "Ok, you an' thet hogleg hol' th' high card," Mav responded, while returning to composure; evaluating Chico's remarks and threatening visage, "I've got th' diary, an', as you said, I need th' map you have. So, it looks like you an' me hafta be *compañeros* an' uh...*amigos*. Th' hitch is thet th' diary's lock'd in th' safe at th' bank in Beaton. They'll not be open 'til tomorrow at ten. Nothin' ken happen 'til then." Mav chances a risky smile.

"What if Chico, he does not believe *Señor* Maverick? What if Chico believes that *Señor* Maverick is trying to trick Chico?" Chico, jaw muscle contractions more rapid, continued his cold level gaze as his *pistola* moved back and forth to emphasize who was in control of the conversation. Presently, Chico reached into a vest pocket and retrieved a square of Hanes Apple Jack plug tobacco and bit off a quid which he positioned between gum and cheek, creating a noticeable cheek bulge. He registered pleasure as the juices from the tobacco began to form in his mouth. After a few minutes, the inevitable occurs, and the floor becomes a spittoon.

As Chico waved his *pistola* back and forth, Mav conceived a plan. "I fancy you searched fo' it when you come. Am I right? An' did you find it? No, you didn't. This here cabin ain't thet large. Killin' me will not find it for you, —and you ain't ne'er git' th' diary. I am a pragmatist, Chico. I reckon, havin' half a fortune's better than no fortune a'tall, —an' bein' shot dead to boot. So, I reckon I'll hafta trust you." Adding as an afterthought, "an' you will hafta trust me." The need for trust between partners now expressed, Mav gambled on his instincts that Chico was greedy but not completely crazy and would not act against his own best interests.

Chico stared at Mav for an extended time while he worked his jaw muscles and tried to decide upon his next step. Finally, he spoke: "Chico, he does not know this pragmarist but what you say is *los veras*...is truth." Finally, with a decision made, Chico announced in a triumphant tone, "*Señor* Maverick, *mi compañero*, we will wait!" and, once again, broke into a wide, insincere smile. His feigned camaraderie did not extend to the sincerity that he would exhibit by his holstering his *pistola*.

"One mor' thin'," began Mav, "th' bank owner will hafta see our pardnership agreement to release th' diary an' th' thousand dollars thet I have on deposit thet will be needed to 'stablish th' pardnership." Mav watched the reaction of Chico as he spoke. Chico's immediate reaction was to straighten in his chair. As he did so, Mav heard the jingle of spurs and Mav wondered if they were the large Mexican-style silver inlaid star rowels so favored by Mexicans of the Southwest. He wondered if Chico also wore a wide concha belt encircling his body.

"You have a thousan' *dólar* on deposit?" asked Chico, then changing his tone to one of anger. "What is this agreement? Why does Chico need some *estúpido*...stupid agreement?" Again, Mav heard the jingle of the spur rowels as Chico shifted his body forward for emphasis. Bubbles of tobacco juice clung to the corners of Chico's lips that had curled downward.

Not reacting to the angry outburst, Mav calmly answered: "'cause th' diary is pledged to th' bank an' a duly signed pardnership agreement will be needed fo' its release. A pardnership agreement needs a uh…a consid'ration, —which means I mus' pay a senior pardner to enter th' agreement for it to be legal, so, yes, we need a thousand dollars to seal th' pardnership to make us able to git th' fortune thet awaits us. Most times, a lawyer writes up sech an agreement." After setting up the deception and dangling a thousand-dollar incentive, Mav waited for a second for it to sink in, then continued:

"But we could write one up ournselves. Thet would work an' save time to boot. Or I could." Chico stared at Mav for a long time as he considered what Mav had told him before venturing his decision.

"You will write it, *Señor* Maverick, so it will be by your hand. I want no trouble at the bank," responded Chico, knowing that he had just trapped Mav into demonstrating theirs was a legitimate business agreement written by his own hand. "You write it," Chico repeated, "I will hold my little frien' then I will read it." Chico waved his *pistola* back and forth in emphasis.

Mav picked up his pencil and reached for a piece of paper saying, "Chico, I will need yor full name to put in th' document. Jes' write in down on this here paper an' I will copy it."

"I will just tell you how to write my full name. I don't need to write it," Chico stated as he pushed the blank page back toward Mav, knowing he is in full control and Mav must do his bidding. "My name is Francisco Alvarez. I am called Chico by my *amigos*…and my best *compañero*."

Cautiously satisfied in the direction events are going, Mav began to write the document:

To Rackley Hall, Pres. Beaton Bank and Trust, Beaton, Arkansas.

Mav Caid — The Complete Story

Subject: Danger: READ SILENTLY and take to Mr. Hall before you do anything else.

This is to notify you that what I am asking you to do verbally is a request that I am being forced to make under the gun of the man with me. The man has killed before and can be expected to kill again if crossed. Have someone quietly notify the sheriff and have him wait outside. Give me the thousand dollars that I have on deposit and any small book about the size of a typical personal diary. Treat this partnership agreement as if I have presented a legal document.

Signed this date: ________ by:

Maverick Caiden ____________________

Francisco (Chico) Alvarez______________

As Mav continued to write the agreement, he asked Chico if he wanted to sign in advance and Chico replied that Mav could sign it for him. While he wrote, he engaged in small talk to suggest that he was now comfortable with their association, even took pains to show some excitement that they would be able to secure wealth as soon as they could recover the diary.

"Well," Mav announced, "this here orta do it. I will sign my name an' you ken sign yorn, but if I am to sign fo' you, I might orta add a line to notify them thet I wuz a-signin' for you. Ok?"

Not waiting for an answer Mav signed both names and pushed the completed document to Chico so he could read it for himself. As he did so, Mav tensed and prepared to overturn the table onto Chico and run for his life if Chico detects his deception.

Chico picked up the paper without inverting it and looked at the upside-down document for a minute, carefully examining it. Presently, Chico's face registered a sinister smile as if he was enjoying a private joke at Mav's expense, and turned the document right side up, staring at it for a minute before holding it up to his new partner, *Señor* Maverick Caiden.

Pointing to the words 'READ SILENTLY,' he asked, slowly, showing again, a sinister smile, "What is this, *Señor* Maverick?"

For a moment, Mav thought his assumption may be wrong, that Chico may be able to read enough to detect the lie. Leaning forward to see what Chico was pointing to while gripping the table edge in anticipation, Mav answered: "Thet is th' name o' ourn pardnership."

Chico continued to stare at the page as Mav watched for eye movement that would suggest that Chico was reading. Finally, Chico handed the paper back to Mav.

"Read it *Señor* Maverick, slowly." Cisco made the demand that was like music. Mav then knew for certain that Cisco could not read; otherwise, he would have sent a serious hunk of lead at Mav's chest. 'The ironic thing about greed,' thought Mav, 'Chico has killed for a diary he knows has a key to understanding the map. A diary that he cannot even read!' For the next several minutes, Maverick ad-libbed legal sounding jargon to his new *compañero*. His partner and best *amigo*.

Mav concluded the matter of their partnership just as dawn broke and sunlight streamed into the small cabin. Mav became more assured that Chico believed in the possibility that incredible wealth was within reach, beginning with a thousand dollars that he must give to the 'senior' partner. Encouragement of their camaraderie is paramount to establishing trust so, as any good host would do, Mav prepared a hot breakfast for himself and his very good *compañero* and new *amigo*, *Señor* Francisco 'Chico' Alvarez.

Four hours later, Mav and Chico mounted up to ride into Beaton for a visit to the bank. An hour following their arrival, Mav stopped by the Arkland office to retrieve his mail.

"I understand that something was happening at the bank today," declared Macy, "what was it all about. I saw the sheriff taking a man to jail. You must have seen what was happening because I was told that you were seen there at the same time."

"Oh, Macy, it wuz jes' an attempted robbery. No one got hurt none, an' th' money is still in th' bank, so there wuz no losses. Thet murderin' snake, Chico, —th' man arrested, —will prob'ly spend some time in th' hoosegow fo' th' attempt. He also will face hangin' fo' killin's he done in Texas, too, so his fate mayhap be to dec'rate some cottonwood tree down in Bandera. If thet be so, I ain't sendin' no flowers!" Mav felt a little shame in not telling the whole story, but the fate of his family and the diary and all was just too much to address with Macy or anyone else at this time.

Macy would ponder the intensity of Mav's words spoken of the man arrested, especially those about murder since no murder had occurred at the bank.

Chapter 11

The Big Dance / Surprise Attack

As the entertainment got underway, Mav, now receiving his first dance lesson and trying to follow the tempo of the music, said to Macy, "Thet fella on th' fiddle ken shor set a pace, cain't he?" After several near collisions with other couples, Mav asked: "May we sit this un out? These new boots…" Smooth soles of new boots always cause clumsiness on a dance floor until they roughen or the wearer becomes more skilled. Everyone knows this.

"Sure can," responded Macy, thinking she may have gotten the worst from the new boots but loving every minute Mav held her in his arms. "Why don't you let me get the punch this time. I won't be long returning. Just tell the ladies that may want a dance that you have promised them all to me."

The idea that other ladies might want to dance with him as clumsy as he believed himself was surprising. Macy must have been teasing him. In spite his initial doubts about the dance, he found himself tapping a foot in time with the music as a fiddle, dobro, and banjo made their melodic sounds. Part way through the evening, additional farmer-musicians added instruments to the mix and a harmonica and a guitar became part of the band. Some of the favorite songs of the night were <u>After the Ball</u>, a waltz in three-quarter time written by Charles K. Harris; <u>The Loveliest Night of the Year</u>, a waltz derived from a work by Mexican composer, Juventino P. Rosas also known by the title, <u>*Sombre las Olas*</u> or, <u>Over the Waves</u>.

By nine o'clock, Mav's anxiety at learning how to dance had transposed to the excitement of discovering new dance steps, and dances like the <u>Cotton Eyed Joe</u>, a unique line dance that was spreading in popularity was readily mastered. The waltz, a staple on the dance floor in Europe, also learned; the two-step, popular in Texas that Mav recalled seeing his parents dance; the polka that had arrived with some new emigrants from Poland who demonstrated its lively steps for the first time in Beaton; and finally, the schottische, from Bohemia, also a newly introduced dance, either tried by Mav and Macy and mastered or tried and failed to achieve proficiency, but retained as a goal for later times. For the polka and the schottische, the music and the rhythm were squeezed from the bellows of an accordion in the capable hands of Hans Werner.

Eleven o'clock came, and the dance floor was becoming an orphan. Couples and singles were beginning to leave for home. Some still had miles to go to get back home. Mav and Macy started their walk back to where she and her pa lived in the house just behind the Arkland office and arrived there about ten minutes later.

"I want to thank you for coming," Macy began, as she turned to face Mav. "There just aren't many fun things to do in a small town like Beaton. Makes a girl sad at times. A girl without a partner at a dance is a sad thing. They can't ask a fella to dance without seeming overly forward and just sitting alone or with other gals just gets them the name of 'wallflower'. I hope you don't suffer from our dance lessons. I think you did really well. Pa is asleep by now."

Mav listened as Macy spoke, thinking that he should say something, but not knowing just what was appropriate. He had never ended a day like this before, nor with a girl before. And what does it matter if her pa is asleep anyway? These are perplexing times. Maybe they should shake hands. He was sorely mistaken in thinking a handshake would be the appropriate way to end his first date, an event that he had not considered putting a description to yet, because as he reached out a hand his hand was promptly and forcefully swept aside and he found himself pressed against the wall while two of the softest, warmest lips that ever graced the face of a human of the female persuasion met his. Needless to say, Mav totally lost his breath, owing to the suddenness and, some might say, aggressiveness, but he darned well loved every moment that it lasted. Just as suddenly, Macy jerked the door open and went inside closing the door behind. From his stand by the door, he thought from the inside, he heard crying. She never shook his hand.

Mav stood on the porch trying to absorb what had transpired, then set his path toward the hitchin' rail where Biscuit patiently waited. Mav and Biscuit will have a serious conversation on the way home. There's something different about dealing with a woman than dealing with a man, and Mav knows he needs to get a little help in figuring it out.

Chapter 12

A Dreadful Storm / A Sheriff Writes

As Thursday arrives, the clouds layer in various shades of gray, the wind gusting through the trees causing limbs to dip and sway and lift as if they seek freedom from their bonds. The sounds of the wind, like some animal moaning in the wilderness from distress that one can only imagine. There is a nervousness in the air that affects all living things. Animals in the pastures and fields mill around in circles lifting heads and tails and bawling, horses whinny and dance in their stalls sniffing the air as if all will be revealed by its scent. The flash of lightning and crash of thunder are fearful things to creatures not blessed with abilities to comprehend nature and make wary humans who do. During his days as a drover for Captain Lytle, storms like this caused severe trouble for the drovers. The sudden spooking of cattle by thunder and lightning can result in a dangerous, chaotic stampede of a herd which cowhands must outpace and turn back upon itself to stop the run. Stampedes were all hands events in which everyone shouldered his share of the task. Every able man mounted up to race into the darkness to get in front of the running cattle and turn them back, skillfully shaping the herd into a continuously tightening circle of panicked animals until there was no path for them to run. Mav first witnessed St. Elmo's fire gratuitously engendered by thunderstorm upon the horns of frightened cattle fifty miles from Ogallala. There are no greater events than thunder and lightning to demonstrate the awesome power of unseen forces and to diminish a man's belief in his ability to assure his own survival. The power of nature trumps all.

In addition to the danger of stampede, the loss of time to round up a fearful herd dispersed throughout some unfamiliar chaparral was of considerable concern. Sometimes, stampedes resulted in the loss of life for both cattle and drovers. A man, alive but minutes before, laying crushed by hundreds of hooves churning beneath eleven-hundred-pound steers standing sixty inches at the shoulder with horns measuring up to one hundred inches tip-to-tip, is a sobering sight. Common myth holds that stampeding cattle will not step on a fallen man neglects the fact that stampedes result from blind panic, and in blind panic even people are known to crush their kind. Although a stampede is of no concern to Mav today, the potential tragedy of a severe storm of this portent is real.

Mav walks to the door and steps out upon the porch to observe the sky and is immediately concerned about the cloud bank to the northwest. No longer does he see layered bands of gray for now, as far as he can see is a solid wall of steel-blue horror. In Bandera people would be calling it a blue norther that would drop temperatures quickly by thirty degrees or more in as little as a quarter hour.

A hard rain is sweeping across the open spaces veiling the landscape in lightning illuminated silvery streaks of fast-falling water, soon changing to fist-sized hail beating upon corrugated tin roofs of house and barn sounding like a thousand drummers banging away on tin buckets while strips of bark peel away from exposed trees. Images of various trees or man-built structures emerge as dark shadows created by lightning flashes. Lemon-bright structures appear in the sky like skeletal trees against the darkness as lightning carves pathways of jittering fire, their ending accompanied by a delayed crescendo of thunderous sound. Mav had had the foresight to bring many of the animals into the barn or into a small containment corral next to the barn, but some had panicked and spread out through the trees. He would have to find them after the storm.

Later that night, the storm's intensity rapidly increased. Winds screamed with a sinister passion, howling like a thousand wolves in pursuit of their prey. As the wind strengthened, Mav's thoughts turned from thunderstorm to tornado, and his concern increased. Survival through such events is the will of God, so Mav offered his thoughts in silent prayer. Trees surrendered large limbs to the wind, that snapped them like finger-sized branches and scattered them below. Loose things on the ground flailed against the walls of the cabin with a determination to pierce to its innards. Windows rattled in their frames behind creaking storm shutters. The powerlessness of one man against the elements brought a feeling of smallness to Mav that he had difficulty setting aside, as six-foot long strips of metal roofing tore away and flew into the maelstrom of swirling, rain infused air, smelling like ozone, that blanketed the landscape and brought a catch to the throat making the process of breathing a conscious thing. A lone pine atop a nearby hill burst into flame following the flash and almost simultaneous loud thunder-clap from the close lightning strike, and he could have sworn he sensed the stench of burning brimstone.

"Thank God it warn't th' barn!" he said aloud, "with all o' th' animals thar, an' Biscuit. Ifn lightn' don't strike us thet toad-stranglin' rain will prob'ly drown us afore mornin'." Mav found that his thoughts of the danger to himself the storm infused into his mind became pale as he realized the storm would find its way to Beaton before the night was through.

"Macy. My God, Macy." Words, spoken into the night, diminished, and silenced by the sheer sound and fury of the of moaning, crying wind, and he could do nothing. Mav spent the longest night of his life waiting for the punishing storm to pass. It seemed to Mav that time twisted in some diabolical way to force him to experience each minute repeatedly until the energy of that malevolent power winnowed away as an echo diminishes, little by little until nothing remains. Morning did come, and Mav who had finally drifted off to sleep from emotional exhaustion awoke to the sound of birdsong and a golden sunrise.

"Wake up Biscuit, we gotta go to Beaton." Mav saddled Biscuit and rode out in the direction of Beaton, riding around the numerous storm-damaged branches and trees littering the ground. As he rode into Beaton, his eyes assessed the devastation. A large tree with a twisted trunk wrenched from the earth lay across the trail into the city. Entire buildings knocked off their foundations, roofs were torn off, and chimneys toppled. Scattered debris littered the streets.

"Oh, God!" he verbalized and urged Biscuit onward toward the Arkland office. The Arkland office stood, virtually untouched, but the house behind it had partially collapsed, exposing a vacant interior and a nearby pile of rubble. His heart stopped for as long as time stood still for him. Quickly, he jumped from the saddle and ran to the rubble looking for what he was afraid to find, searching for the sorrow he feared was awaiting him with each piece of broken wood he thrust aside. Calling, "Macy, Macy, Macy." Tears began to well in his eyes, making it hard to direct his hands to the next board, hands bleeding from the cuts and splinters from his efforts to dig through futility.

Uncounted minutes passed and as a feeling of defeat fluttered in his chest and throat, he heard a creaking sound twenty feet beyond the devastated house where from the soggy earth a door opened, and Macy emerged from a dug-out storm shelter, leading her aged papa out into the brightening day.

"Oh, God! Oh, God!" was all he could say as he ran to her side.

That week, the citizens held services for the fallen in the Beaton Methodist Church and in the First Baptist Church of Beaton and the new Presbyterian Church. Mav attended each with Macy whose hand he found hard to release when Music Director Sutton announced the page of the hymnal to turn to for the next hymn, <u>Shall We Gather at the River</u>, a Gospel song becoming a standard that American poet and Gospel music composer Robert Lowry composed less than a decade ago.

Macy, holding the hymnal turned to page twenty-seven and held the book so Mav could read the lyrics, lyrics that had become familiar to the congregation before he left Bandera. He was amazed at how much he remembered as he lent his voice to the congregation, in alternating verses and a refrain that always brings uplift to the volume from the many voices that are more familiar with the refrain than with the independent verses:

> Yes, we'll gather at the river,
> The beautiful, the beautiful river;
> Gather with the saints at the river
> That flows by the throne of God.[3]

As towns suffer destruction, so also are they rebuilt, and that is the way with Beaton. It took months and a lot of sweat, but the town arose from its momentary defeat like the Phoenix from the pyre. Three people had died on that fateful night and several injured, but the spirit of the town's citizens was undefeatable. Mav and other friends of the small family repaired the Wilson's house and, except for the new paint, it looked much as it did before the storm.

Eugene Stonefield

✳✳✳

"Mav," said Macy on one of his, now more frequent trips into town, "I have a letter for you. It's from that sheriff you wrote to some months ago."

"Much obliged, Macy, I'll read it at home. Is yor papa recoverin' yet from his ailments?" The question was to show concern, not to receive information that would give a person reason to hope for a recovery. By all accounts, his health is deteriorating, and his end may be near. The doc has become a regular visitor to the aged station-keeper but keeps a positive outlook, which is helpful to a fearful daughter.

Mav rode home thinking about Macy and what would happen to her when her papa died. Her papa still draws an income as the station-keeper for Beaton, but it is Macy who performs the duties of the station-keeper. At some point, it will be necessary for the Arkland owners to appoint another to the Beaton station. It isn't likely Macy will be able to receive approval to continue as Beaton's station-keeper. Even excellence in performance does not make the duties of a station-keeper suitable for women in this era. "Biscuit," he declared as he rode, "times are a-gittin' serious."

✳✳✳

Mav arrived at the cabin and opened the letter from Sheriff Partin, hopeful that he will receive answers to his troubling questions about the murder of his family in Bandera. He read:

Mav Caid — The Complete Story

Dear Maverick,

I was happy to get your letter and must apologize for taking so long to answer. I had several people to speak with to get their memory of the sorrowful event that took your family, but they were gone for a time. The story as I understand it to be is that a brother to your ma, your uncle —I now know his name was Wendell Forda —had come to see your mama to retrieve a diary that he had mailed to her previously. Unbeknownst to him, a person known as Chico had followed your uncle who he thought was rich by virtue of some discovery your uncle had made which he recorded in his diary. I don't know for sure how he came to believe that, but others in Bandera knew of it also. Apparently, Mr. Forda had drawn several maps to the discovery, but they were meaningless without the diary which contained some code or key to understanding. Anyway, this Chico confronted your uncle and your ma and pa about the discovery and demanded the journal. One of the victims gave Chico the map in hopes that it would satisfy him, but it only made him angry. He learned of you, Maverick, and became convinced that you must have the diary. Apparently, he learned where you are living from his search of the house in which he found a letter addressed to you in Beaton. In a rage, he killed everyone in the house, and as he was doing it, your uncle broke free and ran to the barn where Chico shot him, apparently as he attempted to retrieve his saddle rifle. Chico then burned both house and barn. Possibly, your uncle had retrieved the diary from your folks and was preparing to leave at the time Chico arrived. Someone found the diary in a saddlebag under the carcass of a horse which protected it from the fire. You should be wary of anyone you don't recognize because Chico is a ruthless killer and will stop at nothing to get what he wants. Before he left Bandera, he revealed to a lady friend, Alicia Nava, what had happened and told her he was going to get the diary from you. Miss Nava recalled reading to him your name and location written upon a letter he gave to her. Alicia Nava was convinced it was in her interest to tell us what happened. She, herself, is fearful of Chico because of his violent nature. Nava said that she has known Chico since before he spent time in some Arkansas jail from which he was recently released. He seeks the diary you now have so you are a target for him if he can find you. Chico may not even be his

Eugene Stonefield

real name, and Alicia could not tell me what it is. That's all I can report. Be very careful. I have sent a warrant for his arrest to your sheriff in Beaton. Don't hesitate to contact him if needed.

Cordially,
C. S. Partin, Sheriff of Bandera Co., Texas

Setting the letter aside, Mav thought about his family and how they had died over a discovery made by his uncle so many years ago that no one even knows if it has value.

"Such a terrible waste," Mav whispered to himself. "Is thar anythin' in this world worth th' takin' of life?" A person is born into life and should have the right to live it however he pleases without someone taking if from him. It's one of the 'thou shalt nots' from the Bible that everybody learns as children. What makes a person want to kill another? After the unanswerable question receded in his mind, the subject turned to his own experience with the murders of his family. Living people, just working to make a place for themselves, and two children who had no chance to learn anything about life – all shot down by Chico. He began to sense the rage come back as it had come to him when he first met Chico. His face began to contort, began to feel hot. Just as suddenly, a coldness swept over his body and the anger ceded to a feeling of helplessness. It was at this moment that Mav realized that he had fought the process of grieving for his lost family for too long, and feeling his exhaustion from that personal battle finally release, Mav crossed his arms on his table and leaning forward, lowered his head upon his arms, and surrendered.

Chapter 13

Decoding the Diary / Epiphany in Beaton

'What strange events,' thought Mav. 'Two people have sought to kill me or threatened to kill me within the last two years.' He recalled that several years before those attempts, one man had verbally threatened him, and that was because Mav had revealed a plot against Lytle, but that threat seems to have gone away after the man on the pinto attempted to shoot him from ambush four miles from his cabin. None have seen the man on the pinto since that time. 'Since he wasn't successful, he probably skedaddled knowing people would be looking for him for his attempt. Still, it may be prudent to remain watchful. How did he find me anyway? Now that's a genuine puzzle.'

Mav, has recovered from the threat of Chico, and has testified against him in the trial for attempted robbery which resulted in a sentence of five years in jail for Chico for the attempted robbery, and he will someday stand trial for murder in Texas. Mav now turns his mind back to the mystery. He is in possession of both the diary and the map, and is ready to learn more about the indecipherable line contained in his uncle Wendell's diary. The children of the ranchers and farmers around Beaton are out of school helping their families get in the crops so he expected a visit to the schoolmaster would not unreasonably impose upon his day. Mav and Biscuit turned toward Beaton early and arrived at the school around nine.

Schoolmaster Marcus Vale was sitting behind the table in front of a slate board used to illustrate ideas and instructions in chalk to the students of Beaton and surrounding countryside. As Mav came through the door, Schoolmaster Vale stood and held out a hand. The offered hand has long, slim fingers that recapitulate the long, slender body of this thirty-something-year-old educator. A sandy colored collar-length hair, frames the elongated face of the schoolmaster, and he looks at Mav from washed blue eyes under thin eyebrows. He is clean shaven. Marcus' credentials stem from an education he received at the University of Nashville in Tennessee.

"Welcome, Mr. Caid. I haven't seen you since the big dance. I trust you have been well."

"Howdy, Mr. Vale, an' I hav' been well," began Mav. "I come to see ifn you might could hep me with interpretin' a line o' numbers an' sech from a diary. I have this here diary, an' it has a writ line that's some kinda key to a hand-drawn map. I've been a-puzzlin' over it fo' a time but believe thet if I am a-knowin' its meanin' I gotta hav' hep from someone who is a-knowin' about celestial navigation." Mav waited for a response while casually glancing around the classroom and remembering his own days in a similar room before he left home.

"If I can assist, I am happy to do so. Could you show me the line?" responded Marcus Vale. "Which hemisphere are we talking about?"

"I reckon I know it by heart, so I'll jes' write it on thet slate board." Mav walked to the board and wrote: 3 4lt-9 4lg (1mt ▲ nw 12dfmnores 12m) (2mt ▲ se 150dfrmnores 3m) (3mt ▲ sw 190dfmnores 15m) D runne>sw. "Oh, an' it would hafta be somewhar near."

"Navigation, you say?" asked the schoolmaster.

"Yessir, I'm a-thinkin' it has somethin' to do with latitude an' longitude but my rec'lection from my own school days, when they larn'd me about them early explorers is dim," returned Mav.

"Well, I have no experience in navigation, but maybe we can break this down into smaller pieces and figure it out. First off, I see what appears to be something shaped like a dunce-hat or triangle which I don't know what it could mean. It could be a symbol, but, if so, its meaning is obscure. But, let's assume the letters are the first letter of a word it represents and we also assume we are dealing, as you have said, with coordinates of latitude and longitude." Marcus placed a hand over mouth and chin as he pondered what the letters and numbers could mean. "So…Let's see, if 'lt' is assumed to be latitude and 'lg' to be longitude then the characters, '3 6lt', could mean some place between 3 degrees and 6 degrees north latitude, and '-9 4lg' could mean a location between 9 degrees west and 4 degrees east longitude which would…let's see," walking to a cabinet Schoolmaster Vale removed a strange elongated object which he immediately expanded into a round balloon-like object.

"My prized possession," stated Marcus Vale, "a Betts Portable Globe! See, it opens like an umbrella into a globe of the world and shows the five continents with lines of latitude and longitude."

Marcus paused in thought for a moment, then resumed. "Now, assuming those numbers are coordinates, that would put a person somewhere about here…Wait, this doesn't make sense. That would be a large area near the north pole somewhere above Greenland. But, what if 3 4lt is 34 north latitude and -9 4lg is 94 west longitude?"

Eugene Stonefield

"Wait! How is it you are a-knowin' from them numbers thet it is west rather than east?" interjected Mav, looking puzzled.

"Well, if a minus sign precedes the number it has to reference a longitude west of Greenwich if you are talking longitude, and a latitude south of the equator if you are talking latitude," replied Marcus. "It is by nautical convention, and was established so navigators would know which area of the globe was referenced." Pointing to the Betts, Marcus shows Mav the prime meridian running pole to pole through Greenwich which represents longitude zero, and the equator representing latitude zero. "As you can see, this convention allows you to find a location in any one of eight possible areas of the globe."

Recovering his trend of thought, Marcus looks for a location on the Betts, "that would put you about here," pointing to a place on the globe near the center of North America. "Incidentally, we are about here, relatively near." Marcus Vale showed his satisfaction with a smile before continuing. "Now, to describe something on a map, landmarks of some kind must be identified, so let's look for descriptions that suggest landmarks." For a moment, Marcus Vale stroked his chin and silently pointed at the characters. "So, now," he continued, "the '(1' and 'mt' – I'm not sure, but let us assume that 'mt' means 'mountain,' and 'nw' could be 'northwest' – a reasonable assumption since we must be dealing with directions. So, '12d' sounds mighty like 'twelve degrees,' and 'fmnores' I am not sure of. The 'fm,' I can't guess, but the following 'nor' could mean 'north,' and 'es' I, also, am not sure of, but the next '12' followed by 'm' could, if taken together build a phrase. We could read: '12 degrees fm (from?) north, 'es' (estimated?) 12 'm' (miles?). If that is true, then the next phrase would be: '(2 – again not sure of, but the rest could be…ah ha! (2 must certainly be landmark number two! So, (1 and (3 are landmarks also. The left parenthesis mark pairs with the following right parenthesis to segregate a phrase. The three phrases mark a triangle!"

Mav Caid — The Complete Story

"Read this:" an excited Marcus Vale remarks while writing quickly on the slate board. Satisfied with his analysis, the statement reads: Landmark 1 is a mountain northwest, 12 degrees from north estimated 12 miles; Landmark 2 is a mountain southeast 150 degrees from north estimated 3 miles; Landmark 3 is a mountain southwest 190 degrees from north estimated 15 miles, D runs northeast to southwest.

"These coordinates describe a triangle lying at or near latitude 34 north and longitude 94 west, which is near where we are. It still needs minutes and seconds to be definitive. If we had minutes and seconds, we could be more certain of its location. What is supposed to be there? What is 'D' that runs northeast to the southwest? A river? Stream?" Marcus looked intently at Mav.

"Well Mr. Vale, for shor, that is whut I am a-tryin' to larn. I wuz giv'n these here directions in a diary to 'splain a hand-drawn map, but nothin' to say whut's there, only thet it wuz thought to be important. I maybe orta go look fo' it. Now, I thank you, mightily, fo' hepin' me understand." Mav shook hands with the schoolmaster and returned to his cabin more knowledgeable than when he left but still lacking in the knowledge of what was there. He wished he still had the strange rocks his uncle sent to him with the map years ago. Those could have revealed a lot if more knowledgeable people could see them.

❋❋❋

Leaving the school, Mav decided to drop by the Arkland office and speak with Macy about something that had been bothering him since the dance.

"Howdy, Mr. Wilson, good to see you up an' around." said Mav as he entered the Arkland office an found the station-keeper behind the counter, "Macy in?"

"Macy's to home right now," he returned, "why don't ya just knock on the dowha?"

"Obliged, Mr. Wilson, I'll do thet." Mav left the Arkland office and walked around to the house behind, now rebuilt from the storm, where he knocked on the door and announced himself.

"Why, Mav! What brings you here?" Macy's surprise was evident, as they spoke across the threshold of her recently rebuilt house.

"Macy, I'm a-hanker'n' to talk to you 'bout somethin' thet's been a-botherin' me. You recall thet dance, an', well, after th' dance I walked you home an' you…" Mav turned scarlet and went silent.

"I recall, Mav. What is bothering you about it?" answered Macy with some consternation.

"Well, Macy…" again, Mav went silent.

"Yes?" responded Macy.

"Well, Macy…Well, Macy, we wuz a-standin' here on the porch an'…an' you…uh…you kissed me." Mav looked as if he wanted to run, and the color drained from his face.

"Mav, should I not have kissed you?" asked Macy from her growing puzzlement.

"Well, Macy…Uh, maybe, maybe, uh, could you do it ag'in?" Mav turned red again.

If a more desirous gift ever fell into the hand of such a worthy girl, one would be hard pressed to name it. Macy felt the exhilaration of a Caesar returning to Rome in triumph. Caesar may have conquered a world, but Macy had captured her dream.

"I could, Mav," she began, "if you want me to, but I would like to try something different." She moved closer to the threshold and Mav.

Mav's scarlet hue turned white. "What?"

"You kiss me, this time." Macy stepped across the threshold onto the porch and faced Mav.

Mav, still a shade pale, answered: "I…I don't know how."

"Don't you remember, Mav? We walked to this porch, and we were talking, and something came over me, and I pushed you against the wall and kissed you. Then I went in because I was afraid that I had insulted you. Mav, this is the wall. Pretend you are me and do what I did."

Epiphany is not the sole purview of God's faithful and Mav just had his. Mav stepped forward and took Macy by the shoulders and pressed her against the wall and found his courage. After this inspiring osculatory embrace, Mav found his courage again.

Chapter 14

An Accidental Proposal / The Catamount

This is the time of year to be planting, and Mav has worked diligently over the last year to clear more field for growing crops. At first, a small garden for needed vegetables was enough, but as Beaton continues to grow, Mav sees an opportunity in producing more than for his personal need. He does not associate the contemplation of opportunity with the effect of a maturing mind. Most of the farming around Beaton is for family. The farmers trade among themselves and take produce to a farmer's market for the needs of citizens of Beaton. Mav wants to fill the needs of those running the hotel and the two boarding houses that have opened to serve the people of Beaton. Recently, Mav struck a sole supplier agreement to supply milk from his dairy cows to baker Keller. He thinks of striking similar agreements with the hotel owners for beef. Often, Mav questions why he seems driven to clear land and plant, when his earlier interests were satisfied by hunting and fishing. Now, he seldom hunts or visits his fishing hole, given the time demands of his growing interests. He keeps hearing in the back of his mind the words of his pa telling him he could not escape his roots. He didn't fully understand when his pa said it to him, now though, he understands. Mav is a farmer, born to farming. He probably will live and die a farmer. Someday soon, he will need to hire help with the chores. Someday, he will have to choose what interest is paramount. His interest in cattle for beef comes from his years with Lytle. Dairy farming began with his need for milk and butter. Vegetable farming, first for himself, now he envisions developing into a true business. Mav's activities grow, but have no focus. What is Mav Caid? is a question that does not enter his stream of consciousness. What does, is Macy Wilson.

Trips to Beaton are more frequent now and usually for goods and services that he might need. More frequent trips give more opportunity to drop by the Arkland office and see Macy. Her papa is more aged, more fragile, and Macy is performing more of the work of the station-keeper.

Today, he travels to Beaton to buy seed for planting and pick up a copy of the farmer's almanac. First, though, call on Macy.

"Good morning, Mav," Macy called out from behind the counter. "Come for your mail?"

The question has become a standing joke long since, but sometimes it is true.

"I come fo' somethin' a might better," Mav returned as he leaned over the counter and kissed Macy on the cheek, then felt his face warm from instant embarrassment.

"Best you can do?" she asked, wide-eyed.

"Right now," he returned. "What more ken you ask of a fella on a workday?" then following, "how's yor papa?"

"About the same, Mav. I am thinking of applying to become the Arkland's station-keeper in Beaton if he should die or become unable to continue. The owners must know he's sinking and I want to get my name in the mix of candidates for the job. I just hope Jess Kinder doesn't want it. He has connections. And I have never heard of a woman station-keeper, even though I have demonstrated my ability to perform all the duties. But, I think, why not? If that one-eyed, hard drinking, Charlie Parkhurst - that woman who masqueraded as a man and drove stagecoaches in California around 1860 can do that, why can't I be a station-keeper?"

"Well, ifn it don't happen as you want, how are you at farmin'?" Mav asked while showing an entirely blank, expressionless face.

Looking up swiftly, Macy looked at Mav and exclaimed: "Maverick Caiden, don't you tease me! That's a question with two meanings! You know I'm not a landowner and have never farmed. I know nothing but how to keep a station running properly. What makes you ask a question like that, knowing that papa and I aren't farmers? Papa was a store-keeper back east before we came here. We've never farmed anything."

"Now Macy, I'm jes' tryin' to be helpful an' offer ideas. You're strong. Farm work is hard sometimes, but rewardin' an' you ken larn. An' th' wife o' a farmer..." The statement's implication triggered the attentive Macy, to interject:

"What did you say? Maverick Caiden. What did you say? Are you asking me to marry you? Mav?" then following: "I can't marry you. I have Papa and...and all this work to do and, I...I...Yes. Yes! I have to go. I have to tell Papa." Macy disappeared through the back door. Mav didn't get another word in, nor did he get his mail. After waiting for a time, Mav shrugged his shoulders and ambled out the door.

Stopping at the S & E General Store, Mav asked to speak with Edna. "Edna, do you hav' any concoction thet soothes jittery nerves? I wuz jes' by th' Arkland office an' Macy has th' jitters somethin' fierce. She scooted out whilst I wuz a-talkin' to her an' ne'er come back."

Edna surveyed Mav's face then responded: "I hav' ergot an' some peppermint oil, an' some chamomile. Chamomile tea is good fo' soothin' anxiety. Peppermint oil helps with sour stomachs. Ergot, well, we ladies know about usin' ergot, but it's good for headaches, too. Which do you think she needs?"

"I shor don't know. Maybe you orta send some o' each?" Mav paid for the concoctions and remounted Biscuit for the trip back home without the seed.

"Well, Biscuit," said Mav as they were halfway home, "I jes' went fo' seed but accidental-like put in a whol' dif'runt order jes' talkin' in generalities. An' I don't know whut got into Macy. She went off all helter-skelter an' forgot to give me my mail. Women are hard to understan' sometimes. What's yor opinion?"

If Mav expected some sagacious comment from Biscuit, he was to be surprised by what happened next. Biscuit snorted loudly and crow-hopped sideways, causing Mav to lurch in the opposite direction of the leap and pull back on the reins. Just off the trail in front of Biscuit was the reason for his reaction. Glittering golden eyes tracked their movement with an unsettling interest. A partly concealed catamount appeared ready to spring, yet declined to do so for an unknown reason. Biscuit, responding to the pull-back on the reins, had stopped his initial jittery behavior but stamped his front hoofs nervously as he eyed this tawny cat just twenty feet away. Mav reached for his rifle and leveled the barrel at the cat. A standoff ensued. The cat retained the posture of one intending to leap while Mav maintained his stance of one ready to pull the trigger. And nothing happened. The cat snarled. Mav scratched his head. A puzzled Mav searched for a cause of the cat's behavior, knowing that a catamount would generally avoid contact with a human unless it was unavoidable or the cat was protecting her young or starving. He could see no kitten, nor could he hear a cry of one, nor could he assess starvation. Silence. Mav urged Biscuit to back up, a maneuver Biscuit knew well and responded while keeping an eye on the catamount. Still, the animal remained and showed no sign of wanting to attack or run, although she did register her disapproval with growls.

"This is th' darndest thin'," whispered Mav under his breath. "What's yor opinion, Biscuit? I think somethin' must be ailin' it. Some reason…Wait! I see it Biscuit. I see it. A broke limb 'cross her back. Could be a broke back. How could somethin' like thet happen to a cat?"

A perplexed Mav Caid discovered a growing sense of pity for the captive catamount, a wild animal, unable to exercise familiar freedom to move about, possibly, even experiencing intense pain. There were times during his days with Lytle that his response might have been to shoot the cat, especially after finding a calf half consumed and knowing it was likely Lytle's calf that one of his cows had dropped in the scrub. Nevertheless, pity assumed the upper hand and Mav backed Biscuit further off and dismounted. The cause became known as Mav drew closer to the catamount lying in a depression under the large branch, front torso on one side, hindquarter twisted with both back paws to one side on the other. Thinking to himself that the cat must have a broken back, Mav lifts his rifle to his shoulder and aims between two golden eyes of the trapped catamount that remained watchful, if not waiting for a conclusion. 'No animal should suffer as this cat must be suffering,' Mav thought, as he took his aim, then finding his finger refusing to obey his command, as if some instantaneous paralysis had asserted control and stayed the hand of the executioner. Mav returned to Biscuit and replaced the rifle in its holster, then untying the whang strings securing his lariat, took the rope from his saddle. Mav circled the catamount to draw all attention to himself and approached the encumbered animal. Her golden eyes followed, but she now remained silent. Mav closely inspected the physical appearance of the catamount occupying that fortuitous indentation in the earth beneath the fallen branch and could see no punctures or cuts on the body.

Eugene Stonefield

"Jes' enough room to trap you without serious harm, but not enough to allow you to crawl free," Mav said to the catamount. Mav stepped closer to the cat where he bent down to draw the rope beneath the limb and tie it, his hands so close to the catamount touching was unavoidable. As his hand hovered near the catamount, he noticed a scorched appearance of the entrapping limb and the catamount's fur. In his mind, he could imagine a sudden lightning strike that sheared the branch and stunned the catamount lying below in a shallow depression over which the branch fell, trapping the cat.

"Lucky gal," Mav said, addressing the silent feline. "Whut ere you goin' to do ifn I free you?" Mav asked the cat as she watched intently over her shoulder and sniffed the air. Presently, Mav threw the rope over a sizeable overhanging branch and drew up the slack. Mav began to pull the loose end of the rope, but the limb refused to lift being heavier than Mav. Changing positions, he tried again to lift the imprisoning branch off the catamount. The result was the same.

"I must be plumb loco," Mav whispered to himself, "but for better or worse, I've made a commitment to this catamount, mayhap a fool's commitment, but I made it anyhow. If anyone e'er said my papa ne'er raised no fool, I might have to challenge thet." As he released the rope a second time, he heard a soft moan, a sound coming from the cat that he had never heard before. I was the sound of despair. A sound never heard from a living creature unless all hope was gone leaving only a sense of inevitability of doom. For a moment, the cat abandoned eye contact and laid her head down as if in acceptance of defeat. Mav walked over to Biscuit and tightened the cinch and patted him on the neck, whispering to him, seeking to engage his trust. "I need you Biscuit."

Returning to the dangling rope leading Biscuit by the reins, Mav picked up the rope and tied it around the saddle horn. Then mounting, he nudged Biscuit to back up. Here was the moment of ultimate truth.

If the cat cries out and Biscuit panics, or if when freed, she turns upon them, pandemonium is certain to occur, with an unpredictable result.

"Back up, Biscuit. Back up," Mav whispers into Biscuit's ear. Suddenly, the limb moves upward and swings back toward Mav and Biscuit. The catamount is free. For a moment, Mav focused his attention on the rope still tethering himself and Biscuit to the suspended branch to determine if they have provided the necessary clearance to free the catamount. Having assured himself of the sufficiency of that clearance, Mav loosened the rope, and the branch fell back to the ground. The cat stands as if assuring herself that she is uninjured and that she is free from her entrapment. Uncertainty of the freed catamount's next move propels Mav to remove his rifle from its holster once again. Again, she turns her golden gaze onto Mav and Biscuit. Mav, for the first time, realizes how large and how strong and how dangerous in her freedom the catamount appears up close. She circles once to the left, then to the right, each time returning her golden-eyed focus toward Mav and Biscuit. For a minute or more she surveys the environment and sniffs the air, then as if responding to a call by her kitten somewhere far, —a call unheard by Mav, —she turns away and quietly ambles off through the undergrowth. Mav again dismounts and walks to the branch and cuts the rope just above the log, recoiling the remainder which he secures to the saddle.

"Biscuit," said Mav, softly as if to himself, "I reckon we mayhap orta keep this ourn secrit. Nobody's gonna believe it nohow."

Chapter 15

Objections of a Papa / Negotiation

Station-keeper Chauncey Wilson rallied from his listlessness when his daughter raced in to announce that she was to marry Mav Caid. While rallied was the term used to describe his return to reasonable vitality for a man of his age, a jolt into disapprobation bordering rage would be the appropriate term for his disposition. Chauncey Wilson is the product of an older tradition and Macy's announcement of such momentous occasion without prior approval, represented a clear violation of the precepts of that tradition.

"He hain't axed me for yor han'!" objected Papa to Macy. "He hain't axed for yor han' a'tall." A true charge made in the argument. "An' wher's th' courtin'? A papa needs to see a wooin' befo'a he gives his only darter to a stranger! What kinda worl' would we be livin' in if a darter could just go decidin' them things herself? What kinda man would come and steal a darter like some thief in th' night? It haint' proper!"

"Papa, Mav is not a stranger. You have known him for a long time. And folks have seen us together at picnics and dances, just this last year. And you know we write letters to each other. How can you say there was no courting?" pleaded Macy.

"Nobody tol' me! I thought you an' Mav wuz jes' good frien's," countered Papa to offset the possibility that he just hadn't been paying close enough attention. "I want to see a courtin'!" Chauncey drew out the statement with an emphasis on each word.

"Ok, Papa. How long?" asked a dejected daughter, still mindful of the frailness of her papa and desirous not to unduly upset him.

"Oh, 'bout a year orta do it," responded the victorious papa, then repeating, 'bout a year orta do it."

"Oh, Papa! A whole year? How about six months?" Macy asked, showing her willingness to be reasonable and end the discussion, yet feeling whipsawed between joy at his showing more will to reengage and despair at her papa's demand she feels could sidetrack her desire to be a wife.

"An' he orta ax me for yor han'," countered Papa, insisting on a papa's prerogative to influence aspects of the life of a daughter.

"Papa! I'm twenty-one years old! He may change his mind. He may meet someone new, or…or, younger." All manner of threats swirled around Macy's mind as she pressed for her papa to recognize a new reality and her right to independence. "It's a new day, Papa. Folks don't follow all those old rules anymore. Six months?" Macy held her breath and laced fingers of her drawn up hands, touching her lips.

"Aw…aw'right! Six month', but not one minute shorter an' he doesn't need to ax me for yor han'. But, darter, I would have giv'n it anyway." Papa received a hug, and a few tears fell onto his whiskered cheek.

"Oh, thank you, thank you," exclaimed Macy as she withdrew from the field of combat, relieved that she and her papa agree. Macy worried about how to tell Mav to whom she had already committed, and decides that a letter will be the best way to tell him. Back in her room, Macy sits down to write a letter that she fears could ensure her future or wreck it. What if he is having second thoughts? What if Mav takes offense at Papa's insistence on a courtship? What if he doesn't love me as much as I love him? What if? What if? She ponders the wording and casts away several attempts before committing herself to these words:

Dearest Mav

Today I told Papa that you have asked to marry me. Papa was not pleased with the manner of the proposal. He is of another era, an era that demands the completion of specific steps before he gives his daughter away. Papa also feels that you should have asked for my hand, formally, as he had asked for my ma's hand. I know it sounds odd, considering how long he has known you and how many times we have enjoyed each other's company, but his ways are set. He demands a formal courtship of six months, so others will ask him about it, and he can play the part of a papa engaged in the long-term welfare of his only daughter. I need at least six months to prepare anyway. He has told me that you don't have to ask him for my hand, which is a big concession for him. I hope you can find it in your heart to comply with his wishes and not think badly of him nor of me who loves you so very much.

Forever yours,
Macy.

After completing the letter, Macy placed it in an envelope addressed to Mav and put the message in his postal box. Keeping a positive outlook, Macy begins immediately to plan a wedding for six months in the future. Something old, something new. Something borrowed, something blue. 'First, make a list,' she thinks, so, she picks up a pen and paper and begins.

✳✳✳

Mav came into the Arkland office on his, now regular Thursday mail-checking day and walked to the window.

"Mr. Wilson, yor lookin' fit today. The whol' town is amazed at how you hav' recovered frum yor ailment," stated Mav, expecting the station-keeper's usual engagement.

Eugene Stonefield

"Mr. Caiden." A decidedly strange clipped greeting delivered by Chauncey Wilson to a perplexed Mav. "I 'spect yor want'n' yor mail." Without making eye contact, Chauncey pushes a letter toward Mav rather than handing it to him as is his usual practice. Chauncey made no attempt to make eye contact with Mav.

"Uh, is everythin' all right?" asked Mav, still perplexed by the changed behavior.

"Right'n as rain, Mr. Caiden." Chauncey turned back to his mail sorting and ignored Mav, who paused for a moment, then left the Arkland office shaking his head.

After purchasing the needed items from the General Store, Mav returned to his cabin and sat down to read his letter which he already knew to be from Macy. A worrying thought crept into his mind that the message may hold news he would not want to hear. 'Maybe she had changed her mind,' he thinks. Bracing himself, he opened the letter and read it.

"Well, I swan! This shor beats all!" he said to himself. "This beats all." Mav sits for a while thinking that he must respond in some manner but certain of what that should be. He will have to sleep on it.

***

Friday morning observes a Sunday-go-to-meetin' dressed Mav Caid and Biscuit returning to Beaton and heading for a new business that had opened earlier in the year. The owner of the business, Willow Spear, arrived in the community two years ago with her husband from far off Cumberland in Northern England. Willow's husband, Randall, was an engineer and a wealthy Englishman who invested in several enterprises in America, one of which was near Beaton. After working for twenty years in engineering, he and Willow left Cumberland and came to Beaton to oversee their investments, then, in an unfortunate accident, Randall died from a broken neck trauma when the horse he was riding threw him into a rocky ravine.

His widow, Willow's, interest is the growing of flowers so she decided to open a gardening and nursery business. Since Willow's wealth was enough to permit engagement in such a risky enterprise, she entered the business and proceeded to grow the flowers herself and be close to members of the community. To sweeten his appeal to emigrate from Cumberland, Randall had had a glass-enclosed building built like what she had in England to grow them in. The greenhouse was her pride and joy, one that she often mentioned that Randall built from plans identical to those used for the greenhouse for Lady Arabella Fitzmaurice Denny in Dublin. Lady Arabella, Willow often mentions, owns a level of fame as a supporter of the Dublin Foundling Hospital for abandoned infants and children, and further for founding the Magdalen Asylum on Leeson Street in Dublin, chartered to recover the lost doves from the streets of Dublin and to lead them in a righteous way of life thereafter.

In one of their previous conversations, Macy had told Mav that they call the structure a 'greenhouse' even though it wasn't green and that the business of growing flowers in greenhouses is common in Cumberland, according to Willow. Mav had nothing against flowers, but he did wonder why one would pay for them and not just grow them themselves. Most of the people around are farmers anyway and in the business of growing things.

Entering widow Spear's flower shop, Mav looked over the displayed bouquets and chose something he thought would be just the right thing.

"Yer al' donned up," Mr. Caid, "deckt oot i' t' best britches an' gallasas! Right fansome, I hafta say. I ain't t' ast fo' perticlers, but, ere ya gon t' jump th' broom?"

"Cain't say, Widow Spear," returned Mav, "time tells all. Right now, I jes' want to git some flowers."

"Joost call me Willow, honey."

"Yes'm. Willow." Mav removed his hat.

"These marguerite flooers are mighty nice, Mr. Caid," asserted Willow, "ere ya ina mind fer some courtin'? I'll ha' some maybelles bloomin' soon."

"I reckon I'm a mind to do thet, somewhut," answered Mav as he paid for the flowers and turned to leave.

"Well, ifn yur chosen lassie be Macy," opined Willow, smiling, "Macy th' fortanach lassie! An' ye'er lassie' aboot as fewsome as a bug's ear."

"Much obliged, Willow," Mav responded to Willow's compliment, as he stepped from the store into the street, pondering what 'fewsome' meant.

Pausing, Mav looked up and down the street to see if anyone might be walking about to see him carrying flowers, an activity that induced a feeling of unease to this young man, well recalling the ribbing given to cowhands so daring as to reveal a tender side. Assuring himself that there was no one close, set his direction toward the Arkland Stage-line office.

Entering the office with his purchase Mav was immediately confronted by Macy who first looked anxiously at Mav, knowing that he had received her letter yesterday, then at the bunch of flowers, he held tightly in his right hand.

"Mav, what are you doing?" asked Macy, a question that Mav ignored.

"Is yor papa in?" Mav asked Macy, who was now even more intrigued.

"I'll…I'll call him." She answered.

As Chauncey Wilson came to the window, Mav thrust a bouquet of daisies toward him with a suddenness that caused Chauncey instantly to hold a hand out to take them.

"Fo' you, Papa. May I hav' yor daughter's han'?" asked Mav.

"I…I… No one never give me no daisies befo'a! No one!" declared the flabbergasted station-keeper, who stood staring at the bouquet of white daisies, unable to decide what he should do.

For a full minute, silence ensued as three people absorb the bodacious action before a crescendo of laughter burst forth from all three, simultaneously.

"Why son, of course, yo' can!" said the most traditional-leaning papa of a modern-leaning daughter to the innovative, prospective son-in-law. "Of course, yo' can."

Chapter 16

A Wedding

Six months passed with speed only half-imagined by any of the three persons involved in the upcoming wedding. Mav proceeded with a proper courtship of his chosen and Beaton town-folk queried Chauncey endlessly as they came into his Arkland office for their mail. All was well in the town as preparations began in September for an end-of-month ceremony. Mav expressed his ideas to Macy, and Macy expressed how it was really to be. All got along better that way. Papa had little to do with that aspect of it and agreed with Macy.

On September 29, readers of the Beaton Gazette were to read in the news of the wedding of Miss Macy Wilson to Mr. Maverick Caiden. The announcement read:

Today, at ten o'clock, attendees at the Beaton Methodist Church at 100 Elk Street, witnessed the joining in Holy matrimony longtime resident, Miss Macy Elaine Wilson, to local farmer Mr. Maverick Caiden. Macy is the beloved daughter of Arkland Station-keeper Chauncey Sidney Wilson. Officiating at the wedding was the Reverend Mr. Smedley. The maid of honor was Miss Stephanie Wile, daughter of Ira and Melanie Wile, owners of the Wileman barbershop on Ebber Street, and best man was Billy Cole, a neighbor farmer of the groom. In attendance were family, friends, and acquaintances of Macy and Maverick.

The lovely bride's Watteau style wedding gown, which she stitched herself, is of white pompadour taffeta, an expensive imported fabric acquired by mail from Johnson Millenaries of St. Louis. The dress with bishop-style sleeves displays pearlescent sequins hand sewn to the cuffs and midriff. Her veil of matching color was also sequined. The bride's shoes were white pumps of fine glove-quality kid leather dyed to match the color of the wedding dress. The bride carried a bouquet of pink carnations from the widow Willow Spear's Flower shop on the corner of Grover and Main.

The groom wore a new set of clothes consisting of Levi Straus denim waist overalls - the new kind with the copper rivets patented by Levi Straus and Jacob Davis of San Francisco; a poplin shirt with red and green stripes - so new that creases from the folds were visible; a Pembrook celluloid collar to add formality to the outfit; and a brown string tie. Galluses of yellow with threads of brown woven throughout was also new from the mail-order catalog of the Hershey Haberdashery in St. Louis. To top it off, Mav wore a five-button brown corduroy jacket with three pockets, a new Boss of the Plains hat from the John B. Stetson company in Philadelphia and new custom boots with stitched designs of cow heads with horns front and back. The boots, stained in black-cherry, the groom purchased from the Curry Mills Boot and Saddle shop in Beaton.

Constance Dade, organist at the Beaton Methodist church, provided music for the ceremony on their new Mason and Hamlen pump organ, with vocals by members of the choir. Selections were: The Bridal Chorus by Richard Wagner, Johann Pachelbel's Canon in D, performed on the flute by new resident Gustav Rosenzweig, a graduate of the Musickhocgschulen in Stuttgart, plus assorted religious music of the day favored by the bride and selected from the compositions of Thomas Hastings and Lowell Mason published in their collaborative work titled Spiritual Songs for Social Worship.

Except for the groom's forgetting which pocket contained the ring, the wedding ceremony was perfect in the eyes of all attendees.

After the ceremony, the bride and groom shared a slice of white wedding cake baked by Harvey Keller and his wife Maribelle who own and operate the Keller Bakery on Main Street. The new husband, Maverick Caiden, personally cut the wedding cake and served the first piece, the bride's share, to his new wife, Macy Caiden. Coffee, tea, and punch were also available in the Community room to accompany the cake.

A rotogravure image of the bride and groom standing before the church appears below. For those unfamiliar with the term, a rotogravure is an image transfer to a rotary printing press from the photographic plate created to commemorate the happy occasion by the newly employed photographer for the Beaton Gazette, Gabriel Hafner. A gilded-framed image printed from the plate will be given to the new husband and wife later as a gift from the owner and publisher of the Beaton Gazette, Mr. Wallace Zentner.

The day was the happiest of occasions and there were many gifts given at the reception. An unusual gift from the widow, Willow Spears for the new bride and groom, was a new ten-volume set of the <u>Chambers Encyclopedia</u> by Scotsman, Ephraim Chambers, published in Philadelphia by J B Lippincott company in 1890. Willow said her late husband, Randall, ordered the cyclopedia for delivery upon printing, but it was not received until after his death. Willow said there was much knowledge to be gained from the cyclopedia, and it will be invaluable in educating children. When the widow Willow Spears made that statement, the new husband noticeably raised an eyebrow. This reporter failed to note the reaction of the new wife.

Following the reception, the new family of two left in a horse and buggy with red trim supplied by Cisco's Blacksmith & Livery on Oak Street and will be honeymooning at the famous Altern hotel in Villon near Hot Springs. When they return, they will reside at the Caiden farm outside of Beaton. All well-wishers turned out to throw rice at the newlyweds and send them off on their hymeneal sojourn in Villon.

Chapter 17

Altern Hotel / A Felon Returns

Villon, like Beaton, is a rapidly growing community in the Ouachita mountain range and is the home of a timber industry, a cotton industry and numerous proprietorships that service the needs of residents of the city and visitors. The Altern Hotel is the crown jewel of Main Street and has forty rooms to rent for overnight or more extended stays. The hotel has become a mecca for newlyweds, vacationers from neighboring communities and for people seeking the health-enhancing mineral waters of the nearby hot springs as it regularly hosts entertainment that ranges from Shakespeare to vaudeville. Traveling entertainment groups from highbrow to lowbrow book dates at the Altern to debut new concept plays such as the great Frank Willard Bacon's rib-tickling old liar, Lightnin' Bill Jones. Performances of Kit, The Arkansas Traveler, are standard fare in the town's opera house since its construction fifteen years ago. Although the 'legend' had gone through many changes since originally conceived by Colonel Sanford C. 'Sandy' Faulkner in 1840 when he was stumping for politicians Ambrose Sevier and Archibald Yell, among others, it shows endurance. Villon historian, Hallie Udall, wrote that both Broadway Veteran, Frank Chanfrau, and his son, Henry, have played the lead part at the theater since 1875. And there are some who swear that the great actress Jersey Lily, whose real name is Lillie Langtry, had been to the Altern for a performance of <u>The Lady of Lyons</u>. They say she was on her way to Langtry, Texas to see her namesake town, christened so by saloon keeper and Justice of the Peace, Roy Bean.

Journalist Thomas Quaid, of the Hot Springs Weekly Bugle, reported that the self-appointed Judge Bean lauded himself as 'The Law West of the Pecos', that sandy, rattlesnake strewn wasteland west of the Pecos River. Some suggested that Langtry was on the same train in 1890 that Judge Bean flagged down by waving a danger signal so he could invite industrialist Jay Gould and his family to visit his saloon, named The Jersey Lilly Saloon in her honor. Knowledgeable people say that the saloon doubled as the courthouse and that Bean selected juries from patrons of the saloon at the time of need and saw no reason to discriminate against a drunk juror any more than a sober one, so long as they were awake to take the oath. The delay in Gould's arrival at destination caused panic on Wall Street from the false report that his delayed arrival was because he and his family had been kidnapped by Mexican banditos and held for ransom. No mention was made of Miss Langtry in news reports, but some suggest that is because Miss Langtry stayed in Langtry for a while. Judge Bean could be persuasive, so some say. Bean had a reputation for harsh justice in the Chihuahua Desert. Some called him a 'hanging judge,' but he insisted that they were easier hung if they were dead of other causes first, and said that it was only proper to fine those lawbreakers what was in their pockets at the time of their demise to pay for final expenses and such. Judge Bean was all for equality, so if a crime merited only a fine, Bean based the fine on whatever a person had on him at the judgment, just as he did with the dead. When asked why Langtry had no jail, Bean was reported in past accounts to have said: "What was the need when all lawbreaking could be handled by fines or dangling?"

"Did you know of Judge Bean?" queried Macy, as she finished reading the brief history of the Villon Opera House.

"I wuz tol' wunst thet Bean lived in San Antonio near Bandera fo' a time but, thet he'd left San Antonio befor' I wuz born, an' his town o' Langtry is 'bout eight days hard ride frum San Antonio. Most o' whut I hav' heard is whut I wuz tol' 'bout him by some o' th' wranglers when I wuz with John Lytle. One wrangler said he wuz fined five dollars by Bean fo' putting those sweaty hands o' hisn on a poster o' Lily thet Bean had put on th' wall o' thet saloon o' hisn. Judge Bean tol' him he couldn't tol'rate no cowpuncher spoilin' her fine dress with sweaty hands so th' fine wuz two dollars. Then Bean fined him three dollars fo' whut he wuz thinkin' when he put his hands on th' poster. Thet wuz jus' after th' judge asked how much money he had on him. Willie, - thet's th' wrangler - said he wuz mighty lucky to hav' five dollars to pay th' fine, knowin' thar wuz no jail in Langtry an' thet th' alternative to a fine wuz hangin'. I understand he ne'er sent any o' th' fines to th' State Treasury, but kept them fo' hissel'."

It was to the Altern Hotel that Macy and Mav went to consummate their nuptials and enjoy the healthful benefits of the natural hot springs. Nearby, on the Ouachita River, is accommodation for swimming and canoeing. Macy and Mav made liberal use of the river accommodation though both had to purchase swimming apparel before doing so. A nearby park had swings, a metal slide, and a teetertotter. While usually, children used the equipment, several early mornings found Mav and Macy on the swings and teetertotter, talking and laughing. At other times, paddling a canoe or enjoying a private picnic under a large oak tree would occupy their time. One evening, as the canoe drifted in quiet water, Macy became thoughtful.

Eugene Stonefield

"Mav, when you were herding cattle on the trail, how did you and the other drovers calm the cattle." Macy waited for Mav to consider her question before continuing: "I have heard that singing to them is common practice. It sounds strange, singing to animals."

"Might strange, I reckon, but th' idee is to let them know someone is thar. Why them cattle might care, I cain't imagine. My reckonin' is thet it is to let other boys know whar you are an' not asleep on the job." Mav looked at Macy as she sat watching him.

"Mav," she began, "you sang a song your papa used to sing when he was plowing. You must remember. It was at the picnic. It was called <u>The Yellow Rose of Texas</u>. Do you know any other songs? Maybe something you sang to the cattle?"

"I rec'lect one I larned from one of th' boys. It was called <u>Streets of Laredo.</u> Jim, wuz th' name o' th' drover thet larned me th' song, an' he had this here guitar thet he would play for th' tune. I think I rec'lect some o' it. It goes:

As I walked out in th' streets o' Laredo
As I walked out in Laredo one day,
I spied a poor cowboy, all dress'd in white linen
All dress'd in white linen an' cold as th' clay.

I see by yor outfit thet you are a cowboy
These words he did say as I slowly pass'd by
'Come sit down beside me an' hear my sad story
I'm shot in th' chest, an' I know I must die.'"

At this point Mav broke off saying: "I cain't remember some o' th' other words, but the last part went somethin' like this:

We beat th' drum slowly an' played th' fife lowly,
An' bitterly wept as we bore him along.

For we loved our lost cowboy, so brave, an' so handsome,
We all loved th' dead cowboy, although he'd done wrong."

Macy sat silent for a moment, then asked, "Mav, do you recall the tune?"

"I think so, Macy."

"Sing it Mav."

Mav thought for a moment then in a rich tenor voice memorialized some unknown cowboy, lying shot in the chest, dying in the dust of Laredo, Texas.

***

Five days into the honeymoon, the joyful newlyweds heard a knock on the door to their room on the second floor. Mav strode to the door and opened it to face a large six-shooter pointed directly at his face. As his eyes focused exclusively on the barrel of the gun, he was unable to recognize the man behind it.

"Good afternoon, Mr. Caid, or, if you prefer, Mr. Caiden. Let me introduce mysel'. My name is Hank Weld, but perhaps you will remember me as Fenner Korn, which I wuz until just recent. My partner here, Henry Slade, whom I know you have met, have an issue ta discuss with you. You may recall thet you innerfeered with Henry's and mine's bizness in Ogallala some years ago which caused me ta waste three years in a Nebraksa jail fo' thet misunderstanding. But I want you ta know thet we hold no grudges fo' th' result of thet innerfeerence. However, Henry and me's here ta collect a just compensation for yor mistake." With that introduction, both men pushed into the room.

"I recall th' incident," answered Mav, "I jes' recall it a might dif'runt. You and yor pardner were a-tryin' to rob Mr. Lytle o' his money from his cattle drive to Ogallala. I might recall to you thet some o' thet money b'longed to th' drovers too. Thet judge was right in sendin' you to jail, an' if Slade, there, hadn't turn'd tail an' lit out like some cowart thet he wuz, he woulduf also. An' ifn Slade hadn't skedaddled like some scalded polecat, y'all woulduf had some'un to talk with fo' th' las' few year! Now y'all get out o' ourn room!"

"Come, come, Mr. Caid. Let us keep everythin' frien'ly an' on a quiet note - seein' that I hav' this here persuader." Fenner Korn waved his gun and pushed Mav into a chair as Macy stood shocked at this unexpected and threatening intrusion. Looking around the room, Fenner failed to see any weapons that could induce Mav to challenge them. Finally, he said: "I fig'er you have a gun somewhar, Mr. Caid. Whar's it at?"

"I'll git it," answered Mav as Slade sniggered his amusement.

"Ah, no, Mr. Caid. Mr. Slade will git it. Now, whar's it at?" Fenner waved the barrel of his Remington forty-four for emphasis.

"Over yonder, in thet drawer," Mav answered, pointing toward the chest of drawers across the room. Slade retrieved Mav's 1847 Colt Walker, but not before he searched through Macy's undergarments. The Walker, he stuck in his belt.

"Whut is it y'all want?" Mav asked. "We hav' very little money."

"Ah, money! Ever'one seems ta think money's a physic fo' all ills and transgressins. No, Mr. Caid, money won't do. Not a'tall. My partner wuz through yor neck o' th' woods a couple o' year ago an' seen you. He asked 'round an' wuz tole thet you had a nice little farm out o' town a few miles. Now thet little farm an' all them items 'sociated with it, I am tol', is fo' sale."

"Well, thet's a bald-faced lie!" responded Mav. "Who tol' you thet?"

"Why, Mr. Slade," Fenner replied, waving toward Slade who stood aside displaying a wide grin. "He tol' me thet farm o' yorn could be akwired fo' a farr price. Surely, Mr. Caid, anythin's fo' sale at a farr price? Wouldn't you agree?" Fenner looked at Mav with a blank expression.

"Why do I get th' feelin' thet y'all are a-plannin' to offer a farr price today?" Mav questioned.

"Ah, you are an astoot person, Mr. Caid. Ass-toot," returned Fenner with a smile. "Let me say thet a farr offer, ta my way o' thinkin', is, umm, one silver dollar an' yor pretty bride's life." Fenner tossed a silver dollar and stared at Caid with a hard look that communicated an abiding hatred.

"Whut?" returned Mav, mouth opened in surprise at the implication. "Y'all wouldn't…"

"Oh, yes, Mr. Caid. We would…after a time," Fenner replied while staring at Macy. Fenner smiled broadly and looked at Slade for his approval. "In fact, Mr. Caid, I have here a contrac' writ proper by my, um…, lawyer fo' yor John Henry. Of course, th' gen'rous offer ta leave yor little wife with her life is a side agreement jes' between us. Th' other stipplation, which I saw no need ta mention b'fore, is thet both of y'all would disappear an' ne'er return ta Beaton. It will become known ta the good people of Beaton thet th' newlyweds up an' decided ta sell their farm at a farr price an' move on ta Californy ta buy some land."

Mav stood in silence, then glancing at Macy and back at the gun held in Fenner's hand, his fully alert mind racing, trying to think of what he should do.

Macy returned the look of Mav with one of her own that asked, what do we do?

"But, Mr. Caid, we are ready ta give you time ta think about th' offer an' consider how gen'rous it really is," continued Fenner, then motioning to Macy, said: "Little lady, why don't you jes' come over here by me, Honey. Maybe us two can convince yor husband thet th' offer is farr an' reas'nable."

Eugene Stonefield

Macy looked at Mav then reluctantly moved over to Fenner. When she came to him, he took her arm and told Slade to cover Mav with his gun. When Slade drew his revolver, Fenner holstered his own and suddenly, seizing Macy, kissed her hard on the mouth.

Mav started to rise from his chair but was stopped by Slade, who raised his gun to face level and aimed it at Macy. Mav returned to his previous position, his face scarlet with anger, his mind engulfed by a growing rage.

"How am I to know thet y'all won't jes' kill us a'ter I sign yor contract?" asked a furious Mav who was taking pains to keep his voice level and his anger in check.

"We're biznessmen, Mr. Caid. We buy an' sell farms and ranches. We don't kill without cause. It's bad fo' bizness." Fenner replied, suddenly giving Macy a shove toward Mav. "We only want ta get a farr deal thet soothes our hurt feelings from th' loss of o'er three-hunnerd thousand dollars in Ogallala."

"Three-hundred thousand? How do y'all git to thet? You wuz one o' the drovers an' drover pay wuz three dollars a day." returned Mav.

"Mr. Caid, I've had three whol' year ta calc'late our loss." Reaching into a pocket, Fenner withdrew a crumpled piece of paper. Holding it up to garner better light, Fenner pointed to lines on the paper, saying: "It's like this: John Lytle druve thirty-two-hunnerd head ta Ogallala whar they fetched twelve cents a pound. Now, each steer weighed 'bout eight-hunnerd pound. So, twelve cents times eight-hunnerd per steer is... ninety-six dollars fo' each steer, times thirty-two-hunnerd steers...yes! Three-hunnerd seven-thousand two-hunnerd dollars!" Fenner offers a wide smile to all around to celebrate his mathematical acumen. "Without yor innerfeerence thet would have been mine an' Henry's!"

"Y'all mangy coyotes!" shouted Mav in an elevated voice. "Thet's all wrong. Th' best Lytle coulda got wuz forty-eight dollars a head.

Mav Caid — The Complete Story

Twelve cents a pound...thet's after th' steers wuz killed an' dressed out fo' th' butcher shops in Chicago an' San Francisco."

"Please don't shout, Mr. Caid. Just sign this here contrac'." Fenner placed the document on the table next to Mav.

"I'd like to talk privately with my wife about this," said Mav, directing his attention to Fenner.

"Of course, Mr. Caid," returned Fenner. "Take a few minutes. We both want y'all ta be happy. Go talk ta thet purdy little lady. Me an' Mr. Slade will be right here."

Mav stood up and led Macy to the corner of the room and whispered: "Macy, these two coyotes will kill us ifn we sign o'er th' home place 'cause they cain't tol'rate us returnin' to Beaton an' exposin' th' fraud. I cain't reckon how good a shot Fenner is, but Slade couldn't hit a wall if it wuz five feet away from him. Fenner is th' one to fear. Slade is th' one who shot at me some time back. I think he has 'possum eyesight an' cain't see thru a empty whisky barr'l ev'n ifn both ends are knok'd out. Now, they won't dare to shoot us here 'cause othern town folk might hear, but they'll want to take us out, to th' river, most likely, or somewhar outen town. I don't cotton thet hap'nin' ifn I ken hep it. Wunst I sign thet contrac', they'll take us from th' hotel. You needst be in front o' Slade when we git to th' street. I'll sign th' contrac' 'round sundown. We hafta delay them fo' a time an' distract them. I want their thoughts to be on somethin' other than killin'. I ain't thought o' how to distract them yet."

Macy was thoughtful for a moment, then whispered: "These are a lecherous pair. I can distract them, Mav. I will change from this dress I am wearing into riding britches. They can't afford to leave the room, so they will watch me change. They will be thinking of things other than killing us for a while."

"Macy, I don't like...I don't want you to..." began Mav only to be interrupted by Macy.

"I can suffer the indignity, Mav. The question is, can you? Can you be still while I distract them? Fenner has already forcibly kissed me so I know I can distract his thoughts. I watched Slade pawing my undergarments when he searched for your gun. I agree that we cannot allow them to take us as far as the river. I know what will happen, Mav. I know."

"Yes, Macy. We, - you 'special, are in great danger ifn we are forced to leave Villon with these two polecats. But they won't dare to hav' their guns drawn as we leave 'cause folks might see an' holler fo' th' sheriff. Their guns will be holstered an' thet'll be givin' us advantage, some. You stay in front o' Slade an' when I ask, 'Where are y'all takin' us,' you scream mighty loud then run as fast as you can but not straight. Run to whate'er cover you see. Slade may draw an' shoot at you, but my reckon'n' is thet he'll only kick up th' dirt ifn he does. As you run, run un'xpect'd. Run like a serpent moves, four or five steps in one direction, then veer t'other direction fo' several steps, then t'other direction again. That serpentine movement will keep Slade from drawin' a bead. I am gonna take thet plug-ugly galoot, Fenner, an' knock him cattywhompus as soon as he is distracted by yor scream. That will draw Slade's lookin' at you back to Fenner an' me. Fenner wears thet holster o' hisn fo' a left-han' cross-draw. Thet means when I face him, hisn gun-butt will be a-face'n' me on hisn right side. Now, I inten' to git thet gun first, faster than a calf ken bawl 'bout a brandin'! Ken you do this? Will you do this? It's a might risky. Either you or me could get shot. I might could be wrong. But, ifn we don't fight, we cain't win." Mav waited.

Macy whispered back: "I can do this, Mav, I love you."

Mav and Macy returned to their previous location, and both sat down at the table. The slant rays of sunlight entering the room through the partially shaded window told them that sundown was upon them.

"Fenner," said Mav, addressing the leader. "We have talked it over, an' I will sign yor contract fo' ourn place. Then you an' Slade ken leave us alone."

Laughing briefly and looking at Slade then back at Mav, Fenner said: "You an' th' little lady will have ta come with us fo' a short ride until we clear town. We don't want you runnin' ta the marshal tellin' him some fanciful story we have ta refute by this here contrac' you signed. We have rent' a couple o' horses in yor name from tha livery fo' you 'n her ta ride. You can return them yorselfs when we part company outside o' town."

"Mav," interjected Macy loudly enough to ensure Fenner and Slade would hear, "If we are to ride, I will need to change into riding britches first."

Fenner and Slade exchanged glances. Fenner said, "well hurry up, we want ta git on down the road before it gits too late." Slade stood near the door grinning.

"I need some privacy," exclaimed Macy, looking squarely at Fenner. Fenner and Slade exchanged glances again.

"Jes' change," said Fenner. "Slade 'n' me, we are stayin' right here. You jes' preten' we ain't here. We'll be watchin' yor husban'."

Macy glanced at Mav and received a subtle nod to continue. "I have to get my clothes out of the chest." Macy looked to Fenner for compliance.

"Git 'em." Fenner motioned for her to continue. Again, Fenner and Slade traded smiles.

Macy walked to the chest of drawers and opened a drawer from which she removed a nightgown and laid it on the bed. Fenner and Slade shifted positions. She pulled out a pair of short pantaloons. Again, a shift. Finally, she laid out her riding britches and a blouse.

"Hurry up," said Fenner, "we ain't got all night. The sun's goin' down." Slade stepped to the wall-mounted gas lamp and lit its flame, adjusting it for maximum light, then returned to watching Macy.

Macy, ignoring Fenner, slipped her hands beneath her dress and found her garter which she slowly slid down and stepped out of. Removing one silken stocking then reaching to remove the other garter and stocking brought both Fenner and Slade to attention. Finally, Macy glanced at both men and implored, "don't look now. I need to finish dressing." Turning her back on the attentive captors, she lifted her dress over her head and threw it toward the bed. Fenner and Slade followed the dress with their eyes as it arced through the room then turned their eyes back to Macy. Her petticoat and camisole followed, and finally, long pantaloons. The smooth pale skin on Macy's body seemed to return the warm glow of the gaslight that Slade had set alight when the sun was setting. Her long auburn hair fell against her youthful skin to add color and texture and siphon the held breath of her captors. She could feel their hot eyes, sense their lewd thoughts as she stood reflected in the dresser's ovoid mirror, a visual echo of Titian's Venus Anadyomene, that iconic image of Venus rising from the sea in all her naked beauty.

Macy very deliberately reached for a ribbon, then arching her back, slowly raised her arms high, her elbows thrust wide and began tying the ribbon around her voluminous hair. In her mind's eye, Macy could envision herself through the lascivious eyes of Fenner Korn and Henry Slade. She imagined she could see her back facing the two men as they watched, and she could see her long auburn hair and sea-green eyes and, most of all, her naked young breasts reflected in the mirror. And she could sense the lust of their two captors. For a moment, she believed she could even feel their hot breath filling the air around her. Finishing, Macy pulled on short pantaloons, then reached for a blouse and slipped it on, buttoning slowly. Finally, when her sense of conquest was at its apex, Macy stepped into her riding britches, tucked in the blouse, and sat on the bed to button her shoes.

As Macy willingly engaged the prurient minds of the two intruders, she thought how the innocent Susannah of the Book of

Daniel, unknowingly, stimulated the lecherous minds of the elders in the garden - wondering if Susannah's unwilling sacrifice of dignity equated Macy's willing sacrifice, as Macy's own husband, Mav, looked at the floor, wishing he still had his forty-four. Her heart had ached for the pain her husband had to have been suffering, but her mind was clear that she was pursuing the greater good.

Fortune has a way of favoring the desperate on occasion, and as Mav sought to avoid seeing the lustful pleasure on the faces of his and Macy's captors, his eyes fell upon his slip-joint knife that had dropped from a pocket when he placed his trousers on the chair the night before. Carefully he slid forward in his chair and extended his leg. For a moment, his foot hovered above the knife, then making a conscious effort to quell his anxiety, he began to lower his heel. Although the knife was reachable by Mav's boot heel, its handle, rounded to better fit the hand, made unpredictable its movement in response to a nudge. Mav said a silent prayer that the knife would move toward him and not in a direction that would put it out of reach. As his heel touched the knife, Mav held his breath and bent his knee, drawing his foot backward. The knife slid toward him. Slowly and quietly Mav pulled the knife toward himself until it rested just behind his boot, just inches away from his hand that now hung near the floor. Mav looked steadily at Fenner and Slade who remained mesmerized by the titillating show. Carefully Mav reached down and retrieved the knife and brought it up to waist level hidden by his hand. Watching the captivated captors, Mav cautiously opened the knife and slid it into his sleeve, blade first, so that when wanted, it would fall handle-first into his waiting hand, breathing, "I wish this wuz my bowie."

Macy, having buttoned her shoes, stood, and turning to her captors said in a musical voice: "I am now ready."

"About time," stated Fenner with some regret. "We gotta go now, but remember we will be right behind an' we still have these here black-eyed-susans." Fenner patted his holstered six-shooter and elbowed

Slade who remained mesmerized in some concupiscent fantasy, saying: "Me first."

Mav nodded at Fenner and stood up, handing the signed contract for the farm to Fenner who glanced at the signature and folded it to fit a pocket where he placed it.

"Let's go." Fenner motioned for all to move toward the door. The hallway was dimly lit by gas lights spaced every twenty feet. Neither Fenner nor Slade was aware that Mav and Macy were maneuvering to position themselves in front of the appropriate person. All went down the stairs and out the front door without meeting anyone on the way.

"The hosses are tied 'cross th' street," said Fenner. "Just min' yor Ps an' Qs an' y'all will be ok."

For five yards Mav and Macy walked three paces in front of Fenner and Slade, stopping only to allow a beer wagon to pass. As they waited, Fenner and Slade drew closer to Mav and Macy, standing just a yard behind. While paused for the beer-wagon to clear, Mav looked back over his shoulder to see the focused stare of Fenner Korn at Macy's shapely body. Anger filled Mav as he thought about the personal disgrace Macy had endured to give him this single moment, to provide this moment of distraction that could be the difference between life and death. His growing, silent rage built into an intense, formidable personal demand to change the direction of this abhorrent plan of these two outlaws.

For a moment, Mav would experience the dark reformulation of the Golden Rule – to do unto others as they would do unto you, but do it first. This, of all moments, cannot be his moment of failure. Tension grew in the mind and body of this young farmer, and every muscle received a message from his determined brain to prepare to act. Adrenalin began to flow like water over Niagara, and the plashing of that adrenalin eclipsed the sound of the passing wagon and the ambient sounds of the town. As the barrel-laden wagon rumbled past the standing quartet, Mav dropped his flexed arm, and from his sleeve, the pre-concealed knife fell into the hand and a hard fist formed around it.

In an elevated voice, Mav asked: "Where are y'all taking us?" and before his last word faded Macy emitted a resounding scream that could have frozen the heart of a catamount and began to run, angling left for a few steps then right, then veering back left, running in a serpentine manner toward the slowly moving beer wagon. Just as immediately, Slade reached for his holstered six-shooter, and drawing it, fired in the direction of the fleeing Macy, but wide enough to not endanger the object of his lust - his bullet, deadly only to a bullet pierced barrel of beer that began spewing its contents onto the street. His action was pure reaction to Macy's scream and race toward freedom, the suddenness not mentally connected to a pre-planned attack. Fenner, equally startled by Macy's scream, started his draw just as a hard farmer's fist smashed into his face snapping his head back with force enough to cause his hat to slide forward over his eyes and his hand to separate from the gun for which he reached. Extending from that farmer's hard fist was a five-inch blade of steel, warmed by its recent sequester in Mav's shirt sleeve and honed by the mental resolve of a man who cannot fail. As quickly as a diamondback strikes, Mav repositioned the knife in his hand to enable a thrust attack which was already in full motion.

The surprise blow from Mav's sudden attack momentarily hindered Fenner from completing his draw, a critical moment allowing Mav to plunge five inches of steel into Fenner's shoulder. Fenner's arm reflexively drew away from his holstered gun and sought the knife in his shoulder, on his face, an amalgam of pain and surprise. Simultaneously, a determined Mav Caid seized Fenner's Remington forty-four, and his aim was true. Slade cried out as Mav's bullet pierced his body under his extended arm in the process of turning from the fleeing Macy to challenge Mav's attack on Fenner. Slade fell, groaning but mortally wounded in the heart by a bullet from Fenner's captured 'black-eyed-susan.' Fenner, with a five-inch blade still embedded in his shoulder, turned to run, and got no more than five paces before his leg folded with a thigh sorely impaired by a bullet from his own smoking gun.

From a darkened doorway, Macy retraced her pathway of escape, omitting its serpentine nature, and ran to Mav to clasp him in an embrace as deserved by any hero, though unsung in any heart save one.

Gunfire has a way of giving focus to a community, and the attention of Villon turned toward the street in front of the hotel as the shots rang out. Both the Marshal Hank O'Connor and his deputy arrived several minutes later and ordered that Mav lay down his weapon that he retained in his hand as his other arm still embraced Macy.

Marshal O'Connor conducted an initial inquiry, after which, he escorted Mav, Macy and Fenner to the marshal's office where he placed Fenner in jail, then called town doctor, Carroll Palmer, to attend Fenner's leg and shoulder injuries. After explaining to the marshal what had transpired both in the street and previously in the Altern hotel, Mav and Macy returned to their room. Slade was taken to the local mortuary where he was installed in a pine box, preparatory to his burial at boot hill. The next morning Mav and Macy appeared before Judge Roy Turner who listened attentively to their explanation of the sorrowful events of the previous night, believed them, and didn't believe Fenner Korn, a.k.a., Hank Weld, nor the legitimacy of his contract.

Upon the request of Judge Turner, Mav and Macy signed a statement documenting the events leading to the killing of Slade and the shooting of Fenner Korn. The judge told them he would hold a trial within three months for Fenner Korn and would write them with the date of that trial so that they could come back to Villon to testify. Until that time, both were free to return to Beaton. Judge Turner determined that the killing of Slade was an act of self-defense, a non-chargeable offence.

***

The carriage ride back to Beaton was anticlimactic in comparison to what they had experienced under the guns of Fenner and Slade and provided a period of recovery from the anxiety brought to its fullness by the machinations of their criminal minds. The weather was that of early fall and color was creeping across the countryside. The air, crisp and invigorating imparted an energy to the returning honeymooners. Several times when finding particularly beautiful views Macy and Mav would stop the carriage and just enjoy the scenery and talk about their feelings and desires. At one particularly inviting cove in a natural lake they were passing, Macy and Mav stopped to enjoy a lunch they had bought to carry with them and availed themselves of a swim in the quiet water of a partially hidden cove. Their swimsuits remained folded and dry in the Gladstone. Macy recalled her previous, unsettling fantasy and smiled.

"Whut ere you a-smilin' 'bout, Macy? Ere you a-smilin' 'bout bein' nekkid outdoor? Thinkin' what yor papa might say?"

"Nothing along those lines, Mav. I'll tell you sometime."

Arriving at Mav's cabin, Macy appraised the small confines of the bachelor's sanctuary with moderate despair. "Well, we'll be a might crowded, but it's good to be home."

Hearing Macy call the cabin 'home' was strange but welcome. "I hav' some ideas 'bout how we ken make improvements nex' year." Mav waited for Macy's response.

"Mav, it will all work out. A little crowded for a time, but it will work out just fine."

"Billy has been o'erseein' th' place while we wuz gone. I see him ridin' in now, so I'll settle up with him an' start gittin' th' routine back to normal," said Mav, while stepping from the porch to greet the visitor.

"Welcome back, Mav," said Billy as he dismounted. "I trust yor new missus is well."

"Very well, Billy. Thanks, fo' o'erseein' th' place. You've been a great hep." Mav shook hands with Billy. Macy stepped outside to wave at Billy then returned inside.

"Mav, I need to tell ya, a couple o' strangers come by jes' after you and Macy left town. They asked where you wuz, but I wouldn't tell them. I did tell them y'all had jes' got hitched an' wuz on y'all's honeymoon, an' thet's when they asked if you wuz married in Beaton. I told them you wuz an' thet it wuz writ about in the Gazette. They rode on off. I hope I didn't do no wrong." Billy waited anxiously for a confirmation that he had not betrayed a confidence.

"No, Billy. You didn't do nothin' wrong," now knowing that their whereabouts was easily discoverable by reading the Gazette. "I don't 'spect they'll be back this-a-way."

Returning to the cabin, Mav found Macy busy sweeping the floor and singing under her breath as the dust swirled around in complete defiance. For a moment, Mav observed the scene thinking how many times as a child he had witnessed the same scene, somewhere else, pursued by someone else. Mav wished his ma and pa could have met Macy. He learned that even when happiness describes his world, grief can revisit to remind him that life has many dimensions. He quietly backed out of the cabin and turned toward the barn to talk to Biscuit.

✳✳✳

Over the following months, Mav and Macy established their individual routines. Macy became the go-to person when it came milking time for the four dairy cows now owned. Hers also is the care of the chickens and the collecting of eggs from the henhouse. Milk that Macy collects beyond their own need, she pours into sizeable metal cans which Mav takes to baker Keller in Beaton along with the excess eggs. Mav spent his days taking care of the land, the crops, the beef, and dairy cattle they have, the swine, and planning a larger home for the family - the real justification for the need not yet known even to Macy. Mav described his ideas for expanding the cabin and getting a better sink for the kitchen and perhaps a larger cookstove and buying a windmill. Macy talked about material for curtains and a new bedspread. It would not be long before she would be mentioning the need for a crib. In the late evening, after she and Mav have completed their chores and dinner finished, Macy washed the dishes, Mav read the <u>Chambers Encyclopedia</u> and reached for the marvels of knowledge. As Mav read the articles, he took special pains to look up unfamiliar words in a new dictionary Macy had bought for him and note how to use them.

Suddenly, winter was in full swing and snow was falling. Mav brought the animals into the barn or holding pen where he watered and fed them, before he returned to the warmth of the cabin. Recently, Macy had bought and hung curtains over windows to shield the cabin from drafts of cold air, and had bought a potted plant from Willow that Willow had promised would bloom in early spring. A new sink was on order, and the well that Mav and Billy had dug was providing sweet water for all their needs. Recently he excavated a stock tank to supply water to the growing dairy herd and water to fill the tank obtained by temporarily diverting a small creek from its natural channel. And lately, Mav had busied himself building a small shed to house a zinc coated steel tub for bathing. Mav's habit had always been to head down to the river when he felt he needed a bath. Macy thought it best to bathe inside where she could heat water to add to the tub of cold well water. Mav said he didn't care as long as he could watch. Macy said he was terrible. Mav recalled how angry he was at the two gunmen and their voyeuristic behavior in Villon and resumed construction of the shed with unusual vigor. Mav ordered a tub from the Beaton hardware store and received it from its manufacturer in Dallas. On Thursday, Mav received a letter from Judge Roy Turner:

Dear Mr. Caiden

While I had hoped to inform you of a date for the trial of Fenner Korn so that you and Mrs. Caiden could come to testify, I am apologetically having to tell you that Fenner Korn was able to escape our custody. He is subject to immediate arrest when he is located. Marshal O'Connor received one report, but it was not confirmed as that of Fenner Korn. You have my assurance that all reports of sightings will be investigated as they occur. The marshal sent bulletins to all surrounding counties in Arkansas and some in Louisiana beyond the location of the initial unconfirmed sighting. While I cannot say that Fenner Korn will seek to harm you or your wife, I cannot promise you that he will not try. Marshal O'Connor said that Fenner has railed against you continually while in his custody and blames you with all the jail time he has endured and for the thigh injury you inflicted upon him in Villon. I would advise you to be alert until such time that he is again in custody.

Cordially,
Roy Turner, Judge, Garland County, Arkansas

Chapter 18

A Hidden Valley / Rainbow Rocks

Two years pass quickly as Mav and Macy build their future. Their responsibilities have increased with the births of two children, Case and Lyla. The home-place has expanded with the purchase of a nearby patch of land suitable for cultivation. Beaton too has grown beyond its original narrow profile with three streets running north to south and four running from east to west and is now a town with a need for a government to manage that growth. Names of newcomers attest to the character of the nation itself. Names of German, Scottish, English, and Irish derivation have become commonplace. Families from other countries have come to open businesses and provide services not conceived of in previous times, and people hear the languages of other lands spoken frequently on the streets and in the shops of Beaton. Some of the older residents have passed on, and younger family members have taken their places at their businesses and farms. The laughter of children has never been so ubiquitous. As for services, there used to be one option, now there are many. Change and excitement are living things as the Gazette announces each new addition to the texture and character of the town.

Twenty years ago, a ceremonial 'golden spike' driven into a railroad crosstie in Promontory Summit, Utah marked the connecting of the east and west coasts by rail, and many independent companies are now building railroad trunk lines to service the need of cotton and grain farmers to get their harvested products to market. Railway trunk lines servicing towns from Gatesville, Texas to Birds Point, Missouri have become a reality, and farmers are planting more crops to ship to faraway places. Today, farmer's expectations are running high. The year is 1892 and the family of Mav, Macy, Case, and Lyla are a part of this hopeful era.

"I've been a-thinkin', Macy," began Mav, musing one morning as Macy prepared breakfast before sunup. "Thet discov'ry by my uncle, Wendell… mayhap we might orta larn more about whut he found. Ifn it's silver or gold or whatever, it might be somethin' of real value an' we might be missin' out every day we do nothin', an' someone else may run acrost it. So, I'm a-thinkin' thet I might orta go out an' take a look-see, mayhap file a claim. The map an' diary is there in th' hidie-hole. What's missin' is for us to find what it's a-pointin' to."

"I don't know, Mav," Macy answered, concern in her eyes. "What about the farm?"

"After th' crop is in, I could ride on out an' search fo' a month or so an' ifn I cain't find it, head on back an' try ag'in nex' year. Ifn I do find it, then we ken plan how to exploit th' opportunity, ifn thar is one." Mav waited for Macy to consider his plan and respond.

"I guess it could work that way, Mav. But I will hate your being gone that long." Macy set what Mav declares are the finest biscuits in Arkansas on the table and sat down. "If anything comes up, I'm sure I could get help from Billy Cole or other folks around."

Mav Caid — The Complete Story

Mav and a couple of hired hands harvested the green bean crop in in record time in September, 1892, and Maverick Caiden saddled up to find the still indescribable discovery of his dead uncle, Wendell. Mav had used some of his free time pursuing information on valuable minerals in the cyclopedia Willow had given them, and time on learning more about discovering where he lives on this big globe that is swinging around the sun.

He has read more about navigation in the cyclopedia. Mav better understands latitude and longitude and how to use the stars for guidance. He understands that longitude calculation is based on time passed from solar noon in Greenwich, England, which by longstanding convention is at longitude zero. He knows an hour of time equates to fifteen degrees rotation of the earth, and that determining the time of solar noon at his current location allows him to calculate the longitude of his position as a measure of how many hours and minutes has passed since it was solar noon in Greenwich. Knowing that he needed to know the Greenwich time when he makes a calculation, he has purchased a second watch set to Greenwich time which he obtained from the telegraph operator. He also understands how to determine minutes of longitude by marking a series of points along a shadow arc cast by a peg on a level surface to provide a finer definition. He understands that a degree of longitude equates to more than sixty-nine miles at the equator and each minute, over a mile. The distances are less, but enough at his latitude to cause a person to miss the destination for which he searches by a considerable amount. Precision is crucial.

Last year he purchased a compass and had practiced using it. He knows how to use the shadow from a stake in the ground to tell him the time at his location. He knows to start finding latitude with a north-south line drawn on the ground. He has built and taken a quadrant with an aiming beam and understands how to use it with a protractor attached to that quadrant to help with angles to reveal latitude with greater accuracy and how to make adjustments dependent upon the time before or after a summer or winter equinox. He is prepared. Mav has said his goodbyes to his tearful family and is now twenty miles from their place traveling toward the sunset. He knows the general area he needs to begin, and he knows that he is looking for a stream running northeast to southwest located within a triangle of landmarks termed 'mountains' in his uncle's diary.

As he nears the discovery location, he believes to be at 34 degrees north latitude and 94 degrees west longitude, he begins to climb the tallest hills in the area to get the views from their height. Where are the other hills? Would they look like mountains from lower elevations? How are they positioned with respect to where he is standing? What would he estimate their distance from each other to be? What streams or rivers can he see? In which direction do they run? Mav answered each of these questions before deciding to move on to another.

Days passed. Two weeks passed. A month passed, and snow is falling on a weary rider riding down the sloping side of a hill into a quiet valley between three mountains. The landscape he views from the higher elevation seems to match the criteria for his search. His destination is a stream about five miles distant that runs in the general direction of the one he seeks. As nightfall descends, the weary rider dismounts and begins to build a lean-to for protection from the elements. Mav gathered wood for a fire and ignited a small campfire with lucifer matches. Rather than hike over to the stream for water, Mav scoops fresh snow from a snowdrift and puts it in his small coffee pot, an innovative invention that has a pierced metal basket for the ground coffee sitting above the water heating below. Once the water begins to boil, the hot water progresses upward through a tube into a closed glass bead on the lid, then cascades through the ground coffee repeatedly until the coffee is fully brewed.

Mav Caid — The Complete Story

Owing to the loneliness of having no other voice to hear, Mav has fallen into the habit of talking to himself just to fill the silence. "Shor, beats boilin' coffee ina pot as we did on th' trail to Ogallala," said Mav to himself, "ne'er did like gittin' th' spent grounds with th' last sip. In those days we jes' called it Arbuckle, an' it wuz brewed dif'runt. Manuel'd roast green coffee banes in an iron skillet an' ground 'em in a hand-cranked coffee grinder, then boiled th' coffee with a fresh egg cracked in it, ifn he had one, until it boiled fo' some time, then put in a little cold water to settle th' grounds, an' thet wuz it." This coffee pot is one of two luxuries that he allowed himself to bring. The other is twice the amount of coffee he will likely use in a month.

As Mav sits beneath the boughs of a fir tree covering his lean-to, he engages in a mind game by listening to the unpredictable melody of the percolator varying its sequence of perks that flummox and bewilder the listener who is trying to predict the next volcano-like eruptions of brewing coffee into the small hollow glass bead on top of the lid. As Mav removes the coffee pot from the fire, the sound of the percolating coffee ceases, and he perceives the strange sound of wind blowing through reeds growing near the water a short distance away. The sounds, varying in tone and cadence, combining, blending into a complex melody, ever-changing as the wind gusts and changes tempo and direction. Mav sat on his saddle spread upon the ground and blessed his good fortune to be Mav Caid, husband of Macy and father to Case and Lyla.

Of the many places he has investigated, this valley appears to conform best to the description in his uncle's diary, and he resolves to search this valley and return home by Christmas. Yet, he still does not know exactly what he is looking for. He has seen pictures of various ores in his cyclopedia, but none of them look the same as what he sees in his mind's eye of the lost rocks his uncle sent to him years ago. Even gold in a matrix of quartz is different.

Eugene Stonefield

Later, his coffee consumed and a belly full of the hardtack and salted pork, Mav wraps himself in his woolen blanket and lays back on his saddle-bag that will be his pillow for the night. Sounds of the wilderness are muffled by the ambient snow which has ceased to fall and is now softly reflecting the light filtering through the departing clouds. Somewhere a wolf howls and others join in the chorus of the wild. Presently, a bright moon transposes the remaining late autumn clouds into a gossamer gown reaching across the evening sky to adorn her skyscape in alabastrine glory.

Mav looks up at the changing sky and finds again the awe that used to permeate his mind as starlight begins to pierce evening's delicate veil. He recalls the times he rode around the herd walking nine hundred miles to market from south of Bandera through Fort Griffith, Vernon, and Doan's Crossing on the Red River, that last provisioning post before crossing into Indian Territory in Oklahoma. The drovers rode horses chosen daily from the remuda and watched for landmarks like Mount Teepee, Big Elk Crossing, and Soldier's Spring to make their way. Along the way, they would occasionally encounter bands of natives waving 'white man's talking paper', a demand written in English for compensation for the grass consumed by the cattle crossing Indian land. These crucial talking papers presented by natives who had learned they could gain concessions from the trail bosses in the form of a few cattle, —bribes to forestall the threat of a raid-induced stampede that could result in catastrophic loss. A gift of two or three head was trail-etiquette and prudent. The cost of doing business was the refrain of the trail bosses. It wasn't always so easy. In bad times, troops from the Washita River Crossing escorted the herds from Doan's Crossing to the Washita River where soldiers from Fort Eliot relieved them and continued the escort.

As for the drovers, these boys and men who experience the hardships and responsibilities of the drive, the risks were different as these, ofttimes naive cowhands, encounter towns along the way.

Mav Caid — The Complete Story

Dodge City, Kansas, one of the crown jewels of the frontier emerges in his thoughts. Dodge City, —a siren, a vixen, a danger to the dusty men of the drive who salivated over the excitement and pleasures of this late-day Gomorrah near the Santa Fe Trail and the Arkansas River. Many thirsty young men with tempers and six-shooters, many who were not aware of the dangers of gambling and intoxication before entering the saloons of Dodge City or the like, found permanent homes in Boot Hill. Like Little Joe, recalls Mav, the boy with the sweetest voice who calmed the cattle, dead of a bullet through the heart at the Long Branch. Of the lights and sounds of the city, the China Doll, that red-hued beacon of distraction, was eschewed by the young Maverick Caiden, whose image of his mother hovered in the forefront of his mind, looking as stern as Gabriel at the Gate, while the admonitions of the severe preacher at the First Baptist Church in Bandera rang in his ears like the very voice of Moses himself standing before the rescued Hebrews chastising them for falling again into the sin of idolatry.

✳✳✳

'Morning and coffee,' thinks Mav, 'what better way to begin a day.' Night had been good, and Mav had slept well. Biscuit and the pack horse were pawing at the snow to see what might be underneath. A bright sun was peeking between two hills in the distance putting green eye-memories in the eyes of Mav Caid who chanced to look in its direction. As the green spots cleared, Mav stood to stretch and get some of the kinks out and began to run through the directions given to him by his uncle in his 'diary of misery' as he had lately begun to refer to it. His family died because of the very existence of this diary, Mav thought, what a great disappointment it would be to find that it was all for nothing. At times over the years, he considered throwing it away and forgetting that it existed, but each time he realized that a haunting will follow if he did. It isn't the diary that deserves the hatred imbued into Mav's heart for its linkage to his family's killing, it is solely the criminal activity of Chico. No, Mav must carry through and find its meaning, vanquish the hold it held over his mind, excise the thorn that is in his heart thrust there by Chico's infamy. Mav walked over to where he had placed the packs from the pack horse. Rummaging through it he extracted a small shovel.

"Jes' in case," Mav said to himself, "I'll dig 'round some over near thet stream if need be."

He approached the stream that lay fifty to sixty yards from his camp. As he arrived, he stopped on the bank to observe it in its run. The water ran smoothly in some areas making it seem slow moving, and turbulent in other areas. Not much different from any I have seen in the past, he thought. But then Mav looked down through the water to the bedrock below. Strange, tear-shaped, and circular pockmarks abound in the bedrock. Small indentations of a half-inch to two inches in depth and two to three in diameter, all tear-shaped depressions carved into the native rock.

"Jes' like uncle Wendell described!" exclaimed Mav to himself. Then, the magic of sudden comprehension flooded his thoughts. Envisioned clearly in his mind are the small stones, endlessly swirling within entrapping dimples in the stone creek channel, constantly gouging and deepening their prisons. But where are the pebbles? He looks closer and sees something small in each of the holes. Reaching through the frigid water, Mav picks out one of the octahedron pebbles and holds it up to inspect it. As he turns this strange stone about between his fingers, the awakened sun sends its own magic through those millions of miles to this small valley to fracture one tiny hand-held stone into a rainbow.

"Whut?" was all he could say in his astonishment. For the next hour, Mav reached in to remove stone after stone from their watery prisons, some so colorless that they all but disappeared in the covering water, placing each in a leather pouch with drawstrings.

Mav spent three days exploring for the headwaters of this tiny stream but was never sure that he had found its beginning because it disappeared underground several times and each time Mav was ready to declare that he had found it, he would look again and see that it flowed on, weaving in and out of the ground as basket laths weave in and out the staves. It was as if the top surface of an underground tube eroded away, here and there, to expose the interior of the tube. 'Strange. But this will have to wait', Mav thinks to himself. 'I need to be home by Christmas.'

The next day, today's explorer is on the ride back to Beaton with a newly drawn map, complete with landmarks that will lead him back next year.

Happiness at his return was uncontainable. Case hung around his pa's neck competing for his attention coming from Lyla who was demanding attention from her crib. Macy stood back smiling at the chaos of sound as each sought an answer to their question or for his undivided attention to what tale they were telling, mostly in baby gibberish. Macy smiled and waited and for the moment, Macy ceded her need for attention. Midnight will come.

"Ifn I tell you whut I b'lieve they are, Macy, you might reckon me loco. Truth is, I don't really know. They are jes' like th' stones thet uncle Wendell sent to me with th' map. He reckoned they wuz important. I reckon I'll hav' to b'lieve it too 'til I know otherwise." Mav shrugged and looked at Macy for her response. Macy shrugged in agreement. Midnight came, and the stones were forgotten.

The next morning, Mav picked up last week's copy of the Gazette to peruse the news of the day. His eye fell on the notice of the death

Eugene Stonefield

of Hunkpapa Lakota chief Sitting Bull by action of the police at Standing Rock Indian Reservation on December 15. His killing occurred during an attempt to arrest him and keep him from joining the Ghost Dance that was sweeping through the reservations and creating fear of an uprising.

A couple of weeks afterward, a tragic incident occurred resulting in a massacre of two-hundred-fifty to three hundred men women and children at Wounded Knee Creek on the Lakota Pine Ridge Indian Reservation in South Dakota. Twenty-five soldiers of the cavalry also died and thirty-nine suffered wounds. Official reports confirm that the incident resulted from efforts to tamp down the Ghost Dance that the natives were beginning to believe was a guaranteed pathway to deliverance from domination by the government in Washington and to satisfy their longing to return to the old ways of life. The Ghost dance, instills in the white settlers the fear of a general uprising and hastens the pull of the trigger.

In this tragic incident at Wounded Knee, a regiment of the 7th Cavalry trained upon the camp the awesome firepower of four Hotchkiss Mountain Guns, —rapid fire weapons unmatched by natives in their camp at Wounded Knee Creek. Witnesses said the episode started with the discharge of a rifle by a deaf tribesman named Black Coyote who was resisting the confiscation of his weapon because he said he had paid for it. The accidental discharge resulted in the 7th Cavalry Regiment under Colonel James W. Forsyth firing into the campsite.

What was it? The Ghost dance was an invention of the Paiute prophet, Wovoka, promising the return of the Messiah, Jesus Christ, in the form of a native who would ensure their deliverance from the white man's dominance. Ghosts of the ancestors would also return, and the white man would disappear from the land, and the herds of buffalo would return. Life of the native would return to the harmony known before the tumultuous coming of the white men. All of this would come to pass if only the people of the reservations would dance the Ghost dance wearing the protective shirts that bullets could not pierce, —shirts imbued with a magical power revealed by Black Elk in his vision. The cost to assure a return to normalcy, was to dance the dance, and believe.

In the International News section, famed artist Vincent van Gogh is reported to have died of his self-inflicted wound suffered several days before at the Auberge Ravoux in Auvers-sur-Oise in Northern France.

Mav folded the Gazette and sat in contemplation. "So much violence, so much blood," he whispers to himself. Such it is with the reading of current news, that seems to sensationalize the negatives and minimize the positives. Bad news appears above the fold, good news below or on another page. 'Is there some written or unwritten rule that makes it so? Are folks more drawn to tragedy?' Mav troubles himself with the thought. 'Perhaps it is the nature of reporting by those whose interests are divided between the desire to show the truth of a matter and the desire for self-aggrandizement. What reporter does not covet the thought of seeing their own name in the byline for a sensational story? Is blood the lubricant for the story? The allure for the reader?'

But there is another kind of reading by which Mav has endeavored to expand his knowledge. It is the cyclopedia, and the books from the small Beaton library that are opening Mav's eyes to the world, and to the world of differences. In their course of providing information, these resources are rapidly reshaping the mind and the language of this rudely educated farmer's son turned drover turned farmer from Bandera. With a desire to be a positive role model for Case and Lyla, the modestly educated Maverick Caiden set his goal to become more knowledgeable in the endeavors of the era and in the promises of the future. In this quest for knowledge Mav cast away no subject as unimportant. No effort, unworthy.

Chapter 19

First Train Ride / Epiphany in Chicago

Winters can be hard in Arkansas, and the winter of 1895 was particularly so for the twenty-eight-year-old farmer. The hardness of this particular winter was that it is the winter of a year of total crop failure resulting from unfortunate weather events that brought hail and excess rain at the wrong time. Crops failed, money was tight, and even the purchase of seed to sow for the next year was difficult. Mav sold most of the beef and dairy cattle months before, and of the few cows kept for their milk, several would be going dry soon. Mav and Macy know that they must find more income or the farm itself will be at risk when the mortgage payment is due in February next year and is the subject of a kitchen table conversation.

"Macy, we done scant little to larn ifn th' discov'ry we checked out two year ago might be useful to us. We still ain't sure ifn thar's money to be had from th' find. I am a-thinkin' thet I should orta go to Chicago an' jes' see whut I ken larn about them stones an' ifn they hav' value. Th' railway now runs through Beaton, an' I ken take it an' be in Chicago ina day or two." Mav finished his statement and waited for Macy to respond.

"Mav, we have been lackadaisical on this, so I would not oppose trying to find out as much as possible. When would you go?" asked Macy.

"I took a look-see at th' runnin' schedule an' ken leave Tuesday. I reckon I'll buy a round trip ticket to return th' followin' week an', ifn it takes longer, exchange th' ticket in Chicago fo' another date." Mav now considers the decision made and gets up to pour another cup of coffee as Macy begins to prepare some broad beans to go with the cornbread and ham for supper.

✳✳✳

Tuesday finds Mav standing on the passenger platform waiting for the train to arrive. In the distance, he sees the dark smoke rising through the bare-branched trees through which the tracks run. A long 'whoo-whooing' tone like one generated by a pipe organ is sounding in the distance as the train gets closer to the station. A bell atop the engine is clanging as the train pulls in only thirty minutes behind schedule and begins to take on water for the boiler. Mav ignores the engine's hissing steam release from the power cylinders that veils the platform with a fleeting touch of billowing white fog as he walks toward the passenger car. Presently, the conductor steps down from the passenger car and sets the portable step on the platform for passengers to de-board, and six passengers get off. Mav picks up his Gladstone bag and walks to the car on which he will be spending the next two days as it winds its way across the white countryside from Beaton to Chicago. The distance is over eight hundred miles on rails snaking through Little Rock toward Memphis, up the western bank of the Mississippi River, crossing the river by the Merchants bridge at St.

Louis, then through Springfield and Joliet in Illinois, and into Chicago, stopping at Grand Central Station.

The train will stop at towns along the way momentarily to leave or take on passengers, mail, livestock, grain, and cotton destined for Chicago and other cities. From some stops, railroad crews will fill the coal-tender with coal, and men with large canisters of oil will walk down both sides of the train spraying oil on the wheel axles or adding oil to the journal boxes to lubricate the axles and prevent the unwanted ignition of friction fires, called 'hotboxes,' beneath the cars as the wheels turn. An exception is that stops at small stations are dependent upon the stationmaster erecting a signal that passengers and freight are waiting. Otherwise, the train will roar through the station at a rapid pace blowing the steam whistle that rises in tone as it approaches then falls just as rapidly once it has passed the listener. Mav has learned from the Gazette that the lowering of tone is called the 'dopler effect.'

Steam locomotives have so captivated the imagination of the populace that folks stand respectfully before a passing train and wave at the engineer who typically waves back or blows the whistle in recognition. The cord or lever operated steam whistle provided flexibility enabling the engineer to customize the sound to his personal liking, some, even to the extent that the sound of the whistle would identify the specific engineer operating the train. The purpose of the whistle is to facilitate communication with others responsible for train operation, and to perform that function, the companies implemented a system of whistle codes like the Morse code used in telegraphy. In addition to the whistle, some communication is visual, conducted by crew members riding in the caboose, using flags and lanterns to signal status from their perspective at the rear.

Postal clerks deliver incoming mail by tossing bags of mail onto the dock as the train speeds by. To bring local, outbound mail aboard economically, an ingenious mechanical catcher-arm aboard the train's mail car snatches bagged mail staged for the transfer from a scaffolding on the station's loading platform. This transfer of mail allows the train to pass through the station without stopping, thereby reducing the cost. Once retrieved, postal employees aboard the train sort the mail in the sorting car as it travels down the rails. The process was an innovation of the Railway Post Office company holding the contract for the Federal Postal Service in Washington. Mav knew much of the process from issues of the Gazette that he had read in months past, and now seeing it in action is astounding. Proper signaling and timing are known to enhance profits for the shareholders of the railway companies, according to the reports, and customers receive a benefit from the innovations by a reduction in cost for their shipments. It is an irrefutable fact that a train that does not have to stop saves money by reducing the amount of fuel used on each run.

Mav has not lost his amazement to the changing times and wonders whether the cattle drive of Lytle is a thing of history. Maybe, he wonders, if all livestock travels aboard cattle cars like the ones he can see in the distance, or will in the future. He is unaware that the last large scale cattle drive along the Great Western Cattle Trail was last year, a victim of the times. Mav, though, knew well that a historical word, 'murrain', —coined from the fifth of seven plagues of Egypt that occurred as Moses sought freedom for his enslaved people had entered the vocabulary of many cattle owners trying to explain why local cattle died rapidly following the transit of cattle from Texas heading to processing plants and railheads north. For fear of this pestilence, Texas cattle can no longer go through eastern Kansas by an act of the legislature. When the last drive along the Goodnight-Loving trail ended may never be known. Similarly, for the others, such as the famous Chisholm from Ft. Worth, Texas to Abilene, Kansas.

Currently, the cost of moving cattle by rail is over-priced, so cattle owners still attempt small scale drives but are encountering increasing difficulty. Westward migration of settlers establishing farms on rangeland with their common desire to control incursion into their crops by passing cattle, is diminishing the open range through which cattle must travel.

Yet it will be the ingenuity of Lucien Smith and Joseph Glidden's improvement upon the original design of barbed wire, or 'bobwire' in the lingo of Texan, Mav Caid, that tilts the path of history away from the trail drivers. Loss of the open range from the cross-fencing of land with barbed wire, and legal prohibitions against a tick-borne scourge of cattle known as Texas Fever, and the increasing availability of rail transportation, will combine to strangle and kill the cattle drives.

Before that metal invention, planting fences of shrub-like trees, its thorny equivalent, was the mode of controlling cattle incursions into planted fields. Farmers enclosed many acres of farmland by close-planted trees known by names such as bois d'arc, horse apple, and Osage orange that bears only a knotty green orange-sized inedible fruit. Natives knew the tree as the bow-tree and eagerly sought its wood for making their bows. Barbed wire was cheaper, faster to install, more certain of a complete enclosure and soon became the solution of choice for farmers and ranchers carving their futures from the free-range. From testimonial letters lauding the durability and cost of the new fencing, potential customers also learned that the benefits of installing barbed wire included economy of space, no adverse effects on soil or vegetation, immunity to high winds, and that the fencing creates no snowdrifts. Today, Mav is well experienced in the use of 'bobwire' to protect his growing crops and corral his animals.

Soon, Mav hears the shouted, "All aboard!" voiced by the conductor as the coal-tender and water tanks are fully replenished, firebox stoked by the train's fireman, and workers have finished loading and unloading boxcars. Encouraged by the loud clanging bell atop the engine now belching smoke through the smokestack, Mav steps up to the lower step of the passenger car and looks back at the dock where iron-rimmed wooden wheels on flatbed wagons are moving their loads around the dock under the efforts of station porters in red hats.

The wagon wheels make successive thumps and clicks as they pass over the cracks between the wooden planks of the platform. Soon he will hear the clicking of the train's iron wheels passing over the joints between rails of polished steel fastened to seven-inch by nine-inch by ninety-six-inch creosoted crossties laid upon crushed stone track ballast to support the tremendous burden of the train. He will hear the steam whistle emit its plaintive wail as it approaches or leaves a rail stops along the way. He will hear the clang of the brass bell that tops the silver trimmed black engine as the train awaits the signal to return to its run. Exhilaration marks his first ride and a first view of the countryside passing by at an astounding thirty miles per hour. How powerful must be the engine to pull such weight as it must be pulling. How rapid its pace to move a rider as far in an hour as a horse can transport one in a day.

Chicago's Grand Central train station on Harrison and Fifth Avenue is a blur of movement, more people moving about than Mav has ever seen in one place, even Kansas City. Six side-by-side tracks received passenger trains under a metal shed measuring over five-hundred feet in length, one-hundred-fifty in width and seventy-nine feet in height. The structure featured a two-hundred-forty-seven-foot-tall tower with a large clock and an eleven-thousand pound bell to chime the hour. The waiting room displays its opulence in marble bedecked floors, its ceiling supported by Corinthian-style columns, its walls with windows of stained glass. The sounds amplified by the enclosed nature of the station seemed surreal to someone used to the openness of the countryside.

Mav Caid — The Complete Story

Mav steps down from the car with his Gladstone bag in hand and walks toward the buildings that he sees in the distance. Stopping a Red Cap station porter along the way, Mav asks how to get to the hotel and is surprised when asked, "which one?" ushering in another amazement that there are more than one to choose from.

As he walked, he began to formulate a strategy for selecting his hotel and finding it. First, he decided, it should be near the business district because that is where he will get his information about the stones which he has brought with him in the leather draw-string pouch. Second, find out how far a walk to the hotel. Third, pray that the trip is not in vain.

The Red Cap he stopped earlier had pointed out a place that he could get a carriage ride or, if adventuresome, a ride on the new electric powered trolley. After considering his option, he set out for the line of buggies and carriages awaiting the next passenger, where he engaged the driver in conversation about the cost of the ride and determined which hotel would be best. The carriage driver proved to be talkative and peppered Mav with a history of the city in a non-stop stream of talk on the way to the hotel.

✳✳✳

Entering the Tremont Hotel on Chestnut, one of the buildings that Mav learned had been raised by several feet to accommodate groundwater drainage troubling the low-lying city on Lake Michigan since its founding in 1780 by Jean Baptiste Point du Sable. Du Sable, a trader who established the first permanent trading enterprise at the mouth of the Chicago River, was a man of Haitian heritage from the French colony of Saint Dominique. Around 1800, for unknown reasons, du Sable sold out and opened a river ferry service on the Missouri river. Mav also learned that the person who lifted the buildings was an engineer and industrialist named George Pullman.

Eugene Stonefield

Pullman, the carriage driver told Mav, used multiple jackscrews inserted beneath the structure and as many jack operators each working a single jack, to turn the jackscrews incrementally, to lift the building smoothly inch by inch. Subsequently, Pullman constructed a new foundation beneath the raised building, then gently lowered the still occupied building, turn by turn, to set the building onto the new foundation. Occupants and staff of the Tremont continued activities as usual during the operation.

Another thing Mav also found interesting about Pullman, was that the train Mav arrived on was pulling a passenger-sleeper car called a Pullman Sleeper, and staffed by Pullman porters, all by convention, addressed as 'George.' Many, according to the carriage driver, were slaves before the Civil War. Mav wondered if it was the same George Pullman. When Mav asked if he was the same person, the driver said that he was and talked about the company town he had built nearby that housed the workers in his plant manufacturing the Pullman sleeper cars. He told Mav about the deadly strike in which military troops intervened at the order of President Grover Cleveland, and that thirty company workers lost their lives in the conflict. His loquacious driver further said that, in addition to the Tremont, that, of the buildings in Chicago raised by a few inches to a few feet, most had been constructed in the years after the great fire of 1871 that destroyed a good portion of Chicago. The fire, he told Mav started accidentally in a barn owned by the O'Leary family. How the fire started is a point of debate. As the buildings were set upon new foundations, builders laid sewage and water lines upon the ground and covered them by dirt to elevate the streets correspondingly. The effort led to the unique basement-style living quarters exhibiting window wells that, before the raising of the roads, had been the first floor of an unraised house or building. 'The ingenuity of man never ceases to amaze,' thought Mav, 'to lift a city!' Then remembering something he read in the cyclopedia about a statement by the Greek mathematician, Archimedes, that if he had a place to stand, he could lift the world.

Signing his name at the check-in counter was the second time in his life that he had that experience. The first was at the Altern in Villon. He recalled how that went. Hopefully, he will not have someone poking a gun in his face this time.

"Welcome to the Tremont. How long will you be staying?" The Front Desk clerk wearing a name tag identifying himself as Weldon Udall, turned the register toward Mav to enable him to sign in.

"Don't rightly know, but a few days. Are y'all need'n' to know now?" answered Mav.

"No. No. Just let me know when you intend to leave so, we will prepare the room for the next visitor," said the clerk as he turned the register around to read his name. "Ah, Mr. Caid, have you stayed with us before?" asked the clerk.

"No, this here's my first time in Chicago," Mav answered while inspecting the cavernous room with the enormous chandelier hanging twenty feet above. At least twenty people milled about the lobby or sat in chairs scattered about for the guests. Many of the women wore clothing styles he had not seen in Beaton and most looked expensive. Many wore full-length fur coats and tall boots. There was no exception, as the men he saw were equally clothed in expensive-looking clothes from hat crown to soles. None seemed to be wearing guns. All seemed to have a scarf around their necks. Many spoke of the entertainment venues that they had enjoyed or planned to enjoy soon.

"Excellent!" responded the clerk handling his registration. "Mr. Caid, my name is Weldon Udall. I am the Front Desk Clerk for the Tremont and you can reach me any time by telephone. When you leave, please check out through me. Your room has a telephone. If you need anything just dial zero for the operator and she will connect you to the appropriate service station. Mr. Lindale, standing just over to your right is the hotel Concierge, who will assist you with any of your needs while you are with us. Your room is number 422, Mr. Caid. I hope you will be comfortable. The dining room is to your left and the lounge to your right. I'll call the bellhop to help with your bags."

As Front Desk Clerk, Weldon Udall ended his instruction monologue, he motioned for a bellhop who had posted up about fifteen feet away. Handing the keys to the bellhop, Weldon announced: "Rick, this is Mr. Caid, and he is to be conducted to room 422, please."

After admiring the opulence of the lobby architecture and the comfortable appearance of his assigned room, Mav gave Rick a tip of appreciation as he left, then tested the bed. "All is well," Mav whispered to himself as he removed his boots and placed them aside. Walking to the window Mav experienced another amazement in the skyline of Chicago, one that exhibited the soaring steel-structured ten-storied building he was to learn was the Home Insurance Company on the corner of LaSalle and Adams street, a building that moved people vertically, floor by floor, utilizing an 'elevator.'

Mav spent a restful night in a steam heated room, and when morning came, he was ready to visit the dining room, then to start his quest for information. His first thought was how different the sounds of a waking city to the sounds of the farm. He was uncertain if he should start at the assay office, the college of natural history, or a jewelry store to begin showing the stones. After asking Concierge Lindale, for directions to each, Mav decided it was closer to a jewelry store than the others so would start there. Chicago is a vastly bigger town than Beaton and Villon, and there are choices to make even about which jewelry store. The Chicago Times newspaper shows at least a half-dozen jewelers in the city. The lobby of the Tremont displays a map of the city for the benefit of the visitors, and Mav began his day by consulting the map.

Mav Caid — The Complete Story

✳✳✳

The Reginal Benoit Jewelry Company and Manufactory appeared on the map as the nearest, so, Mav set out to walk to that store several blocks away on State Street. Chicago can offer a bitter cold during the winter, and a strong wind carrying light flakes of snow chilled his walk. Upon entering, a clerk greeted Mav from behind a glass case displaying various items of jewelry. Rings of every description sat in individual boxes and broaches to neckless surrounded the boxed rings, displaying stones of all colors known to nature.

"How can I assist you?" began the sales clerk at the counter displaying the jewelry that Mav was admiring. "Do you have a gift in mind? A neckless or ring? What is the occasion? if I may ask."

"No. No gift in mind. Neither, an' no occasion," returned Mav. "I hav' here some stones thet I would be obliged ifn someone a-knowin' stones would look at."

"Oh, you seek an appraisal. Well, that would be the interest of Mr. Benoit himself. I will see if he is available." The clerk disappeared behind a curtain.

Returning, the clerk asked, "Would you follow me, please? Mr. Benoit will see you in his office," stated the clerk.

"I reckon I ken do thet," returned Mav as he came around the counter and fell in behind the clerk who conducted him to the office of Mr. Reginal Benoit, owner of the Benoit company that is engaged in the manufacture and sales of moderate to high-end jewelry.

"I understand you seek an appraisal, Mr....?" began Mr. Benoit. "I presume, cut stones?"

"Caid," replied Mav to the question. "My name is Mav Caid an', no, these here stones are as I fetched them up outen a stream." Mav pulled out the leather pouch and passed it to Mr. Benoit.

163

Eugene Stonefield

Mr. Benoit pulled open the pouch and turned it upside down. Small crystalline stones tumbled from the bag to a dark blue felt cloth laying on the desk. After inspecting one of the octahedrons, he drew the stone across a piece of glass, leaving a deep gouge, then, picking up a jeweler's loupe, Mr. Benoit began to look at each stone, weighing and separating them into several small piles on the cloth. "These are interesting, Mr. Caid," said Mr. Benoit. "Care to tell me where you got them?"

"Well, no sir, not at this time," answered Mav, "I hanker to know whut they are an' ifn they hav' value."

"Value, yes," returned Mr. Benoit. "Value is relative to how these stones are used, Mr. Caid. Crushed, many manufacturers use them to grind things in the process of manufacturing and polishing. I use them myself in my manufacturing process. They would have one value for that. But, if, say, I cut them in such a manner as to have flat surfaces in a regular pattern and at specific angles and mounted in gold or silver as jewelry, then they would have an altogether different value, a value that is dependent upon many things. For instance, color, clarity, size of the stone, and whether it has inclusions, —that's internal flaws. All add to or subtract from the stone's value. Now, Mr. Caid, as you should know, my business is manufacturing and selling jewelry, and I would be interested in purchasing these stones from you. You don't have to decide right now. I am sure you may want to show them to others, but I do hope you will give me the opportunity to, say, amend my offer if someone else offers you more." Mr. Benoit went silent as he began to take each stone from the piles and make a line of stones on the cloth. "Oh, yes, they are diamonds, Mr. Caid, diamonds. Crystals for the adornment of the rich and famous."

"Diamonds? Like fo' rings?" returned Mav, still uncertain of the significance of what Mr. Benoit is telling him.

"Yes," returned Mr. Benoit, "for wedding rings, bracelets, neckless, and even dog collars for those who may be vain about their poodles. And, of course, in countries still retaining a monarch, in crowns of their kings and queens. Diamonds are even said to be a girl's best friend! They can warm the heart, lift the spirits of the sad, Mr. Caid, especially when given unexpectedly."

"Uh, how much might I 'spect to sell these here for?" Mav asked.

"Ah, yes. Well, these, in this line, about twelve a carat. Oh, sorry. A carat is a weight that we use in the jewelry business. It is exactly 200 milligrams in weight. So, twelve dollars a carat and I have jotted down the weights of the stones on this line, which is about four hundred carats, so that comes to about forty-eight hundred dollars for these stones. Would you consider…" Mr. Benoit turned to look at Mav. "Mr. Caid, please sit down for a minute. You look faint." Pouring a glass of water from a nearby crystal carafe, Mr. Benoit passed the glass to Mav.

"Now, Mr. Caid," continued Mr. Benoit, "this line of stones is of lesser quality, so I would give you, say, eight dollars per carat and there are 345 carats here, so that is…yes, twenty-seven hundred and sixty dollars. And the last line, roughly 154 carats at five dollars per carat comes to seven hundred and seventy dollars. The total is eight-thousand three-hundred and twenty dollars for the lot." Mr. Benoit pushed himself away from his desk and looked at a very peaked Maverick who was sitting forward on the chair wide-eyed with shock.

Finally, the shock wearing off, Mav said weakly, "I cain't imagine jes' how many carrots I'd hafta grow an' sell to gain eight-thousand dollars."

"Mr. Caid," said Mr. Benoit, laughing, "I would advise you not to talk to anyone or show any strangers these stones. There are people, greedy people, who will kill for them. One other thing, —and please don't take offense, —there are no known diamond mines in America, so, if you found these in America, you have a unique and possibly, significant find. Since I must import all my rough stones from abroad, I am very interested in having a local source, so to speak."

Eugene Stonefield

Mav retrieved the stones which Mr. Benoit wrapped in separate groups so that he would not have to inspect them as closely should Mav decide to sell to him. Walking back to the Tremont, Mav caught himself looking behind to check that no one was following him. "I wisht Macy wuz here," Mav whispered to himself, "I shor long to hav' her advice."

The second night at the Tremont was not as restful as the first. Mav's mind kept returning to the offer made for the stones. He kept thinking of what Mr. Benoit said about the robbery and theft risk he had just because he had the stones. His mind kept wandering back to the time at the Altern Hotel when he opened the door to face a loaded Remington forty-four pointing at his face.

Sunrise came as sharp blades of light between partially closed curtains and Mav dressed with a determination to make a deal with Mr. Benoit. He reasoned that the amount offered is more than needed to pay off the bank in Beaton for the loan against their farm, and a little because he knew where to get other stones like them. Selling the stones, he reasoned, would minimize his risk of losing them in a robbery, not thinking about the risk of robbery for the money he was to receive, which, at this time he believed would be cash.

Rather than walk to the jewelry store, Mav stepped into a chaise that waited for passengers at the curb in front of the Tremont. It was a short ride, but Mav felt no need to look behind himself as he had yesterday. Again, he asked to see Mr. Benoit and followed the clerk to his office.

"Good morning, Mr. Caid," said the surprised jeweler, who had convinced himself that Mav would want to shop for other bids. "Have you made a decision, or are you seeking more information?" Receiving an affirmative answer from Mav, Mr. Benoit weighed and re-inspected the diamonds to assure himself that they were the same as he had bid on the previous day. "My offer of yesterday, —are you happy with that offer?" asked Mr. Benoit.

"I'm a-thinkin' I am, but I got a notion to change it in this-a-way: a value fo' value trade fo' a gift fo' my wife, Macy, ifn, you ain't opposed to it." Mav didn't have to wait long for an answer.

"Agreed, Mr. Caid," responded Mr. Benoit. "If you come with me to the front display case, you may select whatever gift you want. Once you choose your gift, I will go with you to the bank across the street, and you can get the remainder of your money." A short time later, Mav and Mr. Benoit walked across Chestnut Street and over to the Chicago City Bank and Trust where the cashier provided Mav a banker's check for him to deposit into his account in Beaton when he returns home. Mav knew of banker's checks but had never seen one.

"Mr. Caid," said Mr. Benoit, as they stood on the corner of Chestnut and Rush Street, "I will not feel that I have done justice to my interests or to your interests if I didn't ask if you truly have an exploitable source of diamonds like the ones you just sold to me? You, see, I am in the business of cutting and polishing diamonds as much as in the business of selling what others have cut and polished. I must purchase and import the stones that I cut from the De Beers diamond cartel. Predatory pricing and distance from the source make it difficult at times to satisfy the demands of my customers. Many jewelry stores such as in Memphis, Kansas City, Atlanta, and some here in Chicago are customers of my manufactory. As I have previously mentioned, it would be to my advantage to have a reliable source. So, I have a proposal that I would like for you to consider. I would like to have a first-look option. That simply means that I get to look at the stones first, before anyone else, and purchase what I need to supply my business needs. I will always bid a fair price, but you will always be able to reject my offer and sell to another if you feel you can better my bid. Please consider my offer, Mr. Caid. I feel it can be to both of our advantages. For the moment, goodbye, Mr. Caid. Have a safe trip home."

Eugene Stonefield

Mav spent the remainder of the day walking around this fantastic city and purchasing gifts for Macy, Lyla, and Case from Marshall-Field's department store. Having learned about the elevator at the Home Insurance Company, Mav took a chaise to the towering ten-story building and experienced a heart-stopping ride on an elevator to the tenth floor. The following morning, Mav boarded a train at Grand Central to return to Beaton with stories to tell.

Chapter 20

Retiring the Mortgage

Even though the trip to Chicago was brief, the joy of Mav's return home was palpable. Lyla and Case were delighted at the gifts their pa had bought for them. Lyla's was a new doll with a porcelain face and bright blue eyes that move as the doll is moved about. Sometimes it cries with a sound like a real baby. It was a little advanced for her age, but Mav could tell she liked it. Case is happy for the small wooden horse that rocks on curved rails as the rider moves back and forth. He has already named it Biscuit, which he pronounces as 'Bikit.' Macy is still in awe of the colorful sparkles and flashes of diffracted light from the diamond mounted in a gold ring. For the home, a Regulator clock to set on the mantel. For himself, the joy of seeing the joy in his family was enough.

"And to think, this stone is the same that you took to Chicago just a few days ago," Macy said to her husband.

"Well, not th' same but a might sim'lar. It's amazin' how dif'runt th' stones are once they hav' been cut an' polished," replied Mav. "And best o' all, we're a-knowin' where to git more." The next day, Mav hitched his wagon to a brace of horses and loaded up the family for a trip into town where they had business to attend to. When they arrived, Mav and Macy entered the bank with a banker's check for the outstanding sum of eight-thousand dollars and some change.

"Good morning, Mr. and Mrs. Caiden," welcomed the teller, Orin Seacrest. "Are you here to make a payment on your loan? It is a little early." Orin waited for a reply, and Mav reached into his pocket and withdrew the check.

"We are Orin. In fact, we aim to pay it off in full." Mav and Macy watched Orin's face as the check was handed to him.

"Oh, my," exclaimed Orin, "I'll have to get Mr. Burford!" He hurried off to tell Mr. Burford about the payment which brought the president out to the teller window.

"Mr. and Mrs. Caiden, hello." Said Mr. Burford, as he inspected the check. "You mind telling me where you came by this large sum of money? Inherited? Or…."

"At this time," responded Mav, "I'm a-need'n to keep thet to mysel'. It's th' result o' somethin' thet happened 'most fifteen years ago an' I ain't secured it right enough to chance givin' information to anyone right now. I hope you ain't taken no offense."

"No, of course not. Since this is a banker's check, payment is guaranteed so we won't have to wait for the funds to become available. Orin will mark your debt paid and deposit the remainder of thirty-four hundred dollars to your account. For now, good day, Mister. and Missus Caiden." Mr. Burford handed the check back to the teller and went back to his office to ponder.

Finished with such an enjoyable activity, Mav and Macy shopped in several stores for things they had only hoped to buy just one week ago. Their extravagances included a new butter churn, a new ladle for the bucket at the well, some clothes for Lyla and Case, material for a new dress for Macy and a Winchester Model 1873 lever-loading repeating rifle for Mav to replace his aging Henry. Their last stop was to the General Store, where they purchased all imaginable items to fill the cupboard of a cabin that has grown too small for a family of four.

On the way back home, Mav told Macy of the impressive sights he saw along the way, beginning with the electric lights that illuminated the streets in Little-rock, the use of telephones for person-to-person voice communication, water reservoirs that deliver water to houses and businesses by pipes, and the elevator ride he experienced in Chicago.

"I tell you, Macy, I jes' cain't 'magine how anythin' else ken be more impressive. I reckon'd telegraph wuz amazin' when I larn'd about it. But now…So many new inventions, I jes' cain't but wonder if everythin' thet ken be invented ain't already been invented!"

"It sounds wonderful," returned Macy. "I guess someday Beaton will have all of those things. I wonder if it will extend to the farms around Beaton."

"Macy, I 'spect it will. People want things they see thet othern hav'. It's th' nature o' people, I reckon. An', th' schoolin' opportunities! There are schools o' higher larnin' sproutin' up everywhere I looked, even in Fayetteville, I'm tol' there is an Arkansas Industrial University thet larns folks about mechanics an' sech, even science o' growin' crops. You know, Macy, I want Case an' Lyla to grow up knowin' more than jes' how to plant a crop an' take care o' animals. I want them to see Little Rock an' Chicago. I want them to see th' world. I read so much in th' cyclopedia thet I jes' git excited fo' them to know more an' see more." Mav shook the reins to encourage the horses pulling the wagon to go a little faster.

Chapter 21

Recounting Events of 1892 and 1893

Addressing his wife of five years, Mav pondered current and past events that affected citizens in ways not always recognized. "You know, Macy, a lot has happened since Villon. I'm a-wonderin' where th' time has gone."

"Yes, Mav, I feel it too," returned Macy as she rolled out the dough for the biscuits she was preparing to bake. "But we've come a long way in that time. From the four acres to forty acres under plow. More acres purchased for pasture and the herd of milk cows and all of it fenced to contain their wandering into the growing crops. I think we supply at least a fourth of the milk consumed in Beaton now and a growing portion of the beef butcher Ray sells. Case and Lyla are growing like weeds. We have much to be thankful for."

"But it seems like everythin' is speedin' up in th' world these days. So much is happenin'. I found some old Gazettes I'd set aside in th' barn fo' use in th' outhouse an' decided to read what wuz reported o'er thet time. I read in th' Gazette thet in June o' 1892, an oil fire killed one-hundred-thirty people in Oil City, Pennsylvania. I don't recall thet, so I reckon I didn't read th' Gazette at thet time. They mentioned th' Johnstown flood thet happen'd in 1889 thet killed two-thousand people!" Mav straightens the paper and turns the page.

"And here's somethin'. Tennessee had twenty-six inches o' snow from one snow storm. Glad we didn't git thet un. In August, a fella named Thomas Edison received a patent fo' somethin' called a two-way telegraph thet is supposed to hep people communicate with far-flung places over copper wire. Thet' 'minds me thet a few days back, I wuz down at th' train station an' a man wuz sendin' an' receivin' messages on jes' sech a device. The messages are just tapped out, tic-tac, tic-tac, until all th' message is sent. When a message comes in, th' little device receiving th' message just taps an' taps. I couldn't make heads or tails o' it an' told him so. He just laughed an' said it wuz Morse code! Whatever thet is. I asked him about it an' wuz told thet it wuz integ'al to th' operation o' trains, but, he said, telephone service like they hav' over in Little Rock will be even more important to mos' folk, cause with telephones, two folks ken talk natural an' their words ain't needin' no operator to interpret th' code. He said thet th' Western Union Telegraph company had installed a telephone system in Little Rock back in 1879 then sold it to a local company an' by now has o'er eighty customers with them telephones. It is th' third oldest system in th' nation, he said, an' thet it wuz an invention of Alexander Graham Bell. Even my room in th' Tremont had a telephone. I reckon mail will become a thing o' the past. Prob'ly best thet you didn't get thet station-keeper's job." Mav set the paper aside to refill his coffee cup from the pot of coffee on the stove, then returned to resume reading the Gazette.

"Here's one, th' Dalton gang attempted to rob a bank in Coffeeville, Kansas an' all wuz gunned down by th' town folk. I rode through Coffeeville, years ago. It says thet only Emmett Dalton survived, an' git this, —he had twenty-three wounds! It seems thet th' new Pledge o' Allegiance to th' flag wrote by Union Army Captain George Thatcher Balch during th' war between th' states is bein' recited in schools now. They printed th' pledge right here in th' Gazette." Mav fell silent as he picked up his coffee cup.

"That's interesting, dear." Macy placed the biscuits in the oven. "When we get a current Gazette, I want to check the ads. The children will need new clothes soon."

Local retailers will soon find strong competition from a new mail-order company founded in Chicago by Richard W. Sears and Alvah C. Roebuck and named Sears, Roebuck, and Company. Others will follow.

Life had progressed without significant distractions during the first years of the nineties. The births of Case and Lyla were by far the most important things that had happened. Experienced farm-hands now help with the work on the growing farm and Mav is becoming a reader of books on farming that are circulating through a local lending library established through the efforts of the Beaton Women's Association that began in late 1892 of which Macy is a member. They are hopeful that they will soon receive an approval of a library grant from the Andrew Carnegie's philanthropy which has been establishing libraries in Scotland and other places since 1880.

Macy's pa had died in January 1893 from pneumonia, and his funeral was officiated by Reverend Mr. Smedley. His funeral went well, and his burial was on the Caid home-place under a big spreading maple. Her pa had retired from being the station-keeper in Beaton shortly after they were married and Jess Kinder became the station-keeper, but with the railroad's coming, the days for the Arkland stage are numbered.

Eugene Stonefield

In January of 1893, Thomas Edison finished his motion picture studio in the town of West Orange in New Jersey, and knowledgeable sources say that soon people will be able to see events happening in other places just like they had been there themselves. In June, the court found Lizzie Borden not guilty of murder in the grizzly death by ax of her parents in 1892 in Falls River, Massachusetts. In September, brothers Charles and Frank Duryea drove a motorcar on an American road in Massachusetts for the first time. All of this is reported in the Beaton Gazette which Mav reads weekly.

"Here's somethin', Macy. This article tells 'bout a Texas cowboy named Bill Pickett thet showed how to drop a cow jus' by grabbin' by th' horns an' twistin'. Thet hasta be faster than ropein' an' trippin' th' cow so's a brand ken be applied. It sez thet he also bites th' cow's lip jus' like a bulldog does to bring a cow down. Bill is a-showin' how at somethin' called a rodeo. I rec'lect meetin' Bill wunst. When I wuz with Lytle, we hadta grab th' tail o' yearling' an' jerk him off hisn feet then pull hisn tail betwixt hisn legs an' call fo' th' runnin' iron. Sometimes thet calf would put up a fight an' would kick th' fool outen th' cowboy wantin' to throw him an' brand him." Mav tossed aside the Gazette he was reading and picked another from the pile he had brought in from the barn.

"You remember thet time in 1893 thet had all th' banks worried? Well, the Gazette sez thet it wuz b'cause th' stock market crashed in May o' thet year, somethin' 'bout th' failure o' a company called National Cordage. An' here's somethin' 'bout a device to make buttons obsolete on shoes an' clothin'. Th' inventor calls it a 'clasp locker' an' he sews inta shoes to keep them closed jes' like th' hook an' eye does. I saw a picture o' a pair o' shoes with jes' such a device jes' a month ago. All you hav' to do is jes' put yor foot in th' shoe an' pull this little metal tag up an' it closes th' shoe. I bet it could be used on clothin' also."

"That would really be an improvement in women's clothing," interjects Macy, "and for children's clothing. Mothers would applaud it world over, I predict."

"Speakin' o' what folk's world over will talk 'bout, here's an article 'bout women in New Zealand bein' allowed to vote in national elections." Boy, howdy!"

"Shouldn't women have that right here, Mav? I would like to have a say in who runs the government." Macy pauses her task of preparing a meal and looks at Mav.

"I reckon I ne'er pondered much on it, Macy. I don't see no harm in lettin' women vote. Maybe someday you will be able to jes' like th' women in New Zealand." Setting the Gazette aside, Mav took Lyla on his knee and began to jostle her until she laughed. Shortly after, Case came to his papa but stayed only a short time before going to ride his wooden horse.

"Mav, you aren't hanging around the kitchen just to read some old Gazettes to me. You have something else on your mind. What are you planning to do with this day, Mav?" asked Macy, sensing that Mav is not following his normal schedule.

"I thought, mayhap, I would go a-huntin'. I ain't been a-huntin' seems like fo' years. The farmhands know whut they needst to do." Mav waited or Macy to respond.

"Tomorrow?" asked Macy, beginning to stir the batter for the biscuits.

"Early." Mav answered.

Chapter 22

A Hunters Quandary

At first light, Mav is preparing to leave and Macy is preparing to set his breakfast before him. She has cooked Mav's favorite breakfast of ham and eggs with toasted sourdough bread and a lot of fresh coffee.

"You're not taking Biscuit, are you?" questioned Macy. "Biscuit seems to be favoring a hind leg."

"No, I'm a-thinkin' o' ridin' Hardtack. I hope Biscuit don't mind. But I don't hanker to bring harm to Biscuit when he's ailin', an' you are right. Biscuit is favorin' thet leg, now."

The next day, Mav rode out on Hardtack to revisit an activity that had long since faded into a past life as a bachelor farmer.

"Now, Hardtack, I want you to understan' thet when I whistle, you come a-runnin. Biscuit always come when I whistled, an' you don't want to be less attentive than Biscuit, now do you?" Conversation with a horse can be one-sided, but that's not the point.

Eugene Stonefield

The point is to encourage a companionship with another creature sharing your adventure. A snort, a whinny, one can interpret either as an answer. Who is to say what the animal thinks, feels or understands?

"Right over thar, Hardtack. Thet's whar we are a-goin'." Mav moves the reign to signal the direction and stopped about a mile further on, just at the edge of the forested land bordering a narrow valley. "Thar will be firewood aplenty thar an' thet stream will suit you fine."

Making camp for the night was quick and easy, owing to the availability of fuel. Within a short span of time, Mav had the fire built and was perking coffee and readying to cook a meal for the evening. A gentle breeze wafted through the valley and the night portends a bright showing of stars. Mav tethers Hardtack, something he dislikes doing, but Hardtack tends to move further away from camp than Biscuit ever did, so it was a precaution that Mav considers prudent. The next day, he will begin the hunt.

"Hardtack, you stay here until I get back. I'm gonna climb up thet rise over thar an' view th' landscape some."

Mav begins his climb just after he finished breakfast and extinguished the fire. The terrain was rocky but not overly steep, and the foliage moderate. He climbed for an hour before reaching the top where he could overlook the countryside from a narrow promontory jutting out from the high ground. From that vantage he chose the direction he wanted to go. Since this trip up the hill was for observation, his Winchester remained in its holster back in camp. He stands now on a finger of land projecting out fifty to sixty yards from a more densely forested land, a part of which he traversed in getting here. Surrounding this outcrop are severe drop-offs in front and both sides of the promontory. Mav tarried until the noon-day sun stood overhead just admiring the vista beneath him.

"Rouff", the sound no one wants to hear who is standing where Mav is standing at this moment. Mav turns toward the sound. A large black bear stands forty to fifty yards away between Mav and a pathway to safety. The bear is standing and sniffing the air. He remains upon his hind legs for two minutes, then drops down on all fours and begins to move rapidly toward Mav.

"This is not good, Maverick Caiden," whispers Mav to himself. "I reckon I'm in a pickle." He began to search for a pathway that would put distance between himself and the charging bear. With each step he made to the side of the promontory to search for a pathway down, the bear came closer. Sheer cliffs offered no pretense of escape from the dangerous predicament. Move, look down the side. Search. Search. The bear moves within ten yards. Now five. Now four. The bear, rising back upon hind legs, peers at the sky and its far vista. Dropping back down, the bear sniffs the air and shakes his broad head. The prize, no longer visible. For the next quarter hour, the bear walks back and forth on the rim of the promontory sniffing and trying to get a scent of his prey but thwarted by the dispersing breeze that rushed up the side of the cliff and dispersed Mav's scent skyward. Mav, the man on the razor's edge, the man on the cliff with no way down. The Hobson's Choice, that leads to death in either selection. Go up, if even possible, and eight-hundred pounds of teeth and claws waits. Go down, and the sixty-foot fall will be equally fatal. All this, with night coming, Mav ponders as he stands upon a small rock projection twelve feet below the rim.

If there are positive things about his predicament, it is that the night was cool and dry with a gentle wind and the countryside illuminated by a full moon. The direction of the moon that was still low on the horizon projected oblique shadows along the cliffside beneath Mav's precarious stance upon the five by ten-foot rocky ledge - shadows that reveal better by moonlight what he couldn't perceive in bright sunlight when shadows projected downward. As he peered over the edge of the ledge to which he had leaped just two hours earlier, he could see a few similar projections that offered a stairway to safety, if there was a way to lower himself to them from each higher ledge. The first seemed to be only eight to ten feet below his current position, but was narrow, not a shelf to which he could jump, without a possibility of falling outward from the impact of the landing. He is unable to assess how stable the ledge might be. The man on the edge, needed an edge.

As the night progressed, Mav sat upon the ledge and thought of his family and what it would mean to them if he never returned. What misery they would feel. What loss. After a while of pondering the meaning, Mav began to plan how he would use whatever he had to survive. What he had about him was minimal. A light jacket, shirt, Levi Straus 501 denim jeans, a belt, boots, socks, and his Bowie knife. Night ended with the waking sun and Mav set his plan into motion.

"Well, Mr. Bowie, it's jes' you an' me." Momentarily, Mav removed his boots and set them aside. Next, he removed his Levis and belt, which he laid aside. Laying his Levis flat upon the ground, Mav began to cut along the seams of each leg to open the legs into two pieces of denim sixteen inches wide and forty-four inches long, the length from waistband to hem. The waistband became another strip measuring two inches by forty-two inches. Carefully measuring the widths of each cut, Mav cut the pant legs into eight strips: four of full length and four about ten inches shorter. The utility of a rope is never far from the mind of a cowboy on the trail, nor is it forgotten by a farmer who has lived the life of a wrangler and a drover. Each piece of denim Mav rolled and twisted, then tied with a knot at either end. Taking smaller strips of cloth from his jacket, Mav tied a series of knots around the rolled denim to hold the roll in place. Any rope, to be useful to hold hoof or horn needs a honda. One that allows the rope to slip easily through for drawing a loop. Mav picked up a boot and began to cut a half-moon just below the leather loops he uses to pull the boot on when he dresses each day. Noting that the loops are flat by design, Mav placed a small wedge-shaped rock into the loop at the stitched end to force the loop to open and tied it in place by a strip of material from his Levis. Holes cut through the half-moon segment and threaded by the rolled denim then tied completes the attachment of a honda. Mav then thread a segment of the twisted denim through the newly fabricated honda and tested it for its capacity to allow free movement of the envisioned denim rope through the honda. Eventually, he tied each twisted segment of denim together with opposing twists, such that the tendency of one to unroll was countered by the other that would become tighter. Taking a pocket cut from the Levis, Mav filled it with rocks from the ledge and tied it to the honda to add weight. The final step was to tie the rest of the material segments together with strong knots. The result was a rope of dubious strength that measured about twenty-six feet in length.

Along the sides of the promontory grew small to mid-sized shrubs that projected one to three feet from the cliffside and growing in an upward direction. Mav selected one aligned above the small ledge below and offset from the ledge he stands upon. He can reach a similar shrub just above him which allows him to judge its strength. Finding that it had a tenacious enough hold in the cliff, and strong enough to support his weight, Mav then measures the distance from his position to the target shrub. The distance is three or four feet and directly over the lower ledge. Mav's task is to toss the denim rope over the shrub so that the rope falls to the shrub's base emerging from the cliff. The ledge to which he must descend, he estimates, is another eight to ten feet below the shrub. Also estimated, the strength of the ledge itself. Mav pulls the makeshift rope through the honda to create the loop, aims at the target bush and gives it a gentle backhanded toss. The toss is difficult owing to the weighted honda. The rope slaps the cliff about a foot too high and falls away. Mav pulls the rope back up and repositions for another try. On the second toss, the loop is too small and catches a branch too weak to support any weight. Two tries later, the loop tightens around the base of the small shrub. Mav pulls on the rope to test the knots, knowing the material itself could easily tear, not being bound.

Mav contemplates his strategy, whether to trust the makeshift rope and attempt to swing from the ledge and descend the rope by hand to the lower ledge, or jump and use the rope as a tether should he miss the jump or slide off. Taking the rope end in hand, Mav dropped the end to the rocky shelf below to measure its distance. The distance is fourteen feet. He decides to use the rope as a fail-safe tether rather than a descent rope and ties the rope around his chest, using four feet of the cloth rope. Gathering the remainder of his clothing and his boots into a bag fashioned from his jacket, Mav ties the jacket arms together and slips it over his head. It is not known if Mav offered a prayer before he jumped into the uncertainty of a life-or-death descent, but if so, unquestionably it was answered. As his boots struck the ledge, four feet of slack rope remained, slack that he immediately pulled to him as his feet slid upon the small rocks on top of the ledge. Upon impact, Mav felt the outward pull of the abyss, felt his feet slide toward the edge and his body fall backwards, knowing that if he fell from the ledge his destiny was death or serious injury on rocks below if the rope broke from his weight, or to mimic a pendulum and hang from the small shrub until the rope parted from age and weather. His quick gathering of slack arrested his slide and he lies upon his back looking up at the small shrub tethering him to life. Standing, Mav looks up at the weighted honda and snaps the rope several times to begin a loosening maneuver that he trusts will lower the weighted honda into his waiting hands. As each knot reaches the base of the shrub over which the rope rides the descent of the honda stops and Mav must snap the rope again to get the knot over the restriction. Should it hang or break, the rope would become useless.

As the weighted honda descends further, Mav must release more rope and with each jerky descent of the honda, the rope he holds gets shorter. Finally, the rope played out with the honda still a few feet away. Mav must trust that the weighted honda will bring the rope close enough for him to grab as it falls free. Losing this makeshift rope is a death sentence, either by starvation or by a fall to the rocks below. Mav snaps the rope a final time and releases his hold. The honda weight is enough to pull the last few knots over the base of the bush and the rope falls free. As it plunges toward Mav, the rope snags upon a smaller shrub and the honda swings away from Mav where it mimics a pendulum, just out of reach. Successive strikes against the cliff face brings the swinging rope to a stop four feet away. Adrenaline surges as Mav realizes that a working plan for getting to safety is near failure. Mav takes a deep breath and whispers to himself: "Jus' hold thar fo' a spell. Don't go anywhar."

Mav unloads the bag containing the other items of clothing he brought down with him and retrieves his belt. The belt has a standard buckle, a square metal piece with a movable post that goes through a hole in the belt for the buckle to hold fast. Again, a boot gives up a loop to the Bowie and Mav uses the loop to slip over the square metal buckle to hold the pin out as a makeshift hook. He then slips a second loop from his other boot over the belt and moves it to the buckle to give the post support from the other side. Standing as close to the edge as allowed by the shape of the ledge, Mav begins to swing the belt toward the snagged rope to hook the honda and bring it within reach. Standing with his back to the cliff, Mav swings his arm backward toward the cliff and the buckle flashes out toward the honda, only to miss by inches. Mav swings the belt again, three times, four times, five, but the reach is off. He needs more length to reach the honda. Mav cuts between the last two holes in the belt and ties a strip of cloth from his shirttail to the belt, giving him an extra foot of length. Grasping the cloth extension, Mav tries again to hook the honda. On the fourth attempt the post grabbed the honda and Mav gently pulled the captive toward him as he had many times the caught fish at his favorite fishing hole. Holding this vital prize brought a relief to the tension and Mav stood watching his hands shake as the muscles sought to recover their restful state.

After a close inspection of his make-do rope, Mav determined that it had suffered no serious damage and appeared at least as viable as before his first jump. The next target ledge was a bit closer and would not be as hazardous since it was broader than the ledge he was now standing on and not as far as the first. His second jump was successful as was the third, though he suffered a twisted ankle upon landing. The fourth, the last ledge he perceived reachable, was below the top of a large pine growing close to the cliff's base. A large limb projected from the tree toward the ledge. After measuring the distance to the ledge, Mav changed his strategy and decided to trust the rope to lower himself, reasoning that, if the rope failed, he could treat the tree limb as his fail-safe.

Mav selected a reachable anchor bush in line with the limb and slipped the loop over the bush and tightened the loop around its base. Wrapping the cloth rope around his wrist and griping tightly, he began to lower himself from the ledge. The rope holds. Hand by hand, Mav descends. Closer by each release of one hand to the other's grip. The first ten feet passes and the ledge gets closer. Then the break. Mav falls the remaining twelve feet and as he falls, twists to face outward, to face the remaining aegis between himself and a hard landing on the rocks below. His twisting maneuver, near complete, is the margin as he impacts the ledge and vaults forward toward the waiting tree limb. The pine is now the possessor of hunter Mav Caid who holds tenaciously to the limb as his strength diminishes and his thankfulness surges. Mav stays in the tree for the next quarter hour, gathering his thoughts and preparing to drop the last twelve feet to the waiting pine-needle covered earth.

Once standing upon solid ground, Mav looked back up the cliff and from his lower elevation, could see no ledges that had made the difference between life and death. Being fortunate enough to be on the east side of the rocky promontory from which he descended, his trek back to his campsite was relatively easy, even with a painful ankle, swelling in his boot. As he approached, he could see Hardtack grazing.

"Hardtack, did you hear me whistle?" There was no answer.

The trip home was uneventful, and Mav rode up to the house and dropped rein. Climbing the stairs to the porch and entering the house brought no response from anyone. Mav listened and heard nothing so assumed Macy had taken Lyla and Case down to the stock tank to feed the catfish.

Mav was wrong. Both Lyla and Case were taking a nap and Macy, hearing Mav enter, came into the room. For a moment, Macy said nothing, as she stared at Mav who was standing in the middle of the room in torn boots and underwear, bruised and scratched as if he had wrestled a catamount.

"Mav, you never said what you were hunting on your trip. What were you hunting?" asked Macy, without mentioning his state of dress. "Is there any game I need to cook for tonight?"

"Uh…Macy, I brung no game back. Would you like to know about th' trip?"

"Oh, well, it couldn't have been too eventful, since you didn't bring back any game. But you can tell me about it after you give me your Levis, which I assume need washing."

"Uh, Macy? 'bout them Levis…" He didn't get to finish as Lyla awoke with a yell and Macy left the room to get her.

Life progressed, the farm expanded and became more productive under the growing skills of Mav and Macy. Case and Lyla, ages 4 and 3, were becoming great help around the farm, if you give them a little latitude in the nature of their help, but their primary mission will be to grow into responsible people and become more educated than their parents. The world is changing, and people just need to know more than before. But there remained the unresolved issue of the stones. The stones that played a role in the deaths of Mav's family in Bandera and saved the farm in Beaton - rocks that have value in manufacturing and in personal adornment, —still unclaimed, unutilized.

Chapter 23

Windwalker / Keeper of Tears

Much has been written about the gold rush on the west coast that transformed the Pacific-washed territory wrested from Mexican control that became the state of California, and Mav is not unaware of that history because, over the years, he has become a reader of books and, of course, the cyclopedia. But it was a magazine that interested him in the Winchester when he read about Buffalo Bill's Wild West show with his astounding marksmanship with the rifle. Also, there was Annie Oakley, who was known to prefer the Winchester. And everyone has learned that American Colonel George Armstrong Custer and his two-hundred and sixty-seven soldiers and scouts of the 7th Cavalry Regiment were simply out-gunned and out-manned by a confederation of tribes near the Little Big Horn River. While Custer's soldiers carried single-shot carbines into the battle, warriors of the combined Lakota, Northern Ogallala and Arapaho nations under Crazy Horse, Chief Gall, and Sitting Bull had the more lethal Winchester repeating rifles, thanks in part to the industry of the Comancheros and other traders who sold guns and liquor to the natives.

Magazines circulating across the nation tell of William H. Bonney, the teenage bandit from Texas called Billy the Kid, who pursued his violent exploits armed with a Winchester until he met Sheriff Pat Garrett in 1881 and paid with his life for his misdeeds in the dust of New Mexico territory.

It is with his Winchester that Maverick Caiden set out just after the crops were in in the year 1896 to secure his claim to the riches at 34 degrees north latitude and 94 degrees west longitude, or thereabouts. Biscuit, Mav's trusted friend, consultant, and confessor had retired from service two years ago, and his primary duties are testing the quality of the grass in the pasture. Mav is now aback Hardtack, a black gelding with three white stockings and a star on the nose. Trailing behind is a packhorse with the necessities for a trip to the place of discovery some unmeasured miles away. Weeks before leaving, Mav had consulted the official in charge of registering land and mineral claims and is carrying the necessary papers to record specific information needed to register it. For many years, since the passage of the Homestead Acts, people have been settling government owned, vacant land and receiving title to it after a while and the making of qualified improvements. It is with this intention that Mav turns his attention.

"Hardtack," Mav begins, "do you see thet gap between them ridges up ahead? Well, thet's whar we're a-headin'. We should git through them 'fore nightfall, an' we ken camp on th' other side. Thet ok with you?" Once a person begins talking to a horse, it is hard to stop, even though their answers are hard to fathom. Hardtack is not as perceptive as Biscuit was, but he's still young, and Mav and he haven't known each other as long.

Mav Caid — The Complete Story

By mid-afternoon and the gap threaded, Mav made camp about two miles into the little valley on the river with two forks, one of the landmarks Mav had drawn on his map when he came looking for the find back in 1892. Both forks were visible from the gap, which rose several hundred feet above the valley floor. His destination lay on the other side of the river above the farther fork. In the thoughts of Mav who stood overlooking its expanse, the valley had the feel of the idyllic land to raise cattle or crops or both as it had level grass-clad ground, not overly forested, and an abundance of water, plus some shelter from weather extremes. It seemed pristine, a place for the Maverick of yesterday. 'But today,' thought Mav, 'today it must be about Lyla, Case, and Macy. This marvelous place just might be too isolated for them.' Tomorrow he and Hardtack would break camp and ford the river at whatever place they find to be the most natural place to cross. As the sun pinked the wispy clouds hanging low over the hills through which they came, Mav rolled up his bedroll and prepared to travel on toward his destination. Hardtack pawed the ground in anticipation of getting underway, and the packhorse complained about the burden that Mav was loading upon his back.

"Stop complainin'," said Mav to his pack horse, "it ain't thet heavy. 'sides all thet, you hav' paddin' good as a Navajo blanket to pad yor boney spine."

Riding further down into the valley, Mav began to sense an unease as if something he had consumed was not agreeing with his stomach. "Just a touch o' bilious belly," he said to himself, "it'll pass soon." But it didn't.

After fording the river, Mav began to look for an appropriate campsite. His stomach continued to cramp and churn. His head ached as if a falling tree branch had fallen on it. A weakness enveloped him so completely that he knew he could travel no further. 'If I only had brought some of Edna's concoctions,' he thought, as blackness enveloped his mind.

Eugene Stonefield

✳✳✳

As Mav approached his destination, he saw the form of an unexpected native sitting cross-legged on the ground next to the stream, engaging in a slow side to side rocking motion as he sang a song. In his hand, he held a wooden flute which he brought to his lips and began to blow gently into the breath hole as his fingers spread down the extent of the wooden tube. Mav stopped as the plaintive sound of the flute seemed to fill the small valley. He knelt upon the grassy hillock overlooking the scene and listened as the soft notes flowed effortlessly from the flute. He imagined he could hear the voice of the whip-poor-will, the sound of a gentle wind through the trees, the noise of quail scattering from disturbance, water birds in flight, and finally, he sensed the fluttering passing of something significant but unseen. Presently, the strange flutist put his instrument aside but remained sitting beside the running water. Then with a calling motion, said with clarity, while not looking at Mav, "White man! Come in!"

A completely startled Mav did not hesitate, but rose from his kneeling position and followed the command of the grizzled man sitting next to the stream.

"You have returned for the stones, have you not, white man?" came the next question from this strange and unexpected man.

"How could you reckon thet?" asked Mav of the strange being.

"Because it is told to me by the wind. Come sit with me," said the man.

"I am called Windwalker by my people. I walk with *ni´l chi*,[4,5] called wind, in the tongue of the white man, and *ni´l chi* talks to me. I answer by my song. My song is almost at an end. I know why you have come. You were here before, a few winters ago. And a man of your tribe was here before you. Many winters before that. I have

192

waited. Since Wounded Knee, I have waited. And now Windwalker shall wait no longer."

Trying hard to comprehend the words of this intriguing man, Mav sat down facing the man whose eyes displayed the white opaqueness of complete blindness. He was an aged native with deep creases in the parchment skin and hands with ropy veins prominently displayed. His back seemed permanently bowed from the burden of years. He sat cross-legged, shirtless in fringed deerskin leggings, banded at the knee, and loins covered by a breechclout of dyed deerskin. In his hair were feathers of the eagle, held by a twisted yucca leaf band tied around his head of shaggy white shoulder-length hair. On his feet, he wore deerskin moccasins. Oddly, the soles of his moccasins, visible from his cross-legged position, showed no wear. Suspended around his neck was a small deer skin pouch. His flute lay in his lap.

"Where's yor hoss?" began Mav, not sure how to engage.

"Windwalker does not have a pony. Windwalker walks with the wind."

'What strangeness was the answer of the ancient man,' thought Mav.

"What's th' name o' yor tribe?" Mav asked, feeling that this was a more reasonable question.

"Windwalker is of the Apache. Windwalker is of the Quapaw, the Cherokee, and the Sioux. Windwalker is of the Navaho and the Hopi," he expressed softly. "Many say, Windwalker is of the nation of Everyman and speaks all tongues. My totem is the animal that the Apache call *ndú-chú*, the Navajo call *nash-tu-í-tso*, but white men call catamount."

"How old…How many winters hav' you seen, Windwalker," asked Mav.

"Many," said Windwalker, "as many as the stars in *I-kú˙tl bâ-há*, the Milky-way, in white man talk. Windwalker had hunted *bĭ-shĭsh-jik*, the great buffalo, on the great grasslands before the white man came.

Windwalker has flown with *tsá-cho*, the eagle, from all the mountains that hold up the sky, and Windwalker has gathered tears of the Sun from the time the Sun cried. This was many winters ago. Windwalker knows the sorrows of everyman," returned Windwalker.

"What are th' tears o' th' Sun?" Mav asked.

Slowly a boney hand reached into the pellucid water of the fast-running stream and withdrew several crystal pebbles and handed them to Mav. "They are what you have come for, the tears of *Chu-ga-ni-aí,* he who you call Sun," he answered. "It was revealed to me that once, so many winters ago they cannot be counted, *Chu-ga-ni-aí* had many children. And these children danced around the Sun always. 'Round and 'round they danced. Winter through summer. *Chu-ga-ni-aí* told me that there were as many children as the fingers on my hands. *Chu-ga-ni-aí* and his children were happy and did not cry for there was no reason. The children spent all their happy days dancing and singing the songs of the many tribes of the people. Then, one summer a great dark storm came, that had a great brown *sŭsh*, that which you call bear, riding on its back and the great *sŭsh* caught and took away one *châ-rá-shĕ*, one child of the Sun. *Chu-ga-ni-aí* was angry at first, but his anger went away, and sorrow for the loss of his *châ-rá-shĕ* came into his life. He was so sad he thought of making himself go away, to stop shining, but then *Chu-ga-ni-aí* thought of his other children who needed him, so he did not. But in his sorrow, *Chu-ga-ni-aí* began to cry, and tears fell from the sky like *ná-ĭl-tĭ*, like rain, into this valley that the people came to know as the Valley of Tears. For a time *ni-go-stŭˇn*, Mother Earth, took the tears into her heart and hardened them, then began giving them back. All of the people who once came to the Valley of Tears are now gone to the reservation where they have forgotten the old ways, and now only Windwalker comes."

He held up a medicine bag that hung from his thin neck, saying, "There were few medicine bags that did not hold a tear, for a tear of the Sun takes sorrow from its owner to allow happiness and joy to shine as the Sun shines. Now Windwalker is old and shall not come again. But *Chu-ga-ni-aí* told Windwalker to come one more time and welcome a good man and give him this valley and the tears of the Sun to take to his tribe of the white man that they may bring joy to others who will treasure a tear of the Sun just as my people have treasured them. Though my people and your people fight, *Chu-ga-ni-aí* says that it will not always be so and that all children are of the Sun's tribe which is called Everyman, and all need the same things. Windwalker has welcomed the dawn as many times as have fallen the needles of the *ndĭl-chi*, pine, in all the forests under the smile of *Chu-ga-ni-aí*. Now, for Windwalker, the last needle has fallen. Since Wounded Knee, the ways of my people have flown like *tlĭk*, like smoke above the teepee when the fire dies, flown like the last *rush-tá du-tli˘sh*, the bird the white man calls bluebird, before the snow falls. That bluebird shall return no more, but this way, said *Chu-ga-ni-aí*, people of your tribe, too, will know of Sun's sorrow and will learn that from sorrow can come joy. It is a lesson for the enemy as well as the friend. *Chu-ga-ni-aí* has said an enemy is only an enemy for a while and all will change when each walk in the other man's moccasins." Windwalker went silent as Mav tried to comprehend what this strange man told him.

The old native, this ancient shaman, stood and turned his sightless eyes toward Mav and said, "I see that you are a good man. Your new name shall be Keeper-of-Tears. Your totem will be the *ndú-chú*, as is mine. *Ndú-chú* will protect you. You must never again touch the catamount. You shall forever be the only man who shall enter this valley until you see a need to reveal it to another. There are directions to places everywhere, but not to this valley." Windwalker began a slow dance lifting each foot and bringing them down in a cadence flowing from his mind, then raising his flute to his lips started to play to the four cardinal directions, North, South, East, West, then to the sky above and finally, to the earth below - his ancient body bent like *Kokopelli*.

Eugene Stonefield

Taking the flute from his lips, Windwalker said: "Windwalker has talked to all directions with his flute in the language of the Navajo, to *no-ho-kos*, north; to *shŭ-tŭ-ú*, south; to *há-ĭ*, east; to *i-yŭ-úˇ*, west; to *ya-alh-ní-gĭ*, zenith; and to *a-ya-ĭ dĕs-ĕ-ĭ-gĭ*, nadir, and have told them how it must be forever. Windwalker must go now." As he said these words the wizened shaman turned and began to dance away slowly hoping right and left while playing the sacred songs of Everyman, playing and dancing toward the setting Sun, then changing, walking as an aged man walks, and as he walked the tempo of the wind increased, and the sound of wind elevated in tone, and as they grew in magnitude the ancient form of Windwalker diminished into the distance until Windwalker faded from sight and all that remained in the deepening purple shadows of the coming night was the warble of a flute singing the song of the wind as it blew through the reeds growing near the stream flowing through this unusual valley.

✳✳✳

Mav woke to the sound of water rushing down the stream. His clothes, wet from night sweat that must have accompanied his strange dream. He thought about the strange dream that had come to him as he slept. It was one of those vivid dreams that had a feeling of truth. For the next hour, Mav gathered many rough diamonds and put them in a leather pouch with drawstrings. As he started to place the bag in his saddlebag he hesitated, then, taking a thin strip of whang leather from his saddlebag, Mav thread it through the drawstrings of his bag of diamonds and tied it around his neck. "Hardtack," he said softly to his horse, "it is time for Keeper-of-Tears, to go home." As they passed between the two towers through which they had come into the valley, Mav looked back to find that he could no longer perceive the path between the two pillars and only one large pillar stood, solitarily, where two stood before, above a valley that was there or was not.

"Hardtack," said Mav, "I don't reckon we orta dwell too much on whut we seen today. I think th' meanin' may not live in th' mind, but in th' heart."

Chapter 24

Return of a Catamount

Riding home on Hardtack reminded Mav of the ride home from the first trip to the valley except that he knew that its character had changed. The first homecoming was accompanied by the uncertainty in the value of the stones and if they had any at all. Strange rocks. That was all he knew at the time. The feeling of satisfaction was not in bringing back some rocks of unknown character but in the finding the place described in the diary and associated map. But today, the value of the stones, now known to be diamonds, —the baubles of royalty and the vain, —is known. Now, it is their character that has changed. No longer can he think of them as beautiful adornments, but as collectors of sorrow from the despairing hearts of people of the tribes of Everyman. For the people of Windwalker, they were never about ornamentation. They were about healing. About protection from the ravages of sorrow and toward the encouragement of a heart's joy. They needed no cutting nor polishing, nor mounting, only the abiding belief that these tears of the Sun bring healing from the sorrows of life. If a person has a strong enough belief that the future will bring surcease to present sorrow he can endure. Hope is the aegis protecting heart and mind, the bulwark against despair.

Mav ponders: 'Was this belief in the power of the tears of the Sun all that the natives had to lessen the sorrow of being conquered and losing all? Does that power still exist or has it failed them? Did they see their sorrow as something of their own making, such as the white man views sin? Does this belief in the power of a collector of sorrow equate to the faith in the power of the Nazarene to lift the burden of sin from those who will believe in him? Is the willingness to believe in any power, —real or conceived of mind, —that claims to cure the ills of body, mind, and soul, all that anyone has to bring comfort from their sorrow?'

$$***$$

Nearing his, now six-room home outside of the thriving town of Beaton Mav observes a cow on the trail, bawling is if she were looking for her calf. 'She belongs to someone in the area, could even be my own,' Mav thinks, as he rides nearer to determine if she has a brand and to which farmer or rancher in the region, he should return it. The brand showed the cow belonged to a neighbor. Mav took his lariat and tossed the loop over the head of the bawling bovine. He hoped she would follow without complaining, for he neither saw nor heard evidence of a lost calf and felt she was bawling because she didn't know where the herd was to which she belonged. Isolation is a lonely domain for man or beast. Each needs his like. Mav set Hardtack and his pack horse at a walk and tugged the rope. The cow followed easily.

Suddenly, Hardtack snorted loudly and slowed down as if he was thinking of veering in another direction. Mav noticed the pack animal showed similar inclination and the cow became nervous. 'What now?' thought Mav as he pulled back on the reins.

His 'what now' was answered instantly as a man on a chestnut-colored horse moved onto the trail in front of Mav blocking his path. On either side of the trail was an outcropping of rock that stood ten feet above the base. The narrowness of the opening between these pillars made possible the blocking of his passage easy. Mav started to reach for his Winchester, but the leveling of the man's rifle directly at Mav discouraged completion.

"You jes' don't know how long I've been waitin' fo' you, Mr. Caid. Good people hav' tol' me you wuz ta come back at th' end o' th' month, an' here you are. I am for-tune-ate." The voice was familiar to Mav, but he could not immediately place it, and the low hanging branches obscured his face. "If you would be so kind as ta dismount thet cayuse o' yorn," stated the voice.

"You got no call to insult Hardtack, mister. Whut do you want?" asked Mav, fully expecting that the man intends to rob him. "I have little to offer an' you hav' little to gain by robbin' me."

"You don't recognize me, do you, Mr. Caid?" The voice took on a harsher tone as the man moved from behind the branch. "And how is yor lovely wife, Mr. Caid? I have so missed seeing her. Ah, but tomorrow, perhaps, me an' her shall git reacquainted."

"Fenner!" Mav now recognized the voice and the man.

"Ah, Mr. Fenner, please," returned the highwayman.

"Fenner, ere you so destitute thet you've sunk to robbin' folks o' their bedroll?" Mav sought to return a sarcastic reply." Mayhap you want th' cow to boot? Or, have you not yet stooped to rustlin'?"

"Amusing, Mr. Caid. I thought saltin' th' trail with thet cow was a nice touch. Does it not worry you thet I want none o' them things? Thet th' objective o' this little visit may be dif'runt?" Fenner said as he motioned with his rifle. "Stand o'er there," he said, pointing toward a tree. "And, Mr. Caid, please pick up th' rope I'll toss you." Fenner tossed the end of his rope to Mav, saying: "An' this here is gen-u-wine manila rope, an' bran' new ta boot. Bought yestiddy in Beaton. I even tied a fine noose in it fo' th' occasion."

Mav sensed that all the animals were acting more nervous, even the horse Fenner was riding that had commenced dancing. For the moment he will comply but he will have to do something to spook the animals into chaos to distract Fenner, or his life will end at the end of a rope or by Fenner's rifle. Mav keeps his eyes on Fenner as he reaches for the rope lying at his feet. Mav knows that there is an advantage accruing to him from the fact that Fenner prefers to hang him rather than shoot him, otherwise he would already be dead.

"Now, Mr. Caid. Be so kind as ta toss thet rope over thet thar branch above you. Oh, an' then, pull thet rope down an' place thet fine noose around yor neck, if you please. Oh, an' Mr. Caid, be gentle. Don't want you to hurt yorsel' none." Fenner shows pleasure in his minute description of what he wants Mav to do. "Oh, ho! What's thet bag hangin' 'round yor neck? You become an Injun or somethin'? Ere you a shaman? Does thet thar bag have big medicine? Is yor salvation in thet bag? Heh! Heh! Jes' do whut I said, Mr. Caid. Do it now."

"Yeah, somethin' like thet," returned Mav as he bent to pick up the end of the rope and recalled that Fenner had lifted his rifle momentarily as he tossed the rope underneath his rifle to Mav before lowering the barrel again.

'This could be what I need,' thought Mav, as he threw the looped end of the rope over the tree limb standing out about five feet above him. Mav hesitated before placing the rope over his head and watched Fenner struggling to calm his horse that was becoming more agitated.

"Please, Mr. Caid," said Fenner, "do me th' favor I have axed o' you. The rope..."

His command fell incomplete, as Mav suddenly pulled hard upon the rope, immediately increasing tension upon the rope thrown across the tree branch and still tied fast to Fenner's saddle horn. The slackened rope was beneath the rifle, and as it straightened between the overarching tree branch and the saddle horn, it suddenly lifted the rifle which discharged, shooting nothing but a few leaves above Mav's head.

The sound of the rifle's discharge, combined with the nervousness of the animal, caused Fenner's horse to pitch and rotate making Fenner pull back on the reins to regain control. Ten feet away, Hardtack was troubled and was backing away as was the pack horse. The cow began again to bawl loudly and pull against the rope tied to the saddle horn on Hardtack. Mav quickly took advantage of the chaotic scene to run to Hardtack and retrieve his Winchester. Pulling the rifle from its scabbard, Mav levered a bullet in the chamber and drew the rifle to his shoulder to aim at the still struggling Fenner. The urge was to fire and end the drama between Fenner and Mav, a drama that Mav thought had ended in Villon. Fenner realized that Mav had gained an advantage, as Mav had shouldered his rifle and had taken aim at Fenner while he was struggling with his horse. The struggle impeded Fenner from levering another bullet into his rifle's chamber. Dropping his rifle, he immediately reached for his handgun. Mav, though, did not pull the trigger. Nor did Fenner draw.

Neither men recognized that the choice of whether either man lived or died was not in either's hands but rather in the sharp claws and the fierce fangs of an observing catamount. Neither man had seen the catamount that had watched this drama play out on the narrow trail between the two standing rocks. To the contrary, their attention focused solely upon what one man intended to do to another, human reasons the catamount could never fathom. The catamount's focus had been on the horses and on the cow that dutifully followed the pack animal. But from somewhere deep within the catamount's brain, was the memory of a man and the scent of a man who once stopped to aid his natural enemy. Forgotten was the cow. Forgotten were the horses. Remembered was the man, remembered was the scent. Of the two men there, who could reach out and touch the catamount with a fatal bullet, only one did not have the scent. With a sound that only an attacking catamount can utter, the large cat leaped from the rock to the man without the scent, and both tumbled to the hard ground in a jumble of legs, arms, claws, and powerful jaws that can crush a horse's skull.

Fenner Korn uttered a loud scream as he tumbled, involuntarily, from his horse entwined with a full-grown catamount offering no quarters. The tawny cat was some thirty inches at the shoulder, seven to eight-foot long nose to tail, and possibly weighed one-hundred-forty pounds of muscle, sinew, and teeth. Sharp claws and strong muscles assured the big cat a mortal grasp. The catamount's long canine and incisor teeth searched for the soft throat of the fallen man who vainly pounded the sides of the cat with empty hands. His second scream checked, the beating hands stilled, and silence of finality of death soon prevailed as the big cat's farewell to the fight was a lifting of the torso by the throat and vigorously shaking.

For a moment, Mav lowered his rifle in shock at the scene unfolding before him. The animals were in a state of full panic and were breaking away from the trail to dive into the brush, seeking safety. Presently, there was only Fenner, Mav, and the catamount on the trail that had suddenly become somber.

There was no screaming anymore. There was no whinnying of the horses or bawling of the cow. There was only the sound of wind in the trees. The catamount moved off the still form of Fenner whose throat bore the tearing marks of the cat's canines that now bore the crimson stain of blood as she stood on the trail facing Mav, fifteen feet away. The last sound that came from the mutilated throat of Fenner Korn was the rattle of blood-laden air escaping deflating lungs bubbling crimson into the silence.

To the people of the farm and the ranch, a catamount that takes the animals that represent their livelihood, is an enemy to destroy. This goes doubly so for those that are guilty of taking the life of a man. Once they get the taste of human blood, so it goes, killing the cat is the only sensible thing to do. The hunter becomes the hunted until the deed is done. That is the rule. Several times on the trail Mav has gone after a cat or a wolf that had harassed the herd into a stampede, but never had he tracked one that had killed a man. This catamount is different. His attack was not a planned attack upon a beast of prey, but in some measure, an attack to preserve.

For some minutes, man and beast eyed each other. Mav, uncertain at first of the continuing danger from the cat, became concerned about Hardtack, and with unwise distraction, glanced around the trail to discern where Hardtack may have gone. When Mav looked back, the catamount was gone. At once, his mind recalled the words of an ancient shaman saying to him: "*Ndú-chú* will protect you. You must never again touch the catamount." The shock of the sudden event now lessened, Mav wondered, as he had when Windwalker issued his prohibition, —how did he know? Presently, as his eyes scanned the brush to find where the catamount had gone, they fell upon a rotting log lying on the ground with a rotting rope encircling its girth.

Chapter 25

Home Again

"I'm glad you're back, Mav," a welcoming Macy said to her returning husband. "Was your trip successful? Did you find the place again so you can register your claim?"

"I did find it," returned Mav. "As to th' claim registration, I don't reckon it will be needed."

"I guess I don't understand. I thought that was the main purpose you went, to gather the information necessary to complete the claim registration." Macy registered perplexity in her look.

"It's a complicated story, Macy. I'll tell you sometime, once I fully understand it mysel'." Mav looked at Macy and winked.

Mav picked up the latest Gazette, the section on missions to the reservations reading: Missionary Isabel Crawford of the Saddle Mountain Mission reported on a speech by Domot of the Kiowa, who spoke of the life of the Kiowa before the white man came. "…it was a time the buffalo provided food, clothing, housing, and medicine to the Kiowa. Then everything changed, when thirty years ago, the soldiers came and began the indiscriminate slaughter of the buffalo. They killed the buffalo within seven years, and now the people of the plains starve. White men, he concluded are kill-crazy: "The buffalo, they kill, kill, kill. Indians, they kill, kill, kill. Jesus, they killed. What is the matter? Why? Why? Why?" [6]

"Macy, I hav' 'cluded thet thar's a lot about th' Indians thet we might orta listen to, 'specially things like conservin' resources. Some things, wunst gone, are gone forever. What ifn some common thing, like water, thet ifn it wuz all gone, life jes' wouldn't be possible. An' what ifn land itself would not grow crops 'cause somethin' in th' dirt wuz all used up. I reckon we all would be ina fix!"

"Amen, to that!" replied Macy.

Thus, ends the story of the early life of farmer Maverick Caiden who became the Keeper-of-Tears for all tribes in the Nation of Everyman. Tomorrow begins the story of the man in his middle years.

Chapter 26

Looking Back

Years from youth mark today's reality for Mav Caid and as he rides along the trail from the unique valley to which he has traveled so many times to gather the findings known as the Tears of the Sun. Owing to familiarity of the trail, contemplation of sights and vistas fade into the background, replaced by random thoughts on events and times far away.

Mav reflects upon his beginning as a boy in Bandera, whose wanderlust propels him from boyhood to adulthood. Farming alone defined the character of his family, and by extension, the character of Maverick Caiden. He was then, a roughly educated boy, a farmer to be, one who knew the principles of farming, but harkened to the siren call of the trail. His entry into the cattle industry was late in the history of the movement of cattle from Texas to northern markets in Dodge City, Ogallala, and others, but it enhanced the character of the boy from Bandera as it was honing his born nature. He thinks of his work with Captain Lytle as a wrangler, then trusted drover urging cattle to leave their comfortable grazing and carry on to market where death awaits. He thinks about the tragic murder of his family in Bandera, perpetrated by Chico, seeking wealth of unknown character, its location only a coded diary entry could reveal. He thinks about his uncle Wendell, creator of the diary and discoverer of the unusual crystalline stones in the strange valley. Presently, he thinks of his wife, Macy, and the wedding and the threatening honeymoon encounter with Fenner Korn and Henry Slade and the heroic sacrifice of Macy who endured deeply personal self-abasement to provide a distraction that allowed Mav to secure a crucial victory over the evil plan of the two vengeful outlaws. He thinks of his children and the realization that before, Macy and Case and Lyla, he was not living with any true purpose, that he existed only as a wandering entity with a future that would not survive his own life, a recognition that through children and following progeny, something of himself becomes immortal. Finally, he thinks of Windwalker, that strange ancient shaman, whom he met in the valley in a most phantasmagoric manner, and who remains an enigma. What of the encounter with this man? Was it real or imaginary? Was Mav hallucinating because of his untimely illness in the Valley of Tears? Was his illness just physical, or should he worry about being among the insane of this world? He is conflicted in these thoughts. Who can he trust to tell about it? What would they say about the catamount? Would it damage his close relationship with his family if he shared these experiences? Indeed, would one define these strange events with Windwalker and the catamount as knowledge or hallucination? Would Macy accept the report as true, or would she withdraw and worry about him, possibly begin to think of him as a madman? People often withdraw from those who reveal experiences that evoke thoughts of the supernatural. Miracles and unexplainable phenomena such as resurrections and burning bushes on the mountain are things of the ancient past. Do they exist or are they elements of a troubled mind?

Joys and uncertainties fill the mind of Mav Caid on this day in the year 1900. Mav Caid will turn thirty-three this year, a year of changes.

As Mav approaches Beaton his reflections are refocused on a disturbing sight ahead. A fistfight is in progress between two men, one of whom is known to Mav as one who is often present when folks in Beaton witness such scenes. Mitchell Ormsby is unquestionably a rowdy rascal. Recent past contains instances of Mitchell Ormsby's humanity, or, more properly, lack of humanity toward others who he has taken a dislike to. Whatever the issue, Mitchell will be on the most unreasonable side, and will cede nothing, even in the face of overwhelming evidence that his adversary is right. With Mitchell, might makes right. Mitchell lives to fight and often seeks opportunity to start one. Physically, Mitchell is large, weighing about two-hundred sixty pounds. He is a strong man, capable of doing great harm to someone of lesser bulk and stature. His fists are hard and some say his fascination with causing harm to others is the product of his upbringing in a family whose head, his father, focused the same anger on Mitchell and others in the family. No one knows for certain. His usual target is one Mitchell believes he can beat and torment without chancing harm to himself. Today, his fight is with a young Indian who has come to Beaton for reasons unknown to Mav. How he came to be in a fight with Mitchell also is unknown.

"Hey! Fellas. What's this here fight about?" Mav reins in Hardtack fifteen feet away from the conflict.

"None or your damned business!" returns Mitchell as his left fist smashes into the young Indian's jaw who falls to the ground and lays motionless.

"He's on the ground, Mitchell. You've won. Step back." Mav tells Mitchell.

"Like hell, I'm just beginning. Get out of here, Mav Caid. It's not your business what I do with this Injun." Mitchell straddles the vanquished man and begins to punch him in the face. Punch after punch landing hard upon the face of an unconscious man.

From somewhere, right, or wrong, Mav gets the sense that the fact of the young man being Indian is the reason for the fight. Mav's sense of humanity could not let the beating continue. He untied his lariat and enlarged the loop. Two swirls of the lariat above his head and the loop arches through the air on its way.

"Dammit!" shouted Mitchell as the loop tightened around him, pinning his arms to his sides. Just as quickly, Mav loops his lariat around the saddle horn and signals for Hardtack to turn and trot forward, pulling Mitchell backward off the victim of his beating and dragging him thirty feet across the rocky ground.

Reining Hardtack in, Mav shouts: "Mitchell, I reckon you orta remove th' loop o' my lariat from whut might be yor shredded carcass ifn you don't."

"Damned you! You will regret your interference, Mav Caid!" shouted Mitchell Ormsby, while removing the loop and tossing it to the ground. "I will see you later!" continued Mitchell, over his shoulder as he walked away toward a horse grazing near the road.

Mav retrieved the lariat and tied it back to the saddle. Dismounting, Mav walked to the prostrate Indian who is returning to consciousness.

"Can you stand up?" Mav asks, as the young man wipes blood from his eyes flowing from a cut above the brow. "I'm Mav Caid. Whut's yor name an' tribe?"

Rising shakily from the ground, the young Indian stood erect and looked critically at Mav.

Mav Caid — The Complete Story

"Mav Caid. You are Keeper of Tears, is that so?" The young Indian looked steadily at Mav.

"I am called thet, yes. Folks around here call me Mav Caid," replied the startled Mav, still waiting for an answer to his question.

"My name is *Tohnemah* . I am Kiowa. I am from the Buffalo Mountain Mission on the Kiowa-Apache reservation in Oklahoma territory. I come to speak of the work we do for Jesus." *Tohnemah* walked back to retrieve a bundle of belongings that he had dropped on the ground when Mitchell Ormsby began an assault, then returned.

"What wuz th' fight about?" asked Mav.

"*Tohnemah* does not know. *Tohnemah* has learned to turn the other cheek. It is written so in the Jesus book. *Tohnemah* follows Jesus' word. *Tohnemah* is ready to go now."

Looking around Mav asked: "Where is yor horse?"

"*Tohnemah* pony ran away two days ago. Now, *Tohnemah* walks."

Remembering a similar statement by Windwalker, Mav waits for a moment to see if *Tohnemah* says anything more, which he does not, prompting Mav to interject: "*Tohnemah*, I will take you where you want to go." Mav remounted Hardtack and extended a hand to help *Tohnemah* to mount Hardtack behind him.

"*Tohnemah* must go to the camp of Keeper of Tears."

Mav turns Hardtack toward the home place, thinking: 'Well, at least Macy will know that I don't just bring diamonds home when I return from a trip.'

✳✳✳

Mav, with *Tohnemah* riding double rode up to the house and both riders dismounted. Macy heard the two men talking and came from the house with a questioning look.

"Mav?" Macy began her query, "it seems that you have brought a visitor with you."

213

Eugene Stonefield

"This is *Tohnemah* of the Kiowa nation in Oklahoma. *Tohnemah* is with th' Buffalo Mountain Mission an' is one of th' deacons in th' Mission Church. His congregation is plannin' to build a church house near th' reservation."

Turning to *Tohnemah,* Mav said: "*Tohnemah,* meet my wife…uh, *squaw,* Macy." Macy lifted an eyebrow and looked at Mav.

"*Tohnemah* is happy to meet you, Ma-Ce," he replied through split and swollen lips. Owing to the beating by Mitchell Ormsby, the right eye of *Tohnemah* was swollen shut, though he showed no concern.

"Let's see what we can do with your injuries," returned Macy, leading the two men into the house. Ten minutes later Macy washed and medicated the cut above *Tohnemah's* eye and began preparing something for the two to eat. Although curiosity was surging, Macy resisted asking about the reason for his injuries.

The conversation during their meal reveals that *Tohnemah* has come with an appeal to the congregation of the Beaton Methodist Church to assist with the building fund for the church on reservation land in Oklahoma. The missionaries told him that he would find help from Keeper-of-Tears, a name that was not explained to Macy, and one that Mav has still not come to grips with. Hearing the name from the lips of this unexpected visitor, however, provides a surety to Mav that his experiences in the Valley of Tears was something beyond some phantasmagoric event brought on by illness. By what pathway that name spoken first by Windwalker was conveyed and is now voiced by another is unknown. If others know of, and believe in Keeper-of-Tears, then what must that say of Windwalker?

The next day, Mav, Macy and *Tohnemah* made the short trip to Beaton where Mav introduced *Tohnemah* to Pastor Briggs at the Methodist church and set the schedule for his address to the congregation the next Sunday when he would speak of the work of the missionaries to the Apache and Kiowa on the reservation and on their effort to build a 'Jesus House' for the converts from the 'old road' to the 'Jesus Road'. He would stay for a week, the guest of Mav and Macy before leaving for his long trek back to Oklahoma. Mav and Macy attended *Tohnemah's* address to the congregation:

"*Tohnemah* brings thanks from the people of the Buffalo Mountain Mission to the people of Beaton's Jesus community in welcoming me as I speak for my people. The Kiowa and the Apache of the reservation are a poor people who have not yet ceased longing for the old road to walk the Jesus Road. Our lands are unproductive and the buffalo are gone, so we must depend upon the help of others. Our government agent sends us cattle, but it is never enough. Many of our people now starve, when they did not starve when buffalo filled the plains. My people are weak and have not turned away from fire-water and gambling that takes many brothers off the Jesus Road. We believe that, if we had a Jesus house, more brothers would come to Jesus and walk the Jesus Road with those of us who walk it now. We have saved three-hundred and thirty-seven dollars to build a Jesus house. Those who know about building tell us that we must have nine-hundred dollars or more to buy lumber and iron nails and send them to us.

My mission to you is to ask that those of the white community, our brothers in Jesus, help us to build our Jesus house that your brothers in the Kiowa and Apache community may hear the words of Jesus out of the rain and cold. My brothers, I ask that you think of your gift, not as money, but as like the fishes and bread given by Jesus to the hungry followers when he spoke to them on the shore of Galilee, the small offerings that grew to fulfill the need of the many who came to hear the words of Jesus. *Tohnemah* brings thirty-seven cents to show good faith by being the first to give to the Buffalo Mountain Mission from the house of Jesus in the town of Beaton and ask my brothers here today to offer what you can to make Jesus happy and help your brothers on the reservation hear the words of Jesus." *Tohnemah* held up his hand with the money, then sat down to give Pastor Briggs the floor. The appeal spurred congregants of the church to offer gifts of money and pledges to help their brothers in the Buffalo Mountain Mission, of which they had never heard about before this day.

Three more days passed and *Tohnemah* is preparing to return to the mission and to his tribe in Oklahoma. Macy has prepared food and water for him to sustain him on his trip, and Mav has selected a spare horse which is to replace *Tohnemah's* lost horse.

"*Tohnemah*," Mav said, "I reckon th' horse thet ran away wuz a better horse than this one, but she will git you back to th' mission. We are happy thet you come, *Tohnemah*. Be well on yor trip."

"Keeper of Tears, I am glad I came. Your people have been generous to our mission. I go now." *Tohnemah*, jumped onto the horse and rode westward.

"Well, Macy, I don't know what to say. He come a long way fo' whut little he received fo' his Jesus house. I reckon though, thet two-hundred will hep some." Mav became thoughtful.

Macy nodded her head in agreement, saying: "I just worry that something will happen to him on his trip back. Carrying all that money, and him alone. Anything could happen."

"I reckon I want to believe thet God protects his own," said Mav, wondering how he could believe that when he thinks of his family in Bandera, who were good people, too.

Chapter 27

The Evangelist

As the first stones are being laid for the new capitol building for Arkansas in the year 1900, citizens of the world are experiencing crucial events, especially in Europe where the changing expectations of its citizens and established ethical and moralistic norms are in flux. The atmosphere was like the held breath of a circus audience raptly attending with dread anticipation the fate of the sequined beauty on the wire. Victorian certainties were wearing thin, a plethora of possibilities danced upon the horizon as modernism edged out behaviors of the older generation. The world was opening up. The citizen reaction to the fluctuating events was given a French name to identify a movement.

Fin de siècle, the French term for the end of century, specifically, a change from the nineteenth to the twentieth, —a name wrung from the French art scene of the ninth decade of the last century to describe a movement embracing symbolism and modernism in French art and subsequently applied internationally to the cultural and geopolitics of European countries. The movement, was principally a revolt against norms of the day and carried the desire for change. The period was one that encompassed a feeling of despondency, feelings that human decadence was unchained. Feelings that could only be assuaged by a change in humanity itself. Interpretation of that desire by many was that, only a comprehensive change would reverse the course of the decadence of the 1880s and 1890s.

Expression of the movement took on geographic character in some countries. In overpopulated Germany, the concept of *Lebensraum*, 'living space', and subsequent aggressive actions taken by the Imperial German government to provide that space for the German citizens through territorial expansion, would be devastating within a few years in Europe. Countries of Europe sat upon a powder keg awaiting the igniting spark. That spark will come in Sarajevo, on June 28, 1914 with the assassination of Archduke Franz Ferdinand, presumptive heir to the Austro-Hungarian throne, and his wife Sophia, Duchess of Hohenberg by nineteen-year-old Gavrilo Princip under the influence of the Black Hand. The Black Hand was a secret society founded by Serbian military officers seeking to unify countries with majority South-Serbian populaces that were not already under Serbia or Montenegro rule. The chain of events sparked by the assassination would ultimately touch people of America as American soldiers join the embattled soldiers in Europe in the 'war to end all wars', a.k.a., WWI.

But, knowledge of or effects from those political and cultural implications of the changes occurring so far away was not on the minds of citizens of Beaton, Arkansas and the countryside surrounding on this bright day. Today was the newest religious revival offering to the folks of Beaton. Spiritual revivalism, had been a staple of Methodism and Presbyterianism for almost a century, its beginning generally ascribed to a Calvinistic Presbyterian, Charles Grandison Finney, who was a major leader in the Second Great Awakening of the protestant world. His influence upon the folks of Rochester, New York was profound, leading to the closing of businesses thought not in line with Christian mores, —those fundamental values of the citizenry, —and stimulating the engagement of citizens in the pursuit of moral living. For the first time, women were empowered to speak out and pray publicly in contradiction to the familiar command of 1 Corinthian 14:34 that "…women must be silent in church." As the text goes: "They are not permitted to speak, but must be in submission, as the law says."

Finney began addressing attendees at his tent sermons, abrogating the norm, and challenging those who would come to his tent meetings to commit to Jesus openly and publicly, perhaps a reprise of the challenge of Paul to the 'luke-warm' Laodicean church of old as written in Revelation. "Rise up! Get off the fence!" Finney would challenge, and those who sat silently he would accuse, even by name, of "having rejected Jesus Christ and his gospels." Finney's confrontational behavior from the pulpit drew profound criticism from others, but none could deny his influence on evangelistic fervor from that point onward. Men of the same theological cut, like Holiness Movement's Dwight L. Moody, and Presbyterian Evangelist William Ashley 'Billy' Sunday, helped to drive the evangelical movement to new heights. Sunday, whose intensely energetic and physical sermons either appalled or thrilled attendees of his faith-inspired addresses across America.

✻✻✻

Today, in the spring of the century's change to the year 1900, when a sense of change hangs in the air as petrichor from a saving rain, the young family of Mav, Macy, Case and Lyla Caid are riding behind Clarisse and Francine, two gray mules pulling the wagon in which nine-year old Case and eight-year-old, towheaded Lyla are riding in its bed while from the springboard seat, their papa guides the mules and talks.

The distance between the revival outside Beaton and their farm is sixteen miles and the day is crisp but dry as the sun is rising to its zenith, skipping behind cotton clouds adrift in a cerulean expanse. Mav and Macy have attended a few tent revivals in the past, but this revival promises to be outstanding because the evangelist preacher is a star, albeit, a star of baseball. He is none other than the ex-baseball player for the Chicago White Stockings by the name of 'Billy' Sunday, previously, William Sontag, of Story County, Iowa, —a player familiar to Mav from reports published in the Beaton Gazette on the results of games played across the nation.

Baseball in the early twentieth century is a national pastime with many avid followers of the games, the results of which newspapers report, but the joy of listening to play-by-play radio broadcasting of the games will have to wait. It will be twenty years before the first commercial radio broadcast transmits from a radio station. The first will be from a station owned by the Scripps family's Detroit Daily News, in Detroit Michigan, whose radio signals first broadcast under the call sign 8 MK, and two years later under the call sign WWJ. Even then, it will be two years later, in 1924, that the Atwater-Kent battery-powered radios become available for receiving radio signals in farm communities not yet served by electrical power. Once the technology becomes available, family gathering around the radio to hear news, music, and baseball will become ubiquitous. Listening to radio broadcast of events of the day will become a sacred imperative to gather family around the radio and turn ears and minds to the broader world.

But, in this year of 1900, Billy was a star, known for stealing ninety bases in one-hundred and sixteen games. Informed people know that Billy turned down an unimaginable three-thousand five-hundred-dollar annual contract to play baseball in 1891 to work for a Christian organization named the Young Men's Christian Association or YMCA in Chicago for a paltry $89 per month. It was an astounding rebuke to the National League by the speedy outfielder, who had converted to Christianity at the Pacific Garden Mission in Chicago in 1886. But anyone who rejects wealth in favor of serving others must be a worthy person was the popular refrain. If his mission to serve was God inspired, or a personal moral imperative is unknown, what is known is that from his work with this organization, Billy Sunday helped to invigorate a movement of evangelical fervor that will sweep America and Europe in the twentieth century, —this new century. If the decade before nineteen-hundred is known for its cynicism and widespread feeling that civilization itself leads to decadence, the next three decades of the new century is known for rigorous evangelism. While there was pessimism permeating the citizenry of many nations, and a deep ennui in the last decade of the nineteenth century, there is now restlessness and desire for change. From this desire was born the era of big-tent evangelism that is blooming across the nation as people seek to regain a feeling of relevance and comfort in their belief in the benevolence of a higher power. Belief in a God of hope.

Beyond the moralistic, there were the technological and economic changes affecting the citizens of the nation. From the nineteenth century focus on individual production, the country in the twentieth century is moving into an era of consumerism, and the dynamics of everyday life is reshaping, although it is still in the era of a rural majority. Yet, this nation, with exceptions of the citizens living in the major cities, is a nation of subsistence farming, —families who grow crops for their needs and sell or trade to others whatever they may produce beyond family needs. Handcrafted manufacturing of wooden and iron products is common, —products such as guns, furniture, and plows. At this time, large scale manufacturing for the market was still in the future, and Henry Ford was still plowing a field to lay in a crop and running a sawmill on the side. His *Tin Lizzie*, the Model T automobile of his creative industry, and the assembly line manufacturing that he employed, —one that will change manufacturing forever, —is eight years away. And there is a battle for souls waging between the multiple shades of theology.

Billy Sunday's first association as an advance man for the great evangelical preacher, John Wilbur Chapman, had ended in eighteen-ninety-six, when Chapman made a temporary return to his pastorate. The *kerosene circuit*, that circuit of small towns and villages in America that still relied on kerosene lamps for illumination when electric lighting was rapidly becoming the norm in the larger towns and cities, now belonged to this audacious, talented evangelist, Billy Sunday, and other evangelist preachers of the circuit. Coming on the heels of those pioneers of religious zeal of the revivalist preachers thumping their bible and healing body and soul beneath the canvas tents erected across the American landscape, Billy Sunday, Evangelist, born of German emigrants near Ames, Iowa began to perfect the appeal of Evangelism.

Today, Billy has brought his powerful fervor to Beaton to bring the word of the Lord, Jesus Christ, to its citizens. Wagons, gigs, and buckboards from the surrounding countryside are converging on the tabernacle beside the placid lake bearing families wanting to judge, first hand, the talents of this paragon of sermonizing zeal, to hear the message of this paladin for the Lord.

"I feel the same way, Mav" replied Macy, as the iron-rimmed wheels falling into the deeply rutted road jostled the occupants and made the speaker's voice sound like a stutter. "They are workin' hard on the three Rs, —Readin', 'Ritin,' and 'Rithmetic. Schoolmaster Vale gives good reports of Case's progress. Next year, Mr. Vale is planning to teach about geography so his students will know where they are in the world. Someday, he says, he will explain about government so they will understand the whys and wherefores of the work done for citizens of Arkansas by the Governor and legislators over in Littlerock, and understand the working of the President and Congress in Washington."

"I know they're gittin' smarter," returned Mav, "Why, jus' yesterday I said to Case, —who wuz makin' a racket in th' barn, — Whut wuz you poundin' on, Case? And you want to know whut he said? He said, 'Papa, don't say: Whut <u>wuz</u> you poundin' on? Say: <u>What were</u> you pounding on?' Now that's whut…I mean, <u>what</u> he said. So, I said: Did Mr. Vale larn you that? Then he said: 'Not larn! Say <u>teach!</u>'" Mav paused for a minute, then with a chuckle, continued, "he's so smart, an' Lyla is jes' like him. I reckon I'll be gittin' a whol' lot o' correctin' from them two. From the mouths of babes, so they say. I hope I'm as good a larner as they are."

"Say <u>student</u>, not larner, Papa," came the voice of Caid who had been listening to the conversation, bringing a laugh from Mav and Macy.

These travelers spent the rest of the trip from their home to this anticipated tent revival in silent contemplation of what wonders their children may experience in life. Hearts grow big in parents who see great things happening and know that in a few years their children will participate in creating newer and greater things. Pride in children knows no boundaries. Mav and Macy Caid have big hearts and great expectations.

Arriving at the location of the revival, the family of Mav Caid dismounted from the spring seat of their well-used Weber farm wagon and entered the recently built cathedral. Since early comers get front-row seating, many early arrivals have already selected their seats. All others take their chances. As did the others, the Caid family took their seats as near the front as possible near center stage and waited for the entrance of the Reverend Mr. Billy Sunday who eschewed the large auditoriums of large cities in favor of the site-built tabernacle of his design. Beaton's tabernacle is a scaled duplicate of the first built in

Elgin, Illinois to accommodate three-thousand worshippers, and hosting the voices of a three-hundred singer chorus. Beaton, being a growing community, offers the seating for one-thousand in its freshly built tabernacle.

As the seats filled with citizens of the area, excitement grew. Eventually, preliminary addresses to the crowd of the faithful by local religious personages such as Pastor Briggs from the Methodist Church, Pastor Wall of the Baptist Church, Elder Rutherford of the Presbyterians, and other notables who banded together to bring Billy to the people of Beaton, ceded the sawdust-strewn floor and the pulpit to the impressive personage of Billy Sunday and his evangelical fire.

The power of the man filled the tabernacle with awe for some, fear for others as Billy demanded that worshippers look into their hearts and make a commitment to the Lord. His message was two-fold: renounce sin, accept Jesus as your personal Savior. Always before him was his Bible, opened to Isaiah 61:1-3, *The Spirit of the Sovereign Lord is upon me, because the Lord has anointed me to proclaim good news to the poor....'* His delivery of his powerful sermons was often harsh, as he looked out upon the saints and sinners seated before him. He was never shy of using rough-edged vernacular that engendered erubescent faces upon the worshippers, and send every parent home with a parental conundrum, —how to explain to inquisitive children what the words they heard from the mouth of Billy Sunday meant.

The era is one roiled by the works of Charles Darwin on the nature of the beginning of humans that directly challenged the Biblical account in Genesis. In response to Charles Darwin, upon the raised platform, Billy would thunder: *'I don't believe your own bastard theory of evolution, either; I believe it is pure jackass nonsense,"* and attendees would cringe and many voices would lend their amen! His abhorrence to the concept of evolution, a theme in a public argument with Dr. Washington Gladden of the First Congregational Church of Columbus, Ohio who was more open to scientific inquiry. It is an age of conflict between modernists and traditionalists, of revivalists and non-revivalists, of evangelicals and non-evangelicals.

To another statement, even the children would understand his tongue-in-cheek analogy and laugh at his pronouncement that *"Going to church doesn't make you a Christian any more than going to the garage makes you an automobile."* A mainstay of Billy's sermons was the energetic movements of a natural athlete, jumping from the stage to a chair and setting one foot on the podium while leaning out over the congregation pointing and shouting: *"Live so that when the final summons comes you will leave something more behind you than an epitaph on a tombstone or an obituary in a newspaper."* At the end of an energetic sermon, Billy would drop to a softer voice and asked the audience to accept Christ as their Savior and walk the sawdust trail to the tabernacle to make the pledge before all. *"Come to Jesus,"* he would implore, *"Come to Jesus."* He would meet and shake hands with every sinner willing to walk that sawdust trail and commit to renouncement of sin and acceptance of Jesus as their personal Savior.

The subjects of Billy Sunday were wide-ranging and challenged society to correct their errors, errors involving child labor, suffrage, alcohol, that he personified as *Mr. Booze*, as he railed against the sin of inebriation and excoriated sellers of alcohol. *"The saloon is a liar,"* he *would shout. "It promises good cheer and sends sorrow. It promises prosperity and sends adversity. It promises happiness and sends misery. It is Gods worst enemy and the Devil's best friend."* Nor was Billy ever far away from his youth as baseball metaphor laced his sermons: *"The devil says I'm out, but the Lord says I'm safe!"* For the devout or the curious, Billy Sunday would always send one home energized by the power of his words and force of his presence, or send them home troubled of mind and resolved to change. It was the practice of this indefatigable preacher of the Gospel in the profane language of the common man to preach two sermons daily and three on Sunday for as long as six weeks at the same site to hammer, bully, and cajole the comers to his tabernacle to commit and walk the sawdust trail. It is this element of the Revivalist styled sermon of Evangelical Billy Sunday that sent the Caid family home, energized. On the way, Case asked his pa the meaning of *bastard,* to which Mav replied: "Thet's not a word fo' children, so if anyone asks you, jus' say you don't know." Case's response was: "You don't know either, do you, Papa?" Mav asked Macy if she knew what evolution meant. All had something to ponder.

Chapter 28

The Yodeler

Few events are more amazing than the observing of children as they grow and mature. From the small bundles of noise, children pass through many stages of development, stages that adults seldom recall about themselves. Remembering thoughts entertained before the age of four or five is generally impossible except in rare cases, and of those cases, many adults are at a loss to comprehend their meaning.

"Look at them, Macy. How much beauty in their innocence? They amaze me more every day. Lyla looks at Case like he hung the moon and follows him everywhere. And Case, he is so protective of Lyla. They even seem to have a language of their own.

"I know, Mav. I'm with them more than you are and I am just as amazed as you with their desire to learn and experience new things. They seem so happy. I am so thankful. My heart would break if it wasn't so." Macy took Lyla's hand and walked out to the porch swing. Mav followed with Case holding to his hand.

As they arced back and forth in the swing talking about the events of the previous day, Mav and Macy felt the unique joy of satisfaction in their lives. There are no trials or travails facing them now. The farming operation is good as is the ranching business. Family income is enough and growing. New opportunities seem to pop up when least expected. Life is good. The Caids are a happy family.

"Yesterday Lyla wanted to help with the milking," Macy said, smiling at the memory. "She tried hard and was able to coax a little milk from the cow's teat into the bucket, and did she laugh when it happened. It was precious. The little milk maid!"

"Case hankers to ride that new pony of hisn…his but I'm not ready to turn him loose without being with him." Mav said. "He does know how to properly saddle her, so I expect him to ignore my wishes sometime soon."

"I suppose that means that you ignored your parents when you were young?" returned Macy, smiling.

"A might, I reckon," answered Mav, in thought. "There wuz the time I went swimming in the river without anyone with me. That was against the rules."

"What happened?" asked Macy.

"I larned…learned it wasn't a good idea," replied Mav.

"And?" asked Macy.

"Well, Papa walloped me somewhat with a willow switch and made me promise never to do it again.

"Did you ignore him?" asked Macy.

"For a while, I didn't but sometime after, I did an' went swimming in the river again." Mav looked at Macy.

"What happened then?" asked Macy.

"Nothin'," returned Mav. "Papa started to wallop me again, then jes'…<u>just</u> stopped. I think he wuz rememberin' himself at my age. I wuz ten or eleven then. How about you?"

"Never!" said Macy, chuckling. "I was always a perfect angel."

"Uh huh," replied Mav.

✳✳✳

"What is that sound?" a perplexed Macy asks Mav as an unusual sound of a human voice echoes across the post road they are traveling.

"They call it a yodel," replied Mav.

"What is a yodel, and why does one do it?" asked Macy.

"Well, a person makes a low-pitched sound then changes to a high-pitched sound then back again several times while changing that sound he is makin'." Mav answered Macy while snapping the reins to encourage the team to go faster. "It's kinda like a song without real words being sung. Yodelers even change the sound by introducing different words or part of words, so it comes out somethin' like: 'yodel-eedle-odel-eedle-ay' and so forth. I used to think they wuz saying somethin' about some old lady, like 'odelady-odelady-oh' an' 'yodee-lady-yodee-lady-hoo.'"

"Why?"

"In Texas, besides the Mexican citizens and the old timers thet…<u>that</u> came from other states, there are many folks from Austria and Germany. They brought yodeling to Texas from the countries of their birth. Yodeling in a singing voice wuz…was used in the mountains to call in the herds of sheep and to communicate with folks in distant communities, often on the other side of a valley. The sound travels a long distance in the mountains. At least, that is what I wuz told."

"But why would someone yodel here?" continued Macy in her query.

229

"Entertainment, I reckon. Down in places like Fredericksburg and New Braunfels they had yodeling contests an' folks would pick the best yodelers to give prizes to. Some yodelers had such a distinctive yodel thet others could identify who they wuz just by their sound." Mav pulled on the rein as they reached destination in front of the Beaton bank.

"Get down, Macy, quick! Get into the wagon bed and get Lyla and Case down low." whispered Mav.

"Why?" asked a perplexed Macy while moving to comply to Mav's alarm.

"Look what's happening at the bank," replied Mav. "There's a robbery in progress an' there could be some gunplay because there are several men across from the bank with guns drawn. We are between them." Mav snapped the reins to encourage the team to move forward and pull the wagon from their perilous position. Slowly, the wagon began to move as the first shot echoed from within the bank and three masked bandits emerged. An immediate fuselage of shots rained from the men across the street at the bandits.

Sensing their dilemma, two bandits ran along the side of the moving wagon using it for cover. A third bandit fell to a fatal shot. Mav hunched forward as Macy laid across Lyla and Case.

Presently, the fleeing bandits broke from their position of safety and ran down an alleyway. The pursuing men ran after them firing their weapons. One fell by the bandits' return fire and the others took cover. Mav directed the team to the E & H General store, which was to be their second stop on today's trip to Beaton.

"That was close," said Macy as she helped Lyla and Case up and all climbed down from the wagon bed.

"Too close fo' my comfort," returned Mav. "I hope no one wuz hurt at th' bank." As he was expressing his concern, the door from the hospital opened and several people emerged and headed toward the bank, Dr. Turnbull in the lead.

After a conversation with Edna in which Mav and Macy described the event at the bank, Mav gave Edna their order and loaded up the wagon with his purchase. Given the uproar and crowd formation at the bank, Mav decided to wait until another day to conduct his business with the bank and directed his team toward the home place.

"Did you ever try it?" asked Macy.

"Try whut?" returned Mav.

"Not <u>whut</u>, Papa, say <u>what</u>," interjected Case.

"Yodeling. We were talking about yodeling."

"Oh. Thet…uh, <u>that</u> was hours ago. I did, but it's been a long time."

"How do you start it?" asked Macy.

"Well, you just start makin' sounds, low from th' chest, and high from the throat, and there are some nonsense words, like 'yo,' 'loo,' 'lo,' 'lay,' 'dee,' 'lee,' that you sing as you move from high to low and back rapidly. It goes somethin' like this: 'yodel', which is in a low voice, then 'loo', in a high voice, then back to low with another chorus. Here's what you get: 'yodeleedle-laydeleedle-odeleedlelay-odeleedle-odeleedle-loodeleedlelay' and many variations. Why it wears the tongue out, whipping out those 'ls'. On top of that, you are exercising your throat muscles a might."

"Who taught you?" asked Macy.

"Oh, one o' th' drovers who sang an' yodeled to th' cattle on th'…" An odd instance of apparent negligence stopped Mav from continuing. A gate to the home place of Klaus Steiner was lying on the ground with two milk cows milling about threatening to walk through the opening.

"Hold on, Macy. Klaus's gate is down. I think I'll close it b'fore them cows 'scape." Stopping the team, Mav jumped down and secured the belly buster to the post.

"I guess someone just forgot to close it. It wasn't busted or anythin'." Mav remounted the wagon seat the urged the team onward.

"How's this," asked Macy as she belted out a yodel, before breaking into laughter. It would not stop there, as both Lyla and Case gave their renditions to the delight of all.

As the yodeling practice and laughter subsided, neither Mav nor Macy was prepared to hear again the yodeling emanating from somewhere in the wood.

"Mav, there it is again. Somewhere out there someone is yodeling just like when we came in this morning. But it sounds different now. Do you hear it. Doesn't it sound different to you?" Macy looked a Mav and waited for his answer.

"It does sound different. Plaintive, or weaker somehow. I don't know." Mav stopped the wagon and listened again. After a few minutes, Mav answered the yodel with his own.

Again, the distant yodel, presumably in answer to Mav. Once again, Mav yodeled. Again, came an answer. Finally, the yodel changed into a voiced: *"Hilfe. Jemand hilft mir. Hier drüben!"*

"Do you know what he is saying?" asked Macy.

"Sprichst du Englisch?" shouted Mav.

"Help! Over here! Somevone help me," returned an anxious voice.

Mav dismounted the wagon and strode off in the direction of the voice. Following the sounds of periodic cries for help, Mav finally found its source. Klaus Steiner stood against a tree, securely bound with rope.

"Dankeschön, Dankeschön" offered an anxious Klaus Steiner as Mav cut the ropes binding him to the tree.

"Klaus," began Mav, as he began to untie the rope, "what happened?"

The nervous neighbor replied: "Two men to *meins hous. Ein Pferd wurde verletzt*...vone horse vas injured. *Sie forderten ein Pferd.*"

"English." Mav said.

"*Ja.* They *gefordert*…demanded *ein Pferd*…uh, vone <u>horse</u> to replace the injured vone, then brought me here so I vouldn't ride to town for the tsheriff." As his anxiety diminished, Klaus began to message his wrists to restore circulation.

"Bank robbery," answered Mav. "We were in Beaton when it happened. They shot one bandit. The other two must hav' gotten to their horses an' 'scaped. If one was injured, he mayhap hev' been injured from th' gunfire. But, why did you yodel?"

"*Ich habe meinen Sohn und meine Frau angerufen!*" tumbled out the answer, his nervousness renewed.

"Wait! Wait! English…speak English," returned Mav. "We don't understand German."

"*Ja*, of course…I vas trying to *signal meins Sohn or meins Frau.* They vere not around vhen these men came und didn't know I vas taken. They both know *meins* yodel and vould have come to find me. *Danke, dass du mich gerettet hast*…uh, thank you for rescuing me. *Du bist mein Freund für immer*…you are my friend forever! Vhere did <u>you</u> learn to yodel?" asked Klaus.

"Texas," said Mav.

"*Ja!* Thought so," said Klaus. "I'll help you, if you vant."

Mav turned the wagon around and took Klaus back to his home place where he began to tell his family about his ordeal. Mav and his returned to their trip back to theirs.

"What was it that you yelled to Klaus? Something like '*Spritz du English.* Macy glanced at Mav, thinking, 'he always surprises me.'

"*Sprichst du Englisch*? The only German I know. I found it a hep on th' trail." Mav's reply was met with the voices of Case and Lyla shouting to one another '*Sprichst du Englisch? Sprichst du Englisch?*' Time after time.

A half-hour later Mav and Macy unloaded the supplies into the house and unhitched the animals from the wagon. A short time after that, a posse rode in with Deputy Surface in charge and asked what

Mav could tell them about the bandits since they had seen his wagon in Beaton during the robbery. Mav told them he was too busy trying to get out of the way of the gunfire to see much of the bandits. He told them that Klaus Steiner could describe them since they had come to his place after the robbery.

"What's for supper tonight, Macy?" asked Mav. "All this excitement has made me a might hungry."

"Ham, beans, collards, cornbread and buttermilk!" said Macy, who was already preparing the meal. "And I have made some bread pudding for dessert."

"An' coffee. You didn't mention coffee," added Mav.

"And coffee!" returned Macy.

"I'm going to the barn to feed Hardtack and the others. Call me when it's ready."

"I'll yodel," said Macy.

✳✳✳

"Who were you talking with this morning?" asked Macy. "I didn't see anyone we know, but I saw you gesturing as if you were giving directions.

"The old fella? He said his name is John Chapman an' that he wuz…<u>was</u> jes' passing through. He asked something that I couldn't answer. He asked if anyone grew apples in th' area," answered Mav. I told him I didn't know an' he axed…<u>asked</u> if I would like to plant some an' see if they would grow here. He said he would return fo' an answer in a few days. It got me a-thinking about it. Have you ever made an apple cobbler, Macy?" Mav waited for an answer.

"I never have, or an apple pie for that matter," responded Macy. "Are you thinking about that high ground? That was the direction you pointed."

234

"I am. It is a hard place to plow, so I haven't planted anything there in several years. Maybe an orchard would work. He talked about something called an Arkansas Black Twig that he was a-plantin' here an' there." Mav said.

"Where did he come from?" asked Macy, wiping flour her hands.

"He didn't say, but talked about plantin' nurseries in Wilkes-Barre. He jes' said he has planted a lot of apples in his lifetime in places like Indiana an' Ohio. He was old enough to hav' planted them all, in my reckonin'. An' he wuz…<u>was</u> barefooted! But, ifn he has a supply o' them trees, I jes' might buy some an' plant them. That is, ifn you would make me a cobbler."

"I'll look in my Ma's cookbook. She was from Pennsylvania and she talked about apples that she and her family used to cook. I see what recipes she has." Macy went to a cedar chest an began to search for her ma's recipes.

"I reckon it might take some time b'fore it's needed," replied Mav.

"Was that all he wanted?" asked Macy.

"Well, he asked what churches we had 'round here," answered Mav, "he said he was a Swedenborgian, or somthin' like thet…uh, <u>that</u>. That's all he said."

"Do you think he is from Sweden," queried Macy.

"Well, mayhap he is ifn Sweden is in Pennsylvania," answered Mav.

Chapter 29

Heartbreak

Morning came with Mav and Macy, already busy beginning their day on the farm with Macy preparing breakfast in a room lit by kerosene lamp while Mav took care of the animals. The previous few years had brought numerous improvements to the farm and plans made to buy more land that they would fence and run a larger herd of shorthorns Mav had acquired from the estate of Randall Spear that his widow, Willow, was liquidating. The prices to transport cattle by rail is now more reasonable between Beaton and Kansas City, and the hunger of folks in California, Chicago, and New York for beef steak seems insatiable. The enterprising Caid family keep a foot in cattle ranching and farming to supply their own needs and market the rest. Theirs is a small operation at this early stage, one that has potential to expand and grow. As markets are more reachable by transportation improvements, the opportunity for profit increases. Mav and Macy Caid look optimistically to the future. They read of the discord in Europe, but sense nothing of the significance of that discord, nor of the changes coming. Given the history of European wars, the United States government maintains a policy of non-involvement. Most citizens are comfortable with that policy, yet are unable to isolate themselves from news of the events that permeate the newspapers of the day.

News reports about international events and influential people fills the Beaton Gazette. Leaders of the world's most powerful countries are Nicholas II, Tsar of Russia, Wilhelm II, German Emperor and King of Prussia, William McKinley, 25th President of the United States, and long-lived Victoria, Queen of England. During the year, Mav and Macy will read reports of the Boxer rebellion in China, the capture of a Morning Post reporter, Winston Churchill, by Boer forces in Africa, and in America, will read of Scott Joplin's <u>Maple Leaf Rag</u> that will burn like wildfire through the music world of ragtime enthusiasts. On the home-place of Mav and Macy Caid, life will take a turn. It will be an event they will never forget and their hearts will suffer.

✳✳✳

"Mav, have you read the letter you received from the Perciville geologist that wants to look over our land we bought a year ago?"

"I did, Macy. He wants to see ifn there's somethin' called bauxite on it. He tol' me in his letter that bauxite wuz found by Dr. John Branner, the state geologist, on other property near ourn...I mean, <u>ours</u> 'bout three years ago. I don't know anythin' 'bout bauxite so I couldn't tell him anythin'. He said it is some kind o' lightweight metal ore. I reckon it wouldn't hurt none to let him look." Mav went silent as Macy set a cup of coffee before him.

"Well, if he is interested in finding out, I can't say it would hurt us to know it either. He should go ahead and look." Macy sat down

238

across the table, then said: "Mav, have you been noticing how listless Lyla has become lately? She hardly goes outside for more than a few minutes before she comes in to take a nap. She isn't eating well, and she coughs. I just think we need to let Doctor Chesney look at her soon. I can't account for it, and she looks peaked, —her skin almost looks blue, sometimes."

"OK, Macy," returned Mav, "you reckon best in these matters. We will take her in tomorrow to see Dr. Chesney."

That night, Macy awakened to the sound of hard coughing coming from Lyla's room. Macy went in to check on her and found her feverish, her skin ever bluer, and seemingly not able to breathe easily. Macy gave her a spoonful of honey mixed with apple vinegar that failed to control her cough. She had trouble drinking a little water that Macy offered to her. As her fever seemed to grow, Macy became more worried and woke Mav.

"Mav, Lyla is not doing well. I think we need to get Dr. Chesney now." Mav began to dress and was pulling on his boots before she finished speaking.

An effulgent moon aided Mav in his ride to Beaton by helping him avoid danger while running a horse at night. Arriving in Beaton, Mav dropped rein outside the home of Dr. Chesney and pounded upon the front door. After a wait of a few minutes, the doctor opened the door, still dressed in a nightshirt, and took Mav inside. Mav explained why he came and gave a description of Lyla's illness. The doctor looked grave as he absorbed the information then immediately went back upstairs to dress for the ride to Mav's place.

One hour later, Dr. Chesney stepped down from his gig and took his black leather doctor bag into the house where he opened it in Lyla's room. As Mav and Macy looked on with trepidation, Dr. Chesney examined the small child lying in bed beneath multiple layers of blankets as she coughed and sweat from fever. He used his new George Cammann binaural stethoscope to listen to her heart and lungs, depressed her tongue with a wooden tongue suppressor to view her throat, and took her temperature with a thermometer. After waiting a prescribed amount of time for her temperature to register, he read the results then stood and addressed Mav and Macy in his professional voice.

"Well, Mr. and Mrs. Caid," he began while looking grimly at Lyla's parents, "I think Lyla is in trouble. My diagnosis is that she has come down with diphtheria."

"Wha…What does that mean?" asked Macy as her concerned husband stood by her side.

"Diphtheria is a serious illness that is preferably treated in a hospital. It is an infection by the diphtheria bacterium that results in the symptoms you see yourselves. I don't want to scare you, but it can even be fatal. When did you first notice her changed behavior?" Dr. Chesney looked at Macy for an answer.

"I noticed that she refused to eat a favorite food about five days ago. I thought she may have caught something from some folks that stopped by to purchase some chickens about two weeks ago. I recall that one of the children with them was coughing and sneezing a lot." Macy paused in thought before continuing: "I didn't think much about it at the time since the child seemed energetic."

"I think it is in the early stage of infection and since we don't have a hospital in Beaton, we will have to treat her here or at my home where I keep a room set aside for serious illness that needs constant attention and isolation from others. I have no patient there now, so the room is available for Lyla. Now, we need to realize that diphtheria is dangerous and contagious, and we don't want Case to get sick also, so I suggest we take her to my home." Dr. Chesney waited for their decision that came following a long silent look between Mav and Macy that ended when they made an unvoiced decision and began to gather items of clothing for Lyla.

"I'll hitch up the wagon an' bring her in now," replied Mav. Presently, Mav hitched the team and pulled the wagon to the front of the cabin, and while Macy bundled Lyla warmly and carried her to the wagon, Mav placed a mattress in the wagon bed to cushion her during the trip. Macy lay beside her in the bed, comforting her as they rocked back and forth in a wagon shaken as they traversed deep grooves in the road made by the numerous wagons traveling through Beaton.

When they arrived at the home of Dr. Chesney, Lyla was in a state of delirium and Mav carried her upstairs to place her in bed in Dr. Chesney quarantine room at his home.

"Dr. Chesney," began Mav, "do you have anything we can read about diphtheria so we can understand better?"

Presently, Dr. Chesney handed to Mav a past medical journal called the Lancet from London that gave a brief history of the disease. Mav, struggling with words like bacteriology and the several words to identify the bacterium, he was able to derive that two German doctors of bacteriology, discovered in 1884 the linkage between the bacterium and diphtheria and named it the Krebs-Loeffler bacterium. He also read summaries of its darker history, reportedly from the 1613 account of _El Ano de los Garrotillos_ or <u>The Year of the Strangulation</u> in Spain; and of the epidemic in New England in 1735; and that the daughter of Queen Victoria, Princess Alice, plus another princess, Princess Maria of Hesse had succumbed to the terrible disease that shows no mercy to its victims, rich or poor. Mav's and Macy's fear grew as they read and prayed silently for Lyla's recovery, —that they would not have to bury a child, a possibility too horrid to imagine.

Dr. Chesney reentered the room where Mav and Macy waited and took the book back from them, asking: "Is there anything I can explain to you?"

"Will she be ok?" was the only question they had.

"I don't know for certain. I must be honest with you. All we can do is try to keep her airways open so she can breathe and keep her temperature down with aspirin. You may have read about a vaccine under development by the medical community in St. Louis, but it is not ready yet, and if I had it today, it would be too late anyway, since the infection has already set in. Vaccines are given to ward off infections before they occur by creating an immunity to them, not to cure one after an onset." Dr. Chesney pointed to a candlestick telephone sitting upon his desk saying, "I now have a telephone here and I will call some doctors I know in Chicago to see what they would recommend." Dr. Chesney ended with an offer to let them sleep for a while in his guest room while he made those calls. There would be no sleep for Mav and Macy. There would be only fear and trepidation.

Lyla, the precious and beloved seven-year-old daughter of Mav and Macy Caid, would live for another six days. During the week Dr. Chesney made every effort to keep her breathing pathways open, but as the hours fell into history, her blood was carrying the infection throughout her body, affecting heart and kidneys. At four in the afternoon on June 12, 1900, Lyla Caid took her last labored breath and her parents, Mav and Macy fell into an abyss of dark, enduring grief.

The days following were like nothing Mav or Macy had ever experienced. They would get through their responsibilities on adrenalin, then not be able to recall how they had done so. People would offer their condolences and prayers, because what else could they extend to two people with their hearts so torn. Mav and Macy would thank them for their sentiments but would rebel silently at those so insensitive as to tell them that Lyla was in a better place or that because they are still young, they can have another child. *No. No. Lord, no!'* their minds would shout, yet they would remain voiceless. They knew to their soul that the better place for Lyla is alive with her parents! They would want to scream and say that there is no replacement for Lyla, she stands alone in their hearts and in their minds. And they would be angry with God and question his wisdom, question his mercy, question if he cared at all. But in an era when a child death is a reality suffered by many, many of those sufferers knew from their own sorrowful experience what Mav and Macy are going through, and they grieve for them, with them, sometimes communicating their membership in that unwanted community of grieving parents by just touching them while remaining silent. Others who know that time never heals who has lost a child, time only makes the loss more tolerable. For now, for Mav and Macy, time has stopped and the world is upside down.

On June 13, 1900, Lyla Caid descended into her home of eternal rest in the Caid cemetery on the home-place where Macy's papa lies buried, now no longer a lonely occupant of ground sacred to the Caid family. Pastor Briggs, who had succeeded the Reverend Mr. Smedley at the Beaton Methodist Church presided over a well-done funeral and after the interment, as there were no other family members to join them, friends gathered to sit for a meal in the community room where not quite a decade ago Mav and Macy were eating wedding cake and looking outward to a world of happiness.

✳✳✳

Months passed, and grass covered the tiny grave on the hill beneath the spreading oak where Mav and Macy would visit to place flowers or just remember. Case would often go with them but would remain silent, waiting. Change was coming.

"Mav," said Macy, shaking her husband awake in the early hours. "I hear Case. It sounds like he is crying."

Mav sat up in bed, replying: "Yes, I hear him. I'll go see what is troubling him."

Entering Case's room, Mav sets a kerosene lamp on the bachelor chest and goes to Case who is crying under his blanket to muffle the sound. "What's wrong, Case? Are you in pain?"

For a moment, there is silence, then Case emerged from beneath the blanked and looks at his papa. "Lyla. I miss her, Papa. I miss her a lot. Why did she have to die?"

Mav felt a lump growing in his throat. Clearing as best he could for the moment, Mav pulled Case to him, saying: "Case, we all miss Lyla. We all wish she wuz...<u>was</u> still with us. It's just..." For a moment, Mav was at a loss for words to complete his thought. His grief has been so personal that he failed to recognize that Case would also feel the loss. At his young age, there is no comprehension of death and its consequences. Nor is there a way to express the depth of the hurt that he feels, there is only deep disorientation derived from not having enough maturity to have an understanding. Regaining composure, Mav refocused on his grieving son, saying: "Case, people are living creatures, mortal beings, an' all will die at some point, —it is th' way of nature. An illness took Lyla, an illness that we were unable to fight successfully. Life is like that sometimes. We just must recognize that fact an' go on with our own lives. There's no way to go back."

"Papa," asked Case, "Pastor Briggs said we would see Lyla again someday in Heaven. Is he right?"

"Son, I don't know. But we can all hope, an' we can all remember how it was when Lyla was here. We can all remember those things about her that we loved. She does not have to be forgotten." Mav released his hold on Case, who had ceased his crying. "You know," Mav continued, "we can talk about Lyla anytime you want. She was our precious butterfly for a while, but now she is with God. Let us believe in our hearts that it is so."

"Papa, will I die and be put in the ground?" Case asked among the sniffles.

"No. Not anytime soon," answered Mav, "don't you see around you all the older people who are going about their lives every day? There would not be any old people to see if everyone died young."

Mav trusted that his answer would suffice to calm Case's anxiety about dying, but in his heart, he felt anxiety of his own about Case and the many threats Case will face as he grows. Finally, Mav's thoughts changed from anxiety to thankfulness for having Case and Macy in his life, and for the time Lyla was with them. He asked himself what he would be without them and he whispered: "Nothing."

In the coming days, Mav and Macy would have many opportunities to talk with Case about Lyla, and to sense his maturing understanding about life and death, and in those talks, each would sense their own developing philosophy of life, and find their grief change from resistance to acceptance, if not that, then endurance. Mav will contemplate the Christian principles familiar to him since childhood, wondering if a person should believe only in what he can prove to himself as true, or if it is reasonable to believe in unprovable things that give guidance through life's uncertainties. Mav will always be conflicted when such unjust events occur, such as the death of Lyla, a small, innocent child. How can a just God, oversee such an unjust end, and speak not a word to the grieving souls left behind? Some say that God speaks through the mouths of others. But those words often speak to giving comfort, not reason. Given the tragedy inflicted upon his family in Bandera, and Lyla's death to diphtheria, it would be understandable that Mav may feel that there is no deity looking over his creation, that there are only events occurring from unpredictable happenstance. Can hope flourish in either scenario? What value is hope in a world influenced by an indifferent God? What sense is hope in a world governed by happenstance? What, though, do we have without it?

Sunday afternoon, after services at the church, is a time for visiting the graves of Lyla, and the grandfather she never knew, but on this day, Macy noticed something different. Hanging on the marker is an object wrapped in colored paper and tied with a ribbon.

"Mav," questioned Macy, "do you see that? What is it?" Macy pointed to the object suspended from an arm of the cross, marking Lyla's grave.

Mav directed his eyes to the object Macy was pointing to and said: "Macy, I don't know. I've not seen it before." Mav walked to the marker and retrieved the object. Unrolling the enclosing paper, a small carved wooden doll rolled into his hand. Mav looked at the doll for a long moment before handing it to Macy and turning to the unrolled paper. It had a message written in a child's hand in block letters. It read:

Butterfly
You dried your dewy wings
In morning's warming rays
then drew your wings around
the wind and flew away
Come again, sweet Butterfly
Our saddened hearts are true
Come again and flutter by.
Butterfly. We miss you, miss you.

Your brother, Case

Mav read the poem and lowered his hand, looking far into the distance for the longest time without speaking. Finally, he re-read the poem, then choking back a sudden uncontrollable emotion that robbed him of voice, silently passed the poem to Macy.

"Mav. Oh, Mav. This makes me cry!" She moved toward Mav and to his waiting arms.

"Yes," is all Mav said in reply as he enfolded Macy in his embrace.

"Where did he get the words?" asked Macy through her tears. "From the heart," replied Mav, "from the heart."

Chapter 30

The Query / The Source

Today a letter arrived from the geologist for the Perciville Reduction company who has been surveying their property in Saline county for the presence of aluminum ore, known as bauxite.

"Dear Mr. Caid,"- Mav was reading to Macy from the letter he received from the geologist: *"I have completed my geologic survey of your property and can report that I have indeed discovered that a rich deposit of bauxite is present and could be mined if you so desired. I have enclosed a summary report of the survey for your benefit. Now, Mr. Caid, I am a geologist for the Perciville Reduction Company who shipped fifty-five hundred tons of bauxite from nearby mines in 1899 and expect to ship much more in the future. The metal extracted from bauxite, called aluminum, is light-weight and durable and is a metal that has many uses. Many aluminum products are in stores today and many more will be available in the future. Your property, as you know, is in Saline County that the*

St. Louis Southwestern (SSW) Railroad, better known as the Cotton Belt Line, currently serves. This makes mining the property ideal from a shipment cost perspective. I cannot tell you what this deposit may be worth to you, but rest assured, a representative from my company will correspond with you in the very near future to explore the possibilities of purchasing your property outright or of entering into an agreement for the mining of bauxite for our aluminum smelting. For the moment, thank you for giving me the opportunity to survey the property. Goodbye, for now, Mr. Caid. And it is signed by Mr. Hopper of the Perciville Reduction Company." Mav folded the letter and placed it back into the envelope. Presently, he looked over the summary report and put it back into the envelope with the letter. "Well, I jes' don't know what else to say." As there was no official offer from the owners or managers of Perciville in hand, Mav filed the envelope in the vault with other things that have been important to him over time.

✳✳✳

November came and once again, after all the crops were in, Mav prepared to return to the Valley of Tears as he has done each year. Case asked if he could go with him and his papa told him that the trip is too hard for one so young. He accepted his pa's decision reluctantly and vowed to go someday when he was older.

"Will you be careful?" asked Macy, as she packed the items Mav would need for the ride.

"You hav' nothin' to worry about, Macy. Unlike Case, I'm all growed up...oops! All <u>grown</u> up now." He took the packed provisions, checked again that he would have enough coffee, then left to saddle Hardtack. This would be the fifth trip since the strange episode with Windwalker, and Mav wondered if there would be anything of similar nature waiting. He had never told Macy about Windwalker, nor that Mav is known to him as Keeper-of-Tears, still uncertain himself of the reality of his experience, but he had thought of Windwalker many times and wondered if he would ever see him again. He hesitated to hope, recalling how sick he was at the time and knowing that the sick can hallucinate about strange things, things paradisiacal to hellish.

"Well, OK, Hardtack, I reckon you know th' way by yorsel', so let's get a-goin'." Mav threw his leg across Hardtack and settled in for a long ride. A pack horse followed with the provisions for the trip that consisted of food, water, cookware, foul weather clothing, small shovel, rifle, ammunition, and at two-month supply of coffee. Mav looked at the heavy cast iron skillet and thinks about what Mr. Hopper said about aluminum being light-weight.

A week passed, and Mav upon Hardtack were coming to the entry to the valley. His landmark, the great uplift of rock that stood out against the sky as a single, impenetrable barrier to their path. "I reckon we might orta camp here fo' the night, Hardtack. You OK with thet?" Receiving no negative response to his question, Mav dismounted and removed the saddle and blanket from Hardtack, then after removing his bridle, set him free to feed on the unusually tall grass for the time of year. He repeated the process for the pack horse.

The first order of business is always to select a spot and build a windbreak if the weather is threatening, else just a fire. This time, fire is enough, and within a short time Mav had coffee on the fire and was frying salt-cured pork in the iron skillet. Once heated, Mav would remove the meat and make red-eye gravy by adding his stout black coffee to the pan drippings form the pork. This, with some soda biscuits, would be the typical meal unless he chose to take from the bounty of nature a rabbit or deer to provide fresh meat for the meal. He thought of his uncle Wendell walking across Arkansas toward Memphis, sick and in physical distress, hoping that he would find game for a meal. 'It was so long ago,' he thinks as he finishes his meal.

Sundown brought a splendor of color to the clouds widely spread across the sky, and Mav watched them transition from one color to another and watched for the appearance of the evening star that he now knows is the planet, Venus. As the evening progressed, Mav cast his gaze at the brightening sky as a warm wind from the south swept away the clouds. The revealed Milky Way displayed her sparkling splendor across the sky from horizon to horizon, a brilliance enhanced by periodic streaks of fire that crossed before his watchful eyes cast upward from his recumbent position on the ground of a very lonely place near 34.06 degrees north latitude and 93.70 degrees west longitude. The night wore on and somewhere among the consideration of time and space, and the reflection upon his previous visits to the Valley of Tears, Mav fell into a deep sleep, a sleep that woke powers from time past that were palpable but unseen to the farmer from Beaton, the ex-patriot from Bandera, the husband of Macy, and father to Case and Lyla, so soon departed from life.

Revealed in detail are visions of native life, from the peaceful villages emitting smoke from the small thatched homes of the Quapaw, Osage, and Caddo, to the day-to-day endeavor to provide food for the tribes and satisfy the unseen, powerful forces of the spirits who oversee all. Revealed are ancient customs, —rites of passage ceremonies and dances to appease the spirits, to ensure a successful hunt, to rally the warriors charged with the defense of the village, and to shape the weather to the need. Mav sees the deerskin clad French trappers, the white buffalo hunters, even the tall Spanish Conquistadores astride their unfamiliar horses driving the small herds of cattle and swine, kept to provision their quests for wealth. He sees the natives of the plains to the west, roving in bands, hunting the buffalo, —Apache, Comanche, Kiowa, —and, ultimately, the cliff dwellers and adobe villages of Navajo land, Zuni land, and Hopi land. Suddenly, the dream changes, and Mav sees the interface between the natives and the white men with the insatiable demands of the migrating people moving westward, and he witnesses the sorrows of the defeated. He sees the white men with families moving westward with the persistence of a gigantic wave, persistent and unstoppable. Presently, a wind began to blow through the trees, rattling leaves and moaning and Mav Caid, the dreaming man, who sensed that he was dreaming, awoke, —or, at least, thought that he had.

"Keeper-of-Tears," began the voice of a wizened red-hued man sitting cross-legged upon the opposite side of the smoldering campfire Mav had built, "what have you done to heal from your sorrow?"

"It is good to see you again, Windwalker." Mav sat up and assumed the cross-legged posture of his interlocutor. "I find thet sorrow is not curable, but to be endured."

"Yes, some sorrows are forever, but they can be lessened in their power over their bearer." Windwalker became silent as if to invoke an introspection in Mav.

Mav considered the statement for a moment then replied: "It would be well fo' me to know th' secret."

"You already know the secret," returned Windwalker, "it is the power of the tears of the Sun that you must engage." With each statement, Windwalker gestures with his hands.

"I don't understand how to engage their power. Do you mean thet I should be giving a tear to each person as you did in yor day, what, —in all th' world?" Mav showed his perplexity.

"The ways of the past die as the ways of the future are born," said Windwalker, waving his arm in a circular motion. "You have already begun," replied Windwalker. "You have traded the tears, have you not?"

"I hav' sold…uh…traded some fo' money…uh…wampum." Mav's perplexity continued.

"And what have you done with the wampum you received?" asked Windwalker.

"It is in a bank…a safe place…uh…a cache," returned Mav, "an' I have used some to secure my family's wellbeing, —to build a house, uh…a…uh… *kó-wa*."

"And now?" returned Windwalker. "How may the tears of the Sun continue to heal in the future and not be given as in the past?"

"I don't know." Mav stared across into the blind eyes of Windwalker.

"Is not a trade an exchange of value for value? Power for power?" continued Windwalker. "Might not the power to heal be as strong in the wampum as in the traded tears?" The question hung in the silence as Mav absorbed its meaning.

"I reckon I ain't ponder'd about it, but…" before Mav could complete his answer Windwalker interrupted:

"Have you found joy in the growing cache of wampum?" asked Windwalker as Mav began to recall their previous conversation on how each medicine bag contained a healing tear of the Sun. Momentarily, Mav reached for his medicine-bag. He found it still hanging from his neck.

"In th' 'cumulation? Well…I cain't say…I cain't say a growing cache brings joy. It jes' means…more money…more wampum. It only means thet thar's more opportunities to realize from th' trading o' th' wampum," replied Mav, still uncertain of what Windwalker is saying. For a moment, Mav considers the relationship of joy to the receiving and to the giving of something that can change the life of another. "Joy comes from seeing th' results o' thet trade or gift o' wampum. Like a gift to someone," recalling Macy's joy at receiving the ring he gave to her and the joy he felt in seeing her joy. Suddenly perceiving, Mav exclaimed: "It is in th' <u>giving</u>, thet th' <u>giver</u> finds joy, an' in th' <u>receiving</u> thet th' <u>receiver</u> finds joy. That is whut you are tryin' to tell me!" exclaimed Mav.

"Your heart is open. Your eyes see. Only your imagination and will are sleeping," returned Windwalker. "What is the most important quality a person might value in having?"

For an instant, the face of Lyla hovers before Mav and his thoughts cascade. As he attempts to formulate a response,

Windwalker fades from before the campfire and from the now open eyes of the Keeper-of-Tears. The man who thought he was awake, is awake. After reflecting for a moment, Mav tosses a few previously gathered dry limbs on the fire and stirs the ashes. A new blaze engulfs the dry branches as Mav fills the coffee pot for his Arbuckle.

As Mav finishes breakfast and drinks the last swallow of coffee, he stands and extinguishes the fire. Within a short period, all is ready to continue the trip. Mav saddles and mounts Hardtack, talking to him about things Hardtack questions but remains silent to.

While horse and rider proceed toward the valley entrance, Mav notices a change to the skyline. Where yesterday, as they approached the great uplift appearing as impregnable as legendary Masada of which he has read, today, instead of a solitary rock mass, two masses appear as if overnight some gigantic ax had cleaved that single mass in twain. Within two hours, Mav and Hardtack are entering the high gate to the Valley of Tears. He recalls the view from earlier visits. It is as if time had ceased to carve new pathways for streams, expand forests, cover bare ground with new grass. Birds still flew, he sees a few elk grazing at a distance, and the air is still sweet from the scent of blossoms that should not be at this time of year. It was something Mav had not noticed before. Also never seen before is a large white buffalo grazing, an animal known from Indian lore, a symbol of fortune. Moving down into the valley, Mav and Hardtack arrived at a pleasant place to make camp, one near the wooded forest and rushing water of a spring-fed brook.

"Cain't git better water fo' my Arbuckle," Mav announced to Hardtack who merely looked at Mav as he chewed some sweet grass he had pulled up. An hour later the campsite is prepared and a pot of coffee is brewing in the percolator. Mav's interest in coffee had led him to read about percolators in his cyclopedia where he discovered that people have used the device since its invention in 1814 by British physicist and soldier, Sir Benjamin Thompson, better known as, Count

Rumford, a man who hated alcohol and disliked tea so had a great interest in providing an alternative for the troops. For Mav, the great knight of the British realm did the world a valuable service. But it is the innovative design by an Illinois farmer, Hanson Goodrich, whose coffee pot innovation Mav is using today.

As Mav drinks his coffee, he begins to think of the sermon by Billy Sunday that he and his family attended before the tragedy of Lyla's death. Billy said: *"The fellow with no money is poor. The fellow who has nothing but money is poorer still."* On this, he pondered. On another: *"Live so that when your final summons comes, you will leave something more behind you than an epitaph on a tombstone or an obituary in a newspaper."* He felt ashamed that he had not done anything significant for others. Upon reflection, Mav thought of another statement Billy made: *"More men fail through lack of purpose than lack of action."* Mav considers Billy's statements for a moment, then those of Windwalker and murmurs to himself: 'Action is overdue,' and resolves to correct his failure when he returns home.

Mav and Hardtack began a search to find what many would call the mother-lode, the source of the natural wealth spilling from the ground, be it silver, gold, or diamonds. Beginning at the clear flowing stream with the indented traps for the tears of the Sun, they followed the stream upland toward a mountain three to four miles distant. As Mav's uncle wrote in his diary, the stream went underground several times, and several times he again found it a few hundred yards away, but still tracking upward toward the mountain. Finally, Mav approached an enigma. In the distance it appeared that fog or low cloud embraced the pathway forward and as he approached, the temperature grew warmer, the air moister. Mav could hear a gurgling sound, an occasional murmuring, like the rolling boil of a cauldron. The ground became noticeably soggy and warmer as he approached the ground-embracing, whispering opacity. Coming closer, he realized that the obscurity was from steam emitting through a fissure in the earth. The heat became more intense as he cautiously approached the crevice. Looking down, through the barely endurable misty cloud of moist air, Mav could vaguely see a bubbling mass of bluish colored dense material bubbling and rolling within the cauldron, like some thick soup in a stew pot. Every now and then, a more substantial emission of steam would create a belch, and the bluish material with a consistency of clay slurry would eject into a natural pool a few feet below the fissure. From a height above the receiving pool, a stream of water coursed into the pool where the temperature grew cooler and the blue clay washed from around the shiny crystalline stones that now tumbled from the containment into the stream where they rolled and fell above and below ground to the valley miles below. The searcher has found the source!

His purpose met, and bags of soapy-feeling diamonds gathered, Mav and Hardtack left the valley for a return to Macy and Case. The only difference from the previous visits is more knowledge and an unsettled conscience.

As Mav and Hardtack traveled the familiar way back home, Mav contemplated the ephemeral nature of life itself and how happiness and sadness affected serenity. He thought about his family back home in Beaton and how they were deprived of the fullness of a long life. Life is good. Without life, what would be the purpose of the earth, the heavens, all that exists. How many the years from the times of Jesus Christ. How many the years before from the time of the Pharaohs. How many years even before then, when the Bible says God formed Adam of clay, and Eve from the rib of Adam. How many years has the earth existed? Ussher gave a date of all creation as nightfall of October 22, 4004 BC. Who believes that now? How people have tried to make sense of any of it, and now there is this thing of evolution that challenges all the teaching to date. He has seen pictures of the pyramids and the sphinx in Egypt in the cyclopedia. No one can say how old they are. Much is hidden by time. He has seen pictures of little known Dinosauria. When and why did they die? He has seen representations of Jesus, of Moses, Joseph, Mary, and all the people familiar to Christians. He has read of those calling themselves Mohammedans, Hindus, an' Buddhists. They tell a story but what does it all mean? Natives see the world in a different light. Catholics, Mormons, and Protestants are different also. How many others still unknown to him differ in their beliefs in the unseen, the undefinable. Who is right? Who has the knowledge and authority to say? Is he bound by the rules of his childhood? Should he follow what he learned during childhood, or has he the right as an adult to write his own guide in which to believe. Would he burn in hell if he did so? Is being different a sin? Is thinking of these matters a sin?

Contemplation of the meaning of life captures the mind of Mav Caid. He reasons that there must be a God who created all that he sees or he must believe in the ever-being of the material universe. Yet, there are differences. People, animals, fish, and fowl and everything that burrows and slithers are born and experience life but eventually die. Vegetation too, sprouts from the earth, grows, dies, and rots. Rocks do not die. Water does not die. Air does not die. There are differences between the quick and the dead. A difference of permanence and impermanence. What if this creative God is also the power that animates all the living things, causing all things to live and grow? What then if the death of those living things is because they lost that animating power? If when that living, growing thing loses that power and dies, if God is that power, God then, must be the same as life, —that which causes, is.

Preachers speak of God as a person. What if the God we speak of is only a personification of life itself, just a way to speak of life? Do we, worship a separate entity, or do we simply worship life in the guise of God? Preachers, when they speak of God, also speak of the soul and how everyone has one and how the soul must answer to God. But what if the soul is just evidence of the presence of the animating power and is itself, life? Isn't then God, the soul, and life the same? Just different words for the same thing? Preachers say that God is eternal and indestructible. Would that mean that if an indestructible God is life, then life itself is indestructible? But people die! When they die, the preacher says, that the soul goes to Heaven or Hell. If a person is bad then his soul goes to Hell to be punished. If that person is good, his soul goes to Heaven to be rewarded. Is a soul responsible for what a person does in his living years? Why should a soul be tainted by what a mortal person does if that person has free will? Is the soul a leader or a follower or just another personification of life so is neither? Preachers say God is all good, but he is jealous and is brutal if he does not get his way. Can that be right? To kill when displeased? To destroy the innocent to punish the bad? Did not the great flood sweep away the good as well as the bad? But, if God is all good, and if God is life, and if the soul is life, why would a soul be punished for what its mortal vessel did? It would be like God punishing God, life punishing life. It seems to make more sense to say that the soul is life on loan to a mortal person hosting that soul until the body can no longer do so. Then the soul, leaving a dead body is only indestructible life leaving a destructible body and returning to its eternal self. It is more like we borrow life from God, or, perhaps, is evidence of God within us. The continuum then would be: Life begins when a soul enters a human baby at its creation, then it stays with that person until age or trauma destroys the body's viability, then the soul, —life's essence, —goes back to God. A borrowing from God, returning to God! Saying it another way: borrowed life returning to eternal life. Maybe we need each other. What would be the purpose of people if not to host life? And the purpose of life if not to animate people? Overall, do we all just worship eternal life under multiple names? Does it harm anyone to give that eternal life a name? How many names are there for 'eternal life?'

Then, there is the question about ghosts. People say that they have seen ghosts of departed people occasionally. Am I to believe that? If I say no, what must I say about Windwalker? Is he a ghost? Perhaps a ghost is the echo of a person's essence, a persona, that which makes him different from others. Perhaps it survives a death and on occasion can interact with living beings. Maybe a ghost is the soul. Maybe a ghost, or soul retains all that is unique about a person, the thoughts, memories, the record of their life. Perhaps a ghost is something in transition. Is it not true that some people in this world believe in a reincarnation? Reincarnation means the creation of something new from something old. Maybe a ghost plays a part in reincarnation. 'Ah, the mystery!' Mav whispers to himself.

Contemplation of the metaphysics of life is as endless as the quest to find the second boundary of a Möbius strip and no less is the search for theocratic truth. Some things, perhaps, have no answers and are destined to be continuously explored, never to be answered, to forever be veiled in mystery. Would anyone recognize it anyway, if confronted by it today?

Chapter 31

Cabin in the Wood

The trip from the Valley of Tears began with the realization that the valley that occupied Mav's attention for the last several days was indeed, different. As Mav and Hardtack passed through the towering granite gateway, they crossed into winter. Skies were heavy and gray. It is mid-December, and the warm moist air of the Gulf of Mexico four hundred miles to the south is mixing with the dry, cold air from the northern plains. In the distance, blowing snow envelops the countryside and snowdrifts are building across the landscape, covering the remains of autumn's fallen leaves, presenting a vista of bare, skeletal branches that click together as the wind moves through their skyward reach.

"Well, Hardtack," said Mav to his trusted friend, "I reckon this ride back home ain't gonna be much fun." Mav reached out to pat Hardtack on the neck and thought he could feel a shiver in Hardtack, although he made no other response.

Eugene Stonefield

After a three-hour ride through the continuously falling snow, Mav neared the old abandoned cabin he had discovered in the past and turned Hardtack in the direction of the cabin, thinking: 'four walls and half a roof has to be better than anything else in sight, even if the roof may admit some snow.' As Mav and Hardtack rode toward the cabin an unusual and unexpected occurrence disturbed the serenity of the ride. While passing beneath a tree, a small clump of snow broke free from an overhanging branch and fell directly into Hardtacks ear. The touch of the cold intrusion caused Hardtack to pitch wildly and throw his head downward, shaking it side to side, to expel the snow from his ear. His reaction was sudden and violent, but non-continuous and Mav remained securely in the saddle. His only response was to say: "Well Hardtack! What in th' world spooked you? Or are you jes' reactin' to an earful of snow?"

Arriving at the cabin Mav was surprised to find that someone else had arrived first. Tied outside the ramshackle porch was a bay horse, still with a tightly cinched saddle upon which clung a covering of snow. Above the damaged roof, Mav could see a thin wisp of smoke forcing its presence into the air above the fireplace chimney. It is never a wise idea to surprise a stranger who may shoot first and ask questions only after they discern a shot victim is still capable of conversation, so Mav stopped at a distance and addressed the person or persons occupying the dilapidated cabin:

"Howdy, inside th' cabin!" announced Mav from forty feet away. He waited for a response that came tentatively from a woman appearing at the door with a Winchester rifle cradled in her arm. "Who are you?" shouted the woman, looking around to see if there were others about.

"Th' name's Mav Caid," returned Mav, "from Beaton." Mav went silent, waiting for another question.

"What's your business?" came the next query from the woman who Mav could now see was herself, not alone, for firmly clasping her skirted leg was a child of about three or four years old.

"Headin' home from a trip," shouted Mav, now having little concern that the cabin may harbor some desperado. "Y'all object to my comin' in?" asked Mav.

"Are you alone?" asked the voice.

"Yes'm, I'm alone," returned Mav.

For a minute there was silence, and the woman considered the risk, then: "Do you have a family in Beaton?"

"Wife an' boy back at th' home place," shouted Mav.

"You sound like you're from Texas," replied the woman.

"Bandera," returned Mav. "Is it ok ifn I come in?"

"Weather is getting bad, so come on in. I have this Winchester, though," returned the woman as she waved the rifle in Mav's direction.

"Yes'm. I seen it. Comin' in." said Mav as he urged Hardtack up to the front of the cabin. Dismounting, Mav tied the reins to a post and walked to the door. The woman had disappeared into the room but left the door open for Mav to enter. As he stepped inside, the woman held the Winchester level, pointed at the unknown man entering her domain to signal that some distrust remained.

"Good to make yor acquaintance, Miss…uh…Mrs.?" Mav said, fumbling for the proper address to a woman still pointing a rifle at him.

"Winslow. Mrs. Hugh Winslow. And Jeff. Jeff is four." Mrs. Winslow examined Mav closely as if trying to assure herself she made the right decision in giving her permission for him to come in. Her reason for taking the risk, discernable by her conversation. "We are also on our way to Beaton. Do you…do you have any food with you? Jeff here is pretty hungry and hasn't eaten for two days." She lowered her rifle.

"What happened," asked Mav, then adding: "I do have a bit on my pack horse outside. I'll go fetch it." Mav didn't wait for an answer, but stepped back outside to retrieve a bundle containing some beef jerky and some soda biscuits." As Mav reentered the cabin, Mrs. Winslow placed the rifle upright next to the fireplace and began to speak in answer to his question.

"What happened was, my husband and Jeff and I were traveling from Fort Apache in Arizona to Beaton where his pa has a ranch and we had been on the trail for almost two months before we got into Arkansas territory. Unfortunately, some violent men attacked from ambush and killed Hugh with a shot to the back. The men took Jeff and me captive and tied us to the wagon with all our belongings in it. I don't know what they would have done with us, but I didn't want to find out so I began to work on my constraints. That night, our captors began drinking, and when they fell asleep, I was able to get free. I took Jeff and stole one of their horses and rode off, leading the other horses away from camp so they couldn't follow us. The Winchester was in a saddle scabbard on the horse. I didn't know where we were, I only knew to go east, hoping to find a post road, then I found this cabin by accident. The weather, being so threatening, made us stop. I think I am going in the direction of Beaton, but am not sure." Her story came in a torrent of words amidst the sound of Jeff who is registering his need to have something to eat.

"Mrs. Winslow. I'm truly sorry for yor troubles. I'll hep where I can." Mav turned his attention to opening the package containing the jerky and handing a portion to Jeff who begins eating eagerly. Presently, he gave a similar share to Mrs. Winslow.

After a few minutes, her hunger satiated, Mrs. Winslow resumed their conversation: "Mr. Caid…" and at this point, Mav interrupted.

"Mav. Jes' Mav, ifn it's ok," said Mav.

"Ok, Mav. And my name is Constance."

"Constance," began Mav, "I know a Winslow in Beaton, — Harvey Winslow, —yor husband's pa, ifn I ain't mistaken. He has a sheep ranch on the east side of Beaton several miles out. Ifn you don't object, we can ride on to Beaton together."

Mav unsaddled and hobbled the horses in a partially collapsed shed then returned to the house with another load of wood for the fire. Presently, the snow stopped and even though the roof had holes that permitted some snow to fall into the cabin throughout the day, and even allowing for the partial collapsed back wall, the cottage was reasonably comfortable for the three cabin-mates. Weather permitting, they would continue their trip the next day.

Early the next morning finds Mav fueling the fire with newly gathered wood and brewing coffee. Constance woke to the smell of the brewing coffee and Jeff soon after. For breakfast, Mav gave each a portion of soda biscuits and beef jerky. Mav ceded his coffee cup to Constance and drank his coffee from a tin ladle he had found in the shed where Mav had placed the horses.

"Why wuz…I mean, why <u>was</u> yor family movin' to Beaton?" asked Mav.

"My husband, Hugh, was the government's Indian agent at Fort Apache and he had left the service to return home. He told me he was tired of dealing with the Department of Indian Affairs in Washington," answered Constance. "Do you think we can continue on today?"

"I reckon we can, but I am concerned about you an' Jeff. I mean, neither of y'all hav' warm enough clothing fo' what we are likely to encounter on th' ride in. I reckon y'all had to leave everything on th' wagon." Mav looked at Jeff who was still eating.

"Yes, mostly on the wagon. I did take Hugh's coat, but it was blood stained, and I foolishly used it to start a fire in the fireplace. I guess I don't really know what to do. Maybe we should stay here where we can build a fire until…" her voice trails off as she recalls that winter has just begun and there are no stores of food to carry them through even a short period.

Mav responded: "I have my coat, thet is warm enough, an' a poncho. Oh, an' both horses hav' blankets. I suppose one of them would contribute a blanket. We can work it out ok." Mav waited for Constance to absorb what he was saying, then continued. "The blanket is large enough fo' Jeff, I can cut a hole in it to make a small poncho fo' Jeff. You can wear my coat, an' I'll wear my poncho." A decision made, three travelers left the derelict cabin and rode toward Beaton in a softly falling snow.

Chapter 32

A Trip for Three

For a time, the trail they traveled being narrow, the small party rode single file with Mav in the lead followed by Constance and Jeff on her purloined horse, and the pack horse with provisions and a load of diamonds. The weather was not a factor as they descended from the narrow pathway at the higher elevation to a trail that allowed two horses to come abreast, facilitating conversation.

"You said you have a family in Beaton," began Constance, "what do you do there?"

"My wife, Macy, an' a son, Case. We farm a few acres," replied Mav, thinking of the missing member, Lyla and sensing a little guilt in not mentioning her. "Our home place is prob'ly twenty miles from where yor a-heading. We'll get there, mayhap, day after tomorrow." As they rode, talking about inconsequential things, Mav became aware that Constance never said much about her husband. 'It's a funny thing about grief,' thought Mav, 'sometimes it is so personal it must be hidden. This unfortunate woman didn't even get a chance to say goodbye properly, or lay his body to rest.'

A few miles more and sundown approaches. As the lowering sun extends the shadows, Mav pulls up and points to a place near a bluff that provided a rock overhang where they will be able to make camp. Riding to the site, they dismount and begin to collect firewood from the surrounding forest. Mav unburdened the horses and hobbled the pack horse and the horse Constance and Jeff rode to assure they would not wander too far. Mav trusted Hardtack to stay close so he did not hobble him. After they established the camp, Mav picked up his Winchester and disappeared into the wood. A short time later, nature contributed some of her largesse to the needs of the travelers as a medium-sized white-tailed buck fell to Mav's Winchester.

While Mav hunted, Constance and Jeff had gathered pine boughs and fashioned beds for the three that she placed between the fire and the rock cliff. By the time Mav returned, the fire had warmed the enclosure, and a pot of coffee had sweetened the air with its fragrance. Mav set about cutting the venison, providing a welcome change from the jerky that had sustained them for the last two days. Mav separated the venison into three groupings – that which they would cook, that which they would take with them, and the remains for disposal. Mav tied the venison they would take high in a tree to prevent theft by wandering wild animals.

Before they laid down for the nights' rest, Mav sensed nervousness in the animals and, the rock ledge being extensive, brought the horses under its protection. Having only one bedroll for the three, Constance ceded Mav's coat back to him for the night and slipped into the bedroll with Jeff. Mav stoked the fire and as he was preparing to lay down some distance away, Constance motioned for him to come closer to sleep, and the night began with the small group of strangers sharing warmth between the rock and the fire.

Midnight came, and a half-dozen pair of yellow eyes peered from among the trees on the camp's perimeter. Awakening to the horses' behavior, Mav stoked the fire and picked up his rifle, checking to see that it carried a full magazine of 45-70 centerfires. After checking on the horses to make certain they were secure, Mav picked up parts of the carved carcass from the pile of offal and gave each of them a strong toss to the surrounding wolves. The commotion was instant, and the deer remains disappeared into the undergrowth. 'For the moment, they will be happy,' thought Mav as he tossed more wood on the fire and returned to their communal bed.

Morning appeared as a rosy glow and, for the moment, windless. The day promised to be clear and cold. After the trio had eaten breakfast and horses saddled, the three travelers began their next day of travel.

"I heard you moving around last night," ventured Constance as she set a foot into her horse's stirrup and swung into the saddle.

Mav lifted Jeff to his position behind his mother and glanced at Constance. "Oh, jus' a few four-footed visitors. I fed them, an' they went away," answered Mav.

"Those noisy armadillos, I suppose," returned Constance. We had them in Arizona also.

"Yeah. Pesky armadillos," replied Mav, preferring to avoid creating a concern in Constance's and Jeff's minds that dangerous animals are abundant in the forests.

It was the third day of travel from the encounter at the cabin when they approached Beaton. Mav suggested that she may want to stop at his place and freshen up before going on to the Winslow place on the other side of Beaton. Constance welcomed the invitation, so the path was set for the Caid home-place, a few miles southwest of Beaton.

By coincidence, Macy was sweeping the front porch when Mav, Constance, and Jeff rode in and for a moment Macy looked steadily at Constance and the coat she was wearing.

"Mav?" questioned Macy, as Mav helped Jeff and Constance from their horse.

"Constance, this here is my wife, Macy. Macy, this here is Constance. Oh, an' here is Jeff."

"Mav? I mean, hello Constance and Jeff. Did everyone have a good ride?" questions abound with Macy, questions to be answered, mostly by Constance as the two women, with Jeff in tow, disappeared into the house.

As Mav continued to unsaddle and care for the animals, Macy learned of the reason for her and her son being with Mav, and that Constance did not know her father-in-law, Harvey Winslow, and he had never seen his grandson, Jeff. Constance told Macy that Hugh's father had vigorously opposed their getting married that led to a five-year estrangement between Harvey and his son that they only recently resolved. Harvey does not know about the death of his son, Hugh. It is not news that Constance looks forward to bringing to Harvey and cannot guess what his reaction will be.

"Truthfully, Macy, I don't know if Harvey Winslow will welcome Jeff and me after I tell him. He may blame us for Hugh's death. He may tell me that if I hadn't turned Hugh's head that his son would still be alive. I have great fear and don't know what I will do next. All the money Hugh and I had was in the wagon. Jeff and I…we're destitute and will have no place to go since my family is all gone. Our wellbeing is so dependent upon Harvey now." A look of sadness swept across Constance's face.

"Constance, if that happens, you and Jeff come here." Macy took the hand of the desperate woman, thinking: 'There but for the grace of God, go I.'

Chapter 33

A Woman's Plight

The meeting between Constance and her father-in-law, Harvey Winslow, was predictably tense but sad, and the death of Harvey's son, a devastating blow to a father who had only a four-month-old letter telling him that Hugh and his family would be coming home. Harvey had put a lot of pressure on his son, Hugh, to return to Beaton and take over the management of the ranch, events of the past that drove Hugh away from home fully forgiven by both parties. Constance, though, was still an unknown to Harvey, who five years ago disagreed vehemently with his son, Hugh's intention to marry her regardless of her past pursuit of a career in entertainment, a fact Harvey deplored. But it was true that, for several years Constance traveled with a circuit group of actors and singers performing musical theater such as the works of Harrigan and Hart and Gilbert and Sullivan, familiar to theatergoers of New York and Chicago. To Harvey, a career in entertainment was a wasted life, a life that avoided hard work and honorable pursuits such as sheep raising or farming. Harvey had expected to harvest a grand return of his prodigal son, and now, he reaps but sorrow and regret. His opposition to the marriage of Hugh and Constance was still on the mind of Constance, and she recognizes that hers and her son's future forever changed when her husband died. Constance had no living family, only Beaton could offer a place to rest from her travails and to plan a future for herself and Jeff. What that future will be is in the balance. History drives the conversation.

"Constance," begins Harvey, "did you know anything about the men who killed my son?"

"Not personally, but Hugh had told me about a gang of outlaws that were troubling the area, —I think he called them the Cook gang, —the gang from which a young Texas outlaw named Cherokee Bill was hanged in 1896 for his murder of Ernest Melton of Lenopath. Hugh learned about the gang from an Indian Agent he knew who was working with the reservation Indians in Oklahoma. We visited with him for a few days when we came through. I surmised that those who attacked us were part of the gang from conversations about Bill Cook and Cherokee that I overheard as they were drinking while Jeff and I were tied to the wagon." Constance became thoughtful for a moment then continued: "But, I recall they also talked about a Black Jack, —– Ketchum, I think was the last name, —who was in the Hole in the Wall gang that robbed trains in New Mexico, so they may have just been telling tales of things they had heard."

"Did my son give an account of himself?" asked Harvey.

"He had no chance to do anything. They shot him in the back from a distance. It was an ambush." Constance fell silent as Harvey absorbed the information, then added: "I gathered from their conversation that someone named Faren…Caleb Faren was the shooter." Harvey became pensive before venturing to speak again.

"I know you have no living family, so you can stay as long as you like. But perhaps you have a yearning to return to singing?" Harvey rose from his chair and looked questioningly at Constance.

"Mr. Winslow, I left the stage because I fell in love with Hugh. Now, I have Jeff and Jeff is my life. I was single and alone then. I was fortunate to have a singing voice and had to use the skill available to me to survive. I am a good woman, and I intend to continue being a good mother. Now, I have no interest in singing for an audience or to be constantly moving from city to city. The proper home for Jeff's and me is now here if you will have us." Constance waited for Harvey's reply and happily found her trepidation unfounded.

"Your bedroom is upstairs. My grandson's is next to yours. Second and third door to the right." At this terse reply, Harvey turned and left the room.

It will take some time for Harvey and Constance to get to know one another, but for the moment, three grieving people will be able to support each other in whatever way they can.

✳✳✳

At the Caid place, Mav and Macy were talking about the future, and Macy gave Mav a letter from President Danforth of the Perciville Reduction Company that had arrived just before he returned from the Valley of Tears.

"I have read the letter, Mav, and they are proposing an agreement to purchase all of the bauxite that our land can produce for the next twenty years. They mention that the mining of the bauxite is a destructive process and will leave the land scarred. Since we don't plan to live there, it may be something to consider. He is awaiting your acceptance to begin to talk face to face. He also mentions that he will be in Chicago for a few days in March if you are inclined to meet with him. I know you will be going to Chicago to take the diamonds to Mr.

Benoit so, maybe you will be able to meet with Mr. Danforth then." Macy waited for Mav to respond.

"Well, I was a-plannin' to go in February, but March would work also. I'll write to Mr. Danforth today." That settled, Mav poured the last of the coffee.

By the end of January, Mav had settled on the date, time, and place of the meeting with Danforth, and Mav had read about bauxite in his cyclopedia and now felt that he could have a conversation about it and not feel intimidated by the more knowledgeable Danforth. Mav had also consulted his lawyer, Derick Tarr, about the type of agreement that would be equitable, the pitfalls and such that landowners must avoid when entering such contracts.

By the time March rolled around, he was ready to take his annual trip to Chicago, a practice he began in 1895 when he sold the first of the diamonds from the Valley of Tears to Reginald Benoit for his jewelry manufacturing enterprise. Each trip had produced more money, most of which is on deposit with the Beaton bank and has grown to a sizable amount. Fortunately, the farm and ranch income have been enough to keep the Caid place running smoothly and expanding as needed, so the proceeds from the diamonds are untouched. The acquisition of the land now known to have a rich deposit of bauxite was serendipity. A trip delayed by an incident of the train's engine failure near the site of the land allowed Mav to rent a horse from the local livery and tour the immediate countryside while the railway company brought another engine to the train. He found the property that he purchased, much in the manner he found and purchased the home-place. Macy had questioned the purchase at the time, given its remoteness from Beaton, but she did not oppose it. Until the letter came from the Perciville Reduction Company of Pittsburg, she had mostly forgotten about it. Now, it looked like the family would have another source of income beyond farming and cattle ranching.

Mav Caid — The Complete Story

"Macy, I've done some ponderin' 'bout some things Billy Sunday said when he come through Beaton, an' I've done some rec'lectin' what Dr. Chesney said about how Lyla would have been cared fo' ina hospital had there been one in Beaton. The closest one I know of is in Littlerock. That's too far to be useful to folks around here. Dr. Chesney is a good doctor, but with th' growin' town, he seems over-worked. Ailin' folks call him out night an' day. Ifn Beaton had a hospital, it would attract more doctors over time, an' people in th' area would get faster medical care. We have enough money deposited in the bank to git things started. Would you be in favor o' buildin' a hospital?" Mav waited.

"That sounds like a pretty ambitious undertaking, Mav. We would need a lot of help to see something like that to fruition. Who could we get to help?"

"Dr. Chesney, for one. I reckon he might have a great interest in it. It would mean that, 'stead of treatin' people in his home or in th' patient's home, they could git treated ina hospital with othern…uh, <u>others</u>, to help caring fo' them until recovery. He wouldn't have to do everythin' as he does now."

Such was the beginning of Mav's realization of how the power of the tears of the Sun he has collected from the Valley of Tears, can be employed to bring healing to the citizens of Beaton and area around. Dr. Chesney was, indeed, an investor and promoter of the idea, as were the churches, Mayor Bentley, the city leaders, and most importantly, the business owners of Beaton. The hospital will be two years in the planning and construction, but when completed will accommodate twelve to twenty patients, and Dr. Chesney has contacted two doctors that have an interest in joining the staff of the Caid-Chesney Tears of the Sun Hospital of Beaton when completed. Over the years, many people will wonder about its strange name, but it remains the secret of one man, benefactor Mav Caid.

Chapter 34

The Abduction

Tuesday afternoon enfolds a tranquil countryside and reveals an Arkland stagecoach traveling from Oklahoma toward Beaton, a stage-stop on the way to El Dorado and other locations not served by rail. On board are six passengers, three ladies one of whom is middle-aged, the others in their twenties; also, aboard are two men in their forties or fifties, and a younger hard-bitten man who appears not to be an associate of the others, while the others, by their conversation, are.

There are no hangers-on, or rooftop travelers outside, only the Jehu, the stagecoach driver, and a guard, or Shotgun, as many call him. As they arrive in Beaton and dismount, all enter the stagecoach-stop to have a meal and wait for the stage to depart. All except the hard-bitten man who receives a long package from the coach's boot then ambles directly to the livery stable.

Entering the stable, he requests to rent a horse for a few days. He will also need all other accouterments to dress the horse for riding.

"I'll need a horse and all trimmings," said the stranger to the blacksmith who owned and managed the stables.

"I don't know you," replied Sullivan Jade, proprietor. "Ere you new 'round here?"

"Just passing through and wanting to look the place over." The stranger offers no more information.

"I'll need to know who you are," Sulli replied, "and I'll need a deposit of one hundred dollars. And you must return the horse and everything else by noon, Saturday or another hundred dollars is due.

"Name's Caleb Farenthold." With that pronouncement, a one-hundred-dollar bill was handed to Sulli, and Caleb Farenthold walked out the back of the barn to select one from the containment corral. Caleb picked a large, powerful buckskin and led him to the barn where he placed the rented blanket and saddle across the horse. Circling to the other side he released the tied-up stirrup and latigo strap to fall free, then returning to the mounting side of the bay and reaching beneath the horse, Caleb Farenthold threads the latigo through the cinch ring and rigging ring to cinch the saddle tightly, tying the latigo with a four-in-hand tie. Lastly, Caleb bridles the horse. As he works to prepare the buckskin, he mumbles to himself about the center fire saddle that has only one cinch strap: 'This won't hold for nothin' goin downhill!' Finishing, he adjusts the stirrups to the length of his long legs and, finally, affixes the saddle holster for the rifle he had unpacked from the package and belts a 44 Colt revolver around his waist, tying the holster to his leg. Fully armed, the hard-bitten stranger, Caleb Farenthold appears dangerous.

Caleb mounts his horse and slowly rides through Beaton to become familiar with the look and feel of the town. On this short ride, he locates three of the places of most interest, —the sheriff's office, saloon, and a boarding house that rents by the week. Stopping before the saloon, Caleb Farenthold dismounts and wraps his reins around the hitching rail then turns to watch the stagecoach continue its trip to El Dorado. As the stage moves down the post road, he steps up to the wooden platform where he pauses again and surveys the town's main street. Finally, he steps into the saloon where he cautiously studies the people inside. Walking to the bar, Caleb Farenthold motions to the bardog, as men of the west often call a barista, and ordered a shot of Baker's Pure Rye Whiskey.

Caleb brought the shot glass of rye to his lips and downed it. Pushing the glass forward, signaled for another pour. "I'm looking for a place I heard might be hiring ranch-hands. Perhaps you could point me to the Winslow ranch. I'd be much obliged."

As Terry Marcus, the young man behind the bar, poured another rye, he answered: "The Winslow place is about six miles to the east of the post road to Littlerock. You can't miss it. There is a wooden lintel mounted over the gate, the only one within five miles. The lintel is painted red and has Winslow carved into it, painted white. You know the Winslows?"

"No. Never met the owner, only his son, Hugh. I hope our past friendship will help me hire on as a hand for his papa." Caleb downed the second glass and signaled for another.

"Oh, then you haven't heard. Hugh was killed on the road 'bout a year ago. Ambushed by some highwaymen as he was coming back to the ranch with his wife and son. I'm sorry to have to break the news about your friend." Terry showed a face of sadness to the stranger who simply pursed his thin lips and stared ahead at the image of Sheriff Hickatrisk reflecting in the mirror behind the bar as the officer of the law entered the saloon and began speaking with the customers.

Terry looked closely at Caleb, saying: "I wouldn't have taken you for a sheep herder. I would have figured you more the cattle type."

"Sheep? Well…I've worked both. Just looking for an honest buck for an honest day's work." Caleb eyed the new arrival to the saloon who was moving about talking to people he knew and looking at those he did not.

"Well, barkeep, reckon I need to be getting along. Thanks for your directions." Caleb tossed the coins across the bar to pay for his whiskey and turned around while evading the attention of the sheriff who was talking to a card player at one of the tables.

Caleb Farenthold, road agent, bank robber, train robber, cold killer, wanted in Texas, New Mexico, and Arizona, mounts his rented horse, and slowly leaves Beaton riding toward the Winslow place six miles east. Arriving on the road leading to the ranch house, Caleb surveys the surrounding terrain, picks a secluded vantage point then ties his horse to a bush. From his saddlebag, Caleb retrieves a monocular telescope and waits.

For three days he would ride out to this vantage point and wait for hours watching, then ride back to Beaton where he had rented a room in the boarding house called the Sunrise. Each night he would stand in the window and stare at the activity surrounding the saloon, but would not enter again, not embracing unnecessary exposure. On the third day, Caleb observes a ranch wagon bearing a young woman and a boy heading toward Beaton on some errand. He smiles, congratulating himself on his patience. It is time.

As the wagon turned onto the main road to Beaton, Caleb swung a leg over his horse and settled into the saddle. Falling in behind the wagon, Caleb matched their speed until he could see clearly that there were no other travelers on the road before spurring his horse to approach closer to the wagon. Drawing abreast, Caleb shouted: "Skinner, Pull up! Stop your team!" then to emphasize his demand, pulled his Colt and pointed at the driver.

Wherry, the black driver, reined in the team drawing the wagon to a stop. Constance pulled Jeff closer to her to protect him from the perceived threat. She looked into the eyes of evil, hard eyes that seemed familiar and frightening. The eyes of Caleb Farenthold are cold, the color of an unpainted plank of barn wood turns in the sun after ten years. Gray. Hard. Penetrating. Predator eyes, staring steadily beneath strong dark brows on bronzed skin. The thin face sported a drooping mustache of graying hair that reached Caleb's jaw line below thin lips, —a face on which a sinister smile wafted across its sunburned surface for a moment before turning back to stone-cold immobility, with lips a slash with no curvature, up or down. Strait and bitter.

Without a word, Caleb motioned for Constance to come to him and for emphasis, pointed his gun at Jeff. Caleb's threat was unmistakable, and her fear told her to comply without resistance. She stood in the wagon bed and moved toward Caleb, who waited. As she came within reach, Caleb held out his hand to assist her in mounting behind him. Holding Caleb's outstretched hand, Constance leaned over and placed her other hand on Caleb's shoulder, then stepped from the wagon onto the rump of Caleb's horse and slid down behind her captor. Caleb pointed his gun again at the driver, Wherry, and fired. Constance winced, but stifled a scream, hoping this evil man would not turn his aim onto Jeff.

Caleb spurred his horse toward the line of trees paralleling the road then urged his horse back in the direction of Beaton, stopping behind some thick undergrowth.

"My son?" began Constance, her question immediately interrupted by Caleb, saying:

"He's good. My partner has taken him by now to a safe place, for the moment."

"What do you want from me?" asked Constance, trembling at the veiled threat to Jeff.

"Information," responded Caleb. "Information your husband gave you."

"I don't have any…You knew him?" asked Constance, surprise showing.

Eugene Stonefield

"I killed him," replied Caleb Farenthold, a.k.a., Caleb Faren.

Constance turned pale, and felt her heart began to pound even harder than it was beating already. Her face turned cold, and she tried to focus on the meaning of the moment. Why? was a question that she could not answer. 'Jeff has been left alone with a dead man on a hitched wagon with a team that could run wild, or he could be in the hands of another killer. Jeff could get down and wander away, possibly get lost.' All the possible tragic things that could occur are running through her mind. She must get control. She must conquer her fear.

"What kind of information am I supposed to have?" asked Constance, keeping her voice low and conversational, trying hard to control her breathing as her heart raced.

"The location of the Lost Dutchman mine in Superstition mountains of Arizona," returned Caleb Faren, while pulling from a shirt pocket a letter he obtained from a box of packed correspondence Caleb rifled through after the killing of Hugh Winslow. Waving the letter at Constance, Caleb said: "This proves that your husband learned the location of the mine from a reservation Indian when he was the Indian Agent at Fort Apache. He must have had a map. I searched a dead man, but the map was not on his person, nor was it in the contents of the wagon; therefore, you have it. You escaped from our camp while we slept. Only you could have taken the map." Caleb shook the piece of paper at Constance. As he described his analysis of why the map was missing, his voice became shriller, and the words spilled more rapidly. It was the only time Caleb Farenthold stepped from the seemingly rational demeanor to the irrational. Constance became engulfed by a more intense fear for herself and her son. She recalled that Hugh had spoken about the craziness regarding the mine that had affected people in the area in strange ways. Seemingly normal people offered hand drawn maps as collateral on loans or thrown into the pot at the gambling tables, sure paths to wealth, was the claim of fools looking to get rich quickly or looking to defraud. She recalled

Hugh showing her one of the maps found sewn into the lining of the coat of a murdered man who ventured into the mountains, sacred to the Apache, one of many who followed their greed to the grave. She knew her husband often wrote to others about the insanity associated with the legend of the mine. Caution told Constance to deny knowing anything about it.

"I know nothing about it and everything I had at the time was left on the wagon when my son and I escaped," replied Constance. "As you recall, we were tied to a wagon wheel when everyone went to sleep after a day of drinking. Jeff and I escaped at night on the only saddled horse available to us. We took nothing of our own with us."

"You were a long way from here then. Who helped you get here?" asked Caleb.

Constance remained silent, reluctant to give this dangerous man, this killer, any information that could cause harm to anyone. Eventually, she could only think of her son.

Caleb allowed Constance to assume he would permit her silence. Finally, Caleb said: "You may recall, I told you that my partner had your son and he was safe for a while. Well, his safety may rest on my returning with the map. Now, who?"

Constance could not counter the anxiety of her inability to help her son in any way but to comply with Caleb's demand and prey for a miracle. "It was Mav Caid who helped me to get here. We met by chance and came in together. But he knows nothing either because he couldn't have received a map or anything about any Lost Dutchman mine if I didn't have it, and I did not." Constance wrung her hands as she replied, exhibiting both fear and agitation at having a demand made of her that could have such severe repercussions and have no way of satisfying the requirement to tender what she did not have.

Calm returned to Caleb Faren, and he listened patiently to her answer, then answered: "Your words don't convince. Let's go talk to Mr. Caid. I think my partner will be patient, unless, of course, he sees a posse nosing around. Then…my partner…he hates kids. He would probably drop him off somewhere. There are many cliffs in this area, hanging out over the river." Constance shivered at the thought and told him where to find the Caid place.

As events were unfolding within this secluded, brush cluttered copse, a young boy sat crying and calling for his mother in a wagon with a dead man. Within the hour, another wagon destined for Beaton came upon the scene, and its driver took Jeff back to the Winslow ranch where the boy told his story to his grandfather. Harvey immediately dispatched a rider to Beaton to report the shooting and kidnapping of Constance Winslow to Sheriff Lars Hickatrisk, and a grandfather with his grandson followed to make a full report and take the body of the dead driver in to the authorities. By the time they arrived at Sheriff Hickatrisk's office, Deputy Bascom and a posse of local volunteers were searching the area between Beaton and the site of the kidnapping.

Chapter 35

Greed's Captive

Macy was unprepared for visitors riding up to the house at the Caid place as it was known, and would not have thought to take any precautions anyway when she saw Constance seated behind the unknown rider. Her initial response was one of surprise and perplexity. Why would Constance be double riding with another person, and who is this strange tall, hawk-faced man with such a severe visage? Macy wondered as she prepared her greeting.

"Why, Constance! What brings you so far from home? Is everything all right?" typical queries expressed by Macy. Constance, however, did not reply.

Caleb turned and reached around Constance to encircle her in his strong arm and sweeping her from his horse lowered her to the ground. Constance ran to Macy and whispered: "be careful what you say. They have Jeff."

Dismounting, Caleb turned to face Macy and Constance. "Ladies," announced Caleb in a sarcastic voice, as if speaking to a couple of 'fallen ladies' in the bar of perdition, "I would be most pleased if we could go inside for a minute so we may have a friendly discussion. But first, Mrs. Caid, is your husband available?" Caleb is familiar with the sentiment that honey draws more flies than sour milk, but knowing where a potential threat may be, is prudent. The honied tone of Caleb Faren failed to convince his 'ladies'.

Macy looks from Constance to Caleb and replied: "I don't believe I know you. May I ask your name and why you wish to speak with my husband?"

"My apology, Mrs. Caid for my abruptness. My name is Caleb Farenthold, and I wish to speak with your husband about a trip he took a while back at which time he met Mrs. Winslow and accompanied her back to Beaton. Oh, yes, I forgot to mention. Mrs. Winslow currently has a bad case of laryngitis so I will be speaking for her as well." Caleb smiled broadly at Macy and Constance. "But, of course, I am certain that Mrs. Winslow will surely nod her agreement that this matter is one of life or death." Constance looked hard at Caleb but said nothing and did not nod.

"I was prepared to say Mr. Caid is in the barn and will be back momentarily, but I see him returning now," answered Macy to Caleb's question as Mav came out of the barn and saw the trio in front of the house.

"Mav, began Macy as he arrived, "Mr. Farenthold would like to have a few words with you. He and Constance just came. Oh, yes, that new serpentine belt you ordered has come."

For a moment, Mav looked closely at Macy, then turned to address the visitors: "Howdy, Constance. Mr. Farenthold. How can I help you?" Mav formulated an unspoken question, given that he could see only one horse, but didn't vocalize the question. He did look closely at Caleb Farenthold, noting his Colt holster tied to his leg and worn low, gunfighter style.

"Ah, Mr. Caid. Mrs. Winslow and I have been talking about your meeting and returning together to Beaton some time back, and it has occurred to us that you may have received something I seek, perhaps inadvertently, perhaps not. In any case, what I seek is a map of the Superstition Mountain area in Arizona near where Mrs. Winslow and her husband, —God rest his soul! —served as Indian Agent for the Department of Indian Affairs. If you have such a map, I would appreciate your giving it to me now." Caleb Farenthold went silent but rested his hand on his Colt revolver. The implication of danger confirmed to Mav as he saw the look of terror on Constance's face. That Constance had not spoken even to say hello, the single horse tied to the fence post, a stranger, seemingly in charge of the conversation, and the serpentine belt he never ordered, spoke loudly of coercion, and painted a picture of danger.

"Well, now. Let me ponder it. Thar wuz a coat thet Mrs. Winslow…uh, Constance… wuz wearing. As I rec'lect, it wuz a man's coat. Yeah, a coat belongin' to her husband, Hugh, who wuz killed in an ambush. It was blood stained, and Mrs. Winslow was loath to keep it. I do believe thet th' coat was burned in th' fireplace at th' cabin where Mrs. Winslow an' me first met. Perhaps th' coat had th' map. I don't rec'lect knowin' o' one." Mav waited for a response.

"Truly unfortunate," replied Caleb, "I thought this would be so easy, but, perhaps not. Mr. Caid, go get the map, while I converse with these fine ladies."

Mav ignored Caleb's demand and continued: "And then…there wuz th' saddlebags from th' horse she an' her son escaped from captivity on. Since th' horse wuz not hern…I mean, <u>hers</u>, she had no reason to keep th' saddlebags. I rec'lect thet I tossed them in th' loft in my barn an' never looked in them. They're prob'ly still there." Mav began to improvise, to buy time to think, to plan. 'Plan carefully, be patient, be ready and respond with overwhelming force.' A thought familiar to his mind, one written into his constitution since his encounter with Chico and Fenner Korn some years ago.

"Perhaps we are in luck, Mr. Caid. Why don't you and I just mosey down to the barn and have a look? I'm sure the ladies will stay right here where we can see them." As Mav turned away, Caleb gently lifted his Colt and let it ease back in its holster as a subtle warning to Macy and Constance that Mav is his captive. Constance, at least, knows that he will kill.

"We can do thet, I need to let Hardtack, —thet's my horse, —out to graze an' stretch his legs anyhow." Mav walked between Macy and Constance and whispered the word 'serpentine' to which Constance looked perplexed, and Macy smiled, knowing that Mav understood the danger. As Mav, followed by Caleb Farenthold walked toward the barn, Macy told Constance a story of an unusual honeymoon in Villon several years ago.

Arriving at the barn, Mav announced: "Since it mayhap take a while to find th' saddlebag among th' clutter, I'll release Hardtack first." Then, not waiting for a reply, stepped to Hardtack's stall, and led him out into the open center of the barn, while keeping up a friendly-toned dialog about Hardtack and how praiseworthy he is. Caleb listened but kept a close watch on Mav as he led the horse out, patting him on his neck as he moved forward just four feet in front of Caleb. Several times Caleb glanced back to assure himself his 'ladies' had not left.

It was now or never. One seldom recovers lost opportunity. Mav gently guided Hardtack into a desired alignment, continuing to lightly scratch the horse's neck, moving his hand closer to his ear, then suddenly Mav moved his hand, sticking a finger down into the Hardtack's ear and witnessing the explosion of Hardtack's back hooves lash out in a hard kick, right to the body of an unfortunate visitor. The kick was so sudden and so unexpected that Caleb could not have prepared, nor avoided the ruptured spleen and the fractured ribs that befell him. Caleb fell to the ground gasping for air and groaning, a hand holding his side, neglecting the Colt just inches away.

Mav moved quickly to disarm Caleb as the injured kidnapper lay writhing on the ground and trying to recover his breath that now became laborious and painful.

Stepping outside the barn from which Hardtack had just bolted, Mav waved at Macy and Constance to come. As they ran toward him, he returned to Caleb and helped him into the bed of his farm wagon where he tied his ankles and his wrists in preparation for a painful trip to Beaton.

Stopping outside the sheriff's office, Mav began to tell the sheriff of the recent events: "Sheriff Hickatrisk, Constance tol' me thet th' man in ourn…uh, <u>our</u> wagon is th' one who killed her husband Hugh when they wuz… uh…<u>were</u> travelin' back to Beaton. Mr. Farenthold has suffered an unfortunate accident back at my place. Hardtack took exception to something, an' he wuz hard-kicked. Someone might orta tell Dr. Chesney. Constance has…" Constance could wait no longer and interrupted Mav:

"My son, Jeff, has been kidna…" she would get no further as Jeff, was at that time returning from the soda parlor where Sheriff Hickatrisk's wife took him in reward for his telling what had occurred on the road when Caleb Farenthold took his mother and killed Wherry.

As a gentle collision between mother and son occurred, and tears flowed freely, Mav, Macy, and Sheriff Hickatrisk left the room. Once outside, Sheriff Hickatrisk called to a volunteer messenger to ride out and call back the posse.

It was hard to believe how so much could have happened in the space of six hours. Hard too, is the difficulty in understanding how far a greedy person will go to pursue a rumor of riches when they never existed at all. There was no map. Is there a lost mine in the Superstition range? Many died thinking so. The letter? Only a tale of the kind of stories people are acting upon and dying for in the Apache sacred grounds called Superstition Mountains of Arizona. How the Sierra de la Espuma, or Foam Mountains, came to be named 'Superstition Mountains' perhaps is lost in the fog of history, but it is known to be sacred to the Apache, a land that deserved protection from the trespasses of those who would trample upon the spiritual presences known to the Yavapai. If the rich gold mine of Jacob Waltz that he revealed to his boarding house owner, Julia Thomas, from his deathbed is real may never be known. Many searched for it. Many died violent deaths. Whether fact or myth, the tale will continue to appear in frontier fiction magazines by freelance authors seeking to parlay legend into cash. These 'dime novels' found popularity among the reading citizenry who found romance in the tales of the frontier. Perhaps realization of the wealth of the Lost Mine of the Superstition Mountains comes penny by penny in the telling and retelling of the story, a telling by writers who have never been near the mountains, but exercise their imaginations on Oliver Visible Typewriters and the later innovations of the companies, Underwood and Royal.

Chapter 36

A New Day

This is a new day in the year 1902, and the Caid-Chesney Tears of the Sun hospital is celebrating a grand opening. A person receiving medical services in a hospital is rare in Arkansas in 1902. Soldiers and officers of the military have hospitals on the posts of their assignment. For all others, options are more limited. Although in the more populated cities like New York, Chicago, and San Francisco there are hospitals built by private interests, churches or civic organization, most citizens of small towns and rural areas of Arkansas receive needed care at home, —other than one notable exception in Arkansas. That exception is in the treatment of neurological diseases for which treatment a person would be committed to the Arkansas State Lunatic Asylum in Littlerock. Founding of the facility for the treatment of nervous disorders received approval by Governor Elisha Baxter, and the facility opened in March 1873. Admission to the facility was often a one-way trip.

Eugene Stonefield

But for the health of the physical body, to cure disease and illness, citizens relied on four protocols: knowledge gained from personal experience and that of others; the proclaimed skills and knowledge of Indian medicine that permeates the hinterland; an occasional physician with medical training such as Dr. Chesney; and the distribution of elixirs by owners of traveling medicine shows. To many, the owners of the latter, the medicine shows, are known as 'snake-oil salesmen', a pejorative moniker derived from an old Chinese concoction containing fat of the Chinese water snake that purportedly was a treatment for real snake bites. Western medicinal claims based on the inclusion of snake fat or snake venom were mostly false, although an Abilene, Texas entrepreneur, Clark Stanley, made a business in selling his patented elixir named Clark Stanley's Snake Oil Liniment that he advertised in newspapers and sold through apothecaries throughout the nation.

The beginning of the twentieth century was a period of *laissez-faire*, a time when there was no governmental oversight of products, and anything, however worthless or dangerous, could be sold to a willing buyer. 'Let the buyer beware,' was the admonition. Following the well-known adage 'the healthy person has a million wants, a sick person has only one' and the stage is set for 'snake-oil salesmen' to come to the market with miraculous concoctions for all that ails. Alcohol was a far more common component of these elixirs and concoctions, but the inclusion of opiates was not unknown. Manufacturers sold these concoctions, compounds and topically applied rubefacients to treat mild pain and various discomforts. Every human organ known or suspected deserved a specific pill, powder, elixir, or tonic to assure health and wellbeing. Traveling medicine shows promoting concocted salves and potions to cure ailments of whatever description crisscrossed the country, and their businesses thrived on the naivety of the customers and willingness of those customers to attribute natural healing to effects of the concoctions.

False attribution of their curative powers led many to ignore dangerous health conditions, even when scientifically proven medical options were available. Many curable diseases ran their destructive course when, had proven medicines and medical procedures been available and applied, the sufferer may have received a cure. When the citizenry's ignorance or naivety is ripe, the snake-oil salesmen strike. Even with the presence of Dr. Chesney, Beaton was not immune to visits by the traveling medicine shows.

Today in the Summer of 1902, Mav Caid, Dr. Chesney, and various luminaries of Beaton meet on the bandstand near the lake for the official announcement of the opening of the long-awaited Caid Chesney Tears of the Sun Hospital. The local band has welcomed the crowd and the mayor, James Holbrook, has made his statement as have others, and the ceremony is nearing completion at which time, Mayor Holbrook, Mav Caid and Dr. Chesney will walk to the hospital and officially cut the ribbon and open the hospital for a grand tour.

"Well, the path was long but worth it," said Mayor Holbrook, and his sentiment received an agreement from Mav and Dr. Chesney.

"A new doctor is due in within the week. His name is Richard Turnbull, whose medical training is from the Columbia's College of Physicians and Surgery in New York. He will be a VIP in Beaton, I predict." Dr. Chesney smiled, knowing that he was instrumental in getting Dr. Turnbull to commit to moving so far away from his roots. Both doctors are investors in the hospital so share ownership with the Caid family and several others in the Beaton area.

"That is good," agreed Mav, "maybe Beaton will become a mecca to folks around here in time."

"It feels like a new day," added Macy, who had joined the three as they conversed on the bandstand. "It seems that it was just yesterday that the city council approved of its construction."

As they continued their conversation and eventually, their guided tour of the new hospital, a medicine wagon was drawing near to

Beaton. Driving the wagon is the famed Dr. Asklepion, past physician and surgeon for the Emperor Napoleon of France. Dr. Asklepion and his equally notable niece, the midwife, Agnes Agnodice, rode in the springboard and rocked back and forth to the discordant rhythm of the road, bringing their power to heal the ailments of the excellent folk of Beaton.

"Agnes," began Dr. Asklepion, "that last stop wasn't as profitable as I had hoped. I sure hope Beaton isn't as bad. Some people seem to be moving away from our French cures. I think it may be time to bring out the Egyptian cures. What are your thoughts?"

"It wouldn't be hard. We would have to get new labels to paste over those on our present stock of potions and elixirs, but that's not so difficult. We can probably get labels printed in Beaton since it has a press for a weekly newspaper."

"What products would we need to relabel?" said Dr. Asklepion.

"We have potions for the liver, kidneys, and stomach in liquid form, and balms for burns, hemorrhoids, carbuncles, and pills for catarrh, scrofula and rheumatism, of which," replied Agnes, "only the liquid elixirs would need relabeling."

Agnes looks back into the covered wagon bed at the closed container of their new potion for rejuvenation of vitality for folks over forty, or folks over twenty if the crowd is youthful. "The new potion is fermenting now. It should be ready for bottling. What should we call it?"

"I don't know. What all's in it anyway? That will give us a clue," returned Dr. Asklepion.

"I was able to acquire some eucaine, cannabis indica, bear bile and cohosh, but I haven't used the cohosh since we sold some to some expectant women and several had bad results and went into premature labor. Also, I acquired some morphine and heroin, and something called chloral hydrate someone recommended for helping with sleep troubles when we were in St. Louis. I didn't use those though. But I included some laudanum that we got in St. Louis and, of course, I put in some calomel. We can promote the potion as an invigorating elixir that also assures a person regularity and a nice night of sleep. First the sleep, then the invigoration." Agnes was comfortable in her thought on how a person taking the elixir may respond to it in the short run, knowing, of course, the desired response is that they buy it and not suffer after-effects until their medicine show had left town.

"How about Dr. Asklepion's Laudable Potion for the Restoration of Slumber and Vigor," Dr. Asklepion asked his trusted partner while snapping the reins to signal a faster pace.

"A little long in the title, but printed properly in two lines, should be fine." Dr. Asklepion shook the reins again to encourage his lethargic team to step up the pace.

"And, I think I may have added some fennel for flavor, and, of course, an alcohol base as we always use. We are out of whiskey, so this time I used applejack," Agnes continued as she recalled the items brewed into the new elixir.

"That fennel for flavor…what else does it do?" returned Dr. Asklepion.

Agnes thought a minute, then replied: "I don't know. I heard someone say it was good for restoring eyesight. I guess we will find out. Oh, yes, I have some Indian Pink, that destroys worms in children."

"Well, I guess if it is bad for worms in children, it's bad for worms in adults. Put some of that in," said Dr. Asklepion. "Anything else in the wagon?"

"I have some crude antimony, dulcified spirits of salt, ipecacuanha, and ambergris that we could use, and for flavor, licorice," Agnes replied, authoritatively.

"Ipecacuanha? What does that do?" asked Dr. Asklepion.

"I was told that was a powerful emed…no, emetic, whatever that is, but it came from Doc Tate in Waco, so it should be good," returned

Agnes. "Doc Tate sells his own products called Tate-Lax and Tate-O-Rub in shows just like ours throughout Texas. He uses real musicians to open his shows. Some of the musicians are really good and bring in a good crowd. You should remember Doc Tate, he's the one who built that building near Waco out of large chunks of minerals and volcanic glass. The building with all the colors of the rainbow."

Nearing Beaton, Dr. Asklepion and Agnes Agnodice pulled off the main road into a pasture to camp for the night, assuring time to mix and bottle their magic potion and prepare their presentation. Tomorrow they would enter the town of Beaton amidst all the noise they can make to attract attention.

By nine o'clock in the morning, a brightly colored covered wagon unfolds near the bandstand next to the lake. Colorful banners and fluttering flags wave in the trees in the area as a hand-cranked Edison gramophone blares out Sousa's <u>Stars and Stripes Forever</u> from its faux morning glory trumpet while famous Dr. Asklepion and Agnes Agnodice stand upon the platform lowered from the rear of the wagon. Agnes Agnodice stands arrayed in eye-catching colorful clothes as Dr. Asklepion stands in the background in severe black attire, proper for his station; each looking anxiously at the town's morning activity and waiting for citizens to recognize their presence. Dr. Asklepion is artificially aged to give credence to his claim of the physician to an emperor, however preposterous. Within an hour, people begin to assemble in front of the two hawkers of medical miracles and stand, listening to the promotion of their never-fail elixirs. Several people familiar with these medicine shows had come by earlier seeking employment while the show is in in town. It is a common practice by medicine shows to hire local citizens to give testimony on the efficacy of the elixirs offered, and frequently referenced to provide proof of their product's worth. They were always enthusiastic and positive in their testimony.

"Ladies and gentlemen of Beaton," began Agnes, "you and your fine town of Beaton are fortunate to have been selected for this visit by world famous Dr. Asklepion, past physician and surgeon to the Emperor of France, Napoleon Bonaparte, even into his exile until his premature death. But that event, ladies and gentlemen will result in your being able to experience the great healing properties of <u>Dr. Asklepion's Laudable Potion for the Restoration of Slumber and Vigor</u>, that you will be able to purchase today. You will then be able to say that you fully understand how Emperor Napoleon Bonaparte had the energy and superior vigor to command his troops in his campaigns in Europe, and you will understand how Dr. Asklepion has attained his advanced age with the vigor you see before you, and finally, ladies and gentlemen, you too, will be able to sleep well and rise up in the morning with vigor and happiness that goes with good health. Ladies and gentlemen, welcome Dr. Asklepion."

A standard introduction of the world-famous medical man faded into a full-press sales pitch of the most recent concoction brewing in the wagon that he and Agnes bottled, corked, labeled, and sold on the spot. First person testimonials assured the audience that no fraud could occur and that each purchaser would sleep well tonight and awake invigorated by this secret formulation. No one thought to question how this world-famous Dr. Asklepion might have provided services to Napoleon when he had died eighty-one years ago. No, the claim could have been valid, after all, look and this aged man with his gray hair and beard. He seems to be a centenarian himself. Didn't he say he was hundred-thirteen years old? He probably took daily doses of his potion himself. Why would he not? He does attest to the elixir being the reason for his vitality and long life. And there are other testimonials.

Eugene Stonefield

"Have you seen what's occurring near the bandstand?" inquired Dr. Chesney of the new Dr. Turnbull who had recently arrived in Beaton.

"I thought all of this was a thing of the past," replied Turnbull, "it is demeaning to be considered just one of the options for medical treatment, —mothers' traditions, science, Indian, and today, — traveling snake oil sellers!"

The travelers stayed two days, the safe number of days to remain in one place, given the uncertain effect of their products sold to their customers. By Thursday, various folks became less than invigorated. On the fourth day, Drs. Chesney and Turnbull began seeing patients come in with similar symptoms: headache, dizziness, vomiting, nausea, insomnia, severe diarrhea, and muscle cramps.

Informed citizens of Beaton know that just before the turn to the new century, between years 1881 and 1896, an epidemic of cholera occurred, —the fifth wave of the disease since its first occurrence in 1816, —so the initial fear in the minds of Drs. Chesney and Turnbull was that this could herald another iteration of the dread disease. Science has eclipsed the original beliefs in the cause of disease being a punishment of God, or brought by immigrants, or a spontaneous generation, or the miasma theory that diseases ensue from 'bad air,' and was vigorously exploring germ theory as the cause of disease transmission. Research into this theory was still in its infancy. However, the medical communities in Europe were already developing vaccines for smallpox from a similar cattle disease called cowpox, and a potential vaccine for diphtheria is under scrutiny by medical scientists, but most causation theories are searching for proofs. To address the immediate crisis, it would fall to Drs. Chesney and Turnbull to make the diagnosis of this dread, possibly deadly disease plaguing the citizens around Beaton.

"Dr. Chesney," spoke Dr. Turnbull, "the professors at Columbia are looking at a path of transmission of cholera that involves the contamination of water. It looks quite certain."

"Dr. Turnbull," returned his colleague, Dr. Chesney, "people around here get their water from lakes, rivers, and wells. It is unlikely that there is a contamination in all sources in the area, only one or two perhaps. Perhaps we need to find out where the sick folks are getting their water."

"I agree completely, Dr. Chesney," replied Dr. Turnbull. "Maybe we should go further and find all commonalities. Let's write up a list of questions to ask each patient and see if anything else is common."

The two doctors compiled a list of questions to ask of each patient who came to the hospital. The results were that there was a very little commonality of drinking water for folks outside Beaton, great commonality of water for those living in Beaton, but one that stood out above others, —all the sick people had bought a bottle of <u>Dr. Asklepion's Laudable Potion for the Restoration of Slumber and Vigor!</u>

The cure prescribed by the two good doctors was most severe, — stop taking Dr. Asklepion's potion immediately. Many patients left their offices in the new hospital looking sheepish and wondering how they could have been so naive. Though it is doubtful that the elixir, with its fennel, improved a person's eyesight, without question, it improved their hindsight

Chapter 37

The Past Surfaces

Mav Caid and wife Macy sit upon chairs they have taken to the front porch discussing their lives and dreams for the future. In this, they do as all couples do eventually. They have come to that unique point in life where they do not understand where all the time has gone. Both are approaching middle-age. They see the sands of time half-poured from the amphora of tomorrows into the basin of yesterdays. While hope embraces possibilities limited only by the mind's ability to imagine, truth enfolds but one, —fact, and much hope fades to time as they progress through life and confront life's realities. They have suffered the heartbreak of Lyla's death and have experienced the joy of seeing Case take the spelling bee for the first time and win, the result of his virtually memorizing his Webster's Blue-Back book that schools use to teach grammar and as a reader for practicing their learned skill of reading. They, long ago, ceded the hope that there would be more children born to them and have concentrated upon matters at hand. They have had the good fortune to see the purchase of land become a source of income from the mining of bauxite and have helped to build a hospital for the needs of the citizenry of Beaton and rural surroundings. They are successful, altruistic, worthy citizens of Arkansas, and life goes on. As in most families, porch chair conversations, like kitchen table conversations, are planning sessions.

"Macy, I'm thinking of digging another well and putting a windmill on it to keep that stock tank full for the dairy herd. This year's drought has hampered its being refilled by rain." Mav pointed to the place he thought would be the right place for the well and windmill.

Macy followed his pointing, then said: "I think that's a great idea. It would be wonderful if we had electricity to the place and wouldn't have to use a windmill to pump the water, but I know that is quite a way off. I have been noticing the receding water level lately. We could use more rain."

Digging of the well began a week later and was progressing well when Mav discovered an unusual object about two to three feet below the surface. The rust and clay encrusted object showed significant deterioration from its long burial, but was recognizable as an iron cross with the base of the cross constructed to receive a wooden pole, —a Christian cross manufactured for displaying several feet above the head of the carrier. Both Mav and Macy were familiar with the pole-mounted cross from pictures in the cyclopedia.

"What do you make of this?" Mav asked Macy when taking the find into the house.

"I don't know. I have seen no evidence that there was any kind of church here. Perhaps someone passing through sometime in the past lost it," returned Macy. "Does it matter?"

"Matter? Oh, only as a curiosity. How did it get so deep underground? It must be quite old." Mav responded. "Maybe something else will turn up to give us a clue."

And find he did. By the time the well was down to the water table some twenty feet down, Mav had recovered several other items. A large spur rowel that appeared to be of silver. Three coins of age, two seem to be silver, the other of copper, broken arrowheads, and metal parts of some weapon and some buttons. Mav placed all items in a box and stored them in the barn. Resolution of curiosities must always be secondary to needs of the present.

"The windmill will be arriving in a week or two. Billy, Case, and I will assemble and install it, and we should be up and running a month from now," said Mav.

"Don't you let Case get hurt. He's still a boy," admonished Macy.

'Mothers never change,' thought Mav. 'My ma said the same thing the first-time pa put me on a horse.' The old plow horse could not move faster than a walk. Mav smiled at the thought but recalled the horrible way she died at the hand of Chico. Mav will always carry a self-imposed blame for not being at home in Bandera to interfere with the killing of his family, —believing that he would have been able to kill Chico before the carnage, a belief that bears no certainty, but an inevitability. From that belief in the certainty of a positive result comes the self-blame. Mav will also carry self-blame for the death of Lyla, although reason should tell him he could not be at fault for the ravages of disease for which the medical community has no cure. Self-blame, a grip of grief so hard for one to dispel.

"I have been reading about explorers thet came this way many years ago. One of them, Hernando de Soto, came to Florida in 1539 and spent several years exploring th' lands thet are now Florida, Georgia, Alabama, an' Mississippi, then came to Arkansas territory when he crossed th' river, he named th' Rio Grande, a river th' natives called Meschacebe thet we spell as Mississippi. Hernando wuz a hard man, even cruel, an' took natives as slaves on occasion, but others thought he wuz deathless divinity, an image he sought to promote. Like another explorer of th' new world, Ponce De Leon, Hernando may have been searching fo' th' fabled 'fountain o' youth', magical waters thet made a person retain youth, but more likely, searching fo' gold thet he never found. Eventually, he explored th' northwest part o' th' state's current land area then went south where he died around 1541 an' his soldiers buried him in th' Mississippi River under th' darkness o' night to hide De Soto's death from th' natives who believed him immortal. Wouldn't it be interesting ifn them items we found when digging the well wuz hisn...I mean <u>were</u> his?" Mav looked at Macy.

"How can we find out?" asked Macy.

"I don't know yet," replied Mav.

"Where did you read about De Soto anyway?" asked Macy.

"Th' book is titled <u>Hernando De Soto</u> by Pierre Custodio was jes'...<u>just</u> published. It also has an account by Gonzalo Silvestre, one of his captains. I found it at the Beaton lending library. I think they buy any book thet even mentions Arkansas!

The Caid family spent the remainder of the year managing the growing Caid empire now spanning the state of Arkansas where the Caid brand is on timber, mining, farming, and cattle raising enterprises. Case continued to grow and learn and was becoming a real asset of the family. Mav continued to receive instruction from Case on proper language as Case discovered it, and Mav accepted the criticism with an open mind and an enthusiasm for the growing knowledge of his son. Although habits of a lifetime are difficult to change, Mav remained willing to try, to learn, and to entertain the points of view of others, regarding the subject of discussion.

At eleven, Case was managing the hired hands with the cattle, much of the skills taught by Mav. Mav and Macy still jointly manage farm and dairy operations, but there were five farm hands to perform the everyday chores that freed Mav and Macy to do other things in which they had interest. Macy's interests are engaged in tasks associated with the expansion of the hospital, and she spends much of her time working with the doctors and nurses at the hospital to assure its operational and financial well-being. Mav is now more involved in the bauxite mining enterprise that requires more travel to the site or to Chicago where officials of the Perciville Reduction company hold meetings for their Midwest operation.

"Macy, have you read the Gazette this week?" Mav waves the Gazette at Macy.

"No, what has your attention?" replies Macy.

"The Gazette reports that a volcano destroyed a whole city of Saint-Pierre on th' island of Martinique an' killed thirty-thousand people! Only two survived, a jailed prisoner named Louis-Auguste Cyparis an' a Léon Compère-Léandre. The name of th' volcano is Mt. Pelée. Th' article mentions other natural events such as th' hurricane thet…_that_ destroyed Galveston in 1900 an' tells about an earthquake that happened near us in 1811 called th' New Madrid quake that destroyed th' city of New Madrid in Missouri. Damage even occurred in St. Louis over a hundred-sixty miles away. Says here that there were aftershocks into January of 1812, an' resulted in th' creation of a new lake over in Tennessee. I'll bet folks thought th' world was ending." Mav put the Gazette aside to accept a cup of coffee Macy had placed before him on the table.

In just a few years, Mav will be reading of a similar natural disaster occurring in San Francisco in 1906 where nearly three-thousand people perished. From the less tragic news, he will learn that in 1903 the first cross-country automobile trip by drivers Horatio Nelson Jackson and Sewall K. Crocker departing from San Francisco on May 23, 1903, completed their trip to New York on July 26. He will also read that Orville Wright and his brother, Wilbur attempted the first powered aircraft flight at Kitty Hawk, North Carolina. It is an exciting era.

Eugene Stonefield

✳✳✳

"Mav, are you going to Chicago for the meeting with the Perciville executives this year?" Macy pauses to await an answer before continuing her reading on state-provided sickness insurance programs that some countries in Europe are instituting, and in employer-provided insurance in which employees share in the costs. Here in America, there have been some calls for the creation of a national program to ensure people a basic income after they reach sixty-five years of age, calling it Social Security.

"Well, I plan to go. Is there something you want me to do or get for you while I'm in Chicago?" replied Mav.

"No, I just thought that, if you have the time, you could run those coins you found while digging the well by some of the folks at that Chicago Museum, or at that new College founded by John D. Rockefeller and the American Baptist Education Society. Someone knowledgeable may be able to tell you how old the coins are," responded Macy.

"Sounds like a good idea, Macy. I will do that." Mav returned to his reading.

Mav spent the month of July in Chicago in meetings with executives of the Perciville Reduction Company where they asked him to be a member of their board of directors. Mav was surprised by their confidence in him and when they asked him to come to Pittsburg at his convenience to tour the reduction plant and home office where he could meet all the executives, he readily accepted. Many of those officers he had only communicated with by letter or Western Union telegram, so he welcomed an opportunity to meet them in person. After Mav concluded business with the executives, Mav took an electric tram to the University of Chicago to meet with Professor Sebastian Desoto of the College of History.

"Professor Desoto, I am happy to meet you. Thank you for providing the time from your busy day," began Mav, as he held out a hand.

Professor Desoto shook the hand that was offered and said: "Mr. Caid. Not at all. I have a lot of free time during the summer, and I am happy to help where I can. Now, I understand that you have some coins that you found buried on your property in Arkansas and are wanting to know their age and origin."

"Yes, here are the coins. I found them when I began digging a well. They were about two feet under the surface with a silver spur rowel and an iron cross. I know nothing about old coins, but it may give me a clue to the age of the articles found. Here is the rowel. It is much larger than any I have seen." Mav went silent.

Professor Desoto picked up a magnifying glass and began to study the coins, turning them over and over and shifting them in the light to pick up highlights and shadows. After some minutes, he put the coins down in front of Mav and stated: "Mr. Caid, these coins are very old and an unusual find as far inland as Arkansas. They are Spanish coins called reals. This one is a full reals. This is a one-half, and this is a one-fourth reals. They are the coin of the realm of Spain under Ferdinand and Isabella. To find them this far inland, —given the known paths of the early Spanish explorers, —they could only have come from Hernando de Soto's expedition in the sixteenth century. The rowel is silver and of Spanish design that also points to Hernando de Soto. It is the type of rowel Hernando and his soldiers would have worn in that era. The college library has translations of chronicles from his explorations from Florida through the south and into Arkansas recorded by Luys Hernández de Biedma, representing the Crown, with the expedition. The original chronicle is still extant in the royal archives in Spain since 1544, and English scholar Buckingham Smith translated it into English around 1851. Hernando is the only known Spaniard to come into Arkansas during that period, so I seriously suspect these articles are from his expedition. You have a rare find. Oh, yes, the iron cross. The expedition to the new world began with eight secular priests, two Dominicans, a Franciscan, and a Trinitarian, so the cross could have belonged to any of those."

"I am amazed," said Mav Caid, staring down at the coins. "The names…your name is Desoto and Hernando de Soto…coincidence?" asked Mav.

"The same family," replied the professor. "Desotos have a long history from the days of the Muslim Caliphate of Córdoba. Before then, in Roman times, the history is uncertain. I have been there and have seen the Great Mosque of Córdoba, the Mezquita, and the Alcazar. I have stood on the Roman bridge. The Alcantara, that derives its name from the Arabic al-Qan-Tara, meaning simply, 'the bridge.' The Alcantara, spanning the Tagus River is also known as Trajan's bridge, in recognition of its builder, Emperor Trajan who commissioned the construction between 104 and 106 AD. As are most things Roman, it is quite impressive."

"Professor Desoto, please accept my appreciation for the information you have given to me. I won't waste more of your time." Mav again held out a hand to Professor Desoto.

"Not a waste of time, Mr. Caid. I am always happy to discuss history. If you come to Chicago in the future, come by to see how we have changed. We have many plans for the future of this university." With those words, Professor Desoto shook the hand of Mav and walked Mav to the door.

Mav's last visit was to the Benoit Jewelry store that first brought him to Chicago more than seven years ago with a small bag of diamonds. His association with the owner, Reginald Benoit, has proven durable and suitable for Mav and more recently, good for the people of Beaton.

"Good afternoon, Mr. Benoit," began Mav, smiling at his friend.

"Great to see you again, Mr. Caid," returned Mr. Benoit. "I trust you have been well?"

"Extremely," returned Mav. From this beginning ensued a conversation of reminiscence of past visits and talk of the future. Eventually, Mav left and returned to Beaton.

Chapter 38

A Trail Gift

April 1904 finds Mav Caid riding at a moderate pace down a familiar trail linking the Caid place to the post road into Beaton. The day is warm and sunny with a blustery wind from the southeast and Hardtack shows his enjoyment at being on the trail because he knows that when they return, he will receive a special treat of oatmeal. Suddenly, Hardtack pulls up, stopping just before they enter an area of dense verdure and overhanging branches of massive trees. Hardtack snorts and his ears twitch, clearly indicating something that he is uncertain about, something that he feels is threatening. A scent unfamiliar? A sound unheard by his rider? Mav pats him on the neck and asks him what is wrong, then urges him to begin his moderate pace down the trail. There is no hurry. The path they are traveling today is untraveled by anyone but Mav who discovered it several years ago and deduced that it was an old Indian pathway. It is scenic, and Mav enjoys traveling it even though it is a longer route to Beaton. As he rides, he has no worries. Everything is running smoothly concerning the farm, though others are working it. Mav will have no board member duties for the Perciville Reduction Company until June. Life is to be enjoyed. That does not mean it will not change.

"What's the matter, Hardtack," breathes Mav as he senses a growing reluctance of Hardtack to continue into the dense growth ahead. He scans the trail and sees nothing, so urges Hardtack to keep moving, but, recalling another time several years ago when Hardtack's predecessor, Biscuit's, instincts were correct, and danger hid in the undergrowth, Mav pulled his rifle from its scabbard, strapped to his saddle, and levered a round into the chamber, then continued into the shaded pathway following the trail's curvature deeper into the green tunnel. His thoughts returned to Fenner Korn, whose vengeful nature drove him to stalk Mav and confront him in a similar situation only to die under an unexpected attack by a large catamount, —Mav's totem, as Windwalker had told him. Windwalker told Mav that the catamount would be his protector. He will always wonder about it, but the recollection urged Mav to begin looking carefully in the undergrowth for a tawny colored, golden-eyed mountain lion. Presently, something unusual hanging from one of the branches of the tree redirects his attention, something swinging back and forth like a clock pendulum, beginning to emit a high-pitched cry.

"I swan, Hardtack, what have we here?" remarked an astonished Mav Caid. Thoughts of the catamount disappeared from his mind as thoughts of a different nature emerged.

Closing on the swinging bundle, Mav could see that it was a suspended Indian cradleboard containing an infant, securely enfolded by leather flaps, and laced to the board. Mav stopped beneath the bundled papoose, then looked around, seeing nothing. Like finding a turtle on a fencepost, one knows without a doubt that turtle did not get there by itself. Someone must be nearby, yet he sees only trees.

"Anyone here?" shouts Mav into the verdure. "Is anyone here? Where are you?" Again, he goes quiet to listen. Mav hears nothing in return but the wind through the trees and the crying of the restrained infant, now becoming more insistent. There is no answering voice, only that of the papoose. Mav repeats his call several more times, each time, pausing and listening. Birds alight in the trees, then fly off as he shouts, but no human voice answers. Mav slides his rifle back into its saddle scabbard and removes his bowie from its holster, then stands in the stirrups to reach the swinging cradleboard. Grasping it tightly in his left hand, Mav brings his bowie to bear against the leather thongs suspending the cradleboard, and its sharp edge cuts them through releasing the cradleboard and papoose.

Pushing aside an overhanging cloth, Mav reveals dark eyes in a bronze face surrounded by short black hair. "Howdy, stranger!" Mav whispers to the crying papoose. "You, little turtle, seem to have found yourself in a difficult place." Again, Mav senses a nervousness in Hardtack as he begins to dance in place.

"What's the matter, Hardtack? Have you never seen an Indian cub before?" Nor had Mav, for that matter, without the mother being present. Many times, as a drover for Captain Lytle he had seen families of Indians in camps or moving from one campsite to another with children, but he was never this close to a papoose this young and never had he held one. Aside from the crying, Hardtack was ambivalent to the papoose. But not so to the catamount Hardtack sensed watching through glittering, unblinking eyes, from the dense undergrowth. From the other side of the trail, equally obscured by brush, are another pair of eyes, dark eyes in a bronze face with straight white shoulder-length hair, watching, unseen, undetected. A phantom whose mission is complete, turns and soundlessly disappears among the forest trees.

Mav shouted into the forest a few more times, even yelling his own name, so any hidden person hearing his voice would know that he is taking the papoose, then finally concluding that they were utterly alone. Eventual revelation may reveal what tragic event precipitated leaving a papoose in such precarious straits, or maybe not. As a final act, Mav took his bowie and, with a powerful throw, embedded the knife into the tree where anyone returning to the spot where this unfathomable papoose abandonment had occurred would immediately notice. Mav turned Hardtack around and told him: "Let's go home."

Approaching their cabin at the home-place, Mav saw that no one was outside so rode on into the barn where he dismounted, leaving Hardtack saddled. Taking the papoose in the cradleboard, Mav walked to the house and stepped into the large room. Macy immediately appeared from somewhere, looking shocked at the scene before her.

"Mav?" she said, "Mav?" she repeated when Mav offered no immediate answer, as her husband was busily unlacing the restrictions to free the papoose from its cradleboard.

"It's a papoose," replied Mav, finally. "I found it hanging in a tree."

"Oh. Of course," returned Macy, then raising her voice to counter the sound of the papoose's cries, Macy said: "We have some warm milk in that jug. I'll get it ready. We still have diapers from Lyla. There in the cedar chest. Get one, please." Following was a painful activity that brought back memories of a happy time with Lyla, that ebbed and flowed with the horrible, sorrowful time when those earlier times ended. Macy began rocking an Indian papoose, the foundling, thinking of Lyla, the lost. Rocking and remembering, finally, Macy began softly singing a favorite lullaby of Lyla's, and feeling good, and feeling sad, but continuing with tears flowing, and in a sometimes, breaking voice:

"Hush, little baby, don't say a word,
Mama's going to buy you a Mockingbird.
And if that Mockingbird don't sing,
Mama's going to buy you a diamond ring..."

As the soft voice of Macy filled the room, Mav turned away to gather in his rampaging emotions so that Macy would not see the pain they shared since the death of Lyla, an action unnecessary, yet justified in Mav's mind who must be strong, being a man.

Following this seminal introduction of this foundling from the wood, and as she nestled in the warm bosom of Macy Caid, Mav and Macy quietly discussed the event, each making suggestions as to what may have happened, but neither being convinced by the arguments proposed for they all were just too fantastical for belief, as each in their private thoughts imagining what suffering must a mother feel to give up her papoose. Later, after the foundling fell into a deep slumber, Macy laid the sleeping papoose on a pallet on the floor and turned to Mav.

"Mav," asked Macy, "how is it that every time you go out alone, you come home with a girl?" The obvious reference to Constance with whom Mav rode in with from a trip to the Valley of Tears."

Laughing, Mav replied: "I just have this magnetic personality, I guess. The ladies jes' cain't help themselves."

"Should we name her?" asked Macy.

"I think…I think we should name her Já-gĕ, 'Antelope,' replied Mav.

"Já-gĕ?" asked Macy. "How do you know Já-gĕ means Antelope?"

"I don't know, Macy, but that is her name," Mav answered with a finality in his voice as Macy shook her head in visible perplexity.

During the following weeks, Mav, Macy, Case, and all workers at the Caid place were alert to anyone approaching the home place and always told Mav or Macy. Beyond neighbors, no one came and, although Mav had gone back to the site on the trail several times to see if the bowie knife bearing his name that he left remained embedded in the tree, it was always there. Finally, after the passage of a month, Mav returned once more to retrieve the knife and went home.

Chapter 39

In the Eye of the Beholder

Mav enters the bedroom where Macy is seated before her vanity table that Mav had given her as a Christmas gift. Macy was appraising herself in the mirror.

"Mav, am I pretty?" a question from the blue, suddenly asked by Macy as she sits in front of a mirror brushing her hair.

"What?" returned a perplexed Mav.

"Pretty. Do you think I'm pretty?" Macy replied, continuing to brush.

"No," Mav replied with a devilish grin. "But I do think you are beautiful."

"I'm serious! Am I pretty?" The question leaves Mav further perplexed, given that in his lexicon, beautiful trumps pretty.

"Uh…What's this about?" asks a more attentive Mav.

"Mav, look!" returns Macy. "Look at these streaks of gray!" holding out a few strands.

"Ah, yes. Well, Ole Father Time just exchanged some o' th' auburn fo' silver,' said Mav, moving behind Macy's chair. "It's no big thing. I think I'm a little touched by it mysel'."

"But you're a man. Gray hair just makes you look more distinguished! On a woman, just old. I don't want to look old, Mav! I don't want to be old."

"I see. Would it help ifn I told you thet I would love you just as much if you had no hair atall? An' besides, you don't look old, an' you ain't old." Mav waited.

"She was wearing your coat!" interjected Macy.

"What? Who?" Mav returned to perplexity.

"Constance. Constance was wearing your coat when you brought her here several years ago." Macy declared.

"Uh, I don't rec'lect… That was several years ago."

"Constance is pretty. She doesn't have any gray in _her_ hair," returned Macy, turning to look at Mav.

"Umm…" began Mav before Macy interrupted.

"I've been thinking of henna," said Macy, further disorienting Mav with her change in subject.

"Who?" returned Mav. "I don't know Henna. Who is she?"

"It's not a who, it's a thing. A dye."

"Ah, ha! Hair dye!" responded a comprehending Mav. "Why didn't you just ask if I would mind ifn you dyed yor hair?"

"I just wanted to know what you would think of me if I dyed my hair. It would almost bring my hair back to its natural color. I don't want you to think me un-pretty if I dyed my hair."

"I will not think of you as un-pretty ifn you dye yor hair," replied Mav.

"So, you think me un-pretty if I don't?" Macy presented a face registering incredulity.

"Ahhh! I need to feed Hardtack." As Mav escaped his inquisition, Macy smiled and reached for the henna.

Mav Caid — The Complete Story

As Mav brushed Hardtack and began to discuss the nature of women to a horse having only a passing interest, Case captured his attention by riding fast into the barn, shouting:

"Pa. I've been hurt." Case, by his elevated voice, emphasized his apprehension. He had a reason as he slid from the saddle, blood dripping down his boot from a long gash to his leg.

"Case!" shouted Mav, "what happened?"

"Wild razorback! I was stringing a fence, and this wild hog attacked. My leg…" answered Case.

"Let me see," Mav said, walking quickly to the side of his son.

"Looks bad," said Mav. "We better clean it up and bandage it. Let's go to the house."

Mav supported Case in the twenty-yard walk to the house where he retrieved the carbolic acid to cleanse the tusk gash to the leg of the young Case Caid.

Macy rushed to the side of Mav as he was pouring the solution over the wound then left to find a suitable bandage. When she returned, Case repeated what had happened as Mav harnessed the mules to the wagon for a trip to the hospital.

Dr. Turnbull met Mav, Macy, and Case as they arrived and inspected the wound, telling them how dangerous a tusk wound can be if not appropriately treated while praising them for their presence of mind to sterilize it and bring Case into him. It took about twenty stitches to close the wound and would result in a scar that would last a lifetime. Dr. Turnbull instructed them on the following care of the injury and gave a vial of laudanum for the control of the pain as needed and to induce sleep, but "not too much," he admonished.

Being young, Case would likely recover quickly, barring any infection, and would have something to show schoolmates when he returns to school. Wounding by a wild hog, now that is something like a badge of honor to a young boy. He would not know that the fact that there are feral hogs in Arkansas is because Hernando de Soto lost them from his herd of domesticated swine that he drove through Arkansas territory over three-hundred years ago. The touch of the past has a long reach.

"He feels feverish," said Macy, touching her son's forehead.

"Probably normal," returned Mav, thinking of Lyla. Rejecting the idea that this could end the same way. Praying that it does not.

Within two days, the young boy was hobbling around, sore, but showing no signs of illness from the slashing. Macy and Mav were breathing sighs of relief.

✳✳✳

Mav retrieves a rocking cradle from the barn attic and lays Já-gĕ, young 'Antelope,' into her new bed that she finds less restricting than the cradleboard and is busy exploring her hands and feet that are free to move about. Now and then she emits a sound followed by a sigh. 'A baby would be as precious by any other name,' thought Macy.

Macy and Mav, who now consider themselves to be her parents, are growing more hopeful that her real parents do not come asking for her. Both can look upon Já-gĕ as an independent entity, a person in her own right, not an echo of Lyla. They are happy that she came.

"Mav, how old do you think Já-gĕ is?" asked Macy.

"I reckon about sixteen to eighteen months," replied Mav. "Why do you ask?"

"Baptism," returned Macy. "I just think we should get her baptized soon. Missionaries have baptized many of her people. They probably would want it too."

History writes that missionaries came to the natives as early as the soldiers, even earlier. Missionaries, carrying crosses of iron atop poles of wood that reminds viewers of Jesus Christ and his sacrifice. Iron crosses, lost and buried in the muck during a battle between the soldiers of Spain and the Kashinampo defenders of an ancient way of life, a way of life that is fading like the vibrant colors of the clouds spreading eastward of the setting sun.

Pastor Briggs, when asked if he would baptize the papoose named Já-gĕ, just quoted Mark 10:14: "Let the little children come to me, — for it is, to such as these, that the kingdom of God belongs." Já-gĕ, received her baptism into the community of God the following week, in the John Wesley way, by triple immersion. She will have a foot in both worlds, forever.

"I feel good about this, Mav," stated Macy, as she held Já-gĕ in her lap. "Pastor Briggs is really different from Billy Sunday. He seems more… gentle."

"Yes. Much gentler," replied Mav, glancing at Macy, wondering where she was going with the conversation. "Billy got your attention, made you fear tomorrow, made you feel inadequate. Pastor Briggs preaches love, makes you feel you have a home. I guess each of them has their place and have followed their hearts in bringing people to God, but I am much more comfortable with Pastor Briggs' preaching than with Billy's!"

"Billy and some of the others scared me sometime." Macy fell silent in thought.

"Well, Macy, it is good to think about what a person's afterlife may be like, but in the main, one does what he has to do to survive th' present life. If a person stays mostly on th' right side, they'll be all right. I believe that. It's only reasonable, if we have a merciful God."

Chapter 40

Something Rotten in Arkansas

The year 1905 would be the year of promise or despair depending upon a point of view, a location, or the subject. It was the *annus mirabilis*, the wonderful year, for a young German theoretical physicist of Jewish heritage named Albert Einstein. In this year this young physicist would publish scientific papers on quantum physics, describe his theory of relativity, explain both Brownian motion and mass-energy equivalents, eventually leading to the world-changing mathematical equation, $E=mc^2$. It was the year of turmoil in Russia with revolutionary forces rising against the Tsar over the Russo-Japanese war, —now in its second year, —and January 2, 1905, would receive the name, Bloody Sunday, for the indiscriminate slaughtering of peaceful demonstrators led by Orthodox priest, Father Georgy Gapon to Tsar Nicholas' Winter Palace in St. Petersburg, Russia. This and other grievances helped to spark a revolution in Russia that was destined to fail and leave the forces of discontent seething. In France,

Eugene Stonefield

Dutch exotic dancer and courtesan, Margaretha Geertriuda MacLeod, nee, Zelle, —stage name, Mata Hari, —would bring exotic dancing to Paris, then seed intrigue that would one day end her life, convicted of being an enemy spy. The Kangra Valley in India would be devastated by an earthquake, and twenty-thousand people will die. In America, Orville and Wilbur Wright will fly their Wright Flyer III flying-machine for over thirty minutes without touching the earth, stirring the imaginations of those who would seek the stars. It will also be the year that Alfred Einhorn synthesizes procaine, a painkiller used to reduce pain in dentistry and from painful injections of penicillin, and name his synthesis Novocain. Readers of the Beaton Gazette will read of these stories, puzzle over some, have empathy for victims of tragedy, wonder about exotic dancing, be confused over the technical language of the scientific community, but, in general, will get on with their lives as they did the day before and the day before that. The family of Mav and Macy Caid, however, will not.

"Mav! Mav!" shouted Billy as he rode onto the Caid place and dismounted. Mav heard the shouting and came to the front porch.

"What is it, Billy?" asked Mav of the excited visitor.

"Rustlers! returned the breathless friend from the adjacent farm. "The fence is down on your cattle operation beyond my place. It looks like somebody has taken out some of your cattle."

"This is not good news, Billy." Mav mentally calculated the number of cattle on the ranch. "I'll saddle up Hardtack an' ride out to check th' damage. You comin' with me?"

"Yes," returned the long-time friend.

Without a roundup of all remaining cattle, Mav could not determine with precision how many cattle the rustlers stole. He did learn that Wade Pinders, a ranch hand for the cattle operation was missing. Wade had been with Mav for three years and lived in a line shack near the fence cutting. Wade was instrumental in executing Mav's plan to improve the beef cattle herd with the importation of Angus cattle from Scotland. He had been reliable for the duration, but cannot be located now.

"What do you think?" asked Billy.

"Doesn't look good. I can't account for Wade's not being here. It's hard to believe Wade may have gone bad an' is part of th' rustling, but I searched th' line house an' immediate area for him when I found th' downed fence. He should be here. Just looking at th' tracks, I think th' rustling occurred three or four days ago. I will notify th' sheriff an' telegraph th' Cattlemen Association in Littlerock that a rustling event has occurred. Maybe th' rustlers are of a known gang." Mav remounted Hardtack and set out for Sheriff Hickatrisk's office in Beaton. Upon arrival, Mav made the report then returned to the home-place where he told Macy.

"Macy, it looks like we lost some cattle to a rustler. I don't know how many yet, nor do I know th' whereabouts of Wade. It looks as if th' rustling occurred just this week. I'm going to see if I can follow th' trail of th' cattle. It may take a few days." Mav began to pack a few needed items in his saddlebag and picked up a box of ammunition for his Winchester. His last action was to buckle on his Colt Walker, a weapon he has not worn in several years.

"Oh, Mav. You aren't going alone, are you?" Macy showed concern by her expression.

"The trail is cold enough already. I can't chance a rain killing our chances to find where they have taken our cattle," Mav buckled the bag and started for the door. "Tell Case that I will be back in a few days and that he is in charge until then. Have him get some men to repair th' fence. We don't want th' others to wander off."

Arriving back at the downed fence, Mav began to inspect the ground for additional clues before starting to follow the trail. The land showed a disturbance by many hooves of the cattle driven through the constricted opening, but one anomaly stood out, —two straight parallel lines about one foot apart overtopping the tracks of the cattle. Lines that presumed the dragging of something heavy along the ground. The lines disappeared about twenty feet outside the fence line and did not appear again. Disposition of stolen cattle must rely on transportation out of the area by rail or removal to a hidden ranch to become part of a new or ongoing operation's stock. Because of the terrain, there was only a couple of ways a person could reasonably drive the cattle to a railhead. The rustler's intent to take the cattle out of the area by rail is an obvious presumption since the arrival of the railroads, and further, because cross-country cattle drive to market being a practice of the past. One direction would be west toward Hope on the road to Texarkana, the other, east toward Beaton, but Mav would not know which way they went until he reached that point where the rustlers must make a choice. By noon, Mav had reached the spot. Tracks of the rustled cattle led toward a natural level-ground pasturage near the post road between Beaton and Hope, now called Clark County Road 3. Another half-hour passed, and Mav approached CR 3 near the meadow, that was empty as expected. The trail seemed to end there. Reason demands that tracks of the rustled cattle continue in some direction from the assembly point, not just disappear! Where were the cattle tracks? How are they now missing? By what means did the cattle leave?

After inspecting the area where the rustlers temporarily held the cattle, Mav decided to follow the road leading north for a few miles and see if he could pick up a trail. Mav recognized that local cattle owners often drive their cattle down this road when moving them from one pasture to another or taking them to the railhead, which makes it impossible to identify one herd from another without seeing them in transit. About three miles from where he began, he saw a young farmer working his land. He was walking behind a plow hitched to a mule and was cutting a furrow for planting a crop when the time is ripe. As it was unfenced, Mav turned Hardtack toward the man in the field. As Mav neared the man plowing, the sandy-haired man of around twenty-five greeted Mav with a big smile spread across his face.

"Hello," greeted the man, "name's Pehlan. Rich Pehlan. "What's yours?"

"Mav Caid. Good to meet you. I'm a-tracking some missin' cattle an' saw you in th' field. I hav' a question to ask ifn you ain't objectin'." Mav dismounted Hardtack and shook Rich Pehlan's hand.

"Sure," returned Rich, "if I can be helpful."

"Hav' you seen any cattle bein' moved down this here road this week?" began Mav. "Mine were rustled a few days back, an' I hav' tracked them to about three miles back yonder toward Beaton where I lost their tracks. I reckon they wouldn't have taken them to Beaton, so they must hav' come thisaway or mayhap, driven them into th' forest, which don't make sense."

After listening to Mav, Rich Pehlan replied: "It was bizarre, the way they were being driven down the road. The hands were keeping the cattle in a narrow file, —two or three abreast, —so they couldn't leave the road. It was a long string of animals, must have been about fifty or so. If any animal tried to go off the road, a rider would ride up and force it back to the center. I didn't know what to make of it. It was quite a sight. This was really early in the morning, about Thursday of this week." Rich Pehlan stopped talking and waited for Mav's response.

"I reckon I do know what they were a-doin'. They wuz hidin' th' trail by keepin' on th' hard-packed macadam road th' state has built to test its durability. We used to drive a line of cattle past th' boss fo' a trail count when I wuz…<u>was</u> with Lytle. I read about th' road some time back in th' Gazette that discussed th' work of th' Good Roads Association. They're a-treatin' th' soft sides of the road like them furrow fences plowed along th' cattle trails through Kansas to signal to drovers that allowing cattle to walk over a furrow was a trespass an' was subject to a fine. I reckon they felt that ifn the cattle didn't step off th' macadam they wouldn't be detected. They just didn't consider that someone might be a-seein' them."

Mav knew that somewhere ahead was a cutoff where they would move the cattle from the road into a pen for rebranding, then driven to a destination. The rustlers were depending upon the tracks being untraceable in a few days. Mav thanked his new acquaintance and returned to the road to ride further, searching for that point of egress from CR 3. As he continued his search, the atmosphere was becoming heavy, and a scent of rain was in the air. The sky was cloudy with gray clouds, heavy with water that began to spill in large droplets. He knew that he must find the trail now or lose it forever. It was another three miles before he noticed that the grass looked tamped down on one side of the road like many hooves have trampled it.

"Hardtack, this looks 'bout as promisin' as can be. There ain't no similar tracks on th' other side, so cattle crossin' th' road did not leave th' tracks. Let's see where them tracks go." Mav urged Hardtack from the macadam to follow the trail.

Mav and Hardtack followed the tracks for about two miles before arriving at a small ramshackle ranch operation with all the indicators of being temporary. Dismounting, Mav took up a position where he could observe the front door of the dilapidated cabin. The heavy air carried the sound of lowing cattle located somewhere close but just out of sight from his vantage point. After a while, a red-headed man of above average height and weight stepped from the cabin. Mav watched as the man retrieved a bag of Bull Durham tobacco from a pocket and took a cigarette paper from a flat pack of thin cigarette paper that he began to fill with a measured amount of shredded tobacco, distributing it equally end to end. The man rolled the tobacco filled paper into a tube, then lifting it to his lips slid the edge of the loaded paper across the tip of his tongue to moisten the outer edge, then deftly turned the moistened edge over the distributed tobacco to seal it into a cigarette. Momentarily, the tall red-headed stranger retrieved a friction match from a metal canister and drew its flammable end across the wall of the cabin to strike it into flame, cupping his hand to shield the fire from any wind. Bringing the match to the cigarette hanging from his lips, he lit the cigarette, took two puffs, then stepped off the porch. Presently, two more men came from the cabin, following the red-headed man into the scrub behind the cabin. Mav waited for any others to exit, then believing it empty, cautiously walked to the side of the cabin and looked through a window. Finding it empty, Mav crept to the front and entered the cabin. There was very little order inside, a few provisions, an iron stove, and a table. The cabin had the feel of abandonment. On the table, he found a partially completed bill-of-sale for fifty-eight Angus beeves. At the bottom of the bill-of-sale was the signature of the seller. His own!

Following his startling discovery in the cabin, Mav quietly left and returned to where Hardtack was waiting. Mav mounted Hardtack and set out to notify the sheriff in Beaton.

"Sheriff Hickatrisk," said Mav as he entered the office, "I have tracked th' rustlers to a place 'bout ten miles from here. I observed three people there, one was tall with red hair. We may be able to catch them before they move out, but there is a complication. They have a sales contract with my signature, but I didn't sign any such contract."

"Did you see the missing Wade Pinders?" asked the sheriff.

"No," answered Mav, "only th' three mentioned an' they are all strangers."

Sheriff Hickatrisk told his deputy to gather a posse, then went to the Western Union station to telegraph a query to Little Rock about any known rustlers that met the description Mav gave him. Upon his return, Deputy Coggins was still assembling a posse, and Mav briefed the deputy on the location where he found the cattle rustlers. Sheriff Hickatrisk and Mav then became the advance party to the interception and left Beaton immediately to set up observation at the site and await the posse that was to catch up. Upon arrival, Sheriff Hickatrisk and Mav circled behind the cabin and located a rope corral with the cattle. They estimated that there were fifty or more beeves contained in the pen. They saw no evidence of rebranding. Presently, both men returned to the county road to await the posse. Surprisingly, when they arrived, a tall redheaded man was waiting.

"Good afternoon, gentlemen! Sheriff, I am Hannibal Rhodes, agent for Severine Comstock of Chicago. And, good afternoon to you, Mr. Caid, I am pleased to renew our acquaintance." Hannibal offered his hand to the sheriff, then to Mav. Each shook his hand in turn, each puzzled by the familiarity and the quiet confidence the man exhibited. Hannibal continued: "Mr. Caid, I do hope Wade has finished repairing the fence we took down to move the cattle. He was beginning to re-string the wire when we left him. I really appreciate your allowing us to drop the wire since it saved so much time, and Severine is anxious to receive the cattle that you sold to her so she could meet a contractual obligation." Hannibal gave a warm smile.

"Begging your pardon, Mr. Rhodes, but I sold no cattle to anyone this year, an' I have never met you until just now," Mav replied, becoming angry by the unfolding events.

"Oh, certainly you did, Mr. Caid. I don't know how you could have forgotten. Here is the bill of sale for fifty-eight beeves, dated six weeks ago. It has your signature, does it not?" Hannibal waited but looked at the sheriff. He passed the bill of sale to the sheriff who took it and read it.

"Mav," began Sheriff Hickatrisk, "is this your signature?"

"Sheriff Hickatrisk," responded Mav, "it looks authentic, but I never signed such a document."

"Mav, we have to resolve this before we can go forward," returned the sheriff," then turning to Hannibal, said: "Mr. Rhodes, where may we find this, Severine? I must assume you work for her?"

"Only by contract, sheriff. I locate the cattle for her to purchase and deliver to her at the transportation point. She executes a contract with the owner in which I assist, then completes the purchase by telegram just before I take possession for her. Severine then sends the cattle purchased directly to slaughterhouses with whom she has contracts. Unfortunately, Severine is not available just now. I could let her know you wish to speak with her." Hannibal looked questioningly at the sheriff.

"If she is not available, how can you let her know?" asked Sheriff Hickatrisk, handing the contract back to Hannibal.

"Telegram," responded Hannibal, "I telegraph from the nearest station to let Severine know when the cattle are to be shipped so she can alert her buyer when to receive them. We have complete trust in each other, and keep in touch by telegram." Hannibal let the Sheriff and Mav consider what he had to say, then continued, "but, if you will excuse me, my boys and I have to move these cattle to the rail yard for transportation. Hannibal mounted his horse and rode back toward the cabin.

"Mav, I want to believe you didn't sell the cattle, but it is a testimony conflict that must be resolved. Most likely, he will have witnesses, one or more of his 'boys' to support his claim," stated Sheriff Hickatrisk. "Moreover, to your counter-claim, Hannibal will simply say that you have just gotten cold feet about the sale. We need to find Wade before they load the cattle since he seems to be our only eye-witness to events. I sincerely hope he is not an inside partner of Hannibal." Sheriff Hickatrisk turned to the deputy who had just arrived with the posse and told him they should begin a search for Wade Pinders who was still missing. Shortly after the posse began their search, and the sheriff and Mav were riding back to Beaton, a herd of cattle was moving in the same direction toward the cattle loading shoot for the SSW railway station in Beaton.

Eugene Stonefield

✳✳✳

As Sheriff Hickatrisk and Mav came into town, they stopped at the Western Union to see if an answer had come in response to the telegram that they sent earlier asking for information on the redheaded Hannibal Rhodes.

"Ah, no, Sheriff Hickatrisk," said the telegraph operator to the sheriff's question, then turning to Mav said: "Mr. Caid, glad you came in. I received this telegram several days ago that stated it should be held for retrieval by you personally." The telegram read:

Telegrapher: Hold for pick-up by addressee <stop>

To: Mr. Mav Caid, Beaton, Arkansas <stop>

From: Severine Comstock, Chicago, Illinois <stop>

Payment of $23,200 by banker check mailed today <stop>

Thank you for your trust in early delivery of cattle <stop>

"Mav," said Sheriff Hickatrisk, "this does not look good for your assertion. I won't be able to stop the loading of the cattle. I have no cause. All of the evidence is on Mr. Rhodes's side."

The forged bill of sale, the predicted telegram from Severine stunned Mav to the core. He knew a crime was being committed, but could not prove it. Everything suggested a legitimate sale to a willing buyer by a seller who has changed his mind. His rising anger at the blatant fraud tempers as he remembers that Wade Pinders is still missing. Mav knows that they must find Wade. Wade is the witness who knows the facts. His uncertainty is for whom would Wade be witness? He thanked Sheriff Hickatrisk and left for home.

"Hardtack," said Mav to his trusted advisor, "There's something rotten in Arkansas."

✳✳✳

Mav Caid — The Complete Story

Mav returned home earlier than expected, finding Macy, Case, and *Já-gĕ* on the front porch in the porch swing Mav built last summer. Mav's report on the strange events that appear to have defrauded them of their property perplexed Macy, and, seemingly, there was little legal recourse to prevent the cattle shipment to some slaughterhouse. The only person who may be able to shed light on the crime is the still missing Wade Pinders. A posse of citizens has been searching the wilderness area for Wade, all hoping they will find him alive, but have concerns that it would not be the case.

"Macy, I have to go back out to help find Wade, an' trust luck thet…<u>that</u> I can find him in time. I'm still packed for a few days so will go now. I'll come back or try to send word ifn I must stay longer than three days." Mav mounted Hardtack and rode off.

Mav returned to the downed fence and found two men working to re-string the barbed wire. After conversing with them, Mav inspected again the tracks, still bothered by the two lines that overtopped the disturbed ground made by the rustled cattle. Were the lines wider and had they been visible for more than the few feet, Mav would have suspected they were made by a travois. Since these stopped about twenty feet further out, Mav paid additional attention to that area, noticing that two horses had left prints there, then had moved away from the direction of the herd's tracks. In his mind's eye, Mav could see an unconscious man, heels dragging the ground, being placed on a horse for removal from the area. Whether that person was dead or alive was the question Mav pondered. He would have to believe Wade was alive until he knew otherwise. This trail, he would follow.

Riding forward, the ground became considerably rockier and the trail harder to follow making it necessary for Mav to dismount and walk, searching for overturned rocks or chance prints in areas that are conducive to showing them. Three hours passed before he found a disturbance at the foot of an acclivity where it appeared that the two horses stopped and milled around for some time. Why did they stop? Looking further, Mav noticed that the trail of the two horses turned back in the general direction from which they came. Why turn around? Had they met their purpose for coming? A close inspection of the disturbed ground showed that the hoof-prints of one horse were lighter than the other horse, as if one horse's burden was lighter, perhaps, by the weight of a man. Mav began to search the uplift, for clues, finally seeing a small cave near the top of the uplifted ground, but reachable. Climbing to the cave entrance, Mav ventured inside. At first, the transition from sunlight to darkness prevented Mav from seeing the cave's interior. Upon adjusting to the dark, Mav found Wade Pinders, bound tightly, lying against the wall of the cave about eight feet from the entrance, his head covered in dried blood. Mav touched Wade to see if he still possessed the breath of life and, finding him still alive, returned quickly to retrieve his canteen of water. Mav cut the rope by which Wade was bound then poured water over his face. Wade responded to the water and within a few minutes was able to drink some and look around at his surroundings.

"Wade, can you ride double with me so I ken…<u>can</u> get you back to your cabin?" asked Mav.

"I'm weak, Mr. Caid, and my head is throbbing, but I can hang on," returned Wade, thankful of Mav's finding him. "They didn't intend to come back for me, Mr. Caid. They were just letting me die. I haven't had food or water since they jumped me Tuesday."

"I think you are right, Wade." Mav helped Wade to his feet, and they walked to the entrance of the cave. The descent was one of careful placement of foot and hand and an occasional slide down loosened soil. Both men, mounted atop Hardtack, began their ride back. The ride back to Wade's cabin was slow in deference to Hardtack's having to carry two grown men. Once there, Wade assured Mav that he was feeling better and would not need to go to the hospital. Mav cleaned the head wound with carbolic acid and bandaged the injury Wade had suffered, opened a couple of Campbell's airtights of tomatoes for Wade to eat, then began asking questions about the rustlers. Wade remembered that it was Hannibal Rhodes who gave him the wound and forced him into the cave. He knew nothing of a Severine, or of a bill of sale for the cattle. During the questioning, Wade recalled that Hannibal had asked if he had anything showing the signature of the owner of the ranch and had taken the letter Mav had signed specifying how much pay Wade would receive for his services and the responsibilities he was to uphold.

Night was falling, and after assuring himself that Wade had recovered enough to leave alone, Mav decided to go home for the night and ride to the sheriff's office the next day, a picture of an elaborate, sophisticated plot forming in his mind.

As Mav entered Sheriff Hickatrisk' office, the sheriff was reading a telegram he had just received from Little Rock, the answer to his query to the state law enforcement he had sent earlier.

"Morning, Mav," said Sheriff Hickatrisk as he looked up and saw who was entering. "I have an answer to my telegram. It seems that our Mr. Rhodes, a.k.a., Barbarossa, —the alias given to him because of the red hair, —is known. He has used the ruse several times in Texas and Missouri to steal cattle by making it appear to be a legitimate purchase. His objective is to complete the theft before detection, but if detected, then to confuse the law for enough time to avoid arrest. Mr. Hannibal Rhodes, in concert with a Severine, who no one has seen, and possibly does not exist, forestalls the law long enough to ship the cattle and escape. Texas named this gang of a varying number of members the Barbarossa gang. Rhodes is a lawyer by training and a skilled forger who, if confronted, always presents a bill of sale with the signature of the cattle owner. If questioned, he may refer to a pre-transmitted telegram from Severine to the owner that supports the legitimacy of a transaction. The rustling occurs from ranches near railheads where Rhodes can load just before the train leaves and timed to take advantage of a quick loading of the cattle shortly after the theft, often before the owners know their cattle are missing. On two occasions, he and his gang have stopped the train to unload the cattle before it reaches destination. This may have occurred, because Barbarossa suspected the law was aware of the scheme and would telegraph authorities somewhere down the line. On those occasions, gang members robbed passengers on the train while unloading the stolen cattle. The unloaded cattle, he sold to unsuspecting buyers in the area. He has been known to abandon the operation if he senses an unmasking of his scheme and is in danger of arrest before loading the cattle at a railhead. Overall, he is extremely arrogant and prides himself in being able to outsmart authorities and forestall apprehension by knowing the law and picking desirable places to exploit. Also believed is that scouts are employed to find appropriate victims and prepare for Barbarossa to come into the rustling at the last minute to minimize his personal risk. Barbarossa typically uses innocent people whom he hires to take the cattle to the railhead and load them onto the rail cars."

"I wonder if, attempted murder is an escalation to his crime? I hav' found Wade, an' he is ok an' back at his cabin, but Barbarossa intended that he die horribly. Barbarossa took Wade to a cave in th' wilderness an' left him bound to die of hunger an' thirst. He must be caught before he does kill somebody," returned Mav.

"Rhodes said they were taking the cattle to a rail yard for loading. Let's go see what is happening at the stock-loading enclosure at the SSW." Following this conversation, Sheriff Hickatrisk and Mav left the office to check out any activity at the loading shoots. As they arrived, several hands were pushing cattle through the inclined cattle loading shoot into the train's cattle cars. When the train arrives, the loaded stock cars destined for the Chicago's Union Stockyards will be coupled to the string of cars being pulled by the powerful engine. Sheriff Hickatrisk and Mav dismounted and walked to the place of activity. As they approach, the sheriff and Mav recognize the loaders.

"Howdy, boys," began the sheriff, addressing one of the men loading the cattle. "I know you boys to be local, and I'd like to ask a few questions, like: Where did you get the cattle?"

"Oh, hello, Sheriff! These ain't ours. These belong to a lady named Severine in Chicago. Mr. Rhodes, her agent, hired us to load the cattle. He even paid us in advance because he said he had been ordered to ride on ahead." The sheriff's interlocutor fell silent awaiting the next question.

"I suppose you saw which way Mr. Rhodes went after he paid you?" followed the sheriff.

"No, sir," returned the young cattle loader.

"When did you last see Mr. Rhodes?"

"Yesterday morning when he paid us."

"OK, but if you see any of the boys associated with him, come get me." The sheriff ended his questioning and turned back to Mav. "Mav, I guess that somewhere close someone is watching to see if there is any effort to block cattle from leaving. Likely, somewhere ahead, Barbarossa will stop the train and unload the cattle, long before it reaches Chicago. We can let the loading continue and try to interrupt the scheme, possibly arrest Barbarossa, or I will order the loading to stop so you can recover your cattle. It's your cattle, your call." Sheriff Hickatrisk waited for Mav to answer.

"Well, Sheriff Hickatrisk…for me, I want to recover my cattle, for Wade…I want Barbarossa," answered Mav. Sheriff Hickatrisk and Mav waved at the loaders and mounted for their ride back to the sheriff's office.

"Sheriff Hickatrisk," began Mav, thoughtful in demeanor, "I think I would like to be there, wherever there is when Barbarossa is arrested. How can I do that?"

"If you are a mind to do that, I can deputize you, so if anything goes bad, you will be acting for the law and not for yourself," returned the sheriff.

"Do it," replied Mav.

As the loaders locked the stock cars awaiting coupling to the noon train, Sheriff Hickatrisk deputized Mav Caid, and devised a plan. Soon after, the sheriff purchased two tickets for Chicago. When asked if any redheaded man had bought a ticket, the ticket-master informed them that tickets for four people and their horses were purchased yesterday on the noon train that left Beaton on time. Mav sent a message to Macy that Deputy Mav Caid will be delayed in his return home for an unspecified length of time. Macy received the startling message and pondered the new title of 'deputy' for her husband.

"Mav," began the sheriff, "I expect that when we pull out, a confederate of Barbarossa will telegraph to some station stop ahead that the cattle are on the way." It happened.

"Makes sense. Barbarossa, then, will retrieve th' telegram at a pre-selected watering stop, possibly Littlerock, an' will be prepared to stop this train to retrieve th' cattle, possibly even to rob the passengers. Otherwise, they go to destination an' are sold to a slaughterhouse." Mav shook his head and said: "Shor seems like a hard way to make money." With that, both men sat back to await an unscheduled stop. It came midway between Little Rock and Memphis.

"Please allow me your attention, ladies and gentlemen," announced a smiling curly-haired man who had boarded the train just after the train stopped near Brinkley. "Folks call me Curly, and I have been sent to entertain you while we are stopped. We will remain here for a while as my friends unload some cattle. While we wait, pretend you are in church, —sing a song to help with the entertainment. I personally, like <u>Amazing Grace</u>. And, just like being in church, I will be picking up an offering from all of you caring folks. Your offering will be, all money and valuables you have on you or in your luggage which I ask that you put in this bag that you should pass among you and return to me. Oh, and, please no drama. This little lady could get hurt if someone gets cute." Curly reached down and pulled a young passenger from her seat and held her in front of himself as a shield, then rested his hand on his holstered six-shooter, saying: "and I'm really fast." The passengers did not misunderstand the gesture, and the collection bag began the rounds. Several gray-haired ladies began to sing <u>Amazing Grace</u> with voices wavering in fear or because of age.

"What arrogance! I guess this is what we've been waiting for," whispered the sheriff to himself from his seat in the last row of the car. "Now, if he will only walk a few feet down the aisle so Mav will be behind him…." Whispered the sheriff, easing his gun from its holster but keeping it out of sight of Curly.

"As expected," whispered Deputy Mav Caid from his seat in the front row of the car.

Curly showed no intention to move from his position at the front of the car, but without a gun in hand, Curly unknowingly gave a momentary advantage to Deputy Mav Caid. Deputy Mav Caid would take it.

"Curly, here's somethin' you orta see." Mav reached out his closed hand toward Curly, palm down. The unexpected non-threatening gesture from a seated man took Curly by surprise and he automatically held out his hand to receive an object offered by Mav, seated in an aisle seat near where Curly was standing holding the young girl. Immediately, Mav dropped a deputy's metal badge into the Curly's outstretched hand. Curly felt the badge drop into his hand, looked briefly, dropped the badge, and began a move toward his still holstered gun. Curly's alarm was too late, as a strong farmer's hand seized and gripped his wrist tightly, twisting as he began pulling himself to a standing position. To free his other arm Curly pushed away his hostage, but to no avail. From being his shield and protector, the young girl became his impediment and Mav's momentary assistant. As

Curly leaned away from his attacker to free his captured arm, his movement further assisted Mav in his rise to a standing position, and having completed his twist of Curly's wrist, was now standing behind Curly with a tight hammerlock on Curly's arm with the other arm around his throat.

While this was occurring, Sheriff Hickatrisk, gun drawn, was racing down the aisle toward the action. When the sheriff reached the subdued Curly, he took the Remington .44 from Curly's holster and shoved it into his own belt.

"Ever thought of what Curly may have done if he could have drawn his gun?" asked Sheriff Hickatrisk.

"I'm a-thinkin' it now, sheriff. Glad he didn't," replied Mav, then adding: "I hav' an idea for rounding up th' others."

"I'm listening," replied Sheriff Hickatrisk. Following was a description of Mav's idea for the others. The attempted robbery under control, the pair took the subdued Curly to the mail car where postal mail clerks sorted and bagged mail in route to various places. The sheriff ordered the mail sorters to leave the car and go into the passenger car. Finally, the sheriff addressed Curly:

"Curly, this is your one chance to avoid being charged with the murder of Wade Pinders back in Beaton. I'll only tell you one time. This is what you must do. Do it wrong, and you just may be the first casualty when the shooting starts. Try to escape, and you will be dead before you reach the ground." As the sheriff spoke the sobering words to Curly, the sliding mail car door to the outside was opening. Sheriff Hickatrisk told Curly what he was to shout to Barbarossa. Several cars away, Barbarossa and two hands were unloading the cattle, but were within shouting distance of the subdued Curly, and shout he did, as Sheriff Hickatrisk held his gun on him from behind.

"Barbarossa! Barbarossa! Gold! There's gold in the mail car. Forget the cattle. Hurry!"

As Barbarossa and two compatriots started toward the mail car, the sheriff pulled Curly away from the door and stood him by an open bin of packages at the end of the car. Mav positioned himself at the other end, crouching behind the sorting counter. Sheriff Hickatrisk crouched near Curly and waited for Barbarossa and his men to enter the car.

"Where is it?" asked Barbarossa as he and the others scrambled aboard and looked at Curly.

"Right here," said Sheriff Hickatrisk, rising from his hidden position, gun in hand. Barbarossa started to draw his weapon.

"An', right here," said Mav from the other end, holding his Colt Walker.

"Gentlemen," said Sheriff Hickatrisk, "be so kind as to drop your gun belts. No drama, please. It would be so messy.

"I didn't kill that Wade Pinders," exclaimed Curly.

"I know," replied Sheriff Hickatrisk. Nobody did!"

As Mav and Sheriff Hickatrisk secured the gang of rustlers they discussed the events, and the sheriff asked Mav what he would do with the cattle that are now reloaded onto the cattle cars, thanks to the efforts of thankful passengers. Mav said that, since transportation for the beeves to Chicago has been prepaid by Barbarossa, they will proceed to the Union Stockyards in Chicago where Mav knew a buyer who would buy the cattle. The plan was to get off the train in Memphis and telegraph the buyer who would receive the shipment and forward the payment to Mav. Sheriff Hickatrisk, and Deputy Caid would return their prisoners to Little Rock to face the charges of rustling, train robbery, and attempted murder. After that, both Mav and Sheriff Hickatrisk would take a return train back to Beaton.

On the trip back to Beaton, Sheriff Hickatrisk and Deputy Caid discussed the appearance of Barbarossa before Judge Simmons in Little Rock.

"It was the height of arrogance for Barbarossa to claim that his arrest was a mistake and try to present the counterfeit bill of sale as evidence of ownership with you available to dispute it, but I guess desperate people do desperate things to try to change the trajectory of what is awaiting them," stated the sheriff.

"He did seem a bit put out when I thanked him fo' paying fo' th' transportation of my cattle to Chicago," replied Deputy Caid. "By th' way, sheriff, I resign."

Chapter 41

The Problem with Ormsby

On occasion, life seems too easy for comfort and begins to encroach upon those feelings of serenity. The discomfort begins to magnify and move into consciousness.

"Macy, do you git…<u>get</u> the feelin' that things are goin' along too well?" asked Mav as he read the Gazette and noted fewer catastrophic events in the news.

"What do you mean?" returned Macy.

"Jes' things. We haven't had any problems with anything lately. I jes'… I mean, <u>just</u> think it seems odd." Mav returned to reading but was soon disturbed by the arrival of Sheriff Hickatrisk.

"Mr. Caid," began Sheriff Hickatrisk, "I have a complaint against you for assault upon Mr. Mitchell Ormsby. He attests that earlier this year you engaged with him on a road into Beaton at which time you surprised him by roping him from behind and dragging him for several hundred yards over rocky ground causing him injury, pain, and deep humiliation. Further, he claims that, had it not been for his own ingenuity in getting free, that you would have dragged him to death. Mr. Caid, this is a serious charge that Mitchell Ormsby is making against you and I suggest that you get an attorney to represent you. I will have to take you in to my office where you may make your statement, and arrange bail for your release.

"Sheriff Hickatrisk," Mav replied to the turn of events, "I recall the incident. There is a bit of missing information in what Ormsby told you. I'll give the full story in your interview at your office."

"Fine, I'll wait for you to saddle up." Sheriff Hickatrisk remounted his horse to wait.

Following their arrival at the sheriff's office, Mav related to the clerk the event that led to Mav's roping of Mitchell Ormsby. Since Mav is well known in Beaton and has no history of lawbreaking, the sheriff released him on his own recognizance. Mav spent an hour with his lawyer briefing him on the charges made against him, then returned home.

"Mav, what's it all about?" asked Macy when they were sitting at the supper table.

"Mitchell said to me at th' time that he would get even. Mayhap this is what he meant." Mav returned. "Thing is, th' only witness is *Tohnemah*, and he's somewhere in Oklahoma. I guess this is a he-said, he-said situation. Ifn he expected me to be jailed to await a trial, I suspect he is unhappy right now."

✳✳✳

Two weeks pass and Mav having waived a jury trial, now stands before Judge Melvin Norton who is asking:

"Mr. Caid, do you understand that you are charged with assaulting a citizen of Beaton, Arkansas, and that the charges may be escalated to attempted murder if the evidence so indicates?" Judge Norton gazed intently at Mav as he awaited his answer.

"Judge Norton, I admit to th' altercation, but th' circumstances will show that I acted in defense of another person, who was himself being assaulted by Mr. Ormsby, an action that should be covered by th' good Samaritan rule. Th' idea that attempted murder could be supported by th' facts is simply ridiculous." Mav went silent.

"Well, Mr. Caid," returned Judge Norton, "I'm taking your statement to mean that you are guilty of assaulting Mr. Ormsby, but believe yourself not guilty of that assault because you were acting as a good Samaritan. Is that correct?"

"It is, your honor," replied Mav, as Judge Norton returned to reading the information previously given by parties to the case.

"Is your witness, Mr. *Tohnemah*, with you today?" asked the judge.

"Ah, no sir," returned Mav, "He's somewhar in Oklahoma."

"Mr. Ormsby," said the judge, turning to Mitchell Ormsby, "is your witness here?"

"Yes, your honor. My brother, Everly is here." Mitchell sat down, smiling.

"Then let us proceed, gentlemen," replied the judge.

An hour into the trial Everly Ormsby, brother to accuser, Mitchell Ormsby is giving his testimony:

"It was like this, Judge, my brother and I were standing away from our horses talking about Billy Sunday and we were accosted by this Injun and Mav Caid who took offense at our being in the road. Well, the voices got loud and this Injun screamed such an awful war cry that our horses spooked and ran into the wood. I went after them while my brother, Mitchell, stayed behind arguing. When I got back, I saw Mav Caid throw his rope over my brother who had his back to him and begin to drag my brother over the rocks. I shouted at Mav Caid, telling him he must stop. I shouted three times, Stop! Stop! Stop! Just like that. Finally, he stopped and just dropped the rope with my brother still in its loop. It was awful. Mitchell was bleeding everywhere. Here's the rope. You can still see the blood that got on the rope from all the cuts to my brother, Mitchell. After that, that Injun and Mav Caid just galloped on off on Mr. Caid's horse."

Judge Norton asked to see the rope more closely so he could examine the stains. After looking at them he asked: "Do you testify, Mr. Everly Ormsby, that these stains are not cow's blood or pig's blood?"

"I do, Judge, the stains were made by my poor brother Mitchell's blood."

"Well, since this is evidence of a crime, attested to by you, Mr. Everly Ormsby, I'll keep the lariat myself, until a decision is reached.

Following Everly Ormsby and Mitchell Ormsby's testimony, Mav gave his testimony about the meeting on the road and how he interrupted the beating of *Tohnemah*, who was unconscious from the beating so could not see the dragging. He did not deny the dragging, but he denied the presence of Everly Ormsby and he denied the extent of Mitchell's injuries. The judge gaveled the court out of session until Friday, three days hence.

"Macy, this is th' saddest thing. This, Everly, is lying. He was never there an' his story is a complete lie." Mav sips his coffee and reaches for the Gazette to see if the Gazette printed anything about the trial.

"Mav, what if the judge believes his story? What happens then?" asks Macy, her face showing serious concern.

"Well, I reckon I will be th' guest of th' jailer fo' a spell," returns Mav.

"For attempted murder?" asks Macy.

"Hope not," answers Mav.

Judge Norton brought the second court session to order and asks the last witness, Everly Ormsby to stand as he wishes to address him.

"Mr. Everly, as you recall, I retained the rope you brought in as evidence that your brother, Mitchell was the source of the blood that stained the rope. Now, the thing that puzzled me, was that the rope was so badly stained, almost six feet stained. Configured in a loop around your brother, well, I estimate would be no more than four feet. You may recall I asked if the rope was stained by cow's blood or pig's blood. Do you recall that?" The judge looked squarely in the face of Everly Ormsby as he spoke.

"Yes, Judge. I do recollect that you said that." Everly glanced at his brother.

"SO," continued the judge, "I asked Sheriff Hickatrisk to do something for me. I asked him to buy two ropes just like the evidence rope and stain it with blood to the extent we see the evidence rope stained. One was stained with cow's blood, the other with blood from a swine and the sheriff was to measure how much blood it took to stain the rope to the same extent as the evidence rope." Judge Norton paused as Everly showed comprehension of what he said. Continuing: "Now, here's the thing, it took one fourth of a pint of pigs' blood to stain the rope to the same extent, but the same amount of cow's blood only stained half as much rope. How can you account for it? How can the evidence rope be stained to the extent it is, when it appears you used cow's blood?"

"Because, Judge, it wasn't cow's blood, it was pig's blood which covers more rope, just as the sheriff..." interrupting himself, Everly turned to look at his brother, who was holding his head in his hands.

Later that day, Mav spoke to Sheriff Hickatrisk, asking: "Sheriff Hickatrisk, how did the judge know Everly was lying?"

"He didn't, for certain. Mitchel claimed he freed himself. Everly, however, claimed that he was responsible for freeing Mitchell, so there was that difference, but the judge thought the rope seemed too much stained to have occurred from the event described. The stains appeared to have been made by dipping since the stains were throughout the rope, not just on the surface of the outer fibers. Also, he told me that the testimony from Everly was too voluntary. He answered more than either the prosecution or defense asked, —as if he was selling a worn-out mule to some eastern rube. Judge Norton dislikes witnesses that try to play him."

"I wondered about Judge Norton's thinking. I mean, his comparison of pig blood and cow blood was questionable at best." Mav came to his feet.

Sheriff Hickatrisk stood up in recognition that the conversation was ending. "Yes, but the judge believed that any confusion that was presented to Everly would get a response that would be revealing of his attempted deception."

"What if the judge had been wrong, or if Everly had not tripped up answering the judge's question?" asked Mav.

"I'd be locking you up about now," replied Sheriff Hickatrisk.

Chapter 42

Educating a Ko-tá ˘

The response to the growing non-farm responsibilities of the Caid family with its tightening schedules, was to hire someone to take over management of the dairy herd. His name is Clarence Killebrew, from Abilene. He is to handle the herd and manage all production of milk products.

"Clarence, this is Macy, my wife," said Mav, introducing the two, "and this is *Já-gĕ*, our daughter."

"Kinda different, ain't she," replied Clarence, "Antelope, I mean."

"A joy in our lives," returned Mav. "But, how did you know *Já-gĕ* meant Antelope?"

"A mighty cute little Injun," replied Clarence, smiling but not answering the question. "Are you going to send her back to her people? What tribe does she belong to? *Já-gĕ* is an Apache name and there are several different Apache tribes."

"*Já-gĕ* is a foundling. We are now her people, but the tribe into which she was born, is unknown. But I reckon they know where she is and someday may tell us more about her," replied Mav.

"How did you get her?" asked Clarence.

"Oddly enough," returned Mav, "I found her hanging in a tree."

"Ah. In a tree!" said Clarence. "Did anyone ever tell you that the Apache bury dead children in trees?"

"NO!" replied Mav with some shock. "*Já-gĕ*, was laced in a cradleboard in a tree from which I freed her."

"Well, you see, the Apache bury the adults in clefts of rocks with small stones heaped over the body to discourage wild animals from digging up the body. They consider infants too weak for their souls to break through the rocks and reach their sky home, so, they place them in a cradleboard and put a cloth over them and tie them face up in cedar or pine trees. I traded with the Apache for many years, even lived with them for a few, so I had occasion to see how they lived and died." Clarence was satisfied with himself for providing information on the mortuary practices of the Apache.

"Well, they could not have been mistaken in th' case of *Já-gĕ*, because she was a-wailing to high heaven when I found her. There had to be another reason. I just don't know what it is." Mav answered with finality.

"Abandonment of children is not a practice of the Apache," responded Clarence, "I suspect she was meant to be found. They had their reasons. One might question if she was meant to be found by anyone, or just you."

Following a discussion of duties and responsibilities of the job, Clarence Killebrew left the farm and went back to the ranch. Mav and Macy remained on the porch swing talking. *Já-gĕ* slept in a cradle beside them.

"What are your thoughts about Killebrew?" asked Mav.

"I'm not sure yet. Clarence smiled a lot, but he did draw attention to the fact that *Já-gĕ* is Indian, and asked if we were planning to send her back to her tribe. Maybe it was just conversation," Macy responded, the hint of uncertainty in her voice.

A few days later, Mav saddled Hardtack for a trip into Beaton to order a part for the windmill. The day being temperate, Mav again decided to take the longer path to Beaton.

Billowy clouds drifted overhead against a cerulean sky while a gentle breeze swept through the trees causing leaves to flutter and grass to wave in those natural meadows scattered among the forest trees. As he approached the spot within the canopy of spreading trees where he found *Já-gĕ*, he saw hanging from the same tree a rolled-up buckskin that swung back and forth like a clock pendulum. 'Perhaps,' he thought, 'I wasn't wrong in thinking someone is watching over *Já-gĕ* from a distance and that someday we will know her history.' Stopping under the hanging leather bundle, Mav again stood in his stirrups to cut the hide down. Unrolling the hide revealed a series of multi-chrome pictures painted on the cured hide, pictures that he had no experience in interpreting. 'Another puzzle,' thought Mav, 'I wonder who can help decipher these pictures as schoolmaster Vale explained the key to the map uncle Wendell drew.'

✳✳✳

"Macy, I don't know how to read th' pictures on this hide. Come look at them. See if you can draw any sense from them." Mav held the painted hide out to Macy who took it in hand.

"What I see is four circles, segmented into quarters in each corner of the buckskin, that are attached by wavy lines. Inside are four circles containing human-like characters. Between the three large circles are quarter moon shapes, one dark, one light, and four crosses, two that are shaped like a four-blade windmill. The whole must tell a story, yet

351

I have no clue what they mean." Macy handed back the buckskin, shaking her head. "Sorry. Makes no sense to me."

Considering that Clarence lived with the Apache for a time, Mav asked him if he could interpret the leather scroll. Clarence told him that the scroll would be 'big medicine' to the Apache but could give him no understanding of the figures on the scroll, as the medicine man, the *dĭ-gĭ'n*, of the tribe had never taken him into his confidence.

"I guess it must remain a mystery for now. I have no idea where I can get an interpreter for the characters." Mav re-rolled the buckskin and placed it behind the Seth Thomas Regulator clock on the mantel, then paused to wind the spring that was nearing exhaustion. The clock was one of the many items purchased in Chicago when he visited the Beloit Jewelry Manufacturing company's owner to deliver the year's collection of diamonds.

✳✳✳

Three months passed, and Mav has received the part for the windmill. Mav is preparing to climb the structure to replace the part that needs replacing.

"Don't go up there now, Mav," advised Macy, "the weather is not going to hold much longer, and it could be dangerous if the wind gets up, or the gathering storm brings lightning with it." Macy always feels that Mav walks a little too close to the edge.

"I should finish before it gets here. But, ifn I don't come back in within a reasonable time, send Juan to look for me." Mav set out in the farm wagon to the windmill.

Arriving at the site, Mav locked the blades to guard against runaway in high wind and prepared to make the needed repair. He would not have the time he anticipated to complete the repair as a fast-moving front, bearing thunder and lightning swept through leaving Mav lying unconscious on the ground near the windmill that took the lightning strike. Four hours fled, and Mav had not returned home. Strong gusting wind and rain moved across the landscape in bands. Macy would wait no longer and sent Juan to find Mav.

✳✳✳

As Mav lay on the ground, swirling pictures ran through his mind, images of past experiences, scenes of things recognized and unrecognized, pictures of Chico, Fenner Korn, Henry Slade, and Windwalker. There was no intelligible sound beyond that of wind and rain as he lay paralyzed on the ground, unaware of his physical impairment, knowing only that which ran through his mind. Eventually, everything swirled out of existence leaving his mind filled with the sound of a flute rising and falling in tone, and as it diminished, Mav heard the familiar voice of Windwalker.

"Keeper-of-Tears, it is good to see you again. You have called me. You have questions." Windwalker picked up his flute and began to play.   Keeper-of-Tears sat up and looked at the ancient phantasmagoric Windwalker, then saying:

"I want to talk about *Já-gĕ*. I want to know who she is, an' why I have her. I want to know th' meanin' of th' buckskin, an' who gave it to me. Most of all, I want to know what I am to do with th' knowledge." Mav fell silent. Windwalker continued to play. After some minutes, he stopped and began to speak:

"Can you see the buckskin in your mind's eye?" asked Windwalker.

"I see it," answered Mav, and as he looked at the buckskin superimposed upon his mind like characters written upon a schoolhouse blackboard, the first finger of the specter's gnarled mahogany hand began pointing to the images on the buckskin as Windwalker spoke.

353

"In this small circle is *Chalhkĕlh Nalín*, Night Girl and this is *Kútĕrastan*, The One Who Lives Above. Here is *Stĕnátlĭhăn*, Woman Without Parents. These others are *Chuganaái Skhĭn*, Sun Boy; *Chuganaái*, The Sun; *Klĕganaái*, The Moon; *Yádĭlhkĭh Bĭnálzĕ*, Sky Messengers; *Nigostŭn Bĭká Bĭnálzĕ*, Earth Messengers; *Nastĕlh*, Makers of Dreams and Visions, and *Hádĭlhkĭh*, Lightning. *Hádĭlhkĭh* has touched you, that you might speak with me." Windwalker continued to point out all the sacred symbols painted on the buckskin and to tell Keeper-of-Tears what they mean to the Apache, finally saying, "You must take the sacred buckskin to the mountains so that you may learn of *Já-gĕ*."

"But tell me, Windwalker, tell me what..." Mav was being shaken by the strong hands of Juan, saying: "*Signor*! *Signor* Caid! Wake up! Wake up!"

After some time, Mav returned to the reality of the moment, and Juan has brought Mav back to the house where a concerned Macy is scurrying around getting some water and asking if Mav is ok.

"Water?" said Mav, "cain't I just have some coffee?"

"Hound! And I thought you were hurt! You scared me to death!" replied Macy, relieved.

✳✳✳

Days later, Macy came across Mav in the process of packing his saddlebags and laying out clothes for a trip that he had not mentioned to Macy before.

"Mav, what are you doing?" asked Macy. "Are you going somewhere?"

"Yes," returned Mav, "I'm goin' to take a few days an' ride over to th' Ouachita. There is somethin' I need to do."

Macy accepted Mav's answer without inquiring further. It was Mav's decision and she respects his decisions. She is certain that Mav will tell her eventually.

"I'll get together some salted meat, some airtights of tomatoes and such, and coffee that I know you will want," Macy interjected, then set about getting the coffee pot and utensils he will need.

As his last gesture before leaving, Mav took the buckskin from the mantel and walked from the room onto the porch. From there, Mav went to the barn and saddled Hardtack. He expected the trip to take several days, yet there was no certainty.

"Hardtack, we are not going to th' valley this time. This time, we go into th' Ouachita." Hardtack shook his head and started in a trot out the gate and into the wilderness. Two days they would travel before entering the foothills, another to reach the more elevated terrain, and another to reach ultimate seclusion. They would stop and make camp and await the will of whatever power that has directed their pathway to this omphalos of solitudinous wilderness, this sanctuary of the wild.

That night, a full moon rose into an azure sky and continued its path into a dark realm of sparkling stars. Somewhere a hoot owl voiced a plaintive sound answered by a growing wind sweeping the uplifted terrain and whistling through the trees. A wolf, somewhere in the forest howled and from four quarters answers reprised his lonely call. Mav sat patiently, waiting for something he could not comprehend. Finally, for reasons he could not explain, he rose and took the buckskin and began to climb to the pinnacle of the rock uplift. When he reached the summit, Mav bent down and placed the unrolled buckskin before him, its characters illuminated by the full moon's radiant shine, its magnitude enhanced by the clear air. Mav stood overlooking all of nature as if he was the first man to witness its majesty, the first to ponder its meaning, the first to know the 'I am'. All around him were the mountain peaks, illuminated by the full moon. The otherwise darkened forest spread in counterpoint to the expanse of sky showing the vast milky way above. Presently, Mav sat upon the projecting rock citadel, legs crossed, back straight, hands, palm up upon his knees, eyes closed invoking unfamiliar powers. Unseen, just twenty paces away was a catamount of extreme proportion, watching through golden eyes.

"Keeper-of-Tears," came the discarnate voice from out of the night's void. "You have been chosen to teach *Já-gĕ* the ways of the white man. She must know the new ways and not have her heart too tightly bound to the old ways of the fathers, yet she must also know of the *Tzlĭh A Gŏ"*, the people from whom she came. You will be her teacher. She will be ours. The fight is over between our people. We share the wisdom of *Hinmatóoywyalahtqit,* — Chief Joseph of the Nez Perce, who said, many moons ago, 'From where the sun now stands, I will fight no more…forever.'[7]"

Silence ensued for a few minutes, then the voice continued: "The gods have talked as you can see by the lines of lightning reaching from spirit to spirit on the sacred medicine buckskin. I am *Nastĕlh*, an earth messenger, between the spirits and the keepers of nature. The spirits have decided that the way of the white man is the only way of the future for the Apache. Only by becoming one people in the tribe of Everyman will the *Naishandina,* —our people, —the people of *Já-gĕ,* survive."

Each entity is identified by this incorporeal voice and the story of their coming to be. There are some who would say the time passed quickly and some who would say it stood still. Whatever one might say of time, when Mav climbed down from that lofty stone citadel, three moons had risen, and three moons had set, yet he did not know.

Arrival back at the home-place chanced questions that he could not answer without people thinking him a man of bizarre beliefs, a man of extreme hallucination, perhaps a mad man, and so he remained silent. The experience was one of enlightenment. The child, *Já-gĕ*, became less the foundling ward and more the sacred charge. *Já-gĕ*, would grow and learn the ways of the white man, speak the language of the White man but would never wonder what her blood must know, —that she is the daughter of a revered chieftain of the Kiowa-Apache nation, one given into the care of a *ko-tá˘*, chosen from the many by the powers who are.

Chapter 43

Plowing New Ground

Case Caid has just reached his seventeenth birthday and has received new clothes to match his growth for the year. Mav thinks of his own seventeenth birthday, soon after which he left home to join Captain Lytle's cattle drive to Nebraska. He recalls the conversation:

"When will you be back?" asks his ma, as he packs the clothes, he wants to take with him.

"I don't reckon I know," answers Mav. "I jes' want to work with Captain Lytle an' see somethin' of th' country. I'm not gone forever. I'll be back someday." He recalls that it was in 1884, the last time he saw them alive. The experience has given him the uncomfortable understanding that every goodbye is potentially forever and the best one can do is say it with a prayer.

Eugene Stonefield

"Be careful, son, remember your roots," said his pa, as he mounted his horse to ride to a local Bandera ranch where Lytle was recruiting drovers to take a herd of longhorn cattle north to market.

"I will, Pa," replied Mav, thinking how unnecessary the advice. "Why would I not?"

$$***$$

Unlike his pa, Case has no wanderlust and is satisfied with living and working at home with the cattle herd and the farm when needed. He thrives on increasing responsibilities, and he takes them seriously. All the authority to run the beef cattle operation is his, and he spends most of his time ten miles away at the ranch, while Mav and Macy remain on the home-place in their new house built in the same location as the old cabin that was torn down to make room for the new home. Gone are the log walls of the owner-built cabin, and welcome are the walls of sawn lumber from the lumber mill of Carlton and Henson Graves, or the C & H Mills as it is known. Just as in the old cabin, the new home contained a secret vault for valuables and memories behind the mantle. In this vault among various deeds for property in Texas and Arkansas is a mud-stained diary, a lock of auburn hair, and a golden lock of Lyla's, —those touchable evidences of memories.

"Macy," said Mav, "I think we orta…_ought_ to talk to Case about college. He finished his schooling with schoolmaster Vale a couple of years ago with good marks, an' he knows about farming an' ranching, but it's th' business aspects that I reckon he will need down th' road. We ain't…_aren't_ getting younger, an' he needs to be prepared better than I was. Nowadays, everything you do needs to have a contract drawn up before you can do it. Sometimes lawyers write those contracts in such a biased manner they cheat a person, an' it is all legal. It will make it so much easier on Case if he knows more."

"Where would we send him?" asked Macy.

"I read that th' state is building a new agricultural college to be opened next year in Jonesboro on land made available by th' Morrill Land Grant College Act an' is to be called th' First District Agricultural College. He will have to live there, but we can afford it, an' he will gain by th' experience. Since th' war between th' states, higher education ain't…<u>isn't</u> all about Latin an' Greek anymore, its more about learning practical things to help people live more productive lives. They say this will be possible by learning more about scientific farming, an' engineering. When he graduates, he will be th' first in th' family to do so. My pa moved to New Orleans from Carolina at seventeen where he grew up an' had only a modest education. He met my ma there an' my ma had a little more, simply because her folks were more affluent an' paid a private educator up until her fifteenth year. They moved to Texas with a group recruited by Stephen F. Austin. There was little opportunity for getting an education in them…<u>those</u> days. My own schoolin' was lacking in many ways, but th' schoolmasters were not well educated themselves an' were paid mostly with gifts of victuals from parents of the children they taught. College is an opportunity to break the mold for Case." Mav sipped his coffee and opened the Gazette.

"Away from home, Mav?" asked Macy.

"He could come home on holidays," responded Mav. "An', don't forget, he spends most of his time now at th' ranch, so it won't be much different. Jonesville is a railway stop, so traveling by railway is much easier now and it is affordable. He would travel to an' from college in comfort."

The next year, 1910, welcomed the first class on the new campus of the new two-year, First District Agricultural College at Jonesboro and seventeen-year-old Case Caid sat down at his desk prepared to hear Professor Kensington's lecture on the new science of soil management.

"Welcome to your brand-new college," began Professor Kensington. "Today we will be plowing new ground in the science of soil management. I'm accepting that most of you are from farms and are following the lead of your fathers and grandfathers in their tried-and-true farming practices. Beginning today though, you will be learning how to farm more productively using the guidance of the scientific agricultural methods and techniques that agricultural scientists have developed over the years. We will identify people and their contributions as we proceed to an understanding of what soil management is and why we want to participate in it. The first person we will cover is Professor James Jay Mapes, a chemist, and researcher in scientific agriculture. Professor Mapes, who died in 1866, was known as an analytic chemist who was a founder of the National Agricultural Society and held many prestigious posts during his lifetime. He is better known for his study of soil drainage, crop rotation, and seeding, and for the development of fertilizer, he named, —not surprisingly, —Mapes Fertilizer. James Mapes married Sophie Furman, daughter of Judge Garrett Furman of Long Island and they had four children, Mary Mapes Dodge, author of children's books, Sophie Mapes Tolles, artist and teacher of painting, Catherine T. Bunnell, of whom we know little, and Charles Victor Mapes, an agricultural scientist and engineer. Charles Mapes is himself known for developing and promoting Mapes Complete Manure. No laughing, gentlemen! Please! His formula, based on bat guano from Peru was the foundation for his company, The Mapes Formula and Peruvian Guano Company, that he established in 1877. The important thing here is the importance of scientific investigation to the business of growing crops. Fertilized crops on well-drained land where crop rotation is employed along with proper seeding will produce more product for the market and more money in the pockets of the farmer.

Now, is that not the desire of any farmer? Later in the year, we will be discussing animal husbandry, a subject that those of you who are dairy farmers. We will also be covering the subject of engineering and the 'holy grail' of farming, the concept of making machines do the work now done by people. Oh, yes, gentlemen. The days are coming when a farmer plows, plants, and harvests his crops by machines, and when the dairy farmer milks his cows by machine. And it will be people, like are in this class today, that make it happen."

It is an awakening to Case that there are other ways to farm, other ways to raise animals. He also learned that, aside from his study of soil management, he could enroll in classes in industrial engineering and mathematics. The focus of the college, professor Kensington told the students, is to develop knowledge and skills in students to allow them to enter a modern world's labor force with enough understanding of the science of farming to be successful. Some, he told them, would return to their family farms and ranches to manage them. Others would choose to begin their adult lives working in industry, or as scientists themselves. In accepting admission to the colleges opened in Morrill Land Grant campuses, students must receive a level of military training in the reserve officer training corps, or ROTC, and many will choose to accept a commission in the US Army after graduation. Some will go to war.

Chapter 44

Girl Dance at Sunrise

During the preceding years, Beaton has continued to grow and is now the home of a vibrant community of merchants, social and religious organizations, schools, and any other imaginable endeavors that bring people together. On the international scene in this year of 1914, hot discord rages between nations. A war to be known as the war to end all wars, in which millions will die from violence at a level the world has never witnessed before is in the offing. People will see the carnage as recorded on rapidly moving photographic films, viewed in theaters throughout the civilized world, and make people wonder if there is such a thing as a civilized world. On the home-front, between 1914 and 1915, a pre-pubescent *Já-gĕ* learns her lessons from schoolmaster Allison Wexler and learns her history from her *ko-tá˘*, as she knows him, Mav Caid, whom she calls Papa.

Eugene Stonefield

As did *Já-gĕ* learn of Jesus Christ and his meaning to the white man, she also learned of other children of miraculous birth, such as the son of the Sun, *Nayĕnĕzganĭ* and the son of Water, *Tobadzĭschĭnĭ*. She learned of virgins Mary, mother of Jesus, and *Yólkai Ĕstsán*, also known as White Shell Woman, though she did not yet comprehend the meaning. She learned of the sacred symbols of the cross and the crescent. *Já-gĕ* learned of the time of illimitable darkness, before the days of the earth, moon, sun, and stars, and she learned how they came to be through the work of *Kútĕrastan*, The One Who Lives Above, also called *Yŭádĭstan*, Sky Man. She learned of *Stĕnátlĭhăn*, Woman Without Parents. And she learned how, by *Kútĕrastan, Stĕnátlĭhăn, Chuganaái, and Hádĭntĭn Skhĭn*, all things came about. *Já-gĕ* learned much from her *ko-táˇ*, —a.k.a., Papa, a.k.a., Mav Caid, a.k.a., Keeper-of-Tears, —as he learned it first and passed it on. Many were the sessions of learning upon that lonely sandstone citadel in the Ouachita to which, time after time, Mav returned. On each visit, his interlocutor advised him how to prepare *Já-gĕ* to be a woman and he has learned how to get her ready for the Sunrise ceremony, that she may leave youth and become the White-Shell Woman, the Changing Woman.

Youth has always been a fleeting thing and *Já-gĕ*, the young 'Antelope,' owns her share of that fleeting youth. Months and years have flown and even though her actual date of birth is unknown; her body will tell her when she is to abandon childhood and become a woman. That telling came in the year 1915.

On a mid-morning in March, Mav came from the house and sat by Macy who was sitting in the porch swing with a pensive look on her face.

"Perhaps *Já-gĕ* should not run today, Mav," said Macy to begin the conversation.

"Why not?" replied Mav, "she runs well, —truly like an antelope, an' she loves it."

"*Já-gĕ* does run like an antelope," stated Macy, "she seems never to tire, but she is changing now."

Not recognizing the significance of Macy's comment, Mav replied: "Yes, but it is nothing less than what she will need to be able to do in the Girl Dance." [8]

"You have spoken about the ceremony. Tell me more."

"Th' Girl Dance or, *nalín bagúdzĭtash,* is a dance fo' young girls becoming women an' is very important to their prestige an' self-assurance. Th' dance begins at sunrise an' lasts until th' sun is high in th' sky for several days. Participants are eligible when they are aware of th' changes thet…that mark their entry into adulthood. It consists of many dances, songs, enactments, an' demonstrations of physical endurance. Participating in th' ceremony imbues participants with th' powers of White Shell Woman, a spiritual icon of th' Apache. To keep *Já-gĕ* a member of th' Apache that her voice has resonance in th' future, she must engage in this important ceremony," returned Mav.

"I don't think I will ask you how you know this," answered Macy. "Where will the ceremony be held?"

"On the reservation. We will be going there soon, I suspect," answered Mav.

"Yes, soon, Mav. It is time." Macy gave a foot-shove to set the swing in motion.

✳✳✳

Two months later, Mav, Macy and *Já-gĕ* are preparing for a trip to the reservation in Oklahoma, the land of the Kiowa, the tribe of Chief *Ahpeahtone,* the son of Red Otter and relative of Red Cloud of the Lakota Sioux, and Lone Wolf of the Apache. The trip would take the better part of three months.

***

"Why do you wish to go to the reservation?" asked the blue-clad Lieutenant at the Fort where visitors to the reservation must declare their reasons for wanting entrance.

"To visit relatives," responded Mav.

"Your relatives?" asked the Lieutenant, suspiciously.

"No, for our daughter, *Já-gĕ*, who is Apache," answered Mav.

'Do you have any contraband in your wagon?" asked the Lieutenant.

"We do not," replied Mav. "You may search the wagon if you wish."

"Check in with me as you leave. Just ask for First Lieutenant Issa Trailer."

Proceeding onto the reservation toward the village of the Apache, Mav and Macy began to wonder how Indians of the plains survive on this desolate land. The buffalo are gone, and the Apache are not farmers. If asked of the Lieutenant, they would learn that the Apache, as do many other tribes, subsist on the meager allowances provided by the 'Great White Father' in Washington through the Department of Indian Affairs. If they asked the Apache, they would learn that those allowances are indeed 'meager' and that the tribes grow weaker each day. All long for the old days, before the white man invaded and took their land by force and guile; before the buffalo hunters slaughtered the herds and starved the Apache; before soldiers forced them to live on reservations; before Washington forbid ceremonial dancing.

As the three travelers arrived at the village of dome-shaped huts of cottonwood poles covered by grass thatch called *kó-wa*, Mav spoke to a member of the tribe in broken Apache that he had learned from conversations with the messengers and with former trader, Clarence Killebrew who was conversant in the Kiowa-Apache language.

"I am Mav Caid, an' I bring *Já-gě* of th' *Tzlǐh A Gǒⁿ*, —On The Mountain, —tribe to participate in th' Girl Dance."

"Ha!" replied the Apache tribe member who immediately signaled that they should follow him. Upon arrival at a *kó-wa* in the middle of the village, the tribe member directed Mav to enter the *kó-wa* while Macy and *Já-gě* waited in the wagon.

"Welcome, Mav Caid. I am *Que-Tah-Tsay*. White men call me *Ahpeahtone*, — in white-man talk it means, Kills-With-A-Lance." The deference shown to Mav was both unexpected and humbling. For someone unknown to the tribe to be so quickly introduced to the chief of the tribe is an honor.

"The messengers told us of your coming. *Que-Tah-Tsay* shall meet with *Já-gě*," the venerable chieftain told Mav, but first, the honored visitor, Mav Caid, and *Que-Tah-Tsay* must smoke the sacred pipe.[9] It was a tradition of which Mav had heard about but knew little of. For the next few minutes, summonsed leaders of the tribe began to assemble in the lodge and *Que-Tah-Tsay* told them the issue to deliberate is the acceptance of *Já-gě* to participate in the Girl Dance ceremony, a passage rite that many call the *na'íi'ees*, Sunrise ceremony.

Que-Tah-Tsay called for the pipe carrier to bring the sacred pipe for a pipe ceremony with the visitor, Mav Caid. Shortly thereafter, these important tribal members took their seats on the ground in a circle around the fire, each displaying a solemn mien in recognition of the importance of this meaningful ceremony. The pipe is a gift of White Buffalo Calf Woman of legend and everything about the pipe ceremony is symbolic and ritualized. It is solemn and sacred in its entirety; it is a bridge to the spirit world. Participants smoke tobacco because its roots thrust deep into the soil of the earth. Fire to burn the tobacco is no different from fire of the sun, and smoke rising high into the sky, are the reaching words of participants to the spirit world. Through the pipe ceremony, man and the spirits communicate.

Eugene Stonefield

Que-Tah-Tsay began the celebration by smudging himself in the smoke of the fire. Taking the pipe from the pipe carrier and, holding the pipe aloft, —pipe bowl in his left hand, stem in his right, —*Que-Tah-Tsay,* after offering a small amount of the sacred tobacco to the four directions, loaded the bowl with tobacco and lit the pipe with a bundle of grass set to flame by the fire around which the celebrants sat. Taking a puff, *Que-Tah-Tsay* slowly released the smoke with a prayer assuring his appeal will reach the spirit world with the soaring smoke and, as this occurred, *Que-Tah-Tsay* smudged himself again by passing his free hand through the rising, prayer laden, smoke.

Que-Tah-Tsay took another draw on the pipe, holding the smoke in for a few seconds then allowed it to escape upward into the air. *Que-Tah-Tsay* again, waved his hand through the smoke before he spoke:

"I am told, Mav Caid, that you are the Keeper-of-Tears." *Que-Tah-Tsay* fell silent awaiting an answer. After absorbing the initial shock of his knowledge, Mav replied:

"I am called Keeper-of-Tears, *Que-Tah-Tsay.* I did not know you knew this."

Que-Tah-Tsay responded: "I have been waiting for thirteen summers for your visit, Keeper-of-Tears."

Que-Tah-Tsay rotated the pipe clockwise through the four cardinal directions then offered the pipe, bowl first, to Keeper-of-Tears who attempted to copy the manner of smoking by *Que-Tah-Tsay,* but with a different result.

"You cough, Keeper-of-Tears," chided *Que-Tah-Tsay,* amused at the novice pipe smoker.

"My first time, *Que-Tah-Tsay.* Th' pipe is good," Keeper-of-Tears responded as he passed the pipe to the *dĭ-gi˘n,* the tribe's medicine man, called *Tli-chú bu,* or Red Owl. The pipe passed around the seated circle of prominent people of the tribe several times for two hours, each time returning to *Que-Tah-Tsay* from Black Beaver, first son of the chief.

Each participant had his opportunity to weigh in on the issue as the ceremony proceeded, until *Que-Tah-Tsay* made his decision.

"*Já-gĕ* will celebrate the *nalín bagúdzĭtash*, the Girl Dance" *Que-Tah-Tsay* announces to participants in the ceremony as he passed the pipe again to Mav. With each draw upon the pipe, silence ensued for a time in which the person contemplates that that needs contemplation, and perhaps, communicating his thoughts to others.

"It is th' wish of th' powers as I understand them," responded Mav, taking a draw from the pipe, and passing it again to Red Owl, then falling silent. A pause of some minutes ensues as a response is composed.

"Is she ready?" asked *Que-Tah-Tsay*. Again, a pause follows.

"I have been guided well by th' *chĭdn*, th' spirits, *Que-Tah-Tsay*. She is prepared," returned Keeper-of-Tears. "Only her costume is wanting, an' instruction on th' songs an' dances."

"I have been told, Keeper-of-Tears. It shall be done, even though the Great Father in Washington has forbidden the ceremony for many moons and it must be done where there are no eyes and ears of the white man." *Que-Tah-Tsay* continued to smoke and passed the pipe back to Keeper-of-Tears. As the pipe ceremony progresses, Mav Caid, a.k.a., Keeper-of-Tears, senses to his marrow the position he holds in the history of the Apache, and feels his brotherhood with this small band of notables within the natives of the continent, the aboriginals, known to themselves simply as 'the people.'

The pipe ceremony is a deliberative one, hurrying through a ceremony is sacrilege, and each participant had his say as the pipe passes among them. All participants agreed that *Já-gĕ* was welcome to celebrate with others who are ready for this, now illegal, ceremony. *Já-gĕ* will follow tradition and take a sacred eagle feather to place upon the feet of a respected tribal matron who will become the sponsor for the young girl becoming a young woman.

Eugene Stonefield

After the pipe ceremony came to its close, *Que-Tah-Tsay* stood and walked from his *kó-wa* with Mav following behind. Approaching the wagon with Macy and *Já-gĕ*, the chief stopped before them.

"I am *Que-Tah-Tsay*, chief of the Apache. I welcome you *Mā-Ce*, primary squaw of Keeper-of-Tears, and *Já-gĕ*, princess of the *Tzlĭh A Gó*." Immediately following, *Que-Tah-Tsay* turned and walked back into his *kó-wa*.

Soon after this historic welcoming, Mav, Macy, and *Já-gĕ* drove their wagon to the outskirts of the village and set up camp under a cottonwood. The following day brought visitors to the camp, women to begin preparing *Já-gĕ* for the grueling ceremony scheduled four days hence, and *ko-ki*, the tribe members, to visit Keeper-of-Tears, one who is unaccustomed to his elevated status. Macy, the primary squaw of Keeper-of-Tears, wrestles with the surreal experience but graciously accepts her own high state even though she knew nothing of how her husband became Keeper-of-Tears, nor what it means.

Because of the restrictions on dance ceremonies placed upon the tribes by the government in Washington, members of the tribe kept the ceremony secret from the Indian Agent and soldiers. Many prayers sent to the spirit world were asking the higher spirits to protect the ceremony from discovery. Ultimately, the tribe will hold the dance deep in the reservation where the soldiers will not hear sounds from the drums. The dance will commence with all the seriousness of a baptism in the community of the white man.

Songs and dances begin the long ceremony, and several squaws with experience will guide *Já-gĕ* in learning the dances and the songs. Red Owl, the *dĭ-gi˘n*, the medicine man, will play a major role in the dance as he does in any other. As the squaws cut and stitch the whitened deerskin for dress and moccasins, they sing songs to *Já-gĕ* that she will repeat until she knows them by heart. She learns the dances and is given a companion to help her during the ceremony if needed. After three days, all is ready.

Mav Caid — The Complete Story

Já-gĕ will dance the sacred dances daily for four torturous days, each day requiring an increase in the number of hours she will dance. She will demonstrate her physical endurance by running toward the sun at dawn, and toward the four directions symbolic of the four stages of life. She will repeat these runs four times to circle the basket of sacred corn as, each time, the distance increases. She will throw the buckskin blankets toward the four directions; she will lay upon a sacred robe and be massaged by a selected god-mother until she is shaped and reformed into White Shell Woman; and this, all while her face is covered with a sacred commixture of cornmeal and clay that she must not remove for the four days. In her hair she will wear an eagle feather and a white shell. The dance and accompanying songs retell the story of *Esdzanadehe*, Changing Woman, also called White Shell Woman, who survived the great Flood in an abalone shell, then after the waters receded, wandered the mountain, and gives birth to a son named *Nayé˘nĕsganĭ*, Slayer of Alien Gods and *Tobadzĭschí nĭ*, called From Water Born. Through ceremonial reenactment, *Já-gĕ* will receive the spiritual essence of Changing Woman. Finally, *Já-gĕ* will bless the members of the tribe with cattail pollen and will heal them by prayer and touch. Once all completes, *Já-gĕ* will exchange gifts with others of the tribe in recognition of her changed status from childhood to womanhood.

Families of the girls of the celebration provide food and gifts to members of the tribe. Preparation of the food is participatory, and Macy learned much of the way of the Apache. As participants and tribal members exchange gifts, members of the tribe were astounded, but pleased, to receive a tear of the sun, a big medicine of legend, assuring a cure should their hearts fall into melancholy after this joyful day.

On the fifth day, Mav, Macy, and *Já-gĕ* prepared to leave, and as they got into the wagon, the tribe, led by Chief *Que-Tah-Tsay*, gathered before them. Presently the chief stepped forward and placed an eagle feather in the hand of each visitor to honor their participation in a ceremony one in which *Já-gĕ* pledges to renew the fight to restore their right to the dance.

Chapter 45

A Dread Realized

The day is April 6, 1917, and a two and a half year war engulfs Europe. It is a war in which America has sought to remain neutral, but now, American President Woodrow Wilson has acceded to the will of Congress in requesting that Congress declare war on Germany. This action is in response to the growing losses to American shipping from German submarine attacks in the North Sea, a tally of five American merchant ships, lost in March alone. The sinking of the British passenger liner, Lusitania, in 1915 was enough an outrage for former president Theodore Roosevelt, and fellow Republicans to demand that the United States enter the war and they have agitated since for a declaration. Democrat Woodrow Wilson, the current president, had negotiated an understanding with Germany restricting future sinking of passenger liners without first allowing the passengers to launch lifeboats. Subsequently, though, Germany abrogated the agreement in 1917, enraging many in the United States and virtually assuring American involvement. American citizens had generally been approving of non-involvement, but the British interception of a cable from Germany to Mexico, known as the Zimmerman Telegram, proposing an alliance between Mexico and Germany that would assure an attack by Mexico on the United States if the US became engaged, forced the issue. American forces joined on the Western Front, as it was known, in 1918. This new reality for citizens of the United States evokes days of patriotic and fearful conversations within affected families. How many families of German immigrants suffered the trauma of having to choose between their native homeland and their new homeland in America. Their number is legion.

∗∗∗

"Mav, this involvement in the war in Europe has me worried. What happens if we don't win? What if Germany wins?" Macy asked the question on the minds of many.

"I don't know, Macy," Mav replied while reading the Gazette. "We just have to hope that doesn't happen."

"Since the Conscription Act passed last year, most of my concern has been for Case. He's twenty-six, and right in the middle of the age range for conscription, I worry that they could call him up. I just worry, Mav." Macy tied an apron around her waist and began to prepare an evening meal as they continued the conversation.

"What are we havin' for supper?" asked Mav.

"It is a German recipe I got from Mrs. Steiner who wanted to thank me for our finding her husband. It's called sauerbraten and I wouldn't be making it if you had not built the icehouse where it could marinate the meat for three days. I'll have red cabbage to go with it and pumpernickel bread." Presently, Case joined them.

"Pa, I think we need to let those fifty acres of cotton we just harvested go fallow for a year or longer. If not, then do some crop rotation and plant legumes in the winter to help restore the soil." Case sat down across from Mav, then continuing, "There are some ongoing scientific studies at several universities, —one called Morrow Plots at the University of Illinois, Sanborn Field in Missouri-Columbia, and one in Alabama at Auburn University called Old Rotation, that purposely rotates the planting of cotton with legumes and studies the results. I have read synopses of the work and find the results convincing. The study began in 1896 so it has a credible length of time since beginning. We should follow its lead and do our own study."

"What would you suggest we plant?" asked Mav, taking a sip of coffee. "We have had cotton growing on that land for eighteen years at least."

"Soybean or Chickpea. That's what I think we should plant. Scientific studies prove that legumes restore nitrogen to the soil depleted of nitrogen by crops such as cotton. Rotating the planting of cotton with legume crops ensures better yields over time. The nutrients will enrich the soil that's been under cotton cultivation for so many years it is at risk of depletion."

"But, fifty acres? Isn't that a lot to take out of production?" returned Mav.

"But that's only twenty percent of what we have under cultivation now. I'm thinking that if we rotate through by taking twenty percent out of production each year and concentrating the effort on improving the soil, we will be better off in following years. Some farmers are following a strategy of rotation that changes out the crops over a four-year cycle between legumes such as peas or beans; leafy vegetables like spinach or lettuce; fruit bearing, such as corn or squash; and root crops, like beets or turnips. It just takes management, and, it isn't like they can't harvest and sell them or used them to feed our animals. It isn't making the land less productive, but more productive overall." Case looked at Mav and waited.

"Let's talk about this on another day. Right now, your ma and I are concerned with the war and the conscription act. Everyone in the age range twenty-one through thirty-one must register for the draft." Mav showed a concerned face to Case.

"I know, Pa. I've already registered with the Selective Service, and if they call me up, well, it's not like I haven't already had some training. My college had an active program of military ROTC training that was required of all able-bodied students," replied Case. "I am ready to serve my country if called to do so, and should be able to join with the beginning rank of lieutenant."

A month later, Case received a notice to report for induction into the Army. Given his status as highly educated with ROTC training, his request for assignment to the US Army Air Service created by President Woodrow Wilson's Executive Order in 1917, received approval and he is to receive preflight training at The University of Texas in Austin, Texas. Then, if all goes well, he will receive eight-weeks of aviation flight training in the new Curtiss JN-4A Jenny at Kelly Field in San Antonio, Texas. After that, he will be receiving skills training in airborne pursuit, observation, or bombing at one of nine possible fields hosting the specific specialization. After all his training is complete, he will join the American forces across the Atlantic somewhere in Europe.

Second Lieutenant Case Caid completed his three months flight training, receiving his aviator wings as a pursuit pilot, in early October and is home to prepare for his deployment for which he has orders to ship out in two weeks.

"I will be back," promised Case to his ma to assuage her concern. "Nothing will happen to me. I promise to fly safely when I get there." Mav looked on, allowing Macy to carry his concern with hers while trying to show his own fraudulent lack of concern to Case.

Case finished his packing of the few items he will be able to take with him on the troop carrier leaving from New York two weeks from today. He made his exit from the home place amid the serious, fretful, visage of his family, and climbed aboard the wagon Juan had drawn up to carry him to the train station. Two weeks later, Case Caid boarded a troop carrier with three thousand other men embarking for the first time to foreign soil and the turmoil of war. Communication between Case and his family began two months later by letter heavily redacted by military observers.

Dear Ma and Pa,

Arrived on the Western Front and have settled in at [redacted] field in [redacted]. The trip over was rough, and a lot of guys were sick from the constant motion of the ship. All were aware of the possibility of a submarine attack, but no one talked about it much. I have found another flyer I met in college. His name is Raymond, and he is from Littlerock. We bunk together but have different jobs. His is one of observer. Mine is a pursuit of an airborne enemy. The enemy bombers – they call them Gothas – have been bombing [redacted], and it will be our job to stop them. I look forward to the task. I understand that Germany was bombing [redacted] also from Zeppelins, but the enemy seems not to be using them now since the last Zeppelin attack was in August. Apparently, Peter Strasser, German Imperial Navy Commander responsible for Zeppelin operations died when a British pilot shot his airship down during the raid. He was aboard the newly commissioned L 70 Zeppelin as an observer. All is well, otherwise, and I will write when I can but don't know when the next letter should get to you.

Say hello to Já-gĕ and any of my friends you run across. You can send letters to the P. O. box that I have given and they will eventually get to me, but policy forbids disclosure of any identifiable location and Army censors will remove any mention. Several of the pilots have already been sent to units in [redacted]. My place will be where the greatest need lies. The odds are that I and many of the others

I came with will go to [redacted] or [redacted] to support operations on the front. I will write again when I know.

Love all,

Case

Macy was finishing reading Case's letter when Mav arrived. "A letter came from Case," said Macy as she handed the letter to Mav. "I'm relieved that he got across the Atlantic, but I will be sleepless thinking of the task he now has and the dangers involved. Flying through the air just doesn't seem natural, so fast and so high up. I hope Case is flying low and slow."

Mav read the letter but said nothing. He returned to the barn to talk to Hardtack. Although the face he displayed to Hardtack was the stoic face of unconcern, his heart held an unimaginable fear and a wish that he could magically replace Caid with himself, the life of a son, — far, far of greater importance than that of his own.

Chapter 46

Black Beaver

Morning began as any typical morning on the Caid place with a single exception, as riding toward the farmhouse in a dust covered black Model T Ford, is an unknown official of the court.

The sound of the vehicle's arrival brought Mav to the front porch with understandable curiosity. He watched quietly as this unknown person stepped down from the automobile to approach the house.

"Good morning, Mr. Caid?" began the stranger with a lifting of his hat.

"I am Mav Caid," returned Mav, still curious about the man's purpose for coming. "And you are Mr.…?"

"Ralph Haston," replied the man. "I am here to serve an order for you to appear in court in Pine Bluff on the sixth of next month. Please take this summons, Mr. Caid, then I will be on my way."

Eugene Stonefield

A stunned Mav Caid accepted the court summons from Mr. Haston and began to read its notification of a suit initiated in the court to answer for the enslaving of an important maiden from the Kiowa-Apache reservation, one *Já-gĕ*, daughter of Chief Black Beaver of the Kiowa-Apache nation, and the prevention of her returning to her tribe.

After reading the introductory notification, Mav looked down at the waiting officer of the court who had not stepped upon the porch but remained on the ground, two steps lower. "Mr. Haston, I can't say I welcome the purpose of your visit, but you appear to me to be in need of a cup of coffee."

"Indeed, I could accept the offer," replied Mr. Haston, "as I can see that you just may wish to know more about this suit."

Presently, Mav and Ralph Haston entered the house and pulled up chairs to the kitchen table where Mav poured two cups of coffee. "You seem familiar to me, Mr. Haston, have we met before?"

"Well, in a manner we have. I was a law clerk for Judge Simmons who handled the trial of a Mr. Hannibal Rhodes, also known as Barbarossa. Now, this Barbarossa, who was an attorney himself, but lost his right to practice before the court because of his convictions for rustling and attempted murder of your employee, Mr. Wade Pinders, has reemerged as an Indian Agent for the Department of Indian Affairs. I do not know how this happened, however, I do recall that Mr. Rhodes was an expert forger, so his credentials may be fraudulent. If they are, I have reason to suspect that the court did not verify them. Anyway, Rhodes served five years before his release, but is now associated with the complainant, Black Beaver, in his court filing against you. Mr. Rhodes has presented documents to the court citing his standing as a federal Indian agent to participate in this suit, that the judge has accepted. As you will read in the suit, what is sought is the return of *Já-gĕ* to the reservation and one hundred thousand dollars reparation for her enslavement and loss of service to the tribe." Mr. Haston sipped his coffee and waited for Mav to respond.

"Barbarossa should have received a greater sentence, by my reckonin'," offered Mav, then said, "but you are under no obligation to expand upon this suit, so…."

"No, of course not. You will learn all of this when you come to Pine Bluff. And, I'm not stepping over any legal line in telling you that you should take this seriously. There are political dynamics at play, so things are not necessarily as they seem on the surface." His coffee consumed, Mr. Haston stood up and walked to the door where he turned and shook Mav's hand, saying: "Thanks for the coffee. We may not meet again, but, good luck in your defense." At that, Mr. Haston left the Caid place to return to Pine Bluff.

The acceptance of enslavement of vulnerable people for the benefit of others is not a concept that is foreign and, even though the practice is no longer legal in this nation since President Abraham Lincoln emancipated the enslaved people over forty years ago, slavery still exists throughout the world and will so for many years. Society will struggle to control these abhorrent practices into the future. But today, Mav and Macy will deal with the suit in which they are defendants. They have, for the last few weeks, gathered statements from people knowledgeable about the manner of *Já-gĕ* and her arrival at the Caid place years ago. The problem is that there were no first-hand witnesses to the finding of *Já-gĕ* suspended from an overhanging tree limb. The good folks giving their testimony can only testify to what Mav told them. No others witnessed it.

At the appointed time, Mav, Macy and *Já-gĕ* have taken their seats in the courthouse in Pine Bluff to face the charges laid out in the suit by Black Beaver. On the bench is Judge Wilson T. Wilson, who has requested that the court clerk read the essence of the suit to the jury before beginning. Upon completion of this preliminary step, the attorney for the complainants, Mr. Eldridge Lother, has signaled their readiness to proceed. The attorney for Mav Caid, Mr. Felton Wooster, has likewise indicated their readiness.

Eugene Stonefield

The day progressed with the presentation of evidence, hearing from witnesses and the back and forth of lawyers objecting to the questions asked and decisions of Judge Wilson on whether the questions were improper and whether he would allow them or overrule them. At the end of the day, one thing became clear. Judge Wilson had ruled on all objections in favor of the complainants.

"Mr. Caid," began Mr. Wooster, "things are not looking too good for us at this point. If bias is not a taint upon the court, as it appears, then we have stepped into a court that proceeds by rules different from what I know. Now, if we lose, there is always a right to appeal the decision, and there are enough reasons to think we would be successful. The problem is that of time and money to achieve an overturn of the decision. It could be significant. The suit may just be a ruse to force a settlement, because I have here a proffer of a settlement to drop the case that I received at the hotel where I am staying. The complainants are willing to drop the case in return for your ceding ownership of your holdings in Saline County to the complainants. I do not know of those holdings myself, so don't know the significance. In any case, the proffer is good until the beginning of court next Thursday." Mr. Wooster passed the written document to Mav for his reading. Macy looked over his shoulder as he read.

Mav completed his reading and looked across the table to his attorney, saying: "The significance, Mr. Wooster, is that that property is the location of the Caid Bauxite mine. It is worth millions."

"I know of the mine. I just didn't make the connection to you." Mr. Wooster cast a glance at Mav and Macy who was now sitting in a chair pulled up next to Mav. "Something is rotten in Pine Bluff, Mr. Caid. When and from whom did you acquire the property?"

"Let me think a minute. I purchased the property about 1898 and a geologist discovered bauxite within a couple of years. I purchased the property from executor of the estate of Mr. Amos Wilson who had died. Do you suppose?..." Mav and Macy looked at Mr. Wooster.

"I do suppose. I'll check it out. If Judge Wilson T. Wilson is a member of the Amos Wilson family, the whole thing could be a subterfuge to get the property and a valuable mine back. But, of course, Wilson is a common name." Mr. Felton Wooster immediately left to begin some research to discover the possible connection while Mav and Macy remained to ponder the events of the day.

The pondering on the newly discovered suspicion would last for a short twenty minutes as the telephone rang in their room. Mav picked up the receiver and spoke briefly to the caller and hung up the telephone. Turning to Macy, Mav said: "*Já-gě* has been taken."

Macy sat, an astonished look upon her face. "Mav! *Já-gě* just left an hour ago to do some shopping. Who was that who called?"

"He gave no name, only saying that *Já-gě* is well, but under lock and key. He said I had the key to her release in my hand and that I was to tell no one about it. He said he would call again soon." Mav looked at Macy, expressing one word, "Barbarossa."

"Mav, this is crazy. Barbarossa would have to know this won't work and he will spend more time in jail. And, Judge Wilson, he must know that what he is doing won't withstand an appeal if he rules against us. What is their game?"

"I can't know for sure whether it is all greed for money. It could be revenge. *Já-gě* is the insurance they need to force the ceding of the property to them and to keep us quiet. If we accept their proffer of settlement, they will submit it to the court as an agreed settlement to drop the case. The judge will immediately approve and halt the trial. If we refuse, we will lose the case on decision of the court and the court will order the payment of a significant amount of money in the judgement. In addition, if revenge is a motivation, I can expect a following criminal charge for the thinly-veiled abduction of *Já-gě*."

"What about *Já-gě*," asked Macy. "What will they do with *Já-gě*?"

"I think, for the moment, they need her, so she will be ok. If Black Beaver is her real papa, unless he is craven, he will not harm her.

I don't trust Barbarossa. I don't know for how long, or if her fate depends upon which option we take." Mav remained sitting; a pensive look displayed upon his face.

Two days pass and no further contacts came from the caller. Mr. Wooster has returned with information about the judge and his relationship to the deceased Amos Wilson.

"Mr. Caid, the situation as I know it now is this: Amos Wilson, whose estate from which you bought the land, was estranged from his wife, Millie Kitteridge. They had one son who was living with his mother at the time. My informant was not certain of the name of the son nor where his mother and he lived. He thought the son's name may be William. He was certain that Amos had a brother, and the given name of the brother, he thought, was the same as the last name. The coincidence is notable. How many people have the same first and last names?" Mr. Wooster went silent.

"Ok, so the fact that Amos had an heir, who, likely did not know of his father's death because of the estrangement, allowed the executor, his brother to sell the property and keep the money himself?" Mav waited for a reply.

Mr. Wooster nodded his agreement in Mav's understanding of the information before adding: "Right! With the wife and their son in ignorance, the deceased man's brother had a free reign to engineer the sale in his favor. As executor to the estate, he had full authority to dispose of the property for the benefit of the rightful heir. Instead, he stole the proceeds from the sale. But there's more. No one liked Amos. Apparently, he was a difficult person to deal with. Even his brother Wilson, and Wilson's son, Andrew, hated him. I don't know the reason."

"This sounds incredible!" interjected Macy, before saying: "oh, I didn't mean to say…"

"No, that's ok, Mrs. Caid. It does sound strange, but not as strange as the next thing I was told."

"Who is this informant you have spoken to?" asked Mav.

"A barber. Mr. Berryman, down at the barbershop on Main. Very informative. Seems to know all about people here in Pine Bluff." Ralph Wooster allowed himself a quick chuckle, thinking of the adage that if you wish to know the scuttlebutt you just need to get a haircut and a shave.

"You mentioned that there was something else." Mav looked directly at his attorney.

"The best of all. Andrew, the son of our Judge Wilson T. Wilson had political aspirations. At the time of Amos' death, both Judge Wilson and his son, Andrew, were chasing donations for Andrew's campaign that fell off upon the sale of the deceased Amos' property. The campaign still had six months to go before the elections, the barber told me, but Andrew's quest for donations had dropped in intensity. He was not asked for a donation after that point."

"What office was Andrew seeking?" asked Mav as an afterthought.

"District Attorney," returned Ralph Wooster. "The current District Attorney."

"You mean, a district attorney for the state of Arkansas, with power to indict a person on criminal charges?" asked Macy.

"The very one," stated Mr. Wooster.

"Mr. Wooster, there is something you need to know. I have received a telephone call saying that our daughter, *Já-gĕ*, has been kidnapped and I was warned about telling anyone about it. The price for her release, just as in the proffer you received, is the property in Saline County with the Caid bauxite mine." Mav waited for a response from his attorney.

"Mr. Caid," said Felton Wooster, returning to a more formal manner of speaking, "you are in jeopardy. Unquestioningly, *Já-gĕ* is also."

"Mav, what are we going to do? Someone may arrest you at any time on a criminal charge of kidnapping *Já-gĕ* and you would have no defense for the accusation other than a handful of testimonials that say that you alone told how you found *Já-gĕ*. If the court and the district attorney are in cahoots, how can we win?"

"We can't win, Macy," admitted Mav. "We have to disturb their plan by doing something unexpected. What we must do is talk to Black Beaver and find out how he is involved. It may be a reach, but maybe he will drop the case."

"But, Mav, —wouldn't that be improper to have that conversation without the lawyers?"

"Technically, perhaps, but in the interest of negotiating a settlement, I think it would pass muster. Besides that, everything they are doing is improper. Black Beaver is a wild card. Someone unexpected. Someone, perhaps, to lend his name to an improper suit for money. He may be as much a victim as what they are trying to make of me. I just don't know. I met a Black Beaver years ago. I don't know if he is the same man."

"How will you find him? We have to have an answer by Thursday or the proffer to settle will expire and Judge Wilson will rule." Macy had asked a question that yet had no answer. "Besides that," she continued, "we have to wait for *Já-gĕ's* kidnapper to call. He told you to wait."

Mav nodded his head at Macy, then returned to a pensive posture, saying nothing more. Macy left the room.

Returning an hour later Macy witnessed a strange scene. Mav had moved the table to the wall freeing the middle of the room in which he sat, cross-legged and shirtless. Around his neck hung a leather drawstring bag. In the bag is a natural diamond, a Tear of the Sun. Mav sits, motionless, with eyes closed and seemingly, his attention focused elsewhere. His mind, the seat of the faculty of reason, reaches for a far plateau, descending through the levels of conscious and subconscious thought, —surfing the waves called gamma, beta, alpha, theta, and delta, —transgressing the subliminal into a region without a name, a region where all is possible.

After observing for a time this strange scene, Macy quietly left the room, perplexed, but feeling that when and if Mav wants to tell her why she is seeing what she is seeing, he will tell her.

✻✻✻

"I heard your call," said Windwalker. "Tell me what you need."

"*Já-gĕ* is being held captive by some evil people, Windwalker. Black Beaver knows where she is and I wish to speak with him. I think he has been led astray and does not know what he is doing in the white man's court," answered Keeper-of-Tears. "The man, Barbarossa, who has influenced Black Beaver, is an evil man. Black Beaver has been led astray by Barbarossa, whose tongue is like that of the snake."

"I will talk to Black Beaver." Windwalker faded to the shadows of coming night, as Keeper-of-Tears began to stir.

✻✻✻

Thursday arrives and all parties are in court before the judge. As Judge Wilson takes his seat, all are asked to rise and the court is gaveled into session. As all eyes turn toward Judge Wilson, Black Beaver suddenly stands to address the judge in an impulsive manner. He does not ask permission to address the court.

"I wish to withdraw my complaint," states Black Beaver. Mr. Lother, Black Beaver's attorney, appears stunned. Black Beaver's request was a complete surprise, and one that Judge Wilson was unprepared for. He immediately begins looking around the courtroom for Barbarossa who is not in the room.

Black Beaver walks over to the table where Mav and his attorney, Mr. Wooster sat and leaned in to speak quietly to Mav.

"Keeper-of-Tears," said Black Beaver, "I did not recognize you. Many summers have flown since you came to the reservation with *Já-gĕ* for the ceremony. I am chief now. I have spoken with Windwalker and I am wiser now. I did not know that the man, Barbarossa, spoke with the tongue of a snake. Mr. Rhodes, the man called Barbarossa, told me that *Já-gĕ* had been taken from the man entrusted to care for her. I thought you were her captor, not her *ko-tá˘*. I suffer great embarrassment for my being tricked. *Já-gĕ* is in this building, in the room behind where the judge sits at this moment."

Judge Wilson, as shocked by the turn of events as much as others in the room, gavels the court out of session and immediately rises to go into his chamber. Judge Wilson's movement toward the door was late in its execution, as Mav Caid jumps to his feet and runs to the door leading to the back room, adrenaline rising. Arriving at the door, Mav bursts through without knocking. Inside he finds *Já-gĕ* tied to a chair with her mouth covered. Her black hair, tangled, but her eyes bright and her demeanor, calm. Barbarossa, taken by surprise is standing next to a window, but whirls around as Mav bursts through the door.

"Ah, Mr. Caid. So happy to see you. I take it that you have accepted my proffer." He would not have the opportunity to continue the conversation by verbal means.

"Barbarossa! You are <u>not</u> happy to see me," a statement accompanied by a powerful strike to the jaw of a red-haired kidnapper and would be extortionist. Barbarossa's arms flailed to the side as his, now unbalanced body fell backward through the window to the boardwalk outside the courthouse. The crash and succeeding tinkles of shattering glass attracted the attention of passersby who are witness to the sight of a graying man of middle age emerging from the shattered window with a focused intent of continuing his kinetic conversation with Barbarossa.

"I've never seen the like," said a witness to the deputy sheriff. "No, never."

"That man was like a raging bull before a bull-fighter," said another.

A third simply said: "That redhead was like a Raggedy Andy doll, his head snapping this way and that way. I bet his nose stays as flat as a pancake for the rest of his life. I've never seen a beating so thorough. I have to wonder what he had done to deserve it."

"I have been informed by Mr. Wooster standing over there that your name is Mav Caid. Is that correct?" asks the just arriving county sheriff.

"Yes," replied Mav.

"Well, you will have to come with me, Mr. Caid. You are under arrest for this disturbance. You can tell me your story down at the jailhouse.

"Yessir," returned Mav, "an' ifn possible, you might want to invite th' US Marshal to th' confab."

Chapter 47

A Gathering Concern

By late 1918, Germany is on the defensive and as the world waits for the war to conclude, so awaits the Caid family. *Já-gĕ* continues her studies and will complete her schooling within the year. With Macy's influence on the direction of hospital care in Beaton, and the numerous times *Já-gĕ* has helped Macy with her speeches and presentations, *Já-gĕ* is showing an interest in entering the medical care field herself. Mav and Macy have queried schools of higher learning about their nurse training. Because of the need for nurses for the war effort, Vassar College in New York had established a three-month nurse training course followed by practical training at a local participating hospital. Vassar College Admissions has answered the letter, telling the Caid family that their daughter, *Já-gĕ*, would be welcome at Vassar next year for the fall semester. They mention that she should enroll using her real name rather than *Já-gĕ*, her obvious nickname.

Eugene Stonefield

"I don't know," mused Mav, "do you think they would rather like the translation?"

"Antelope?" replied Macy. "I think, perhaps, we will just have to educate them on her name, and hope for the best. To say she is a foreigner would be untruthful at its core."

Several times over the years 1917 and 1918, *Já-gĕ* visited the reservation to gain more insight into the traditions, beliefs, and language of the Apache. During these visits, *Já-gĕ* taught the Apache about the ways of the white man and spoke to the value of farming. She could not assuage the longing of the Apache to return to the traditional way of life when the buffalo provided most of their subsistence, but she could help them ease into a new life. She never forgot her pledge to regain the rights to the dance and, in this effort, wrote many letters to many politicians in Washington, lobbying for the restoration of the rights to the natives. Letters flowed between Tennyson Berry, an important chief of the Apache, and *Já-gĕ*. The initiative will not be realized until all Native Americans, —those most people of the day call Indians, —will be considered by law to be 'citizens' of the country of their birth with rights of expression. It will not happen until 1924 when President Calvin Coolidge signs the Indian Citizenship Act into law.

Mav picks up the Gazette and begins to read the articles about the war but finds a distraction in an article describing an influenza outbreak at an army base in Kansas. Several soldiers have come down with an illness called 'Spanish Flu.' The article continues to report that military personnel here and abroad have contracted the disease and many have died because of the infection, the cause of which remains unknown. Because of security concerns, reporting of the outbreak in many countries is restricted, making it impossible to see the scope of the pandemic of this severe and deadly disease. Unlike similar respiratory infections, the Spanish Flu seems to kill the youngest and the healthiest.

"Macy, have you heard of the Spanish Flu?" Mav began his conversation and laid the Gazette aside to accept a cup of coffee from Macy.

"It was being discussed in the last board meeting at the hospital," returned Macy, "and because of its high mortality rate, the doctors are worried about its coming into Beaton. A decision was made to gather as much information as could be found on the infection and prepare for treating it should it come to this community."

"People in official positions in the government are saying that the end of the war is near. I hope they know what they are talking about. There has been fighting in Europe for four years, and it is time for it to end and let everyone go home. Since the War Department censors all the letters now, we don't know for sure where Case is right now." Soon after, fate smiled upon this worthy family.

Chapter 48

Return of Case

Mav and Macy arrived in their new Maxwell Mascotte Touring automobile and waited for the six-o'clock flyer to round the bend bringing Case home. Mav bought the Maxwell in Chicago when he met with officers of the Perciville Reduction company on their annual trip to visit their Midwest operation. Two of the officers gave mention to its sturdiness and dependability and Mav decided that it was time to move with the times. The automobile cost seven-hundred dollars. Today, he will demonstrate to Case that he is a modern person. As the train arrived, Macy and Mav stepped onto the passenger loading platform and continued their wait.

"Case! Case! Over here." Macy could not contain herself when she saw Case step down from the passenger car carrying his bag. He looked larger than life to her. Mav met Case half-way and took Case's bag from him then turned back to the car freeing Case to receive a welcoming hug from his ma who could not make herself wait in the car.

"We've missed you Case," began Mav, "it's good to see you've come home. I trust you are as glad to be home as we are to have you back."

"I am Papa. It seems like it has been a long time, even though it hasn't been two years." Case turned to his ma saying: "Ma. You've grown younger and prettier, I see."

Laughing, Macy replied: "Case Caid, you sound like your papa! I'll bake you the cornbread I know you're angling for. You don't have to butter me like I know you will the cornbread!"

Within minutes, the three headed toward the home place with Macy in the back seat listening to all the questions and answers about the Maxwell that were passing back and forth between the two men in the front seat. She was in heaven.

"I have taken your advice and planted legumes on the fifty acres we discussed before you left. I'll show you the schedule I plan to use for the other acres." Mav knew Case would be appreciative that his pa took his advice seriously.

"That's good, Pa. We can look that over. I know it will be fine. I do need to tell you about something that came up before the army released me to come home. Some officials from the postal service came to talk to the flyers about jobs that are available flying postal routes between cities. The airmail service,[10] as they call it, they have begun to build it already. They already fly regularly between New York and Washington with a stop in Philadelphia, and they need all the pilots they can get to build the service throughout the country. It's almost like new discovery to open a new service. I'm thinking about it seriously." Case went silent as he waited for Mav to respond.

"My papa told me when I went to be a wrangler for Captain Lytle that a man has to make his own way in this world, and he ought to have the right to make it in his own way. We would hate to see you leave again, but would understand." Mav looked at Macy who was near tears and trying not to show it.

"Think about it a while, Case. You haven't even had your cornbread yet. Surely, you have some time to decide such a serious thing." Macy turned away, so Case could not see the tears forming in her eyes.

✳✳✳

Over the next several months, Mav and Case worked on their strategy for rotating their crops. "I think this will work for us, Papa," ventured Case as he read the plan Mav had written down while Case was in Europe. "Have you thought of buying machinery to help with the harvesting?" he continued.

"What have you heard about it?" asked Mav.

"When I was in college, there was talk about some company in Iowa that was building a threshing machine on wheels that a farmer could take to the fields and thresh the grain there. The inventor called his company the Waterloo Gasoline Traction Engine Company, as I recall. A John Froelich owned the company and some grain silos, and had invented a steam-powered threshing machine earlier which he used to thresh grain for farmers for a fee. Eventually, he sought to put one of his machines on a moveable platform. He envisioned moving the platform around under gasoline power. We ought to look at buying one for the farm. I can't imagine it would be any harder to operate than the Maxwell you drive now." Case waited for Mav to respond.

"Will you be around to operate it?" asked Mav, revealing what is constantly on his mind since Case spoke of the airmail service.

"Papa, I don't think so. I want to fly for the postal department. I have learned something about myself. I love to fly." Case studied his papa to judge his reaction.

"I know, Case. I guess I was just hoping to be wrong. Your ma will be sorrowful. You should tell her soon." Mav stood up and placed his hand on Case's shoulder, then left the room, a sad man.

Case did as his papa had asked and told his ma of his decision. Macy tried to hide her disappointment by getting the necessary ingredients from the cupboard to bake something special for Case. She will allow her sorrow to have its way in the privacy of her bedroom.

Case left for Washington the following week.

Chapter 49

The Advocate

Vassar's enrollment of *Já-gě* in nurse training was not without some controversy. The typical student had never seen a real native up close. Out of her class of twenty-three student nurses, only one had had the opportunity to engage with a native, and that, only because she was the daughter of an army officer who once served reservation duty when she was younger. The family had lived near the Pine Ridge reservation in South Dakota for two years. That girl, Melanie Wofford, became a close friend of *Já-gě*. Some of the others were apprehensive, one even asked a teacher if she was in danger of being scalped while she slept. Her concern was that her hair was naturally curly and she was fearful that, if she suffered a scalping, when it grew out it may not be curly. The teacher assured the girl that she was at no risk of anything like that happening, and chose not to tell her that in a real scalping, should one survive, the hair does not grow back.

Vassar established the program to support the war effort by providing more nurses. The ending of the war in Europe and the return of the forces terminated the need for the moment.

"Mav, listen to this." Macy was reading from a letter they had just received from *Já-gĕ*:

"…so, on the twelfth of February, we were all seated at dinner when a fire-bell rang. Everybody thought it was a fire-drill which we have now and then. But this time it was a real fire! There was a lot of screaming and shouting and running about to get out of the building. Not long after that the firemen from the Poughkeepsie Fire Department raced in and began to attack the fire. To get the water they needed they had to chop holes in the ice covering Sunset Lake. They did what they could to save the personal effects of the students by throwing their clothes and things out the windows for the students to retrieve later. The girls formed chains from the main building to pass furniture and files and other important documents to safety in Rockefeller Hall. The fire started in the kitchen flue and spread to the back where the house cleaner and kitchen staff lived. Unfortunately, the fire destroyed the main building as well as the housing for the house cleaners and some staff. It was amazing how the girls shouldered the responsibility and well they did. Regardless of the discord and damage, classes began on time the next day. We are planning to form a committee to raise funds to replace the losses that the house cleaners and staff suffered.[11]

On a happier note, I want to report that my studies in nursing are going well. My test scores are in the top ten percent of the class. I hope to finish my training and return to Beaton by summer."

Macy lowered the letter and looked at Mav.

"Mav, this could have been horrible. I'm so glad it didn't happen at night when all were asleep." Mav shook his head to acknowledge Macy's statement and took the letter to read it himself.

Mav Caid — The Complete Story

Summer came and *Já-gĕ* returned to Beaton with nurses' credentials. Her first job was with the hospital and it would last for only one year.

***

Nineteen-twenty began like most years, with expectations that positive things would happen in a world still adjusting from the hot fires of the war. Mav returned from his trip to the Valley of Tears and will travel to Chicago in May.

"Papa, could I speak with you a minute?" asked *Já-gĕ*.

"Of course," said Mav, setting aside the Gazette. "What's on your mind?"

"Papa, I want to read law. I want to work on restoring the Indian rights to celebrate. I know I can help them if I learn more about the law." *Já-gĕ* sat down across from Mav and waited for his reply.

"Have you spoken with your ma about this?" asked Mav in a typical strategy to delay giving an answer. "It's a big step to take when there is no need to do it," returned Mav, thinking about her recent success in her job at the hospital.

"But there is a need, Papa. I told them. I told my Kiowa family at the Sunrise Ceremony that I would work to get their rights restored. Now I want to make good on that promise." Whether she knew that that one answer is the only answer her papa, her *ka-ta*, could have no objection to will remain unknown. But it is the bedrock belief of Mav Caid that a man's word defines his character more than anything else. How could he deny it to his daughter?

The following week, Macy, Mav and *Já-gĕ* drove to Beaton to discuss the plan with his attorney, Derick Tarr.

"Well, little lady," began Derick Tarr, pointing to a shelf of books on the laws of the nation and Arkansas. "Given the reasons you have expressed, I think you need to start with reading about the constitution

403

and constitutional law. Read a chapter then come to me to discuss it. It will be good for both of us."

"Yes sir. I will begin tonight." *Já-gĕ* took the book Derick handed to her. Later that night, *Já-gĕ* would be found with her legs curled beneath her on the sofa with a book in her hands.

August 23, 1922

To the Honorable Henderson Jacoway
United States House of Representatives
Washington, DC

Dear Representative Jacoway,

I wish to introduce myself as an advocate for Native American rights. My name is Já-gĕ Caid, and if you are puzzled about the name, it means Antelope in the Kiowa language. I am of the Kiowa-Apache nation, though I have been the ward of a white family since infancy and have received an education at Vassar from which I graduated with honors in 1918. I have a foot in each nation, so to speak, I am Kiowa, and I wholeheartedly feel that I am American as well.

Many years ago, Washington restricted the Kiowa, as well as other tribes from pursuing their social and religious ceremonies that involved dancing and singing. It is my contention that these harsh restrictions have served their purpose and Congress should rescind those restrictions to allow the people of the tribes to follow their cultural roots. There are no risks to anyone from restoration of these rights. I request that you sponsor a bill to submit to a vote in the U S House of Representatives that would rescind the laws and all associated policies that interfere with the rights of the natives to pursue Life, Liberty and Happiness just as are afforded others living within the borders of this great country. In fact, an even more just solution would be served if full citizenship rights would be codified into law immediately. Lady Liberty pleads for the recognition that the aboriginal inhabitants of these United States ought to receive the equality they deserve.

Sincerely,

Já-gĕ Caid, Kiowa-Apache Advocate

This advocate for Indian rights is not alone in her efforts. Just this year, Ruth Muskrat Bronson of the Cherokee Nation, age twenty-four and recent student at the University of Oklahoma is working at the Mescalero Apache Reservation in New Mexico and destined for scholarship to complete her education at the University of Kansas. History will record that Ruth continued her advocacy of Native Americans until her death in 1982. Born in 1897, Ruth saw first-hand the disastrous effect the Curtis Act of 1898 had upon her people of the Five Civilized Tribes, the Cherokee, Choctaw, Chickasaw, Creek, and Seminole, when the act mandated allotment of the communal lands belonging to the tribes and instigated a damaging pattern of detrimental land transfers to unscrupulous buyers.

Chapter 50

They were Young Then

There are never enough letters from children far away from the protection of home. Today proved to be a day of pleasure as happy parents are reading a just received letter from Case.

Dear Ma and Pa,

I have completed my first postal flight for the new service and flew one-hundred-forty pounds of mail from Washington to New York. I flew from the old Polo grounds in Washington's Potomac Park, to Bustleton Field in Philadelphia then to Long Island's Belmont Park in New York. The modified Curtiss JN-4D Jenny like I flew in Europe has an extended range, but Philadelphia is a scheduled stop so I refueled there. The Jenny's designation is now the JN-4H with the supplementary fuel tanks, and replacement of the forward seat and controls by the mail compartment. The replacement of the original engine with the 150 horsepower Hispano-Suiza gives it more power.

I was not lucky enough to be the first. All of that happened back in May of '18. Those honors went to Lieutenants George Boyle, Howard Culver, and James Edgerton, Torry Webb, Walter Miller and Steven Bonsal. Major Rueben Fleet, charged with getting the service in operation picked the four experienced pilots who had not committed to go to France. They were Lieutenants Culver, Webb, Miller, and Bonsal. Postmaster Burleson picked Edgerton and Boyle who had just graduated from pilot training in Ellington Field in Texas, so they had limited experience.

Boyle had a mis-fortune when he ran out of gas and had to land in a field. His Jenny flipped and broke the propeller. Luckily, he suffered no injuries. He said that he became lost and flew in the wrong direction, following the wrong railroad tracks. 'Flying by rail' is what we call flying from town to town by following the tracks. Landmarks are all we really have to navigate by, since there are no maps yet. I understand that mapmakers are now working to rectify that for the future. Until then, all we pilots can go by are rivers, rails and coastlines, and a general knowledge of where a city might be. We have a compass to help, but without maps, the help it gives is minimal. We call it 'dead reckoning' navigation. In general, it means estimating where you are now by knowing where you were some minutes or hours before then calculating where you should be, — given your direction of travel, your speed in flight, and the number of minutes in flight since you knew where you were by the landmarks. The complexity is that the speed that one travels on the ground is not the same as the speed they might travel through the air because of the effects of wind. Sometimes a pilot can fly against a strong wind for an hour and not travel an inch with respect to the ground. I'll explain it better the next time I come home.

I hope all is well with the farm. The farmland I fly over is beautiful. It was the same in France. You get a different perspective from the air. When I see folks plowing their fields or harvesting their crops, I get nostalgic and wish I was back home working alongside Pa and the farmhands. But then,

I think how much I love to fly and how important the mission to expand the airmail service to the country.

    Say hello to Já-gĕ and ask her to write me and tell me about what she is doing now. The last I heard she was reading law.

    I need to go now and get some sleep. I will write again soon.

Sincerely,
Case

Months passed as Case helped to open new mail routes and build his dream. *Já-gĕ* read law with Derrick Tarr for two years before hanging her shingle notifying the citizens of Beaton that a new law office is open for business. The year is nineteen twenty-three.

Dear Ma and Pa and Já-gĕ,

    My bosses at the postal service promoted me and now have the responsibility to bring air postal delivery to another area of the country. The other news is that I will be coming home for a few weeks for a vacation and expect to be there on the Flyer at Beaton station at noon on the thirteenth.

Sincerely,
Case

"Mav, I feel I just can't wait for Case to come." Macy smoothed her apron and turned back to the roast she is preparing to cook for dinner.

"It will be good to see him and hear all about what he has been doing and what he will be doing in the future to expand the air postal service." Mav spread the Gazette before him on the table and took a sip of coffee. "His crop rotation is being followed to the 'T' and I know he will want to know what we think about it now. All the farmhands that we employ understand the concept, of course, not all of them agree. The older ones are set in their ways to look at the crop rotation with some doubt."

"Are we set in our ways, Mav?" asked Macy.

"Oh, I guess to some degree, we are. It's from age and familiarity with the routines of living. Folks don't like to have to learn new ways of doing things when they are comfortable doing those things by familiar means," replied Mav, as he put his glasses on to read the Gazette. "By the way, *Já-gĕ* told me that she is getting some support for her lobbying effort on the restoration of tribal rights. She said our congressman is working to garner support for a bill he is writing. She is excited about the prospect that it will pass when it gets a vote. *Já-gĕ* also said that her law business is gaining new clients."

"She still comes by the hospital from time to time. Did she ever mention a Doctor Fannin?" Macy glanced at Mav who concentrating on some article in the Gazette. "Mav? Did you hear me?"

"Fannin? When did he become staff?" replied Mav.

"He came about the same time *Já-gĕ* began as a nurse there. I guess they became friends, both being new. I thought you knew of him." Macy placed the pot on the stove.

"I guess I have been away from the operation of the hospital too long," returned Mav. "Do you think she goes to see him?'

"They have been seen together. Constance saw them at the ice cream parlor last Thursday." Macy sat down across from Mav.

"Mav, that name, Fannin, sounds familiar. Have we ever known anyone by that name? I can't think of one, but the name…" Macy is interrupted by Mav.

"Well, I don't recall anyone in recent memory, but I do recall there was a Fannin that played a part in the Texas Revolution." Mav looked to Macy to ask the next question.

"Tell me about the revolution. What was it about?" asked Macy, satisfying Mav's expectation.

"Papa told me a lot about that when I wuz…<u>was</u> young. It seems that Mexico originally belonged to Spain, dating back to Spain's original exploration. Then about 1810 a revolution started in Mexico to gain their independence from Spain. It was successful, but th' leader in Mexico, Generalissimo Antonio Lopez de Santa Anna overthrew their constitution an' declared himself Mexico's dictator. He recognized, though, that Mexico's territory north an' west of Texas, that is, California, plus Arizona an' New Mexico were not well populated. He was fearful that th' United States would attempt to take it from him so he devised a plan. The plan was to encourage migration of people from th' United States into Mexico. He thought that with land grants an' special favors, th' emigrants would become loyal citizens of Mexico. He didn't count on th' people maintaining some allegiance to their roots. They continued to speak English an' grouped together. Some folds, like Steven F. Austin brought in people by th' thousands. Austin brought in up to twenty-five thousand. Well, eventually th' governance of th' territory became more strict an' caused stresses. A revolt, I guess, was inevitable. Anyhow, Santa Anna ordered his soldiers to go into Texas an' disarm th' citizens which he had now begun to fear. He went to Gonzales an' attempted to take a cannon that th' city did not want to give him. Th' citizens of Gonzales thwarted his pressure so th' soldiers retired. As th' anger rose throughout th' territory, a few men holed up in a mission in San Antonio. The name at th' time was th' Mission San Antonio de Valera which we now call th' Alamo. One-hundred eighty-three were supposed to delay Santa Anna long enough for Sam Houston to build an army. Other things had happened, such as a massacre where officers of Santa Anna forced prisoners to display a bean they had blindly taken from a sombrero. His order was to execute every tenth man out of th' one-hundred seventy-six captives. There were seventeen black beans mixed with th' white. Santa Anna executed all those who had a black bean including their leader, Colonel Fannin. 'Bigfoot' Wallace escaped execution because he drew a white bean. But at the Alamo, all were killed, when th' walls were breeched an' th' fightin' became hand-to-hand. Jim Bowie, th' designer of th' knife I have in th' other room, Colonel Travis, Davie Crocket, an' many dedicated people died there, but it allowed time for Houston to recruit his army. The soldiers of Houston an' Santa Anna met later down at San Jacinto, an' Houston won. Texas became a new republic from that point on. Most of the unowned land is still claimed by the state of Texas, but some of th' land that went as far north as Colorado was ceded for one reason or another. Th' one thing that stood out above all others in Texas was th' number of free or wild longhorn cattle that roamed th' countryside. Fellows like Oliver Loving, Jesse Chisholm, John Lytle an' many more began rounding up those free cattle an' moving them north to sell from Kansas to Canada an' all points in-between. I got in on the last days of those long trail drives.

"Did your papa know Austin?" asked Macy.

"Austin recruited him to come to Texas from New Orleans," answered Mav. "I reckon it was about 1829."

"Hmmm." Macy hummed, but ventured no opinion. A few minutes later Mav observed Macy take a rotogravure photograph in a gold frame from the fireplace mantle to look at.

"They were young," mused Macy.

"Who?" replied Mav.

"Mav and Macy, in this picture. They were young."

"Yeah," replied Mav.

✳✳✳

Youth is a fleeting thing that begins with a cry and ends too soon for some, withers slowly for some, and lasts forever for another.

Youth may be best left to the heart to define. Those remaining young at heart see more the beauty of life, enjoy more the pleasures, and better memories are its rewards. Philosophers throughout history have opined about youth and have sought to define it, frequently with a sprinkling of cynicism. Someone once said that by design, youth is to be disillusioned and when he is no longer disillusioned, he is no longer young.[12] Another said that the future of a happy life depends upon youth not believing in the impossible. There is no requirement that a person must recognize the passing of youth and that person retains the right to enjoy the attitudes and ambitions for as long as they please. Explorers and alchemists have sought the secret of eternal youth and have failed because they always looked externally rather than internally; the secret of youth lies in the heart. For Mav Caid, old age has no meaning, yet old age is knocking at his door.

Chapter 51

A Nation in Trauma

For the Caiden family in the third decade of the twentieth century, the weakening economy is just another facet of life to endure. Mav's history to date has seen the end of the great cattle drives and the expansion of rail transportation of cattle to markets. He has sunk farmer roots deep into the Arkansas soil and has taken to wife, Macy, and has fathered two children and raised a foundling. He has endured the killing of his family in Bandera when a young man and has engaged with the strange native known as *Windwalker*. Mav, with his wife, Macy, has helped to build a needed hospital and has beaten the criminality of Francisco 'Chico' Alvarez, Fenner Korn, Henry Slade, and Caleb Farenthold.

As a couple, the Caiden's have unconsciously aligned themselves with the worthy citizens of the world, though not of the scale of philanthropist Andrew Carnegie, who built libraries throughout his native land of Scotland and his chosen country, America. Carnegie will continue giving support for educational pursuits until he distributes ninety percent of his wealth in benevolent gifts. Nor of the scale of John D. Rockefeller and son of the same name, Julius Rosenwald, Margaret Olivia Slocum Sage, Edsel Ford, and Henry Ford, —people of money and heart. But these are the people with whom Maverick and Macy Caiden stand in spirit.

The conservative-minded Caiden family were fortunate that their only exposure to risk was their money on deposit at the bank. Their main assets consisted of land and the produce from that land. The Caiden family are affluent, having achieved their wealth from farming, beef and dairy cattle, mining, and timber. Long-standing diamond sales continued to fund the Caid-Chesney Tears of the Sun Hospital. Altruism toward others became second nature. The Caiden philosophy became, help your neighbor, help your community.

The decade of the 1930s was one of deprivation and an intense need for many citizens of the nation and the world as the great depression that began in the United States with the stock market crash of October 23, 1929 that created a wave of panic among investors. The following days of October 28 and 29, known as Black Monday and Black Tuesday, cast their shadows on the economy, and gave birth to long bread lines in the cities as breadwinners lost jobs, and pantries went bare. The reasons for the economic instability are many but include consumer over-confidence, lack of bank regulation, and inflexibility to respond to the growing crisis due to the government's fiscal and monetary policies.

Investors, who measured their wealth by ownership of company stock, had unrecognized risk exposure. Many of the more affluent investors used margin accounts to purchase common stock at a fraction of the stock's value, effectively borrowing the rest from their broker. Profit expectations relied on a rise in the value of the stock to give them a gain on resale and liquidate their debt to their broker. The stock market by 1929 had been in a long period of rising values, a 'Bull Market' in the language of the market, and had drawn in unsophisticated investors, believing the run would never end. Working with common stock was a 'buy low', 'sell high' strategy. However, as stock values declined, brokers called for cash infusions from their customers to bring those margin accounts back into balance. Many could not meet those margin calls without deep pockets and ready cash, so their brokers sold the stock into a falling market, thereby flooding the market with stock for which there were few buyers. Wealth vanished within hours on Monday October 28 and Tuesday October 29, 1929. The 'bull' market rapidly became a 'bear' market with sellers far outnumbering buyers.

Efforts of the Republican Hoover administration were tepid and ineffective. An economic downturn spread among the populace, and rich and poor suffered. For the more affluent, the financial assets counted upon to insulate from want failed as banks closed, and the stock market fell to dismally low values. Swept away in their entirety were great fortunes as unmet margin calls went out to those heavily invested in speculative stocks. Investors lost over $30 billion in value and economic depression followed. Creators of quotable quips coined lines like; 'When America gets a cold, the world gets the flu.'

International trade fell by fifty percent. American GDP fell, and unemployment rates soared as high as twenty-five percent. Manufacturing stagnated. Bank depositors in need of cash, and those fearful of bank failures, began runs on banks, demanding the return of their deposits, which at the time, had no insurance protection. Banks failed. Confidence in the economy fell. Hunger in the cities rose.

Even larger banks, imperiled by withdrawal demands, began to run short of cash to meet the requirements and began calling in loans. A loan to a borrower is an asset to the bank. Many loans to customers are callable or become so for some infraction of the terms. Borrowers in rural communities, especially debt-loaded farmers, could not meet repayment demands from bankers. As a result, over nine thousand banks failed by 1933, unable to liquidate enough assets to pay back their depositors demanding a return of their savings.

Eventually, a deflationary spiral that increased the value of the currency began in 1931, making it possible for citizens to buy more goods for the dollar. Still, a man without a job, —without income, — could buy nothing. Cash strapped buyers delayed purchasing significant items, such as automobiles, depressing production in the industry. Lack of buyers stimulated a weakening in prices for goods and services making the plight of citizens, especially debt-loaded farmers, more acute. In some regions, the cost of getting farm and dairy products to market exceeded the return to the farmer. To deliver food to markets in the cities was to lose money. People with cash, began hoarding their money at home, the result of their fear of losing it in a bank failure, and for its potential to rise further in value because of the deflationary spiral pushing the value of the dollar higher.

The credit was tight for those who needed to borrow to continue or improve their operations. Farm income fell as crop prices fell, and long-term drought in the country's mid-section launched a great migration of desperate people searching for work. Many went to cities in the north, others ventured west. The orchards and vegetable fields of California gained a golden aura of salvation for many from the failing farms in the heartland. Ultimately, the promise failed to deliver as the labor supply soon outstripped the actual number of jobs available. Average economic returns on a day's work fell below survival needs for a worker in the orchards and fields. Getting any job was highly competitive. For people over the age of forty-five, employment was non-existent.

For the reading public, the era witnessed the publication of books such as The <u>Grapes of Wrath</u> by John Steinbeck, describing the horrors experienced by the 'Okies,' those Oklahoma farmers exiled from their farms in the Dust Bowl of Oklahoma by years of drought. Many pondered if these were the 'grapes of wrath' prophesied in Revelation 14: 19-20, of the Holy Bible. For what reason was this 'wrath' visited on the people? Also, spawned by these tragic events, are the Woodrow Wilson 'Woody' Guthrie's folksongs documenting the results of this era of economic discord.

Closer to home, debt-ridden Arkansas suffered as corn and cotton crops production diminished, and meat became challenging to purchase. Hunting wild game became a necessity for some, and the rabbit acquired a new name of 'Hoover hog,' referring to President Herbert Hoover, who many blamed for doing too little to fix the economy. The country was in the mood for change.

The election of 1932 brought Democrat Franklin Roosevelt to the presidency, on a promise of a 'New Deal' for the citizens. His intended policy was to get money into the hands of citizens to meet their needs. During his presidency, his administration established many public works programs to get people working again.

As the years progressed, younger Americans had had their fill. Reacting to the somber mood of depression-era America, youth took a holiday. The now-ubiquitous ownership of the phonograph of Thomas Edison was known to all America. The demand for the hard-lacquer disks hiding music in thin grooves became a focus of multitudes of young people. Music blossomed in every parlor and every barn in rural America that had a phonograph or a radio. Any place with a makeshift dance floor, the young began to move their feet to the rhythms of the day. In the larger cities, the young turned to ballroom entertainment. Big bands set the tone, and people began to dance to new tempos. Swing music replaced the sounds of the 1920's jazz. By 1936, band leaders and arrangers, Count Basie, Duke Ellington, and Benny Goodman were making themselves known. Individual artists, Artie Shaw, Lionel Hampton, Harry James, Ella

Eugene Stonefield

Fitzgerald, Billie Holiday, Frank Sinatra, Jimmy and Tommy Dorsey, and Peggy Lee were making their horns and voices familiar to listeners everywhere. Radio carried their sounds into communities throughout the nation. Eclipsed were the musicians and voices of jazz of the previous, 'Roaring Twenties.'

✳✳✳

It is January 23, 1933 and the telephone rings at the home of Mav and Macy Caiden. Waiting on the line is the President of the Beaton Bank, George Insley.

"Mr. Caiden," begins the conversation, "this is George Insley calling from the bank. I have a serious item to discuss with you if you have a moment."

"I have the time, Mr. Insley. How can I help you?" Mav takes a seat to receive whatever information is on the mind of the bank's president.

"Mr. Caiden, we are in a difficult place with the economy being as it is." Mr. Insley pauses before continuing. "Some of our depositors are demanding a return of their deposited money for reasons that suggest that they are fearful of what is reported in the news. If the 'some' becomes 'many' then, if we are to meet their demands, we will have to begin calling in the loans from customers that have done business with the bank since we began operations. If we can't liquidate those loans for cash to cover the depositor's demands, the bank could fail and everyone would be affected." Following this serious admission of impending danger to the bank and its depositors, Mr. Insley went silent to allow Mav to assimilate what he told him.

"But, Mr. Insley, we don't have any outstanding loans at this time," Mav answered, but finds the reason for the call baffling.

"It's like this, Mr. Caiden, you, and Mrs. Caiden are our largest depositors, consequently, have the most to lose if things go badly as

420

they have for so many banks across the country since Black Tuesday. I am calling to assess your grit in weathering this financial storm. There is no question in my mind that if you seek a return of the money you and your wife have at the bank, we will founder. This is serious. I must reveal that I am the second largest depositor. All my wealth went into buying the bank years ago and I am at risk of losing all. I, and hopefully you and Mrs. Caiden, will want to prevent fear from creating financial havoc here as it has in so many other places. Frankly speaking, I am asking for your help."

"Well, Mr. Insley, we are aware of the depositor runs on banks across the nation and know of the hardships caused by bank failures. If your bank failed, we would lose a lot of money, but not our farm as would many of my neighbors who have mortgaged theirs. I can speak for both of us, we will stay with you on this. There will be no requests for a return of our deposits." With that decision, Mav and Macy Caiden protected many friends and neighbors from loss. The bank was able to meet all demands and fear subsided in the area served by the Beaton Bank.

Chapter 52

Colorado Interlude

The call is short. "What are you saying? When? Oh, God! I will come now." Macy replaces the telephone earpiece back in the switch hook on the telephone. She immediately calls for the foreman to bring the farm truck to take her into Beaton. The ride seems to Macy, interminable, the passing countryside, a blur to her watery eyes, her hands nervously wringing a scarf, her heart in her throat. Her mind is in turmoil. In another's, only the comfort of remembering life on the trail.

✳✳✳

The white peaked mountain panorama glows rose-gold in the rising sun as the eighteen-year-old Mav Caid saddles his horse, Trencher, an Appaloosa mare from the remuda of his employer John

423

Lytle. The Appaloosa, a horse showing leopard spots, is called a Nez Perce pony because it is the preferred of the Nez Perce tribe in the northwest, the tribe's homeland. Trencher is dark bay with spots covering her hindquarter, rather than the whole animal as some do, and weighs close to a thousand pounds.

Having delivered the consignment of one thousand fifty-five beeves to a purchaser in Walsenburg, Colorado, in the foothills of the Sangre de Cristo Mountains, Mav, Tucum, and several others are free to follow their travel urges in their return to Texas. The town of Walsenburg is near the Spanish Peaks called by the Spanish, *Huajatolla*, meaning 'breasts of the Earth.' To a boy from the middle of Texas where high land is unknown, the tall peaks of Colorado strike awe into the mind of the young cowboy. Mav and Tucum have chosen to discover the beauty of the country of mountains. The others are to follow a different path and are returning to Texas via Raton pass, that narrow mountain passage between the 38th state and the New Mexican Territory annexed by the United States in 1850. The autumn leaves of Aspen trees are in full color, the air brisk and showing the freshness only the mountain air can provide. The two riders are preparing to ride from Walsenburg. They are talking about nothing, the subjects ranging from weather to landscape.

"Shor is enticin' country with all them peaks hoverin' o're them valleys," said Mav to his friend Tucum, who was putting the final touch to saddling his horse.

"Well, I was born and raised near the Tucumcari Mountain in New Mexico, and any mountain can be cantankerous at times," returned Tucum.

"How'd you come by thet name o' yorn?" asked Mav, who has wondered about it since they first met on the trail.

"It was given to me by missionaries who cared for me from the time I was a baby until I was old enough to care for myself. I don't know my real name. I was just an infant when the Apache killed my folks near Tucumcari Mountain, and the missionaries couldn't find anyone who knew my real name. Some folks call me Cari, but the drovers prefer Tucum. I don't care. Either will do." Tucum gave a last tug to snug the cinch beneath his horse's belly. Swinging into the saddle, Tucum turned to Mav and said: "Which way do you want to head?"

"I'm reckonin' we orta ride over thetaway an' see whut's thar." Mav pointed to the south-west and turned Trencher in that direction. Their ride will generally follow the railroad tracks for the Denver and Rio Grande railroad line once they intersect them. Tucum nodded his agreement and followed suit. The riders spent the next several hours in silence as they rode into territory unknown to themselves but historically, crossed by Spanish explorers claiming the land for the Spanish crown and naming it Colorado, after the Rio Colorado, —the 'red river.' Two centuries later, Major Zebulon M. Pike entered the territory and gave his name to the peak that stood sentinel over the gold rush, beginning in Denver in the 1850s and terminating in the 1890s at Cripple Creek.

"What about yours?" Tucum asked as they rode toward Alamosa, a young town that grew from a tent city to a railhead for the Denver and Rio Grande Railroad about ten years earlier.

"My whut?" returned Mav

"Mav. How did you get your name? It sounds like it could be short for Maverick. I think of a maverick as an unbranded calf."

"It is." Mav told him the story about the Maverick brand in Texas and how events of the day introduced the name into the culture of Texas.

"So, are you branded?" asked Tucum.

"Whut?" Mav looked questioningly at Tucum.

"Hitched to anyone. Married!" returned Tucum.

"Nope. Ne'er reckon'd 'bout it. Don't hav' no sweetheart back home nohow. How 'bout you?"

"Naw. I travel light. Don't see that I would have time, anyhow."

The two companions traveled west toward Alamosa as the sun lowered itself behind the horizon and the temperature dropped toward their norm of around twenty degrees. Little thought was given to the events occurring across the nation and in the world.

$$* * *$$

On the fourth day of their ride, Mav and Tucum approached Alamosa. The day is sunny and cast sharp shadows on the snow-covered ground; the cold air moved by a brisk wind. Both riders are looking forward to a hot cup of coffee and a hot meal which they expect to find in the town. As they enter Alamosa, Mav points to an unpainted building with a sign reading: 'Gold Nugget Saloon.'

Seeing no other signs to suggest food could be obtained there, Mav said: "I reckon we orta stop thar an' see whut we ken git."

"Yep. Looks like that's all that's available," returned Tucum.

Upon entering, Mav and Tucum noticed the absence of customers, something they didn't expect to find in a mining town. The man behind the bar watched as they entered and asked: "What can I get for you, gentlemen?"

"I reckon we hanker fo' some Arbuckle an' some grub," Mav replied.

"Boys, didn't you see my sign outside? It says, saloon, not restaurant! I got no coffee! I serve whiskey and suds. There are some pickled eggs in that jar at the end of the bar. The price is fifty cents an egg." The saloon keeper waited for a response.

"We hav' a need fo' mor' than a pickled egg. Is thar a restaurant in town?" Mav asked.

"Can't say. What will you have?" returned the saloon keeper.

"I reckon we'll jes' be lookin' fo' someplace else," Mav replied as he and Tucum turned to leave.

"Hold on, boys. NO one comes into my place without buying something!" replied the saloon keeper as he reached below the bar.

"Whut do we hafta buy?" asked Mav.

"A bottle of your choice." The saloon keeper kept a steady eye on the two, as he placed a shotgun onto the bar.

"I reckon I'll take one o' them, then." Mav pointed to a bottle on the shelf.

"That's Old Overholt Rye, and the price is two dollars." The saloon keeper retrieved the bottle and pushed it toward Mav.

Mav gave him two dollars and took the bottle. Mav and Tucum left the saloon and remounted to continue their search for a place to eat. As they neared the end of the street, Tucum pointed to a building from which several people were emerging. It had no sign to identify it as a restaurant, but the smell of cooking food permeated the air.

Mav and Tucum dismounted and entered the building. Several people sat at tables eating, and the two hungry travelers took their seats at an empty table. Presently a waitress approached.

"You boys hungry?" asked the petite girl of about seventeen, dressed in a gingham dress overlaid by a white apron. Her hair, a dark mahogany color that hung in long curls framing her face. She had light brown eyes that sparkled in the stream of sunlight entering through the front window. Her lashes were dark and long, with a slight upward turn. Her cheeks showed a pleasing blush and the hint of dimples.

"Coffee?" asked Mav.

"By the gallons," replied the girl.

"I want a steak with potatoes, greens, baked bread, an' lots of coffee." Tucum just nodded his agreement on Mav's order.

"How come y'all hav' no sign?" asked Mav.

"Mayor won't permit it unless the proper fees are paid." returned the girl.

"Who is th' mayor?" asked Mav.

"The mayor is Kirk Everson. He pretty much runs the town. He's the saloon owner up the street, and the last restaurant that hung a sign without paying the fee burned down the day they hung it. The fee is expensive. My ma owns this place and won't take a chance of hanging a sign. She says everyone around here knows about her restaurant anyway." The waitress turned to place the order with the cook in the kitchen.

Addressing the waitress when she returned with their order, Mav told her: "We stopped at th' saloon as we come inta town, an' it was empty. Thet seems unusual."

"Oh, no one goes there unless Alice it there," replied the girl, laughing.

"Does she entertain th' customers or wait tables?" asked Mav.

"Nope. She gambles. They call her Poker Alice. Her last name is Duffield, and she used to gamble in Silver City in New Mexico territory. Her parents came from England when she was about twelve and sent her to finishing school in Virginia. She and her husband Frank moved to Leadville sometime after she finished her schooling. Frank Duffield was a mining engineer working in the mines and was killed in some accident with dynamite in Leadville. He taught Alice how to play poker. She's a high-dressing looker and wins a lot of money from the miners and the railway folks. All the gamblers want to sit at the table and try their luck against her. Kirk is sweet on Alice and wants her there every day, but she won't work on Sunday." The young waitress turned to go to the next table where new arrivals had just seated themselves.

Mav and Tucum finished their meal and prepared to leave. Presently, the young unnamed waitress collected the fare for their lunch, and as they stood to leave, she pointed to a table across the room. "There is Alice."

"I reckon I ain't seen a gambler as pretty," said Mav.

"Amen," concurred Tucum.

Mav Caid — The Complete Story

Before they left, a man arrived and looked around. Seeing Alice at her table, he walked over and stood in front of the attractive gambler.

"You took my money last night. I want it back. No woman can be that good at poker unless she's a shark. You owe me seventy dollars." The man leaned forward, placing his hands on the table as Alice reached for her purse, hanging on the chair back next to her.

Alice opened her purse as if to comply with the man's demand but withdrew a forty-one caliber Remington Model 95 pocket pistol, which she leveled at the surprised man.

"Calling a card-player a cheat is a serious charge, mister. Would you like to retract that?" Alice's face was impassive. "Your ante is your unfounded accusation. I have two rimfires to raise your ante. Do you want to call? Show your cards?"

For a minute, the man stood looking at the twin barrels of the pistol, then carefully, straightened to a stand. "I guess I was mistaken." As Alice and the rest of the customers in the restaurant watched, the man slowly turned and left the room. Alice went back to her meal.

Mav and Tucum resumed their movement toward the door and left the restaurant. Outside they observed the man riding out of town. Presently, Mav and Tucum mounted up to continue their ride to Durango.

"Well, I swan, thet Alice ken take care o' hersel'!" said Mav.

"Amen!" returned Tucum.

Neither Mav nor Tucum could know that her success at poker eventually will return a quarter-million dollars, most of which she will spend on clothes in New York. Nor did they know that she previously dealt cards in a Creede, Colorado saloon owned by Bob Ford, the man who killed Jesse James just three years prior, in 1882. Nor could they predict that during her advanced years, she would be pardoned by South Dakota Governor William J. Bulow for her killing a soldier who became enraged by her 'never on Sunday' rule. Neither could they imagine that she would get through the long hours in jail by reading her Bible and smoking cigars. Life on the frontier was not for the humble or the squeamish.

✳✳✳

Eight days into their impromptu adventure, Mav and Tucum entered the town of Durango. Throughout the town, men and women went from place to place pursuing their daily lives, lives drawing its sustenance and energy from the split rocks of the surrounding San Juan mountains, measured in silver and gold. For the last three years, the Denver and Rio Grande Railroad has operated trains on narrow gauge tracks through the town to connect Durango with Silverton and Chama, New Mexico. Durango town is becoming the locus of a major smelting industry for the mined metals.

"Hav' you e'er thought 'bout diggin' fo' gold or silver, Tucum?" asked Mav of his young partner.

"Not me," replied Tucum. "I have a reluctance to being underground, considering that when my time comes, I'll have ample time to spend there. I don't want to get an early look," replied Tucum. "What about you?"

"I like sunlight an' wind. Not so much on rain an' lightnin' though. Guess I'm like th' cattle on thet." Mav drew Trencher to a stop, and Tucum immediately reined in his horse, Cloud.

"Why are we stopping?" asked Tucum.

"Jes' to look at thet sunset. Hav' you e'er seen anythin' like it?" returned Mav.

"Well, we had some beauties around Tucumcari when I was there, even saw some Injuns watching us. Some, just like those over there." Tucum pointed toward a group of five mounted men a hundred yards away.

"Do you reckon them frien'ly?" asked Mav.

430

"At least they're not painted up," replied Tucum. "I think they may be Kiowa or Cheyenne. My guess is they are curious about us."

"You know anythin' 'bout them?" asked Mav.

"A few stories about the Cheyenne. The missionaries I lived with told me a story about a massacre at Sand Creek in which Colonel Chivington and his Colorado Volunteers killed one-hundred and fifty or so, mostly old men, women, and children. I was told that there were no Dog Soldiers in the village to fight back and that the village flew both a US Flag and a white flag of truce at the time. This was back in 1864. Chivington hated Indians and would kill any Cheyenne or Arapahoe he could." Tucum gave a pat to Cloud.

"The Indians were of Black Kettle's tribe of Cheyenne, so he decided to move his tribe into Wyoming to join the Northern Cheyenne. On the way, he raided settlements and forts but was never captured. Black Kettle was a man of peace, but events like the Sand Creek massacre can push any man too far."

"I shor hope I never git pushed thet far." Mav nudged Trencher forward toward the group. "Let's go meet them."

As Mav and Tucum rode toward the small group, they could see that a conversation ensued and assumed by the gestures that it was about Tucum and himself.

"Howdy," Mav said, extending his hand toward the foremost horseman. "Mighty fine horses!" No one took his hand.

For a moment, several of the Indians exchanged words in their own language, then the one to whom Mav spoke returned Mav's greeting.

"My name, *Ba'-chú*. It means Wolf in white man talk." This said as *Ba'-chú* slapped his chest to emphasize his identity. "Here are my brothers of the Kiowa."

"Mighty proud to meet you, Wolf!" returned Mav.

Bá"-chú reached back to one of his tribal brothers and took a rifle, which he immediately displayed to Mav and Tucum, causing some trepidation.

"You have bullets?" asked *Bá"-chú*. "We hunt, but have no bullets." *Bá"-chú* looked at Mav and Tucum, waiting for an answer.

"Whut do you think, Tucum?" asked Mav. "You reckon we orta give them some? His rifle is a Henry, jes' like you an' I hav'. I hav' a few extra forty-four rimfires."

"They seem friendly enough," Tucum answered, remaining wary.

"Whut do you hunt?" asked Mav while digging into his saddlebag for bullets for the Henry held by *Bá"-chú*.

"We hunt *bí"-nal-dé˘*, that you call elk." Wolf reached for the bullets, then returned the rifle to the owner along with the bullets. Turning back to Mav, *Bá"-chú* said: "My brother wants you to have this in return," and extending his hand, dropped a gold nugget into Mav's hand. "We go now."

Mav and Tucum watched as the five Indians rode away toward the forest.

"Whut do you make o' thet, Tucum?" asked Mav.

"Worthy men," answered Tucum. The rest of the day was spent riding westward then veering southward in a random meander.

Chapter 53

The Prognosis

In the office of Dr. Furnham a conference is underway between Dr. Furnham and Macy:

"At this stage, it is difficult to say if the injuries are too severe to expect a full recovery. Right now, your husband is in a deep coma resulting from the severe blow to the head he suffered in the accident. He suffered a fractured leg and lacerations, which, as you can see, have been addressed." Dr. Furnham spoke quietly to Macy, who sat before him with great concern showing. Lying in the next room is the man she has loved since she was eighteen, a man she can't do without. Mav Caid, husband, and father to two children, now with the remainder of life hanging in the balance. Today, he sleeps, perhaps he dreams. So much is unknown about brain injuries in 1935.

"But, Doctor Furnham, is there anything you can do to bring him to consciousness?" her question asked from fear that an end to her happiness is near. "I must talk to him. I must tell him how much I love…"

"I'm sorry, Macy," replied Dr. Furnham, "only time can do that. His brain must heal from the damage before he returns. I wish I could be more positive, but I can't at this time. Head injuries are uncertain. We must wait."

"Who brought him in?" continued Macy.

"The railroad people brought him in shortly after the accident. We were told that his automobile seemed to have lost its brake and, although he tried to turn to parallel the tracks, he was too late. The automobile he was driving hit the train engine as it was crossing the road. He was fortunate that he was not thrown under the wheels. But he was thrown from the car into the side of the train's engine. That is all they said." Dr. Furnham stood up and told Macy that he would keep her informed if his condition changed.

As Macy left Dr. Furnham's office at the Caid-Chesney Tears of the Sun Hospital, the comatose patient relived times past when he was a young man, learning how to live as an adult, far from the home of his youth in Bandera. The trip to Walsenburg was his first completion of a cattle drive beginning on the Western Trail with Captain Lytle and his first experience at being completely free to choose his future.

✱✱✱

"Tucum," said Mav while pointing into the distance. "Whut do you make of thet? Ifn my eyes ain't deceivin' me, thar's buildin's under thet rock overhang."

"I see them, Mav. I don't see any people, though." Returned Tucum.

"Thet prob'ly is to ourn advantage, considerin' th' builders had to be Injuns. Mayhap they warn't so frien'ly." Mav slapped Trencher and encouraged a faster pace toward the rock roof of the abandoned village below the rim. An hour later, both cowboys were climbing down a discovered ladder descending to the abandoned village.

"I have seen adobe pueblo villages over in the desert lands, but adobe buildings built into the cliffside is unbelievable," mused Tucum as birds responded to his voice and took flight. "Do you suppose they moved to some reservation?"

"Shor don't know," returned Mav as he peered into the interior of a multi-storied structure. Soon after, Mav stooped to retrieve a small leather pouch that he found inside a crack in the rock wall. Inside were various objects: a claw from a catamount, a button-sized knob of some dried vegetation, the severed foot of some bird, and a blue-green stone shaped like an owl. "Whut do you think this here is?"

"Around Tucumcari mountain, some Injuns tied them around their necks. I was told they were called medicine bags." Tucum inspected the contents. "Musta had some meaning to them."

Mav tied the medicine bag around his neck and turned to Tucum, saying: "How's this? You reckon I look like a Injun?"

The return to the top of the mesa was not the easy task expected. The ancient ladder, that had permitted their descent, was not up to the task of allowing their return without penalty. Mav ascended without difficulty. Tucum did not, and his fall was sudden and could have been fatal, were it not for a small tree growing from the rock cliff that he was able to catch and arrest his fall.

"You ok, Tucum?" asked a shocked Mav, peering from the top.

"I think I broke something."

"How bad?"

"Bad enough. My ankle. I think it's busted."

"Hold on, Tucum, I'm a-comin' down."

"Naw, Mav. The ladder fell away when I fell. I can't stand to set it up again."

"Thar cain't be jes' one way down," replied Mav. "Thar's got to be another somewhar. I'll find it."

"Hold on, Mav. It's nearly dark now. You can search for it tomorrow, and I'll be ok down here. It will be cold without a fire, but I'm ok with it. Toss down my bedroll, though." Tucum looked up at Mav, who was peering over the rim of the canyon about thirty feet above.

"I'll drop some jerky an' lower yor canteen an' bedroll with my lariat. Tomorrow, I'll look for another way to get down." Mav disappeared to get the food and water for Tucum. The next day he found the second place the cliff-dwelling Indians had used to get down to the village but found that the ladder was missing. Returning to the rim above Tucum, Mav shouted to Tucum that he would have to try to bring him up by rope. By tying his and Tucum's lariats together, he had a length of rope long enough to reach Tucum with some to spare.

"Tucum! Tie thet rope around..."

"How're you gonna pull me up by yourself?" returned Tucum.

"I ain't. Trencher will do th' pullin'. I'll do th' guidin' o' th' rope. You ready?" Mav finished tying his end of the rope to Trencher's saddle horn and led him around a tree so he could hold Trencher's rein and control the rate of extraction of the injured Tucum.

Within a quarter-hour, Tucum was above the canyon rim, and Mav was tying a splint around his broken ankle. An hour later, following breakfast of water-biscuits and jerky, the two travelers began their return to Durango, their plans for returning to Texas by a circuitous route interrupted by the need for medical services.

Arriving back in Durango, Mav and Tucum searched for a sign identifying a doctor's office and found that of Dr. Pool. Dr. Pool was well known to people in the area as a specialist in repairing broken bones, a common occurrence in mining operations. Amid some pain and trepidation on the part of the patient, Dr. Pool prodded, twisted, and finally, re-splinted Tucum's ankle to enable the bone to heal correctly. Dr. Pool gave Tucum a crutch to help him walk and avoid further damage to his ankle. The cost of the service, including the crutch, was seven dollars, about two days wages for a cowhand. The cost of their disappointment was inestimable, as it demanded a redirection of their travel back to Texas with its attendant hardship of traveling with an unhealed injury.

✳✳✳

The ride back to Alamosa from Durango was uneventful but necessary. From Alamosa, the pair will ride to Trinidad then south to Raton, in New Mexico. By that time, Tucum's injury will be completing its first two-weeks of healing. Dr. Pool told them Tucum could expect the healing time to be four to eight weeks.

As they neared Alamosa, Tucum voiced his desire to order another meal at the restaurant they visited on the way from Walsenburg.

"Mav, do you think that pretty girl waitress will be there?" Tucum looked at Mav questioningly.

"I reckon. She said she wuz th' owner's daughter." Mav stiffened in the saddle as he observed a shadowy figure walking down the side of the building carrying a kerosene can. As the sun was beyond the horizon, the light was too dim to reveal much more.

"Thar's someone a-sneaking 'round th' corner o' th' restaurant." Mav pointed in the direction. "It looks like he's a-carryin' a can o' kerosene."

"Oh, he probably bought it at the general store for his lamp and is heading home. I'm hungry. Let's go in," said Tucum. The inside seemed to have frozen in time to the two travelers. Poker Alice is sitting at the same table where she sat when she pulled her pistol on her accuser. The young waitress is taking her order.

"Welcome back, strangers." The waitress signaled her recognition of Mav and Tucum. "Looks like you may have gotten a splinter in your leg, or maybe your horse threw you."

437

"Broke ankle," replied Tucum. "Fell and broke it about a week ago. Uh, by the way…you got a name? My name is Tucum. My friend is called Mav."

"Glad to meet you, Tucum and Mav. Yes, I have a name. It's Sam."

"Sam?" asked Tucum.

"Samantha," responded Sam.

The two hungry travelers placed their orders, and as they waited for the food to come, Mav told Tucum that he was going to visit the outhouse and wondered where he would find it.

"You can ask Sam when she comes back," Tucum advised.

"I cain't ask a girl a question like thet." Mav colored.

"Why not?" asked Tucum.

"It wouldn't be proper. I'm a-goin' to walk aroun' back and look fo' mysel'." Mav left the restaurant and turned the corner heading to the back of the building to find the privy. As he neared the rear of the building, the hissing sound of a lit fuse and its brilliant glare refocused Mav's attention.

"Lordy!" Mav exclaimed aloud. Although darkness kept him from seeing where the fuse ended and to what attached, intuition told him that by the direction of the burn, the restaurant and all occupants were in danger. Mav ran toward the burning fuse.

A few minutes later, Mav returned to his seat at the table, carrying a can of kerosene encircled by sticks of dynamite, which he set down by his chair.

"What in tarnation is that?" asked Tucum.

"Kerosene an' dynamite," answered Mav.

"What? Why did you bring it in here?" asked Tucum.

"It's safer in here than out thar with th' owner," returned Mav.

"Where did you get it?"

"Oh, it wuz underneath th' buildin' 'bout whar Alice is right now."

"Oh. Did you find the outhouse?"

"Don't need it now."

"Why not?"

"Hadta put out th' fuse b'fore it blowed Alice up."

✳✳✳

Riders, Mav and Tucum, were on their way to Raton from Trinidad discussing events they had experienced since leaving the drive in Walsenburg when sunset suggested they make camp for the night. The weather was cold, and the desire for a fire is strong. The place they selected offered protection from the elements by a ten-foot-high ridge. Soon after stopping, a fire was boiling a pot of Arbuckle's.

"My guess is that we will have snow by morning," ventured Tucum.

"Shor looks like it," answered Mav. "Do you see thet flock o' turkeys over there?" Mav pointed to a small rise just behind Tucum.

"You reckon to shoot one?" asked Tucum, twisting around to see where Mav pointed.

"I ain't pondered on it none," responded Mav, "but they shor recall to me Thanksgiving back home in Bandera. Ma would cook us one with all th' trimmins'. I miss thet. Ma always had mincemeat an' punkin' pies too."

After a while, the travelers ate their trail food, and Tucum got up saying that nature was calling him and that he was going to wander over beyond a line of trees not far from their campsite. Given his ankle injury, he retrieved the crutch that he had brought from Durango and began a slow hobble across the uneven terrain. Mav poured himself another cup of coffee and sat down to enjoy the setting sun. His enjoyment was brief.

"Aieee! Owooooh! Owooooh!" a scream of pain emanating from the line of trees brought Mav to his feet.

"I'm comin' Tucum. Keep a-yellin' so I ken find you!" shouted Mav, reaching for his Henry and levering a bullet into its chamber as he ran, thinking Tucum had encountered some wild animal.

"Over here, Mav. Over here!" shouted Tucum.

As he ran around the scrub growing beneath the taller trees, he collided with the perpetrator of the current mayhem, —an adolescent native attempting to put distance between himself and the screaming Tucum. Both fell to the ground with Mav falling atop the Indian boy, who immediately began to struggle to get free.

"Whoa! Hold on!" shouted Mav. "I mean no harm. Hold on."

Mav remained atop the boy until his struggle subsided. Rising from the ground, Mav held a hand to the boy who rejected the offer and stood by his own effort. Instead of attempting to flee, the boy stood facing Mav as if expecting some punishment for the collision.

"Me, hunt *tá-zhi*! Me no shoot…" the young hunter's explanation was interrupted by Tucum, who came toward them crawling on hands and knees.

"He shot me, Mav. I got an arrow in my fanny! It hurts, Mav. You gotta do something." Tucum shouted as he continued to crawl toward Mav and his captive.

"You speak some English. Whut is yor name an' tribe?" asked Mav of the boy. "Are you Cherokee?"

Spitting on the ground, the boy said: "Me, Apache! Me no Cherokee! Cherokee, bad!"

"Whut do they call you?" Mav asked again, eying the boy.

"Me called *Tsá-cho*. You say, eagle."

"*Tsá-cho*. Good! I am called, Mav, an' Tucum, here, an' me are proud to meet you," returned Mav.

"You might speak for yourself," interjected Tucum from his four-point position. "And, you might think about pulling this arrow out."

"Uh…sorry, Tucum. I jes' got distracted frum th' situation." Mav gave a contrite apology to Tucum as *Tsá-cho* looked on, not showing signs of wanting to leave. "Let me see th' damage." Mav inspected the wound, saying: "Yep. Thet thar arrow orta come out. I'll jes' give it a yank. Hold still now."

"Aieee! Stop. Stop!" screamed Tucum as Mav pulled at the arrow.

"Nope! Looks like it will hafta be cut out," said Mav.

"Uh, Mav? You recall that bottle of rye that saloon-keeper made you buy in Alamosa? You still have it?" asked Tucum, sweat forming on his face and neck despite the cold.

"I plumb forgot! I do still hav' it. I ain't open'd it. But you might orta get back t' th' fire b'fore th' sun's full down," advised Mav.

Tucum continued his crawl toward the camp about twenty yards away, groaning as he went. *Tsá-cho* followed behind, watching his embedded arrow whip back and forth as Tucum crawled.

Pulling out his Bowie knife, Mav instructed Tucum to face away from the fire so he could have better light on Tucum's butt and the injury.

"Hold on to somethin' whilst I cut thet arrow out o' yor…" Mav is interrupted by Tucum, showing great concern.

"Now <u>you</u> hold on, Mav Caid! Hand me that bottle first!" demanded Tucum.

"You gonna drink this stuff?" asked Mav while passing the bottle to Tucum, who takes the bottle.

"Well, it ain't all going to go on that end. Some is going to go down my gullet before you start carving!" answered Tucum, who steadies himself on one hand and twists his torso to raise the bottle of rye to his lips.

"Me want some," said *Tsá-cho*, holding a hand out.

"You don't want any, *Tsá-cho*! Yo're too young," replied Mav.

"Me not too young! Me, warrior!" replied *Tsá-cho*.

"An' I'm yor papa!" said Mav in exasperation.

"You not my papa! Me son of *Tli-chú-bu*! White man say Red Owl! He great warrior! Have many horses. He own two squaw," replied *Tsá-cho*.

"Wal, *Tli-chu-bu* would not permit yor drinkin' fire-water. I know thet!" countered Mav.

"*Tli-chú-bu* drink fire-water. He great warrior. Me warrior," a questionable argument given in reply.

"I don't care! <u>No</u> fire-water, an' thet's <u>final</u>!" returned Mav.

As the argument between Mav and his new-found warrior friend continued, Tucum continued pouring rye down his throat until the course of the alcohol made its presence known. Finally, Tucum slowly sank to the ground, head across the arm still holding the partially filled bottle and butt lifted high in the air. Mav retrieved the bottle and poured half of the rye on Tucum's wound and began to carve.

Tsá-cho watched Mav cut the arrow out then announced: "Me take arrow now."

"I'm reckonin' Tucum would say 'good riddance' since it's yor arrow in th' first place." Mav handed *Tsá-cho* his arrow.

"*Tsá-cho* take fire-water now. Give to *Tli-chu-bu*. He great warrior." *Tsá-cho* reached for the nearly empty bottle, but Mav brushed his hand aside.

"No fire-water, *Tsá-cho*. Go home. I hear yor mama callin'."

"She not my mama. She *Tsé-skŭs-si*, you say Squirrel. She *Tli-chu-bu* number two squaw. Me 'fraid of Squirrel. Great Warrior, *Tli-chu-bu*, he 'fraid of Squirrel. Me big trouble. No kill *tá-zhĭ*." *Tsá-cho* waved at the woman in recognition of her call.

"Who's *Tá-zhĭ?*" asked an exasperated Mav.

"*Tá-zhĭ*…he, you say turkey." *Tsá-cho* picked up the bow he dropped when he and Mav collided and trotted toward the calling woman.

As fading light and distance closed around *Tsá-cho*, Mav whispered, "Farewell, great hunter! I wish you many horses. An', stay away from firewater!"

Chapter 54

Campfire Tales

Time heals most wounds, and Tucum is well into the process as he and Mav stop for the night near Tucumcari, Tucum's home for many years. They have camped on the shore of Lake Conehas.

"So, this is yor homeland?" asked Mav.

"Yes, until I left home three years ago."

"Yor folks are still here, I reckon." Mav stirred the fire under the Arbuckle.

"No, they moved to Arizona territory. I have a few friends still in Tucumcari though," replied Tucum. There is this Padre Ortega at the mission…" Mav interrupts.

"I ne'er met a Padre. What's he like?" asked Mav.

"Well, he is a good man and a true believer in the mysteries. He taught me about things his church members believe and…" again, Mav interrupts.

"You're Papist, then?" asked Mav.

"Not so you would know it," replied Tucum. "I have trouble with mysteries. I guess I'm a skeptic about those kinds of things. Padre told me a story once about a young girl who had taken her vows in Spain and was a cloistered nun. That means she could not leave her convent. Anyhow, the Padre said that she would often appear in this area and in Texas and Arizona territory to teach the natives about Christianity. This was in the seventeenth century; just as Spanish missionaries were coming into the southwest with the explorers. He said some of the missionaries reported back to their church superiors in Spain that when they first contacted the natives, some of them were asking that the padres baptize them. They were saying that is what this 'lady in blue' told them they should do. Then, he said…that is, Padre Ortega, said that the superiors upon hearing this were so astounded that they investigated. They searched in Spain for nuns wearing gray habits with blue cloaks, which was the way the natives described her and found her among a Franciscan order called the Sisters of the Poor Clare. What they found was that this sister in the convent would fall into a trance on occasion and would be unresponsive for hours and sometimes, days. Then, when she came out of it, she would report that she had been teaching the natives in a faraway New Spain." Tucum ceased talking to load his plate with rabbit stew they had prepared for their supper, the rabbit being a generous gift of Tucum's Henry.

"Thet shor sounds strange. Kinda like Saul bein' stuck blind on th' road to Damascus when he wuz persecutin' th' Lord. Mayhap, more like Jesus appearin' befor' th' apostles after hisn resurrection. Jes' outen th' blue, thar he wuz!" averred Mav, shaking his head in wonder. "Whut else did th' padre say?"

"He said her name was Maria. Sister Maria de Jesus de Agreda, as she was known in her home town of Agreda, but her given name was Maria Fernandez Coronel. Padre Ortega said she told her superiors about the people and the landscape of the southwest and that she had come over five hundred times. They were amazed. How could she have known? It remains a mystery. But Padre Ortega also said that Jumanos in Texas, Piro natives near Socorro, and Tompiro all tell stories to this day about that 'lady in blue' who visited their ancestors.

"Well, thet's a good tale. I reckon folks will be writin' books 'bout thet." Mav replied as he reloaded his plate.

"You got any good stories to tell?" asked Tucum.

"Aw, I don't know. Hav' you e're heard about a Chupacabra?"

"Naw. What's a Chupacabra?"

"Folks down Texas way hav' told stories about this here 'goat sucker' animal thet roams around Texas. Folks say th' Chupacabra is a animal with sharp teeth an' claws an' scaly skin with red eyes thet shine in th' moonlight, an' standin' 'bout four feet tall. They say it preys on goats - thet's why they call it a 'goat sucker.' Anyhow, when one's been aroun', they always find some o' th' goats drained o' blood an' dead as ken be. But I reckon a better story is th' one 'bout *El Muerto*. Hav' you heard thet one?" asked Mav.

"No. Tell me."

"So, thar wuz this here bandit…a Mexican named Vidal who stole horses. Wal, one night he stole this horse frum a ranger. It wuz Ranger Creed Taylor, back 'bout mid-century. Anyway, th' ranger went to find hisn horse an' ran 'crost a ex-ranger by th' name o' Bigfoot Wallace. Now, he an' Bigfoot teamed up to find Ranger Creed's horse an' found it in th' hand of this Vidal an' his band o' horse thieves. Now, these two rangers had no love fo' horse thieves an' killt them all. But then, Bigfoot cut off th' head o' Vidal an' put it in hisn, —that is, Vidal's sombrero, —an' tied th' sombrero an' Vidal's headless body to Vidal's horse an' let him go. Some say it wuz a wild mustang, but whatever horse it wuz, it roamed around scarin' folks an' causin' trouble. Sometimes after, some cowboys caught an' released thet por horse frum hisn burden an' let it go. Whilst thet headless Vidal wuz roamin' folks started callin' them, —thet is, th' cut off head an' headless Vidal hissel', — callin' them *El Muerto*. Folks still say thet they seen *El Muerto* on moonless nights jes' ridin' an' ridin'."

"That's a good one, Mav. I sure wouldn't want to meet *El Muerto* on some dark night out in the wilderness like where we are now." Tucum stirred the fire to bring some life back into it and threw more wood upon the recovering flames.

After a pause of some minutes, Mav began again as he recalled another story.

"There's another story a Mexican farmhand tol' me wunst thet he called *La Llorona*, which he said meant 'crying woman,' an' it went like this: A young woman fell in love with this *hidalgo*, —thet means a important man, —who she met dancin' at the Saturday night fandango an' over time bore him two childern. Now, she wuz a poor woman with no fam'ly to hep her an' she had two childern to raise by hersel'. So, one day, she went to thet *hidalgo*, —hisn name wuz Estevez, —an' tol' him thet he must marry her an' help her raise them childern o' hisn. But Estevez refused an' tol' her, —her name wuz Maria, —he said: 'Maria, I'm not marryin' you 'cause I'm marrying Jacinta,' which means 'flower' an' only Injuns ken hav' two wives. Well, Maria wuz heck-bent fo' revenge an' ina rage, she killt them two innocent childern by throwin' them in th' river whar they drownded. Later that night, Maria realized whut she done, an' went back down to th' river an' screamed an' cried fo' th' childern who would never come back. She walked th' river day an' night, wailin' an' cryin' until she died on th' bank of th' river wearin' her white gown. Now, thet should hav' been th' end o' th' story, but it wuzn't, cause not long after thet, her ghost began to roam an' folks started to see her in thet white gown o' hern, cryin' an' searchin' fo' them every night. She would cry out: '¡Oh, mis hermosos hijos!', —whut means, 'Oh my beautiful childern!' An' sometimes would cry: '¿Qué les ha pasado a mis hijos?', —whut means, 'Whut has happened to my sons?' She would walk accrost th' water as if it wuz solid ground. Eventually, grief an' bitterness took over an' she, thet is, her ghost, became a fearful thing fo' folks. Soon, they started callin' Maria's ghost *La Llorona*, an' warnin' childern not to go out at night else *La Llorona* would grab them an' pull them inta th' dark water o' th' Rio Grande." Mav ended his story, saying: "Wall, I reckon we orta turn in fo' th' night."

As the two trail-hardened hands started to bed down, they heard a heart-stopping, piercing scream coming from a brush-choked arroyo about thirty yards away. The blood-curdling sound repeated every few minutes as two travelers took rifles from their holsters and levered bullets into each firing chamber.

"You hear that," asked Tucum.

"I hear it. Whut do you reckon?" asked Mav.

"Panther, I guess. I hope," returned Tucum. "What does a Chupacabra sound like?"

"I don't reckon I know," answered Mav.

"Think I'll move the horses closer," said Tucum.

✳✳✳

The day is cold as the two riders decamp and return to the long ride back to Texas. Tucum is sitting better in the saddle than before and is not muttering about *Tsá-cho* or *Tsá-cho's* arrow, and his ankle is mending well.

Three hours pass and they have veered toward the area known as the Llano Estacado and are in the Blackwater Draw in New Mexico near a site called Clovis that is currently being prepared for the railroad.

"I'm ready fo' a cup o' Arbuckle," stated Mav.

"Here is as good as any other place," replied Tucum, and the two saddle-weary cowboys dismount. Within a few minutes, a fire is heating water from the stream and coffee added.

Mav picks up a piece of flint from a small mound rising a few yards from the water.

"Whut do you make o' this?" Mav asks, showing Tucum a six-inch blade with fluted edges. "Looks like th' hand o' man made this, but it's different than whut I e'er seen b'fore. I reckon this here is some kinda knife or spear point some Injun made." He passes the blade to Tucum.

"It's different, all right. I sure am glad *Tsá-cho* wasn't hunting with one of these," returned Tucum, unconsciously rubbing his still-healing wound.

✳✳✳

Mav and Tucum continued their ride toward Bandera, a town still almost five-hundred miles away. At the rate of twenty-five miles a day, that equates to eighteen to twenty days. The food they brought with them from Tucumcari is running out, and the travelers must rely on the game they find along the way. The talk of hunting and food is a daily part of their conversation.

"Did I ev'r tell you 'bout th' time my friend Elfrin Tiddle went a-huntin' fo' turkey an' returned with a turkey he didn't shoot?" Mav was asking Tucum.

"So, what was he doing, leading it at the end of a rope?" Tucum responded, laughing.

"Naw, this here's a serious story. Elf…we jes' called him Elf, an' it wuzn't called thet 'cause he wuz small. He wuz as big as a elephunt. An' strong too." Mav pulled up Trencher, and Tucum followed suit. Both dismounted at the stream to water their horses.

"Elf had bought hissel' a new shotgun. It wuz one o' them Anson and Deeley boxlock shotguns thet didn't hav' no external hammers like th' older shotguns. Anyways, Elf wanted to try it out an' went out to hunt turkey. He made camp an' set thet shotgun o' hisn shotgun next to this tree an' crawled inta hisn bedroll. He said he wuz a-sleeping really good an' havin' a nice dream when, suddenly, in th' middle o' th' night, bang! Hisn shotgun went off. He said it nearly skeert him to death, an' he thought he wuz under a attack. It wuz pitch dark, an' hisn fire had gone out in th' night, so he couldn't see anything. Wal, th' nex' day, Elf went a-lookin' fo' hisn shotgun an' found it at th' base o' th' tree he had leant it on. He jes' looked, an' thar it wuz on th' ground with a dead turkey smack-dab on top o' it."

"It just went off in the night?" asked Tucum.

"Wal, 'cordin' to Elf, —which he figgr'd by th' animal tracks 'round th' tree, —this here band o' raccoons come upon hisn shotgun an' found it interestin' enuff to inspec' as they do, an' somehow got a foot on th' trigger. Now, they wuz this turkey thet had roosted in th' tree, so it got shot by th' raccoon whilst it slept."

"That's a good story. Maybe when we get back to Bandera, we can buy us a shotgun and get us a raccoon to hunt the turkey, then we can just lean back against some tree and wait for the raccoon to bring us the turkey. And, if we could get the raccoon to cook it too, we would be in paradise," responded Tucum.

As the two friends jawboned at the stream, talking about what they would eat that night, had they had it, a giant turtle came toward them and was as welcome to the two tired travelers as manna to the Hebrews. That night they had a tasty meal consisting of turtle, hearts of cattail pulled from a nearby swampy cove, wild carrots, wild onions, and pigweed found growing in the area.

It took twenty-seven days to return to the Lytle ranch, where both were reemployed as cowhands for the Lytle operation in its planning for the next drive up the Western Trail.

Eugene Stonefield

Mav, told Tucum that in his younger years, he became fascinated by the description of trail drives told by legendary men of Bandera. The stories of Amasa Clark, Ben Batot, George Hay, and Seco Smith never failed to inspire a young farm boy by the name of Maverick Caiden, and he looked forward to joining an outfit that moved cattle to northern markets. When he and his pa took a wagon into San Antonio to purchase supplies needed on the farm, Maverick would without fail, engage anyone coming into the general store, or wherever they may have gone to talk to them about the trail. The trail had a mystique about it that grew larger with each discussion, each related experience, and undoubtedly, each bare-faced lie that a cowboy could fashion to amuse and inspire a young farm boy. Having been on one, he now looks forward to another. This next drive, Mav hoped would be all the way to Ogallala in Nebraska.

Chapter 55

The Second Cattle Drive

Dr. Furnham stood up as Macy entered his office and motioned for her to take a seat. Macy thanked him and sat across from the doctor.

"Has there been any change?" Macy began, looking hopefully at the doctor and trying to perceive his thoughts before he spoke them.

"I'm sorry. No, Mr. Caiden hasn't shown any improvement since he came in. It will take more time. The good news is that all his vital signs are positive. He has no infections from the cuts he received, judging from his temperature, which is normal. His heartbeats seem normal, strong, in fact. I'm hopeful still that he will respond within a day or two." Dr. Furnham waited for Macy to respond.

"I guess I am just anxious," replied Macy.

Eugene Stonefield

"I understand," returned the doctor.

"Captain Lytle, ifn it's ok with you, I hanker to work with the remuda." Mav's appeal to Lytle came from his long-held fascination with 'all the pretty horses,' a description he had given to a passing herd of mustangs when a child of six in Bandera. Maverick had asked his papa if he would get him one for his birthday but was told that he could ride Bernice, the plow horse when he was a little older. It was never satisfactory. A plodding plow horse, the color of dirt was not comparable to the beautiful horses he saw in that passing herd. They were haughty and proud. They ran with heads held high, tails and manes streaming in the wind, or dancing up and down with the pace of the running herd. In his eyes the horses were raw power and showed dignity in their running; majesty in their pride. He promised himself that someday he would ride a horse like those he saw. In his mind, he imagined himself atop a magnificent chestnut or rich brown stallion, or maybe even a palomino as it runs with the abandon of wind.

After listening to young Maverick Caiden's appeal, Captain Lytle said: "I do need someone to work with Charlie. Come with me, and I will get you set it up with Charlie Hale." Captain Lytle and Mav walked to the corral. They spoke with Charlie, and Charlie agreed to introduce Mav to the intricacies of breaking horses and training them for working with cattle. Mav was to replace Herman Jo, a bronc-breaker whose body had suffered too many traumas to continue, so Herman was offered the job as a cook for the drovers. Herman Jo, whose independent nature gave him a reason to be angry for the loss of his long-time responsibilities, was mollified by the higher pay that a cook receives, and the higher status inherent in the position. Cooks often served as the *Segundo*, or second in command, on the trail if the trail boss had not named another. Life's changes do, sometimes, have favorable consequences he decided and set out to be the best cook the outfit had ever known. Lytle had no reservations in picking Herman for the cook since Herman was an excellent cook already and had substituted for the regular cook on several occasions when the other was ill or injured.

Mav spent half the next two months in the air above a pitching horse and the other half on the ground with dust billowing around him and hooves flashing above. But he learned, and learned well, if not with abundant pain. Bruises, sore muscles, sprains, lacerations, embarrassment, constant ribbing from his cowhand friends, and no broken bones were his rewards.

As Mav and horse drew each other's measure, cowhands of the Lytle brand were rounding up Lytle's cattle to drive to market, and receiving herds from others to join the trail north. The trusting of valuable animals to trail drivers for trailing to market was common. The purchase of herds by trail drivers equally common, though payment for those cattle was often deferred. Trust, goodwill, and credit were the lubricants of the business. A man's reputation and his handshake, its guarantee.

By May, the trail brands had been applied to all cattle, supplies purchased, and loaded into the chuck wagon. The trip began on May 11, 1886. There were thirteen drovers, one cook, Mav Caid, —the horse rustler, or wrangler, for the remuda of one-hundred and four horses. Managing the drive was trail boss, Alliance Nelson, who had been with Lytle for thirteen years. Alliance is not an employee, per se, of Lytle. Instead, more a business partner since Alliance brings with him his own cattle from his operation just north of Brownsville on the Frio River.

By seven am, the herd was on the move from the assembly point south of Bandera. As the herd passed through the small community, Mav thought how he would like to stop and see his family three miles on the other side of town. It was not possible, given the need to move up the trail and get the cattle and remuda across the Medina River, which they planned to cross near Kerrville. From there, they would drive to San Angelo to bring along a previously assembled herd waiting in that town.

The day proved to be a typical day in Texas in May. The temperature was pleasant, and the skies were clear, but the trail dust was pervasive owing to the lack of rain for the last two weeks. To Mav, caring for the remuda is a far-sight better job than riding drag on the herd where all the dust settles on the riders. Riding drag had been his first job on his first trip up the trail to Dodge City, where the boss diverted part of the herd to Walsenburg in Colorado. This time, their destination is beyond Dodge City, where the trail boss will deliver the whole herd to rancher, Branch Storm, who will fatten the cattle on his ranch then send them on to market via rail at the appropriate time.

"Mav, I tell you, that horse I drew from the remuda today was the most cantankerous cayuse I have ever tried to ride. He just would not do what I wanted him to do for the entire day. One of the other boys told me he wouldn't ride him either for the same reason." He pointed to the horse that was milling around among the others in the remuda. "My thoughts are that, if you can't bring him around, he should be sold at the first opportunity."

"Thet one?" asked Mav as he picked up a lariat to lasso the offending horse. A few minutes later, he was leading Biscuit out of the rope corral, preparing to saddle him. Biscuit leaned his head toward Mav and whinnied as Mav patted him on the neck. Mav continued to pat and scratch Biscuit's neck and talk to him in a soft voice. Biscuit seemed to be listening and would snort or whinny now and then as if the conversation was to his liking. Mav gave Biscuit a chewy treat of grain and molasses that he brought with him. Presently, Mav saddled Biscuit and rode him to the herd that was bedding in a field a short distance away. As he rode around and among the cattle, Mav noticed how well Biscuit responded to the knee signals Mav gave him and decided that with a little more work, Biscuit could become an excellent cutting horse. Within a year, Biscuit would be able to identify Mav's intent and cut the intended animal from the herd with little additional guidance from Mav. Biscuit became Mav's horse exclusively from that point onward.

The drive was in its fifth day from Bandera and would cross the Concho River north of San Angelo. Rain, falling onto the northwest watershed of the river, promised high water by the time they arrive, so Alliance has ordered the drovers to utilize every bit of sunlight to move the herd closer before bedding them down for the night. In the winnowing light of day, the herd bedded down, and the drovers began to collect around the chuckwagon for a well-deserved meal. Time following is a traditional period of story-telling by the drovers, wranglers, and visitors alike. Each teller would try to top the others where wisdom of the trail suggests that the 'taller the tale, the taller the Texan telling it.' Clyde Cole told an interesting story about San Angelo, or just Angelo, as most called the town. Clyde said that there was a social club in the town owned by a Miss Hattie where drovers, soldiers from Fort Concho, and menfolk of the town visited on occasion to engage in a little 'rest and relaxation' with the women employed by Hattie. Clyde said that visitors to the club, from the soldiers of Fort Concho to visiting cattle drivers, entered Hattie's establishment by the front door. However, visitors from the Angelo community entered through the Hausenfluke Bank, which, conveniently, had a tunnel between the bank and Miss Hattie's place. Prominent persons in the town say that it is just gossip, that there is no tunnel, and that their visits to the bank simply attest to their success in their various businesses. Whatever the reason for its denial, traveling to see Miss Hattie via the 'non-existent' tunnel, kept peace at the home-places of innumerable San Angelo husbands.

Gathering around chuckwagons to tell stories, sing songs, and just talk was not a characteristic of trail driving until the days of Charles

Goodnight. Chuckwagons are not the long-standing method for feeding the drovers. Until Charles Goodnight's invention of the chuckwagon, the cowhands carried their own food in saddlebags. The typical foods found in those saddlebags were dried meat, beans, hard cheese, dried fruit, hardtack biscuits, and coffee. Goodnight's innovation changed all of that since the 1860s when he bought a Studebaker manufactured Army wagon and added a pantry box with a drop-down door to the rear of the wagon. Food, cooking utensils, tools, and all manner of useful equipment was loaded onto the wagons, even to the firewood needed for the cooking. The wood, collected along the way, was stored under the wagon in a sling made of cowhide or canvas to keep it dry. By the day of the current drive, Studebaker had begun to manufacture wagons for the general market. It was just such a wagon that accompanied the cattle drive from Bandera.

A chuckwagon moves at a more rapid pace than the trailing herd, so Herman, now known as 'Cookie,' after breakfast, would take the wagon, pulled by two teams of strong mules to a rendezvous some miles ahead of the herd and begin preparation of the next meal. Perhaps the most welcome item on every menu was the boiled coffee that he provided for the cowhands' pleasure. Evening meals were heavy on beans since beef is more challenging to keep in the wagon due to spoilage. On occasion though, a pot of 'son-of-a-bitch' stew - or, for the more language sensitive, 'son-of-a-gun' stew would find its way on the menu should an animal suffer an injury on the trail requiring it to be killed. Sourdough bread, a staple of any meal, was a pride of the cook, and he would take special pains to protect the sourdough keg containing the crucial ingredient for making pancakes or biscuits. Victuals that because of rapid spoilage or delicacy, the trail boss would purchase from owners of farms and ranches encountered along the way and from supply stores in towns the herd happened to be passing as they moved up the trail.

***

Trail hands had unhitched the mules and set them to graze when the complaints from the cattle rose to a level of concern. Clouds gathering overhead became dark and threatening. Occasional lightning between clouds could be seen a few miles to the west, and the scent of rain was in the air. As the storm drew closer, the loud crashes of thunder began to unnerve the cattle further. Alliance told the hands to be ready for the animals to stampede or start to drift before the rain, should it come. About eleven in the evening, a particularly loud thunderclap spooked the cattle, and they began to move about, lowing into the darkness. As the claps grew more frequent and gathered in intensity, the animals started to run, pell-mell into a night darkened by cloud, and periodically illuminated by lightning flashes. Immediately, the drovers mounted their horses and urged them into a gallop with their riders having one charge, —to outpace the herd and turn them. "Roll 'em in!" and "mill 'em," was the shouted instructions as the hands turned the leading cattle back toward the direction they came. In time the rolled herd became a circling mass of horns and tails milling around with no place to go. That is the strategy. That is the fix to a herd of stampeding cattle. Eventually, calm would return; no stampede lasts forever. When it occurs, though, a stampede is an 'all-hands-on-deck, even-the-cook' event. As such, all hands are expected to take their share of the task, and their share of the risk, which is considerable.

Mav, riding Biscuit on this night, races through the tumultuous herd to reach the leading cattle running in wild-eyed panic where he waves his hat and shouts at the herd. Crowding the leaders, Mav and Clyde Cole re-direct their movement leftward. After the herd had run for a mile, both drovers fired their six-guns near the front of the herd to counter the fearful noise from the sky with a dreadful noise in the front. Tucum and another hand soon joined them, reinforcing the efforts, — crowding, crowding, shaping the run of the leaders who are being followed by the stampeding herd until they flow into an ever-tightening circle. Control is regained. For the moment. The night-watch riders are again able to circle the heard at thirty or forty paces to help keep the herd calm and watch for predators. Predators, like wolves, coyotes, and catamounts, also called panthers and 'painters' by many who are familiar with the scream of that big cat that sounds like a woman in distress.

Night passes. The storm passes, and sleep-deprived hands, soaked to the skin, come to the chuck wagon where a pot of steaming Arbuckle's coffee awaits. On the fire, sourdough biscuits are baking in a Dutch oven. Nearby, Cookie is slicing the salt-cured bacon to be cooked and served with the eggs scrambled in a large iron skillet over the open fire. Eggs are luxuries on the trail. They usually are purchased from farm and ranch owners along the way or from provisioning stations such as Doan's at the Red River Crossing.

Cookie opens the conversation, asking: "You boys sleep well last night?" and is met with several scowls.

One hand, taking the bait, mumbled: "best I ever had on back some panicked, wild-eyed cayuse who'd rather be sleepin' hissel'."

✳✳✳

Alliance called to Mav to have a word with him. "Mav, we will be at the Colorado by tomorrow. Crossing the Medina and the Concho was a fording. Swimming these brutes across the Colorado is bad enough if it is running low, but a high-running river is no picnic. I want a couple of hands over on the other side to receive the herd when they cross. How are you at swimming?"

"Biscuit an' me are ok with it. Are you sendin' the chuckwagon o'er ahead o' th' herd?" Mav asked, thinking forward to the tasks that will have to be accomplished.

"I may do that, but I want you to scout out the best place to cross if the shallow-water crossing north of Angelo is choked by another herd. I aim to get my herd moving through Indian territory as soon as possible, and we're still a distance from Doan's store up in Wilbarger and we still have the Brazos to cross." Alliance broke away to converse with his *Segundo*, his second in command. Rich Bacon is a competent man with a name that drew any number of humorous wisecracks, — out of earshot, of course. Mav turned his responsibility for the remuda over to Tucum and rode out to locate a secondary crossing.

Fate chose the secondary crossing with its deeper water for them when Alliances' first choice, offering shallow water, was found to be fully engaged with one herd and another waiting. The cattle for Lytle were moved east, and the crossing began at seven am on May 18. Mav and Tucum took the remuda across first and contained them in a rope corral. With the remuda were the mules for the chuckwagon.

The water flowed swiftly, but a crossing was considered manageable, provided the chuckwagon could raft across. Cookie caulked the wagon to repel the water from entering the chuckwagon as it mimicked a raft in its' crossing. To control its drift while in the water, a long rope was tied to the front and back of the wagon, and the ends were wrapped around trees on either side of the river from which it was played out slowly to keep the wagon aligned. The strategy worked, and the wagon gained the other side of the river where a waiting Mav Caid and Tucum re-introduced Cookie's mule team to bring it out of the water onto dry land. Shortly after, the first of the herd went into the water to begin their swim to the other side.

As a precaution, Mav rode upstream to watch that a danger to the cattle was not heading in their direction as they crossed. The threat that floating trees might drift into the herd was real, and animals could be lost should it occur. Fate was on the drovers' side that day, and the herd crossed without a loss.

Chapter 56

Troublesome Foundling

At the Caid-Chesney Tears of the Sun hospital, Macy Caid again confronts Dr. Furnham. "What is it about head injuries that keep an injured person in a coma?" Macy asked of Dr. Furnham as she entered his office.

"We don't know a lot about injuries to the brain, but believe that hard blows to the head can cause swelling of brain tissue that prevents the injured person from regaining consciousness. We believe that he can hear someone speaking to him, and he may even know all that occurs around him. He cannot respond. I have seen some who have not had head injuries but lose their ability to communicate by voice or by writing. Most times, they get over it in a day or two. It's a transient condition. In those cases, the patient is not in a coma. The point I am trying to make is that whatever causes the brain to stop responding does not mean it is permanent. I recommend that you talk to Mav. Perhaps his will to answer will somehow force a breakthrough," Dr.

Furnham replied. Following his advice, Macy entered Mav's room. She began talking to him about the events of the day, keeping conversational, and not allowing her emotions to taint the communication. As she spoke to the seemingly unconscious man, Macy worked thread with her crochet needle to fashion a doily in a pineapple pattern.

On the trail from the Colorado crossing to Doan's store, the weather again showed its troublesome nature and set the herd to drift. Unlike stampedes, the epitome of chaos, a drifting herd is a more an organized movement of cattle following a leader. As such, trail hands will accompany the herd to assure the cattle don't get scattered. A scattered herd is a time-waster and hours, sometimes days, can be lost locating and bringing in the cattle to reform a cohesive herd. Often, when drifting cattle stop their drift, among those are cattle lost from a herd previously passing through the same region or those belonging to ranchers in the immediate area. Trail bosses are duty-bound to return those found cattle to their rightful local owner if possible. However, if trail-branded, those cattle are intentionally taken with the herd for return to the rightful owner should they catch up with them later in the drive.

Alliance sent the order around to search for strays. For the most part, the herd had stayed together, so the hands found few strays, but they did bring in one heifer that had strayed from a previous drive. The brand was one known to Alliance.

Speaking to Mav, Alliance said: "Mav, this heifer belongs to Jim Bob 'Whisper' Bales who took a herd up the trail a month ago. We may run across him coming back if he takes the same route." The idea that they could run into an owner returning home after a drive north is not so far-fetched, given the propensity of all cattlemen to visit a chuckwagon of the advancing herd to get reacquainted with friends and share a free meal while they talk cattle.

"I'll keep an eye out fo' folks comin' this a-way," returned Mav, looking at the brand that was not familiar to him. Mav mounted up and started the heifer toward the herd, only to witness the heifer stop and bed down as if night-time had overtaken her mid-day.

"Git up ya malingerin' cuss! Yur jes' dodging yor responsibilities," a command ignored by a nine-hundred-pound animal that began to chew cud and slap flies with her tail. Now there are several ways to get a critter to stand and more ways than that to fail to get it done. Mav tried twisting her tail with no result. Hard slaps with his lariat only seemed to amuse the beast. Twisting and pulling on her neck was equally unproductive.

Similarly, there are two results from a successful effort in standing up a large bovine, —one that makes them think it is their idea to get up, and another that infuriates enough to warrant getting up so a proper attack can be made upon their tormentor. No cowhand has ever been born who enjoys seeing a half-ton, angry critter with five-foot horns charging with intent to do him harm, especially when that cowhand's only immediate salvation is his ability to run. Reachable corral fences and big trees are golden. Sagebrush and prairie grass are not. Nevertheless, an animal refusing to rise is a concern because cattlemen know that a cow suffers serious health issues if it is lying about for too many hours. It is imperative to determine the cause if possible and correct it if possible. Cause, such as illness or broken bones, are often not easily defined. On the trail, the luxury of spending time trying to determine the cause is not available. Generally, the choice is to stand on all fours or die by the gun and become stew meat.

The herd was putting distance between themselves and the malingering heifer. Since Mav had other duties to perform, he called to one of the drag riders passing on his way to the herd and asked for help in getting the heifer up. Ralph Perkins slid from his horse and untied his lariat. Moving to the front end of the heifer, Ralph looped the rope around the heifer's front leg next to the ground. Next, he walked around the animal to the back, threading the rope below the back legs and around the body, pulling the rope to bring the lassoed front hoof close to the body. Stepping around the heifer and bringing the rope across her hindquarter, Mav took hold of the rope, and both men pulled to force the front leg up closer to the body into the normal position that the animal would assume when standing up. Hopefully, the heifer would get the drift of what was wanted and bend the other knee and roll up on her front knees, then stand up on her back legs. Coming to a full stand then should be a natural thing, —except that it didn't work. Several other attempts tried by the men failed. The recalcitrant heifer just looked at the two, unconcernedly, and continued chewing her cud.

"Perk," began Mav, "I reckon this here heifer ain't worth th' effort. I'll see ifn Alliance will let me put her outta hern misery. Mayhap, Cookie will find a use fo' her." Presently, Mav mounted Biscuit and rode off to find Alliance.

"Mav," said Alliance to the question, "that heifer is lost to Whisper already. When I see Whisper, I'll tell him what happened and pay him if need be. Let Cookie know when you do it. All the boys will welcome some 'sonofabitch stew!'"

Returning to where the heifer lay and reporting his conversation to Ralph, Mav prepared to shoot the animal. As he chambered a round and turned to face the heifer, she was getting up. Mav re-holstered his gun and, shaking his head, remounted Biscuit. Arriving at the herd with the heifer now rapidly moving to join the herd, Mav noted Alliance looking at him quizzically. He shrugged his shoulders and kept moving.

"My mouth was watering for some 'son-of-a-bitch' stew that ornery heifer could have provided with a little help from Cookie," Perk told Mav and a couple of boys around the campfire.

"Mine, too," said a voice nearby.

"And mine," said another.

"Cornbread, beans, bacon, rules the day. I'll jes' hav' some coffee," stated Mav.

✳✳✳

The next day the herd neared Doan's store on the Red River. Doan's was the last place to re-provision before crossing into Indian territory. The Indian Intercourse Act of 1834 had established the boundaries of Indian Territory. By the 1880s, however, it had shrunk considerably, owing to the various Organic Acts of Congress that carved future states out of the unorganized territory. Washington policy encouraged White citizens to organize, form governments, and sue for statehood. Although many Indians were on various reservations by the eighties, the land that was still belonging to the aboriginal owners was primarily concentrated in what would become Oklahoma. It was into this territory that boss Alliance Nelson, horse wrangler Mav Caid, 'Cookie' Herman Jo, and drovers Tucumcari, Ralph Perkins, Clarence Paige, William 'Willie' Paige, Manuel Arredondo, Jose Borrego, Clyde Cole, 'Hondo' Duarte, Gary 'Little Joe' Plagens, and Rogelio 'Rogue' Perez, would enter upon crossing the Red River.

"Cookie and I have finished provisioning," said Alliance to Mav, "so, tomorrow we will cross. I want the remuda to cross first. Still, you need to be watchful because there will be Indian eyes watching, and they like nothing better than taking horses. They collect a fee for allowing a herd to enter the territory. I'll take care of that. You make sure the horses are safe."

"Tucum will give me a hand with the remuda, and one of us will guard the remuda while the other helps with the cattle as they come

467

across." Mav signed to Tucum to come over so he could tell him what Alliance wanted.

The horse remuda crossed the Red River and was constrained in a rope corral Mav and Tucum fashioned for them. Tucum stayed to guard the horses while Mav went back to help with the cattle. The entire herd was across by nightfall and bedded down two miles from the river. There were no losses in the crossing, although two steers managed to find a soft bottom and became bogged down. Jose and Hondo freed them with all the attendant effort required to extract them from the muck. They both were pretty mad about their situation and charged the men when freed from the mire. Both men were able to elude the charging animals.

The next morning as breakfast was being prepared, four Indians rode into camp motioning that they wanted to eat with the drovers. Cookie was ready for such an occasion and fed the four along with the drovers. The fare for today was flapjacks with syrup, and the visiting natives so enjoyed the syrup given to them by Cookie that they howled and shouted like successful hunters at the buffalo hunt as they left camp.

As the drovers prepared the herd to move out, Deja-vu visited, and a certain heifer remained on the ground as the others stepped around her. As the last of the cattle continued up the trail, Mav dismounted Biscuit to confront the unruly heifer.

"Hardcase, my powder's still dry, an' th' boss done tol' me I could shoot yor lazy self ifn you don't start behavin'. An' I shor ain't a-lookin' ta make th' boss consider shootin' me 'cause I didn't shoot you." Mav stood looking down at two black, unconcerned eyes staring at him from a piebald face. The heifer twisted her head to bring the tip of horn against her flank to scratch and gave a sigh. Mav returned to Biscuit to remove his rifle from its saddle holster. Returning to face the heifer, Mav levered a shell into the chamber. "See this?" said Mav as he shook the rifle at the heifer that was still showing unconcern.

Mav walked back about ten feet and turned back to face the heifer. Hardcase rolled her massive body into a kneeling position and stood up.

"Good choice," said Mav. "Now, git!" The heifer began trotting in the direction the herd had taken.

***

The day was uneventful, then nightfall came. The bedded cattle were content. At two in the morning, the horses became restless. Mav was on watch for this period, so he became alerted to the disturbance among the horses. Having ridden Biscuit all day, Mav had given Biscuit the night off and put him in the rope corral with the other horses. Mav walked around the corral looking for any threat but found none. The horses continued to mill around and sniff the air. An hour passed, and Mav went back to camp to wake Tucum, who was to take the watch until sunup. When he returned, four horses were missing, including Biscuit. Mav immediately sounded the alarm that brought the hands up to face a threat. Mav told them of the theft as he mounted a horse to follow whatever trail he could find. Darkness provides excellent cover for such raids, and it would take sunlight to reveal the direction the Indians had taken.

The first task of the morning is to locate the Indians with their stolen horses, a difficult one considering that the rustlers have had several hours head start. Since the Indians had ridden over ground not disturbed by a cattle herd, Mav was able to follow their tracks. Three hours passed without sighting anything promising. Suddenly, as Mav topped a hill, he was amazed to see Biscuit slowly following three other horses heading toward the herd. Had he not seen evidence of an intrusion by someone who stole the horses in the first place, he would have suspected that Biscuit and the others broke out themselves and just went on a wander. It would always be a puzzle, for he will never witness Biscuit tossing the first rider into the dirt as he attempted to mount him. Nor will he see Biscuit charge the other three horse thieves knocking two of them to the ground. Nor see Biscuit, corral the other horses to force them back to camp, nipping them on the hind-quarter if they veered in the wrong direction. That will be a tale only told in horse-talk by those with first-hand knowledge, a privilege of equine brotherhood.

Chapter 57

Perriman Maas

Crossing Indian territory proceeded smoothly for several days, and there were no attempts made to steal any of the cattle or horses. One unfortunate heifer stepped into a gopher hole and broke a leg. She provided the 'son-of-a-bitch' stew the boys had been pining for since the first opportunity did not pan out. Cookie's recipe for the stew did justice to the loss by the inclusion of tongue, tripe, kidney, heart, liver, and sweetbread from the slaughtered cow. Vegetables used were onions and potatoes brought from Doan's store, wild carrots Cookie found at the last stop on the trail. Water, salt, pepper, and some ingredients Cookie would not reveal, all that went into the pot with the other ingredients to bring forth a royal feast for the tired boys on a night in June. A full moon and calm weather allowed complete rest and relaxation for two days.

The herd was moving in the third hour when Hondo told Alliance that he had seen a rider following the herd. Alliance told him to keep him in sight until they bedded the cattle later in the day. At sundown, the stranger rode into the camp and dismounted. Walking to the chuckwagon, he motioned to the coffee pot boiling on the fire and asked Cookie if he could have a cup.

"Stranger, you got a name?" asked Cookie.

"Yup. Name's Perriman Maas. Down from Kansas City," answered Perriman. I ran across your trail a few miles back and thought I might talk a spell with your boss."

"His name is Alliance Nelson, and he'll likely be along soon. My handle is Herman Jo, by most call me Cookie," returned Cookie.

The introductions over, Perriman took his coffee and sat down on a log next to Mav. Not long after, Alliance rode in. As Alliance dismounted, Perriman Maas stood up and advanced toward him.

"Mr. Nelson, allow me to introduce myself." Perriman touched his hat brim in a typical westerner's signal of greeting.

"How can I help you?" returned Alliance.

"I would like to join up with you if possible. I lost the chuck I was carrying in an unfortunate meeting with an Indian band, so I'm looking to trade. I'll work at whatever you want me to do for the chuck. And, of course, some of your cook's great coffee." Perriman gave a broad smile as he ended his appeal.

"You are down from Kansas City, but heading back toward it. What took you south?" asked Alliance, trying to elicit as much from Perriman as needed to help him decide if he wants to offer a job to him.

"I was down in Texas visiting family there. I still have folks living there."

"I start all of my new hands riding drag, Mr. Maas. Does that change your mind?" Alliance waited for an answer that came quickly.

"Done that often, Mr. Nelson. I'm good with it." Perriman smiled again.

"I don't like to see a man go without chuck, so come along with us. I'll move our current drag rider to the flank." The matter settled; Alliance ambled off to speak with Rogue Perez.

"Whut outfits hav' you been with?" asked Mav as Perriman sat back down on the log.

"I wrangled mostly for Blocker, down around Austin. And did some wrangling for Littlefield. I've been around some." Perriman offered no more information, and Mav asked no more questions. Though he expected Perriman to ask him about Alliance or even himself, it did not happen. Both men finished their coffee in silence.

At breakfast, the next day, Alliance introduced Perriman Maas to the hands as the new drag rider. Perriman revealed very little to the hands about himself but gave some information about his time with Blocker and Littlefield. One of the hands watched Perriman with a strange intensity. When Perriman mounted up to take up his assigned position, Clarence Paige whistled softly and shook his head. Standing up, he ambled over to where Mav was standing, preparing to mount Biscuit.

"Mav, have you ever heard of a man called Mannen?" Clarence waited for Mav's answer.

"No." Perplexity showed upon Mav's face.

"This Perriman is a dead ringer for Emmanuel, or 'Mannen' Clements," said Clarence. "He's a killer, Mav. A cold-blooded killer. He is the father-in-law of Jim Miller, himself called 'Killer Miller', and is a cousin to John Wesley Hardin, a prisoner at Huntsville, Texas right now. Hardin is in prison for killing two lawmen. Hardin is bad, Mav, and so is Mannen. I know this because I come from a branch of the Clements family. I don't think he recognized me, though. Alliance needs to know." That night, Mav and Clarence told Alliance about Clarence's suspicion about Perriman.

Eugene Stonefield

Two days later, Clarence was riding watch on the herd and heard someone call him. He could not get a clear look at the man until he stepped out from the scrub.

"I've seen you before. Your name is Clarence. Am I right?" Perriman asked Clarence, causing him a measure of fear at the pointed question from someone who is known to be dangerous.

"Ah…Yes, my name is Clarence. What do you want?" asked the nervous hand.

"Nothing. I just wanted to get a closer look." Perriman turned and disappeared back into the scrub.

Later that day, Clarence approached Mav. "Mav, I was scared. He suspects me. He thinks I know who he really is, and a man who takes on a different name is running from something." Clarence looked nervously over his shoulder.

"Aww, ifn he thought thet he prob'ly would hav' done somethin' right then. He jes' thought you looked like someone he's run accrost sometime in th' past." Mav tried to quell the concern of Clarence while thinking, Clarence may be right. "Course, he'll keep a-thinkin' 'bout it 'till he remembers, I reckon."

***

"Mr. Nelson," began Perriman, "I saw a small party of Indians just a mile or so back. I'd like to take a look-see if you can spare me for an hour or two. Might give us some idea if they have plans to cause us trouble."

"I'll give you four hours to check them out. Don't start anything. This is their territory, and they may just be passing through." Perriman accepted the answer and rode out as Alliance motioned for Mav to come to him.

"Mav, Perriman has asked to leave the drive to look for a band of Indians he saw. I don't know that I believe him. Follow him and see what he does. If he's as bad a character Clarence said he is, he could be communicating with compatriots who are planning to steal some cattle themselves. Stay out of sight. Come back when you can tell me something."

Mav mounted Biscuit and rode out in the direction Perriman had taken a few minutes before. Perriman rode for a mile back down the trail over ground they had already passed, then veered west for a few minutes, then back again in the direction the herd was taking. His parallel ride lasted until he got ahead of the herd, where he selected a position on a rock outcropping where he could see the herd as it approached. Perriman took his rifle from its holster and lay it beside him as he assumed a prone position on the outcropping.

Mav dismounted Biscuit behind a thick band of scrub and crept to where he could watch Perriman from the side. He waited for some minutes but knew of the approaching herd by the numerous bellows from the cattle. He could feel his heart move to his throat as he realized that Perriman did not watch for Indians, but waited for the herd, and very likely, Clarence. Sweat began to run down his neck. As the sounds from the herd came closer, he could see Perriman's attention become more focused.

Mav returned to Biscuit and took his lariat and his rifle from its holster. As a last thought, he cut two whang straps from his saddle and brought them back to his observation post. Removing his six-shooter, he crept about twenty feet away to a tree and tied the pistol to a branch that reached in the direction of Perriman. Next, Mav tied a loop in the whang strap and looped it over the trigger, stringing the remainder of the strap around the tree where he tied the whang strap to his lariat. Reaching up to the revolver, he cocked the hammer. Returning to his original position twenty feet away with the rope laying loosely on the ground, he waited for the herd to come closer. Twenty minutes later, he could sense them very nearby.

Perriman picked up his rifle and levered a round into the firing chamber. For a while, he just looked in the direction of the herd. Finally, he began to take aim.

Mav checked that his own rifle had a bullet in the chamber, then reached for the lariat. As Mav sensed Perriman was ready to fire, he pulled the rope, and the revolver sent a bullet in the direction of Perriman. Immediately, Mav fired off several rounds in Perriman's direction, levering the cartridges into the firing chamber as quickly as he could and moving away from the position of his last shot. He took no aim at Perriman, though it would have been easy, and maybe prudent to do so; Mav was not a killer. As the last round left the muzzle of his Henry, Mav gave out his best rendition of an Indian war-whoop as he could imagine one to be. Immediately, he ran to another position in the other direction. Firing again, he saw Perriman jump to his feet and run to his horse a short distance away. He did not remain in the area long. Mav retrieved his revolver and lariat and remounted Biscuit to join the others who were busily riding to turn a stampeding herd set in motion by an apparent Indian raid.

The stampede stopped after a three-mile chase, and Alliance ordered the hands to bed the herd down for the night. Cookie began to prepare the beans, cornbread, and bacon for the night's meal. Mav sat down with a cup of coffee.

"Mav, I haven't seen Perriman since he left five hours ago. Did you trail him?" asked Alliance.

"Yessir, I trailed him a bit. He kinda looped 'round th' herd an' got ahead o' you." Mav sipped his coffee then continued: "Last I seen o' him he wuz headin' yonder to th' east at a gallop."

"Would that be before the Indian raid, or after?" asked Alliance.

"Well, sir, I'm a-thinkin' it wuz sorta during thet raid," replied Mav.

"I never saw the Indians that caused the stampede. Did you see them?" asked Alliance.

"No, sir. Not even one." Mav replied, reaching for a plate to load with beans and cornbread.

Chapter 58

Tragedy on the Trail

Dr. Furnham entered the room and closed the door before beginning his conversation with Macy and Case.

"Last night, your husband showed some positive signs," said Dr. Furnham to Macy. "The nurse reported that he stirred some and mumbled something unintelligible." He could come out of the coma at any time. It doesn't seem as deep as over the last several days."

"Thank you, Dr. Furnham, that makes me feel much better." Macy left the doctor's office in higher spirits than what she brought into the hospital.

***

Today is the thirty-first day of the drive, and the fourteenth time Mav has had to level his Henry at a heifer that, periodically, refuses to get up with the rest of the cattle. For her malinger, the heifer had been awarded a name by some of the drovers. Dodge. It amused the hands to talk of Dodge dodging Dodge, Kansas, where she is sure to be sold. Mav just treats her recalcitrance as a quirk to be overcome now and then. If truth be told, Mav has developed an affection for the beast.

Alliance is addressing the hands as they prepare to resume the drive, saying, "I reckon all of you have seen the clouds gathering to the northwest. Those who are on their first drive may not be aware of the threat they pose. Lightning strikes during these storms are our worst nightmare, and I have never heard of a way to avoid it. All I can say at this time is, if this storm reaches us, expect anything. A stampede is likely, so be ready to get out front as fast as possible. We don't need a herd charging off some cliff."

If his words sounded prophetic, they were. They made it through the day without any significant event and bedded the cattle in grassland. The storm rolled across them at one in the morning. Beginning with a loud thunderclap, followed by several lightning strikes near the herd, was enough to set three-thousand beeves in motion driven by blind panic. The hands already on watch raced with the cattle attempting to reach the leaders of the running herd to turn them. Other cowhands, troubled in their sleep by the words of Alliance, arose from their bedrolls and mounted quickly to join the chase. Twelve thousand hooves pounded the ground as three million pounds of beef raced wildly into the night illuminated only by flashes of light in the clouds above and fearful cloud-to-ground strikes. Less than twelve miles ahead are the banks of the Cimarron River that the herd must cross tomorrow. Cattle are much like bison in running ability. They can run seven miles in the span of an hour, and most troublesome, they are endurance runners. Horses can gallop at a speed of twenty-five to thirty miles per hour, but can only maintain that speed for a short amount of time. Riding at break-neck speed in the middle of night with the threat of being thrown from a horse beneath those beating bovine hooves, or being dragged to death with one foot caught in a stirrup, or being knocked off his horse by tree branch, or being struck by lightning are the everyday concerns of every cowhand given the dubious opportunity of going up the trail in the eighth decade of the nineteenth century in America. Every cowhand has a personal story about stampedes; if he has been up the trail, most have more than one. Many will remember the names of those who paid the price.

After a five-mile run, the herd was turned into a ball of frightened cattle, bawling, and milling with wild eyes while St. Elmo's fire danced upon their ears and horns. As the herd began to regain composure and settle down, the hands continued to ride around the herd to monitor the shaky equilibrium between panic and peace in their bovine brains. Eventually, as calm was restored, hands began to return to the chuckwagon.

Finally, the storm moved on to the south leaving clear skies and a landscape that began to be illuminated by a yellow sun rising in the east overtopping the clouds of the receding storm. As sunlight reached the backs of the rain-soaked cattle, steam drifted upward from their drying backs.

"Anyone missing?" asked Alliance.

"Clarence. Clarence is missing," stated his brother Willie.

"Find him," responded Alliance, and all sleep-deprived hands in camp mounted up and rode back from whence they came.

An hour later, Manuel Arredondo returned to the chuckwagon with the broken body of Clarence Paige.

"Willie," began Alliance. "Manny found Clarence. I'm sorry. He's dead. It appears that he and his horse were struck by lightning. His horse is also dead."

Willie Paige went over to his dead brother, now laying on Clarence's bedroll that had been retrieved from the trail wagon. He stood staring down at his own, his mentor, his protector throughout his twenty-one-year life, —his face, a white mask of disbelief. After a few elongated minutes, during the self-imposed silence of the saddened cowhands, Willie walked slowly out behind a crop of trees.

Burials along the trail are not unusual. The deceased is necessarily buried without a casket, their bedroll, a shroud, silence, their lasting companion. People die on the trail as they die at home and in the towns and cities everywhere. Yet, it is the solemn thought of leaving family or friend in the lonely ground with no permanent marker, and no one to visit to ponder the life of the lost cowboy that wrenches the heart of every cowhand on every trail since the beginning of those great movements of cattle up the trail.

The herd stayed in place for the next day as the trail boss and cowhands laid Clarence to rest upon a nearby hilltop. It fell to Alliance to say a few words over the grave of this unfortunate cowboy, and he proceeded by choosing a passage from the Bible that Cookie kept in the chuckwagon. As all the hands gathered around the grave, he opened the Bible to Second Corinthian 5:1 and read:

"For we know that if the tent that is our earthly home is destroyed, we have a building from God, a house not made by hands, eternal in Heaven." And he followed by Romans 14: 7-9: *"For none of us lives to himself, and none of us dies to himself. For if we live, we live to the Lord, and if we die, we die to the Lord. So then, whether we live or whether we die, we are the Lord's. For to this end, Christ died and lived again that he might be Lord both of the dead and of the living."*

When he finished, Alliance reached down to take a handful of black earth from the pile excavated from the grave, and holding it above the shrouded body of Clarence, let it fall with the paraphrase of Genesis 3: 19, the words: *"Ashes to ashes, dust to dust."* Brother Willie, and each of the trail friends of Clarence followed suit, and the grave was closed. As a final service to the departed friend, the hands collected rocks and placed them upon the grave to impede the disturbance of the body by any wild animals that might perceive the grave below.

"I guess you may want to head on back home," Alliance was saying to Willie. "You can catch a train in Dodge."

"Ain't nobody left to tell," answered Willie, "besides, my brother would have wanted me to finish the job."

Chapter 59

Death in Dodge City

The evening and night were quiet, and the cattle settled in. Cowhands on night watch were walking their mounts around the perimeter of the herd humming, occasionally singing some preferred song. From whence came the songs? The short answer is, from everywhere. Early colonists from England, Holland, —from wherever people lived, who sought a different life in a far-away land. Colonial songs, like <u>Young Johnny</u> or <u>Springfield Mountain</u>, told a story of death by snakebite. Some songs grew from the bleeding of Christianity into the slave communities in the south that blended Christian themes with African rhythms sung in Gullah and Sea Island Creole dialects. Songs like <u>Come by Here,</u> later to be called <u>Kumbayah,</u> the word 'yah' meaning 'here' in Gullah. They arrived from Scotland with the men and women forced from their homes during the Highland Clearances of the eighteenth and nineteenth centuries, known by the Scots as the *Fuadach nan Gàidheal,* or the expulsion of the

Scots. From these expelled Scotsmen came the <u>Skye Boat Song</u> memorializing the battle of Culloden and the escape of Bonnie Prince Charles from the clutches of the Duke of Cumberland. Many religious songs came from Spain with missionaries. Some of the songs were laments of lost loves, many were sea shanties, brought to America by seafarers. Songs of the American Civil War, like <u>The Battle Hymn of the Republic</u> by Julia Ward Howe, and <u>When Johnny Comes Marching Home</u> by Patrick Gilmore, its melody taken from a drinking song called <u>Johnny Fill Up the Bowl</u>. One favorite song is American born and is a lament that tells the story of the longing of some fur-trader for the daughter of Oneida Chief Shenandoah. The lyrics are:

> *"Oh, Shenandoah,*
> *I long to see you,*
> *Away, you rolling river.*
> *Oh, Shenandoah,*
> *I long to see you*
> *Away, I bound away,*
> *'cross the wide Missouri.*
> *Oh, Shenandoah*
> *I love your daughter*
> *Away, you rolling river.*
> *For her I'd cross*
> *Your roaming waters*
> *Away, I'm bound away,*
> *'cross the wide Missouri."* [13]

The voice was that of Little Joe, a boy from Missouri. A sweet singer who was willing to sing songs by request from hands around the evening campfire. He knew many songs and had a harmonica and a guitar that he jealously guarded against the elements. Having lived along the river until he was called to the trail, he had learned many songs that were written and sung by men of the waters, —sailors, bargemen, fishermen, and those of the ports around the world. He learned them from his father, William, who was a sailor from Baltimore turned riverboat owner on the Missouri River. William, son of a sailor from Liverpool, learned them from his father, who taught him many songs if the seas. One of Little Joe's favorites - one he was often asked to sing - was <u>Goodbye, Fare Thee Well</u>. The lyrics go:

> *"We're going away to leave you now*
> *Goodbye, fare the well*
> *Goodbye, fare the well*
> *We're going away to leave you now*
> *Hoorah, me boys, we're homeward bound*
> *Oh, give me the girl with the bonny brown hair*
> *Your hair of brown is the talk of the town*
> *So, fare you well, we're homeward bound*
> *Homeward bound to Liverpool town…"* [14]

Feelings around the campfire in the second month on the trail after listening to Little Joe perform his repertoire were happy but nostalgic for home. The nearer it got to the destination, the more anxious the younger of the hands became. For some, the ride back to Texas would be a dull repeat of other returns. For some, the first ride on an iron horse rolling down the shiny rails.

Dodge City, the first significant town on the trail to Ogallala, and the beginning of the threats to the green boys who had never experienced the wildness of a city of saloons and bordellos, nor played the games of chance offered non-stop to all.

Little Joe, nineteen years old, a babe ripe for fleecing by the master of a deck of cards.

"Mav, you gotta come with me. They are playing a card game that I am an expert at playing. I can win a lot of money for us. More than we will get at the end of the trail. Come with me." Little Joe was adamant in his appeal. He knew he could win, but Mav was uncertain.

"Naw, Little Joe," returned Mav, "I reckon I'll stay with th' herd to make shor no rustlin' happens."

For a while, Little Joe won, hand after hand, until he had a sizable stack of clay poker chips. Then the celebrations with free shots of rye whiskey, and the cheating began. Little Joe lost hand after hand until he detected the trick. Red-faced with anger, Little Joe stood, facing the cheater, shouting at him, and decrying the deception, until he made a fatal error by dropping a hand to his gun.

Self-defense was the decision of the sheriff, based upon witness testimony at the scene. "Nothing to see here, folks," the sheriff said to the Long Branch crowd, "go on home."

Home for Little Joe is Boot Hill. Notification of next of kin is the requirement of the moment, and Alliance Nelson discharges his duty to the parents of the deceased boy via telegram at the local telegraph station:

To: H. H. Plagens <stop>
Hannibal, Missouri <stop>
From: Alliance Nelson <stop>
Dodge City, Kansas <stop>
Son Little Joe killed yesterday <stop>
Burial Dodge City Boot Hill <stop>
Condolence sent by all <stop>
Alliance Nelson <stop>
John Lytle Company <stop>

Burials at Boot Hill followed a pattern. Gravediggers dug the grave for a body delivered by wagon. Around the grave stood the drovers who knew Little Joe. Alliance Nelson engaged a preacher from the town to officiate at the gravesite. The preacher stood at the gravesite to offer a prayer for the fallen and advice to the sinners attending the funeral.

"What is his name?" was the question from the preacher who had not bothered to introduce himself.

"Joseph Plagens. We jes' call him Little Joe," answered Mav.

"Age?" asked the preacher.

"Nineteen, I think," answered Alliance.

"Are there any kinfolks here?" questioned the preacher.

"No kin, just friends." Alliance's answer satisfied the preacher, who stepped to the grave.

"We are gathered here to say farewell to a friend. Joseph 'Little Joe' Peg … uh..., Paguns…Pagan…PLAgens, at nineteen, was a young man in the prime of life, cut down by the sinful pursuit of wealth promised by a deck of cards. But, as we all know, God will deal with all men, of whatever nature, whether good or bad. It is not our place to judge, so we do not. Today, Little Joe Plaga…Plagens, be he sinner or saved, he is now in the hands of God, our Father in Heaven." Opening the Bible, he announces the 23rd Psalm, and reads:

> *"The Lord is my shepherd.*
> *I shall not want.*
> *He maketh me lie down in green pastures;*
> *He leadeth me beside quiet waters.*
> *He restoreth my soul;*
> *He guideth me in the paths of righteousness*
> *for the sake of His name.*
> *Even though I walk through the valley of the shadow of death,*
> *I will fear no evil.*
> *For Thou are with me;*
> *Thy rod and Thy staff, they comfort me.*
> *Thou preparest a table before me*
> *in the presence of mine enemies.*

Thou anointest my head with oil;
My cup overflows.
Surely goodness and mercy will follow me
all the days of my life,
And I will dwell in the house of the Lord forever.
Amen."

The unnamed preacher continued from the 23rd Psalm through the 27th, and the eyes of several drover friends of Little Joe filled with tears for their friend.

As the preacher's voice trails off into the final 'Amen,' six voices repeat the word and step forward to take a handful of dirt to toss into the grave. One after another, each man passes by to drop their handful of dust onto the unpainted pine casket displaying the bright nail-heads securing the lid on Little Joe Plagens' eternal, sunless chamber. The clods thump upon a crudely made pine box, drumming a final farewell to another young man who could not beat the odds at the Long Branch.

Chapter 60

Passage Negotiation

The initial heavy feeling at leaving a friend in Dodge City began to lift as the herd pushed on toward Ogallala. As drives go, it had been more relaxed than some, harder than others. Only two stampedes were significant, and only one life lost to stampede. Placing Little Joe Plagens in this place, at this time, had nothing to do with his killing. Blame must rest on unrealistic optimism, ignorance of the risk, bad choices, and the hand of unfeeling fate. All are elements of human existence. How one handles them, does much to shape the successes and failures in life.

The forty-second day of the drive and the Smokey Hill River is a half-day's drive out from their current location. Hondo, scouting for the next bedding ground for the herd, encounters a long furrow fence. The furrow fence is a legal fiction. There is no fence. Only the representation of where one would be if there was one. Beyond the plow-lines are cornfields, —crops a farmer wants not to have destroyed by a cattle drive. To address the complaints of farmers, the legislature has constructed the fiction and has given the farmer's power. Cattle invading a growing crop are subject to a fine, levied upon the owners of the offending cattle. The fines could be significant. Farmers mark the land by plowing the ground around the legally protected acreage, and the law expects the drovers to honor the fiction or pay the fine. Alliance and Mav, having ridden for several hundred yards along the plowed ground, decide to cross and ride to the sodbuster's cottage they see in the distance. Their purpose is to discuss driving the cattle across the portion of the field not planted.

"Mr. Farmer! Hello." Alliance called to the occupants of the small sod cabin. His wait was not long as from the cabin came a diminutive man in overalls and heavy boots. From the door peered a woman with a shawl.

"You're on my land Mr. Cattlemen!" the farmer advanced several yards toward the pair before continuing, "did you see my plow line?"

"We did. And we came to see if we could cross that part of the land that has no growing crops." Alliance and Mav started to dismount but interrupted their dismount with the next statement from the farmer.

"It means horses, too." The farmer stood with a determined posture and an attitude that told Alliance and Mav that negotiating passage could be difficult.

"You have a plow line that extends all the way to that forest in the distance but you only have a small portion cultivated. We have three-thousand beeves to take to Ogallala and can pass over your fallow land without damage to the corn growing here in this area. Taking the herd in any other direction will cause us trail-days that would be difficult to make up later. Not being able to cross your unused land seems unreasonable. We can do that by tonight, and the cattle will be controlled," replied Alliance. "All we need is your permission."

"I would have to have twenty-cents per head to let you pass over my land." The farmer asks for the moon.

"You won't be feeding the animals; they will just be walking across. I think five-cents per head is about right." Alliance leaned forward in the saddle.

"That many cows will trample the ground and make it hard to plow next year. Why should I take your offer if I must work harder to plow the ground next year? Besides, they tend to leave things when they cross that people step in," replied the farmer.

"Fertilizer! It will make your crops better next year. If I were selling those cow chips to you, I would have to ask three cents a bushel. This way, you get them free.

"Well, I wouldn't pay more than a penny!" replied the farmer.

"What is the penalty for violating the trespass law in this region?" Asked Mav.

"Fifty cents a cow," replied the farmer. "You aiming to violate it?"

"Not unless necessary," returned Alliance, showing some exasperation.

"The last herd that crossed my land paid more than you offer. Why should I take less?" returned the farmer.

For a moment, Alliance was silent, giving Mav a moment to interject his thought.

"Is that your mule I see over yonder? She looks a might puny." Mav said, and as he pointed, Alliance got his drift. The drive began with four mules to pull the chuckwagon. They need only two from this point on.

"She is ailing a bit with a sore back." The farmer looked back at his mule. He knew she was getting old.

Alliance made his pitch: "Let's agree on this: I give you a good mule to replace your ailing one, and you get all the cow chips that we leave in our crossing. How does that sound?"

"Ok." Said the farmer who turned and went inside to tell his wife of the great deal he made.

"How much do you figger thet mule o' yorn is worth?" asked Mav.

"About one hundred-twelve dollars. And, before you ask, the chips ain't worth nothing to me. To the sodbuster, the value is in the heat they will generate this winter."

"Well, the trespass fee would have been about fifteen-hundred dollars," Mav replied.

"Yeah, I figure we saved a bit. Now," said Alliance, with a straight face, "now, someone probably will need to collect the chips so we can count the number of bushels so we can report to Lytle the real cost of the agreement. Would you…"

"Th' remuda needs a little more attention," said Mav.

"Thought so," returned Alliance. Both men turned their horses back toward the advancing herd.

Chapter 61

Arrest of a Horse Thief

U nable to contain her fear, Mach turns to Dr. Furnham: "It is so hard to take, Dr. Furnham. It has been five days, and he has done little beyond what your nurse told you on Thursday. How long? Is it possible that he will never wake up?" Macy asks Dr. Furnham, showing her fear that this is the future.

"Macy, I just can't tell you anything with any certainty. He could wake today. Or he could wake in a week. I think it is too negative to think he may never wake again. Too negative. I urge you to resist those thoughts and concentrate on more positive things."

Macy accepts Dr. Furnham's advice, knowing that thinking negatively is a street to despondency. Still, the advice is hard to follow as the dreadful consequences that are possible loom over her mind like the fabled sword hanging above the courtier, Damocles, in the court of Dionysius II of Syracuse in the 4th century BC.

Eugene Stonefield

✳✳✳

"You are gonna hang, Mr. Oates!" stated Sheriff Harper of Hitchcock County, Nebraska. "Folks around here don't tolerate horse thieves."

"But my name ain't Oates, sheriff. My name is Maverick Caiden, an' I come up with th' Lytle company's herd. Th' herd is bedded down jes' two miles south. Anyone thar will tell you who I am," answered Mav, looking out between bars of the jailhouse door.

"Don't need to, Mr. Oates. One of our most respectable citizens has pointed you out while you were in the general store. I suppose you meant to rob the store too!" Sheriff Harper drew closer to look at Mav through the bars, then, after a moment of uncertainty, pulled a pair of eyeglasses from his vest pocket and put them on. Once again, the sheriff peered at Mav, finally saying: "Well, I can't say I completely agree, but the witness is a respectable member of this community, so I'll have to take that into consideration. Good night, Mr. Oates. Sleep tight. Judge Sedgerow will be here tomorrow to arraign you for thieving that horse." That night, Mav spent a sleepless night in jail.

"Judge Sedgerow," began Sheriff Harper, "I arrested Mr. Oates yesterday for stealing a horse belonging to Tiffany Coddles. Mr. Woodrow Coddles swore that Mr. Oates took his daughter's horse about five in the afternoon two days before. He saw it happen from a distance but swore the thief was Iver Oates. When he saw Oates in the general store, he told me, and I arrested him. No one has seen Iver in these parts since the townsfolk ran him out of town for his behavior over three years ago. I suppose he thinks we don't remember." Judge Sedgerow turned his eyes from Sheriff Harper to Mav.

"Where is the horse now, Sheriff Harper?" asked the judge, looking intently at Mav, assuming to assess the character of the man before him.

"Down at the livery," responded the sheriff. "I have already sent word to Mr. Coddles that I have the horse, and he can pick it up at any time."

Turning to Mav, Judge Sedgerow asked: "Mr. Oates, how do you plead to the charge against you?"

"I ain't guilty of nothin', judge. This here's jes' a mistake. My name is Maverick Caiden, an' I'm up frum Texas with a herd o' beeves a-headin' to Ogallala. Th' herd is only a few miles outten town, an' anyone thar will vouch fo' me. An' thet horse b'longs to Mr. Lytle." Mav waited for the judge to continue.

"I'll have the sheriff do that right away, Mr. Oates. But for the moment, I'll send you back to jail, so you won't get any ideas of leaving." The judge ordered Sheriff Harper to check out the prisoner's assertion. Sheriff Harper nods his receipt of the judge's order but makes no move to follow it at the present time.

As Mav turned for the sheriff to take him back to jail, a man entered the courtroom and spoke to the sheriff, then to the judge, saying: "Is this the horse thief? I hear he says he's not Oates." He turned to look at Mav, saying: "Is that true? You look like Oates." He drew close to look at Mav more closely.

Mav said nothing but looked over his accuser carefully. The man appears in his early fifties with salt and pepper hair, handlebar mustache that turns down at the ends. His skin is typical for a person that spends a great deal of time under the sun, and sky-blue eyes behind thick eyeglasses. Turning back to the sheriff, Woodrow Coddles announced that he would take the horse back to his daughter.

Mav could no longer be silent and interjected: "I don't think thet's a good idea. Biscuit won't let no one but me ride him. A young girl could git hurt."

"We will let Mr. Coddles be the judge of that. He will take his horse back to his daughter as he wants." The sheriff closed the conversation.

"Judge, may I suggest thet someone here in town ride Biscuit befor' takin' him to Mr. Coddles' daughter? I shor don't want to larn o' her gittin' hurt. Biscuit ain't mean, he's jes' pertic'lar 'bout who rides him."

"I'll ride that horse, myself," interjected Coddles, "whether I ride my horse and lead hers, or ride hers and lead mine makes little difference." The judge nods, and both Sheriff Harper and Woodrow Coddles leave to get Biscuit from the livery stable. Mav and Judge Sedgerow remain in the courtroom looking at each other as Deputy Wilbur Knott remains in charge of the accused horse thief, Iver Oates.

"Whut now, Judge?" asks Mav.

"Well, seeing that the stolen horse has been recovered, we may not hang you. Course, that's for the jury to decide," returned the judge.

"Yessir. Thet's good news." Mav sat down to wait for his return to jail. Within a few minutes, a commotion erupted outside, and Woodrow Coddles burst through the courtroom door, followed by the sheriff. Woodrow walked toward the judge brushing the dirt from his coat and adjusting his glasses.

"Judge Sedgerow, that horse damn near killed me. He was all friendly when I led him from the livery, but when I mounted him, he tossed me so high, if I hadn't been able to catch on to the sign hanging out over the street, the fall itself might have been fatal. He sure can't be the same horse my daughter had. My daughter's horse is as gentle as a lamb." Turning to the sheriff, the respected Woodrow Coddles said: "I think someone ought to spend some time finding out whose horse Mr. Oates stole!" His statement finished; Woodrow Coddles withdrew from the courtroom.

"Judge Sedgerow," said Mav, "ifn a horse ain't a stolen horse, how ken it's owner be a horse thief?"

"But you look like Mr. Oates, and Mr. Oates is a known horse and cattle thief. We have you in our hoosegow now, and we didn't the day before, so, as Mr. Coddles said, the sheriff just needs to find the owner of the horse you have stolen. We already have it on good authority that you are in possession of a stolen horse. When he finds whose horse it is, we can proceed to trial. Of course, if he doesn't find out right away, you can expect to stay with us for a while."

"Wal, I reckon thet jes' might cook th' goose o' any stranger thet finds hissel' lookin' out th' bars o' yor jail cell." Mav turned from the judge, shaking his head, then turning back, continued: "Ifn y'all would jes' ride out to th' herd an' ask about me y'all would git th' answer about Biscuit an' me."

The strong arm of the law sometimes is not willing to discard an assumption previously made, so the inclination is strong to contort the logic to accommodate the erroneous assumption. If the crime does not fit the identified perpetrator, find a crime that does. One is seldom accused who is not guilty of something. Why take the word of the accused against the credence of a witness you know, which could waste time in achieving justice for the accuser, especially if he has social status? The accused always say they are innocent anyway.

Presently, Sheriff Harper takes hold of Mav's arm. "Mr. Oates, you could make it easier on yourself to tell me where you are living now. If there are no stolen horses or cattle there, it might persuade me to recommend that the judge just fine you for trespass or something and let you go. But if we find anything stolen, well…" Sheriff Harper let the statement end there.

"But Sheriff Harper, I don't live nowhar…" Mav started to explain again that he was with a trail drive when the sheriff interrupted.

"Mr. Oates, don't waste my time. You won't go anywhere until you tell me where you live." With that pronouncement, the sheriff led Mav Caid, the denier of being Mr. Oates, back to jail.

Mav sat on the bunk in the cell, wondering if the sheriff would ever ride out to the herd to check out his story. If he did not, and if the herd passed on by, he could be in for an extended stay as the guest of the small town of Coddlesville.

Eugene Stonefield

✳✳✳

Preparations for moving out are underway as Alliance and Tucum discuss the missing Mav Caid.

"Mav has not returned from scouting the route, and I'm not willing to wait any longer. If he doesn't intersect our path, he will just have to follow our trail." Alliance tossed the rest of his coffee into the dirt and signaled that he was ready to proceed. "If you want to look for Mav, fine. You can follow our trail just as well." With that, Tucum mounted up to find the missing Mav Caid. On a hunch that Mav may have gone into town to buy something he needed, Tucum decides to begin his search in the nearby Coddlesville.

The herd was now up and waiting for the signal to head 'em up; move 'em out, while Hondo was talking to Jose Borrego.

"I don't want to do it. Will you do it?" Hondo holds out the rifle to Jose.

"I can't do it. Let Manuel or Rogelio do it." Jose turns away as both Manuel and Rogelio shake their heads that they would not do it either.

The issue is Dodge. Dodge has decided that her nine-hundred-pound self would stay exactly where she put it the evening before. After Hondo had queried all hands on their willingness to execute the recalcitrant heifer and gaining no takers, he informed Alliance about the impasse.

"Why not?" asked Alliance.

"We all kinda feel that Dodge is Mav's heifer, and no one wants to kill her," Hondo said to an incredulous Alliance Nelson. "Besides that, no one would eat the 'son-of-a-bitch' stew Cookie would make from her anyhow. They just wouldn't feel right about it."

"Maybe 'Boss' doesn't mean what it used to mean," said Alliance to himself. "Ok, leave the critter for the next herd to pick up. Let's get this herd moving!"

As the herd moved forward on a trail that would circle Coddlesville, Tucum was riding into the town to look for Mav. The smallness of the town limited the places to search, and upon seeing a familiar horse tied to the hitching post in front of the sheriff's office, Tucum knew his search was over. Tucum rode to the office and tied up next to Biscuit, who was waiting for a return to the livery stable.

Entering the sheriff's office, Tucum asked the deputy if the owner of the horse outside was somewhere around. The deputy looked suspiciously at Tucum then called out to the sheriff, who was at that moment, returning from a visit to the outhouse. "Make yourself at home," he told Tucum, "Sheriff Harper will be in soon."

"Sheriff," stated the deputy as the sheriff came in, "This man, Tucum, is looking for the owner of that troublesome horse out front." He motioned toward Tucum as an introduction.

"You want to see Mr. Oates?" began the sheriff.

"No, I'm asking for the owner of Biscuit, the horse tied out front," returned Tucum.

"Humm. You know that horse?" said Sheriff Harper. "And you know its owner?"

"Yessir. The horse is Biscuit, and the owner is Mav Caid." Tucum waited for the next statement from the sheriff.

"That's curious, Mr. Tucum. Mr. Oates, who claims to be this Maverick Caiden says the horse belongs to a Mr. Lytle. Lytle is not someone who is known around here. So, are you saying the horse doesn't belong to Mr. Lytle?"

"Well, the horse, —he's called Biscuit, —is from the remuda that is owned by Mr. Lytle, but no one other than Mav can ride him. Biscuit won't tolerate other riders. All of us drovers of Lytle's herd consider Mav is the rightful owner."

Sheriff Harper looked over Tucum for some time, then spoke to his deputy: "Let him loose. He's not Oates." With that, he turned and went back out the back door, the stress of the situation clearly wreaking havoc with his digestion.

Once outside, Mav spoke to Tucum: "Tucum, I think we are 'bout even on favors, —yor leg an' my neck." His verbal equation brought a questioning look from Tucum, who shrugged and remounted his horse.

Tucum told Mav that the herd had left to go on up the trail, and they would have to catch up. As they left Coddlesville, the sun was high in the sky.

Following the herd was easy; just follow the chewed ground, and the 'meadow muffins' dropped by the beeves. As Mav and Tucum rode toward the herd, they experienced a rare occurrence of a strange Deja-vu. Coming down the trail to meet them rode Mav Caid on Biscuit.

The approaching rider stopped before Mav and Tucum, the rider staring at Mav and Biscuit; Mav and Tucum equally fixated on the other horse and rider. For a moment, there was silence.

"I 'spect yor name is Oates," said Mav to the stranger who registered an odd questioning look on his face. Neither Tucum nor Iver Oates said anything, they just pulled aside and rode on their separate directions. After a few seconds, Oates turned his horse around where he stopped and continued to stare at the receding doppelganger, the strangely met 'oracle' who knows all.

For a quarter-hour, Mav and Tucum rode in silence, then Tucum asked: "Did you know that fella?"

"Ne'er met him," replied Mav. "He was the spitting image of you. And his horse looked almost like Biscuit." Tucum looked intently at Mav.

"Yep," replied Mav.

Chapter 62

Rescue by Friend

Cade looks at his mother with concern and speaks. "He'll be ok, Ma. I've been up to see him. I know what you are thinking. But I just know he will be all right. He just needs more time. Pa is tough. He'll wake up soon, you'll see." Case makes his best attempt to lift the spirits of his ma, Macy. He knows that she is scared. He, too, knows that this uncertainty must come to a conclusion, and he is fearful that the outcome will deprive him of a pa. The accident happened two weeks ago, and the anxiety grows daily.

When Mav and Tucum finally caught up to the herd, Hondo met them at the chuckwagon, where they all poured themselves some coffee. Hondo spoke first: "We had to leave Dodge back down the trail, Mav. She just wouldn't get up. Alliance said the next trail boss could deal with her, however manner he chose."

Mav became thoughtful, then said: "I reckon I'll jes' head back down th' trail an' look fo' her a spell. Ifn I ain't back by sunrise, I'll catch up later. Tell Alliance." With that, Mav mounted Biscuit and turned back down the trail they had just traveled.

Trying to find a single heifer in the middle of the night is generally a losing cause. Still, Mav was hopeful that he would be successful. The moon that had shown good light for most of the ride was now behind a cloud, and ignoring his diminished visibility, he continues his search. Off to his left, he hears a loud bovine bawl that could be Dodge, but had as much chance of being one lost from another herd or belonging to someone in the area. Biscuit, upon hearing the insistent bellow, veered toward its source. Mav gave Biscuit his rein and the two rode toward the bawling animal. The sound got louder as they approached, and ceased as they stopped before a standing Dodge, the problematic heifer that immediately knelt then fell on her side.

"Thar you are, Dodge, you cuss. Don't do thet." Mav dismounted and walked around the heifer's bulk to face her. "You git yorsel' up, right now!" He could have saved his breath. Dodge began to calmly chew her cud. After a period of staring at each other, Mav went back to Biscuit and retrieved his Henry. Walking back to face Dodge, Mav said: "This is it, Dodge. You git yorsel' on yor feet, or yor trail ends right here!" Levering a round into the firing chamber made the signature click that had been the motivation for Dodge since their first introduction back down the trail. Dodge looked at Mav as Mav lifted the rifle to his shoulder and uttered a snort, then began the laborious rise to get up on four legs. A rising bovine rises to a standing position from a reclining one in a four-step process: the animal first folds its front legs back and pushes up onto its knees. Next, the animal gets up onto its back legs in a half-stand. Then, shifting slightly and straightening one bent front leg after another, pushes up into a full stance from a kneel. Mav showed patience as the complaining Dodge brought herself to a stand.

"Good decision!" said Mav to Dodge. Soon, all were heading up the trail to rejoin the herd. Previously occurring but unknown to Mav, as Mav and Biscuit searched for Dodge, a desperado at camp nearby awakened and, fearing the sheriff was searching for him, had mounted his horse in preparation for leaving.

As sunup came and Mav with Dodge neared the camp, an unexpected event unfolded. The 'Mav Caid' doppelganger came upon them, pistol drawn. "Get off your nag," said Iver Oates. Mav saw the serious end of a forty-four pointed at him and decided a discussion on the propriety of his demand would be useless, so he began to dismount. Without warning, Iver Oates was suddenly propelled sideways as nine-hundred pounds of longhorn barreled into the side of his horse, sending both horse and rider sprawling onto the ground. Oates' revolver jarred from his hand as he fell, leaving him with no ready weapon to pursue his intended crime and leaving his fate to the goodwill of a heifer with a horn spread of five feet. Mav, still in a mid-dismount, through his leg back across Biscuit to regain his seat in the saddle, and looked down at the struggling horse, that was seeking to get back on its feet. Iver Oates, with one leg beneath his horse, was pounding the ground in anger while Dodge looked on with ultimate unconcern.

"I don't know whut got inta you Dodge, but whate'er it wuz, it got into you at th' right time." Finally, turning his attention back to Iver Oates, Mav said: "Mr. Oates, thars some folks whut wants to talk to you back in Coddlesville, an' ifn thet leg o' yorn thet got itsel' between yor horse an' Dodge is broke, I'll ride in an' send somebody out to hep you with it. Ifn it ain't broke, well, I suppose you ken take care o' yorsel'." Oates declined to have anyone from Coddlesville come to him.

Mav and Dodge rejoined the herd, and a sleepless Mav Caid had a long day and daydreamed of drinking a lot of coffee.

∗∗∗

"What will you do with Dodge when we get to Ogallala?" asked Tucum.

"She ain't my heifer," said Mav, "you might rec'lect she b'longs to Whisper Bales, an' we wuz only trailin' her fo' Whisper."

"But you and Dodge seem to have this understanding. What about that? Besides, if you look behind you, you will see Dodge trailing you." Tucum broke a wry smile as Mav's head whipped about to see the truth of Tucum's claim.

Animal behavior is a strange subject to contemplate. Everyone knows about horse and dog behavior. When similar behavior is found in bovines, it is nothing short of amazement. Cattle are expected to display no characteristics that would likely endear a person to the animal. Yet, here is Dodge, acting more like a somewhat cantankerous horse or a dog than a walking porterhouse.

Looking back again, Mav saw his bulky longhorn friend walking calmly behind. "Good Dodge. Good Dodge," exclaimed Mav, with a laugh.

Chapter 63

The Trail Ends

On a day in September 1886, the herd is approaching Grant, Nebraska, due south of Ogallala. Weather is bringing colder temperatures to the area and at night is nearing forty degrees. There is activity in the area as surveyors crisscross the land, marking the new route for the Chicago-Burlington-Quincy Railroad line. Early comers are beginning to build various structures for businesses that will be needed to support a trunk line to the network of rail lines spiderwebbing the nation. The herd has been pastured three miles distant to rest the cattle before the scheduled delivery in early October in Ogallala to the Armour & Company. The new owners will winter the beeves until next year then transport them by rail to Omaha, where their main meatpacking business operates.

"Alliance, we picked up a couple of stray horses for the remuda when we came through Kansas. They don't carry any brand I recognize. Are they to be taken back with us with the chuck wagon and remuda?" Mav has a clear memory of the horse-stealing accusation by Woodrow Coddles leveled against him earlier and is not anxious to have another.

"We'll keep them with us until we find some authority in Kansas to hand them off to and be done with it," replied Alliance.

The cowhands were beginning to prepare for an end of trail celebration, that they anticipate launching as soon as they deliver the herd in Ogallala. To that end, some have even begun to spruce up. Several months on the trail grows a lot of beards and a lot of hair. Since part of the duties of the cook is to make repairs, care for the ill, treat injuries, pull teeth if needed, shaving and haircutting are expected. At this moment, Mav is sitting on an upturned bucket talking to Cookie as Cookie begins to use the shears to lighten Mav's load of long hair

"Cookie, I ne'er mentioned this b'fore, but I hope you didn't take no offense when Alliance give me yor job with th' remuda." Mav sat still, looking out at the landscape of waving prairie grass.

"Mav, are you suggesting that I miss being tossed around like a rag doll by some devil horse wishing to do me harm? I had my day with the remuda. They were good days, and I enjoyed them as you are enjoying them today. I was second in charge of cooking on earlier drives and substituted for sick cooks and those who left unexpectedly, so I knew the ropes."

Cookie began recalling that he <u>was</u> angery at the time by his being replaced by Mav and that it was only the better salary and heightened prestige that kept him with the company. As he thought about it, as he snipped hair, his anger returned, and he snipped more hair. Cookie had no mirror to show the results of his haircutting expertise, so Mav was unaware of the unique trim Cookie had given to him as he sat on the bucket. In short, the cut given Mav was so unique that it could only have had a French origin, therefore, be described more appropriately as a coiffure. Given his sparse beard, a shave was not needed. As Mav walked through the camp, stares and muffled laughter followed. Once discovered the reason for their mirth, Mav had to accept the assumed prank played on him by Cookie and devise a plan to return the compliment.

A week passed as the animals took advantage of the grass and continued to acclimate to the cooler air. Fortune had been with them, and there were no thunderstorms to frighten the animals into a stampede. Now the day had come to move on to Ogallala. Cookie and a couple of hands were gathering dry chips to load the firewood sling for the fuel needed at future camps. Mav checked the remuda and brought out the two mules that had been kept with the horses and led them to the chuckwagon. Whether inattention on the part of Cookie or the fact that a giant longhorn standing six feet at the shoulder blocked Cookie's view of the mule team, could not be determined. Whatever the reason, Cookie experienced some shock as he rounded the wagon to mount the driver's seat and found himself looking at two harnessed mules standing backward in their traces and staring back at him. There surely were some who knew who did it, but all were somewhere else when it transpired. So, they said.

Mav was becoming the go-to hand when Alliance needed something to be done quickly, or with certainty, it would be done right. Previously, Alliance had tendered ownership of the herd to the Armour & Company agent, and Alliance accepted a company check for the purchase. As Alliance was preparing to visit the bank to receive the payment, he turned to Mav, saying, "Mav, I want you to go with me to the bank. I'll be bringing back money for the boys. I would feel a bit better if I had someone with me to keep an eye on things."

"Are you 'spectin' trouble?" asked Mav.

"No, but being careful is prudent. I'll be carrying most of a year's salary for each hand, and a lot of people, some not so high on honesty, know it," returned Alliance. An hour later, both men ride to the Cattlemen's Bank of Ogallala.

Alliance presented the contract for the sale of the herd of some three-thousand-forty head to Armour & Company of Omaha. He asked that he be given thirty-seven hundred dollars in gold for return expenses and drover pay, plus a banker's check for the remainder. Ten minutes later, Alliance and Mav are riding back to the camp.

All cowhands lined up to receive their pay for the several months on the trail. Each dealt with the thought of what they intended to do with the money, plans developed over the months, now subject to immediate revision. All hands prepared to go to town to celebrate before boarding a train to return to Texas, or before riding back to camp for the long ride back with the remuda and chuckwagon. Since several horses were lost to drowning or injury during the trip up the trail, the remuda is smaller. Mav, being in charge of the remuda, will return with Alliance, Cookie, Hondo, and Tucum. All the others will experience their first ride on the 'iron horse,' an experience of breathless expectation.

"Well boys," said Alliance, "the trail ends. It has been long. Someday, not long from now, there will be no trail to follow. We all saw it on the way up. The range is becoming smaller, portioned up by farmers plowing furrow-fences around hundreds of acres of grazing land, putting it off-limits to us cattle drivers. Some even had the wherewithal to erect metal fences with barbed wire. Laws are being enacted that favor the local citizens and impede the movement of cattle through a free range that is no longer free. Railroads are being pushed into places a few years back would be considered unimaginable. Someday soon, cattle will be driven to local rail stops, and their cattle transported a thousand miles away by rail. Times are changing. A new day is being born before our eyes. The boys coming up before us had Indians to contend with, but the ranges were open to all. These were different issues for certain, but our issues aren't curable." Men of the small party listened to Alliance. Yet, none saw a different horizon from that which branded them the last of the breed of tough, ambitious men following a way of life that will soon be a subject of history. Three days later, the small group of seasoned trail drivers began their ride back to Brownsville in south Texas over twelve-hundred miles away.

"What are you plannin' to do when you get back?" Mav was asking Tucum and Hondo.

"Me? I have this girl over in San Antonio," replied Hondo. "We talked about getting married when I got back. Her papa has a hardware store, and he said he would take me into the business. I guess I'll be selling things folks want to buy."

"Oh, I suppose I'll continue to work with cattle in some manner. Some of the old cattlemen I'm told are setting up operations they call 'stock farming,' so, maybe I'll look in that direction. I've saved a bit of money over the years and can buy a little land." Tucum said no more, and the three rode on with silent, private thoughts.

Chapter 64

Prairie Fire

Waking one morning in Kansas brought a realization that the day was not a normal one. Smoke drifted through the air from a fire that was sweeping across the plains somewhere nearby. The small group broke camp quickly and started out in a southward direction. The smoke got heavier as they moved.

"Can anyone see the fire?" asked Alliance. No one spoke up.

"Thar's a tall tree on thet little hill. I'll climb it an' take a gander." Mav rode toward the tree and dismounted Biscuit as he arrived. Climbing about half-way, he could see the flames about a quarter-mile away, moving in their direction. Returning to the others, he reported: "Looks like it's comin' to us. Ifn we veer east some we ken git around it."

The party turned east and picked up the pace as a precaution. Within the hour, the smoke had lightened enough to check again where the flames were, and Mav climbed another tree to look. The flames were definitely behind them so they could return to the more familiar path. The party turned due south from their easterly direction.

Their two-mile ride brought them to another patch of smoke drifting across their path. As Mav climbed to a higher elevation to gain another view, he could hear shouting from a man and the panicked screams of a woman from somewhere hidden by the smoke. He waited to see if a clearing wind would reveal the location of the people so obviously distressed. A splash of color through the grayness of smoke told him that a few hundred yards to the west, someone was going to die. Mav dropped to the ground and jumped aback Biscuit, bringing him to a gallop toward the flames that he could perceive easily as they came closer. Biscuit continued his run, the fire getting closer, their heat beginning to be felt. Thicker smoke blowing in the wind made breathing difficult, and Mav lifted his kerchief to cover nose and mouth. Biscuit suffered but continued his run. In minutes the fire had moved to close the path from which Mav and Biscuit had come. Mav and Biscuit were within a crescent of flames rapidly moving northward. Glimpses of color was Mav's only compass to whatever destiny awaited the endangered people. Screams became louder, smoke thicker, shouts weaker. Mav turned toward the screams. Suddenly, a woman with a crying child in her arms, standing barefoot upon the bed of a farm wagon about thirty yards from a burning farmhouse, came into view. She was looking back toward the approaching flames and crying, her anxiety, fearfully displayed.

"Lady. Lady. Get down. Come with me." Mav shouted above her screams.

"My husband! He's back there! He went to bring the mules. I don't hear him anymore! Help him! Please!" Her pleas, the agony of hope against all odds. Her husband was gone, a victim of the flames.

"Lady, it's too late. You and yor child gotta come with me. Now!" Mav shouted to her. The terrified woman turned, tears welling in her eyes. Clutching her child, she started to climb down from the wagon that was beginning to burn. Mav urged Biscuit closer to the wagon as flames threaten to encircle, to close the diminishing crescent, the only ground not burning. She leaned outward and handed her blanket wrapped child to Mav, who had removed his foot from a stirrup for the woman to use. As Mav looked down, he saw flames beginning creep up the calico dress she wore. "Git outten thet dress, it's on fire!" shouted Mav. The terrified woman looked back at the hem to see the flames spreading, its hungry tongues lapping up the dress. She began to feel the scorching heat on the backs of her legs and knew she had no option but to comply. Grasping the cloth encircling her throat, she began to pull against the buttons securing the dress together. Tearing at her clothes, the woman had but one thought: live for her baby! As the dress fell into the wagon bed and exploded into flames, the almost naked woman reached to take Mav's hand and set foot in the freed stirrup to mount Biscuit behind Mav.

Mav turned Biscuit toward the opening in the wall of fire, now closing in, engulfing the wagon. The race from the flames was desperate. Thick smoke filled the air, impeding their vision and making their pathway to safety uncertain, their direction mandated by fires threatening from three directions. "Run, Biscuit. Run like you've ne'er run b'fore." Mav urged Biscuit. One mile. Running, running. Pain growing from the inhaled smoke affected all. Biscuit slowed his pace but resumed as Mav again urged him onward. Flames licked at Biscuit's flashing hooves, singing the hair on his ankles. Run, Biscuit. Run. Two miles. The greatest of horses, wherever they may be, whenever they may have lived could not have run with more heart, nor with more determination, than this horse, on this day, with this load upon his back. The woman's tears had stopped, and a realization was forming in her mind that today was the last day of her previous life as the proud wife of a Kansas farmer. She had accepted her fate.

Mav, still holding the child, looked ahead, not at flames as he could see on either side and could feel creeping from behind, but at the charred ground, just a hundred yards ahead. Biscuit ran onto the charred field and, from somewhere within his brain, knew that safety had been found. Safety. Life. Biscuit began to slow his pace.

As they reached the blackened ground from the previous fire that had now grown cold, Mav reined in Biscuit and helped the woman down, then handed her the bundled child.

Dismounting Biscuit, Mav said: "I'm sorry fo' y'alls loss, ma'am. I'm truly sorry." The woman opened the covering blanket to reveal the face of a child with dark hair.

"It's a boy," is all she said. After a moment, she began to cry softly, knowing her husband would not be coming to her again.

The soot-covered trio and the exhausted Biscuit remained in the charred sanctuary watching the advancing flames die out as the last grass between the previous fire and the new was consumed. Biscuit's heaving sides returned to normal as he recovered from the hard run, but continuing were the periodic snorts issued to clear the smoke from his nostrils.

"Ma'am. I reckon we orta be goin' o'er yonder. Th' fire ain't likely to start up now thet its fuel is all burned up." Mav said as he stood up from the blackened ground and held a hand out to the lady, whose name he did not know.

"Mister, I don't know how to thank you for saving us. We would have died. Please accept my thanks and that of my baby, John. That's his name. He is named after his papa. My name is Felicity. Felicity Olsen." Mav followed suit and introduced himself to the family of two. As they waited for Biscuit to recover, a young mother unashamedly offered a breast to her hungry child as Mav watched and remembered similar scenes of his ma nursing his brother Travis and sister Sara. In the strangeness of the moment, Mav Caid, imagined a Madonna before him.

The trio remounted Biscuit and began to walk back to the east toward the place Mav expected to find the others.

Mav Caid — The Complete Story

Alliance, Tucum, Cookie, and Hondo stood, mouths agape, watching a ghost ride toward them with an unknown passenger, who they soon were to find is two passengers. A few hours later, seven people surrounded a new grave on the prairie for a farmer with unfulfilled dreams. The ground from which the grave was dug, radiated warmth from the fire; the air, still acrid from the smoke.

Returning to the campsite following the burial of John Olsen, everyone welcomed the supper prepared by Cookie and settled in for a night of needed rest. The men, as usual, slept on the ground; Felicity and little John slept in the chuckwagon where room was made by unloading some of the articles and personal items carried in the wagon. Everyone, being extremely tired from the day, slept deeply, un-wakened by sounds of nature. Eventually, sunrise changed all that.

"Huh! Wha…" the first sounds uttered by Mav Caid as he opened his eyes to see a mound of longhorn lying beside him and staring at him as her jaw worked back and forth while she chewed her cud. Mav immediately jumped to his feet. At some point during the early hours, Mav's cantankerous friend, Dodge, had arrived and bedded down next to Mav.

"You wuz left in Ogallala," said Mav. "How in tarnation did you git here?" Mav's exclamations awakened the others, each of whom registered wry smiles.

"Boys, is there anything you want to tell me?" asked Alliance of the small group of guilty-looking cowboys.

"Well, you see Boss, it was like this: We saw how much Mav loved this heifer and figured he would be just too lonesome without Dodge. So, when you and Mav went to the bank, we pooled a few dollars and bought her from the buyer of the herd. She's been trailing us ever since. She just finally caught up. I reckon Dodge will have a tale to tell about how she trailed us all the way from Ogallala to Bandera." Tucum looked at Mav, whose face was showing one of surrender to unchangeable fate. 'Some folks, just have dogs,' thought Mav with a sheepish grin.

"In a way, Felicity was fortunate that her folks lived close to where Mav found her. Their home was in Garden City, a town that is growing rapidly since the Atchison, Topeka, and Santa Fe Railroad selected it for a railway switch station. But after losing everything, she couldn't have stayed on their place any longer." Hondo was expressing his analysis of Felicity's plight. "Mav shared his clothes with her until we took her home. She looked just like any one of us, in those trousers and shirt, although she had no boots, and the bonnet made a strange sight. The moccasins Tucum made for her worked just as well. Tucum said he might like to go back to see her if he happens up this way on another drive."

The drive of 1886 was one for the memories of all the participants, and the road back to Bandera was uneventful, a characteristic that all the returning men welcomed. Riding, making camp, sharing stories, building upon friendships developed over the previous half-year, are events and pleasures to last a lifetime. Each will go his own way over the next few months, and someday in the future, he may join again in another drive if there are to be any. But most likely, they will continue following separate paths into old age, where they will tell their stories to sons and daughters.

Chapter 65

Back in Bandera

Alliance retrieved mail that had been received for the hands since they left on the drive and began to distribute letters to those who had returned with him. One was for Mav.

Dear Son,

Your pa and I have leased the farm out for the year and are going to Louisiana. My mama is very ill and needs someone to care for her. We are taking your brother and sister with us. If you get back before we do, please check on things at the farm. Mr. Thomas is our tenant. He is a good man and will tell you anything you want to know. Our address in Thibodaux will be the Acadia Plantation, Route 3, Thibodaux, Louisiana.

Your pa said to tell you hello. So do Travis and Sara. Well, that's all I can tell you right now.

Ma.

Mav folded the letter and put it in his warbag with his other letters and personal items, his disappointment not revealed to the others around him.

Two months later, Alliance received a second letter which he gave to Mav. For a moment Mav shows puzzlement, then he reads:

"Dear Mr. Caid,

When we met back in Kansas, I was in such a state of shock by the tragic events that, looking back, I am not sure that I even thanked you for your kindness. If I did, it could not have been enough, given the circumstances. I was hungry, and you gave me something to eat; I was thirsty, and you gave me something to drink; I was a stranger, and you took me in; I was naked, and you clothed me. You did the work the Lord asks, Mav Caid, you are an angel. I pray that someday we will meet again. Until that time, should it ever be, I thank you from the bottom of my heart.

I love you if I may say that without embarrassing you. I know you know what I mean.

Felicity

Mav folded the letter as he had the letter from his ma and put it in his warbag for keeping. For the months November through February, Mav worked with the horses. He was expert at breaking new horses and in training the broken ones in what is expected of a cutting horse.

✳✳✳

"Mav," began Alliance, "I want you to meet this fella from over in Williamson County. His name is Bill Pickett, and he's been showing

520

the hands how he bulldogs a critter for branding. His method is quick and effective. Let him tell you about it."

"Howdy, Mr. Pickett. I reckon showin' orta be better than tellin' so why don't you an' me jes' head on o're to th' corral. Thar's several two-year steers in thar now." Both men left the ranch house and walked to the corral.

Pickett threw a leg across the corral fence and dropped to the ground inside the corral. Pickett mounted a saddled horse while another rider waited for him to give a signal to start chasing one of the steers from the left side while Pickett raced alongside the steer from the right. As Pickett closed the gap, he removed his outer foot from the stirrup and leaned across his horse to reach the steer running just a yard away. Suddenly, Pickett grasped the closest horn with his right hand and leaned across the steer to grip the opposing horn that he intends to cradle in the crook of his left arm for the throw. Pickett slid from the saddle to the ground next to the steer that continued to run, now encumbered by Pickett's heavy body. Working quickly, Pickett slid his left arm beneath the far-side horn and twisted the neck of the steer. The neck twisting and Pickett's encumbering weight, caused the animal to stop. As the steer stopped, Pickett drew himself to a stand and quickly threw his body backward to unbalance the steer causing it to fall upon its side. Pickett demonstrated his technique several times to the observers. If the steer failed to fall, Pickett would lean across the steer and bite the lip of the animal, 'bulldog' style to complete the take-down. Mav was convinced that Bill Pickett knew what he was doing.

After one such demonstration, Mav told him: "Well, I'm a-guessin' them steers cain't be too mad at a-bein' throwed, seein's how they are gittin' kissed at th' same time." Bill Pickett stayed with Lytle's outfit for a while, then rode on off to demonstrate his unique skill to regular folks who are being introduced to a new form of cowboy skills exhibition called <u>rodeo</u>. He and four brothers referring to themselves as the <u>Pickett Brothers Bronco Busters and Rough Riders Association</u>, would be seen in county fairs throughout the southwest for many years. Bill Pickett, a man of African and Cherokee blood, born in Travis County, Texas, will someday be lauded as the 'Father of Rodeo.'

Chapter 66

Generalissimo Obregon

Several days had become several weeks and Macy has prepared herself to be disappointed, "How is Mav today, doctor?" asked Macy of Dr. Furnham. Is there anything I can do to help? The question asked, while knowing the answer to be 'no'. Today she will be surprised.

"There has been some change. The nurse told me that last night he became restless and moved around a lot. She said he began to mumble as if troubling things were occurring in his mind, but unlike before, his voice was stronger and more intelligible. She said that he called out the name, Felicity. Is anyone in the family or friends named Felicity?" asked the doctor.

"No. No, Felicity is not a family name," replied Macy, a thoughtful expression on her face. Presently, a notion sent her home to look through an old saddlebag with a wallet that Mav told her years ago contained nothing but old letters and documents he saved just in case they may be needed.

After a half-hour search for the old saddlebag, Macy found it behind a stack of Beaton Gazettes Mav had saved. For a moment, she hesitated to open the bag, trying to get control of a feeling that she was invading Mav's privacy, perhaps invading a secret that is best left alone. Macy pulls down some of her graying hair and inspects it. Grayer, she decides. After a while, her curiosity wins the argument, and she opened the bag to retrieve the wallet. Near the middle of the stack of letters tied in a bundle, Macy finds the letter from Felicity. For a moment, her heart beat at a faster rate. She wanted to know, and she did not want to know at the same time what the letter contained.

Macy retied the letters and replaced them in the wallet. When she left the barn, nothing was any different to the eye.

"Mav, Tucum," said Alliance, "the remuda is in perfect shape for the next drive. I want both of you to go down south to help assemble the herd for the next drive in May. We will be taking a mix of two and three-year-old cattle to Utah." Mav and Tucum left the next day for Brownsville in deep south Texas. Ten days later, they approach the Rio Grande a few miles from Brownsville.

"Hav' you e'er been to th' Rio Grande?" asked Mav.

"Naw, I spent most of my younger years around Tucumcari Mountain, though once I went due west to Albuquerque, and another time I went east to Amarillo. There was mostly desert to the south." The Rio Grande flows through Albuquerque, so I saw it there, but never down in Texas, where it flows between Texas and Mexico. Tucum urged his mount to a faster pace.

"Well, thar it is!" said Mav as he pulled back on the rein. "We jes' hav' to follow th' river a bit till we come to Lytle's spread."

It was early afternoon when they came upon the river across from several vaqueros on the far side riding in the same direction they were heading.

"See those boys yonder?" Mav pointed to the group.

"I see them," replied Tucum. "What about them?"

"They are a-lookin' like they're in some hurry to git somewhar, that's all." Mav continued to watch the vaqueros as they rode fast toward some unknown destination. Neither Mav nor Tucum is aware that a low-water crossing is just ahead.

A half-hour later, as the two riders topped a hill leading down into a shallow valley, they also rode into trouble. Fourteen vaqueros closed around Mav and Tucum with guns drawn.

"*Señores*," said the apparent leader of the group, "you must come with me." He pointed his *pistola* toward the low-water crossing they had used earlier to cross into Texas from Mexico.

"Why orta we do thet?" asked Mav.

"Because, *Señor*, we are the revolutionary forces under the command of Generalissimo Juan Arabula Obregon, and he wants you." Immediately, the leader signals that they are to re-cross the river, and the small band of captors and captives rode across the shallow water into Mexico. Presently, their captors blindfolded Mav and Tucum and tied their hands before they plunged into the Mesquite and rode toward the generalissimo's secret encampment.

After a half-hour ride, the group came into the camp of Generalissimo Juan Arabula Obregon and his revolutionaries. At the time, Obregon was trimming his moustache and closely examining his appearance in a small mirror. For several minutes, the captors and captives, who were no longer blindfolded, waited for the generalissimo to acknowledge their arrival. The generalissimo adjusted his mirror and began to check his teeth. Finally satisfied that his appearance could not be improved, turned to face his visitors.

"*¡Bienvenidos señores!* Welcome, sirs!" were the first words of the fastidious general of the revolution. "I am Generalissimo Juan Arabula Obregon, leader of the Texico revolution." As Mav and Tucum awaited further explanation, the generalissimo returned to his personal inspection. He re-inspected his even white teeth closely in the mirror. After combing through his ample black hair, he turned to face Mav and Tucum a second time. "You have questions…yes?"

"Why are we here?" asked Mav as Tucum looked around the camp at the forty or so men sprawled upon the ground smoking, chatting, and taking liberal swigs from a jug of tequila.

"*¡Silencio!* Silence! *¡Haré las preguntas!* I will ask the questions! What were you doing in Texico?" returned the general.

"We wuz in Texas, on th' other side o' th' river. We wuzn't in Mexico," Mav replied.

"*Señores*, my revolution does not recognize Texas or Mexico. This is Texico. You are spies, no?" replied the general.

"We are wranglers fo' Captain Lytle. We ain't no spies," Mav said as he looked at Tucum. Tucum nodded his agreement with Mav.

Generalissimo Obregon stared at Mav for a moment then concentrated his stare on Tucum. "Which of you is the leader?"

"Thar ain't no leader. We come fo' some cattle an' thet's all. Now ifn it's ok with you we'll jes' ride back 'cross th' river an' git on with whut we wuz a-comin' to do," stated Mav.

"No, no, no, *Señores*. Not before my interrogation is complete," returned the general, slapping a riding crop against his leg. "*¡Lléveselos!* Take them!" ordered the generalissimo.

Soldiers of the generalissimo took Mav and Tucum further into the camp and pushed them into a make-shift prison of ocotillo limbs and lariats. Soldiers of the revolution tied Mav and Tucum to mesquite trees and removed their boots to make escape difficult. Scattered around the makeshift prison were limbs of the ocotillo and their spiny deterrent to bare feet.

"He speaks English, this Generalissimo Obregon," Tucum said to Mav while inspecting the ropes binding his hands.

"Yep," replied Mav, "I jes' cain't reckon why they went to all th' trouble to bring us here."

Two days pass, and hunger, thirst, and heat are wearing on the captives. Both men are sitting, backs against mesquite trees. These reluctant guests of the generalissimo were given little food and just enough water to keep away the more severe effects of thirst. It seems the generalissimo is aware that a man with a swollen tongue cannot talk well, but a hungry man may be persuaded. Mid-morning was approaching when two revolutionaries came to take Mav to the generalissimo for interrogation. Tucum remained tied to his tree.

"*¿Cuál es su nombre?* What is your name?" The generalissimo shouted at Mav as he walked back and forth before him.

"Maverick Caiden," answered Mav.

"Where were you born?" asked the generalissimo.

"Bandera."

"Bandera?" The generalissimo stopped walking and peered at Mav more closely. He seemed lost in thought for a moment, then vigorously slapped the makeshift table with his riding crop. The table, built from dried ocotillo limbs tied together with rawhide strips shook under the impact, its hollowness reverberating the sound.

"*¡Espía!* Spy! You are familiar with the name Lamelas?" demanded Generalissimo Obregon. "Everyone knows that name."

"Wall, I reckon I'm th' exception, 'cause I don't know no Lamelas," replied Mav, wondering what the name has to do with their being held captive.

"How about Rosalez? Eh? Eh? Ro-<u>sa</u>-lez?" Generalissimo peered closely at Mav.

"I reckon I don't know thet one neither."

"Think carefully, spy. Refugia Alfrido Lamelas Rosalez …does that name ring any bells?" the generalissimo looked intently into the eyes of a perplexed Mav Caid.

"I cain't rec'lect a-knowin' any Lamelas or Rosalez fam'ly a'tall."

"You're lying!" shouted the generalissimo.

"No, sir! I don't lie. Who is she?" asked Mav of his captor.

"Refugia Alfrido Lamelas de Obregon! She is my *senora*," returned the generalissimo.

"Is she a revolutionary like yorsel'?" Mav asked

"Only against me," replied the generalissimo. "You have come from her, yes? You have come to find me for her. I *sabe* her tricks." The generalissimo began to walk quickly back and forth behind the table, separating himself and Mav, showing intense agitation and slapping his tall boot with his quirt.

"Maybe, spy, I should send you to her with a message of my own. What do you think of that?" Generalissimo Obregon pointed at Mav with his quirt and looked at Mav with a grim expression, one that suggested a devious plan is developing in the curious mind of the self-proclaimed revolutionary.

"I reckon Tucum an' me might could take a message to yor *señora*," returned Mav, thinking a messenger sounds better than spy.

"Now, tell me what she told you to tell me." The generalissimo demanded in a voice more measured to entice an answer.

"She didn't give me no message, 'cause …" The generalissimo interrupted Mav.

"*¡Caramba!* Ha! Of course! That's what she would do, —send a messenger with no message." The generalissimo showed a grim smile as if he knew that an adversary had a momentary advantage. "Ah, that *señora* is a sly one! I should answer! Maybe for emphasis, I should send her an ear along with the message. That would tell her she can speak to the ear, but there is no one to listen. Ha! I like that!"

Mav Caid — The Complete Story

"Ifn you mayhap will pardon me fo' sayin' so, thet seems extreme. Cuttin' yor ear off to make a point jes' seems…" once again, Generalissimo Obregon interrupts Mav.

"Not my ear, Spy. I'm thinking about that other spy. Tucum, is his name?" asked Generalissimo Obregon, who then shouted for a guard to take Mav back to his prison.

Tucum looked up at Mav as a revolutionary pushed Mav back into the enclosure. As the guard moved away, Tucum asked: "Well, what did the generalissimo say?"

"He is a-thinkin' 'bout takin' one o' yor ears to send to thet wife o' hisn," returned Mav.

"What? Take my ear?" A jolted Tucum asked.

"Well, either thet or hang you fo' bein' a spy," returned Mav. "I'm a-thinkin thet hit don't matter much to th' generalissimo ifn he takes yor ear b'fore th' hangin' or aftern." Tucum unconsciously touched his throat, then his ear.

The day ended, and darkness enclosed the countryside, interrupted only by the crackling of a small campfire that was burning down to embers and the creaking of crickets.

***

The morning after, Generalissimo Obregon released Mav, who is now on his way to Bandera carrying a donkey's ear wrapped in a kerchief. Mav considers his taking a donkey's ear to the *señora* rather than one of Tucum's was a stroke of good fortune.

His morning started when a revolutionary soldier woke him before dawn and took him back to the generalissimo for instructions on where to find the generalissimo's *señora*. In his conversation with the generalissimo, Mav suggested to him that a donkey's ear was a stronger message since it would convey a donkey's characteristic stubbornness with the message of one who will not listen. The generalissimo finally agreed that it was stronger, and Tucum's ear was spared from the knife, all to Tucum's great relief. Tucum, however, would be a guest of the, now benevolent revolutionary for the duration. Mav was to deliver the message and return with whatever message from Refugia Alfrido Lamelas de Obregon wished to convey.

The generalissimo's parting words to Mav were: *"Señor* Caid if you have a notion to not deliver my message, I want you to remember that your *amigo* is my guest, who is still considered a spy. The revolution cannot tolerate spies, so if you fail me, it will tell me that both of you are spies, and your *amigo,* Tucum, will have a painful death. First, I will take his ears. Then his nose. Then I will…." At this point, Generalissimo Obregon broke off his threat and gave Mav a smile.

"I savvy. I will get yor message to yor *señora,* then I will come back for Tucum. It would not be good for you, ifn he cain't return with me to Texas." Mav refrained from saying more. It was the first time he could recall making a threat of any kind.

Mav addressed his horse as they forded the river: "Biscuit, I reckon we orta hurry a bit, 'cause thet generalissimo o' th' revolution is not a-playin' with a full deck. I'm a-keepin' my eye out fo' a ranger."

Five days into a ten-day ride, Mav discovers a man coming in his direction with a load of merchandise destined for merchants in Brownsville. The waggoneer told Mav that he regularly traveled between San Antonio and Brownsville and was familiar with the Lamelas family living between San Antonio and George West. He told Mav that the family is well respected and has lived in Texas since long before the revolution that severed Texas from Mexico. He gave directions to the Lamelas *hacienda* on their *Rancho del Sol.*

On the morning of the seventh day, Mav and Biscuit are approaching the Lamelas' *hacienda,* the ancestral home of the *Senora*

Obregon's grandfather. Several children spot them approaching and begin to run alongside Biscuit from the gate to the ranch house. As Mav dismounts, a Mexican servant comes to the top of the stairs of the veranda five feet above the ground level and waits for Mav to mount the stairs.

Addressing the servant, Mav said: "*Buenos, dias.* My name is Mav Caid, and I'm a-needin' to speak with *Señora* Obregon, *por favor.*" The servant appraised the visitor, trying to recall if he had seen him before. Deciding that he had not, he questioned why Mav wanted to see the *señora*, and Mav told him that he carried a message from her husband, Generalissimo Obregon.

"*Si,*" he said, rolling his eyes, then motioned for Mav to follow him into a room near the entry door and left to find the s*eñora.*

Mav was ushered into a large room to wait for the *señora.* As he waited, he inspected his surroundings. The room's furnishings are of the last century; the walls hosting large paintings of ancestors of the Lamelas family. One large painting was of the family's founder Eduardo Villarreal Lamelas on horseback, dressed as a conquistador. Rich carpet covered the floor. Mav had never seen such opulence.

Mav would like to have studied more of his surroundings, but *Señora* Refugia Alfrido Lamelas de Obregon's entering the room captured his attention. The *señora* was striking, a tall woman who commanded attention as she swept into the parlor dressed in a vibrant silk dress died royal purple and overlaid by a crocheted shawl wrapped around her shoulders. Her eyes were dark, almost black below arched eyebrows on smooth caramel-colored skin without a hint of blemish. Her hair was long and black, worn in a thick rope, twisted into a bun that rested on her neck just above her shoulders. The senora's lips were well-shaped and colored like strawberry, that, when she spoke, revealed small, white teeth.

"I don't often get such distinguished-looking visitors, Mr. Caid. Could you tell me the reason for your visit?" *Señora* looked intently into the eyes of her visitor.

"Yes, ma'am…uh, *Señora.* I'm a-bringin' a message frum yor husband, Generalissimo Obregon, who camps in Mexico on th' other side o' th' Rio Grande." Mav held out the severed ear of the donkey that he had wrapped in his kerchief. "Yor husband sent this to you."

The *senora* did not reach for the wrapped object, but stared intently at Mav before asking: "What are you giving me?"

"Well, *Señora,* it's a message frum a donkey, thet yor husband said you would savvy." Mav continued to hold the wrapped ear toward the *señora.*

"You speak the truth, Mr. Caid, that husband of mine <u>is</u> a donkey!" The *senora* smiled at Mav, considering that they both had the same opinion of the generalissimo.

"No, *Señora.* I didn't mean thet. Yor husband is more than a donkey. He is a revolutionary. Th' best I ken reckon is thet he reckons to capture Texas an' Mexico to form a new state of Texico thet he will lead." Mav dropped his hand with the ear to his side.

"Revolutionary! He's no revolutionary, he's a madman who is angry with his *señora.*" *Señora* Obregon motioned for Mav to take a seat. When he took his place, she sat in a chair across from him. "My husband, the…ah, generalissimo, stormed from the house several months ago and took several *vaqueros* with him. He was angry about his pet. I will not tolerate that animal in my *hacienda. ¡Nunca!* Never!"

"No, *Señora.* A troublesome pet ken be a problem. I had a worrisome pet heifer thet foller'd me frum Ogalalla to Texas. The main thing is, yor husband is a-holdin' my friend, Tucum, hostage until I return with a message frum his *señora.* He said we, —thet's Tucum an' me, —are spies! Then he said thet we are messengers from you, an' when I tol' him we wuz not, he said thet it wuz jes' like you to send a messenger with no message jes' to cause him to worry about whut you wuz a-thinkin' when you didn't send no message. Now, on thet, I hav' my doubts. But since he is a-holdin' Tucum, I had to come with his answer to yor message thet you didn't send. So, Ma'am…I mean, *Señora*, would you take this here message an' giv' me one to carry back to him sos I ken git my friend Tucum back?" Mav leaned forward and reached out again to the *señora*, his hand holding the wrapped message.

"A message is spoken, Mr. Caid, or written. What you are trying to hand to me is neither. Can you tell me what it is?" The *señora* looked intently at Mav, awaiting his explanation.

"Well, *Señora*, the generalissimo said thet 'a messenger with no message must return to its sender a message thet says thet the generalissimo is a man who is stubborn as a donkey when it comes to listenin' to a messenger with no message.'" Mav paused before continuing: "So, he sent you this here ear sos you would know."

"Ha! So, he sent me one of his ears!" The *señora* laughed loudly.

"Well, no, *Señora*. He sent you a <u>donkey's</u> ear," Mav replied, attempting to clear up her misunderstanding.

"Please, Mr. Caid. Don't talk in riddles. Which ear did he send?" asked the *señora*.

"Uh…*Señora*, I cain't rightly say. It coulda been th' right, or it coulda been th' left. I didn't notice." Mav looked perplexed, wondering why that matters.

"NO, Mr. Caid. I mean, <u>which</u> donkey lost his ear? The generalissimo, or some poor beast that will never look at himself in a mirror again." *Senora* looked exasperated.

"Well, this'n here is long an' kinda hairy." Mav wonders where this inquiry is to end.

"Ah, bless the beast, the innocent victim of Generalissimo Donkey! *Señora* called for a servant to receive the donkey ear from Mav, telling the servant to dispose of the ear.

"Ma'am…uh, *Señora*… whut kinda pet? Mav's curiosity about the type of pet that could cause such severe discord slipped out.

"Raccoon. His pet is a raccoon. That nosy animal gets into everything. He tore up my *mantilla*. He chewed up my favorite tortoiseshell comb. Before I threw the pottery and broke the mirror, he opened the drawer to my dressing bureau and was sleeping on my…Oh, never mind. The animal had to go. The generalissimo…I, mean, my husband said if Ringo, —that's the raccoon's name, — couldn't stay, he couldn't either. So, that donkey is planning to start another revolution! Mr. Caid, my family was with the Texians in eighteen-thirty-six, and I plan to stay with them. I'll give you a message to take to the 'generalissimo' so you can rescue your friend.

✳✳✳

"Biscuit, I'm a-thinkin' thet this here message frum th' *señora* ain't likely to hav' a positive effect on th' generalissimo. I'm a-thinkin' thet we need another plan. Soon as I gin' this here raccoon tail to the generalissimo, I'm a-thinkin' th' revolution will start right then, an' neither Tucum or me will hav' th' Alamo to hunker down in." Mav ponders the ways that the generalissimo might behave if he thinks the tail belongs to his pet. And even though Mav knows that the tail is from a coonskin cap that one of the *señora's* servants had, Mav feels almost certain the generalissimo would not believe him.

As Mav and Biscuit near the Rio Grande, a thought occurs to Mav that he could get help from the Texas Rangers, and there is a ranger station in Brownsville. Mav rode into Brownsville about ten miles from the location he was to meet the generalissimo upon his return. At the ranger station, Mav asked to speak with the ranger in charge and an orderly introduced him to Captain Lucian Grady, to whom he explained the situation with the generalissimo across the Rio Grande in Mexico. Captain Grady informed him that the rangers could not legally make incursions into Mexico since Mexico would consider their presence an invasion into Mexican territory.

"Well, Captain Grady, I shor reckon thet we wouldn't' want another war with Mexico, but I'm concerned about my friend, Tucum, an' I don't want him hanged fo' bein' a spy which he ain't," said Mav. "Mayhap ifn th' generalissimo comes back inta Texas? Could y'all do anythin' then?"

"If the generalissimo or any of his revolutionaries set foot back in Texas, I will arrest them for threatening violence against Texas citizens," replied Captain Grady.

"I'm a-thinkin thet I might git them to cross over tomorrow," Mav said, "mayhap y'all could be thar when they come?"

"How many revolutionaries are there?" asked the captain.

"I'm reckon 'bout forty," Mav answered.

"I'll send one o' my rangers." Captain Grady stood up and walked Mav outside.

Thinking about the captain's response, Mav ventured the question: "Beggin' yor pardon, Captain Grady…yor' a-plannin' on sendin' jes' one ranger?"

"Well, there's just one revolution, isn't there?" Then the captain smiled.

An hour later, Mav visited the local general store, where he purchased some items that he would need the following day. Next, Mav rented a room for the night at a local Brownsville Arms hotel. After putting the purchased items in his room, Mav went to a *cantina*.

"*Hombres!*" began Mav, "might any o' y'all like to make five dollars tomorrow fo' a few hours work?" Several young men stood up and went over to Mav, who told him what he wanted them to do. Five men agreed to meet him outside the hotel and go with him for the half-day ride. Mav returned to the hotel to work on the plan.

The morning broke as Mav, and five men mounted their horses for the ride. Arriving at the Rio Grande, Mav began pulling items from his saddlebag. Within a few minutes, a makeshift flag was flying from a long pole one of the men had cut and trimmed. Painted on the flag was the word 'Texico' in bright red paint. The men on horseback began to come, one by one, to Mav standing beneath the flag and speaking for a minute, then remounting to ride behind a hill nearby. By mid-afternoon, each rider had rotated between Mav and the hill several times, each man changing shirts to appear to be a different man. Each rider made a lot of noise as each shouted his question: "Is this here the recruitment station for the Texico revolution?"

✳✳✳

"What?" asked the generalissimo when informed about the activity on the Texas side of the river. "Who dares to recruit for my revolution? Who are these *hombres?* They have no right!" The generalissimo, clearly distraught, shouts to his men: *"¡Revolucionarios, cabalguen rápido!* Revolutionaries, mount up, quickly!"

The resulting activity by Generalissimo Obregon became apparent as the first riders charged into the shallow waters of the Rio Grande. Mav signaled for the men, whom he had already paid on their last rotation, to return to Brownsville.

"What do you think you are doing?" shouted the generalissimo to Mav as he and his men surrounded the Texico flag. "This is my revolution!" As the generalissimo recognized Mav, he put his thought aside, dismounted his horse, and asked: "what is the *señora's* message?"

Mav looked around at the men circling the flag and saw Tucum, who the revolutionaries brought with them.

"Generalissimo Obregon, you untie Tucum an' I'll give you yor wife's message."

"Take down that flag!" shouted the generalissimo, at which command Mav immediately pulled the pole from the ground, the signal previously agreed upon by Mav and Captain Grady as the signal for his intervention."

"Boys," shouted Captain Grady, "Y'all's revolution is over. We rangers have you surrounded. Throw down your arms. Put them in a pile and step back."

Whether the fame of the rangers as a tough breed of men that do not back down was an influence, or if the generalissimo's interest had waned is not known. Whatever the cause, all men of the revolution sheepishly placed their rifles and sidearms in a pile near the site where the Texico flagpole once stood.

"Captain, I hope y'all treat these revolutionaries gentle like. An' 'specially thet generalissimo. Thet *señora* o' hisn tol' me he ain't no revolutionary nohow. She tol' me he wuz jes' mad at her 'bout his pet raccoon, an' jes' a might *loco* ta boot. Ifn you jes' show him this raccoon tail he'll run home to see ifn thet raccoon of hisn is all right. She tol' me her husband is jes' *loco* at times, but he gits over it."

"Raccoon?" returned a laughing Captain Grady.

"Yessir, an' I reckon Generalissimo Obregon will tell y'all all 'bout it."

Riding away in the direction of the Lytle spread, Mav turned to his rescued friend. "Tucum, do you reckon we'll be fired fo' bein' a month late to Lytle's spread?"

Chapter 67

The Awakening

On the morning of the seventeenth, Macy arrived in the hallway outside the room in which Mav continued to lie comatose. She entered to find Case sitting at Mav's bedside.

"Ma," asked Case, "have you heard that Pa called out to you last night?" He rose from his chair as Macy entered the room.

"Who told you that?" returned Macy, removing her bonnet.

"The nurse was leaving when I came in. She told me, but she also said that it occurred when he appeared restless. Then he settled down, and nothing else happened. She wouldn't say that it indicated that he was waking up." Case returned to his seat as Macy sat down.

Shortly after, Dr. Furnham came in and gave Mav a cursory glance before addressing Macy and Case.

"The night nurse recorded that Mr. Caid called out to you, Macy, last night. I would like to assure you that he is nearing consciousness, but I know from experience that this kind of event is not a good predictor of what is to happen. His mind is running over various periods of his life, and he is speaking to them on occasion. We still must wait and see. I wish I could be more positive." Dr. Furnham waited for some response from Macy or Case.

"Thank you, Dr. Furnham," replied Macy.

"Yes, thank you," said Case.

"Thanks for what?" enquired Mav.

For a moment, silence ensued. Next was a rush toward the bedside of the wakeful Mav Caid.

"What kind of mule kicked me?" asked Mav. "He must have kicked me six ways from Sunday, considering what my head feels like. I'm hungry. And I feel like I haven't had any coffee for a whole day!"

"Three weeks," replied Macy.

"What?" Mav responded, looking quizzically at Macy.

"Yeah. Three weeks," said Case.

Mav remained in the hospital for another four days upon the recommendation of Dr. Furnham, who wanted to assure himself that Mav was indeed out of danger.

"I feel a bit weak still." Mav's walking was tentative, and he leaned on a crutch Macy and Case had brought to him upon release from the hospital. Mav was slowly recalling the reason for his being in the hospital for the three weeks following the accident. He recalled that he was on the way to get Case at the train station when his brakes failed. Case told him that his Maxwell was a total loss.

Later, Mav and Macy were seated in the reception area of the hospital waiting for Case to bring around transportation, for which he had gone to acquire an hour before.

Unknown to Mav and Macy, Case stopped by the local dealership for Pierce-Arrow automobiles and purchased one for his pa. As they waited, Case returned to the hospital to pick Mav and Macy up for the ride back home.

"This is a fine machine, Case. Are you planning to drive it back to Atlanta?"

"This isn't my car. This is your car, to replace the Maxwell." Case shifted into the next gear, smiling, and looking in the rear-view mirror at his pa, who sat in the back seat to provide more space for his broken leg that remained in a plaster cast.

"I don't know if your pa should have a new car, Case," interjected Macy.

"Now, Ma…Pa knows that when you get thrown, you must get back in the saddle right away. Isn't that right, Pa?" Case glanced again at his pa riding in the back seat.

"That's been my experience," returned Mav, squeezing Macy's hand that she had reached toward him from the front seat.

"Where is *Ja-gé?*" asked Mav.

"She is in Washington. We called her, and she will be coming in on Thursday." Case pulled up in front of the house and shut the engine off.

Entering the house, Mav received the full force of his weeks-delayed homecoming from the staff. These are the dedicated workers that endeavor to keep the Caid household supplied with the wants and needs of a successful entrepreneur. Their return to the home-place brought a crowd of farmhands to welcome Mav back home. Loraine, the cook for the family, brought out a just-baked apple cobbler and a large bowl of home-made ice cream.

"Welcome home, *Señor* Caid," came the voices of Juan and Anita, who quickly followed up with a question: "What else can we get for you?"

"Coffee?" replied Mav.

"Thought so," returned Anita. "Here it is! Enjoy it with your cobbler."

"Apple cobbler?" asked Mav. "Where did you get the apples?"

"From the orchard, you planted on the high ground several years ago," replied Macy. "It's my ma's recipe."

"I didn't plant an orchard," answered a perplexed Mav.

Chapter 68

Toward a Darker Horizon

ooking back ten years, by nineteen-twenty-four, the Caid operation had changed. Mav and Macy, now in their fifties, have secured their needs and have decided to reduce their activities. The cattle raising is a business of the past, one that they sold to Billy Cole two years ago, and the Caid bauxite mine sold the following year to the Perciville Reduction Company. The farm is now the primary interest.

"Seems like a long circular road that we have traveled," began Mav in conversation with Macy. "We started as farmers, and we are still farming. All the other things seem like something I'm reading about someone else."

"Yes, it does. Selling the timberland to the Graves sawmill allowed us to expand the farming operation at an opportune time, and the finding of bauxite had already expanded our wealth considerably. We have been overly fortunate. Our work to build the hospital seems like a gift, considering that the money to put into the hospital came from the diamond sales. We have been blessed." Macy became pensive.

"We went through some strange days, though," said Mav, thinking of Fenner Korn, Slade, Barbarossa, and others whose paths crossed with theirs and worthy of forgetting. Others, such as *Windwalker* and John Chapman, those worthy of pondering.

"What's next?" asked Macy. "Oh, there's the telephone. Would you answer it, please?"

"Hello. *Ja-gé!*" exclaimed Mav, then turning to Macy, said: "it's our daughter, calling from Washington.

"Yes. No, I have not heard the news. What is it?" asked Mav.

"Incredible! So, it was signed into law. Congratulations! You have worked hard for this. We are proud of you. When are you coming home?" Mav paused for a moment as he listened. "We will see you then." Replacing the earpiece on the candlestick, Mav turned back to Macy.

"Indian citizenship is almost a guarantee. Congress passed the Snyder Act [15] that the natives can become full citizens with equal rights if the states follow the lead of the federal government." Mav poured a cup of coffee and sat down to drink it and read the Gazette.

"Mav, when is she coming home?" asked Macy.

"Day after tomorrow," replied Mav.

The period since Washington forced the natives onto reservations and banned the dance is a half-century-long. Earlier rulings that governed the awarding of citizenship, such as marriage to a current citizen, or service in the war, were small steps. Denial of citizenship for those natives having more than one-half Indian blood is now overridden by the new law. The limiting factor now rests with the states.

"Was the trip comfortable?" asked Macy of the returning *Ja-gé*.

"A Pullman Sleeper ride makes a lot of difference," returned *Ja-gé*. "We traveled through a huge storm part of the way. It was exhilarating at night. The darkness, shattered by the lightning, was just wonderful. I was glad that I was inside the coach. I can just imagine how the old-timers on the trail would have thought about such a night."

"Humpf! Well, I can tell you some of what an 'old timer' would have thought about it on the trail," interjected Mav. "He would have been thinking about the herd that just went into a panic that he was riding fast into the night trying to outpace the leaders to turn them back and stop the stampede. He would have been afraid of the lightning strikes going on all around him that could take him at any minute. He would have been thinking about his horse stumbling and tossing him beneath the hooves of three-thousand cattle. That's what he would have been thinking about."

"Do you miss it?" asked *Ja-gé*, smiling at her *ka-tá*, her pa.

"Sometimes, I do. But it's mostly the people that I worked with and lived with on the trail. Did I ever tell you about Dodge?" asked Mav, thinking about the recalcitrant heifer on a drive to Ogallala.

"Dodge? You mean Dodge City, Kansas?" asked *Ja-gé*.

No, not Dodge City. I'm talking about Dodge, a hei…" Mav is interrupted by news from the radio station WHO-AM transmitting from Des Moines, Iowa, since the spring. Reported in the news is that the first transcontinental airmail service between New York and San Francisco has been completed.

"He did it!" exclaims Mav. "Case and his folks in the post office department have delivered the mail across the country! Remember, he talked about the concrete compass rose to help pilots calibrate their compasses and the large concrete arrows that pointed to lighted beacons leading a pilot across the country? How pilots could follow the arrows to each beacon and know that they were on the proper course? It's amazing. When I was on the trail, we used the sun to tell us if we were traveling in the right direction. Each night, cookie aligned the wagon tongue to point in the direction we wanted to follow just in case the morning was cloudy, and we couldn't see the sun. We'll have to ask Case what pilots do when the ground is covered by fog or blowing dust."

✳✳✳

News reports from the beginning of the century through the decade of the 'Roaring Twenties' were reports that did not penetrate the minds of the average citizen of the United States but had tremendous impact on the governments of Europe.

In 1917, Tsarist Russia was overthrown by violent revolution and was now a communist dictatorship. The Bolsheviks had murdered tsar Nicholas and his entire family. The fear of similar 'workers revolution' throughout Europe resulted in strong activity from the right wing of the political spectrum and Fascism blossomed at the expense of even the most moderate political theories.

In Italy, Fascist leader, Benito Mussolini came to power in 1922 and formed a government at the request of King Victor Emmanuel III. By 1932, Benito, then known as 'Il Duce,' would receive sixty-five percent of the vote of parliament and would force the king to share control of the military.

In Germany, the year after Mussolini's October 1922 march on Rome, Austrian born Adolph Hitler attempted a similar feat in what became known as the 'Beer Hall Putsch,' but failed to topple the government. In a sham trial in Bavaria, Hitler received a five-year prison sentence for high treason. Nine months later he was freed. During his imprisonment, Hitler completed work on his manifesto titled, *Mein Kampf*, or My Struggle, with its main thesis, 'the Jewish peril.' Ask anyone after 1945 if they know what 'holocaust' means.

546

Mav Caid — The Complete Story

From Japan, radio listeners and newspaper readers learned of the assassination of the prime minister of Japan by ultranationalists. By 1937, Japan, mired in a war with China, will cast off its experiment with democracy following the demise of the Tokugawa Shogunate. It will begin looking back to past glory and becoming more nationalistic, more militaristic. But Japan is far away. China is far away. Japanese atrocities in China will leave three-hundred thousand Chinese citizens in their graves. What threat could Japan offer America when their focus is on China? Ask an American on December 7, 1941 if any of that mattered.

From more remote locations, by 1932, they may have heard of Mecca falling to the forces of Ibn Saud of Arabia. And that the ultra-conservative elements in the kingdom, known as Wahabists, reserve the right to determine all religious issues. Many will shrug and say: "Why should that matter to me, what religion teaches in Arabia?" Ask that question after September 11, 2001, of anyone.

During the decade of the 1930s, people of the United States will ponder the differences presented by differing political and philosophical thought between Communism, Fascism, Socialism, and Democracy. "What difference does it make?" many will ask, "if they don't bother us, now that the 'war to end all wars' is over?" Few people see the world getting smaller, neighbors getting closer, nationalism growing in Europe.

Today, in America in 1935, most certainly, they will hear that Amelia Earhart flew solo from Hawaii to California. They will read that the FBI killed the 'Ma' Barker gang, including Ma Barker. And, that Richard Hauptman was convicted in the kidnapping and murder of the child of famed flyer, Charles Lindberg, Jr. Some will read that Adolph Hitler has ordered a re-armament of Germany in violation of agreement of 1919 known as the Treaty of Versailles, and later that he has ordered resumption of conscription to fill the ranks of his *Wehrmacht*. Many will read about the great dust storm affecting the states of New Mexico, Colorado, and Oklahoma, on a day to become known as Black Sunday. They may read of records being set. Records like Sir Malcolm Campbell's three-hundred-one miles per hour run in Bonneville, Utah; Howard Hughes' three-hundred miles per hour flight in his H-1 Racer; Babe Ruth's final game, playing for the Boston Braves; possibly, Louisiana's Senator Huey Long's fifteen and one-half hour record-breaking speech.

On a more somber note, in 1935, people will mourn the passing of humorist Will Rogers and aviator Wiley Post in a crash in Alaska; poet, Edwin Arlington Robinson; author and hero of Arabia, T.E. Lawrence in a motorcycle accident; Nobel Peace prize winner, Jane Addams; American painter, Childe Hassam; American Suffragist, Laura M. Johns; and Huey Long, politician.

On New York's Broadway, audiences applauded the dancing skills of Ginger Rogers and Fred Astaire in an Edward Everett Horton musical comedy, <u>Top Hat</u>. The following year they will enjoy the Victor Moore musical comedy, <u>Swing Time</u>, again with Fred Astaire and Ginger Rogers.

Of all the events following the Great Crash on Wall Street of 1929, is a focus on the succeeding decade of economic depression suffered throughout this nation and the world.

Chapter 69

The Shadow of Deception

On an afternoon in June 1934, Mav was called to the door by a sharp knock. He had no preparation for the arrival of a man seeking a conversation on a serious matter. The message he brings is a shock.

"Mr. Caiden, I am from a group of citizens who are interested in good governance for the state of Arkansas. It is my pleasure to inform you that you are of interest to this group as a potential candidate for public office. Please give me a little time to explain. My name is Ralph Teagarten, and the group I represent is the Arkansas Committee for Positive Growth, the ACPG. We have been watching the things you have accomplished in your lifetime and believe we, —that is, — Arkansas, would benefit from your candidacy for Governor." The speaker stopped talking to allow Mav to consider his appeal and answer.

"Well, this is a surprise, coming unexpectedly, and something I have never considered before. Governor? Bit of a high aim, wouldn't you say, considering that I have never held public office," returned Mav, trying to place if he has heard of the ACPG.

"Mr. Caiden, it is a simple as this: the two foremost candidates, Lamar Koch, and Herkimer Judd, are not right for Arkansas. We want someone fresh, someone, not tainted by events and positions of the past. If Arkansas is to move fully into this century, it must have new blood at the top. Your reputation is well known across Arkansas. We believe that you can provide the pathway for a new Arkansas if you will only say yes. There are rich and powerful people behind this appeal to your sense of duty to this great state. I can promise you sufficient funds to launch a viable campaign as a third-party candidate and continuing help as the campaign moves forward." Ralph smiled at Mav, showing even white teeth beneath full lips topped by a neatly clipped mustache.

"Mr. Teagarten, would you like a cup of coffee so we can discuss this more?" answered Mav. "By the way, I have never heard of the ACPG."

"Not surprising," stated Ralph, "we prefer to work quietly behind the scene. Some might call us 'kingmakers,' I suppose. Our members are content to work that way and not have to answer so much to the press, which can impede the serious work of serious people. It can distract from our purpose and muddy the water."

Pouring coffee for his unexpected guest and himself, Mav replied: "What is it, exactly, about my experiences that attract the attention of your group?"

"Ah, yes. Well, your experience with the aluminum industry. And, of course, your benevolence in founding the Caid-Chesney Tears of the Sun hospital. And, of course, you are a farmer, a man close to the soil. Arkansans, or Arkansawyers, if you prefer, relate to farmers better than anyone else, so many are engaged in farming themselves.

Industry, altruism, a man who stains his hands in Arkansas dirt, — three important credentials for a governor in this modern age," returned Ralph Teagarten. "Of course, I know you will want to talk it over with your family before giving us an answer. So, thank you for the coffee, and I will take my leave. Here is my card with the number where you may reach me."

"I will talk it over with my wife, Macy, and will have an answer for you in a few days." Mav walked Ralph to the door. A few minutes later, Macy entered the room.

"Macy, some folks want me to run for governor. Can you believe that? I don't know what to make of it."

"You would make a good governor, Mav. I believe in you and think you can do whatever you set your mind to. So that's what I think of it! But what do you want to do?"

"This Mr. Teagarten says that I would be running as a third-party candidate. He didn't mention the name of that third party, but from the way he spoke, I surmised it would be called the Progressive party or something similar. I only know of the Republicans and Democrats. If what I read in the Gazette is true, the Democrat has a small edge in their support. Another thought is that I haven't voiced my opinion or given any public support to either party. How could they suppose that I would be a fit for the policies they support? Teagarten said that the fact that I have not expressed opinions in public is an asset since no one could attack me for something I said in the past. I would be a new face with new policies to promote. Maybe that's true, it seems logical. I just don't know. This is far too strange. I will have to know more about the policies they want to promote and who these ACPG members are." Mav became thoughtful as he poured another cup. "I think I will explore this." A few days later, Mav called Teagarten.

"Mr. Teagarten, this is Maverick Caiden. I promised to give you an answer to your question about my running for governor. I must admit that I don't have a yes or no for you today. What I have is a need to meet your group and have a discussion to see if the policies they wish to promote and my beliefs match. Can that be done soon?" Mav held the speaker to his ear while holding the candlestick telephone near his mouth.

"Tuesday will be fine. Where do you want me to come, and what time?" Mav asked.

The following Tuesday, Mav drove to the Garton Hotel in Beaton to meet with the group calling themselves the ACPG. As he arrived and walked down the hallway toward the suite specified, a man exited the room, putting on his Stetson, which shielded his face. To Mav, the shielding seemed intentional. He apparently saw Mav and quickly changed his intended direction leading to the elevator, then disappeared down a stairwell. Mav obtained only a brief glimpse of the man as he turned into the stairwell and only the shadow of the man wearing a Stetson projected upon the wall by the stairwell light. Mav knocked on the door and entered the suite.

"Good morning, Mr. Caiden," began the greeting from Ralph Teagarten. "Let me introduce our members. Mr. Axel Sabin, Mr. Walter Hamilton, Mr. Carlton Fisk, and Mr. Louis Milton. Of course, you already know me." After Ralph finished all introductions, a question-and-answer session followed with each person giving a statement of objectives and characteristics they wanted in a candidate. After each had had his say, Mav realized that what he heard was that everyone believed in the sanctity of motherhood and apple pie. There was no depth. Only platitudes. Overall, though, members of the ACPG advocated nothing that would violate the personal beliefs of Mav Caid. The meeting ended with a request that Mav decides to join their efforts to form a third party for the next gubernatorial election. As he previously surmised, the party is called the Progressive Party. The one curious thing to Mav was that none of the attendees were local, but hailed from different regions of Arkansas.

"Macy, my read of these people is that they are not forthcoming in what their objectives really are. They want me to believe that they are serious in funding a candidate because the other candidates don't meet their liking. Still, a third-party candidate is a long shot at best, so I think that they really want a spoiler. Someone to draw off votes from one of the other candidates. They seem to be looking to split the votes for the Democrat, which would give the Republican candidate an edge." Mav was thoughtful for a moment, then continued: "Of course, it could be just that it is so new to me that I am suspicious of motivations when I shouldn't be."

"So, you think that they want to use you to help their candidate by damaging the chances of the other?" asked Macy.

"I don't know, but that is what my thoughts are now. I mean, let's face it, these people are the quintessence of conservatives in their manner of dress and demeanor. In my mind, they would normally rally to the Republican candidate. What is it about that candidate they don't like?" Mav sat down and picked up the Gazette and began reading. "There is to be a rally for the Republican candidate this coming week. I think I'll look in on it. Maybe he has horns, and the ACPG hates horns. I'll check that, and I'll check his feet too, just to make sure he stands on feet, not hooves."

Tuesday, the next week found Mav standing in a crowd of supporters of the candidate. The rally followed the script for all political rallies, and Mav spent his time looking over the crowd. At last, he saw something interesting and familiar. A man wearing a Stetson. He asked a man in the crowd who the person in the Stetson was Mav learned that his name is Buster Palmer and that he is the campaign manager for the Republican candidate. Mav observed the man for a few minutes to assure himself that he was the same person he saw leaving the suite at the hotel when he went to meet the committee members of the ACPG. Of course, Stetsons adorn the heads of many people wherever they live. He could still be wrong.

Eugene Stonefield

"Macy, it was strange, seeing this man, Buster Palmer, at the rally for the Republican candidate after thinking I had observed him leaving a meeting of the ACPG. If true, why would a campaign manager of one party be associating with members of an organization that opposes both candidates? It may be that he was trying to change their mind about running a third candidate. I just don't know." Mav showed his consternation. "More and more, I think that I need to keep my eyes open on matters regarding the ACPG."

"Sometimes, it is best to follow instinct and not be too trusting of those you do not know," Macy replied. "So, what are you going to do?"

"I'm not sure yet, but I'm leaning to giving it a whirl," replied Mav.

Several weeks went by, and several meetings with the ACPG assuaged Mav's initial concerns about their motivations. He worked with the ACPG to write policy statements on child labor, labor unions, and women's suffrage, to which all agreed. One issue, that of school funding, remained unresolved because of conflicting views among the members of the ACPG. Mav decided to give this more time for the members to resolve among themselves but assured Mav they would bring Mav in to determine the appropriate strategy for the campaign. Mav has given his views on the subject but knows the importance of presenting a well-conceived message, so he is willing to wait.

Several months passed, and the campaign for governor progressed as well as expected for a third-party candidate with no state-wide name recognition as a politician. Mav was attentive to the way Ralph Teagarten managed the campaign and kept a close eye on Buster Palmer when he knew he was nearby. All seemed reasonable and creditable until an unusual occurrence two weeks before the election placed Mav and Buster Palmer in the same hotel in Littlerock. Just as the first time he laid eyes on Buster, Buster once again was leaving the hotel room of Ralph Teagarten. He did not see Mav as Mav was leaving his own room to visit Ralph for a planning session for the campaign rally at the coliseum.

"Good morning Ralph," said Mav as Ralph opened the door to Mav's knock. "Anything unusual happening that I need to know?"

"Not that I know of," replied Ralph.

Mav looked intently at Ralph for a minute before saying: "I just saw Buster Palmer leaving your room."

"Oh, no. Not Buster. But there is a man who looks much like Buster just down the hall. I have seen him also. He probably was walking by my room as you arrived." Ralph revealed nothing in his demeanor.

'I'm not wrong,' thought Mav. 'Why would Ralph lie to me?' Sitting down at the table to begin a discussion about tonight's address of supporters and onlookers did little to allay Mav's concern that Ralph is keeping something important secret.

"Polling across the state are in for the week," began Ralph, showing the front page of the Littlerock Bugle. "It is a curiosity. It appears that you are drawing supporters equally from both camps. We expected that you would draw votes from the Democrats alone. We may have to change the message."

"You didn't mention how I am polling. Mav waited for a reply.

"Actually, you are very near both other candidates. The polls show a near three-way tie. You need five points to top the Democrat and three points to top the Republican. It wouldn't surprise me if one camp or the other would be asking for you to drop out and support their candidate," replied Ralph.

"So," stated Mav, "the Republican camp is less likely to win without my withdrawal and appeal for my voters to move to the Republican candidate?"

Ralph studied Mav for a time, then began: "Now, Mav...I think..."

"I think," Ralph, "you already have that request in your pocket. Am I right?" For a moment, Ralph again looked intently at Mav, wondering if his question did not reveal that he knew that Buster had visited just before Mav arrived.

"No. Oh, no. I have nothing of the sort. But it begs the question. What would you say if someone did make that request?" asked Ralph.

"Oh, I might ask if that was the original plan, —that my running would draw enough votes from the Democrats to assure a win for the Republican candidate. Then if it looked like I had a shot of winning, to encourage me to leave the race and throw my support to the Republican. Perhaps my drawing near enough to suggest that I could win outright was unexpected."

"Don't read too much into my question. As your campaign manager, I need to know what you're thinking. Of course, you must know that there are powerful people who seek the defeat of the Democratic candidate for economic reasons." Ralph pursed his lips as he ended his statement.

"Their bull would be gored if the Democrat won?" asked Mav.

"Severely," replied Ralph.

"Do you have some back-channel knowledge of what is at stake?"

"School funding. The Republicans object to the idea that they should fund public education. It is their opinion that if communities want public education, they should ask their citizens to pay for it. The state should stay away from it altogether. The democratic candidate is aggressive in this matter and would not veto a bill to secure funding through the taxing authority of the state." Ralph went silent.

"And, of course, land ownership, being the basis for taxation, affects large landowners the most," returned Mav. "What does the ACPG say?"

"Well, they are all wealthy people," replied Ralph.

"Macy, my initial concern about the governor's race has returned. The ACPG is vehemently against public education. I never received more than tepid support for my opinion on it. I'm getting a glimpse of a plot to assure the Republican will win if it looks that he will not win without my tipping the scale in their direction." Mav took a sip of his coffee and looked at Macy. "What would you say if I withdrew this late in the campaign?"

"Mav, I would say that I fully support your decision if that is what you want to do. How would you do it without looking like you are part of the plan?"

"That is the problem. There are voters out there that believe in me. I don't want to let them down." Mav reached for the Gazette.

"Education should be for all," replied Macy. "Not just for those families who have money to pay for private educators."

"Yeah."

One week before the election, Mav stands before members of the press who are reporting the race to their readers throughout the state.

"Supporters of my campaign, gentlemen of the press, citizens of Arkansas. I have endeavored to bring my message to you in an honorable and forthright manner as I could, and I believe that I have done so. However, I have recently become aware of something that I feel all citizens that plan to vote in this election should hear about. In keeping with my belief in truthfulness and transparency, I am revealing today what I have learned recently. I sought election as your governor when I had never held office before, because of the encouragement of the ACPG, who you know is an acronym for the Arkansas Committee for Positive Growth. I believed in the motivations of this committee because they seemed to align with my own beliefs, at least, ostensibly. However, I have become aware that there is a darker motivation, which is contrary to the goals they have presented to me." Mav stopped talking to allow himself time to judge the attention of the crowd.

"The truth is, fellow citizens, that this dark motivation is predicated upon a supposition that a third-party is unlikely to win the office. Consequently, it will draw votes from a candidate that they most want to defeat. Words, ladies, and gentlemen are sometimes cheap. The ACPG assumed a 'grin and bear it' posture and structured the message, —my message, —to align more closely with the message of the Democratic candidate. To that end, the ACPG gave support to my campaign in the expectation that I would draw from the Democrat candidate alone. A strategy does not always work in the manner expected, and sometimes that third-party candidate draws equally from each of the other, shall we say, mainstream candidates. An event of this kind threatens the result desired by perpetrators of the deception. In this case, the ACPG. I reveal this, to avoid deceiving voters who have pledged support for my campaign, and to unmask those who have sought to deceive my voters and me. The ACPG expected me to draw votes from the Democrat to ensure the Republicans would win and were willing to infuse my campaign with hard cash to make it happen."

Mav took a sip of water before continuing. "Under the circumstances, I feel obligated to tell you of the plot against my candidacy and my thoughts on withdrawing. At the same time, the election date being too near to print new ballots suggests that I do otherwise. Those of you who would typically vote for the Republican candidate, Lamar Koch, stay with me, I could win, still. And for those who would typically support the Democrat, Herkimer Judd, feel free to stay with me, —as I just said, I could win, still. But if you choose to switch to my Democrat opponent, feel free to do so. You will be changing without rancor or hard feelings from me."

A rumble of voices swept the room. Mav looked across to see some familiar faces leaving through the back door. Picking up the thread of his presentation, Mav continued.

"In closing, I want to say thank you sincerely for your trust. And for the ACPG, I renounce your support for its deception and for the taint against myself and my campaign by its sordid intent. Thank you all for coming." Mav stepped down from the podium to answer the many questions reporters are now shouting to him. All members of the ACPG have quietly left the venue.

One week later, voters went to the polls and voted their trust in the Democratic Herkimer Judd. Mav Caid came in second and the Republican, Lamar Koch, a distant third. While the results were being reported in the Gazette and many other newspapers, Mav sat at the breakfast table talking to Macy.

"Well, Macy. I think I'm glad that the voters have made their choice. I have no regrets. And maybe school funding will be assured. I guess I was a bit naïve in listening to Teagarten."

"You did the right thing, Mav. Perpetrators of fraud should not be rewarded. Honesty will always be the right path. Integrity wins."

"I can't agree with you more, Macy. If we don't have honesty in our political leaders, we can't have a country that matches the vision of the country's founders."

Chapter 70

A Parkland for Children

It is 1935, and a sixty-eight-year-old Maverick Caiden and his wife, Macy, are being honored for their continuing support of the Caid-Chesney Tears of the Sun Hospital in Beaton. The hospital they started has grown to be a major regional hospital for the area. Mayor Richard Laramore has awarded the keys to the city jointly to Mav and Macy at a public ceremony that has just ended.

"Mr. and Mrs. Caiden, the city of Beaton, will always be indebted to your generosity and continuing support for public needs for the citizens of Beaton and those frequent visitors to the city. I would be failing in my duties as mayor if I did not mention another growing need. That is a need to provide a park for the entertainment of children, and of course, adults. There is a large area with lake shoreline that most of the council believe the city could develop into a park with equipment for children to play upon and get their exercise. The possibilities are exciting, the funds to develop such a vision is decidedly lacking. The city does not have the budget for development but could donate the land. We, that is, the council and I are asking if you might consider working with us on this issue?" The mayor smiled at Mav and Macy, hoping that their generosity will be the key to the realization of the stated vision.

"Mayor Laramore, we can't give you an answer at this moment, but I will assure you that we will discuss it and get back to you soon," Mav answered with an agreement from Macy in the form of a nod.

✳✳✳

"Macy, I have been thinking about the mayor's appeal for money to develop a parkland in Beaton. Children do need a place to have fun and exercise their bodies. What are your thoughts on it?"

"I agree. What are you thinking of doing?" Macy has known for a long time that if Mav spends time thinking about something and talking about it, he is a step away from doing something about it.

"I have been reading about some of the things they have in places like Chicago, and I think they can be replicated on a small scale in Beaton. They have little electric bumper cars called Dodgems that allow drivers of these little cars to drive around in an enclosed area crashing into each other. Kids can have great fun. And there are carousels, miniature trains, Ferris wheels that lift riders high into the sky, and all manner of structures to climb, to swing on and slide down. I can envision folks starting businesses to supply food and drinks for the people coming to the park. Macy, I think we ought to help with this." Mav waited for Macy to respond, knowing that she feels the same way about children.

"We would just write a check to fund all of it?" asked Macy.

"No. We will match, dollar for dollar, other donor contributions. The city donates the land, donor solicitations made of others for the equipment, and we would match the pledges. We know that the mayor wants this, but we don't know what the citizens of Beaton want. If they are of a like mind, they will vote for it with their contributions, which we will match. What do you think?"

"Well, that would give an incentive for others to get engaged. How soon could it be done?" returned Macy.

"Perhaps a year, maybe two years. It depends upon how quickly the other donors can be engaged and encouraged to contribute. We could do it ourselves, but I think it is important that others step up and become part of the effort. It means more then." Mav poured himself another cup of Arbuckle, still his brand of choice. "I have sent information requests to the Max and Harold Stoehrer company, the manufacturer of the Dodgems, and to the Lusse Brothers that make a similar car called an Auto-scooter. I want to get information on the miniature trains next and..." Macy interrupted Mav saying:

"Didn't they do something like this in Chicago some years ago?"

"On one of my early trips to Chicago, back in 1893, Chicago was putting on a World's Colombian Exposition to celebrate the four-hundredth year of Christopher Columbus' discovery of America. Funding for the construction was from the public. I recall some of the names of the major donors. Marshall Field, —he founded the store bearing his name that I bought gifts from for you, Lyla, and Case. Philip Armour, —Lytle did business with Armour for years. Philip founded his Armour & Company meat-packing industry in Chicago. Gustavus Swift, —he was another meat-packer that Lytle sold to. And there was Cyrus McCormick's company, although by then his company had merged with another and is now the International Harvester Company. We bought a harvester from the company several years ago. Charles Yerkes was a financier who helped with the effort. Then there was a banker named Lyman Gage. He raised several million dollars in a twenty-four-hour period to tilt the decision to build the exposition in Chicago rather than New York. Congress was to make the decision on location, and a group of influential fellas like Cornelius Vanderbilt,

J.P. Morgan, and William Waldorf Astor wanted it in New York. Anyway, the exposition featured an amusement park with various rides for visitors. And a civil engineer, named George Washington Gale Ferris, Jr., built his ride on a large wheel that he named a Ferris Wheel. It was the first. An amusement park in Beaton could be similar, just not as large as the exposition." Macy could see Mav's excitement grow as he spoke of the exposition.

"Mav, how do you remember all of those details?"

"I don't know, Macy. Astounding events, —and large projects like the Exposition did astound me at the time, —just stuck in my memory."

✳✳✳

"Mayor Laramore, Macy, and I have talked over your proposal, and here is our decision. Macy and I are prepared to meet the donations of all others on a dollar-for-dollar match. Here is the information I have collected on a few of the amusements that we think could be core to the amusement park. After you meet with the council, perhaps you will let me know of their decision to move forward with donor solicitations. We should be able to help with them also." Mav handed his information to a pleased mayor.

"Mr. Caiden, I am grateful for the decision you and Mrs. Caiden have made, and I will take it up in the next meeting." Mayor Laramore smiled. "Is there anything else I can tell the council?"

"Well, since there will be many other donors, I hesitate to make a demand, but it would not displease us if the park was named 'Lyla's Joy Playland.' Mayor Laramore shook hand with Mav and left, too young to know the history of Lyla and too uncertain in his ignorance to ask.

Lyla's Joy Playland saw its opening in the spring of 1937. Within a year, donors added a small zoo that brought the citizens of Beaton into contact with seldom seen animals. Visitors could see animals previously only seen as pictures in books and cyclopedias.

Chapter 71

Last Visit to Chicago

Macy and Mav arrived in Chicago in the fall of 1938. They came to see the sights of the city; which Mav had told Macy of following previous visits. His earlier visits had been his trips to bring diamonds to Reginald Benoit and to meet with executives of the Perciville Reduction Company. Their first stop is to visit Professor Desoto at his office in the History department of the University of Chicago, a pleasure Mav had engaged in for many years. Professor Desoto is nearing retirement and expresses delight at meeting the wife of his old friend Mav Caiden.

"I am so happy to meet you, Macy. Your husband had spoken of you many times when he came by for a visit."

"Professor Desoto, I too am pleased to finally meet you." Macy shook hands with the professor and added: "Mav has told me that you came from Spain. He told me a story about a lady who dressed in blue and played a role in the work of the missionaries in the early going of the missionary contacts with natives in the southwest. I wanted him to ask you about it since the story is so unusual and interesting. Now I am privileged to ask you in person." Macy waited for Professor Desoto to answer.

After a period of thoughtfulness, the professor said: "Oddly enough, I do know a bit about it. About six years ago, I received a letter from a colleague who had heard the story from some Jicarilla Apache in West Texas. He was working then with the tribe doing research on the Athapascan language. I knew nothing about a blue lady at the time but I had planned to travel to Rome on a sabbatical the next year, so I investigated the story from a historical perspective. It turns out that the archives of the Vatican have documents from the Inquisition about such an occurrence that took place during the years 1620 through about 1624. There was so much speculation about it at the time that the office of the Inquisition became interested. They did their investigation to determine if some type of demonic possession or witchcraft was at the root of the apparent instances of teleportation. The nun…your 'lady in blue'…occasionally fell into trances during which time she swore that she had come to Nueva Spain, the territory of Texas to Arizona. While there, she worked with the natives acquainting them with the story of Christianity and to prepare them to meet the missionaries who were beginning to arrive here." Professor Desoto fell silent.

"Then, the story is true?" asked Mav.

"Well, who is to say? It was a long time ago and, well, sometimes different people have different motivations in recording a story. The investigation by the office of Inquisition would have been different from the type of investigation that would occur if done today. Theirs would have been tainted by their belief in witchcraft, heresy, demon influence, things that would not be a factor today. All I can say about it is that my friend insists the Jicarilla believe in the story and treat it as we Christians treat the resurrection of Jesus. It is odd though that the natives sought out the missionaries to ask for baptism and came to them displaying handmade crosses and rosaries," replied the professor. "From whom did they get the knowledge?"

"It is a strange story," averred Macy.

Mav and Macy spent the afternoon touring the campus with Professor Desoto before making their leave to return to the Tremont hotel, where they registered when they arrived. That night they attended a stage play, featuring the famous John and Ethel Barrymore of the renown Barrymore thespian family. The play was Romeo and Juliet. After the end of the performance, Mav and Macy enjoyed a late dinner at the Won Kow referenced in John Drury's guidebook, Dining in Chicago.

The next day, Mav and Macy went to the Marshall Field's store to shop for some clothing. They would have gone to the Benoit Jewelry store to visit with Mr. Benoit, but upon Mav's inquiry by telephone of the aging man, Mav was told that he had died three months ago at age sixty-nine.

"It is sad that he has passed on before you could meet him. He was an honest man and always treated me fairly. If I were still bringing diamonds to Chicago, I don't know where I would be going." Mav picked up a gray Stetson and put it on his head. "How do I look?" he asked.

"Distinguished," Macy answered, smiling.

✳✳✳

Tickets to Wrigley field were selling quickly as fans of the Chicago Cubs baseball team were becoming more confident that they would see their team in the World Series. Mav has long been a fan of baseball, and Macy, though less engaged, accompanies Mav on trips to the ballpark to watch the Beaton Bees play. Today they will witness an event that will go down in the annals of great baseball moments. On

September 28, the game between the Cubs and Pirates was tied at five runs. Because of the coming darkness, the umpires made the decision to end the game in the ninth if it remained tied and replay the entire game the following day. Charles Leo 'Gabby' Hartnett, catcher for the Cubs, was at bat in the bottom of the ninth inning. The pitch, delivered by Pittsburg Pirates' pitcher, Mace Brown, and with two strikes already against the batter, Cubs' catcher, Hartnett, sent the ball into the left-center field bleachers. The walk-off home run became known as the 'Homer in the Gloamin', its description a word-play on the popular Irish song of the day, 'Roamin in the Gloamin.'

"I have to say, that was some game!" said Mav, as he assisted Macy into the Yellow Cab.

"I doubt Hartnett will ever be able to set foot on the ground after the way the fans erupted onto the field and accompanied him around the bases. He had to have been floating!" interjected Macy.

Events will be hard on the Cubs later as they fall to the New York Yankees in the World Series, the fourth time the Cubs have lost in ten years. Events disappoint, hope is eternal, and the Cubs lost no fans in Chicago.

Chapter 72

Benevolence

Macy set the Gazette aside as Mav entered the room. "Mav, have you read this story about the family in Beaton whose home was destroyed in a fire last week?" Macy relished being able to be the one asking if the other had seen something in the Gazette. On a typical day, Mav gets the Gazette first and does the asking. It is Mav's way of eliciting a question from Macy about a subject he wants to tell her about.

"No. What is the story?"

"The home of William and Caroline Kearney burst into flames overnight and was completely engulfed by fire by the time the Beaton Voluntary Fire brigade got to the scene. Their pet dog woke them to the flames, and they were able to escape. They have three children, ages seven, five, and two years old. The leader of the brigade, Clyde Efferson, said that the house was being wired for electricity at the time and is thinking it could have been started by an electrical short circuit. They lost everything. William works at the feed store. The article says that they have no kin in the area. If they belong to a church, perhaps they can get some help there. If not, …" Macy is interrupted.

"Macy, I count five people who need a place to live right now. Do you suppose their church would find some accommodation? I mean, if they belong to one."

"I don't know an answer to either question. The family is at the Garton Hotel right now, but William's wages aren't enough for them to stay there for very long. The mayor has made an appeal to others to help them." Macy placed the Gazette on the table before Mav, who immediately picked it up and began to read.

"Macy, do you recall our setting up an account at the bank for emergencies? We have never had to call on it, and there is a lot of money just sitting there."

"Are you saying that the Kearney's plight is a qualifying emergency? But we don't know them." Macy waited for an answer.

"Do we need to? Know them, I mean?" returned Mav.

"Well, no. I guess knowing the Kearney family is secondary. Easing their misfortune is more important." Macy points to the telephone on the telephone stand and says: "You should call Insley."

After a moment, Mav rose from his chair and went to the telephone.

"Doris, this is Mav Caiden. May I speak to the president at Beaton Bank?" Mav waits for President Insley at the Beaton Bank to come on the line.

"This is Mr. Insley," began the recipient of the call. "How may I help you, Mr. Caiden?"

"What is involved in establishing a trust to hold real estate, and how long does it take to create one?"

Within a week, Insley establishes a new trust to acquire and hold real estate assets. Mav and Macy's emergency fund provides the funds to purchase real property with the Beaton bank serving as trustee. Immediately, a representative of the trustee begins the search to find available houses to buy. In the mean-time, an anonymous person or persons have paid the bill at the Garton Hotel for a family of five.

A week later, the trust purchased two houses. One is in a move-in condition, and the trustee is getting the other repaired and painted for occupancy. Presently, Mr. Insley placed a telephone call to the Garton Hotel, room 23, occupied by William Kearney and family.

"Mr. Kearney," spoke the caller, "We haven't met, but I have been following your plight since the tragic fire, and I believe I can offer you some assistance. My name is Insley. I am president of the Beaton Bank but am acting in the capacity of trustee for a benevolent trust. The trustor has asked me to ask you if you would be interested in moving into an available property of the trust to help your family get back on a more secure footing?" Mr. Marion Insley waited while William Kearney considered how many ways he could say yes. The next day, Mr. Insley handed the Kearney family keys to the house to enable them to begin again.

There were questions asked of Mr. Insley. Questions like: How much is the rent? Are there other obligations that must be met? How can I repay the trust? The answers were easy. There are no deposits, fees, or rents to be paid. However, to show good faith, you should pay what you can to the trustee until you are financially stronger. After that, decide if you want to purchase the house at a favorable price and favorable interest. Whatever amounts you have paid will be applied to the purchase. A date for your decision will occur at a two-year interval. Keep the property in good condition for the next occupant should you decide not to buy. Have good thoughts for your benefactors and promise to help someone else down the line that has suffered tragedy as your family has.

✳✳✳

As the years recede into the past, the value of the philanthropic trust named 'The Long Road Benevolent Trust,' grows as transfers of wealth continues to flow from one account to another within the brick-and-mortar walls of the Beaton Bank.

Chapter 73

Tennessee Valley Authority

The day begins, as usual, Mav is reading the Gazette, which is now a daily publication, and drinking coffee. Macy is reading the ads and making mental notes of who is selling what she needs for the family.

"What do you make of the Tennessee Valley Authority that some senator from Nebraska pushed so hard to get Congress to pass a few years ago? The Gazette says that the purpose of the legislation was to bring electricity to the folks in the region of Tennessee, Kentucky, Alabama, and Mississippi. Construction on dams throughout the region is continuing, even though Eminent Domain laws are forcing some people out of their homes to make way for the construction. Do you think that is something the Federal government should be involved in?"

"Mav, I don't know. I guess it depends upon a lot of factors. How many people will it help? What are the underlying problems? What is the full scope of the act?"

"Well, it says that it will provide better river navigation, flood control, and electricity to areas that are not now served. Also, it will allow for fertilizer manufacturing and expand the economic development of the area." Mav folded the Gazette and took another sip of his coffee.

"Mav, it sounds like a positive objective. Most of the people in that region are likely farmers just like we are. They deserve to have electricity at a minimum. Arkansas could benefit from a similar program. I know Governor Bailey favors electric cooperatives in Arkansas, but I haven't seen any results yet. I understand some are talking about hydroelectric dams on the White and Ouachita rivers. If building hydroelectric dams is the answer, then why not? But didn't they have some electricity already?"

"Yes, in some areas. Much like Arkansas. The problem seemed to be that the private electric utility companies were, basically, monopolies and could charge what they wanted, with no regulations to protect the public from overcharging. Some in the government, like this Senator George Norris of Nebraska, thought a correction was needed. So, the idea he promoted was that the government will start the process of development and turn the whole operation over to a corporation, which is the Tennessee Valley Authority, or TVA, as most refer to it. Hoover vetoed his first attempt, then Roosevelt signed the bill when it came to him. The TVA has eminent domain authority to acquire the land, and when fully built out, the operating expenses will be from sales generated from the sale of electricity and from fees from the recreational areas that will be built. There should be no taxpayer funding in the future. It should pay for itself."

"Mav, what happens to the private companies when the Federal government begins to compete for their business?" asked Macy, getting more interested.

"According to the article, the Public Utility Holding Company Act, PUHCA for short, addresses that and they purchase the ongoing utilities which are folded into the TVA. Some, of course, won't sell and will likely go out of business if they can't compete on price. There is little doubt that the TVA will be favored."

"I guess I still don't understand why a senator from Nebraska was so interested in the Tennessee Valley region. Why do you suppose?" asks Macy.

"Perhaps he is doing his job and is trying to do something that benefits the nation. The Gazette says that after World War I ended, serious problems plagued the region. Thirty percent of the population of the Tennessee Valley developed malaria, for instance, and their income was so low that some were existing on as little as one hundred dollars per year! Farms had been over-farmed for years and couldn't produce good crops. You recall what Case said about crop rotation? Well, these folks didn't know about it, and their land became depleted of the necessary minerals needed to support good production. Farms in that area of the country are far older than those in Arkansas. The best some families could do is generate six-hundred thirty-nine dollars per year in income. That is not enough. I can't imagine how we would survive on that. President Hoover, who had an opportunity to do something about it, said it was socialism, which he doesn't support. Roosevelt made it part of his 'New Deal' that he campaigned on. I reckon I am leaning toward Roosevelt's policies to change the path the nation is on."

"I recall," began Macy, "that Roosevelt's 'New Deal' also proposed a program to give some financial help to people who are too old to work or disabled. What about that program?"

"I think it is front of Congress right now. The way the Social Security program works is that workers pay into the program from their salaries during their working years, then receive back a lifetime income from the government during their retirement years. The current legislation is to add some disability provisions should a person get injured or injured and can't work. It will go a long way toward helping old folks, like us, to maintain their independence." Mav smiled at Macy.

"Old, my foot! You take that back, Maverick Caiden!" replied Macy in mock anger.

"Aw, you're not old, Macy, but you are beautiful. Even when you're angry." Mav ducked the chair cushion that was arching across the room in his direction.

∗∗∗

"Mav, do you see what I see over there by the gate? Is that Melvin Ware?" Macy points to an old man standing by the gate looking over as if trying to decide if he would be welcomed if he came through the gate.

"Macy, I think you are right. He certainly looks like Melvin. What do you suppose he wants? He left the dairy operation we had at the time and left for parts unknown. You remember how we wondered at the time why he left. He had been with us for several years. If he is here looking to get back in our dairy business, he will be disappointed."

"Yes. Maybe Melvin is just passing through and wants to stop by to say hello. If that's the case, he will be knocking on the door soon."

A few minutes later, a knock came at the door.

"Hello, Mr. and Mrs. Caiden. You remember me, Melvin Ware?"

"We remember you, Melvin. How many years has it been?" asked Mav. "Are you passing through or…"

"Looking for work, Mr. Caid. I've been sick some, and unable to return to the work I was doing. I found myself back in the area, and I remembered that you always treated me right…"

"But you left us in a lurch as I recall. You just up and left," returned Macy.

"Yes, Ma'am, I did, and I am sorry about that. It was that the job that this fella offered me, and he said I needed to start it right then, and the employer wouldn't wait. I had to go then." Melvin attempted to explain. "Maybe you have something?"

"Melvin, we don't have a dairy operation anymore, just a milk cow for our own needs. All our business is farming now. How are you at operating machinery?"

"I can operate some machinery. It depends upon what it is." Melvin looked nervous and despondent.

Macy, who had been observing Melvin as he talked, said: "Mav, could I speak with you for a moment in the other room? I think Melvin will give us a minute while he drinks his coffee."

When in the next room, Macy asked Mav: "Mav, did you notice his hand? His left hand? He doesn't carry that hand naturally. I don't think he can use it."

"I didn't notice it, but I'll ask him about it. I don't think we can use a one-armed man around the equipment," replied Mav.

"And Mav. His color is not good. He shows a pallor and doesn't breathe easy. I think he is sick somehow."

"Melvin, it looks as though you may have had some hard luck with your left hand. Tell me about it."

"I have, Mr. Caiden. One day while I was on the job and I got this awful headache. It caused me to lose consciousness, and I fell to the floor. Others found me and took me to the doctor. He told me I had suffered a stroke. The stroke affected the left side of my body, mostly my hand and arm. I can't use it for much." Melvin looked down at the floor.

"Do you have family around here?" Mav asked to change the subject.

"No, nowhere now. My family died years ago in a fire. I never was married. It's just me now." Melvin set his cup down and stood. "I guess I'll head on out. It is good to see both of you again."

"So, where are you going?" asked Macy.

"Just down the road to Beaton. See what I can find," returned Melvin.

"Uh, Macy? You know that cabin we picked up when we bought that farm from Ellery a couple of years ago?"

"Yes. I recall it. What are you thinking, Mav?"

"The roof is good, and the windows are tight. It may be dusty, but maybe Melvin won't mind that. I think we can accommodate him, and it is getting late in the day. What do you say, Melvin?"

"Ah, Mr. and Mrs. Caiden. I could rest my bones there. It won't hurt my feelings that it may be a bit dusty."

Macy set about collecting items that Melvin would need to sleep for the night, saying that anything else they could handle in the morning. Before they left, Macy handed Melvin a basket with food for the night. Mav drove Melvin to the cabin and bid him goodbye until the next day. Mav was thoughtful in his drive back to the home place, thinking about his family in Bandera and how they died, and how Melvin's family died.

"Mav, what are you thinking?" asked Macy as he sat quietly in the porch swing.

"How we can employ him," replied Mav.

✳✳✳

For a time, Mav found activities for Melvin that helped to restore Melvin's feeling of self-independence. But, as time continued, troubling signals began to accrue that all was not well with Melvin. Hard, sustained coughing, breathlessness, blood in sputum.

"Melvin, your cough is getting worse. Macy and I both think that you need to go into Beaton and visit Dr. Slater." The next day Mav drove Melvin to Dr. Slater's office.

"Mr. Ware," began the doctor after his examination, "I have made a diagnosis. Unfortunately, Mr. Ware, it is not good. You have contracted tuberculosis."

Melvin Ware sat for a moment in silence as he sought to absorb the full meaning of the diagnosis, finally asking: "Doctor Slater, are there medicines for it?"

"Treatment for TB is uncertain at best," replied Dr. Slater, "but it is best treated in a sanitorium. There are several to choose from, — one is Booneville."

"What treatment do they give there?" Melvin is calm, though he is aware that the diagnosis is dire.

"Well, fresh air is important, so the state constructed Booneville to take advantage of Arkansas' fresh air. And a milk and egg diet are helpful. And, they prescribe acetylsalicylic acid. Sometimes a pneumothorax is performed under anesthesia…" Dr. Slater is interrupted.

"What is a new-mo-throw-axe…" asked Melvin.

"Pneumothorax is a collapsing of the lung by surgical means to help the lung heal from the infection." Dr. Slater waited for the next question.

"How…uh, how much does it cost? The sanitorium, I mean?" asked Melvin.

"Currently, about ten dollars weekly. You receive housing, meals, and treatment for as long as needed," replied the doctor.

"And, how long is that?" asked Melvin.

"Well…" responded the doctor.

***

"I guess I wasn't wrong when I said Melvin's pallor was bad. What do you think he will do?" asked Macy.

"Macy, what else can he do? Treatment today is based on aspirin outside the sanitorium. Inside, he may have a better chance of surviving. I understand some people do get better, even beat the infection, and live out a normal life. Nobody really can predict with accuracy the survival of a single individual. The group maybe five to ten years."

"Do you think he knew? I mean before he came? Mav?"

"I don't know, Macy. He could have known that something wasn't right with him. He admitted to being unusually tired."

"He was happy here when he worked with the dairy herd. He left because he thought he would better his income and status in life. I can't fault him for that."

"Do you think he came home to die?" asked Macy.

"Home?" asked Mav.

"What else do you call a place where they will always take you in?"

***

A week passed, and preparations completed to take Melvin to the sanitorium at Booneville. Mav drove to the cabin to get Melvin for the trip. A short time later, Mav returned home and entered the kitchen, where he found Macy.

"Where is Melvin? I thought you would be bringing him here before leaving for Booneville."

"He won't be going, Macy, he's dead."

"Dead? What happened?"

"Don't know for sure, Macy. I found him sprawled on the floor next to his bed. I think, maybe, another stroke."

Chapter 74

The Poet

Time on hand begs the filling. Since all non-farm businesses owned by Mav and Macy Caid have been sold, Mav has concentrated on reading books and publications by writers carving their credentials through prose and poetry. Mav has read the prose and poetry of both England and America. American authors, F. Scott Fitzgerald, Sinclair Lewis, Ernest Hemingway, William Faulkner, John Dos Passos, Margaret Mitchell, Jack London, and John Steinbeck are providing notable prose though writers from earlier times are still famous and avidly read. Some examples are, humorist Samuel Langhorne Clemens, more popularly known as Mark Twain; transcendentalist authors Henry David Thoreau and Ralph Waldo Emerson; transitionary author Walt Whitman who bridged the gap between realism and transcendentalism; romanticism's Herman Melville; Nathaniel Hawthorne and James Fenimore Cooper.

Eugene Stonefield

Poetry appreciation in America has roots in Phillis Wheatley, a black ex-slave whose poems spread beyond American shores before the year 1800. Interest in poetry was later re-awakened by poets, Emily Dickinson, Walt Whitman, and Edgar Allen Poe. Mav read other popular poets, such as the internationally acclaimed Henry Wadsworth Longfellow; Modernist poets Ezra Pound, E.E. Cummings, T.S. Eliot, and James Joyce; lyric poets Robert Frosts and Sara Teasdale; beloved Chicago poet, Carl Sandberg; Langston Hughes of the Harlem Renaissance; and poet, novelist, and dramatist, Steven Vincent Benét. The lists cannot do justice to the importance of their contributions to American culture.

"This, I like," whispers Mav as he finished a book of poems by Edward Arlington Robinson. Then, continuing in thought: 'The pictures he paints with words make me feel like I know the subjects personally. I think I may try my hand at writing a poem. What kind of poem should I write? What was that line from a Lord Byron poem? She walks in beauty, like the night of cloudless climes and starry skies? Yes. That's the line. Oh, Byron placed no private brand on beauty. Others see beauty as well. Should mine rhyme? What about the conversational poetry of Coleridge? Should that be the style of the poem? What was that poem…<u>Aeolian Harp</u>…was that it? Coleridge didn't rhyme that poem. Why try for rhyme at first? Why not *vers libre*, the unrhymed free verse? T.S. Eliot's <u>Wasteland</u>. I read it in <u>The Dial</u> down at the library. That was free verse. I'll try to write in *vers libre*. Conversational *vers libre*!'

Following came a sequence of writing lines, reading them for effect, discarding them for their failures, and trying again. After days of effort, Mav decided that he needed a subject that his heart and mind could lead the hand and found that only Macy could best fulfill that demand. So it was that he began again to write about Macy and himself, to record feelings that he never felt competent to say aloud. Mav had the material that he could write about based on over forty years of marriage, plainly enough to drag out some creative ideas. As Mav reviewed their life together, he found that the difficulty is not in having enough to write about, but in selecting the most remarkable things about their life together. Things like the sharing of love, closeness, experience, the sharing of hope, happiness, and tragedy. Finally, the thoughts emerge from their sanctuaries in heart and mind:

> *I watch you sleep – You find peace in dreams.*
> *The clock chimes. Years melt away. Thoughts*
> *reprise the days when life's sweet breath filled,*
> *edge to edge, billowing white sails of joy;*
> *when there was but the present and future;*
> *when the past was but a footnote afloat*
> *upon ripples on the boundless river of time.*
> *Then you were new, I was new, love was new.*
> *Came then the writing of our history.*
> *From two, who in unity, became four,*
> *then three in never-forgotten heartbreak.*
> *Now the voyage of life nears its ending.*
> *As our love bathes in the glow of life's joys,*
> *though poets promise unending bliss,*
> *and religions promise eternal life,*
> *crystal truth teaches only death endures.*
> *Life and love flame only for a moment,*
> *to be cherished, —held all the more dear.*
> *Two joined people, aswirl in the vortex*
> *of life, now pledged to become as one. So,*
> *the story plays out. I know your thoughts*
> *even before you voice them, and you, mine.*
> *Silent talk between two halves of the one;*
> *Mute conversations of the all. Tell:*
> *Do you hear these thoughts while you sleep?*

Eugene Stonefield

Mav is happy with the results of this initial attempt to write a poem, yet he is reluctant to share it with Macy. She might consider his efforts silly or immature. 'The poem isn't perfect,' he thinks to himself. 'For Macy, it should be perfect. But what is perfect? What is perfection in the eyes of one who had dedicated her entire life to you?' Mav does not know, so his poem is undelivered. Later he will try again.

Several days later, he makes good his promise to himself and searches for a subject for another poem. His thought turns back in time to their beginning and to the dance. He thinks of how vital the dance is to the natives, how different the nature of the dance of non-natives between today and yesterday. There was no such dance as the Charleston, Lindy Hop, or the Black Bottom, with all that slapping of a dancer's backside, in the days Macy taught him how to dance. Other than those like the Polka, the older dances were slower, more conservative in their steps. It makes one wonder just where society is going with it. Mav recalls his clumsy efforts to learn each new dance step Macy sought to teach him. He recalls Macy's attempts to avoid the penalties befalling her from her efforts to teach a young man with new boots with slick soles sliding upon a slickened dancefloor. The poem must focus on the dance. He remembers that it was after that seminal dance that Macy declared her love with a kiss, one that was unexpected by Mav, impetuous and similarly unexpected by Macy. In his nostalgia, with skepticism about the new styles of dancing, Mav set about to write another:

Our dance steps may be old,
But our music never is
And holding you is ever new -
Like our first uncertain kiss

Mav Caid — The Complete Story

Tendered in those greener years.
In those greener years, —years
When spring seemed eternal;
When we were immortal.
Now, winter slows our pace
As age rimes our hair;
Carves lines upon each face.
Well, ok.
So, let our dance be old, —
Just let the music play.
I'll hold more tightly in the turns,
Dance more closely,
Love more deeply, —
While the music plays.

"What are you doing, Mav?" asks Macy as she enters the room where Mav is busily writing.

"Writing."

"What?"

"A poem."

"What?"

"A poem."

"About what?"

"You…us. What else." Mav looked up from his writing to see Macy shake her head in disbelief. "You always surprise me, Maverick Caiden. You always have."

Some months later, while coming from the funeral of their longtime friend, William Cole, Mav, and Macy express their thoughts.

"Billy was a good friend, possibly the first person I met when I came to Beaton," said Mav as they drove back to the home place.

"Well, I'm confident he has found peace in Heaven." Macy responded, certain in her theology.

"I guess. I can be hopeful on that matter," averred Mav.

"Don't you think so?" asked Macy.

"It's just…just that I can never be sure of the truth. What people considers to be true changes over time. How can you trust what you think you know is true when history shows that it changes? I've read somewhere that sometimes you must take things on trust, that life is too short to work out everything with mathematical certainty. Maybe that itself is a truth, but maybe it is saying that we should not try to discover truth. I couldn't agree with that. I think being a creature that thinks demands the pursuit of knowledge. Must everything have an opposite?" Mav looked at Macy who was taking in his answer.

"You don't believe in Heaven?" she asked.

"I think, its more that I don't believe in Hell. I can't rationalize a Hell existing if God is a forgiving deity. But if there is no Hell, what does Heaven mean? Everything seems to need an opposite to have meaning. If one doesn't exist, maybe the opposite can't." Mav went silent.

"What about God and the Devil? What are your thoughts on them?" asked Macy.

"Once again, opposites. Good versus evil. Good loses an 'o' and we speak of a God. Evil gains a 'D' and we speak of a Devil. Opposites. Dualism, —each must exist to give contrast to the other. I'm in a different place than where I was before Lyla died. I have wondered if whom we call God is really a person or only the personification of life we know, —a conceptual face to the reality in which we are familiar. Each person has an image of God in their mind, but no one sees God, only an image suggested by artists. Show me a person who has had a talk with God where it wasn't a one-way conversation. If a personification is true, then all the rest must be the imagination of people living long ago. Words of the prophets? Maybe nothing more than the thoughts of men considered to be 'wise' by others in their community. There is no equality in the level of understanding among people. Wisdom, perhaps, is just the recognition of greater enlightenment. Prophets make prophesies. If the prophet's words prove false, the prophet is false and suffers ridicule. If what he said proves true, the prophet is lauded and gains stature. Was it an actual communication of God's commands to Moses that resulted in the Ten Commandments, or was it the wisdom and inspiration of Moses of the rules needed to ensure peace among neighbors? Did the message drive the prophet or the prophet drive the message? In any case, the words have more weight when people believe them to be God's words to Moses. Is that claim no more than a tool that the powerful have used from the beginning to control others in the community? Yet, I want to believe in the story of Christianity. The story is beautiful in its telling, amid the tragedy, there is hope. Yet, I still see great injustice in events that harm the innocent among us. What good comes from injustice? Lyla…."

"I know, Mav. I know."

As time moved on, Mav continued to ponder the meaning of life, the character of God, and continued to write poems, some about his days riding up the trail with the Lytle company, others that found themselves upon Macy's pillow or in her favorite chair. If they were good poems, nobody knows. Only Macy.

Chapter 75

Metamorphosis

Having lightened his workload over the previous decade with the sale of the mine, timberland, cattle operation, and retrenched from working on the farm, Mav and Macy are retired. Macy makes various items usable in the home, such as bedspreads, table cloths, curtains, doilies, and some clothing. Mav devotes hours of the day listening to news and sports on the radio and reading. Mav is an avid reader with interests that go beyond what his appetite has been in the past. Poetry, philosophy, art, and the words written about them, Mav devours daily.

"What are you reading, Mav?" asked Macy as she enters the room and finds Mav drinking coffee and reading.

"Just something I ran across at the library. It is a collection of poems translated from Latin. It makes me think that there is so much in life that is unknown. Mysteries involving powerful entities we call 'gods.' It seems that anything that happens that can't be readily explained, people consider the business of some god. It appears that that is the way it has always been. Mystery, magic, and medicine go hand in hand. When what is mysterious becomes explained by growing knowledge, the powers of the gods diminish, and the power of man increases. This book tells of changes that the gods of the ancient world engineered. Some of the changes, or metamorphoses, are punitive, and others are to protect or reward those who were victims of some outrage. One that I just read was written by a poet living around the time of Jesus. His name is Publius Ovidius Naso, who is famous enough to be known by a single name, Ovid. A few years before Jesus began his ministry by curing the sick and raising the dead in the Holy land, Ovid was writing poetry for his pagan society in Rome. In his times, people believed strongly in a pantheon of gods and goddesses and in the limitless power that they possessed. Every god had adherents who worshipped them in temples. They held the power of life and death over all living things, man, and beast alike. And they had the power to change people into other things and elevate people to the heavens as they pleased."

"You mean his poems are about ordinary people who were changed into something else, like animals?" asked Macy.

"Yes, and flowers, trees, reeds, and other things. One story is about two young lovers named Pyramus and Thisbe. They were neighbors prohibited from associating with each other by strict parents. A wall separated their properties kept them apart physically, but a hole in the wall allowed them to converse. One day they rebelled against their parents' prohibitions. They made plans to violate them by running away and meeting after the parents had retired for the night. The young girl, Thisbe, arrived first at the designated rendezvous but danger lurked nearby. A lion roamed the vicinity, so Thisbe hid. But as she ran toward her place of safety, she dropped her cloak, and the lion found the cloak. The lion, having just finished killing and eating his prey, chewed on the cloak leaving it stained with blood. Pyramus, arriving late, found the blood-stained cloak and believing Thisbe dead, could not handle his guilt for not being there earlier. He ultimately killed himself with his sword beneath a mulberry tree that, at that time, produced white berries. Thisbe, sensing that the lion had left the area, came out of hiding, and found Pyramus. Thisbe couldn't bear the thought of not having Pyramus, so she took his bloody sword and leaned upon its sharpened point, killing her as it had killed Pyramus. Their blood had splashed upon the tree with its berries and stained them, and soaked the tree to the root. The tree changed to memorialize the tragedy. The gods made it so, and now and forever, the mulberry tree shall produce red berries. Shakespeare has told this story in one of his plays that I read some time ago. <u>Midsummer Night's Dream</u>, I think it was. Although, in this play, it was a comedic play within a play. It also has some relevance to the story of <u>Romeo and Juliet</u>, star-crossed victims of a feud, that is resolved by their untimely deaths." Mav pauses before continuing.

"Another is about two strangers who went to a small village and went house to house trying to find someone who would ask them in, to have them as guests. Well, they couldn't find anyone willing to take them in except for an aged couple of poor means. Their possessions were few, their house, small and shabby, but their sense of brotherhood was great. So, they invited the two strangers in for shelter. They fed and entertained to the best of their meager ability and made beds for them to sleep upon. Anyway, after a while, the old couple became fearful because the wine jug seemed always to be full when they started with so little. They began to suspect that there was more to their two guests than they imagined. In those days, encounters by gods and mortals frequently occurred, usually to the detriment of the mortals. The aged couple expressed their fear, for meeting gods was always a dangerous encounter. The two strangers finally admitted that they were the gods Jupiter and Mars, Jupiter's son. The gods told the couple that the town folks, who had failed to show them hospitality, were to pay for their insult. Presently, the gods took the aged couple to a mountain where they could watch the retribution the town folks were to suffer for their unwelcoming behavior. A god-engendered flood engulfed the town, rising to the modest home of Baucis and Philemon, the aged couple. As they watched, their modest home began to change, to transform into a marble and gold temple for the worship of Jupiter and Mars. Baucis and Philemon, though saddened by the fate befalling their neighbors, asked Jupiter and Mars to make them priests, to live out their days serving them in the new temple. The two gods saw merit in their request and granted them their wish. Then, the aged couple asked one favor more. It was that they perish together, that when the time came that one should die, the other would die also, so neither would have to bury the other. As priests of the temple, Baucis and Philemon fulfilled their duties well. Then, one day, as Baucis and Philemon were tending the grounds around the temple, Baucis saw leaves begin to sprout from the body of Philemon. Philemon looked to see leaves beginning to sprout from the body of Baucis. New branches with new leaves grew from their bodies, and skin began to transform to bark. Their feet became rooted to the ground. Before bark covered their faces, they said goodbye to each other as they were metamorphosed into an oak and a linden there on the temple grounds."

"Why that's a sad but beautiful story," returned Macy, "are there any others as beautiful?"

"There are many, maybe not as appealing, but commendable. Ovid's tales make me think of other stories I have heard in the past, like that one about the 'lady in blue.' That's the one you asked Professor Desoto about.

"I remember. That is a good story. And gives me goosebumps when I think of it." Macy put aside her work in crochet and continued: "What do you think of mysteries such as those?"

"Mysteries are real, Macy. There are things that none can explain. But mysteries are temporary. As I read articles on discoveries, I see an evolution in knowledge. Concepts such as poor choices made by people bringing about godly punishment such as disease, evolving into knowledge of a bacterial cause. Advances in knowledge calls into question <u>all</u> suppositions of cause. The one that puzzles me the most is who or what we really worship. God. Who is God? I can't decide if HE is real. I know what the pastor says, but is it true? I want to believe that there is a higher authority who cares about people, but if I don't see any evidence, how can I believe completely. Maybe God is just a way of speaking about life. Life, is everything. There is nothing without life. It's valueless. Life has value. I can see people worshipping life. If God is life, it makes more sense. I just don't know. Maybe I will know someday. Maybe folks want a god so they won't feel so alone, so vulnerable. Someone said if man didn't have a god, he would invent one. Maybe he did."

Chapter 76

Sinister Changes

On an evening in 1938 in the home of Mav and Macy Caiden, Mav turns on a lamp and opens a book which he begins to read. Macy enters the room and views a scene that she has found comforting over the last year. Living has been easy for the small family, even though the difficulties of the world are severe. At home, there is serenity.

"What are you reading now, Mav?"

"Oh, I'm reading George Chapman's translation of the <u>Odyssey</u>.

"Didn't you read his <u>Iliad</u> translation recently?" Macy asked, taking a seat across from Mav in the living room.

"Yes, it is also in the book, <u>The Whole Works of Homer</u>. The Beaton library has it. When Willow died, she willed hers and her late husband's library to the Beaton Library. They had several thousand books. This is one of them."

"What is the <u>Odyssey</u> about?"

Eugene Stonefield

"Well, Macy, it is an epic poem about the difficult return of a major hero from the battle of Troy. Odysseus was a wealthy man from Ithaca who had been fighting on the side of the Achaeans in their war with the Trojans over the abduction of Helen by Paris, the son of King Priam of Troy. Helen was the wife of Menelaus, who was the king of Sparta. Menelaus was the brother of Agamemnon, the king of Mycenae who was in command. After the Achaeans sacked Troy, the Greek forces of Agamemnon, went home. Odysseus started for home but was delayed time after time by life-threatening events for which he had to use his superior intellect to survive. People highly regarded Odysseus for his intellect and courage, and he was a contrast to the anger-driven Achilles. Aside from normal challenges, temptations, and the like, in his return, Odysseus incurred the enmity of powerful sea-god, Poseidon, the brother to Zeus and Hades. That enmity threatened Odysseus and his crew of sailors throughout their journey home. He was not without a friend, though, because Athena, Goddess of Wisdom, helped Odysseus at crucial points in his journey. She also aided Telemachus.

Odysseus was gone from Ithaca for twenty years, and during that time, his faithful wife Penelope had to fend off numerous greedy suitors for her hand, many believing that Odysseus was dead. Odysseus' and Penelope's son, Telemachus, was too young to eject the suitors who were consuming the wealth of Odysseus in daily revelry at his estate. Knowing the war with Troy had ended, the suitors sought to make Penelope choose one of them, and conspired to kill Odysseus should they be wrong about his death. Odysseus, advised by Athena, returned to Ithaca in the guise of an old man, —a man to the suitors of Penelope worthy only of scorn."

"Mav, it sounds like a great story. Who was Homer?"

"Homer was a Greek poet who lived at a time when an oral tradition governed how legends and tales were publicly told, either by the epic poet-singer, called an *aoidos,* or by a *rhapsode,* a professional performer like actors of today. These poets would take the legends of the people and weave them into memorable lines of poetry so they could be faithfully retold. Bards of the day circulated throughout festivals in Greece reciting the poems and competing for prizes of wealth and fame. Eventually, someone committed those legends to a written language. Some believe that Homer lived in Ionia in the 8ᵗʰ century BC, which was an enclave of Greeks on the shores of Anatolia, the land of the Trojans. I guess nobody knows who first committed the poem to written text, but the <u>Iliad</u> and the <u>Odyssey</u> have had a major influence on western culture."

"Those tales of gods and man interacting seems fantastical to me. People don't think that way now." Macy picked up a work of tatting that she was trying to finish as a gift to a friend.

"Oh, I don't know. I think it has always been so. Gods and man interacting, I mean. In Homer's Greece there were many gods and goddesses. They were immortal, and enjoyed independence of action, but were subservient to the powerful Zeus who held the aegis. Sometimes, actions of a god would be parried by those of another god or goddess, but could not be reversed. Sexual relationships between the deities and humans produced heroes and demigods. Their system worked for them but lost favor to the one-god doctrine of Christianity. But the world gained much from Greek philosophers."

"What about the <u>Iliad</u>? Was it a bloody war?" asked Macy.

"A horrible war. Troy was under siege for ten years, and so many tragedies unfolded. Heroes fought toe to toe, like Hector of Troy who Greek hero, Achilles, killed. Fathers mourned sons, wives mourned husbands, families were destroyed. God forbid we ever see the like!"

"What happened to Troy and to the citizens?"

"Macy, I guess the survivors just went back to the countryside to learn how to live. Although, one main warrior, Aeneas, escaped the burning Troy carrying his father on his back and leading his son. I haven't read the book yet, but a Roman poet, Virgil, in his <u>Aeneid</u>, tells of Aeneas' travels that takes him to the land now called Italy. I will read it next, because I find the stories compelling. I wish I knew Greek and Latin so I could read them in their original languages." Mav laid the book aside and looked at Macy. He has been concerned that she looks pale.

"Are you ok, today?" asked Mav.

"Oh, I guess it is just my worrying about the plight of so many people affected by this depression. And news from Europe seems so dire. I just worry. If somehow there is a war, would they call Case?"

✳✳✳

Macy's concerns are valid as the world sits atop a cauldron of unrest. During the third decade of the twentieth century, newspapers report daily notable developments on the world stage with worldwide implications. For many in America, the import was not recognized.

In Germany, Adolph Hitler, Chancellor, and the most powerful politician in the government, has an agenda. His plan is to defy the Treaty of Versailles and rearm Germany. By abolishing the War Ministry and creating the office of *Obercommando der Wehrmacht*, —the ultimate commander of the army - Hitler assumed full military control. In his portfolio of aggressive plans to achieve *Lebensraum*, or 'living space,' is a plan named *Fall Grün*, or 'Fall Green,' to expand influence over the Sudetenland currently a part of Czechoslovakia. World powers become alarmed by the historical and current public statements of Adolph Hitler confirming that he favors an aggressive foreign policy. It is a policy in conflict with the articles of post-World War I agreements. The Enabling Act elevates Adolph Hitler to dictator of Germany. Later, Hitler became *Führer,* leader of the country.

In England, Sir Anthony Eden resigns his position as Foreign Secretary in a clash with Prime Minister Neville Chamberlain, who favors appeasement of Germany. This tilt toward the appeasement of

German demands calls into question the strength of an existing French and English defense pact with Czechoslovakia. Czechoslovakia, with legal authority over the Sudetenland touching three of her four borders, perceives an existential threat from German influence and is seeking assurances from international partners.

After demanding more Nazi participation in the Austrian government, German troops charged into Austria. The Austrian parliament approves their annexation by Germany, and German power expands. Tepid pushback by European powers to the aggressive behavior of Germany, emboldens Hitler to makes new German demands regarding the Sudetenland, land occupied by German-speaking citizens who have lived in the borderlands of Bohemia, Moravia, and Czech Silesia, dating to the Austrian Empire. Hitler wants them under German control.

The Soviet Union, a border country to Germany, following the philosophic pathway of Vladimir Lenin and Karl Marx, has a left-leaning communist government under the iron hand of Joseph Stalin. Stalin, becoming alarmed by the action of Hitler's Fascist Germany, proposes a joint defense pact to the United States, which Secretary of State, Cordell Hull, rejects. America is not ready to engage in another European war, so soon after the first world war ended.

A concerned Soviet leadership under Joseph Stalin inspires a declaration of Soviet support for Czechoslovakia. The fuse for a clash of powers is set. Soviet troops assemble on the border with Ukraine demanding free passage across their territory into Czechoslovakia, so they can protect the Czechs from Germany. Ukraine, refuses, but neighboring Rumania approves of the Red Army passage.

Fascism is on the move throughout Europe. Duce Benito Mussolini becomes Field Marshal in Italy, gaining equal power over the military with Italian King Victor Emmanuel III.

Eugene Stonefield

In Spain, a civil war is in progress since 1936 between the Nationalists led by Francisco Franco and the Republicans, supporters of the Second Spanish Republic.

On the other side of the world, China is attempting to counter the rapid advancement of Japanese troops in the continuing Second Sino-Japanese War. In 1938, an attempt to slow Japanese progress, the Nationalist Government of China creates an artificial flood of the Yellow River, killing over four hundred thousand people.

A concerned English politician, Winston Churchill, is suggesting to Prime Minister, Sir Neville Chamberlain, that England bolster the defense of Czechoslovakia. His vision is to bring the United States and the USSR into some form of support for the existing defense pact between France, England, and Czechoslovakia. His assumption on the readiness of President Roosevelt to commit was premature, and Sir Neville Chamberlain has contrary inclinations that he wants to pursue through a personal meeting with Hitler.

Within the year, American support for Czechoslovakia will confuse the public. American Ambassador William Bullitt declares American solidarity with France implying a joining with the French in war with Germany should Germany invade Czechoslovakia. Shortly after, Americans hear President Roosevelt declare neutrality.

In Czechoslovakia, President Edvard Benés, hoping to defuse the tension with Hitler, is showing a willingness to accede to some demands of the German government and German-speaking citizens of Sudeten. His requirement is that the Sudetenland remains within the Republic of Czechoslovakia.

By September 24, Neville Chamberlain, who is personally negotiating the fate of Sudetenland and Czechoslovakia with Hitler, ends with Neville Chamberlain's acceptance of Hitler's demand on the Sudetenland. He transmits the <u>Godesberg Memorandum</u> to the Czech government for concurrence. The Czechs reject the agreement, as does Chamberlain's own cabinet, and likewise the French who begin mobilizing the military for war with Germany.

Chamberlain, after meeting with French Premier Ĕduard Daladier and Foreign Minister Georges Bonnet, informs the Czech president, Edvard Beneš, that England would not go to war to defend Czechoslovakia from Germany. He advises Benés to mobilize.

Hitler calls a meeting in Munich with Mussolini, Daladier, and Chamberlain before the October 1 deadline to resolve the Sudetenland issue. Although it was of vital importance to Czechoslovakia, Hitler excludes the Czech government. The negotiated Munich agreement provides for the annexation of Czech territories by Germany. Neville Chamberlain returns to England, claiming he has achieved peace. On October 1, 1938, German troops began to occupy the Sudetenland. In a secret memorandum, Hitler orders his *Wehrmacht* to prepare to occupy all of Czechoslovakia. Within a year, war will again rage in Europe as Hitler turns his eye on one country after another.

Meanwhile, in England, Winston Churchill calls for western countries, specifically the United States and Britain, to prepare for an evitable war with Germany.

On October 18, 1938, the expulsion of Polish-born Jews from Germany began. A month later, the 'night of broken glass' or *Krystallnacht* started the reign of horror, leading to the Holocaust.

In Japan, militarists turn their eyes toward Hawaii and the American naval forces at Pearl Harbor. By December 7, 1941, Americans will know why.

In America, a secret project, known as the Manhattan Project, begins. Six years hence, people the world over will learn about Hiroshima and Nagasaki as the nuclear age begins.

Chapter 77

When the Music Stopped

On the Sunday night of October 30, 1938, citizens across America tuned their radios to a Mercury Theater broadcast of unique content. By this date, radios were in two-thirds of all households in America, and many of those tuned to the CBS network featuring the Edgar Bergan and Charlie McCarthy Show at 8:00 pm. Others found the Mercury Theater that had scheduled a dramatization of a science-fiction fantasy book. This production under the direction and participation of Orson Welles, featured the book <u>War of the Worlds</u> by H.G. Wells. Orson Welles, was twenty-three years old and destined to set records for excellence on stage and for cinematic productions. But on this day in 1930, listeners were fascinated by the broadcast or terrified depending upon whether they had tuned in at the beginning to hear Mercury Theater's announcement of purpose, or later in its progress. The reaction of listeners demonstrated that people were willing to entertain the idea that citizens of Earth are not unique in the universe. The uniqueness of life has always been the teaching of all religions. That belief found its test as fictitious onsite reporting of other-worldly attacks alternated with popular music of the day.

"What do you make of this, Macy?" asked Mav, who was trying to decide what he felt about the subject of life existing somewhere other than upon the Earth. "I think this kind of broadcast is foolishness. How could anyone be interested in it?"

"Maybe it is something young people find interesting. I mean, speculating about life somewhere else in the universe. I think the pastor would turn his radio off and so will I. I'll mend some socks. You can listen to it and tell me about it later." Macy left the room.

For the folks who tuned in later in the broadcast, the reaction was unexpected and severe. Many readers of H.G. Wells and Jules Verne were fascinated by the pseudo-science of the literature that broadened imagination. Readers of John Wood Campbell's magazine <u>Astounding Science Fiction</u> yearned to know if there were hidden truths awaiting discovery. Confronting listeners of this broadcast was an affirmation of extraterrestrial life or its plausibility. But the concept that unknown entities with advanced technology could be an existential threat, was also present, recognized, or unrecognized. Especially if these 'extraterrestrials' traversing the distance from Mars to Earth should be compared to citizens of Earth who could not match that feat. The threat was sobering. In many cities and countryside across America, mass hysteria made an appearance. The fictive event, situated in Princeton, New Jersey, traveled instantly, through the airwaves upon radio signals to the far reaches. Fear of dying at the hands of extraterrestrial invaders was more significant than the fear of dying by any other means. Churches and public buildings filled with anxious people seeking solace and praying for deliverance. Many anguished to the point of a nervous breakdown. To some, it was like the coming of the End Times of John's Book of Revelation and most felt unprepared.

Mav Caid — The Complete Story

✳✳✳

On the morning of October 31, 1938, Mav was driving his Pierce-Arrow toward Beaton. As he neared the town, he found the road blocked by cars and trucks surrounded by several men holding rifles. Mav pulled over to the side of the road and watched for a few minutes trying to decide if the men were friend or foe, given the uncertain nature of the roadblock.

"Hey, fellas! What's the roadblock about?" Mav yelled.

"Mr. Caiden! Come on in. Hurry. They're coming now," shouted a returned answer.

Exiting the Pierce-Arrow, Mav walked to the barrier and circled to the other side, where he found six or seven armed men in various parts of World War I attire.

"Hello, Mr. Caiden," said one of the men. "Did you bring a weapon? We've been here all night."

"What's it about?" asked Mav, still not comprehending.

"We are under the command of Major Fenroe over there, and we are part of the militia formed to meet the invaders from Mars." The interlocutor, a man known by Mav as Herbert Issa, a shopkeeper in Beaton, held up his 1903 Springfield rifle to show Mav that they are prepared.

"Ok, I understand. All of you heard the broadcast from the Mercury theater last night on the radio." Mav suppressed a smile.

"We did, and we're ready. The roads are blocked on the other side of Beaton also." Herbert pointed back toward town.

"It's not real, Herbert. I heard the broadcast also. I heard them say it was a dramatization of a science fiction story. Y'all must not have heard that part." Mav waited for his words to register with Herbert Issa.

"We were all at the Mule Kick, and the owner turned on the radio. We heard where and when the attack began. Now you are saying it is not true?" Herbert looked bewildered.

"Not true," returned Mav. "I thought the Mule Kick Saloon was closed down because of Prohibition."

"Aw, Mr. Caiden! You're pulling my leg. I know you know they repealed prohibition in 1933! But folks can still buy the 'white lightning' liquor they began to distill out in the hollows during prohibition. One fella is distilling a really good recipe he calls 'Speakeasy,' and that's how buyers order it at the Mule Kick. It ain't exactly legal. Still, the authorities seem to prefer it to the commercial brands, so some folks 'speakeasy,' so to speak, and others look aside. They get it from that bootlegger out in the hollows." Herbert waved all around to signal multiple directions. "You ought to get some and try it."

"I have never had liquor of any sort, though I bought a bottle once at the suggestion of the saloon owner with a shotgun. But I had to use it not long after." Mav then asked to talk to the major.

"Major Fenroe," said Mav, keeping a straight face. "I think there has been a mistake about the invasion by Martians."

"Maverick Caiden, right? Mr. Caiden, we all heard the broadcast and are bound to take action to protect our town and our families. Will you be joining us?" Major Fenroe looked serious about his heavy responsibilities. "These Martians are big and ugly, and we mean to give an account of ourselves even if we die trying!"

Mav then told him what he previously had told Herbert, and the major dispatched a man to return to Beaton to call state authorities for an update on the invasion. Believing all would soon resolve, Mav prepared to return home and not attempt to drive around the barrier, which would likely damage his prized Pierce-Arrow. Before he could leave, Herbert Issa approached.

"What happened? You said you had to use the only bottle of liquor you ever bought. What happened?"

"It was a long time ago. I was, maybe, eighteen, and my friend Tucum and I stopped at the only building displaying a sign in Alamosa, Colorado. It was a saloon with no customers at the time. I guess the owner was superstitious about having at least one sale, so he insisted that I buy a bottle. I did so because it was easier than dealing with the trouble it could have caused if I refused. I put the bottle in my saddlebag then Tucum, and I found a hotel with a restaurant down the way where we bought a meal. Later, Tucum's tuckus got transfixed by an errant arrow shot by *Tsá-cho,* a young Apache who was hunting turkey. We poured the liquor on Tucum's tuckus. Well, some of it we did, but Tucum did drink a bit of it to dull the pain of the arrow and what I was going to cause by cutting it out." Mav smiled at the memory, wondering what became of Tucum. Time slips away.

✳✳✳

An hour later, the man dispatched to check on the errant assumption that the Martian invasion was real, returned to report to the major. A few minutes later, the militia members assembled to hear the major order the men to take down the barrier. Mav waved goodbye to the militiamen and turned the Pierce-Arrow around to head back to the home-place. When he arrived, he found Macy suffering.

"What's wrong, Macy," asked Mav, showing great concern. "In what way are you ill?"

"My belly, Mav. I have terrible pains, and it seems swollen." Macy looked at Mav and shook her head. "I don't think things are right with me. I need to see a doctor soon."

"Where do you feel pain?" asked a concerned Mav.

"Upper left side, just under the ribs. And I feel a fullness, even when I haven't eaten for a while. I have been tiring more easily, just doing my usual activities. I don't know. I just don't feel well. I thought, maybe I have some liver problems and have been taking those Carter's Little Liver Pills, but they don't seem to help."

A week later, Macy and Mav received a diagnosis of Macy's illness. Leukemia.

Chapter 78

Sunset at the Dawning

It is early in the day in January of 1939, and Dr. Trevor is talking to Case and *Ja-gé* at the new hospital wing in Beaton. They are sitting on a sofa in the office of Dr. Trevor as he explains the reasons for having two patients admitted to the hospital.

"The situation is this: Mr. Caiden has a severe case of pneumonia that I understand he acquired shortly after pulling a calf from frigid water. I understand that the calf had wandered onto the ice covering the stock tank and fell through. Mr. Caiden received a severe chill at the time, and it progressed into pneumonia a few days later. He has been in the hospital since Friday. My prognosis is, at best, guarded, given his age. As for your mother, Mrs. Caiden, as I know you have already been advised, is suffering from leukemia. The hospital admitted her just a day after your father and is in serious condition. I am, reluctantly, giving a less than positive prognosis for her. I wish I could be more positive. I am glad that both of you could be here."

"Has he said anything or asked for anything before we came?" Case asked.

"No, the nurse from last night said that he seemed to have fallen into delirium. She said that he was talking to no one in the room and calling out several names. She heard names like Fenner Korn, Slade, Little Joe, —just several names of people from his past. He also said something about a *To-ne-mah*, and a *Windwalker*, and something about the valley. I didn't know what he was saying, but it must have meant something to him. Do you know?" asked the doctor.

"Some of the names I have heard, but, no, I don't know anyone named *Windwalker*. I do recall that there was a valley he visited every year somewhere west of Beaton, Pike County, I believe," answered Case.

Would it be possible to place them in the same room?" asked *Ja-gé*. "I know they would welcome each other's company."

"It would, and if all agree, I will order it today." Dr. Trevor wrote the order on the chart for Macy as he receives Case's agreement with a nod.

Later that day, the nurses moved Macy to Mav's room with her bed placed close enough for the patients to reach out and touch hands if they desired.

✳✳✳

"Mav," began Macy as she perceived that he was awake. "How are you doing today?"

With difficulty, Mav responded in a weak, raspy voice: "I just want to get out of here and go home. But they are treating me well so I shouldn't complain. How about you?"

"Oh, you know, they are treating me as best they can. Leukemia is…" Macy's words are drowned out by Mav.

Mav Caid — The Complete Story

For a minute, Mav became engaged in a series of hard coughs that prevented him from speaking. Finally, his cough subsiding, Mav said weakly: "Take my hand Macy. Take my hand. I want to touch you." Mav stretched his hand toward Macy who took his hand.

"Have you seen Case and *Ja-gé*?" asked Mav.

"Yes. Case and *Ja-gé* came by together. They told me that they both were in Washington when they received the call and were able to come by train together." Macy began to register pain.

"Are you hurting, Macy? Is it bad?" asked Mav.

"Just a bit, Mav. I'll be ok. The nurse will be by shortly to give me my medication." Shortly following, Mav drifted into a deep sleep.

✳✳✳

If an inquiry into the meaning of *Windwalker* could reach into the mind of Mav Caid, the answer would astound. As this could not happen, only a few words mumbled by the deathly ill man could be reported by an observer.

"*Windwalker*, how good to see you." In his dream, Mav Caid welcomes an old friend.

"Keeper of Tears, it is time for my visit. We must talk." *Windwalker* assumed a cross-legged position facing Mav sitting at the campfire beside the rushing brook. "You are troubled by questions you cannot resolve."

"I have questions I cannot answer, yes," returned Mav. "Questions about the nature of God…uh, the Great Spirit."

"This is not unusual, Keeper of Tears, when only the mind leads. Enlightenment comes slowly and it will ever be so. This is because there are truths that cannot be understood fully until the pathway has been walked. A man has two guides. One is the mind. The other is the heart. The pathway to the village of the Tribe of Everyman will always be found, yet it is the one who follows the heart who finds it

615

with least effort. Those who follow only the mind must go down many roads to find the one that's true. But it will be found because the Great Spirit is merciful and has willed it so. In the village, all is known."

"But, the Great Spirit…" Mav is interrupted by *Windwalker.*

"Is known by many names, Keeper of Tears. It is of no consequence. A tribe may have one name or many to speak of him. It is of no matter. There is a beginning and an end and all are welcomed into the Tribe of Everyman. Your tasks are finished and the portal to the Valley of Tears is closed until *Timewalker* decides to open it to all."

"*Timewalker?*" asks a perplexed Keeper of Tears.

"Some will see an apple as a whole. Others see an apple as the sum of many parts, —stem, seed, skin, flesh. Each part a different name. Great Spirit, Wakhán Tháŋka, Gitche Manitou, Elohim, Yahweh, Jehovah, Zeus, Jupiter, Allah, Ahura Mazda, Timewalker, …what is a name?"

As Keeper of Tears considers what has been said, *Windwalker* brings his flute to his lips and begins a tune of eternity. Mav Caid awakes in the light.

✳✳✳

Dawn broke over Beaton, and two patients at the Caid-Chesney Tears of the Sun hospital are again holding hands. Macy is speaking to Mav in the breaking light streaming through the window to their room.

"Mav, there is a question I always wanted to ask but never did. Why was Felicity naked?"

Receiving no response, Macy asked: "Mav, would you squeeze my hand? Please?" She received no squeeze, no answer.

With anxiousness growing, she spoke in a louder voice: "Mav? Mav?" But only the silence spoke. "Oh, Mav. Oh, Mav. I love you

616

so. Oh, I love you so. I love you so. I…Oh. Oh! OH!" A wrenching pain, a fear, a release, a joy.

Quietness filled the room as Nurse Silbey entered to bring the medication prescribed for Macy. After a moment, she called the doctor on duty.

Later that day, Dr. Trevor speaks to Case and *Ja-gé*: "It sometimes happens that couples who have been together a long time leave near the same time. I think that when two people share so much of their lives, the heart cannot contain the stress accruing from the loss of their partner. Pneumonia took Maverick. Leukemia did not take Macy. Her heart simply burst from grief…or, overwhelming joy. Only God knows."

Four days later, upon a sun-bathed hill near the graves of Macy's father, Clarence, and of Lyla, the beloved daughter taken by death too soon, a single grave receives two people, joined in death as they were joined in life, joined now for eternity beneath the entwining limbs of the oak and the linden.

Chapter 79

Epilog

Steady the cadence of the bell that chimes
minute by minute, hour by hour, by year,
by millennia since heartbeats began; an
Un-sensed rhythm amidst the progression
of time, marking soul's gains and losses, made
manifest by twists and turns attendant
to soul's never-was-to-ever-more trek;
The time between the first cry and last sigh.

Those who would counsel against the bell -
Who struggles against the fading light
Gain most by accepting its binding chime
and fashion a meritorious life
worthy a simple epitaph: 'Beneath
this stone rests an exemplar of the best.'

Eugene Stonefield

As long as the Earth has been the home of 'the people', there have been born occasionally, a Maverick Caiden. One, whose life includes no greatness for which fatherhoods of life-changing movements are named. But instead, one whose life is nuanced by gentleness and caring by which families are built in the broader sense, —the family of mankind, the Tribe of Everyman. These unique men dedicate their living years pursuing knowledge and self-improvement to ensure they are living life to its fullest measure. In their hearts, there is a goodness welling from the purest of natural urges to enjoy all that one can savor from life and to help others do the same. A meditative thinker might say that existence precedes essence and would not be wrong. Mav Caid began his existence as a rudely educated boy desiring to experience and learn, and earned his essence. Inherently he knew that for one to suffer ignorance, they must agree with their suffering. That he could not do. Without fanfare, without excessive recognition, Mav Caid followed the rules taught by his caring parents in Bandera. The rules governing prudence, courage, temperance, and justice, —the active measures of humanity.—he followed unconsciously, guided by moral and ethical codes steeped into his being. Some truths he learned, some he knew intuitively, of others he was of two minds. He never reconciled his uncertainties in the metaphysics of being and of knowing, nor in the uncertainties in the nature of the one called God. But in his heart, he believed that, with just a little more knowledge, those too, would be resolved. The questions of 'Who am I?' 'What am I?' 'Where have I been?' and 'Where am I going?' took root early in the mind of Mav Caid and embodied an old proverb that states: "No matter what path a human might take, it is _my_ path; no matter where they walk, it leads to _me_." Whether the journey is from God to God, or from Life to Life may be nothing more than shades of perception.

Endnotes

1 The story of the name 'maverick' is told by Luther A. Lawhon in the book Trail Drivers of Texas, published by Cokesbury Press in Nashville, TN in 1925. The book is a compilation of first-hand stories of trail drives in the building of the cattle industry in Texas from the early beginnings. The book was compiled and edited by J. Marvin Hunt and published under the guidance of George W. Saunders, President of The Old Time Trail Drivers Association. Copyrights in 1924 by George W. Saunders and 1925 by Lamar & Barton, Agents.

2 Song 'Oh Promise Me' copyright 1889 by Reginald De Koven. The song, a love song often used in weddings was used in the score of the opera, Robin in the 1890s. Music score and lyrics viewable at Digital Media Repository at Ball State University. See also: Wikipedia contributors. "Oh Promise Me." Wikipedia, The Free Encyclopedia, 25 Jun. 2017. Web. 13 Nov. 2018

3 Song 'Shall We Gather At The River', is a traditional Christian hymn written by American poet and music composer Alan Lowry (1836-1899) and named 'Hanson Place' in honor of the Hanson Place Baptist Church in Brooklyn, NY. See also: Wikipedia contributors. "Shall We Gather at the River." Wikipedia, The Free Encyclopedia, 13 Jan. 2019. Web 9 Mar. 2019

4 Note on the language of Native Americans used in the dialog of Windwalker: All language examples are taken from the publication, North American Indians, Vol 1 by Edward Curtis, copyright 1907.

5 Pronunciation key. names and words used in this book:
>   a - as in father
>   ă - as in cat
>   â - as aw in awl
>   ai - as in aisle
>   e - as ey in they
>   ě - as in net
>   i - as in machine

ĭ - as in sit
o - as in old
ǒ - as in not
ô - as ow in how
oi - as in oil
u - as in ruin
ŭ - as in nut
ü - as in German hütte
ụ - as in push
h - always aspirated
q - as qu in quick
th - as in thaw
w - as in wild
y - as in year
ch - as in church
sh - as in shall, sash
n - nasal, as in French dans
zh - as z in azure
' - a pause

6 Speech by Domot recorded in the book: Kiowa. The History of the Blanket Indian Mission by Isabel Crawford. Published by the Fleming H Revel Company in 1915.

7 Surrender speech of Chief Joseph of the Nez Perce: "I am tired of fighting. Our chiefs are killed. Looking Glass is dead. Toohulhulsote is dead. The old men are dead. It is the young men who say yes or no. He who led the young men is dead. It is cold and we have no blankets. The little children are freezing to death. My people, some of them, have run away to the hills and have no blankets, no food. No one knows where they are – perhaps freezing to death. I want to have time to look for my children and see how many I can find. Maybe I shall find them among the dead. Hear me, my chiefs. I am tired. My heart is sick and sad. From where the sun now stands, I will fight no more forever."

Wikipedia contributors. "Chief Joseph." *Wikipedia, The Free Encyclopedia*. Wikipedia, The Free Encyclopedia, 29 Oct. 2019. Web. 1 Nov. 2019.
8 Apache Girl Dance:
Reference publication North American Indians, Vol. 1 by Edward S. Curtis, first copyrighted in 1907 and is in the public domain.
Reference also information available on the internet.
https://encyclopedia2.thefreedictionary.com/Apache+Girls%27+Sunrise+Ceremony
http://www.webwinds.com/yupanqui/apachesunrise.htm#Introduction

9 Sacred Pipe Ceremony:
Reference information available on the internet:
http://www.native-americans-online.com/native-american-pipe-ceremony.html
http://www.muiniskw.org/pgCulture2f.htm

10 Airmail service history.
Reference information available on the internet:
https://www.mavericksofthesky.com/the-air-mail-pilots/
https://www.historynet.com/airmail-service-it-began-with-army-air-service-pilots.htm

11 Fire at Vassar occurring on Feb. 12, 1918.
http://vcencyclopedia.vassar.edu/notable-events/fire-of-1918.html

12 From 20,000 Quips and Quotes by Evan Esar, Barns & Noble Books, New York, NY. Copyright 1968 Evan Esar. ISBN: 1-56619-529-2

13 Song Shenandoah: Origin is unknown but generally considered as originated by Canadian and American voyageurs plying the Missouri River in their fur trading pursuits. Eventually, the song was circulating among mariners as a sea shanty. The lyrics tell of a fur trader who longs to marry the daughter of Oneida Iroquois chief, Shenandoah.

Eugene Stonefield

See: Wikipedia contributors. "Oh Shenandoah." *Wikipedia, The Free Encyclopedia*. Wikipedia, The Free Encyclopedia, 28 Oct. 2019. Web. 29 Oct. 2019.

14 <u>Goodbye, Fare Thee Well</u>, is a traditional English song that became popular as a capstan shanty that sailors sang as they walked around the anchor capstan to weigh the anchor. The ballad was first published in <u>The Book of Roxburghe Ballads</u> in 1847 by John Collier; from ballads collected by Robert Harley, 1ˢᵗ Earl of Oxford and Mortimer; and later by John Ker, 3ʳᵈ Duke of Roxburgh.

15 Snyder Act of 1924 was an act to give citizenship primarily to Native American veterans for their service in the military during the WWI. It was signed by President Calvin Coolidge on June 2, 1924. There were limitations to citizenship that were not removed until as late as 1948.
Re: https://www.archives.gov/historical-docs/todays-doc/?dod-date=602
See also: Wikipedia contributors. "Indian Citizenship Act." *Wikipedia, The Free Encyclopedia*. Wikipedia, The Free Encyclopedia, 25 Oct. 2019. Web. 30 Oct. 2019.

General: Historical events mentioned regarding international affairs were selected from years 1928 through 1939 as referenced in: Wikipedia contributors. "19xx." *Wikipedia, The Free Encyclopedia*. Wikipedia, The Free Encyclopedia, 9 Jan. 2020. Web. 17 Jan. 2020.

Chapter 1 Market Crash and Great Depression
<u>https://honors.uca.edu/wiki/index.php/Great_Depression</u>
<u>https://pocketsense.com/causes-effects-1929-stock-market-crash-1401.html</u>

Chapter 2 Poker Alice:
https://en.wikipedia.org/wiki/Poker_Alice
Wikipedia contributors. "Poker Alice." *Wikipedia, The Free Encyclopedia*. Wikipedia, The Free Encyclopedia, 25 Jul. 2019. Web. 1 Jan. 2020.

https://www.legendsofamerica.com/we-pokeralice/
http://thewildwest.org/cowboys/wildwestlegendarywomen/206-
pokeralice

Chapter 4 Legends
Chupacabra:
https://www.chupamacabre.com/chupacabras/legend-el-
chupacabra/
https://www.livescience.com/24036-chupacabra-facts.html
https://www.nationalgeographic.com/news/2010/10/101028-
chupacabra-evolution-halloween-science-monsters-chupacabras-
picture/
http://www.animalplanet.com/tv-shows/lost-
tapes/creatures/chupacabra-history/
El Muerto:
https://www.onlyinyourstate.com/texas/urban-legends-tx/
https://www.americanfolklore.net/folklore/2010/07/el_muerto.htm
l
https://www.legendsofamerica.com/tx-elmuerto/
La Llorona Legend:
https://en.wikipedia.org/wiki/La_Llorona
https://www.legendsofamerica.com/gh-lallorona/

Chapter 21 Blue Lady:
https://www.desertusa.com/desert-people/lady-in-blue.html
https://www.eastmountaindirectory.com/publishing/Historical/227-
The-Legend-of-the-Blue-Nun.html
http://socorro-
history.org/HISTORY/PH_History/201206_blue_nun.pdf

Eugene Stonefield

ABOUT THE AUTHOR

626

Eugene Stonefield writes fantasy-fiction, employing historical references to highlight the time and events of the era in which the story unfolds. He is a native Texan and a Liberal Arts graduate of the University of Texas at Austin. He currently resides in San Angelo, Texas. His career choices have included service with the US Air Force, and employment in computer technology by federal and state governments. It is his sincere desire that the books he writes are read and enjoyed by the reader

Mav Caid — The Complete Story

Other books by this author

Mav Caid The Early Years:
The story of Mav Caid is a fantasy-fiction about a naive farmer's son who leaves Bandera, Texas at seventeen to experience life beyond the farm life into which he was born, and to find his niche in the world. After spending five years as a wrangler and drover for Captain John Lytle driving cattle up the Great Western Cattle Trail, Mav strikes out on his own, arriving in Beaton, Arkansas where he obtains some land and settles in to live off the largess of nature. His plan is to be short-lived when he finds that he cannot ignore his roots as the son of a farmer. Nor can he ignore the magic of Macy, the Arkland Stageline station-keeper's daughter. This is the story of Mav Caid's maturation following the tragedy of his family's murder in Bandera. During the years 1889 through 1899, Mav is faced by a series of threatening situations in which he employs courage and native intelligence to survive but is eventually forced to violate his natural abhorrence to killing to protect his new wife and himself. His story is also one of how he became the 'Keeper of Tears' in the nation of Everyman and built a legacy. Mav Caid is the first of a three-book trilogy, The Life and Times of Mav Caid.

Mav Caid The Middle Years:
The story of Mav Caid The Middle Years is the second book in the fantasy-fiction series The Life and Times of Mav Caid. The book continues the tale about a naive farmer's son who leaves Bandera, Texas at seventeen to experience life beyond the farm life into which he was born, and to find his niche in the world. After spending five years as a wrangler and drover for Captain John Lytle driving cattle up the Great Western Cattle Trail, Mav strikes out on his own, arriving in Beaton, Arkansas where he obtains some land and settles in to live off the largess of nature. His plan is to be short-lived when he finds that he cannot ignore his roots as the son of a farmer. Nor can he ignore the magic of Macy, the Arkland Stageline station-keeper's daughter. The first book, Mav Caid The Early Years, was the story of Mav Caid's maturation following the tragedy of his family's murder in Bandera and covers the years 1889 through 1899. This second book, Mav Caid The Middle Years, begins in 1900 and continues the story of Mav Caid as a farmer and entrepreneur in Beaton, and the unpredictable events that occur, such as the responsibility thrust upon him to be the educator and mentor to Ja-ge, an Apache foundling.

Mav Caid The Later Years:
The story of Mav Caid The Later Years is the third book in the fantasy-fiction series The Life and Times of Mav Caid. The book continues the tale about a naive farmer's son who leaves Bandera, Texas at seventeen to experience life beyond the farm life into which he was born, and to find his niche in the world. After spending five years as a wrangler and drover for Captain John Lytle driving cattle up the Great Western Cattle Trail, Mav strikes out on his own in 1889, arriving in Beaton, Arkansas where he obtains some land and settles in to live off the largess of nature. His plan is to be

short-lived when he finds that he cannot ignore his roots as the son of a farmer. Nor can he ignore the magic of Macy, the Arkland Stageline station-keeper's daughter. The first book, Mav Caid The Early Years, was the story of Mav Caid's maturation following the tragedy of his family's murder in Bandera and covers the years 1889 through 1899. The second book, Mav Caid The Middle Years, begins in 1900 and continues the story of Mav Caid as a farmer and entrepreneur in Beaton, and the unpredictable events that occur, such as the responsibility thrust upon him to be the educator and mentor to Ja-ge, an Apache foundling. This book, Mav Caid The Later Years continues the story from 1920 onward but begins with a lookback at the events occurring in Mav Caid's life as a young man driving cattle up the trail.

Adventures of Angus Mach Eraclee:
Angus Mach Eraclee, a young man seeking to become a merchant in Massachusetts, suffers the tragedy of a kidnapped wife at the beginning of his efforts to build a life for himself and Felicity during the mid-eighteenth century. The sorrowful episode places Angus on an odyssey to find Felicity somewhere in unfamiliar, foreign lands, beginning with the finding, and interviewing the woman pirate, Flora Burn, last observed taking Felicity from their cabin near Marblehead, Massachusetts in the year 1755. Angus begins his search in the Caribbean where he meets his future mentor, Imlac Azar, a plantation owner with connections world over. Imlac offers Angus a job finding and buying rare manuscripts which Imlac plans to use in building his dream, the recreation of the House of Wisdom library of Baghdad that invader Halugu Khan destroyed in AD 1258. Angus travels throughout the world buying manuscripts and historical documents and searching for Felicity. His only lead is that Flora sold Felicity to an Emir in Arabia. His disappointment is that she was subsequently taken by the young son of the Emir who fell in love with the beautiful Felicity. Angus' search engages him in unexpected and unusual life-threatening episodes that ultimately leads him to experience a severe emotional breakdown. This book is a prolog to The Saga of MacHeracles, a fantasy-fiction that completes the story of the life of Angus Mach Eraclee.

The Saga of MacHeracles:
The Saga of MacHeracles concludes the story of Angus Mach Eraclee from the previous book, Adventures of Angus Mach Eraclee. It is a fantasy-fiction of a delusional Angus Mach Eraclee who, believing himself a raccoon, is taken aboard a tramp merchant vessel off the coast of Scotland in the late 18th century. It is a tale of his adventures throughout the world where he becomes a special agent for the captain of the Okeanos, a decommissioned warship owned and sailed by tramp-merchant captain, Master Nebbleston Glaucus. The crew of the Okeanos are chosen from a plethora of out-of-work entities from mythology plus those of imagination. Angus MacHeracles, in his delusional character, interacts with animals and historical people, such as Thomas Jefferson, Fletcher Christian, Alessandro Cagligostro, and Fra Diavolo, in efforts to carry out the wishes of Captain Glaucus. The intrigues embody danger and humor and, although some of the people and events are

historical, they interact with the hero, Angus MacHeracles to advance the story. History anchors the time and place of action. Animal characters met in the tale have human characteristics and are capable of human interaction. A non-omniscient narrator tells the story of MacHeracles which is commented upon by an omniscient chronicler whose involvement is not appreciated by the narrator. During the narration of the tale, periodic word-battles break out between the narrator and the chronicler.

Fantasia for Adelaisa

Fantasia for Adelasia is a story of a young boy in Poggibonsi, Italy during the nineteenth century whose dream is to become a virtuoso on the violin. As a young student he is mistreated by his teacher, Maestro Bianci, a temperamental, ego-centric instructor. A quiet observer of his mistreatment, a man with a mysterious demeanor, Professore Tchort, engages Pietro, suggesting he could better teach and manage his progress to realize his dream. Adelaisa, a beautiful young admirer of Pietro's violin playing attracts Pietro's attention but he draws back proclaiming their relationship can only be platonic. Professor Tchort, a sinister man of wealth and unknown history, is a violin advocate, and guides Pietro to realize his dream of wealth and fame with some unique requirements. Pietro is beloved by Adelaisa who waits for Pietro to recognize romantic love. Through an intercession of a strange client, Adonai Sapiente, Pietro recognizes his deferred, romantic love for the loyal Adelaisa and rushes back to Poggibonsi. He learns of Adelaisa's decline and breaks his promises to Professor Tchort which has serious consequences. Adelaisa's last plea is that Pietro play an opus for her which ends in an epiphany for Pietro.

DeFinis Storm　　　　　　**His Story**

DeFinis Storm found his calling to law enforcement in Texas just following the end of the Civil War. DeFinis was a privileged son of a union between his Anglo father, Acton Storm, and his African-American mother, Luella. He was privileged in the sense of being afforded the same education as his half-brother Heston, and half-sister Alicia, and treated equally. He was not afforded the same equality in the eyes of the law that declared a person black if he had black parent or ancestors, so was not able to receive a just apportionment of the plantation when Acton died. DeFinis, at nineteen, chose to leave the plantation and find his own way on the frontier at the site of Fort Concho where the community of Santa Angela was being settled. As he travels toward the frontier, DeFinis meets, Angela Byrne, a young girl fleeing with her mother, Emma Byrne's abusive husband, Caulder Byce. At first recruited into an unpopular Reconstruction police force, DeFinis later joined into the ranks of the Texas Rangers where he met many challenges. This is his story.